Praise for E

"One of the best of a new
who have driven the genr

"Kelton's explanation of these men—cowboys without a future—is the strength of his writing. He understands them well, and his descriptiveness is simple but complete. There is a rhythm to his writing. . . . [The cowboys] are so familiar to him, so universal, their dialogue is seamless."

—*Fort Worth Star-Telegram*

"Elmer Kelton is to Texas what Mark Twain was to the Mississippi River." —Jory Sherman, author of *The Barons of Texas*

"[Kelton] never shrank from bending the rules of the genre. . . . He devoted himself to explaining and defending the cowboy's way of life."

—*The Wall Street Journal*

"A masterful Western author."

—*Lubbock Avalanche-Journal*

"You would be hard-pressed to find a better Western fiction author than Kelton. . . . A true master of the Western literary form."

—*American Cowboy* magazine

"One thing is certain: as long as there are writers as skillful as Elmer Kelton, Western literature will never die." —*True West* magazine

FORGE BOOKS BY ELMER KELTON

After the Bugles
Badger Boy
Barbed Wire
Bitter Trail
Bowie's Mine
The Buckskin Line
Buffalo Wagons
Captain's Rangers
Cloudy in the West
Dark Thicket
The Day the Cowboys Quit
Donovan
Eyes of the Hawk
The Good Old Boys
Hanging Judge
Hard Trail to Follow
Hot Iron
Jericho's Road
Joe Pepper
Llano River
Long Way to Texas
Many a River
Massacre at Goliad
Other Men's Horses
Pecos Crossing
The Pumpkin Rollers
The Raiders: Sons of Texas
Ranger's Trail
The Rebels: Sons of Texas
Sandhills Boy: The Winding Trail of a Texas Writer
Shadow of a Star
Shotgun
Six Bits a Day
The Smiling Country
Sons of Texas
Stand Proud
Texas Rifles
Texas Standoff
Texas Vendetta
The Time It Never Rained
The Way of the Coyote

Lone Star Rising
(comprising *The Buckskin Line*, *Badger Boy*, and *The Way of the Coyote*)

Brush Country
(comprising *Barbed Wire* and *Llano River*)

Ranger's Law
(comprising *Ranger's Trail*, *Texas Vendetta*, and *Jericho's Road*)

Texas Showdown
(comprising *Pecos Crossing* and *Shotgun*)

Texas Sunrise
(comprising *Massacre at Goliad* and *After the Bugles*)

Long Way to Texas
(comprising *Joe Pepper*, *Long Way to Texas*, and *Eyes of the Hawk*)

TEXAS RIFLES

AND

MASSACRE at GOLIAD

Elmer Kelton

A TOM DOHERTY ASSOCIATES BOOK • NEW YORK

TEXAS RIFLES AND MASSACRE AT GOLIAD

A Forge Book
Published by Tom Doherty Associates, LLC
175 Fifth Avenue
New York, NY 10010

www.tor-forge.com

ISBN 978-0-7653-7050-1

First Edition: March 2013

Printed in the United States of America

0 9 8 7 6 5 4 3 2 1

CONTENTS

TEXAS RIFLES

1

Cloud almost rode upon the Indians' grazing horse herd before he realized it.

The summer sun had been bearing down upon him for hours now, sapping his energy, stealing from him the vigilance that he normally never lost while riding across these fringes of Comanche country. In this unrelenting heat it was easy to drowse in the saddle, to let one's mind roam the thousand miles and more to the smoky battlefields of Virginia.

There, even now, angry cannons thundered and men died in the blast of shellfire.

But here, in these rolling hills that marked the western edge of the Texas Cross Timbers, it was still and quiet . . . so very quiet.

He saw the horses and yanked hard on the hair reins, pulling his sorrel back into the green cover of post oak brush. Suddenly wide awake, he whipped his rifle out of its beaded deerskin scabbard. He stepped down quickly to the summer-dried grass and held his hand on the sorrel's nose to keep it from nickering. Cloud's heart hammered, his breath came short.

Gradually he eased and got his lost breath back. Those Indians must have been as heat-sleepy as he was. They hadn't seen him.

That was just a shade too close to heaven! he thought.

He was a medium-tall man, crowding thirty. He was broad of shoulder, strong of back. Three days' growth of beard was beginning to blacken a face already browned by sun and wind. His large hands were leather-tough, for they had known the plow. Yet his legs showed a trace of a bow, too, because he had ridden a horse ever since he had been old enough to lace his fingers into a mane and hang on. He wore a sweat-streaked cotton shirt, buttoned at the loose-fitting collar to keep the sun from baking his breastbone. He carried a Colt revolver high on his right hip and a seven-pound Bowie knife on his left, encased in a scabbard made from the hide of a buffalo's tail, the bushy black switch still hanging as a tassel.

Through the screen of brush, Cloud studied the loose-held horse herd and the Indians who slacked in the shade of scattered trees around it. Comanches, mostly squaws. He could see only one man, on the near edge of the herd. The warrior slouched on a bay horse that showed the marks of a collar and a white man's brand on the hip. He hadn't spotted Cloud because he was giving his attention to a slender young squaw who sat as close to him as her black-maned dun would get. The warrior was laughing and talking with the woman while he rolled a fresh-made arrow shaft between his teeth, taking the sap out of it.

These were horses a stray band of Comanche raiders had been picking up in the Texas settlements, Cloud reasoned. Now the wily thieves were working their way north to the safety of those trackless stretches of open grass on the Staked Plain, where they would lose themselves like a whirlwind that suddenly lifts and disappears into air, in a solitude so vast that white men drew back in dread.

Counting in fives with tiny moves of his big hand, Cloud estimated that there were eighty or ninety horses. Many a farmer and cowman had been left afoot to walk and curse. More than likely, a few had lost their scalps as well as their horses. To the Comanche warrior stealing down from his stronghold on the high plains, warfare was a game to be played and enjoyed—an end in itself. To steal a *Tejano*'s horses brought material wealth and a considerable measure of honor. To count coup on the hated *Tejano* and bring back his scalp greatly increased the honor and raised the warrior's status in the eyes of the tribe.

Cloud could still see only the one buck, and he wondered where the rest were. He counted six women, young squaws who remained physically able to make the long forays with their men, to do the menial chores and hold the horses and glory in the fighting manhood of their warriors. That there were six women didn't mean there were only six men, however. Many of the bucks never brought women on these trips. They didn't have to, for a Comanche warrior fortunate enough to have a woman with him thought little of lending her to a needful friend.

The other men must be off somewhere trying to

gather up more horses, Cloud reasoned. They must feel sure of themselves, leaving only one man with these squaws to watch the ones they already had. Either they had whipped back their pursuit or they considered it too far behind to worry about.

High time to h'ist my tail and get out of here, he thought. *Only, which way had I ought to run? Wrong guess and I'll butt heads with Lord knows how many Comanches.*

He was no stranger to Indian warfare. He'd had his scraps, and a deep scar on one shoulder to show for it. But he saw no sense in riding headlong into a one-sided battle where overwhelming weight of numbers was sure to grind him down.

There was a time to fight and a time to ride away. Without question, this was a time to ride.

He heard the heavy roar of a rifle from somewhere over the next hill, and he jerked involuntarily. The blast was followed by the staccato rattle of smaller guns. The horses lifted their heads, their ears pricking up in the direction of the gunfire. The buck and the squaws turned too, listening. The buck shook his head confidently to the young woman beside him. Telling her, Cloud judged, that it wouldn't take long.

Cloud eased back afoot until he could no longer see the horses, and until he hoped the Indians could not see him. At least now he knew where the rest of the band was. Good chance to get away.

But he was held by the sound of battle. Somebody across yonder was putting up a good fight.

The trouble with being a reasonable man was that reason all the time wanted to argue with a man's emotions. Reason told Cloud to mount up and spur out of there while he could. But emotion made him wonder and worry about whoever the Comanches had bottled up. How much chance did those people have?

Cloud skirted through the post oak, circled the horse herd and made his way up the off side of a hill, the rifle across his lap. Staying within brush cover, he climbed until he could look out across a clearing at the farmhouse below. It was pretty much the usual Texas frontier farmer's log cabin. Actually, it was almost two cabins, its two rooms built under one roof but separated by a narrow, open "dog run." Each room was buttressed by a heavy rock chimney. Man with a family, Cloud figured. And most of them shooting.

Defending fire racketed from three places—from each section of the cabin and from a heavy post oak corral. The settler must have had a little warning, time enough to get his horses into the corral and shut the gate. To get them, the Indians were first going to have to kill him. Even then, they would be under close fire from the cabin. Heavy smoke rose from the man's position in the corral and drifted slowly away in the hot breeze.

They sometimes said of Texas gunpowder that if the bullet didn't kill the enemy, the smoke would choke him to death.

He's in a good spot long's his powder holds out, Cloud thought. *But there's four or five horses in that corral, and them Comanches can almost taste 'em.*

He tried to rough-count the attacking Indians,

but it was hard to spot them all. Some had found good cover in the tall grass. Others lay behind downed trees that the settler hadn't yet put into his fences. Ten or twelve, Cloud judged. A few were firing rifles. Most used bows. He could see the straight, quick flight of arrows, although at a distance he could not hear them strike the cabin or the timber that made up the corral.

He saw an Indian sprint toward the house, then jerk in midstride, pitching headlong to the ground. That angered the others.

They're determined now, he thought. *They'll stay till they've got the job done.*

He might be able to hit one or two of them from here with the long reach of his rifle, but he wasn't likely to change the situation much. They would dispatch a few warriors to take care of him while the rest went on after the people in the cabin. No use in a man selling out that cheap.

He thought then of the horse herd.

There was this about Comanches: they liked to fight, but they didn't care for suicide. If they saw they couldn't win, they usually pulled back. Cowardice was one thing, good judgment was another. Badly as they wanted those few horses in the corral, they probably would leave in a hurry if they thought they were in danger of losing the others they'd already taken, he reasoned. His one rifle wouldn't do a lot of good here, but it could cut a big swath out at that horse herd.

"Just hang on down there, folks," he muttered, backing away carefully. "The dance ain't over yet."

In the saddle again, he circled back the way he had come. Using the brush to hide him, he made his way to the place from which he had first seen the horse herd. He stepped to the ground, taking his stake rope loose from the saddlehorn and working to the end of it, tying it about his waist with a slipknot. The other end was looped around the horse's nose beneath the bridle.

Dropping to one knee, he steadied the rifle against the trunk of a post oak tree and drew a careful bead on the lone buck. He started to squeeze the trigger but hesitated, hating to. The thought of back-shooting sent a cold chill through him. But he knew the Indians didn't fight by rules.

His sorrel chose that moment to stamp flies. The buck turned, bringing up a big old rifle. Cloud felt the man's eyes touch him, and he fired.

The little squaw screamed as the man pitched forward on the horse's neck and slid to the ground. The horses nearest the shot shied into the rest of the band, creating a shock ripple like a stone dropped in water. Cloud drew his six-gun and fired once from where he was, then moved a little, staying in the brush. He aimed over the heads of the squaws on the far side and fired again. Now the horses were on the move away from Cloud. In panic, the squaws began pulling back. Waving their hands excitedly, they screamed at one another and hurried northward. Cloud fired a third time with the pistol.

He knew they thought they had been found by a group of angry *Tejanos*. He sent another shot plowing into the ground near them, to keep them running.

The horses were running now too, in a southerly direction. Cloud stopped to reload the rifle and put fresh charges in the pistol. That done, he coiled the stake rope and stepped onto the sorrel, the rifle slung over the saddlehorn, the pistol in his hand. He spurred in after the horses, firing occasionally, hollering, keeping them on the run.

Ahead lay the heavy post oak timber. Get these horses scattered in there and it would take hours for the Comanches to round them up.

A few of the horses split off to one side. Cloud elected to let them go, lest he allow the others to slow up and fall back into the hands of the Indians. He pulled up a moment to listen. The gunfire over the hill had stopped. Hearing the noise up here, the warriors probably had pulled back from the house and would be on their way here as fast as they could move. Cloud spurred up, yelling and firing the pistol, pushing his horses into a dead run that the Comanches couldn't stop.

He made it. Looking back as he rode into the brush, he saw that the few horses he had lost were slowing down. But the bulk of the horse herd broke into the heavy timber just moments before the Indians bobbed up over the hill. Under cover, Cloud stepped down again with the heavy rifle in his right hand, the stake rope in his left. Again he looped the free end of the rope around his hips. He dropped his reins and trotted to the end of the rope.

Held close by the reins, a horse might shy at the roar of a rifle and jerk away, leaving its owner afoot. But when the shooter stood off at the end of the stake rope, a horse with any training usually took it with comparative calm. Should the horse begin to run and drag him, Cloud could yank the slipknot and free himself. But that was unlikely, for he had taught the sorrel to stand with the nose hitch.

Dropping to one knee and leveling the rifle barrel over a limb, Cloud aimed at the Indian in the lead. He saw the dust puff in front of the man's horse. The Indian jerked the rein so hard that the horse stumbled and almost went down.

Cloud moved twenty or thirty paces and took a long shot with the pistol. He didn't expect to hit anything at the range, but he could raise dust. The Indians hauled up and milled uncertainly. They plainly thought there were several Texans in the brush. He fired again with the pistol and took advantage of the moment to pour a small measure of gunpowder out of his powder horn into his palm. He followed this with a poured-lead bullet and a thin buckskin scrap for a bullet patch. He rammed it down tight, hardly taking his eyes off the Indians.

For a moment it seemed they were going to come on down his way. He leveled the rifle again, drew a careful bead and squeezed. A horse went down, thrashing.

That was enough. One of the Comanches reached down and pulled the unseated Indian up behind him. Then the whole pack put the heels to their mounts and began to run. They picked up the few horses Cloud had lost, but they were giving up the others.

Cloud loaded the rifle again before he moved, and put fresh charges in the pistol. It looked clear now, but a man never could tell. That was likely to be a mighty mad bunch of Comanches. Losing a battle at that house yonder, losing their stolen horses. Now they would have to sneak back into camp like a bunch of squaws.

Cloud coiled the stake rope as he moved toward his horse. He tucked the coils under his belt, where he could yank them out into use if there came a sudden need for the rope again. He eased into the saddle, still watching warily the dip in the hills where he had seen the Comanches disappear. The only thing a man could know for sure about Comanches was that they were likely to do what he didn't expect. Since he didn't expect them to come back, it was a good idea to watch.

Staying in the brush as long as he could, he angled across toward the cabin he had seen. Good chance the Indians—some of them, anyway—were hanging back to see how many Texans were in that timber. An Indian might not be able to read, but he could blamed well count.

Two hundred yards from the cabin the timber had all been cut away. Besides giving the settler material for his house and fences, this also afforded him a clear view of anyone approaching. It cut down the chance of surprise. But the farmer had left some of the tree trunks where they had fallen, and these had given the Indians some protection from rifle fire. Cloud would bet it wouldn't take the man long to drag these up into a pile.

Moving into the clearing, he could feel the rifles

trained on him, even though he couldn't see them. Two dogs set up an awful racket. "Hello the house!" Cloud called, keeping his hands up in clear sight and making no quick moves. Nobody answered him at first, but he saw a slight movement at a glassless window. Then a man stepped out from inside the corral.

Cloud's sorrel snorted and shied away from a dead Indian the others had been in too big a hurry to pick up. Cloud stopped twenty paces from the corral. The two men stared at each other. Cloud finally opened the conversation with, "Howdy."

The black-bearded man who stood there was in his late forties—fifty, maybe, for streaks of gray glistened in the sun. He had the broad, strong body of a blacksmith, the homespun clothes of the pioneer. He studied Cloud, the rifle still high and ready in his hands. Distrust lingered in his brown eyes. White renegades were not unheard of in this country. Now and again there was talk of such men riding with the Indians, turning against their own kind. For all this man knew, Cloud could be one.

"Howdy," the man finally said, evidently satisfied with Cloud's looks. "You one of the bunch that was doin' the shootin' across the hill yonder?"

"I *was* the bunch."

Incredulous, the man lowered the rifle and stood with his mouth open. "You mean to tell me you're by yourself?"

"It ain't the way I'd rather've had it," Cloud replied, getting down.

The settler grunted an oath and shook his head. "Luck. Just puredee luck. But give me luck and you can keep your money." He stepped forward, hand outstretched. "Name's Lige Moseley. Elijah, you know, like in the Bible." The man began to grin, the tension leaving him.

Cloud grinned too. "Sam Houston Cloud. I don't reckon the Bible had much to do with my name, though."

"You must be a sure-enough born Texican to be named after old General Sam."

"My folks always thought a heap of the general."

"Then I reckon you live up to your name. He always was a scrappy old booger."

Moseley turned toward the cabin. Cloud dropped his reins over a post and moved along beside him, looking over this ruddy-faced, bewhiskered settler. Steady as a rock, Moseley showed no sign he had ever been scared.

"Indian-fightin' don't seem like it bothers you none," Cloud commented.

"Fit 'em ever since I was a button. Started back in Tennessee, fit 'em all the way west. Reckon I'll fight 'em clean to the Pacific Ocean."

"You mean you expect to keep on movin' west?"

"What other direction is there for a man to go? Got to move now and again, git to a fresh, unspoiled country. Man sits in one place too long, he just naturally goes stale. Are you a movin' man?"

"Have been, kind of. Ever I find me a place that suits me just right, though, I'll probably light and stay there."

They reached the cabin. Moseley spoke through the open window. "Everybody make out all right?"

"All right," came a woman's voice. Moseley moved on to the other side, beyond the dog run. A boy of thirteen or fourteen stepped out with a rifle in his hand.

"How about you boys?" Moseley asked. The boy, whittled from the same oakwood as his father, stared with open curiosity at Cloud. He said, "We done fine." He frowned then. "Now that we got 'em on the run, Pa, don't you think we ought to chase after them and give them a real proper chastisement?"

The old man proudly laid his big hand on the boy's shoulder. "I reckon if they want to fight some more, they'll come back."

To Cloud, Moseley said, "Raise 'em right, they don't panic at the sight of a few Indians. I've taught 'em this is a white man's land. The Lord meant it for crops and cattle, not for painted heathens and the buffalo. The Lord'll see to it that the Christian man comes out all right, long as he keeps his faith."

He motioned with his rifle. "Downed a couple of them out yonder. We better make sure they're dead. Don't want 'em sneakin' up here cuttin' our throats while our backs are turned."

Cloud said, "I saw one of them as I rode up. He was dead."

Moseley grunted. "Other one's over thisaway, then. Want to go with me?"

Pistol in his hand, Cloud walked along beside Moseley, carefully watching the grass.

"Tall grass, it give them redskins a little of an

edge on us," Moseley said. "It was hard to see them. I'd've burned all this off, only I been afraid I'd burn the house down too."

They found the Indian lying on his back, his chest still heaving up and down. He had dragged himself partially under the dead foliage of a downed tree, trying to find shade from the blistering sun. His open eyes were glazed. Fresh blood made tiny bubbles on his lips. Cloud could see a gaping hole in the Comanche's belly.

"Done for," he said quietly. It seemed proper to speak quietly in the presence of a dying man, whether he was Comanche or not.

The old frontiersman nodded. "No easy death, either. It'd be God's mercy to go ahead and put him out of his misery."

"I reckon it would," Cloud agreed. "He's yours."

Moseley raised his rifle and held it a moment. There was no sign the Indian was even aware of what was happening. Moseley raked his tongue over dry lips. The old man slowly lowered the rifle.

"I can't do it. How about you takin' care of him for me, Cloud?"

Cloud was silent a moment, his hand cold-sweaty on the grip of the six-shooter. "I can't either. I can shoot at a man when he's shootin' at me. But one like this . . ."

Moseley shook his head. "He can't bother us none, the shape he's in. So I reckon now it's just between him and the Lord. He ortn't to've been here, that's all."

The two turned and started back toward the

cabin. Moseley said, "I'll have to set the boys to diggin'. Job like that can't wait very long in this kind of hot weather."

"There's another one over the hill," Cloud said. "But I expect the Comanches carried him off. They generally do, they get the chance."

The Moseley boys were out poking around now for Indian souvenirs. They picked up the dying Indian's bow and arrows and the bull-hide shield that lay where the man had fallen. They held it up and looked through the bullet hole in it.

Moseley stared at Cloud with unabashed curiosity. "Been tryin' to figure you out. Most fellers that's been through here lately has been yellow bellies headin' west, tryin' to git out of havin' to go fight the Yankees. You don't look like that stripe to me."

"Well," said Cloud, "I'm not on the run."

"What *are* you doin'?"

"I'm huntin' for Captain Barcroft's company of the Texas Mounted Rifles. I'm supposed to join it."

"One of them new Ranger outfits, eh? Out to help save the home folks from the Indians while the rest of the boys go whip them Yanks?"

"Not Rangers, exactly. State troops, more like. But you got the job right—patrol the frontier, keep John throwed back."

"John" was a frontier nickname for the Indian—any Indian.

Moseley grinned. "Well, looks to me like you've done started to work. If that Barcroft asks you for any references, just tell him to come and see me."

The cabin door opened in front of them. A woman

stepped back out of the way. "Go ahead in, Cloud," said Moseley. Moseley's wife stood in the middle of the plain room, staring at him. She was a gaunt, wide-hipped woman in her early forties, shoulders bent by a hard-lived life of work and strain, face dried by sun and wind. But there was a strong set to her jaw, a sturdy determination in her eyes. Moseley might be a strong man, but he would be no stronger than this woman he had married, thought Cloud.

It took this kind of woman to stand beside a man and keep pushing west, to hold ungiving against a harsh daily existence in a raw land, to stand firm in the face of the savage red tide. She wasn't much for looks maybe, but looks didn't count for much in this country.

"How do," she said. "I heered what you told Lige. You really come by yourself, mister?"

"Yes'm." He had his hat in his hands.

"Well, that's really somethin'. Really somethin'."

Cloud heard a knocking and looked around him for the source of it. Mrs. Moseley said, "Like to've forgot about the youngsters. Would you kindly he'p me move this chest, Mister Cloud?"

The three of them scooted a battered oak chest out across the packed-dirt floor. Beneath it appeared a wooden trapdoor. Moseley grasped an iron ring and swung the squeaky door up. "You-all can come out now. One at a time, don't be a-steppin' on one another's fingers."

One by one, children of various sizes began to appear from the depths of the hole. Cloud reached down and helped each one make his way out. The kids were dirt-smeared from rubbing against the sides of the narrow tunnel. Each of them eyed Cloud warily. They weren't used to strangers.

One of the boys, who looked to be about five, complained, "Why don't you let us stay down there, Mama? It's cooler than up here."

"That's just for the needful times. Snoopy redskins see you-all playin' around the escape hole outside, they'd know what it was. It wouldn't do none of you any good then. Git on outside now, and brush that dirt off of you."

Last up was a girl of seventeen or so, carrying a two-year-old boy in her arms. The girl glanced quickly at Cloud with pretty hazel eyes, then handed the baby to her mother. "It was scared," she said. "Had a hard time a-keepin' it from cryin'. I was a-feered them Indians might hear it and find the hole."

Mrs. Moseley took her baby and rocked it in her arms. The harshness in her face faded to a mother's gentleness. "There now," she soothed the child, holding its cheek to hers. "Everything's all right now. Nothin's goin' to hurt our baby, nothin' atall."

With Cloud's help, the girl finished the climb out, watching Cloud timidly. Self-consciously she began to brush the dirt from her clothes.

"Outside, Samantha," Mrs. Moseley said. "We don't want none of that dirt in the house."

Cloud couldn't help wondering how it would ever be noticed, the floor being of dirt anyway. But that was woman's business, and none of his.

Moseley showed Cloud the escape tunnel. "For the kids," he said, "case the Indians ever swamp us. Comes out in a little clump of brush yonder. Gives the kids a chance to git away. We cover it with that big chest, so the Indians'll never even know it's there."

A chill worked up Cloud's back. Anytime Lige Moseley and his wife put the kids down that hole and moved the chest back over the trapdoor, they were committing themselves to fight to the death.

"Just such a tunnel as that one saved my life when I was a button in Tennessee," said Moseley. "Pa and my uncle, they put Mama and us kids into the tunnel and shut the door behind us. Indians killed them and set fire to the cabin, but they never knew about us. It ever comes to that, my kids're goin' to have the same chance."

Cloud looked at the Moseleys and wondered what it all led to. It wasn't just Moseley, for there were others like him, all up and down the western line of the Texas settlements. This was the kind of life Moseley and a great many others had lived since boyhood, treading on the thin edge of disaster. They didn't follow the frontier, they led it. They were the "movin' kind," always on the go, always looking west. Most men who moved west talked of a better life ahead, and Moseley probably talked that way too, when a man sat him down and started him putting his dreams into words. But it wasn't really the better life that motivated Moseley. It was the search itself that gave him his satisfaction.

What would Moseley's kind do when there was

no longer a frontier? Cloud wondered. They were a breed apart, a breed for which civilization had little place once it had benefited from their sacrifice.

Moseley looked out the open window at the distant hill. "We sure gave John a whippin'. He won't forget us."

Cloud frowned. "He won't, and that's a fact. They'll remember this place like a thorn in their foot. You watch, some of the young bucks are liable to be back one day, tryin' to even the score up."

"Let 'em," said Moseley. "We'll be rested and ready."

Mrs. Moseley found out Cloud hadn't eaten anything all day but a little bit of broiled bacon and some dry, hard biscuits he carried in the "wallet" slung across the back of his saddle. She said, "Samantha and me, we'll fix you up somethin'. We're a mite short on flour, but you're goin' to have some fresh bread anyhow. We got coffee if you can drink it without sugar. And there's enough venison to finish fillin' you up."

Cloud protested at their cooking up all the flour when there were so many young ones around, but they did it anyway. Almost every time Cloud glanced in the direction of the girl Samantha, he found her covertly watching him. Her shy gaze would quickly cut away.

He felt sorry for her, a little. She was a nice-looking girl. Chances were her mother had looked like this, once. The girl could be pretty, perhaps, if she lived in a settlement where she could have good clothes and shoes and perhaps some bright ribbon for her blond hair. It was her hair that caught Cloud's eye. Tied at the back of her head, it hung far down below her shoulders. It looked silky and soft, and he found himself wanting to reach out and touch it. If the girl had any vanity, living far out here away from other people, it must have been her hair. Cloud could tell that it had been brushed a lot.

He said to Moseley, "Your kids miss a good many things, not livin' near a settlement."

Moseley shook his head. "They miss learnin' a heap of devilment. Ma, she teaches 'em to read and write, and they get all the schoolin' they need, just a-readin' from the old Bible." Moseley reached up onto a shelf and took down a huge and heavy old family Bible. He set it down on the table in front of Cloud and opened the cover. "Got all the kids' names in here and the dates they was born. Two that died, they're in here, too. We had to bury them where they was—no markers or nothin'. The only thing in God's world to show they was ever born is this here page in the old Bible."

He paused, his mind running back into memory. Then he asked, "Are you an educated man, Cloud?"

Cloud shook his head. "Not much. Never had time for schoolin', or a place to go, either. I can read easy enough; my mother taught me that. And I know figures."

"That's a-plenty. Too much learnin' is just a handicap to a man out in this country—puts him to yearnin' after things he can't have. Just know how to read, and know enough figures so them settlement sharpers can't skin you out of nothin'. No, sir, my kids don't git the chance to fool around the settlements there. Settlements, they got all kinds of wickedness and sin—things a young girl like Samantha don't need to know nothin' about. Someday there'll be a young man come along—man like I was a long time ago—and he'll marry her. She'll learn what else there is that she ought to know."

He frowned then. "You married, Cloud?"

Cloud fidgeted. "No, sir."

"Promised?"

"No, sir."

Moseley eased again, an obvious thought playing behind his brown eyes. "You ought to have you a woman, you know. Woman's a heap of comfort to a man—helps take the load off of his back."

"Someday, maybe, when I'm settled down. A man's got no business marryin' as long as he's ridin' around over the country chasin' Indians. He needs to be able to provide her a home."

"A town woman, sure. But you take a girl that's been raised up away from the settlements—one that ain't a-goin' to throw a screamin' fit at the sight of a feather—one that don't mind pushin' a plow and choppin' the wood when her man's got to be gone—she'd be a good wife for a man like you, Cloud. A good woman's the makin' of a man."

He paused, watching Cloud for any sign that the message was taking hold. "You know, my girl Samantha's that kind."

"Yep, I expect she is," Cloud said nervously, wishing the subject would change.

Moseley's oldest son, Luke, pushed through the door, rifle in his hand. Cloud noticed that most of the kids had biblical names. "Riders comin', Pa."

Moseley sat up straight, looking at his own rifle in the corner. "Indians?"

"No, sir, whites. Rangers or Minute Men or some such, I think."

Cloud and Moseley walked out the door and stood waiting. There were twenty or twenty-five men in the bunch. They rode tired horses, and the riders' shoulders sagged with weariness. But most of them held rifles or shotguns balanced across their saddles, ready for instant action.

Riding out in front was a dark-skinned man Cloud took to be a Mexican. Almost even with him came a tall, lean, somber-looking rider who quickly caught Cloud's eye. Instinctively he knew this was the leader. His bearing showed it without any questions asked. Cloud remembered what the colonel had told him when he had handed him his orders.

"Aaron Barcroft is the captain. You'll know him when you see him, for there's not another that looks quite like him. He's a tall, nervous whip of a man, with black eyes that bore through you like an auger. You'll think he's the grimmest man you ever saw, and he probably is; he's had some grim things happen to him. He'll drive you till you hate him, but you'll always respect him, for he drives himself harder than any man."

Captain Barcroft rode up to within four or five

paces and stopped. He took one long, unhurried glance about the place and seemed to miss nothing.

"I see you've had trouble," he said. "Anybody hurt?"

Moseley said, "Nobody but Indians."

Barcroft said, "We've trailed that band since yesterday. They had a sizeable bunch of stolen horses with them. Now we find those horses—most of them, anyway—scattered out in that brush. What happened?"

Moseley explained in colorful detail what Cloud had done, adding a little fiction for good measure.

Barcroft's black eyes dwelt heavily on Cloud. Unaccountably, there was annoyance in them. "Who are you?" Barcroft demanded.

Cloud told him. He handed Barcroft the letter the colonel had given him. "I been huntin' you, Captain. I'm supposed to join your company."

Barcroft didn't take time to read the letter. He shoved it in his pocket. His voice had a sting to it. "I'm not sure why you're here, Cloud. From what you did, I gather you might be one of those who joins the Rifles looking for glory and adventure. Well, you'll get little glory here. Or maybe you've come to the frontier to get out of going against the Yankees. If you have, you'll find a steel knife and a stone arrowhead can kill you just as dead as a Yankee cannonball. Might even be slower and more painful.

"I'll warn you right now, this is no place for the lame or the lazy. If you go with this outfit, you'll ride sometimes till you're so weary you can't see. Then you'll get off and fight and climb back up to ride some more. You'll go on short rations and tighten your belt and suck on a pebble because you had no water. You won't enjoy it. No one does."

Angering, Cloud said, "I've fought Indians before, and I ain't huntin' no glory! What I did here today I did because it looked like the only thing."

Barcroft said gruffly, "It might have been better if you hadn't. Those Indians didn't know how close we were. If they'd stayed here a while longer, we would have caught up with them. We could have wiped them out. As it was, you ran them off. They'll be hard to catch now."

Lige Moseley's face flushed red. He shoved into the exchange. "Sure, you might've caught them. But it might've been a shade late for me and my family. Besides, between us we dropped three of them, and Cloud scattered their horses. What the hell else you want?"

Barcroft eyed him coldly. "I didn't ask you, but now that you've spoken out, I'll tell you something. You're a fool even to be here. You're miles from any kind of help. Your very presence is a temptation to any stray band of braves that passes through."

"It's a free country. I can settle where I want to."

With bitterness Barcroft said, "And endanger that family of yours? No man's got a right to do that. You load up and move back to where it's safer."

Moseley said, "I been stopped a few times, Captain, but I ain't never been pushed back. I don't start now. Not for the Comanches and not for you!"

Moseley's family had stepped out and stood lined up behind him now. Barcroft looked at them. Particularly he looked at Mrs. Moseley and at the little girls. Cloud thought he could see pain in the captain's eyes.

Barcroft shrugged. "I can't force you, Moseley. I would, if I had the right. If you don't move back, you're a fool. Too many men have gone off to war. Too many families have pulled back to safer ground. Don't you know those who stay will be a better target than they've ever been before? You're staying because of pride, and pride can be a good thing in its place. But look at your womenfolks, your kids, and ask yourself which you value the most—your pride or their lives."

Moseley said, "You got a family, Captain?"

Barcroft was slow in answering. His voice dropped a little. "No . . . no family."

"Then how can you tell me what's best for mine?"

Barcroft said, "I know, Moseley. Believe me, I know too well."

He pulled his horse back. "Come on, Cloud, if you're joining up with us. We'll catch fresh horses out of that timber and go on after the Indians."

Cloud said, "Right, sir." He started to salute, but he didn't know for sure how proper it would be. He'd never been in a military outfit before. He let the salute drop, and Barcroft didn't seem to notice.

Cloud paused a moment to shake Moseley's hand. "Take care of yourself, Lige. And maybe you ought to think over what the captain said. Sure, he's an educated feller, but it sounds to me like he makes sense."

"I ain't movin'," Moseley spoke calmly. "Anytime you're ridin' through, you'll find us here. Be sure you stop; we'll be tickled to see you." He glanced back at his daughter. "And don't forget what I told you about a man needin' a good woman."

"I won't forget," Cloud promised. He swung into his saddle and found Captain Barcroft already leading out. Cloud fell in at the rear of the company and looked back once, waving his hand.

The girl Samantha waved back.

2

Waving his hand in a circular motion, Captain Barcroft called to his men, "Fan out and catch fresh horses. Leave the ones you have. We'll round them all up when we come back."

He moved hurriedly, yet without excitement.

It didn't take long. Some of the men formed loops in their stake ropes and cast them over horses' heads. Others, who couldn't rope, rode up beside loose horses and dropped the end of the rope over an animal's neck, then reached down and caught the rope end from beneath and drew it up, making a loop. Most of the men took some care in their selection of remounts. A few had no real idea what to look for.

Watching a few like these, Cloud thought he could understand the captain's bitterness over some of the new men. These were not frontiersmen. Men like these were the shirkers, here to keep out of war.

Cloud left his sorrel and caught a good-looking brown that had strong legs and a deep chest and looked as if it could hold out in a long run. He knew the brand on its hip. It belonged to a ranch far to the south and east. Quite a circle these Comanches had made.

In moments the men were mounted. Barcroft signaled to the Mexican, who struck out in the lead, following the trail of the Comanches.

Cloud looked around him as he rode, appraising these other members of the Texas Mounted Rifles. There was no uniform. Every man dressed as suited him—or more likely, as he could afford. Money was scarce in Texas, and always had been. Some wore homespun, some wore store cloth. A few wore buckskin. Some had high-topped, flat-heeled boots, and several wore shoes.

Cloud had seen a copy of the orders setting up a regiment of the Rifles. It required that each man should have a Colt six-shooter, if possible, plus a good double-barreled shotgun or short rifle "if convenient." He was supposed to have a half-gallon tin canteen, covered with cloth, and a good heavy blanket to sleep on.

Every man Cloud saw had a pistol on his hip. And as per orders, each carried either a shotgun or rifle across his saddle. The rifle was good for distance, but a shotgun was unbeatable in close combat. The state didn't furnish the armament. In this outfit a man brought his own weapons or didn't join.

A grinning young man with rust-red hair edged over next to Cloud and stuck out his hand. "Guffey's my name. Quade Guffey."

Cloud took his hand. "Sam Houston Cloud."

Quade made no remark about the name. It was not unusual for boys in that day to be named after

General Sam. "Captain there, he gave you a pretty stiff initiation speech, but don't let it worry you. You get used to him after a while."

"You do?"

"Yep, and then you hate him even worse."

The riders passed the horse Cloud had dropped out from under one of the Comanches. Minutes later they went by the spot from which he had stampeded the herd. Cloud rode off to one side to look. He found a spot of blood where the buck had fallen, but the body was gone.

One less hole for Lige's boys to dig.

The men settled into a long trot, occasionally pushing the horses into an easy lope for a way, then pulling them down again. The Indians had a long start. But they had been pushing their horses hard when they left. The mounts would inevitably tire. By conserving their own horses all they could, the Rifles had a better chance of catching up.

Cloud soon found himself riding near the lead. It was not his way to bring up the rear. Barcroft glanced at him, appraising Cloud and his equipment. But the captain had nothing to say. He glanced toward the sun every so often, measuring the rate of its descent. Cloud knew what the man was thinking. They'd better catch those Indians before dark. Give the Comanche horses a few hours of rest and they would be as fresh again as the ones the Texans rode.

The tracks freshened. The Indians were slowing down. The Rifles came upon a horse, its throat cut. Exhausted, and killed by the Comanches so the white men couldn't get any use from him.

A little later the Mexican up front signaled and pointed to the ground. Riding up, Cloud saw the stiffening body of the Indian he had shot. It lay in the buffalo grass, abandoned by tiring Comanches who could no longer carry it.

"Crowding them," Barcroft said matter-of-factly to those near enough to hear him. "They're getting desperate when they leave their dead."

He raised his hand and gave the signal for a speedup. Then he spurred into an easy lope and overtook the Mexican scout before the scout knew of the order.

To the west, the sun was rapidly sinking into a latticework of dry summer clouds, pretty to look at but devoid of rain. The pursuit had broken out of the brushy country and onto the open grassland that rolled for mile upon unbroken mile, toward the faraway escarpment of the Llano Estacado—the Staked Plain. Here and there a scattering of mesquites stood in low areas where the rainwater tended to run together, and the shadows of these trees were lengthening, reaching across the grass prairie like grasping fingers.

Ahead lay a creek, lined with brush. Barcroft raised his hand for a slowdown while the scout moved out to look it over. He was almost to the scrubby oaks when a rifle exploded. The ball missed the scout and sang by the men behind him. The Mexican spurred his horse sharply to the left, hitting the brush a hundred yards upstream from the source of the shot. Cloud could hear pistol fire.

Barcroft veered the command sharply to one side, upstream from the scout. When he hit the brush, he reined downstream and spurred out. Thus the Texans outflanked the Indian rear guard. Ahead of him Cloud saw the Mexican scout on one knee, aiming a six-shooter. He fired once, then the Rifles swept by him, yelping, and the scout almost lost his horse in the excitement.

Four warriors had been left in the creekbed to slow the pursuit. Two of them fired rifles, then threw the rifles down and began to run. Two others stood their ground, loosing arrows as quickly as they could pull them from deer-hide quivers and draw the bows. Cloud heard a horse go down, the rider cursing as he slid on his belly through the grass.

The Indian stand was hopeless. The troops swept over the warriors like a storm wave breaking over a lakeshore. Within the span of thirty seconds, all four Comanches lay dead. A couple of young recruits were gathering up bows and arrows as souvenirs. More practical, a pair of older men recovered the Indians' two rifles and relieved the bodies of shot and powder.

Barcroft turned in the saddle and looked back upstream. Here came the Mexican scout. He was flanked by two other riders who had held back from the battle and now rode in white-faced and shaken.

Barcroft gave his first attention to the Mexican. "Are you all right, Miguel?" The Mexican nodded. Then Barcroft faced the other two. They seemed to shrink, even before the captain spoke to them.

"What were you doing back there? Why didn't you stay up with me?"

One of the men stammered. "W-w-we thought we'd better help Miguel."

"He didn't need any help. You were trying to stay back out of the fight!" Face cloudy, Barcroft shook his fist at the two. "There's one thing in this world I hate worse than a Comanche, and that's a coward. Next time we're engaged, I'm going to see to it that you two are right up in front, or I'll shoot you myself! Is that clear?"

The two only nodded and looked at the ground.

Barcroft turned away from them. "Anybody hit?" he queried. One man had a flesh wound; nothing serious. A couple of men were out catching an Indian mount for the man whose horse had gone down. The Mexican scout was on the ground with a Bowie knife, grimly scalping the dead warriors. He held up a bloody scalp and shook it. It jingled.

"Looky there, Captain," one of the other men said, "got little bells tied in it. Ain't that the funniest thing you ever seen?"

Cloud didn't see much funny in it and turned away.

"Come on," Barcroft said impatiently, "we've lost time enough."

As scout, Miguel Soto was supposed to take the lead, but Barcroft was crowding him now in his restless haste, staying close behind him. Cloud rode almost abreast of the captain. He could see excitement building in Barcroft's face now—an eager anticipation.

Moments before sundown they spotted the Indians, strung out in a long, tired line. There were more than Cloud had supposed when he had first looked down at Moseley's, and he was doubly glad he hadn't fired into them instead of merely running off the horses. The Indians saw the pursuit and began whipping up their horses. At the distance Cloud knew most of the stragglers were squaws. Some of the bucks began dropping back to protect them, but some were trying to get on out ahead, even at the expense of the squaws.

Most Comanches took pains to protect their women and children, but once Cloud had seen a warrior pull a squaw down off a horse and take it for his own getaway. They could be as cold-blooded about it as some white men.

Ahead lay a stretch of oak timber.

"Spur out, men," Barcroft shouted. "If they make that brush, and dark coming on, we'll lose them."

He used his leather quirt. The riders with the best horses began pulling forward in a ragged line. Those on poorer mounts, and those who didn't really want to be in the thick of it, began falling back. Barcroft looked behind him, searching out the men who had held back in the last skirmish. "You two—Holmes, Ulbrich—get yourselves up here and fight! Spur up, I tell you, or I'll have you shot!"

Somehow the two got extra speed out of their horses.

Their mounts fresher, the Rifles rapidly closed the distance between themselves and the Indians. A few of the newer men wasted a long shot or two that picked up dust far from the Comanches.

Barcroft shouted, "Hold your fire till you can hit something." He used the quirt some more.

One of the warriors stopped his horse suddenly, reined about and raised a rifle. It spat fire. The man named Ulbrich screamed and tumbled from the saddle. Barcroft didn't even look back. Pistol in his hand, he bore down on the Indian and pulled the trigger. The Indian fell. Galloping by, other men fired at the Comanche, making sure he was dead.

From here on it was an easy butchery until the lead Indians got into the brush and scattered like quail. One fell, then another and another. Spurring past, Cloud looked down at one broken body and realized it was a squaw. Regret gripped him, but he knew there was no sense in worrying about it. In a running fight, it was sometimes hard to tell a squaw from a buck.

As Moseley had said, *she just ortn't to've been there.*

The sun was gone, the dusk quickly deepening. The troops were far into the brush, and firing had stopped. The Indians had vanished. His horse sweat-lathered and breathing hard, Barcroft called out, "Assemble! Pass the word, assemble!"

Cloud reined in beside the captain and took the opportunity to reload his six-shooter. His breath was short from the hard run, and his heart was thumping from the excitement. He looked at the captain and saw the man's chest heaving. Barcroft was almost out of breath, yet there was exultation in his face. Pleasure showed in his black eyes as he looked down upon the body of a Comanche warrior.

The Mexican scout dismounted and said, "With your permission, *Capitán*?" He had his knife out and ready.

Barcroft said, "Help yourself."

Something cold passed through Cloud as he watched. Barcroft caught the look. "Bother you, Cloud?"

"Can't say as I like it."

"Indians scalp their victims, or don't you know?"

"They're savages. We're white men."

"We're fighting a savage foe, Cloud. If we're to survive, we need to become as savage as he is."

"Can't say as I accept that, Captain."

Firmly Barcroft said, "*I* accept it, and I'm the captain here."

Cloud glanced sharply at him but said nothing more.

The men gathered and took count of each other, anxious to know if friends had made it through all right. Only one man was lost—Ulbrich. He wasn't much of a loss, Cloud heard Quade Guffey remark. It had been a one-sided fight. Barcroft eyed his men with satisfaction. He turned to the scout Miguel. "How many would you say got away?"

Miguel Soto shrugged. "Ten, maybe. Mostly squaws. The bucks, they try to fight and we pretty much kill."

"Do you think the survivors are heading for an encampment, a rendezvous of some kind ahead?"

"*Quién sabe, mi capitán?*" Soto shrugged again. "Somewhere up yonder, more Indians come together, I think. Most of the time these bands they split up to make the raids. Later they meet somewhere in this open country, where the white man don' go. The little bands they make one pretty good-sized band. They sing and dance and celebrate. Then they all go home together."

"And where is home?"

"Far. Very far, yonder," he said, pointing northward, and a little west. "Up there, no white man ever go."

Barcroft stood a moment chewing his lip, looking northward into the dusk, a wish in his black eyes. "Someday," he murmured. "Someday . . ."

He finally turned back to his men. "We'll move out of this brush while we can still see. First light of day, we'll start again, following tracks. If there's an encampment up yonder, and it's not too big for us to handle, we'll kill us some more Indians."

Soto frowned. "*Mi capitán*, maybeso it *is* too big. Then what we do?"

Barcroft said evenly, "You men will do what I tell you. And I'll do whatever looks best at the time."

The company stopped at the edge of the brush to build fires and make coffee. Some of the men had dried beef to eat, and some broiled bacon on sticks. After supper they would move on, camping for the night in another spot well away from the glow of dying embers, the possible scrutiny of Comanche eyes.

Captain Barcroft never really relaxed. While the other men prepared their supper, he strode restlessly among them, looking them over, searching for no-one-knew-what. Finally a man named Elkin motioned to him, and Barcroft went to Elkin's fire, where Elkin had prepared a little supper for the two of them.

Cloud took Elkin to be Barcroft's second-in-command, although nothing had been said about it. Elkin was a quiet, blocky man well into his forties, a man who went about his business with a quiet competence. Here was a man, Cloud thought, who knew what he was doing and didn't seem to feel he had to prove it to anybody. Elkin had stayed right up front in the running skirmish. A time or two when Barcroft was at some distance, Cloud had seen Elkin give signal commands to some of the other troopers, and they had taken them.

Barcroft quickly ate his beef and drank his black coffee, as if eating was a chore to be disposed of as hurriedly as possible. That done, he stretched his long legs out in the curing grass and took from his pocket the letter Cloud had given him. He held it down close to Elkin's small mesquite-wood fire and read it in the flickering flame light. With a nod of his head he motioned Cloud to come to him and sit down.

"Letter says you know this country, Cloud."

Cloud shook his head. "Not very well, but I've been over part of it. Had me some cows in the country a little east of here. Comanches ran most of them off, and I rode over a lot of this area here huntin' for 'em."

"Find them?"

"No, sir. About all I found was experience. It just about finished me in the cow business."

Barcroft's chin pointed to the letter. "The colonel says here you can track, read signs and know something about Indians. He thinks you'd make a scout if the company needed you for that."

Cloud said, "I didn't read the letter."

"Miguel could use some help, all right. We had another scout but lost him in an ambush. Indian rose up out of the tall grass and put an arrow so deep into the scout's belly that the point came out of his back. Do you want the job?"

Don't sound like there's much of a future to it, Cloud thought. But this day in time a man didn't get a lot of choice. "You're the captain."

Barcroft had a stern gaze that made a man fidgety, made him want to get out from under it. "You've worried me a little, Cloud. I watched you in action today, and you made a good account of yourself. You didn't strike me as a glory hunter, or as a shirker either. It doesn't take long to tell the counterfeits. I gathered you're not here because you're afraid to fight the Yankees. Then you must be here because you don't *want* to fight them. I'd like to know your politics, mister. Are you a damned Unionist?"

Uncomfortable, Cloud studied a moment before he tried to answer. "I'm a Texican, Captain. I was born here in '36, durin' the Runaway Scrape. My ma, she had to drop out of a bunch of refugees on account of me, and I was born just a few miles ahead of old Santa Anna and his Mexican troops. My folks always thought of themselves as Americans, and they were tickled to death when Texas was annexed. That's the way I was brought up.

"Sure, I'm a Southerner, and I think the Yankees have done us a heap of wrong. I think we got some scores to settle with them. But war ain't no proper way to go about it. You boil it down, Captain, they're white folks same as us. They're Americans, and so are we—whatever we might be callin' ourselves right now. I got to agree with old General Sam Houston, that secession was one mighty bad mistake. There must've been a better way out than goin' to war against our own people.

"If there's fightin' to be done, I won't shirk my share of it. But I'll do mine here, at the edge of the settlements, where there's an enemy I can recognize as one."

Cloud could see anger in the captain's face. "A lot of people in Texas seem to feel the way you do. Some have even slipped off and joined the Union Army."

Cloud shook his head. "That'd be even worse. Far as I'm concerned, this war is a mistake for both sides. I don't want none of it, either way."

Barcroft said, "If the yellow-leg Yankee cavalry had ever done to you what it did to me, you'd think differently. I'd be up yonder fighting them now, except that they need somebody to do this, and I hate Comanches even more than Yankees."

He stood up, and Cloud followed suit. Gravely Barcroft said: "Normally, a man's entitled to think as he pleases, Cloud. But this is wartime, and in wartime a man has to forgo a lot of rights. There are several in this command who have the same Unionist ideas you do. If you and the others weren't so badly needed here, you'd probably be hanged. So just remember this: you're in the Confederacy, like it or not. Keep your ideas to yourself and we'll get along. But I'll allow no traitorous talk in this command!"

He turned away and said to Elkin, "Let's move!"

By the time first sunlight spilled out across the dry prairie, the company had eaten its meager breakfast and was a-horseback again. Barcroft motioned to Cloud and pointed forward.

"You go up with Miguel and help him scout."

Cloud nodded and spurred his horse into a lope, overtaking the Mexican well forward of the command. Miguel Soto looked him over as he rode up. "The man who steals horses so good," Soto said, a trace of a smile about him. The Mexican was short and wiry and all muscle. He was not an old man, but Cloud could not make even a wild guess at his age. He rather thought Soto was young, although his face was weathered. A long scar down one cheek helped give him the appearance of age.

Cloud had watched the Mexican with some wonder last night. The other Texans had treated Soto as one of themselves. There had been no sign of resentment or dislike. Most Texans of that day cared little for Mexicans, for they had been enemies in two wars and countless border skirmishes, and even a Texas-born Mexican was likely to be regarded as an alien. That the group here so readily accepted Soto indicated he had already proved himself.

"Maybeso the *capitán*, he don't like you," Soto commented with a grin. "Maybeso he send you up here to get kill, eh?"

Cloud saw little to grin about, but he tried it anyway. "Don't look to me like you're in any place to smile. You're up here too."

Soto shrugged. "Long time now the Comanche, he has try to kill Miguel. But I have live with the Comanche. I know how he thinks, what he's gonna do. This Mexican, he gonna die in bed, a long time from now."

The sun was still low in the east, and a cool morning breeze searched across the rolling prairie as if seeking a place of refuge from the coming heat. Cloud and Soto passed the spot where they had fixed supper the night before, the burned-out campfires only spots of gray ash amid the carpet of short grass. They cut the trail left by themselves and by the Indians in yesterday's running fight. Here and there lay a stiffened horse, a dead Indian. Cloud shuddered. This was something a man never got used to.

Soto stepped down to recover a bow and a quiver of arrows.

"You don't look to me like a souvenir hunter," Cloud remarked.

Soto shook his head. "I already got my Comanche souvenir," he said, pointing to the long scar on his face. "But maybeso we come to a place where we got to kill quiet, and don' want no gun. The arrow, she don't make much noise."

Suddenly Cloud reined up and pointed. "Miguel, look yonder."

An Indian woman was dragging herself along in the grass, trying to crawl away from them. A hundred feet behind her lay a blanket and a blood-splotched patch of ground where she had fallen in the skirmish.

"Must've laid there all night," Cloud said.

They rode up to her carefully. Cloud held his pistol ready. It wasn't likely the squaw would have a gun, but it was foolish to take chances. Miguel unstrapped his canteen and stepped down. He spoke to the woman in the Comanche tongue. She stopped crawling and turned over on her side. Hatred shone through the pain in her dark eyes.

Cloud put the pistol away and swung to the ground. The woman was young. It might have been the squaw who was sitting beside the buck he had shot yesterday, at the horse herd.

Miguel held his canteen out to her. She refused it at first. Miguel took the lid off and let a little of the water trickle out into the grass. The woman's reserve broke. She clutched at the canteen. Talking quietly to her, Miguel held it for her while she drank thirstily.

Cloud dropped to one knee and looked at the shoulder wound that had brought her down. He gritted his teeth and turned away.

Afraid she was drinking too rapidly, Miguel withheld the canteen a moment. She begged for it, and he let her drink again. Fever, Cloud thought. She's all dried out.

The rest of the company caught up to them, Captain Barcroft in the lead. He asked no foolish questions. He stared at the woman without either hatred or pity.

Cloud said, "Looks like this complicates things,

Captain. Was we just to leave her here like this, she'd die."

The captain said, "She's obviously in no condition to go anywhere, either afoot or on horseback. We couldn't take her with us."

"We could leave a man to take care of her till we come back."

"Leave a man out here alone, with other Indians possibly about? Besides, Cloud, we can't spare anyone—not even one man. We don't know what we'll run into up yonder."

Cloud nodded. "Sir, this is a woman. I don't see any other way out."

Evenly Barcroft said, "There's a way out, Cloud. A very simple way."

Cloud froze in shocked disbelief as Barcroft drew his pistol and leveled it at the woman. He saw terror in the squaw's brown eyes, and he shouted, "Don't!"

The pistol flashed and the woman fell back. Cloud dropped to one knee beside her. But he knew at a glance that she was dead. Trembling in rage, he slowly pushed to his feet and turned to face the captain. He felt a strong impulse to drag the man out of the saddle, but he knew that could get him shot. He struggled for words, and they wouldn't come.

Barcroft said, "Don't say anything that'll get you in trouble, Cloud. When you think about it a little, you'll know it was the best way out for her and for us. Now go on, you and Miguel. Take up your positions again."

Cloud glared at him through a red haze, his fists doubled.

"Cloud!" Barcroft spoke again, a sharpness in his voice this time. "Don't ask for trouble. You heard my order."

Miguel tugged at Cloud's sleeve. "You better do what he says, my friend."

Cloud lingered a moment more, his eyes still burning on the captain. But the quick blaze of anger died down in him, leaving a smoldering coal that would turn into hatred. He pivoted on one heel and swung into the saddle. He spurred out in a lope.

3

As the sun climbed, the summer heat bore down unmercifully. Cloud sweated hard, his shirt sticking to his back. The wind itself turned warm, but now and again it felt pleasant as it made the wet shirt cool against his skin. In this country there was nearly always a little wind through the daytime. Without it, the sun would be almost unbearable.

The surviving Indians had ridden far into the night. Finally, they had paused to rest a little while, starting again by daylight. At first they had made no effort to conceal their tracks. Now their panic was subsiding. Judgment was getting the upper hand. They were covering their trail.

Cloud was a good tracker. As a boy he had developed the art from trailing lost cattle and horses, and he had learned to watch for Indian signs. But now and again he would lose the Comanches' trail. Miguel Soto always found something to set the pair of scouts right again.

"You follow them like another Indian," Cloud observed in admiration.

"I *was* an Indian. The Comanches, they make me one."

"How's that?"

"Long time ago, when I was a boy in Chihuahua, the Comanches come. I am eight, maybeso ten years old. They kill my mother and father and my big brothers, strike them down with their lances and their arrows. With these two eyes, I see them take the scalps. The two sisters I have, the young warriors carry them away. My baby brother and me, some others take us along. The baby, he cry all the time, so they smash his head on a rock. Me, I am strong and healthy, and they keep me to work.

"It is a hard life, I tell you. They beat me all the time. Even now, I have on my back the many scars. But I don' cry. Sometimes when they beat me I fight, and they like that. All the time I work hard, so they don' kill me, and I tell myself someday I get my chance. Someday I will get even with them for what they do to me, to all my people.

"Finally they decide I make pretty good Comanche myself, and they don' beat me no more. They raise me like Comanche boy, teach me what they teach all Comanche boys. They think I forget all the bad things, but I don' forget. I all the time remember, and I tell myself—wait, one day the time will come.

"Sure enough, when I get to the age, we go on big raid against the *Tejanos*. This is my Chance. The old warrior who always beat me the most, he is there. I get him alone, and I cut his throat." Soto made the sign with his finger, and grinned with a grim satisfaction as he did so. "I laugh at him and I spit on him while he is lie there, lookin' up at me and dyin'. Then I take coup. I still have the scalp."

He reached back into his saddlebag and drew forth a piece of rolled-up oilskin. He unrolled it and showed Cloud a scalp, tanned to keep. "This," said Miguel, "I keep with me always, so I don' never forget. Here, feel of it. Good piece of work, eh?"

Face twisting, Cloud shook his head. "I'll take your word for it."

Miguel rolled the scalp back into the oilskin. "Sometimes when I go into battle against the Comanche, I think of some of the boys who were good to me, and I begin to feel sorry. Then I look at this scalp and remember all the bad things, and I don't feel sorry no more. I got plenty to hate for."

He frowned then, looking back over his shoulder at Barcroft's company, far behind them. "My friend, there is much you don' know about the *capitán*. You think he is a bad man, and maybeso he is, a little bit. But it is not because he wants to be. He is like me—he has much to hate for. *Quién sabe?* Maybeso one day you understand."

Cloud said sharply, "Some things, there ain't no understandin'."

All that day they rode without once sighting an Indian. But they came across Indian signs, tracks headed north. There were the hoofprints of many horses, even the trail of travois. No longer was there any apparent effort by the Comanches to hide their tracks. This was farther than *Tejano* pursuit usually came. Ahead, for the Indians, lay unviolated sanctuary.

Only once all day did the company come across a waterhole. Barcroft and Elkin saw to it that every canteen was filled before the horses were allowed to move in and water.

"Every man should drink up good while he's here," Barcroft said, wiping the sweat from his face. "Conserve that canteen water as long as you can. No telling how long before we find more."

Grudgingly, Cloud admitted to himself that the captain's order was a wise one. Men had ridden out horseback on searches into the open Indian country, only to drag back to the settlements on hands and knees, tongues swollen, lips parched, begging for water.

Through the heat of the afternoon they rode on, but slowly now, for Barcroft was trying to save the horses. These mounts would have to get them to wherever they were going and carry them home again. From here on, there was likely to be no chance for a change.

Late in the day they came upon a dry creekbed lined by a scrubby growth of brush and dying grass. Cloud dismounted and poked around, shoving his ramrod deep into the bed and drawing it out. He felt the rod and found mud clinging to the end of it. "Been water here," he said. "I expect if we was to dig holes in it, we could water the horses by mornin' from what seeps in."

Spotting a cottontail rabbit, the Mexican took down the bow he had picked up earlier. The captain had given orders against gunfire. With the first arrow, Soto pinned the rabbit to the ground. Cloud whistled. "They sure taught you good."

"Supper," said Soto, holding up the rabbit. "We share it, you and me."

The company scattered up and down the dry creekbed, building tiny fires behind the banks to hide them from searching eyes. Some of the men already were complaining that they were out of meat, that it was time to turn back. Those who still had food left shared it with those whose supplies had run out.

Cloud was grateful for the rabbit, though he was still a little hungry when he finished his half of it. Cottontails didn't grow very big.

The rusty-haired young man named Quade Guffey had sat down beside Cloud to chew on a piece of cold jerky. He enviously eyed the rabbit, cooking over a small bank of coals, but he refused Cloud's offer to split his share with him.

"Ain't hardly enough there for *you*," Guffey said. "Man in this outfit gets used to the lank days anyhow. Trouble with this Indian-huntin' ain't so much the danger you run into once in a while. It's the meals you miss and all the times you go thirsty because the waterhole you counted on was dried up, or it wasn't where you thought it was after all. Feller learns after a while to do like the Indian does—stuff your gut when you can get it, and don't go complainin' when you can't."

Guffey had such a happy-go-lucky attitude about

it all that Cloud was curious. "How'd you come to join this outfit, Guffey?"

"Been wonderin' myself." He grinned. "The call went out, and I asked myself what the hell. Spent my whole life workin' for the other feller anyhow, ridin' the other man's horse, plowin' the other man's field. Figured here was a chance to get a little fresh air, be where the noise was bein' made, maybe shoot me an Indian. And git paid for it too."

The grin faded. "There was somethin' else. I knew that pretty soon they'd come callin' for me to go fight them Yankees. I had the same feelin's on that score that you did." To Cloud's questioning glance, Guffey explained, "I heard what you told the captain last night. I was curious about you, so I plopped myself down where I could listen. I don't want to shoot no Yankees. Far as I'm concerned, this is a rich man's war, only they want the poor man to do all the fightin'. My folks never had nothin'. I never owned a slave and never will, so it ain't no skin off my nose if Abe Lincoln wants to take the slaves away. Might even make a poor white man's wages better. But these rich plantation folks, they want us to fight and keep their slaves for them. Way I see it, if they want to fight, let 'em do it theirselves."

Cloud looked about to see if the captain was within earshot. He wasn't. "Guffey, there's a sight more to it than just slaves."

"Not as far as I'm concerned there ain't. They make a heap of fine talk about other things I don't even understand, but all I see in it is slaves."

That's the way it is these days, Cloud thought. *Most people look at it head-on and make up their minds one way or the other. Secession or union. Slave or free. White or black, and no compromise between.* He wished it could be that simple for him. He had pondered over it a long time before he had made his choice. Even after he chose, he continued to worry about it, wondering if he was right. He still wondered, sometimes.

Without knowing why, he wanted to argue with Guffy now, and he realized his argument would be in favor of the Confederacy.

Who can say what's right and wrong, he asked himself, *when there's so much argument to make for either side?*

Morning, and restlessness stirred the company. The water that had seeped into the holes dug in the creekbed was so muddy the men couldn't drink it, and most of the horses wouldn't either. Some of the canteens were nearly empty, and many men were out of food. A few of the horses picked up in the brush at Moseley's had not proved out.

The company had discipline enough that the men would take orders from Barcroft. But it was not so strongly disciplined that they wouldn't give him their advice. These were free men. A majority had lived on the frontier, or not far back from it. They thought for themselves and said what they thought. Barcroft listened patiently enough to their complaints, but gave no sign that he was convinced. He walked up to Miguel Soto.

"What do you think, Miguel? Are we close to an Indian camp?"

Miguel frowned. "Who can say? By the signs, I think maybeso."

"How big would you say it might be?"

"That, *mi capitán*, I cannot say at all. The sign say pretty soon now the Indians come together. Maybe many, maybe not so very many. We see when we see."

That didn't satisfy the captain, but it was all he could get. He glanced a moment at Cloud as if expecting Cloud to offer advice too. All he got from Cloud was a half-hostile stare. Barcroft turned back to his graying lieutenant, Elkin.

"We've gone this far. It's wasted unless we go a little farther."

"What will we gain, Captain?"

"We can kill some more Indians."

Elkin said, "There may not be any water ahead, and there's little chance of food. It'll be a long, dry, hungry trip back out."

Barcroft replied, "Any man who thinks this is too hard on him can ask to join the Confederate Army instead. Maybe he'll like Virginia better."

He gave the signal for mounting up, then motioned for Cloud and Soto to ride out first.

This was a hotter day than yesterday. Even early, the sun began to blister. Cloud nursed his half canteen of water carefully, afraid it might have to last a long time. He tipped it up, taking just enough water to wet his lips and tongue. Later he put a pebble in his mouth and kept it there. It helped, some.

Looking behind him at the company, he could see it straggling out.

"Captain's goin' to lose half the command if he don't make 'em close it up," he said to Soto. "Better still, he ought to call a halt."

"He is a stubborn man."

"Stubbornness won't take the place of food and water and fresh horses."

Earnestly, Soto said, "Stubbornness takes the place of many things."

Cloud's eyebrows lifted. "Every time I say somethin' about him, you take up for him. You really believe in the captain, don't you?"

"Up to now, the *capitán* he never disappoint me. Until he disappoint me, I believe in him."

The noon stop was made on schedule, but it was more for rest than anything else. Little food was left among the Rifles. Those who still had it shared it among the others. The captain gave all of his own food away, not eating anything. He roamed around looking at his men, surveying their horses. His dark eyes were restless, his face sad beneath a covering of dust, a growth of black beard.

Studying Barcroft, Cloud sensed a driving urgency about the man. There was a devil in him someplace, a black torment that would not leave him be.

Elkin finished the little he had to eat, then stepped up beside Barcroft. "I'm afraid the company's about finished, Captain." He said it with the gentle manner of an older man trying to give advice to a younger one without being insistent. "There's not another day left in them."

Barcroft looked off to the north. "Perhaps not a day. Then *half* a day. Surely we can get that much out of them."

"We've got to save something for the trip back."

Barcroft shook his head. "The trip back will take care of itself. A man on his way home can always find the strength to keep going a little longer. The hard part is this, the search."

Cloud heard complaining as the captain pointed the scouts ahead after the noon rest. But looking back, he saw the captain silently ride out, his grim eyes fixed straight ahead. And the whole command followed him.

Cloud said, "I don't know how he can keep drivin' 'em on."

Soto replied, "He don' drive them, my friend. He *leads* them."

The smell of woodsmoke was the first sign. Cloud and Soto caught it at the same time, and they reined up to sniff the wind.

"There's water up yonder someplace," Cloud said. "You notice how them buffalo trails been anglin' closer together all the time? They're pointin' in to water like wheel spokes point to the hub."

Miguel nodded. "Water and smoke. And Comanches."

Cloud squinted, but he could see nothing ahead except the continuing roll of the brown-grass hills. As the two men waited for the company to come up, their horses began to paw impatiently. They smelled water.

The captain had caught the scent by the time he reached the scouts. His shoulders had squared, and an eager light began to show in his eyes. He ran his tongue over dry, cracked lips. The solid grip of confidence was in his dusty face.

"Where there's a village, there's bound to be water," he said.

Dourly, Cloud reminded him, "And there's bound to be Indians."

The captain ignored Cloud's dislike of him. "I'll hold the men here out of sight while you two go on and scout out the village. See how the camp is laid out. Try to estimate how many Comanches there are. And Miguel . . ." The Mexican lifted his chin to listen. "Miguel, see if there are children."

Cloud asked, "What if there's too many Indians for us, Captain? We've got awful close to water to turn back now."

"Sometimes you just have to depend upon Providence."

"Providence is all right," Cloud responded dryly, "but I'd rather depend on somethin' I can see a little plainer."

Together the two rode out while the Rifles dismounted to rest their horses and check their guns. Like the captain, the men showed a lift to their shoulders, a new vitality that had come from within. The smell of water had even perked up the horses a little.

Cloud and Soto rode into the wind, rifles balanced

across their laps. Soto had the bow ready, too, the quiver slung across his shoulder Indian-style. They angled between the gently rolling hills the best they could, trying to avoid being skylined. An Indian could tell the look of a *Tejano* hat almost as far as he could see the rider.

The smoke smell became stronger. The two men passed between two hills and found a line of brush leading out through a summer-parched swale. Cloud nodded toward it, and they silently edged into the brush for cover. A horse nickered somewhere ahead. Cloud's horse almost answered, and Cloud had to drop quickly to the ground and stop him. He stood there a moment after it was all over, still gripping the animal's nose, his heart high in his throat. He looked up at the grinning Mexican and tried to say something, but it wasn't there. Cloud wiped the cold sweat from his face as the tension slowly ran out of him.

Soto swung down, the bow in his hand. He and Cloud led their horses through the brush, careful to make no noise. Finally they could see the village ahead. There were twenty-five or thirty buffalo-skin tepees, strung out down a green-banked little creek fed by a spring somewhere above. The openings all faced east, away from the afternoon sun. Smoke curled from several outdoor fires, for in this hot weather the cooking was being done outside. Under a scattering of brush arbors, the bucks and most of the squaws loafed in the shade. Children played under the arbors and around the tepees. A few splashed in the creek.

"It's quiet down there," Cloud observed. "Maybe

too hot for them to stir much. Don't look like a very happy camp to me."

"Those Indians we chase, they bring bad news. This is a waitin' camp. Here is where the raidin' bands, they split up to go south. Squaws and children, they mostly stay here. A few young squaws, they go to watch. Later on, the raiders meet here again. I think not all the bands have come back."

"How many fightin' bucks you reckon is in that camp?"

Soto squinted as he gazed off in the direction of the pony herd, loose-held down the creek by a couple of young boys who loafed in the shade, their own horses cropping the green grass of the creekbank.

"Hard to say, except by the pony herd. Not too many for us, I think."

Brush crackled behind them. They whirled, wide-eyed. They saw a Comanche warrior at the moment he saw them. Afoot, he had a bow and arrow and a string of three or four dead rabbits he was taking into camp. For just a moment he stared in surprise. Then he opened his mouth to shout.

Cloud brought up his six-shooter but realized suddenly he could not afford to shoot. He saw a blur of movement from Soto, then heard the slap of a bowstring, the solid plunk of Soto's arrow driving into the warrior's body. Instead of the shout, there was only a groan. The Comanche sank to the grass and died.

Quickly Cloud looked back toward the village again, sweat breaking on his forehead. There had been little noise, and he doubted that it had carried to the camp. But you never knew. . . .

He saw no change in the village, no sign anyone had heard. Not even a dog barked.

Soto motioned for him to pull back. Cloud took one last wishful glance at the creek. "I'd give my eyeteeth for a drink of that cool water."

"And your hair too?"

It took a while to get back to the company. Miguel briefly told the captain what they had seen. Cloud could see the men's faces light up as Soto told about the creek, about the racks of meat they had seen drying.

"Nocona band, you say?" the captain spoke. "And you saw women and children in the camp?" Cloud saw anxiety in the man's eyes.

"Sí, Capitán."

Barcroft's hands trembled a little. He turned to the men who had gathered up close around him. "There's one order I want all of you to hear. I don't want any of those children hurt, do you understand? Not under any circumstances. If you have to pass up a shot at a warrior to keep from hitting a child, then pass it. And as we charge in, take every pain to keep from running a horse over a child. Is that understood?"

He turned back to the Mexican scout. "Now, then, let's draw a plan of that village here in the dirt." Soto did, with help from Cloud, who otherwise had said nothing and offered nothing.

The captain nodded over the crude map. He glanced up at the sun. "We'll have to get on with it to be finished and out of here before dark. But it doesn't look too difficult, so long as we can take them by surprise."

He glanced up at Cloud. "You seem to be good at stampeding horses. I want you to take a couple of men and run off that horse herd. That's for diversion. Make plenty of noise. It'll draw the warriors out into the open. The rest of us will work around the other end and outflank the village. As you hit the herd and the bucks come running out, we'll ride in and make a fast, clean sweep straight down the line of tepees. A minute or two, that's all it should take. I want every warrior dead."

He stood up and looked around him. "When that's done, we'll go back and circle the village. Chances are the women and children will scatter like quail. I want them rounded up and brought back in, all of them."

Cloud stiffened. In a hostile voice he demanded, "What you aimin' to do, Captain, shoot all the squaws?"

Barcroft's eyes flamed. For a moment Cloud thought the captain was going to hit him. He wished the man would.

Crisply Barcroft said, "You were sent here under my command, Cloud; don't you forget that. What I did yesterday was out of necessity. I don't kill squaws unless I have to."

"But you don't seem to mind doin' it." He turned away from the captain. "Guffey, how about you comin' with me? Bring somebody you know."

The three split away from the company and

followed the route Cloud and Soto had reconnoitered. The last part of the way they made afoot, carefully working down into the brush overlooking the village. The horse herd was still where it had been, and the same two boys were watching it. But now the sun had lost some of its heat, and the boys were out in the open, sliding up and down on their gentle ponies' backs.

Cloud said, "We'll wait a spell, give the others time enough to get ready. I'd hate to ride off in there and find out I was by myself."

Guffey was hungrily eyeing a meat rack down in the camp. "I just hope some fool don't ride a horse into that rack and spill all the meat."

Guffey had brought along a boy of seventeen or eighteen named Tommy Sides. The youngster was not old enough to have grown any whiskers of account during the days of march. He said, "Guffey, that there's Indian meat. Flies been all over it. You mean to tell me you'd actually eat that stuff?"

"Boy," said Guffey, "if I was hungry enough, I'd eat the Indian hisself."

The boy swallowed, wondering whether to believe it. Cloud smiled. The kid was green, but he had nerve. He was putting up a brave front even though he was light-skinned and suffered terribly from sunburn. There were some who said this Texas sun wasn't meant for a white man.

Finally Cloud said, "They ought to be ready by now." He brought up his rifle. "Guffey, let's you and me shoot the horses out from under them two boys yonder. Ain't no sense in hurtin' the boys. Then we'll run the horses down the creek, away from camp and out of the hands of any bucks that might get through."

He went to the end of his stake rope, as did Guffey. They leveled their rifles across tree limbs to hold them steady. "Now," said Cloud. The rifles spoke together. The two horses fell. One boy was pinned down. The other scrambled away from his kicking pony. Quickly then, Cloud and Guffey ran back to their horses, coiling the ropes as they went. They swung up and spurred out after the herd.

4

They fired their pistols and squalled loudly. The Indians' horses broke into a hard run down the creek. One of the herd boys was still trying to fight his way out from under his fallen pony. The other shouted angrily at Cloud. He stooped and picked up a rock, hurling it and striking Guffey's horse.

In the village, every dog was awake and barking. Men shouted. Squaws screamed. Cloud slowed and looked back over his shoulder. Comanche men came running out from under the arbors and from the tepees. A couple or three who carried rifles fired futilely at the *Tejano* horse thieves. Several braves came running afoot. Two had horses staked near their tepees. These swung up and struck out after the horse herd, short-bows in their hands.

"Guffey, Tommy, look out," Cloud shouted. He stopped his horse and wheeled about as the first of the braves came riding. Cloud's rifle was empty, for he hadn't taken time to reload. He fought his mount to a standstill, held up his left arm and steadied the pistol over it with his right. He fired and saw the Indian go down.

The kid was on the ground and running to the end of his stake rope, rifle in hand. He brought up the rifle just as the second Indian rider let loose an arrow. The arrow pierced the boy's arm and he went down with a cry of pain. Guffey turned around and stepped off his horse, grabbing up the boy's rifle. As the Indian brought down his bow for a second shot, Guffey fired. The Comanche's mount fell kicking. The arrow plunked harmlessly into the creek mud.

The Indian scrambled to his feet and grabbed up the bow. He pulled another arrow from the quiver and was fitting it to the bowstring when Cloud spurred back by him, pistol in hand. The pistol flashed. The Comanche fell.

By then, gunfire had erupted at the far end of the village. The Comanche warriors who pursued the horses afoot turned and faced the terror that came galloping at them, twenty shouting *Tejanos* with guns ablaze, sharp hoofs cutting deep into the foot-packed sod. Barcroft was in the lead, pistol spitting fire. Warrior after warrior fell beneath the savage hail of bullets.

On either side of the creek, women and children ran for the brush, screaming, crying for help. Some warriors followed suit, only to be cut down by a relentless wave of angry Texans.

Cloud saw Barcroft signal the men to swing about and circle the outside of the camp. Cloud then spurred out around the horse herd and began slowing it down. With Guffey's help he soon had the horses milling. Slowly the pair of them started the horses back toward the village.

Gunfire had stopped. The surprise had been complete. So had the victory.

As the horses came up even with the fallen kid, Cloud signaled Guffey to hold them up. Then he rode out to the boy and dismounted. Tommy Sides sat on the ground, face twisted in pain. He held the wounded arm, blood flowing out around the wooden shaft.

Cloud examined the stone arrowhead. "Went clean through." He realized the boy knew it well enough without his saying it. With a sharp Bowie knife Cloud whittled the shaft off well above the head.

"Now," he said, "I'm goin' to pull it out. Yell, cuss, do anything, but just see that you hold still. It ain't goin' to be fun."

He yanked, and the bloody shaft drew out. The kid gave a sharp cry of pain, then sobbed quietly. In a moment he managed to stop. "I'm sorry," he choked. "I'm actin' like a baby."

Cloud shook his head and gripped the boy's knee with a touch of pride. "When a man hurts, he's just naturally got to make a little noise. That takes the edge off of it. Grown men cry too, so you don't need to worry over that. Now the bleedin' ought to've washed that hole clean. We got to stop it before it drains the life out of you."

He had nothing to wrap with except the handkerchief in his pocket. It was dirty, but he had to use it. He bound the wound tightly.

"Come on," he said, "I'll take you in and see if

somebody's got somethin' better to do the job with." He turned back to Guffey. "Think you can hold them horses by yourself?"

Guffey nodded. "I've got 'em. You take care of the kid."

Tommy paused, despite his pain, to pick up the arrowhead and the whittled-off shaft. Something to show his grandchildren someday, if he lived to have any.

In the village, Texans were rounding up the women and children, moving them into the center of camp. From the far side of the creek, from out of the brush, they came herding the crying squaws and squalling children like so many cattle. One Indian boy five or six years old hit a trooper in the face with a rock. The trooper swung down and grabbed up the boy. He bent him over his uplifted knee and thrashed him as he would his own.

Passing the bodies of their fallen men, the squaws would drop to their knees and begin to cry out a painful chant. The Rifles would let them carry on a moment or two, then would make them get up and go on with the others.

Cloud rode up to the captain. "We got a hurt boy. Anybody here better than average at fixin' 'em up?"

Barcroft motioned with his chin. "Back yonder somewhere. Walt Johnson's a doctor of sorts. He's taking care of the wounded."

Young Walt Johnson had his hands full. A Texan shot low in the chest lay dying on an Indian buffalo robe Johnson had spread out beneath a brush arbor. Other men with lesser wounds sat patiently waiting while Johnson gave his attention to the dying man.

Tommy Sides, pale from shock, said, "I'll make it, Mister Cloud. You don't have to worry about me no more."

Cloud touched his shoulder. "Good boy." He turned away.

By twos and threes, the men were moving up the creek to water their horses and drink a fill for themselves. One corner of the meat rack had gone down, just as Guffey had said, but most of the meat still hung above ground. The Texans were taking it. In some of the tepees they also found Indian pemmican tied up in gut casings.

Captain Barcroft looked over the group of women and children. There must have been fifty or sixty women, and even more children than that.

"Are you sure this is all of them?" he asked Elkin.

"All that've been found, Captain."

The captain turned to Miguel Soto. "Tell them to form a line. I want to look over these children."

Soto barked something in Comanche. The women were slow to comply, and he said it again, rougher this time. They strung out in a long line, clutching their children to them. Some of the women wailed as they stood there. A plaintive chant began.

"They think we shoot them, *Capitán*," Soto explained.

Barcroft nodded grimly. "They know that's what would happen if we were Comanches and they were white women. That, or worse." He stepped forward. "All right, Miguel, let's see these children."

Cloud stared in wonder as Barcroft started at one end of the line, carefully looking over the children. Seeing Elkin nearby, Cloud edged up to him and said, "What's he up to?"

"Looking for captive children," Elkin replied. "Any captives, but especially his own."

"His own?" Cloud's mouth dropped open.

Elkin nodded. "About three years or so ago, it was. The Comanches captured the captain's wife and his three-year-old daughter. He found his wife later, up the trail. She was dead." Elkin dropped his chin, staring at the ground. "He never did find his daughter. But he's still looking, Cloud, still looking."

Cloud turned back toward the tall, grim man who slowly moved down the line, examining the children. Cloud let his own gaze streak swiftly ahead, at the rest of the line. There wasn't a fair-skinned child in the bunch. But the captain wasn't letting himself do it that way. He was looking the children over, one at a time. He probably already knew; his child was not here. But he wasn't admitting it to himself. He was slowly, painfully working his way down this ragged line, avoiding as long as he could the admission that he was looking for something he would not find.

Cloud felt his throat tighten, and he turned away. This, then, was the torment he had seen in Aaron Barcroft.

"Miguel," he heard the captain say, "this girl doesn't look Comanche. I think she's Mexican."

Cloud faced back to see. Stark fear lay in the black eyes of a girl seven or eight years old. A squaw had a tight grip on her arm. Miguel touched the squaw's hand and spoke sharply. The squaw loosened her hold, and the girl suddenly ran forward, throwing her arms around the captain's legs. She began to sob out something in Spanish.

Barcroft leaned down and touched his hand to her hair and looked to Miguel. Miguel listened to the girl cry out her story. Finally he said, "She is captive, *Capitán*, many months. She begs for us to take her home."

"Where is her home?"

"Mexican settlement west of San Antonio. The Comanches they take her last spring."

What Cloud saw then made him shake his head in disbelief. A tear worked a thin trail down the captain's dusty cheek. Barcroft's voice went soft. "Tell her we'll get her home."

The captain didn't finish looking at the children. He seemed to know he wouldn't find what he had been searching for. He stood with his eyes closed, his hands gentle on the shoulders of the little Mexican girl.

Cloud turned and walked away, wondering how he could so misjudge a man.

Later, when the men had eaten and filled their canteens and drunk all the water they wanted, the captain said, "We'll catch fresh horses and take that herd back with us. But first, search out all these tepees. Anything that can be used for a weapon, bring it and pile it up here."

In short time there was a small pile of lances, bows and arrows. What rifles and other firearms the men found, they kept for their own use.

Miguel brought out a hide bag of poor gunpowder he had found in a tepee. He poured this over the pile. The captain said, "Is that all?" No one had anything else to add, so he said, "Burn it."

Miguel fired his pistol into the powder and set it ablaze.

As the flames licked up into the pile of weapons, the captain turned to Elkin. "Originally I had thought we'd burn all the tepees and make it a clean sweep. But with all their men dead, I suppose we can afford a little mercy for these women and children."

"Maybe it will teach them to have a little themselves," Elkin commented.

"Never," Barcroft gritted. He moved away from the fire and walked toward the arbor where Johnson had been taking care of the wounded. Hesitantly, Cloud followed after him.

"How're they doing, Johnson?" Barcroft asked.

The young medic replied, "Rough in spots, but I suppose they'll be able to travel. All except one. He just died."

Barcroft nodded grimly. Then he looked at Tommy Sides as he said, "It won't be easy, but a man can take a lot when he's riding in the direction of home."

Pale, his eyes sick with shock, the kid managed a weak smile. "Yes, sir, I'll make it."

"Sure you will. You've made a good soldier, son."

"Thank you, sir," the boy whispered.

As Barcroft turned away, Cloud said uncertainly, "Captain, I'd kind of like to have a word with you." He motioned with his chin. "Over here someplace."

The stiff reserve was still in Barcroft's eyes as he looked at Cloud. But he said, "I suppose so. Why not?"

They walked together out away from the tepees. Barcroft found a place on the green grass of the creekbank and sat down. Cloud squatted on his heels. He fumbled a little, hunting for the words.

"You see, sir, well . . . I sort of got started on the wrong foot, so to speak. I think maybe you got an apology comin'. What I mean to say is, I said some hard things. I thought some things even harder than what I said, after what happened about that squaw. I sort of got the notion you had a big chunk of lead instead of a heart . . . or somethin' like that.

"I didn't know about your wife and your little girl then. Man goes through a thing like that, he sees things different from other folks, I guess."

Barcroft didn't look at Cloud. A vague wall still stood between them. Cloud guessed it always would.

"Cloud, killing that squaw was a thing somebody had to do, and I did it. I took no pleasure in it. But I've not let it haunt me, either. What *does* haunt me is the way my wife looked when I found her. It wasn't the bucks who finally killed her. They turned her over to the squaws. It was a terrible death."

Barcroft rubbed his face, and Cloud could see the bone-weariness that had settled over the man. Barcroft said, "They're still women, and I try to avoid killing them when I can. But if I have to do it, I don't back away. When I look at a Comanche—man or woman—I can still see my wife the way she was that day."

Cloud pulled his gaze away from the captain's face. "What about the little girl? Have you ever found any trace of her?"

Barcroft shook his head. "Never a trace. The federal government had an Indian reservation in Young County then. I trailed my wife's killers back onto the reservation. The Indian agent and Yankee troops turned me back at the line. They said I was wrong, that none of their Indians had been out. I tried to slip in, to hunt for my little girl. One of those Yankees shot me." Hatred colored his voice as he spoke. "A little later a bunch of the Comanches jumped the reservation and headed for the high plains to join the wild tribes. If my little girl was still alive, they had her with them."

He paused a little, remembering. "She's six now, if she's living. She was so little she probably wouldn't even remember anything about me, or about her mother. She probably wouldn't look the same. Maybe I wouldn't even know her." He clenched his fist, then let it go. "Sure, she's probably dead. Most likely they killed her early and left her somewhere. In a way, I guess I hope they did. But I don't *know,* Cloud, that's what drives me crazy, I don't *know.* I keep thinking to myself, *maybe* she's still out there. I wake up in the middle of the night seeing her face. *Maybe* if I look long enough I'll find her."

With his thumb and forefinger he rubbed the bridge of his nose, his eyes closed tight. "I've got Miguel down there now, questioning those squaws. Someday perhaps we'll find someone who knows something. Someday . . ."

He broke off and looked away, down the creek.

Cloud stood up. Uncomfortable, he started to say something more, reconsidered and backed off, leaving the captain there alone.

Cloud caught the slight movement beyond a fringe of brush, far out in the grass. He didn't believe it at first. He tried to find it again, and it had disappeared. The wind, he thought, a glimpse of shadow as the grass bent aside. Then he spotted it again, just for an instant.

A squaw? A buck who had gotten away? It didn't seem reasonable. The Texans had made a good search of the whole camp.

The third time he knew it was more than a shadow, more than just the play of the wind. He caught his horse and moved out that way for a closer look. Whatever it was, it was a good three hundred yards from the village.

Tensing, he drew his six-shooter, holding it high and ready. At first, it was hard to tell where the thing had been. Then he caught it—something light brown—out there in the sun-cured grass. An animal—a dog, perhaps?

Suddenly it leaped up and began to run. A woman—a squaw with a bundle in her arms—a baby.

"How in the . . ." Cloud choked off the question and touched spurs to the horse.

Rapidly overtaking the woman, he shouted, "Stop there!" He didn't know how to say it in Comanche, but he figured she would know well enough what he meant. She kept running. He put the horse in beside her and slowed it down. "Now looky here, woman. . . ."

She jerked away from him and suddenly headed off at an angle, fleet as a deer.

"Whoa there," he shouted. "There ain't nobody goin' to hurt you." He reined after her. For an instant she looked back over her shoulder at him. That was her undoing, for she tripped and sprawled in the grass. The bundle went rolling, and Cloud heard a baby's plaintive cry.

He slid his horse to a stop and jumped down. He reached the baby before the mother could get up. He unrolled the blanket for a quick look. He carefully examined the small brown head, the arms, the legs.

"Don't seem like he's hurt none, 'cept his feelin's," he said, knowing as he spoke that the woman couldn't understand him. She dropped to her knees and examined the baby for herself. She grabbed it up then, wrapping the blanket around it and smothering its cries. She turned her blazing eyes on Cloud.

Cloud gasped. They were blue eyes!

For a moment he just stood and stared at her, struck dumb. Then he said haltingly, "Why, you're . . . you're a *white* woman!"

She drew back from him as if she understood nothing. She held the baby tighter against her breasts and looked at him with defiance flaming in her eyes.

"L-look, ma'am," Cloud stammered, "d-don't you understand? You're a white woman, like I'm a white man. You're not no Indian."

He took a step forward, and she stepped backward, her eyes wide.

Crazy woman. Cloud thought then. *That's what she must be, a crazy woman. She's forgotten about her own kind.*

"Look, lady," he tried again, "I just want to help you. Help you. Can't you understand?"

She trembled, but she held her ground. A question formed in her eyes. She tried once to speak, but nothing came. Then she said haltingly, "Help? . . . Help me?"

A long breath went out of Cloud, and he smiled thinly. "Well, you do know English after all."

"English." She studied the word a moment. "Yes, I know English."

The words came hard for her, as if she were reaching somewhere far back to find them, somewhere back in distant memory.

"How long have you been with the Comanches?" Cloud asked.

"How long? Very long. Very long."

Cloud reached out to grasp her arm, to start her toward the village. She pulled away again, frightened. Patiently he said, "Look, ma'am, I told you I ain't a-goin' to hurt you. We're goin' to take you back—back to your own people."

"People?" Again the question in her eyes. "My people? My people here."

"No, I don't mean the Indians. I mean white folks—*your* folks."

"No white people mine. I am Nocona. Nocona."

Nocona, Cloud thought. Sure, that's one of the

Comanche bands. He shook his head, pitying her. He studied her face. She was so brown from the sun that she could pass for an Indian unless a person looked closely. But there were the blue eyes, and her hair was only brown—not Indian black. She did not have the typical round face one usually found in the Comanche. Hers was oval, a white woman's face. Very likely an attractive face, if it had had the chance. But a silent tale of hardship lay in her eyes, the sun-parched skin, the work-rough hands.

"Come on," he said gently, "let's go back to the village."

Plain enough that English was hard for her. He had heard it was that way with people who were in an alien land and never used their own language. With time, they lost it.

Miguel can talk to her in Comanche, he thought. *Then maybe we can find out something. Maybe she'll understand what we're going to do for her.*

"Come on," he said again. "Don't be afraid."

No one paid much attention as they first came in. Just a stray squaw Cloud had found. Then the word spread like wildfire. White woman!

Captain Barcroft came on the run. He shouldered roughly through the crowding circle of curious men. "Where is she?"

Cloud said, "This is her, Captain." He motioned toward the pitiable little figure who stood fear-stricken in the center of this group of staring men. Afraid of the other Texans, she somehow moved toward Cloud for protection.

The captain saw the fear in her eyes. He removed

his hat, bowed from the waist in the old Texan style and said quietly, "You've got nothing to be worried about from now on, ma'am. You're with your own kind now." When she made no reply, Barcroft glanced at Cloud. "Who is she?"

"I don't know, sir."

"Who are you, ma'am?" the captain asked.

Hesitantly she said something in Comanche. The captain looked puzzled. Miguel Soto spoke up. "She use a Comanche name, *Capitán*. It mean Little Doe."

"But I want her *white* name, her real name."

Cloud spoke up. "Maybe she doesn't remember it, sir."

Incredulous, the captain demanded, "What do you mean she doesn't remember it? How long has she been with these Indians, anyway?"

He reached out and uncovered the baby's face. He stepped back in shock. "That's not her baby. It's an Indian baby."

Cloud said, "I reckon it's her baby, all right. She's been with these Comanches a long time."

Slowly the shock in the captain's face turned to revulsion. "My God," he breathed. "A white woman, an Indian baby. My God!" He stepped back again, shaking his head. "Why didn't they kill her when they took her? She'd have been a lot better off."

Cloud said, "She's bound to have people somewhere. They'll be glad to get her back."

"Will they?" the captain asked, bitterness in his voice. "Will they?"

The men parted to make way for him as he walked off. He strode out to the creek and stood a while looking down into its clear water. Cloud watched him, wondering what Barcroft was going to do. Then he watched the woman, watched how she tenderly rocked the baby in her arms to quiet its crying. He remembered how he had seen Mrs. Moseley doing the same.

Presently the captain came back, his head bowed. "I've decided what has to be done," he said huskily. "It's hard, but it's the only way. Miguel, she seems to know Comanche better than English. Tell her we're taking her back to her people. But tell her she'll have to leave the baby here."

Miguel hesitated. "*Capitán*, she is the mother."

Sharply Barcroft said, "I gave you an order, Miguel! Tell her!"

Miguel spoke quickly, plainly hating what he had to say. The woman cried out and clutched the baby tightly. She tried to break away, but stopped at sight of the Texans standing behind her. She broke into English. "No, no. My baby! My baby!"

Barcroft could not bring himself to look at the woman. "Cloud, take the baby and give it to one of the squaws."

Cloud stood with his fists tight, anger swelling in him. He didn't move.

Barcroft's voice lashed at him as it had at Miguel. "Doesn't anybody here understand an order?"

"She's the baby's mother," Cloud argued, his face darkening. "You don't just pull a mother away from her own child that way."

"It's for her own good, don't you see? How will she be treated when she goes back to civilization with an Indian baby in her arms? She'll be cast out like a leper."

"She might prefer that to losin' her baby. You ought to know how it is, Captain, to lose a baby."

That hurt. Cloud could see the pain of it in Barcroft's dark eyes. Some of the anger went out of the man's voice, but the resolve was still there. "Yes, I know. I know better than any man here what it's going to cost this woman. But in the end, she'll know it was for the best. When she's back with her own, she'll forget all this. Perhaps she'll marry a good man and have more children, and she'll forget this one was ever born."

Cloud argued, "No woman ever forgets a baby."

Seeing no one else would do it, the captain stepped up to her and said, "Let me have the child."

She cried out, but he took the baby from her arms and turned away. He walked between the silent men, pausing long enough to say, "Get ready, men. We'll be riding in a minute."

A wrinkled old squaw walked forward to meet the captain. She took the baby and folded it tenderly to her bosom.

Cloud saw the woman's eyes pleading with him.

Stop him! a voice cried in Cloud. *Stop this thing now, before it's too late!*

"Ma'am," he said, "there's nothin' I can do."

She fell to her knees, sobbing in anguish, and the heart went out of him. He said it again, for his own benefit rather than hers:

"There's nothin' I can do."

5

The wind had cooled and the edge was well gone from the day's heat when the Rifles swung onto their horses and splashed out across the hoof-muddied creek, driving with them the whole horse band taken from the Indians. Gone was their weariness, swept away by the eruption of violence and the taste of victory.

Riding an Indian saddle, the white woman twisted sideways and looked back. On the hoof-pocked bank of the creek, the old squaw stood shoulder-slumped, the infant in her arms. Tears glistened on the white woman's cheeks. She forced herself to turn forward in the saddle again, straightening, her chin high, her face stony. There were no more tears. It was as if she saw nothing, felt nothing.

They rode a long time that way, heading south and a little east, the cooling north wind to their backs. Covertly, Cloud watched the woman, and he knew the other men were watching her too. She held herself rigidly aloof. Whatever turmoil might have boiled within her, she gave no outward sign of it.

Captain Barcroft called no supper halt. The men had wolfed food in the Indian camp, and he figured they needed no more. It was a long way home. He wanted to put all the miles he could between them and the Comanche village before they quit for the night.

The time of the full moon had passed. Now a thin slice of moon, fragile as a pine shaving, provided the only light by the time Barcroft decided he had pushed horses and men as far as they would go. He held up his hand to halt the men in front. In the darkness, some of the riders bumped their horses against those in front of them before they knew of the halt.

"Far enough," the captain called. "Picket your horses. Elkin will assign guard duty."

Picketing was out of the question for the Indian horse band. Elkin had to set up an extra guard to take care of it. Cloud drew first guard. Before going out, he untied the blanket from behind his saddle and took it down, bending the roll over his arm. He sought out the woman. Barcroft had assigned her a place inside the circle of men to discourage her from trying to get away.

"Ma'am," Cloud said, "that old blanket you got don't look like much. Thought maybe you might like to use mine. I won't be in need of it noway."

She gave no sign that she had heard him. He tried to hand her the blanket, but she put her hands behind her back, her eyes defiantly avoiding him.

Cloud swallowed. He stood waiting uncertainly a moment, wondering if she might relent. Then he knew she wouldn't. This was how it would remain.

"Sorry, ma'am. Reckon I can't blame you none." He spread out the blanket anyway and walked off, leaving it for her. He didn't look back, but he felt she was watching him.

He stood his tour of duty. It was difficult because of the near-darkness and a tendency of the horses to drift. His time done, he stretched out on the ground, leaning his head against his saddle. It was a hard, ungiving pillow, but better than the brittle grass tickling the back of his neck.

Cloud was deeply weary, his body aching and crying for rest. Yet he could not sleep. He kept thinking of the white woman he had found.

Who was she? Where had she come from?

He began trying to compare her with women he had known, and none seemed to fit. He found himself linking her with Lige Moseley's daughter, Samantha. There was much that was alike in them. Not town girls, either one. Yet both might be comely women if given the chance. The Comanche captive appeared to be older than Samantha by three or four years, but it was hard to tell. The harsh life of the nomadic Comanche would age a woman before her time. Still, there wasn't anything easy about the life of the Moseleys and their kind, either.

There was one big difference between the two. He had seen a wide-eyed innocence in Samantha Moseley. He knew he need not expect it in this woman. Kids grew up in a hurry around the Indian camps, for privacy was unknown, and initiation into adult life came early.

This line of thought brought him around to what

worried him most—the baby. Sure, she had probably been taken by the Indians when she was too young to know much about white men's ways, white men's rules. And she was probably married, too, insofar as Indians could be married in the view of the white man. A man couldn't blame her for what had happened. Even a grown woman, taken in captivity, could not help herself.

Well, he told himself, it wouldn't happen anymore. He had found her, and she was safe now.

Safe—but at what a price!

Listening in the night, he thought once he heard her sobbing. But he finally figured out it was young Tommy Sides, tossing in fevered sleep. The woman was through sobbing now. She had that much Indian training. They would probably never hear her sobbing again.

The first flash of dawn came, and someone called for the captain. Stirring, Cloud heard a quick rise of excited talk. He arose stiffly from his bed on the grass to see what the trouble was. Sleep still clung stubbornly to him, for he had taken a long time to drop off.

"Beats me how she slipped away," he heard someone say. "I was sleepin' no more than six feet from her, and I never heard nothin'."

The captain was speaking angrily. "Someone must have heard her. She couldn't just slip out and not stir up somebody."

"She's an Indian, Captain," someone replied.

"She's white!" the captain declared emphatically. "Don't you ever forget she's a white woman!"

Calmly, Elkin said, "The men were all dog tired, Captain. Once they went to sleep, wild horses couldn't have stirred them out. I imagine you were just as tired yourself."

Barcroft cooled a little, his face twisting wryly as he caught Elkin's subtle suggestion. Elkin added, "Might be we just ought to let her go, Captain. We all know she won't be happy with her baby stayin' back yonder."

Evenly Barcroft said, "A white woman has no place in an Indian camp. And she has no place with an Indian baby in her arms. Cloud, Miguel, I want you two."

Cloud sensed the mission, and he felt a sharp regret. He wanted to say, *If that's what she wants, let's just let her go*. But he said, "What'll it be, Captain?"

Barcroft's dark eyes were sharp. "You know she's gone?"

"Figured that from the conversation."

"I want you and Miguel to go find her. She seems to have left afoot. Take her horse and bring her back."

"What if we can't find her?"

"Out on this prairie? You can find her if you want to. If you don't find her, I'll charge you with dereliction of duty. Now get yourselves a little breakfast and start out. We'll move on at an easy pace. You should be able to overtake her and then catch us."

Cloud started to turn away, then stopped. "Captain," he said thoughtfully, "I was the one found her, and I thought I was doin' her a favor. But she must've wanted to go back awful bad. And after all, we don't own her. Maybe we ought to let her do what she wants to."

Sternly Barcroft said, "Find her, Cloud!"

In that thick carpet of dry grass, it was hard to see an individual track. But most of the time, by taking a sweeping look across the prairie ahead of him, Cloud could make out the faint trace—an elusive pattern of shadow where the grass had bent down and had not come all the way up.

"Path's like an arrow, Miguel," Cloud said. "She must've took a sight on a star and followed it."

"She go straight to camp," Miguel observed, pointing. "She don' need no compass."

"That baby's compass enough. A mother that way, she's got an instinct."

The sun came up and started its long rise, heating the wind. This was going to be a scorcher of a day, thought Cloud, wiping his forehead on his sleeve. The climbing sun made the trail harder to follow, for the shadow pattern was less pronounced as sunshine spilled more directly into the bent-over grass. At times the two lost it completely. But they knew the direction and kept going. After a while they would come across a trace of the trail again.

"If she'd walked, we'd've caught her by now," Cloud said. "She must've trotted along, half-runnin' most of the time. Pushin' hard."

"She know when sunup come, we come too. She know she got to hurry. Else she don' get to camp before we catch her."

"Rate she's goin', she'll kill herself in the heat."

Gravely Miguel shrugged. "Maybeso that would be the best way. *Quién sabe*, she maybe want it like that, to kill herself."

"Don't say that, Miguel, don't say it."

Cloud tried to put the idea out of his head, but he couldn't. *She might*, he thought, *she just might. And it'll be on my shoulders, because I was the one found her.*

Then another idea came to him, and he straightened. A wild idea it was, but it might work—just *might*. "Miguel," he said, "we *could* let her go. We could tell the captain that when we caught up to her, and she saw we was fixin' to take her back, she killed herself with a knife."

Miguel pursed his lips, considering the idea. "Not bad, my frien', only where she get the knife?"

"She could've stole it from somebody as she left camp. There wouldn't be nobody own up to it noway. The captain would believe us, I reckon, if we was good enough liars."

Miguel shook his head. "You ever try to tell the *capitán* a lie?" Then he answered his own question. "No, you don't. Is not easy to look him in the eyes and say what is not true. But I let *you* tell him. Me, I don't say nothing."

Cloud still wasn't sure of himself. "Trouble is, I can't help feelin' like maybe the captain's part right. She *is* white. She's got no business in a heathen camp thataway. If it wasn't for that baby . . ." He frowned. "Miguel, you reckon a white woman really could love a baby, knowin' its daddy was an Indian—love it, I mean, like she would if it was white? Her own kind?"

Miguel was a while in answering. "My frien', in Mexico many times the parents, they say who get married. The boy, the girl, sometimes they don' know each other, don' love each other. Maybeso they both love somebody else, and they don' even want each other. But by and by comes the baby, and they both love it.

"With the Indians, most time a woman she is sold for wife. Man want her, he got plenty horses, he trades for her, just like that. She marry because she is squaw and has to do what the father say. Man, he marry because he want a woman. Maybe he don' even care which one, if she is pretty—just a woman. I bet my boots this is what happen to this woman. She have a foster father, and he sell her somebody for wife. The woman, she got no say. She is for work, and to have the babies, *no más*. Maybe she don't like the man, but she will love the baby. That is woman's way."

Cloud chewed his lip, feeling the whiskers with his teeth. "Chances are her husband is dead. If we didn't get him on the trail, we likely laid him out in the camp." A cold feeling came over him. "You reckon if we let her go back to them Indians, the same thing'll happen to her all over again?"

"Young, pretty squaw, she don' stay widow long. Another man take her."

A knot started drawing up in Cloud. "Captain's right, then. Ain't Christian of us to let her go back to that. Come on, we better pick up some or she'll outrun us plumb to that camp."

There was no place for her to hide in the open, rolling prairie. When they first sighted her, she was looking back over her shoulder. She must have seen them first. Already moving at a trot, she broke into a run. Cloud and Miguel touched spurs to their horses. She ran as fast as she could. She fell once, pushed onto her feet and ran again.

They came up even with her, and Cloud swung to the ground, dropping the reins. He grabbed at her. She eluded him, only to stumble and fall. She rolled over onto her side and came up onto her knees. Sun flashed on the bright blade of a knife in her hand. Getting to her feet, her eyes stabbing in anger, she desperately brandished the blade at Cloud. He parried with his hand, drawing a thrust. He grabbed her arm and twisted it sharply. She gave a quick cry of pain and dropped the knife. Still holding her wrist, Cloud reached down for the knife and shoved it into his belt.

So she had *stolen one after all*, he thought.

He let go of her wrist then. "I didn't go to hurt you, ma'am. You made me do it."

She dropped to her knees, gasping for breath, and Cloud saw how thoroughly worn out she was, how she had been running. Defeat lay heavy in her eyes, but she wasn't crying. She just knelt there, her back and shoulders heaving up and down as her lungs fought for air.

Cloud took off his hat and held it in both hands.

"You made an awful good try," he said with admiration. "Too bad we can't just let you go."

She didn't try to answer him until she had her breath. Then she turned her face up to him, her blue eyes pleading. "Please, please, that is my home." She spoke slowly, the words still difficult for her. "My baby is there. Why can't I go? You took no other woman."

"You're a white woman, the only one there was."

"I am not white woman. My face is white, my eyes are the eyes of a white woman. I have often been ashamed of that. But my heart is Nocona. My baby is Nocona. Why do you want me?"

Cloud looked to Miguel for help and got none. "But you *are* white," he said, knowing it wasn't answer enough. "That's all the reason there is." Now it was Cloud who pleaded with his eyes, pleaded for her to understand. "Ma'am, you grew up with the Indians, so there's a lot you can't know. There's things a white woman just don't do. You get back to the settlements, and live awhile with your own folks, you'll understand what I'm tryin' to tell you."

Despair colored her voice. "I don't want to go to the white people. I want to go to my baby. It is a weak baby, a sick baby. It needs me."

For a moment Cloud thought she would cry. His throat tightened in sympathy for her. Again he looked to Miguel and got no help.

"Miguel," he said, "ain't there nothin' you can say to her?"

Miguel shook his head, and Cloud could see in the Mexican's eyes a dislike for the task they had to do. "There is nothing to say. We follow the order, like it or not. The *capitán* say she come, she come."

Cloud looked at the bereaved woman and wished he had never seen her. He turned away, flexing his hands.

There *was* a way, he thought suddenly.

He turned back. "Miguel, how far you reckon it is to that Indian camp?"

Miguel shrugged. "She come pretty far. Two, maybeso three more miles."

To the woman Cloud said, "What if we went with you into that camp to get your baby? Would you come out with us again, and no fuss?"

The woman looked up quickly, sudden hope in her face. "You would let me get my baby?"

Miguel pointed out in argument, "The *capitán*, he don' like it."

"I don't care. It just ain't natural to take this woman away from her baby, no matter what color it is."

"He raise plenty hell with us."

"But he can't turn back anymore, and he can't just leave the baby out on the prairie."

Miguel shrugged. Cloud could tell he wasn't keen about the idea. "Whatever you say, my frien', I go with you. But we have to watch those squaws. They get the chance, they cut us to pieces."

"We'll watch." To the woman he said, "How about it? Promise to come out with us again and not give us no trouble?"

Tears of joy shone in her eyes. "I promise. I promise."

He reached down and took her hands and helped her to her feet. The warmth of her hands stirred him, and for a moment he held them. She pulled the hands away, letting her blue eyes briefly meet his with their glow of gratitude. "You have good heart, *Tejano*."

"I got a conscience," he told her, "and for a little while there, it didn't like me much."

He helped her onto her horse, and they headed toward the village. Miguel moved out a little in the lead, watching ahead of them nervously. Worry rode heavy on the Mexican's shoulders.

Cloud tried to watch the prairie too, but most of the time he watched the woman. He watched the graceful way she sat the Comanche saddle, her back straight, her shoulders square. She would glance at him and catch him looking at her, and she would look away again.

"You know somethin', ma'am?" he found himself telling her. "Get you back to civilization, put some good clothes on you and do your hair up settlement-style, you're goin' to look pretty—right pretty." He felt a flush of embarrassment then and wished he hadn't said it. But she didn't seem to have understood. He could see the eagerness in her eyes, and he knew she was thinking only of the baby.

He rode a while farther before he finally asked her, "What's your name, ma'am? Your white name, I mean."

She shook her head. "My white name? Easter. Easter Rutledge." A look of wonder came into her face. "It has been a long time since I have said that name.

Easter Rutledge. Easter Rutledge." She spoke the name slowly, almost as if she were carefully tasting something that had a strange new flavor. "It sounds . . . I don't know what to say . . . funny. It is like the name of someone else."

"Don't reckon you've had much chance to use it. How long you been with the Comanches?"

"Long ago they took me—many, many years ago. I was' a little girl. I do not remember much—the shooting, the screams. My white father—I am sure he died. My mother . . . I can't remember. It has been so long ago." She looked down, frowning, trying to recall the far-distant past. "I was given a new father and mother in the Noconas. With them I was not white. I was Nocona. Always I have been Nocona."

Cloud observed, "You're gettin' better with your English. You must've had some practice on it."

"There was a white woman with us many years. Slave. Always she called me Easter. Always she spoke English. She said I must never forget my English, must never forget I was white. I told her I was not white—I was Nocona. But I spoke English with her. She died two or three winters ago. Since then I have not spoken with a white person. I have not spoken English."

Cloud was a little hesitant about the next question, and he waited awhile before he asked it. "You have a husband?"

She shook her head. "He is dead."

"Was he . . . I mean, did you love him?"

"Love?" She seemed a little puzzled by the word. "He brought me food. He gave me my son."

"But were you in love with him?"

She frowned. "I don't know what you mean."

Cloud nodded, satisfied. "You weren't, I reckon, or you'd *know* what I meant." The thought made him feel better, somehow.

They rode awhile in silence, following Miguel. They were into the rolling hills now, not far from the creek where the camp stood.

"Soon now," Cloud heard the woman speaking softly, more to herself than to him. "Soon now." Her face was happy.

Easing up a rise, Miguel Soto suddenly stopped. The way he stiffened in the saddle, Cloud knew something was wrong. Miguel held up his hand in a signal for the other two to halt. Cloud did, for a moment, then he and Easter Rutledge moved slowly forward, drawing abreast of Miguel.

Somberly Miguel turned to her and said, "Very bad luck, señora. Very bad luck."

He pointed. Cloud could see the riders down yonder, strung out in a dusty line along the creek, pushing a small bunch of horses straight toward the ravaged camp.

"Comanches," Cloud breathed. "Another raidin' party just comin' in. And way too big for us."

He turned regretfully to the woman, to tell her what this meant. He saw despair drive the glow from her face.

He didn't have to tell her. She already knew.

6

Brush Hill was not much of a town, even as frontier settlements went. It had been built with little view toward permanence and no view at all toward beauty. Money scarce the way it was, few people could afford to buy much in the form of niceties or comforts. Either they built what they wanted out of what was at hand, or they did without.

Besides, there were the Comanches to worry about. No use in a man spending months of labor and breaking his heart building something the Indians might burn down in minutes. Main thing at first was to put up something with a roof on it to keep the family in the dry, and something that would provide a man a solid wall to stand behind with his guns in case the Indians came. There would be a time later to build the fine homes the womenfolks dreamed of, a time when there was money in circulation and no longer any need to worry about "John" sneaking in on a moonlit night to put it all to the torch.

Cloud had seen a lot of settlements like Brush Hill, although he had not been in this one before. It was a loose scattering of picket and log houses, for the most part, each having its garden and shed and outbuildings, its cedar-stake corral to hold the stock. Oldest house—by the aging of its logs Cloud figured it to have been up six or eight years—was built next to a spring which percolated out of a rock outcrop and formed a deep, clear pool. From the pool flowed a small creek, winding its erratic way down through the grassy hills, seeking a level spot it wouldn't find.

The newer the houses, the farther down the creek they sat.

Approaching the settlement, Cloud had seen the plowed fields, the crops mostly burned now under the barren heat of the summer sun, the moisture-robbing search of the dry wind which moaned down from the high plains. He had seen the settlers' cattle, scattered over a hundred hills and more.

Here lay a land of promise, a fresh new land which had seen far more of the Indian than of the white man, far more of the buffalo than of the new spotted cattle, a land which for the most part had still not felt the rip of the plow. Small wonder, thought Cloud, the Indians hated to see it go.

But he felt, as most settlers did, that the Indians had no solid claim upon it. They had come only now and again in search of game, touching lightly like the wind, leaving no mark upon the land, neither building nor tearing down.

Judging from the widely scattered houses he had seen, Cloud would estimate there were fifteen or twenty families in Brush Hill settlement. He saw one large log building he took to be a store. There wasn't much a frontier store could handle except the barest essentials of life, for its customers had a hard enough time buying even those. Here a man earned his daily bread by raising the stuff that went into it. If he didn't raise it, he didn't eat.

Mighty little room in a settlement like this for the riffraff that so often gravitated to the land beyond the law. To make a living here they would have to work for it. Plain to see there wasn't any loose money floating around.

Cloud wouldn't have expected the Rifles to attract much of a crowd here, because there just weren't that many people. But it seemed everybody was out to watch the men bringing in that big string of recovered horses. Children ran and shouted, and chased afoot after the horsemen. Men grinned as they recognized mounts they had lost.

"Hey, Elkin," someone shouted, "did you get back that blue roan of mine?"

Elkin called to him, "We're fixin' to pen them down at the camp. Come along and look them over."

As the horses passed, eyes of the watchers touched first upon the little Mexican girl riding alongside Miguel Soto. Then, inevitably, they would find the buckskin-clad woman of the brown hair and the blue eyes, riding beside the dark-bearded man named Cloud. Cloud could see people pointing to her. Though he couldn't hear them, he knew they were talking about her. And by the way she rode with her chin down, her eyes half closed, he knew she knew it.

White woman, the word raced down the road. *They've rescued a white woman.*

They passed by the store, and Cloud could see the aproned proprietor with three or four other men, standing on the narrow front porch. Atop a low, slender flagpole flew the Texas flag. Cloud stared at it.

The red-haired Quade Guffey said, "They used to fly the United States flag, but come secession they hauled her down. Ain't nobody out here got a Confederate flag, so they use the old Lone Star in its place."

Captain Barcroft had been riding up at the head of the column, out of the dust. Now he dropped back, holding still while the horse herd moved past him. When the last of them had gone by, he cut in behind and signaled Cloud to stop.

His glance went to the woman, then just as quickly left her. Cloud had seen Barcroft look at her this way many times since he and Miguel had brought her back to the command. There was an uneasiness in his manner with the woman, almost a distaste. The captain had avoided any unnecessary conversation with her, except that he had asked her once if she had seen a little white girl with the Indians. She told him she hadn't.

Since then, the captain seemed to have gone out of his way to stay away from her. Yet he often glanced at her, as if in the grip of some fascination he wanted to avoid.

"Cloud," he said, "Miguel will take the girl to a Mexican family at the edge of the settlement. I thought we might bring Missus . . . Miss Rutledge here to these people at the store. I think the Lawtons will take care of her until we can find out more about her and get in touch with her own people."

Without exactly saying so, Barcroft seemed to have delegated Cloud to be Easter Rutledge's guardian. When the captain was around, she would stand steadfast and stare straight ahead, as if she could not see or hear him. But she somehow seemed to accept Cloud, to look upon him as something of a buffer against the tall, dark-eyed officer with the grim voice, the unsmiling face.

Maybe he looks on both of us as outcasts, Cloud thought. *Figures we make a pair.*

Easter Rutledge had not talked since their failure to get into the Indian camp, except to say the things that had to be said. She had not offered to tell any more of her past, and Cloud had not tried to question her. As he saw it, when she felt like talking, she would. You couldn't expect much from a woman who had just been forced to give up her baby.

The captain rode past the front of the store. The proprietor, heavyish and balding, with an old man's step, moved off the porch. "Welcome back, Aaron," he spoke to the captain, a genuine gladness in his voice. But his eyes were on Easter Rutledge.

"Thank you, Mister Lawton," the captain responded. "Is Mother Lawton at home?"

"Just go on back," Lawton said.

The Lawton house behind the store was a double cabin, somewhat like Lige Moseley's had been, with a dog run in the center and an extra lean-to on one side. A young woman stood on the dog run, watching the three riders approach, the old proprietor following along afoot. As Barcroft stepped down and dropped his reins over the cedar-stake fence, she hurried out to meet him. He moved through the gate and stopped.

"Hello, Hanna," he said.

She reached out as if to put her arms around him, reconsidered and drew her hands back against her body. "Aaron," she said softly, a catch in her voice. She summoned up strength and said, "Aaron, it's good to see you back. We were worried."

She was tall and slender, a strongly handsome woman in her early twenties. At first Cloud thought she could be Barcroft's sister, but he decided against it when the captain said, "We came to see your mother."

Still at a loss as to what she should do with her hands, the young woman finally crossed her arms. Cloud thought he could see a trace of tears in her eyes. Tears of relief, he thought. "She's in the house," she said. "I'll call her." She walked back toward the cabin and called, "Mother, Aaron's home."

An elderly woman stepped out through the open cabin door onto the dog run, her hands wrapped in an apron, her eyes wide in joy. "Aaron! You're all right? Not hurt or anything?"

"Just fine," he told her. She walked to him, gripped his arm and pulled him down to kiss him on the cheek. For a moment the captain seemed to soften. Then he glanced at Cloud and Easter Rutledge, still sitting on their horses outside the yard fence. He regained his stiff composure. "Mother Lawton," he said, "I've brought someone who is going to need help."

For the first time the two women in the yard noticed Easter Rutledge. There was a moment of shocked silence as they looked her over, taking in the buckskin clothes, the fringed moccasins, the Comanche braids in her long brown hair.

Then the older woman stepped to the gate, lifting her hands as if to help Easter down. "You poor child," she said with concern, "you must be completely worn out. Come on in with us."

Cloud swung down from his saddle and turned to help Easter. She glanced at him desperately as if asking him what to do.

"It's all right, Easter," he told her, not even conscious of speaking her first name instead of the "ma'am" he had used so much. "These folks are goin' to help you."

Mother Lawton's gray eyes were wide with anxiety as she looked the girl over again. "Those clothes! Land sakes, you've been held by those Indians, haven't you? You poor child!" She bit her lower lip in an unconscious gesture of sympathy. "I'll bet you're glad to be back among Christian folk again. It's God's blessing that our Aaron found you."

Easter Rutledge looked at the ground. Her shoulder jerked in the beginning of a sob before she could catch herself. Mother Lawton put her hands on the girl's shoulders and spoke gently, "There now, there's no need to cry anymore. Everything's fine now, just fine."

Captain Barcroft said quietly, "Before it goes any farther, Mother Lawton, there's something you should know. She's lived among the Indians so long she doesn't feel she's really white. We brought her against her will."

The gray-haired woman looked up sharply. "Against her will? I don't believe it." Her gaze dropped to the girl again. She shook her head slowly. "Then she's more to be pitied than ever. Only God knows how many kidnapped girls there are out yonder like this one, slaves to the heathen."

She took Easter's chin in her hand and looked into the young woman's glistening eyes. "You won't be unhappy long, child. You'll get used to the ways of your own again, and you'll be able to live as a Christian. You'll be glad you came back."

Still Easter did not speak. Barcroft said, "One more thing. You'll learn it soon enough, so I'll tell you now. She had an Indian husband. And she had a baby—an Indian baby."

The old woman's eyes went wide again. "A baby?" She paused, absorbing the idea and finally accepting it. "Well, where is it?"

"We left it behind," said Barcroft.

"You *left* it?" The sharp rise of her voice seemed to surprise Barcroft a little.

"We thought . . . *I* thought it best not to bring it. It'll be hard enough for this woman to readjust herself to white people's ways without having a half-Indian child along. You know the stigma it would attach to her."

Easter dropped her chin again. She closed her eyes, but not before a tear squeezed out and ran down her cheek.

The old woman stood in silence, the anger rising

in her face. Then she blazed, "Aaron Barcroft, sometimes you're the smartest man I know, and sometimes you're a fool. This time you're a fool!"

The younger woman named Hanna spoke up in protest. "Mother . . ."

Anger came into Barcroft's face. "I thought it would be better for her in the long run. I still do."

"And you're still a fool!"

Hanna Lawton stepped quickly to Aaron Barcroft. "Aaron," she said, "Mother's sorry. She says things she doesn't mean."

"She means it, all right," Barcroft replied tightly. "But when she thinks about it some, she'll know I'm right. It was the only way, the only right and proper way."

Mrs. Lawton paid little attention. Her arm around Easter's shoulder, she guided the girl toward the cabin. "Come on into the house, child. Come on in with me."

Hanna Lawton stood by the captain and watched her mother take Easter inside. Her fingertips were white as she unconsciously dug them into her crossed arms. Her eyes were plainly sympathetic to Easter, but she seemed hesitant to say anything that might hurt Barcroft. "It's going to be hard for her, Aaron. Perhaps you don't know what a sacrifice you've forced her to make."

Pain tightened the captain's face. "Hanna, you—above all people—ought to realize what I know about sacrifice."

She reached out and touched his arm, then pulled her hand away. "Yes, Aaron. I'm sorry—I shouldn't have said it. Sometimes a man has to do what he thinks is right, no matter how hard it may be."

Barcroft left the yard, turning back a moment at the gate. "I'll be back tonight, Hanna, when I've had a chance to clean up some. By then your mother may feel more like talking to me."

"Please do that, Aaron."

As he swung into the saddle and started away, she said again, "It's good to have you back."

Barcroft glanced then at Cloud, as if he had forgotten him. "Never did introduce you, did I?" it occurred to him. He studied a moment and said, "You'll come back with me later. That girl seems to have decided she can trust you. Maybe you can get her to tell us where her home is."

Cloud nodded, glad somehow that he hadn't seen the last of Easter Rutledge. "I'll try, sir."

Riding away, he glanced over his shoulder. Hanna Lawton still stood in the yard, watching them. Cloud said, "You've known these folks a long time, Captain?"

"A long time, Cloud. A long, long time." Barcroft's face was grave. He seemed to reach far back into memory a little while, then he said, "My wife was a Lawton. The old folks there, they were her mother and father."

"Then the one you called Hanna . . ."

Barcroft nodded again. "Hanna was her sister."

The store was closed and dark when they rode back in the dusk. At the cabin in the rear, a lantern glowed on the narrow porch, showing the way to the door.

Cloud and Barcroft swung down from their horses and dropped their reins over the stake fence. Cloud stepped to the gate first and held it open for the captain. He rubbed his clean-shaven chin.

"Miss Rutledge may not know us now, sir," he commented. "Bath in the creek, clean clothes and a shave—I don't hardly know myself."

The captain never even attempted a reply as he walked through the gate.

Hanna Lawton had heard the horses. She stepped out onto the porch, into the yellow glow of the lantern. As the captain moved up to her, she held out her hand. He gripped it a moment.

"We've been expecting you, Aaron."

"How's your mother?"

"She has her temper under control. But she hasn't changed her mind."

"I'll not argue with her," the captain said. "Nobody can."

Hanna Lawton's gaze rested on Cloud, and curiosity was in her eyes. Barcroft said, "Hanna, this is Sam Houston Cloud. He's a new recruit in the Rifles. I've put him up as scout with Miguel Soto. It was Cloud who found the white woman."

Hat in his hand, Cloud bowed from the waist. "Ma'am."

Hanna Lawton said, "It's a pleasure to meet you, Mister Cloud." It wasn't just something she said because it was customary. Cloud got the feeling she honestly meant it. In this sparsely settled country, strangers didn't remain strangers long. Frontier dwellers lost the veneer of cool reserve that people so often held to in heavily settled country. A new face was always welcome, unless it brought trouble.

Cloud asked her, "How's she feelin'—Miss Rutledge, I mean? She makin' out all right?"

Hanna Lawton shook her head. "It's hard to tell. She's a little bewildered yet. And sad, too. She won't say so, but she's thinking about"—she glanced quickly at the captain—"about her baby."

The captain asked, "Has she told you anything about her home—where the Comanches stole her from?"

"Nothing, Aaron. But we haven't pushed her. We thought it best to try to make her feel as much at ease as we could, not upset her with a lot of questions."

"Well," said Barcroft, "the questions will have to be asked, sooner or later, if we're to get her back to her home. May we go in?"

"Surely, Aaron. I didn't mean to keep you standing around outside."

She motioned toward the open door. Cloud and the captain stepped up onto the rough-hewn porch. Cloud stamped his boots to get the dust off. He had an idea from the looks of the outside that this cabin would have a plank floor, and he wouldn't want to get it dirty. Barcroft went in first, as befitted an officer. Cloud trailed, pausing to motion for Hanna Lawton to go in ahead of him.

He saw Easter Rutledge then, and the sight of her brought a quick stab of surprise.

The Indian clothes were gone. Although her face was burned a deep brown by the sun, she was unmistakably white in a rather plain sort of homespun cotton dress that fitted tightly around her slim waist and flowed full to the floor. The braids had been taken from her brown hair, the hair washed and rolled up into a round bun at the back of her neck. A simple white ribbon had been tied around the bun.

"By Ned!" Cloud breathed, "I don't believe it!"

Protest formed in the captain's eyes. He turned to Hanna Lawton. "That dress—is it—"

She said quickly, "It's one of mine."

Barcroft nodded then, relieved. "I thought for a minute . . ."

Mother Lawton stood beside the girl, proudly looking over the changes she had been able to accomplish since afternoon. "Aaron," the old lady said, "you still have all of Celia's things packed away in that big leather-bound trunk. They'll do no one any good there. This girl could certainly use some of them. Why don't you—"

"No," the captain spoke sharply. "They were *hers*! I'll give them to no—" He broke off, for he had said more than he intended to. The quick anger settled, but a trace of it remained in the hard set of his mouth. "We'll leave her clothes in that trunk!"

Mother Lawton turned away, face tight. "Anything you say, Aaron."

After an uncomfortable moment, the captain introduced Cloud to the Lawtons. To old Henry Lawton, puffing calmly on his pipe, Barcroft said, "I noticed Cloud looking at your Texas flag on the store. I think he had rather it was still the Union flag."

Cloud flinched. *That was sure putting it out in the open.*

Barcroft said matter-of-factly, "He's not the only one in my command who still fancies the Union more than the Confederacy."

He's not ever going to forget that, Cloud thought darkly.

He could tell by the Lawtons' faces that they disagreed with his politics. But after a moment Mrs. Lawton said, "Well, at least Mister Cloud didn't shirk his call to duty. He joined the Rifles. There are others in this section who see things the way he does." She smiled then to set him at ease.

Henry Lawton drew thoughtfully on his pipe, eyes narrowed as he stared at Cloud. "You a native of Texas, Cloud?" When Cloud nodded, the old man reached out and shook his hand. "That's all right, then. Long's a man keeps his rifle pointed at the Indians instead of at us, I'm inclined to let his politics alone."

Cloud felt better. He knew he could get along fine with these folks.

Barcroft nodded toward Easter Rutledge and abruptly changed the subject. "We came to see what this woman can tell us about her people. We need to find out where she's from so we can return her there and get her off of our hands." He turned to Easter Rutledge. "How about it?" he asked her brusquely. "Where was your home?"

Her eyes stabbed at him, then she turned away to stare sullenly at the cabin wall. She did not reply.

Stiffly the captain said, "It's not for *my* benefit I'm asking you this. It's for *yours*."

She was silent a moment. Then, not looking at him, she spoke with an edge of hatred in her voice. "I do not talk with you, Captain. I will talk to the other man"—she pointed her chin toward Cloud—"but I do not talk to you."

Barcroft's face darkened. He rocked back hesitantly, unaccustomed to being spoken to this way. He started to say something but bit it off short.

Henry Lawton said, "Aaron, maybe it'd be better if you left. Let Cloud talk to her."

Barcroft spoke tightly, "Are you running me off, Mister Lawton?"

Mother Lawton said, "Nobody's running you off, Aaron. But under the circumstances, it just looks as if you might better leave."

Barcroft backed toward the door. "As you wish, then." He glanced at Cloud. "Take over, Cloud. I'm going back to camp. He paused a moment, and it appeared he was more hurt than angry. "Good night, Mister Lawton, Missus Lawton. Good night, Hanna."

Hanna said, "I'll walk out with you, Aaron."

Cloud stood first on one foot, then on the other, feeling that he was caught in the middle. When the captain had gone, he said to the Lawtons, "He don't seem to realize how hard he's treatin' Miss Rutledge. Got a blind spot toward her, seems like."

Mrs. Lawton looked toward the open door through which Hanna had followed Barcroft. "Not the only blind spot he has," she said pensively.

Easter Rutledge still stared at the wall. Wanting to put her at ease, Cloud said, "Why don't you sit down, Easter . . . Miss Rutledge?" He pulled out a chair for her. She sat, but her blue eyes were still grave.

Cloud tried to appear cheerful. "Well, now, these folks have sure fixed you up pretty. I told you you'd look mighty good wearin' a white-woman dress, your hair all done up nice. You do now, and that's a fact."

Henry Lawton said, "Been a steady stream of people to the store, hopin' to catch a look at her."

Mrs. Lawton nodded. "But we've kept her pretty much out of sight. No use gettin' her all nervous with a lot of people starin' at her."

Easter had shown no response, and Cloud turned back to the Lawtons. "Sure good of you folks to take her in this way."

Mrs. Lawton shrugged away the compliment. "We're puttin' her over in the other side of the cabin, in the room with Hanna. She's welcome to stay just as long as she wants to."

"You hear that, Easter?" Cloud asked the girl. "You're goin' to like it when you get used to white people's ways. These are good folks. And they'll take real good care of you."

Easter looked at him a moment, her eyes softening. Then she said, "But there is always the captain."

"The captain, he's been through a lot, Easter. He don't really mean to be hard. He just doesn't think, sometimes."

She said firmly, "He is a bad man."

Mother Lawton sat down beside the girl and put a wrinkled hand on her arm. "Not a *bad* man, honey, a *driven* man." Easter looked blankly at her, not comprehending. Mrs. Lawton said, "Never mind, you'll understand by and by. Right now this young man has come to talk with you, to try to find out some things so he can help you."

Easter Rutledge dropped her chin. "Help me?" She slowly shook her head. "There is only one way to help me—get me back my baby. I tell you, it is a sick baby. It needs me. It has always been a weak baby. The women, they say it is the white blood. Without me it may die!"

Cloud swallowed. "It's too late for you to go back now. Look, ma'am, you've likely got folks someplace, white folks. We'd like to find them for you."

Her lips were tight. "My people are to the north. The Noconas are my people."

Rubbing the back of his neck, Cloud looked around helplessly at the Lawtons. Scouting Indians was something he could handle. Trying to talk soft words to a heartbroken woman was out of his realm.

Mrs. Lawton gently took the girl's hand. "Easter, he means well for you. We all do. You don't belong out there where you were. You belong in Christian company, with your own family."

Bleakly the girl said, "I belong with my baby."

Mrs. Lawton's voice was soft and kind. "God forgive him, that was a bad mistake on Aaron's part. But there's no way we can correct it now. We'll just have to go ahead and do the best we can to make things up to you, to help you. Won't you help *us*?"

For a long moment Easter Rutledge didn't answer. Finally she said, "You are good people. And you"—she looked at Cloud—"you tried to help me." She bit her lip. "I have lost all that mattered to me. I have nothing more to lose. I will tell you everything I remember. . . ."

7

It didn't take Cloud long to find out that soldiering was about one part action to ten parts routine—even frontier soldiering.

Headquarters was a heavy log house a mile or so down-creek from the store. The man who had built this house had put it up large and sturdy, a small fort atop a brush-cleared rise where Indians would have a hard time sneaking up unseen and where they'd have a harder time breaching the bull-stout walls. Bullet holes and splintered wood, darkened now with age, showed they'd tried it more than once. But eventually they'd caught the settler far out from his fortress and had left him to die in the open grass, his knife-carved body bleeding in the sun.

Now the long-abandoned house served as command post for Captain Aaron Barcroft and his company of the Texas Mounted Rifles. Rebuilt corrals held the horses, when they weren't in use or weren't being loose-herded on the prairie. Dust-grayed tents were staked in straight rows on either side of the log house, their canvas sides rolled up to let the summer heat escape, as much as it could.

On the hot days, Cloud wished the settler had left some trees for shade in which to pitch the tents. But the man had traded the shade for a better chance to keep his life.

A pole stood in front of the building, the tamped earth still fresh around its base. It was short for a flagpole, but tall trees weren't to be found in this country. Besides, the company didn't have a Confederate flag yet anyway. It had the pole, just in case a flag ever came.

A flat area below the house served as a drill ground. Here Barcroft regularly brought his well-thumbed copies of Hardee's *Light Infantry Tactics* and the U.S. Army's *Cavalry Tactics* to put the men through instruction and drill. Actually, he didn't really need the books anymore. He'd learned them by heart. Because he'd never been a soldier before—much less an officer—he'd studied hard to learn the things he needed to know. What Aaron Barcroft learned, he never forgot.

Part of company routine was to keep up a picket system along the frontier, one link in the state's chain of posts which extended all the way from the northern extremity on the Red River to the southern line on the Rio Grande. At regular intervals Barcroft dispatched men to work out in either direction, meeting riders from other companies and joining the chain. As they rode, these riders watched closely for Indian signs. Any time the Indians made a raid, they had to cross the patrol lines ridden regularly by the Texas Mounted Rifles.

The Rifles also watched for signs of white men moving west. Often these were war-evaders trying to escape service in the armies of the Confederacy. On the occasions when the Rifle patrols met such men, there was usually little they could do about them. These service-evaders usually traveled in parties big enough to stand off the Indians—or the Rifles.

Anyway, Indians were the main reason the Rifles were organized. The "scalawags" had to be put up with, like an incurable disease. Long as they didn't bother anything, the patrols usually left them alone.

Cloud found that Barcroft had a simple but effective method of getting rid of the occasional laggard or coward who found his way into the command. He worked the man's tail off or put him in the most hazardous duty. Usually it wouldn't be long before the man turned up missing on morning roll call. Though he was supposed to, the captain never sent a patrol after such a deserter to bring him back. He was afraid he might have to put up with the man again.

As to antisecessionists like Cloud, Barcroft had no clear-cut policy, other than to keep them busy. Occasionally some little animosity flared between Unionist and staunch Confederate, but most of the men kept their politics to themselves. They agreed it was more worthwhile to fight Indians than to fight each other.

An exception was a ruddy-faced, belligerent farmer

named Seward Prince, who stood up for the Confederacy proud and loud, and was constantly daring any "black Republican" to say him nay. He had whipped just about every Unionist in the company, including Quade Guffey, and he kept challenging Cloud. Finally Cloud got a bellyful of it.

He walked with Prince down to the creek, out of sight. Here, completely alone, the two took off their shirts and wrestled and slugged for the better part of an hour. They kept it up until both men could hardly move. The only thing they settled was that one was about as tough as the other.

From then on, respecting one another but with no friendship between them, Cloud and Prince kept their distance as best they could.

Barcroft got wind of the fight. Afterwards, he kept Cloud assigned out on patrol duty most of the time. No sooner would Cloud drag in wearily from one scouting trip than he would get orders from Barcroft to go out on another. The only consolation was that Barcroft was working Seward Prince about as hard. Whichever way he sent Cloud, he sent Prince in the opposite direction.

Often Quade Guffey was assigned with Cloud. Riding out one day into the dry country to the west, Quade commented, "Ever seem to you like the captain's got all of us picked as has any sort of Union leanin's? Keeps us bumpin' our tailbone agin a saddle all the time. Don't give us no chance to sit around camp and talk treason."

"Keep us out of trouble," Cloud commented. "Man opens his mouth wrong these days, he can get hung for it. Maybe he's doin' us a favor, keepin' us too busy to talk. Anyway, I'd rather be out on scout than in camp havin' to drill."

Quade agreed. "Drill looks to me like a heap of foolishness. Who's goin' to ride in a column of twos—or march along in step—into a battle with the Indians?"

Cloud shrugged. "Give the devil his due; Barcroft knows what he's about. You take this drill now, it teaches discipline. Most of us in this outfit never took no orders before. Somethin' comes up we don't like, we want to stop and argue about it. But you get in a fight, you got to know how to follow an order. That's what this drill is for."

If Barcroft worked and drilled his men until they dragged, he fought for them, too. Cloud and Guffey happened to be in camp, resting from a long patrol, the day an inspector came out from Austin headquarters to look things over. He was a paunchy little man with a big nose and a quarrelsome voice that started complaining as soon as he rode up in his hack. For an hour he made the rounds with Captain Barcroft, criticizing first one thing, then another.

He pointed to Cloud and Guffey and said crossly, "I see men sitting over yonder in the shade, Captain. Orders call for plenty of drill. I suggest that you should have them out at drill instead of lounging about."

"These men are fresh in from a long scout."

"Perhaps you haven't heard, Captain, but we're at war. This is no time for weakness in men. We must be strong and hard, ready to sacrifice."

Barcroft had tried hard to contain his anger, but that was too much. He pointed to the man's soft belly and gritted, "*You* haven't done without anything, that's plain to see. Time and again you politicians have promised us what we need to carry on our job here, and time and again you've turned a deaf ear to everything I've asked you for. It's all I can to do keep these men fed. Times we don't have enough powder and lead to do our job. It's been two months since these men have been paid. You stand there fat and comfortable and talk to me about being hard, about accepting sacrifice?"

The fat man sputtered. "Captain, I'll remind you who I am—"

"I know damned well who you are, and I know *what* you are! If you press me, I'll tell you what that is. And if you don't like it, I'll let you choose your own weapons!"

The inspector was backing away. "I'll have your commission! I'll tell them back in Austin!"

"You do that! Tell them for me that they're just a bunch of grasping politicians with their fingers so deep in the pie that they don't care if the whole house is afire! Tell them that if they don't send us what we need, I'll turn my back on the Indians and lead this company to Austin! We'll do some housecleaning there, I promise you!"

The inspector didn't even wait for supper.

Cloud and Guffey tried to hold back their grins as they watched the politician's hack pull away.

Barcroft said sharply, "You two get out of my sight or I'll set you to drilling!"

* * *

Now and again, when he had the chance, Cloud would drop by to visit Easter Rutledge at the Lawton home. Indoors much of the time now, she was beginning to lose much of the dark-brown color the outdoor life had given her. Her skin appeared to soften. Some of the grief lines had faded from around her eyes. She seemed now to be prettier than he had first thought.

The first time he saw her smile was one day when she asked him about his name, Cloud.

"Cloud," she said, then repeated the name, listening to the sound of it. "Sounds like an Indian name. You're not an Indian, are you?"

She smiled then as he assured her he was not. After that, she smiled with him more and more often.

And now that he had seen her smile, he went back to visit her more and more often.

One day, freshly bathed and shaved after a long patrol, Cloud rode up to the house behind the store and tied his horse to the fence. Mother Lawton was out sweeping the yard clean. There was no grass, so the old woman took pride in keeping her yard swept bare as her floor.

"Hello, Cloud." She smiled. "I reckon you came to see me!"

He grinned back at her. "Sure I did. Who else?"

"I couldn't imagine. But you'll find her down by the creek. Took her slate with her. She's practicin' writin'."

Cloud's eyebrows lifted. "Learnin' fast, isn't she?"

"Hanna's work. Hanna's a natural teacher. She teaches all the kids around here, and Easter's an apt pupil."

Cloud said, "I'm glad. Maybe she'll find her way easier than we thought she would." He frowned. "How's she doin', otherwise?"

Mother Lawton shrugged, leaning on her broom. "As well as could be expected, I suppose. I mean, you couldn't expect miracles, tearin' her away like that from the people she knew, from . . . But there's times she acts almost happy for a little while."

"The people around here, they've taken to her pretty good, haven't they?"

"Most of them. She was a real curiosity at first. Everybody wanted to come and look at her. They scared her some. But she got over that—sort of come to accept it, I guess. And people liked her—most people, anyway."

"Some didn't."

"Cloud, there are always a few who won't understand. They say she's a white woman, and she ought to've killed herself rather than live with the Indians that way—take one for a husband—bear his baby. One woman even told her that, to her face."

Cloud looked sharply at Mother Lawton. "Did it hurt her?"

"Didn't hurt her as much as it made her mad. And when she gets mad, she gets Indian-mad." She smiled. "That woman never has come back. Not even to the store. Just sends her husband when she needs somethin'."

Cloud nodded. "Good for Easter."

Mother Lawton took hold of the broom again. "Well, I've got work to do. Go on down to the creek. You'll find her."

Walking down toward the water, Cloud could hear children talking. When he spotted Easter, she was sitting in a rude outdoor chair in the deep shade of cottonwood trees, several youngsters gathered around her. She was showing them the letters she had made on a slate. "Is that all right?" she asked. A little girl said, "It's fine, except the bar needs to be straight on the T. Here, I'll show you."

Cloud watched silently, smiling, until the children noticed him and Easter turned around to see what they were looking at. Cloud took off his hat. "Howdy, Easter."

"Hello, Cloud." She stood up and faced him. The children waited around until they could tell their visit with Easter was over. Then the girl who had corrected Easter's writing said, "Well, we'll be going, Miss Rutledge. We'll see you later."

"Come back, children."

Easter watched them go, and Cloud could see the faint smile that lighted her face. "Good children," she said quietly.

"Nice to see you've found you some friends."

"Children are always the same—white children, Indian children . . ." He watched the sadness drift into her eyes again, and he knew she was remembering.

He pointed quickly to the slate. "Looks like you're doin' fine."

She looked at the letters she had made. "The Noconas have a picture writing, but it's not like this. Here you can write anything you want to say, any word." She looked away, to ward the children disappearing from sight. "It makes me feel foolish. I am so much older, yet they teach me."

Cloud smiled. Easter no longer had difficulty in talking. English had come back with use. Before long she would be reading and writing it.

"You're doin' fine," he said again. "Study with Hanna Lawton and pretty soon you'll be readin' and writin' a sight better than *I* can. I never had a chance for real schoolin' myself. Just had to pick it up the best way I could."

"I study and practice hard. It keeps my mind busy. I don't have so much time to think . . . about other things."

"But you *do* think about them."

The sadness lay dark in her face. Cloud knew it was never far beneath the surface. She said evenly, "I know it's useless, but there are things you can't forget. You even wake up, dreaming. . . ." She bit her lip. "Cloud, do you really think you'll find my family—my *white* family?"

Cloud nodded. "Maybe we will. The captain sent word down that way to see if there's still some Rutledges around."

"I hope there are. At first I didn't want to go. But now I want to see them. Maybe if I find a new home, new people, I can stop thinking so much. At least I can try, Cloud, I can try."

He saw then how much hope she was building

up. She was grasping desperately for something to cling to.

"Do you think my people will be ashamed of me?" she asked worriedly.

"Ashamed? Why?"

Pensively she said, "I am a grown woman, but I don't know the things a white woman should know. I can't read, I can't write. I don't know much of the white man's God. Every day I make mistakes. All I know are the Indian ways. Maybe my family will be ashamed."

He reached out and took her hand. "Easter, don't you worry."

"Some people here have said I should be ashamed, living with the Indians when I am white, having an Indian husband. Do *you* feel that way, Cloud? Does that thought bother you?"

"Now, don't you fret yourself thataway," he said quickly. But his voice wasn't as firm as he wanted it to be. Truth was, it *did* bother him a little, even yet. He let go of her hand. "Easter, if they're your folks, they won't bother about what's past. They'll just take you and be glad you're back."

"I hope so," she said softly, "I hope so." She looked up at Cloud then, gratitude in her eyes. "You've been good to me, Cloud. I wish you could come here oftener."

"The captain keeps me awful busy."

"If he doesn't find any of my people, I won't have anyone, Cloud—no one but you and the Lawtons."

"You've got lots of friends here."

"It isn't the same as your own people." She looked

down. "I hope they come soon. If they don't, I don't know how I can stand it."

"I been hopin' they wouldn't come *too* soon."

Her eyes narrowed. "Why not?"

"Because you'll be leavin' then, and I'll miss you."

She gave him a faint smile and touched his hand a moment. "I won't forget you, Cloud." She studied awhile, then asked unexpectedly, "If none of my people come, would *you* take me, Cloud?"

He stepped back, swallowing. "What?"

"I would have no husband, no people. A woman is not meant to be alone."

He stammered. "Look, Easter, among white folks . . ."

She nodded. "I know, they must have the papers and be married. It is like that among the Indians, except without the papers. But I would marry you. Would you marry me, Cloud?"

He swallowed again, and no words came. Hitting him that way all of a sudden . . . she hadn't learned the devious manner of the white woman yet. She still had the direct, devastating way of the Indian.

Looking down, she said, "Or maybe you wouldn't want to. Maybe you'd remember that before you there was an Indian husband."

Tightly he answered, "Easter, you're a good woman, a pretty woman. Any man'd be proud. The Indian husband hasn't got nothin' to do with it. It's just that I hadn't given no study to gettin' married, no study atall."

Yet even as he spoke, he knew he was half lying to her. He knew the thought of the Indian husband *might* stay with him. He knew this: that he wanted to reach out and pull her to him and kiss her. Yet he realized too that every time he touched her, he might remember there had been another man, a savage who had traded for her like he would swap for a brood mare.

He clenched his fist and wished to God he knew what to say.

As it was, he didn't get the chance to say anything. Captain Barcroft came striding down the creekbank toward him, his back straight, his dark eyes somber.

Cloud turned to meet him and stood half at attention. Half was about as far as he ever went. Figuring Barcroft was about to send him off on another long patrol, he asked wearily, "You lookin' for me, Captain?"

"Looking for both of you." The captain's eyes dwelt a moment on Easter Rutledge. Cloud saw no softness in them.

He hates that girl, he told himself.

Easter Rutledge stood up stiffly and faced the captain, her eyes turned suddenly hard.

And she doesn't like him any better, Cloud thought.

"What business do you have with me, Captain?" Easter asked, her voice crisp.

"I have some news for you, Miss Rutledge," the captain replied. "I've just gotten word that they've found a brother of yours down south. He'll be here in a few days."

Easter suddenly swayed. "A brother . . ." The words came in a whisper. She dropped her chin, and

Cloud saw her lips go tight. She blinked, trying to stop a sudden rush of tears. Then she looked at the captain, her voice no longer steady.

"Only a brother? There are no others?"

The captain shook his head. "I couldn't say. The message spoke only of a brother."

Easter sat down limply in her chair. "My own people . . ." she said wonderingly. "My own people . . ."

Cloud took her hand and patted it gently. "That's sure fine news, Easter. I'm glad for you." But he knew he really wasn't. He felt something sinking inside him.

The captain turned his gaze to Cloud. "I'm afraid I have something for you too, Cloud. Miguel Soto has come in with a report of Indian signs—raiding party south of here. I'm preparing to take out the company."

Cloud nodded. "All right, sir. I'll be right with you."

The captain tipped his hat to the girl and said, "Good day," as if he had just casually met her strolling on the street. He turned on his heel and walked back up the creekbank.

Gripping Easter's hand, Cloud stood a moment looking down at this woman, wishing he knew something to say. But there weren't words for what he really felt.

"Easter," he spoke quietly, "I got to be goin'. But as to what you said to me a while ago—what you proposed—I felt honored that you asked me, sure enough I did. But I wouldn't go tellin' Mother Lawton about it, was I you. You see, white women sort of beat around the bush on things like that. They don't just come out plain that way. They get what they want from a man, but they make him think it was *his* idea. Mother Lawton might not understand."

Still dazed by the captain's news, Easter said, "I will remember. Be careful, Cloud."

"I will. And don't you go leavin' here till I get back."

He squeezed her hand, then turned away to follow the captain.

8

Lancing in below Brush Hill, the Indian raiding party had struck out in an arc northeastward. Plenty of settlers in that direction, and plenty of horses. Good strategy for the Indians. Coming in from open country to the west, they could go out to the north without having to retrace their steps, without running head-on into aroused white pursuit.

The raid caught Barcroft's company short, many of his men out on scout and patrol duty. He sent quick word to those he could reach in short time. The others he would have to do without. To those who could get the message, he set a rendezvous point so the rest of the company would not have to wait in camp. Two hours after the alarm was raised, the company was riding out in a column of dry dust, spurs jingling, saddle guns jostling in leather scabbards. Silent men sat straight, shoulders squared, a battle-eagerness in their faces.

Out in the lead rode Cloud and Soto, the Mexican led by his unerring instinct even though they hadn't yet struck the trail. He knew which way it had headed—where they were most likely to cross it without riding unnecessary miles. He rode to it like a bee to the hive.

As the small company moved along, some of its men began catching up and falling in from other duty, adding strength. At the appointed rendezvous point, Barcroft called a short halt for rest. And while the men waited, others showed up as instructed.

Barcroft looked with Miguel and Cloud at the trail the Indians had left. "About fifteen of them, you think?"

"Sí, mi capitán," said Miguel. Cloud nodded agreement.

The captain glanced back over his men and nodded in satisfaction. "Fair match, then, I'd say. Let's go."

The Indian tracks were several hours old, but the Rifles were pushing their horses as hard as they dared, yet saving strength for a long chase if it developed.

At length the company came upon a spot where the Indians had reined up and milled around as if in conference, then had scattered. Cloud raised his chin and sniffed. "Smoke, Captain, I do believe."

Barcroft took a long breath and replied, "You're right. Let's find it."

They rode out, and the smell grew stronger. Cloud glanced at Miguel, then swung his rifle around in front of him on the saddle, where he could get at it in a hurry. He could see the smoke now through a line of brush which clustered along a summer-dry watercourse. Breaking through the brush, he and

Miguel saw the still-crackling ruins of a cabin, the roof tumbled in among the charred sidelogs. They reined up to give the scene a long look from some distance.

"Been a spell since they left, I reckon," Cloud commented in a moment. "We better look around; might still be somebody alive."

Even as he spoke, he saw a movement in the brush at the other side of the cabin. He gave the rifle a quick jerk, freeing its leather thong from the saddlehorn. Then he let the rifle ease down again.

"By Ned," he breathed. "A woman and kids."

From out of the brush came a woman and several children, a couple of them boys of ten to twelve. The woman carried a baby in one arm, a rifle in the other. One of the boys also held a rifle. The woman walked up to the two advance scouts as the rest of the company broke out of the timber behind them. She looked them over a moment before she spoke.

"Howdy. Be you fellers Rangers?"

Barcroft spoke, "We're the Mounted Rifles. It appears you've had some unwelcome company."

"Well," she replied slowly, "they wasn't invited."

"Anybody hurt?"

"No, sir, we taken to the brush in time. Husband, he was out cow-huntin', and he ain't got back yet. He's goin' to be some mad when he does git back. They got all the horses we had, 'cept the one he's on."

Barcroft said, "Do you have any neighbors you can go to?"

She nodded. "We got neighbors pretty close, only

seven-eight miles. We'll go over there soon's my husband gits in." She frowned. "You don't reckon them *national assassinators*'ll be a-comin' back?"

That was a name some people on the frontier had given the Indians because of the federal reservation that had afforded some of the marauders sanctuary between raids.

Barcroft said, "I doubt they'll be back this way. They came in one direction, and I'd judge they'll go out another." He looked at her children, and Cloud could read the thought in the captain's troubled eyes. "Just the same, ma'am, I'd take care. It would be wise of you to move to a settlement and stay there."

She shook her head, much as Lige Moseley had done when the captain had made the same suggestion to him. "No, thank you, sir, we lived in one of them settlements once. There's things worse than Indians."

Barcroft shrugged. People like this, you couldn't scare off. "It's up to you. I wish we could stay and help, but we've got to keep moving."

"We'll make it all right."

"Maybe we'll recover your horses, ma'am. We'll try."

Moving out, they began to cross land that was vaguely familiar to Cloud. After a long time they broke out of the big thicket and came into sight of old Lige Moseley's double cabin. Cloud's heart quickened. The Indian trail led straight that way. They had hit Lige, too, sure as thunder.

The cabin was still standing, though Cloud hadn't seen any sign of life around it. He held up his hand to slow down the rest of the company until he had a chance to ride in and show himself.

"If that old fire-eater's still alive," he told Miguel Soto, "he's a crack shot. We don't want him makin' any mistakes."

Lige's dogs set up an awful racket as Cloud rode in alone. Lige Moseley stepped out from the corral, waving his left hand. His right hand was weighted down by a rifle big as a cannon. Cloud glanced over into the corral. Just as the last time, Moseley's horses were safe inside.

The settler's bearded face broke into a wide grin. "Well, you boys come too late. Excitement's done over."

Looking around, Cloud saw little sign of battle. These raiders evidently had been smarter than the last bunch. They hadn't tried to go up against Moseley's solid walls. "Get you any Indians?"

Moseley shook his head. "Can't say as I did. But we didn't lose no horses, neither. Comanches has got to git up awful early in the mornin' to steal anything off of this outfit."

The rest of the company rode in after seeing it was all right. The captain, dusty now with whiskers beginning to darken his face, nodded at Moseley. Mrs. Moseley and the children filed out of the house to see the Mounted Rifles. The captain's gaze dwelt a long time on the children, especially on a little girl of three or so named Joanna.

Same age as his was, Cloud thought.

Barcroft said, "It appears you've been lucky again, Moseley."

"Ain't just luck, Captain," Moseley replied, patting his big rifle. "Keen eye down the barrel of one of these is better than luck. And keen eyes just naturally run in the Moseley family." He pointed his chin at his wife and at the boy Luke. "You-all care to stop and rest yourselves a mite?"

The captain shook his head. "Can't. The Indians lost a little time here, and they lost some at another place back down the way. If we *don't* lose any we'll be able to make some gain on them."

Moseley agreed with a nod of his head. "I'm a right fair shot, Captain. I'd be tickled to go along and he'p you, if you'd care to have me."

Barcroft shrugged. "Suit yourself. But what about your family?"

"Them Indians won't be back. Besides, Luke'll be here. He's as good a shot as I am."

While Lige saddled his horse, Samantha Moseley came farther out into the yard. She stood silently watching Cloud, her eyes soft with a longing she probably could not even understand.

The dogs followed for a way as the company rode out. Cloud turned once in the saddle to see if they had dropped back. He saw Samantha still standing there, watching him.

Miguel Soto glanced at Cloud, his eyebrows raised. "Pretty girl, that one," he commented pointedly. "A most pretty girl."

The Indian trail was not hard to follow. Besides their own mounts, there were the several extra horses the Comanches had picked up. An hour or so from Moseley's, Cloud and Miguel, up front again, came across one of the Indian horses limping along painfully. Dirt was caked on its chest and along one side. It evidently had fallen and lamed itself, and its rider had transferred to one of the stolen horses.

"Still sweatin' a little," Cloud observed. "Them redskins ain't too awful far in front of us anymore."

Shortly afterward, he thought he heard the distant sound of gunfire, drifting in the north wind. He stepped out of the saddle and handed Miguel his reins. Then he walked out a little piece to listen, where the squeak of saddle leather wouldn't bother him.

He listened a minute or two, turning his head first one way, then the other, his face drawn into a deep frown. "I'd of sworn I heard it," he said, shaking his head. He rode back to report it to the captain, then regained his lead with Miguel. "You ever hear anything, Miguel?" he asked.

The Mexican shook his head. "Maybeso you got better ears."

"Or a better imagination."

They were in and out of the brush for an hour before they suddenly came in sight of a single wagon, sitting at the edge of a big post oak motte. Part of its canvas cover had been burned away.

Cloud sucked in a short breath. "Caught 'em a mover. Bet they didn't leave much of him."

Then he saw movement at the wagon, and he got a glimpse of a man with a hat on, the quick flare of a skirt. "Looky there, Miguel. Them folks must of scrapped their way through it."

He spurred into an easy lope, Miguel close beside him. He reined up just short of the wagon and took a quick look. He saw one gray-bearded man and two women—one old like the man, one young. The man had his left arm wrapped in a white strip of cloth, evidently torn from a woman's underskirt. A blotch of red showed through it. The older of the women stood close, hand red with blood from the bandaging. The younger woman stood a little to one side, the clutch of fear still strong in her dust-smeared face.

Cloud dismounted, flipping his loop rein over his horse's head and keeping hold of it. "You folks must've put up a dandy fight to've run them off." He didn't say it, but he thought it would have taken a lot to have discouraged a bunch of bucks if they had seen the young woman. "You didn't lose anybody?"

The old man shook his head. "They got off with our team, but we got off with our lives."

Cloud glanced at a rifle leaned against the wagon wheel.

"That the only gun you got?" he asked incredulously. "Don't seem like one gun would've held them off long."

"We had a pistol too. Wife used the pistol."

Cloud glanced questioningly at Miguel. Three people with only two guns between them, and a prize like that young woman with her long brown hair. Didn't seem reasonable.

He looked at the household goods piled in the wagon and said, " 'Pears you folks was movin' someplace."

The old man nodded. "We was. But we can't git far now without horses."

The fear still lay live and fierce in the young woman's face. "Ma'am," Cloud said to her, "you don't need to be scared no more. They're gone, and I don't expect they'll be back."

She tried to speak, but the words stuck in her throat.

"My daughter-in-law, mister," the old man said quickly. "She got a bad scare. She'll be all right."

"Where's your son?" Cloud asked.

The old man hesitated, "Why, he's off in the army—the Confederate Army."

"And you was movin', just the three of you?"

"That's it, that's all there is to it." The old man was plenty nervous, and so was the old woman. Cloud thought that was natural, considering what they had just been through. And yet . . .

Then he saw the tracks, a set of boot tracks that didn't match the ones he saw around the old man's feet. And Cloud knew.

There was somebody else with this wagon!

Barcroft rode up with the rest of the company. As was his way, he wasted no time with foolish questions. "Nobody killed?"

The old man shook his head. "No, sir, no damage except a little scratch on my arm, and the fact that them red thieves run off with our horses."

Like Cloud, Barcroft found it hard to believe these three had stood off that raiding party alone. "How did you do it?"

The old woman spoke up for the first time. "We

seen them Indians comin' and knowed we couldn't outrun them. We got our wagon up here and piled off and took out into that brush yonder. They didn't try too hard to come in and git us. They just cut the team loose and left. They set the wagon afire, but we put the fire out before it did us much hurt."

The captain looked at the young woman, and he gently shook his head. Watching him, Cloud knew the captain was thinking the same thing the scout had.

The captain said, "How about showing us where you made your stand?"

The old man argued, "Now, soldier, there don't seem to be no reason for that. 'Pears to me like you fellers would be most interested in gittin' out after them Indians."

"I'd just like to see how you fought them off." Cloud could see suspicion in the captain's eyes.

Then Miguel bent over and examined the foot tracks. "*Capitán!*"

Catching Miguel's eye, Cloud quickly shook his head. But it was already too late. The captain said, "What is it, Miguel?"

Miguel glanced again at Cloud and shrugged. "It is nothing, *Capitán*. We forget it."

"You've found something," the captain pressed. "What is it?"

Hemmed up, Miguel showed Barcroft the tracks. The captain said grimly, "I knew something was wrong here. I just couldn't put my finger on it." He turned to the old man and pointed out into the brush. "Who's in there?"

Trembling, the old man said, "Nobody, sir, nobody. You're mistaken."

The captain declared, "There's no mistake. You're hiding someone. Who is it?" When he got no reply from the old man, he turned sharply to the young woman. "Your husband, perhaps? What is he, a deserter? A conscription dodger?"

Tears rolled down the young woman's cheeks, leaving trails in the dust that lay heavy on her face. "Please," she begged, "please."

Barcroft turned to his men. "Dismount and fan out. We'll push through that brush until we find him."

Miguel eased up close to Cloud. Quietly he said, "I'm sorry. I speak before I think."

"Can't help it now."

They moved out in a walk, a ragged line of men filtering through heavy brush. Cloud could hear the young woman sobbing behind them. She was following. He turned once and told her, "Ma'am, you better go back."

She kept coming, and he let her alone.

A jackrabbit jumped up and skittered away, and half the men in the group jerked their rifles up in sudden reflex before they realized what it was.

Then a man somewhere ahead of them shouted, "Stay back, all of you! We've got rifles here!"

Cloud saw a movement. It wasn't one man; it was two!

"Stay back!" the voice shouted again. There was a shot that clipped the leaves out of a post oak above Cloud's head. Then came the sound of a quick struggle and a second man saying sharply, "Put the gun down. It's no use."

Two men stood up in plain sight, their hands in the air. Cloud broke into a trot toward them. He was one of the first men to reach them. Behind him came the young woman, crying, "Don't shoot them! Please don't shoot them!" She dodged in front of Cloud and threw her arms about one of the men, sobbing. The man lowered his chin and pressed his cheek to her hair, his hand gently patting her back.

Barcroft moved up to them and said solemnly, "You're under arrest."

"What for?" one of the young men asked.

"Desertion, possibly, or flight to avoid conscription. Whichever it is, we'll find out."

The woman turned her face toward the captain. "What'll happen to them?"

Evenly the captain said, "They fired upon a Confederate company. I'd say they'll likely hang for that."

She cried out, "No!" and clung tightly to her husband.

The younger of the two men said, "I was the one fired the shot, not *him*. Besides, I didn't shoot at nobody. I just fired over your heads. Hoped I'd scare you off."

It was easy to tell that the two men were brothers, both in their twenties, both tall and strongly handsome with the broad shoulders of men who know well the ax and the plow.

"What happens to you will be up to a military court," Barcroft said.

Seward Prince growled, "Unionists, I'd bet, the

both of them. Hangin'd be just about right, if you was to ask me."

Curtly Cloud said, "Nobody asked you."

The Rifles walked back out to the edge of the timber, with the two men in front of them and the young woman leaning tearfully against her husband. The old couple stood slumped helplessly, hopelessness in their tired, grieving faces. They sat down on their wagon tongue, and the old man pleaded:

"Captain, it weren't none of their fault. I was the one made them run. It's this damned war. It's not *our* war. We didn't ask for it, and we don't want no part of it. I got no slaves and don't want none. I say if these rich landowners and slave men want a war fought, let them fight it theirselves, and leave us poor folks alone!"

Cloud thought he could see sympathy in the captain's face, which surprised him a little. But he knew the captain was not one to be swayed from duty, even by sympathy. The captain asked, "Where were you going?"

"We was tryin' to git to Mexico."

"That's a long way."

The old man nodded. "It is that, but we had nothin' much else but time anyway. We wasn't goin' to hurt nobody. We was just tryin' to find us a neutral ground. Is that a sin, Captain?"

The captain slowly shook his head. "Too bad, old-timer. If your boys had stayed out in plain sight, we never would have thought much about it, might not even have asked any questions. But they hid, and that changed things. When they fired on us, that sealed the warrant. We'll have to take them with us."

The people were silent a moment. Then the old man asked, "And what about us? What're we goin' to do?"

The captain had no answer. Lige Moseley spoke up quietly: "I got a cabin south a-ways. Back-trail us, and you'll find it. If we don't git your horses back from the Indians, maybe I can swap you a couple. There's lots of things me and my family needs, and maybe you got some of it we can trade you out of."

While the two young men said their tearful good-byes to the family, the captain had a couple of pack-horses stripped so the prisoners could ride them.

"You'll have to go bareback," he said to the pair, "but that's the best we can do. And we've got to take you with us because we can't spare anybody to stay back and guard you."

Lige Moseley frowned. "I'd guard them, Captain."

The captain smiled. "That's a kind offer, Moseley, but I don't know you that well. Being a friend of Cloud's, you might even share a little of his Unionist feeling, for all I know." Despite the smile, Cloud could tell the captain was dead serious. "No offense, but I like to know my guards."

Moseley turned his palms upward and shrugged.

They moved out again, quickly leaving behind them the wagon, the old man and the women. For as long as the raiders remained in sight, the trio watched motionless—three tragic statues standing in the grass.

•

The Indian signs were fresh now. Captain Barcroft signaled Cloud and Miguel to speed up. But darkness came, and the Indians had not been caught. Reluctantly, Barcroft called a night halt. The men ate supper and stretched out to rest. Barcroft had the prisoners' hands tied to the trunks of trees, and set a special guard to watch over them through the night.

Long before daylight, the men were up. As soon as they could see tracks, Cloud and Miguel were out a-horseback, far in the lead of the company.

Before long they came to the place where the Indians had camped. The ashes were still warm. Cloud nodded in satisfaction at Miguel, and the pair moved out. It wasn't hard now to keep the company at a strong pace. If anything, it was hard to hold them back.

Late in the morning Cloud and Miguel rode into sight of the Indians. They reined up quickly and gave the Indian sign to the company behind them. Barcroft spurred forward in a lope. He took a long look, then signaled the men to spread out and charge. The sound of pounding hoofs carried ahead to the Indians. Cloud could see the alarm rush through the bunch like the sudden sense of danger spreads through a herd of buffalo. The Indians pushed their horses into a hard run.

Way ahead of them lay a stretch of timber. The Indians made for it. Cloud spurred hard, the captain riding right along beside him. Glancing at Barcroft, Cloud could see the man's grim anticipation. Truly, here was a man who hated with all his soul, who took a fierce pleasure in seeing Indians die.

Realizing they could not make the timber, the Indians did a strange thing. They stopped and turned around, letting their stolen horses go. They formed a rough line and came running straight back toward the Rifles. Lances bristled. Cloud could see bows swung into readiness. He caught the glint of sunlight off a rifle barrel.

Most of the Texans drew their pistols, for this was going to be sudden and mean—and close up. With the pistol they would have six shots instead of the one they could get from a rifle.

One of the two prisoners pulled up beside the captain. "For God's sake, sir, give us a gun so we can defend ourselves."

Barcroft said something unintelligible, then there was no more time, for the Indians were upon them. The Indians fired first, arrows sailing ahead of them, flame blossoming from stolen guns. A Rifleman's horse went down, and Cloud heard a man shout in pain as an arrow plunked into a leg.

The Texans hauled up on the reins—most of them—and fired back with their pistols. A couple of Indian horses went down, and an Indian was chopped off of his mount as if he had run into the low limb of a tree. The rest of the Indian force passed by and went on beyond, carried by the momentum of the rush.

Suddenly, then, Cloud could see that the Rifle

force had been scattered. The captain was far out to one side. The Indians wheeled their horses around and came back for another desperate try. An early shot from one of them brought the captain's horse down. Cloud saw the animal fall, saw the captain's gun sail out into the grass. The captain tried to slip out from under the animal, but he could not move. He was pinned.

Cloud yanked his horse around and spurred out toward the captain. But the oldest of the two prisoners was closer. He raced to the captain's side and stepped down from his horse, letting the mount run on without him. The prisoner grabbed up the captain's fallen gun and threw himself to his belly in the grass, beside Barcroft.

A handful of Indians, seeing the two men down, peeled off from the rest and swept down toward the pair. Cloud saw the prisoner grab the captain's rifle out of the saddle scabbard, even as he handed the captain the pistol. Leveling the rifle over the dead horse, the man took careful aim and fired just as the nearest Comanche drew a bow into line. The Indian rolled in the grass and went limp as an empty sack.

By the time Cloud got there and stepped off beside the captain, the Indians had hauled up. Cloud fired once, bringing down one of the horses. The Indian, left afoot, reached up for help and got it from one of his friends. He swung up behind another Indian and rode away.

It was a rout now, the remaining Indians abandoning the stolen horses and everything else in an effort to get to the timber.

Most of the Rifles followed after them awhile, managing to bring down one more. They stopped short of the timber, for that was likely to be like a beehive.

With his own horse and rope, Cloud managed to pull the captain's dead horse over and free Barcroft. The captain stood up shakily. The young prisoner loosened the cinch and got the captain's saddle loose.

That done, Cloud walked back to Barcroft and asked, "Everything all right, sir?"

Barcroft was rubbing his leg. "I guess. There doesn't seem to be anything broken." He glanced at the prisoner. "I was in a bad spot for a minute," he said to the man. "If you hadn't come when you did, they'd have ridden over me, more than likely. And they wouldn't have left much."

The prisoner was trembling a little now, the nervous aftermath of the quick battle. He didn't say anything.

The captain observed, "It might have been better for you if you'd let them get me."

When the young man said nothing, Cloud put in, "Captain, it just goes to show you the kind of man he is. He couldn't let a thing like that happen to you, even if standin' back might've given him a chance to go free."

Barcroft said evenly, "Cloud, you should know better than try to change my mind."

"Wasn't tryin' to change nothin', Captain. I was only thinkin' maybe this might make you show some extra consideration."

"Damn it," Barcroft argued, "I'm a soldier. I can't

allow personal feelings—personal gratitude—to stand in the way of my duty."

"Can't you, Captain? Ain't nobody knows about these boys but us. What other people don't know won't hurt them none."

The captain said sharply, "I already feel badly enough about this. Don't make it any worse for me." Turning away, he said to Miguel, "Take a few men and go bring that bunch of stolen horses up here. Some of us need remounts."

He walked on out across the grass, halting just once to look back.

Cloud said with satisfaction, "It's eatin' at him. That's a good sign."

The older prisoner said, "Truth of it is, Mister Cloud, I wasn't really thinkin' much about the captain when I done it. I could see that gun lyin' out there, and I didn't have one. I wanted that gun. I didn't care about the captain."

Cloud held down a grin. "For God's sake, don't you tell *him* that!"

Later that afternoon they came back by the abandoned wagon. Footprints showed the old man and the old woman had gone on to Moseley's, as suggested. The captain let the two brothers hook their recovered horses to the wagon and drive it. The company camped for the night at Moseley's place.

Several times Cloud saw the captain looking at the two brothers and their family. With Lige Moseley, he discussed the uncertainty he could see in the officer's face.

"Lige, I think he's about made up his mind. Only

question is, how can he do it and get by with it. You got a couple of extra horses you'd be willin' to swap to that old man—a couple of *fast* horses?"

Lige Moseley pulled at his whiskers. "I don't want you gittin' the idea I go along with your Union leanin's, 'cause I don't. But I kind of took a likin' to them two boys." His white teeth showed in a smile. "I just *might* have a pair of horses, sure enough."

Presently the captain came over to Moseley. "Mister Moseley, yesterday you offered to guard our prisoners. I have a lot of tired men needing rest. Would you still consent to do it—to guard them tonight?" While Lige considered, the captain added pointedly, "Now, I wouldn't want you to go to sleep. Of course, you being a civilian, I couldn't do anything to you if you did. You *would* stay awake, wouldn't you?"

Lige grinned. "Sure, Captain. You can count on me to do what's right!"

Next morning Lige and Elkin walked up to the captain just at daylight and shook his shoulder. The captain turned over on his blanket and raised up on one elbow, blinking.

Lige said, "Captain, I'm afraid them two prisoners has gotten away!"

"Gotten away?" Barcroft asked with little show of surprise. "Now, I wonder how they did that?"

"Reckon I went to sleep, Captain, even after the promise I made you. Tireder than I really thought. Boys taken a couple of my horses and headed south. Must've gone sometime early in the night."

Elkin asked Barcroft, "Should we go after them?"

The captain shook his head, a shadow of a grin about him. "They have too much of a lead on us now. There'd be no use in it."

Elkin began to understand, humor playing in his eyes. "We *could* notify some of the companies to the south of us."

The captain looked at the smiling Cloud, then cut his gaze back to Elkin. "Yes, I guess we could. I'll write a letter to Austin—first time I think about it."

9

Indian raids excepted, it was one of the most exciting days Brush Hill had ever known. The word came in that Easter Rutledge's brother was due to arrive. Down at the Lawton house, Mother Lawton and Hanna and several other women bustled about in good-natured confusion, trying to get Easter prepared for the meeting. But if anything, they were just making her more and more flustered, more and more nervous.

Cloud went down to see what was happening and found Hanna working with Easter's hair while Mother Lawton sewed one of Hanna's dresses, taking it up to fit Easter. Other women were cooking up a feast—or such a feast as an isolated frontier community could ever have.

Looks like they're fixin' to feed fifty people, Cloud thought. *Ain't but one brother, is there?*

Without any patrol duty to perform, and somehow getting the feeling he was underfoot in all this feminine company, Cloud rode off down the south trail alone and took up a station in the shade of an oak. Loose-tying his horse, he sat on the ground. With one eye watching the trail, he idly sketched maps in the sand, then wiped them out and started over. This, to him, was a worthwhile pastime in that it helped firm in his mind the outline of the various parts of the country he had ridden in.

Tiring of his mapmaking, he finally settled down to watching the trail, looking for a sign of a rider. He asked himself a dozen times what kind of man Easter's brother would turn out to be. He asked himself if Easter would really be happy when she found her own family. Maybe she would. He had seen the glow in her eyes a while ago. She had been depending strongly upon this, for there was little else she *could* depend upon anymore. She had left so much behind her. . . .

Cloud almost wished they had never found her brother. Again and again her words came back to him: *Would you marry me, Cloud? Would you marry me?*

He clenched his fist. *Why didn't I tell her yes? Why couldn't I be man enough to forget about that Indian?*

Now, he knew, it was too late. This was a big country. Once she went south, chances were he would never see her again. He might not even be able to find her if he tried.

A man can be a fool sometimes. If he really loves a woman, he ought to be able to forget about everything else. Why couldn't I?

He saw the wagon a long time before it reached him, and somehow he knew this would be the man.

Slowly he stood up and stretched himself, then stood stiffly and watched the wagon approach. As it neared, he stepped out away from the tree and toward the trail. He held up his hand.

The man hauled up on the lines and spoke to his team. "Whoa, there, whoa-a-a." The dust from the wheels swirled up around him and then drifted out leisurely on the breeze from the north. The young man twisted his face at the taste of the dust, then turned toward Cloud and asked, "How much farther to Brush Hill?"

Cloud eyed him carefully, looking for some resemblance to Easter. "You're almost there." The man was perhaps a couple or three years older than Easter. He had the skin of a man used to staying indoors. Storekeeper, perhaps. But there was something about his eyes that showed he was related to Easter, no mistake about that. "Would you by any chance answer to the name of Rutledge?"

The young man nodded. "I would." He quietly looked Cloud over from head to foot. "And what might be your business with me?"

Cloud shrugged. "No business, I reckon. I just rode out to get the first look at you, and help you find your way in. Cloud's my name." He extended his hand. Rutledge hesitated, then took it.

"Kenneth Rutledge is mine. Ken, better known."

A vague reserve still held the man, as if he somehow distrusted Cloud. "Did they send you out to meet me?"

"Came on my own. I was the one found Easter . . . Miss Rutledge. Got kind of a special interest in her, I guess you'd say. Wanted to be sure her brother didn't have no trouble findin' where she's at."

Rutledge seemed to be looking a hole through Cloud. "You can stop worrying about her now, Mister . . . what was it . . . Cloud? She'll be my responsibility from now on."

Uncomfortable, Cloud stepped back. "Well, I expect you'll be wantin' to get on in to the settlement."

"It's been a long trip," Rutledge acknowledged. "But tell me, how does my sister look?"

Cloud blurted, "She looks mighty good to me." Then, realizing how awkward that sounded, he corrected himself. "What I mean is, she's in good health. Folks here've taken fine care of her."

Kenneth Rutledge nodded. "That's nice of them." He looked ahead of him, up the trail. "Shall we go on?"

He doesn't think much of me, seems like, thought Cloud. "Sure," he said, "Why not?"

Rutledge started his team as Cloud walked back to his horse and swung into the saddle. Cloud spurred to catch up, then pulled his horse to an easy trot alongside the wagon.

"Kind of a surprise to you, I reckon," he spoke, "findin' out after all these years that she was still alive."

"A real shock. I'd given her up for dead—we all had—a long time ago. Ever since the word came, I've been wondering—worrying—how she was going to be."

"Well, you sure don't have to be a-worryin'. She's fine, and you can take my word for that."

Cloud felt Rutledge's eyes appraising him, and he got the notion Rutledge didn't accept his judgment as amounting to much.

I look a little like an Indian myself these days, he thought, seeking the reason. *All that ridin', all that sun . . .*

He pulled up at the Rifles' camp, and Kenneth Rutledge sawed on the reins, stopping his wagon. Looking at the man's dusty face, the dark shadow of whiskers, Cloud said, "I expect you'd like to clean up and maybe shave before you go on to see Easter."

Stepping down from the wagon, Rutledge said, "I'd appreciate it."

"I'll introduce you to Captain Barcroft. Then I'll ride on down and tell the folks you're here, so they can be ready."

Rutledge held back a moment. "Cloud, tell me one thing. Have the years in captivity done much to her? I mean, I've been wondering how she would fit in. We have a tight-knit little community back home now. Settled folks, churchgoing people. Good-hearted and all, but sort of set in their ways, you understand. Easter's going to be a real curiosity to them. They'll have their eyes on her." He frowned. "It wouldn't be her fault, of course, if she made a few mistakes right at first. After all those years among the savages . . . you couldn't expect perfection."

An oddly cold feeling touched Cloud's stomach. "Don't you worry none about Easter. She'll do fine."

The women could tell by the look on Cloud's face as he walked up to the Lawtons' door.

"He's here?" Mrs. Lawton asked, her hands clasped tightly against her bosom.

Cloud nodded. "Yes'm, he's here."

Other women began to talk all at the same time and ask so many questions he couldn't keep up with them. Cloud looked about for Easter and found her standing toward the back of the room, face pale from excitement. Her lips were drawn tightly against her teeth, and she was making a strong effort not to cry. She smiled a weak smile at Cloud, but she could not hold it long.

Cloud walked to her. He wanted to take her hands in his, but not in front of all this company. Besides, what good would it do now? She would be going soon. "Easter," he said, "he'll be along directly. He stopped off at the camp to clean up a little."

It was a painful effort for her to speak. "Cloud, what is he like?"

Cloud shrugged. "He's your brother. He looks a little like you."

"Is he nice?"

Cloud hesitated. "Why . . . he'd have to be, bein' your brother."

Easter looked around for a chair and sank into it. Cloud could see she was trembling. She said, "Stay here, will you, Cloud?"

"Sure, I will, Easter. Just as long as you want me."

Mother Lawton came over, trembling as badly as Easter. "Now, child, don't you be nervous." The absurdity of her own words struck her funny, and she began to laugh. Easter laughed too, and some of the tension was gone. Mother Lawton took Easter's hand

and patted it fondly. "Everything's going to be all right, you watch."

Easter said weakly, "I know. I won't be nervous."

The old woman kept patting Easter's hand. Cloud watched her and thought, *Thank God for a woman like Mother Lawton. It would be a poorer country without her.*

Hanna Lawton stayed close to the front door, watching. It seemed like hours before she turned and said tensely, "They're coming. Aaron's bringing him."

Cloud saw Easter stiffen. Quietly he spoke to her. "Easy now, girl." Mother Lawton stood up and took Easter's hands, gently pulling the girl to her feet. The old woman tried hard to smile and reassure Easter, but she had begun trembling again herself.

Aaron Barcroft stepped through the door, glanced quickly around, then made a sweeping motion with his hand, bidding Kenneth Rutledge to enter. Hat in hand, Rutledge walked in. His blue eyes made a rapid search around the hushed room, then fell upon Easter. His tongue came to his lips, and his chin quivered. He said almost in a whisper, "Easter?"

The girl tried to answer, but no sound came. She lifted her slender hand to her throat, then nodded. The hand shook. Her head went back a little, and the tears broke.

Kenneth Rutledge strode slowly across the room toward her. At arm's length he stopped a moment, looking down at the girl. Then he put his arms around her and pulled her against him, dropping his hat to the rough wooden floor.

Cloud turned and stared out the open window,

his throat drawn into a knot. He heard Mother Lawton move slowly to the wall beside him. She was looking up at a framed picture of Jesus.

"Thank the Good Lord," he heard her breathe. "Thank the Good Lord!"

Most of the crowd had gone. Darkness had come, and the Lawtons and their company sat in the front yard, enjoying the coolness of the night. Henry Lawton and Mother Lawton sat in the chairs on the porch. Easter and her brother had pulled chairs out into the yard. Captain Barcroft stood to one side, Hanna Lawton near him, stealing glances at him.

Cloud sat on the ground, a stick in his hand, idly scratching marks that he couldn't even see. He was unusually edgy, knowing Rutledge was about to take Easter away. He watched the captain and Hanna.

If the captain had any imagination atall, he'd take Hanna for a walk, he thought. *That's what she wants. What does it take to make him see?*

Kenneth Rutledge was talking quietly. "There aren't but two of us left now, just my sister Flora and me. And Easter here makes three, of course. Mother died several years ago. Can you remember Mother, Easter?"

"A little. Just a little."

"She never was quite the same after the Indian raid. The rest of us gave Easter up for dead a long time ago, but not Mother. To the last day she lived, she said Easter was still alive. Got tired of listening to her sometimes. I guess a parent never can really give up."

Cloud glanced quickly at Aaron Barcroft and saw him draw up a little. Hanna touched the captain's arm.

Kenneth Rutledge said, "I was about nine or ten when it happened. You were about six, weren't you, Easter?" When Easter appeared confused, he said, "Of course you wouldn't know anymore. I don't suppose time means much in an Indian camp."

Irritably Cloud thought, *It'd mean a lot if you was a captive!*

"Yes," Rutledge went on, "I was about nine or ten. I stayed home that day to chop wood. Dad and our older brother went out afoot to work on a rock fence they were building. Easter wasn't supposed to follow after them, but she did. First we knew of the Indians was when we heard shots. Mother hustled Flora and me into the house and barred the door. I guess she knew, even then, that the others weren't coming back. She got down the old rifle, and she took up a stand by the window.

"After a little while the Indians came to the house a-horseback. They wanted in, but they could see Mother there with the rifle. They shouted threats at her, but she poked that gun out, and they knew she meant business. Then—I'll never forget it—they brought up Easter. One of them had her in front of him on a horse. And they had two fresh scalps. They waved them around and made signs like they were going to take Easter's scalp, too.

"It broke Mother's heart, but she couldn't help Easter, and she couldn't let them in. They'd have murdered us all if she had. None of those Comanches wanted to be the one she killed with that rifle. So finally they left, and took Easter with them. Neighbors followed their trail later, expecting to find Easter's body somewhere along the way. They never did, but everybody told Mother she was bound to be dead."

He turned to his sister. "I'm glad they were wrong."

Mother Lawton spoke from the porch. "So are all of us. You've got a wonderful sister there, Mister Rutledge. You'll be proud of her."

Cloud asked something that had been bothering him all day. "What kind of plans you got for her, Mister Rutledge?"

"No real plans, Cloud." No *Mister* there. "I'll just carry her home and more or less let nature take its course. I'm sure there are lots of things she'll have to learn after spending all those years among the savages. Between Flora and my wife and I, I'm sure we can teach her. And, after a proper time, we'll begin introducing her around. That country is settled up, and there are lots of eligible men down there now. Who knows?"

Cloud clenched his fist. "You say *after a proper time*. You mean you're aimin' to keep her hidden till you're sure she's civilized enough to meet folks?"

Cloud's impatient tone drew a spark from Rutledge. "I didn't say that. What I said was . . . well, we want to be sure that she's ready before we take her out into public too much and risk embarrassing her. It's for her own good. Later on, then, she'll have nothing to look back to in shame."

Fist still clenched, Cloud wished he had voice for

some of the angry thoughts that raced through his mind.

Not hard to tell he wouldn't like her associating with the likes of me.

Captain Barcroft had said little this evening. Much of the time he had spent just looking at Kenneth Rutledge, as if trying to gauge the man. At length he cleared his throat and spoke:

"There's one thing about your sister that I doubt anyone has told you yet, and I think you should know it."

Cloud felt it coming, and he steeled himself. *Why doesn't he keep quiet? Rutledge will find out soon enough anyway.*

Rutledge sat up straight, glancing sideways at Easter. He saw Hanna turn away from the captain, and he was instantly suspicious. "What is it, Captain?"

Barcroft frowned at Hanna and hesitated a moment, evidently wondering how best to say it. "It's a thing you've probably considered already but haven't wanted to ask about. Your sister is a grown woman, an attractive woman, and she's long past marriage age from an Indian viewpoint."

The captain paused again, and Rutledge cast another wide-eyed glance at the silent Easter. "Captain, are you trying to tell me . . ."

Barcroft nodded. "She had an Indian husband!"

Cloud pushed himself to a stand. He put in angrily: "It wasn't none of her fault, Rutledge. Woman don't have nothin' to say about it. He bought her like you'd buy a heifer. He swapped a string of horses for her. She couldn't help it!"

Rutledge sank back in his chair, face twisted. He didn't say anything for a while. Then: "I guess I realized somehow that it had probably happened, but I didn't let myself think about it." He looked at Easter a long moment. "Easter, you *couldn't* help it, could you?"

Easter had her hands clasped tightly, and she was looking straight ahead, into the darkness, frozen motionless. "It was the Indian way."

Rutledge rubbed his forehead, trying to puzzle his way through. "I don't suppose we have to tell anybody. What they don't know . . ."

Barcroft said, "There's one more thing. The word will get out sooner or later, so it's best to start with the whole truth. She bore a baby by that husband."

Rutledge seemed to wilt. "A baby?" He shook his head, trying to reject the thought. "An *Indian* baby?"

The captain said, "That's right."

Rutledge didn't look at anyone for a while. He just sat there as if he had been struck by the flat side of an ax. Finally he asked weakly, "Where is it?"

For a moment Cloud feared Easter would break down and cry. But she didn't. She sat stiff and silent, unblinking.

The captain said, "We left it behind."

Rutledge had his eyes closed. A long breath escaped him, and he said, "Thank God for that!" His hands trembled a little as he swayed forward in the chair. "But people will find out anyway. They always do about something like that. What're we going to tell them? How can we ever explain?"

Cloud moved forward stiffly, stopping beside

Easter. "They're frontier folks, ain't they? They'll understand."

Rutledge shook his head. "The frontier passed us by a long time ago. We live in a settled community. We have churches now, and church people. They live by the Book."

Cloud gritted, "And don't that Book tell about Christian charity? The Lawtons here, they're Bible-readin' folks, and they understood. They never held nothin' against Easter, not for a single minute."

Rutledge didn't even seem to hear him. "How will I ever explain this?" he said, almost pleading. "What can I ever tell them? The name of Rutledge means something there. We've *made* it mean something. But what will it mean after this?"

Fists tight, Cloud stepped in front of Rutledge. "What kind of a man are you?" he demanded. "Here you've got a sister who's been through hell, and you're not even thinkin' of *her*—you're only thinkin' about yourself!"

Rutledge sat back in his chair, drawn up within himself, something akin to panic holding him in a tight grip. Finally he said, "You can't blame me. If I'd only known, if I'd even thought . . . You have to admit, it's an awful shock to spring on a man all of a sudden, an awful shock."

I got a worse one I'd like to spring on you! thought Cloud. *But it'd hurt her as much as it would you. . . .*

Rutledge stood up shakily and got a grip on himself. Without a glance at Easter, he said to the others, "I'm going back to the camp. I'm tired, and I have a lot to think about."

Mother Lawton asked anxiously, "We'll see you tomorrow?" Rutledge only nodded without looking back as he walked out the gate.

Mother Lawton quietly arose from her chair on the porch. She walked out and stood by Easter, her hand on the girl's shoulder. "It's all right, Easter," she said quietly, "it's all right."

Hanna Lawton leaned against the cabin wall, face buried in her arms. She turned to Barcroft and demanded tearfully, "Aaron, how could you do it?"

The captain replied, "It wasn't easy, but it had to be done."

Hanna cried, "It didn't! It didn't!" She whirled away from him and ran into the cabin. Barcroft took a step after her, his face unreadable in the darkness. Cloud heard him call, "Hanna!" Then he turned around without speaking to anyone else. He walked out the gate, following Kenneth Rutledge.

Next morning, while Cloud sat cross-legged on the ground cleaning his rifle, the captain walked up to him. Cloud gave the captain a quick glance but no greeting. He kept working with the rifle.

"Cloud," said Barcroft, "I'm afraid I have to give you an unpleasant duty this morning."

Ain't the first one, Cloud thought darkly, still angry about last night.

"Go down to the Lawtons' house and tell Easter Rutledge that her brother has gone!"

Cloud almost dropped the rifle. He set it down on

a blanket he had spread out before him. He stood up stiffly and said, "Gone?"

"Got up before daylight, caught his team and left."

Cloud's lips were suddenly dry. "You sure he didn't take Easter?"

"Guard watched him leave. He didn't stop anywhere. He headed straight south."

"That dirty . . ." Cloud bit his lip and looked off toward the Lawton house, which was well out of sight. "And what about Easter? What happens to her now?"

The captain had no answer.

Cloud turned on him angrily. "It was your fault! You didn't have to tell him!"

Barcroft shook his head. "I had to tell him. Before I had talked with him twenty minutes, I knew what kind of man he was—a narrow-minded, egotistical fool."

Cloud thought, *Now look who's callin' somebody narrow-minded!*

Barcroft said, "I knew right then what he was likely to do when he found out. Better to have it happen here than on down the road somewhere, or back in her own town. At least here she has some friends."

Angrily Cloud charged, "You did it to spite her! You're as bad as Rutledge. You've had a contempt for her right from the first! You've hated her all along!"

"*Hated* her?" The captain seemed surprised at the thought. "Cloud, I never hated that girl. What gave you the idea I did?"

"The way you've treated her, the way you've

avoided her. The times you've been over to the Lawton house, you haven't even looked at her. You've turned your head away. From the day we found her, you've wanted to be rid of her. If that's not hatred—if that's not contempt—I'd like to know what is!"

Barcroft sank to his heels and looked off into the distance. "It wasn't hatred, Cloud, or contempt. I've felt nothing but pity for her."

"Then why have you made it such a point to avoid her?"

Pain came into the captain's face. "Because of the things I saw in her every time I looked at her, Cloud. Things I wanted to put out of my mind but couldn't when she was around. I looked at her and I saw my own daughter. I thought to myself, my daughter—if she's still alive—will live the same life this girl has lived. She'll grow up a savage, as much a Comanche as if she had been born one, and she'll know no better, just as this girl knew no better. When her time comes, she'll take a Comanche husband, just as this girl did. And she'll bear his children, Cloud—my own daughter—bearing his children just like any red-skinned squaw!"

Cloud saw the bleakness of prairie winter in the captain's dark eyes. After a long while he spoke. "Captain, I'm sorry for anything I said to you."

The captain said, "You'd better go tell Easter."

10

Easter sat in her rocking chair, dry-eyed but stunned as Cloud told her. Cloud shifted restlessly from one foot to the other, knowing her torment, knowing how she struggled to beat back the tears. He wanted to touch her, wanted to reach out and take her in his arms and shield her from hurt. But he couldn't shield her from this. He couldn't even help.

"Easter," he said quietly, "I know you've come to depend on findin' your family, to make up for what you'd already lost. But it don't mean the world's come to an end."

Face stricken, Hanna Lawton had walked out of the room when Cloud started to tell Easter what had happened. Mother Lawton stayed. Now she moved to Easter's side and spoke gently, "The young man's right, Easter. You've got friends here, and a home just as long as you want it."

Easter gave no response. Cloud put his hand over hers and said, "Easter, remember what we were talkin' about the other day? *I'll* give you a home, and I'll give you a family too. I want you to marry me, Easter!"

Cloud sensed Mother Lawton's approval, but he didn't glance at the woman. He looked down tensely at Easter, wondering if she had even understood. "Easter," he said again, "I want to marry you."

Presently Easter said in a hollow voice, "Because you feel sorry for me?" She shook her head. "I don't want it to be that way."

"It's *not* that way. I *want* to marry you. I love you, Easter!"

"A few days ago I asked *you*, and you said no. Nothing's changed since then, except that now you feel sorry for me." Again she shook her head. "Thanks, Cloud, for asking. But now *I'll* say no."

"Easter . . ." He realized then that it wouldn't help to argue with her now. Maybe later, when time had eased the hurt.

Easter said, "Cloud, would you please leave me alone now? I have a lot of thinking to do."

He squeezed her hand. "Sure, I understand. I'll come back tonight. Maybe by then you'll see your way through. And Easter"—he lifted her chin and looked into her desolate eyes—"Easter, please think about what I said. I *do* love you."

Outside, Hanna Lawton stood on the porch, a handkerchief gripped in her hand. Tightly she asked, "What now, Cloud? What now?"

He shoved his hands deep into his pockets and stood with his bleak gaze to the ground. "I don't know, Miss Hanna, I swear I don't."

"Aaron caused this," she spoke bitterly. "He's

caused all her misery. Why couldn't he just have left her where he found her? She'd have been better off!"

"The captain never has done anything he didn't believe was right."

Odd, he thought, that he should ever find himself having to defend the captain to Hanna Lawton.

She demanded, "What ever gave him the idea he had the right to decide for others, a man who hasn't even been able to find his *own* way?" She choked and brought the handkerchief to her face again. "I wish I'd never seen him!"

Cloud said, "No you don't, not really. Maybe one day he'll see *you!*"

She looked up quickly, but Cloud walked away.

He went back that night. Hanna Lawton met him at the door, her face grave. He found all the Lawtons strangely quiet. "What's the matter?" he asked, alarm rising in him. "Where's Easter?"

"She's down by the creek," Hanna Lawton spoke, almost in a whisper. "She wants you to go down there."

Henry Lawton arose from his chair and drew on his pipe, his brow furrowed with worry. "Cloud, we've had a long talk with her. We don't like what she wants to do, but we can't talk her out of it. Maybe you can." He took the pipe out of his mouth and stared at it. "But if you can't, then for God's sake help her. She can't do it alone."

"Do what?" Cloud felt the blood draining from his face.

"Just go talk with her, Cloud."

He hurried down the creekbank, running into a cottonwood limb and knocking his hat off. He went down on one knee, then pushed to his feet again. "Easter," he called. "Easter, where are you?"

He heard her voice to his right, a calm voice. "I'm over here."

He found her sitting in the willow chair, staring out across the creek. "Easter," he said, the excitement riding high in him, "what're they tryin' to tell me? What is it you want to do?"

She turned to him, and he saw that her face was calm, the calmest it had been in a long time. "I've done a lot of thinking today. I've made up my mind. Cloud, I'm going home!"

"Home?" He sucked in a short breath, and he knew what the Lawtons had been trying to say.

"I've been trying to fool myself. I've thought if I could find myself a family, I could forget all I left behind. I found that family, and it wouldn't have me. It *wasn't* my family, I can see that now. They weren't really my people, not anymore. My real family is that baby, Cloud, and it's far up on the plains somewhere. My people are there, too, the only real people I have. So I'm going back to them. I'm going home."

He took her hands and held them tightly. "You're tired, Easter, and you're all upset. You're not thinkin' straight."

"I'm thinking straighter than I have in a long time. It's the only answer, Cloud, the only way."

"Easter, listen to me—"

"I *have* listened, and I've thought over all you said. But now I'm listening to my heart. And it says, go find that baby."

She leaned toward him. "I think I love you, Cloud. If things were different, maybe . . ." She shook her head. "But they're not, and there's no use talking about it now. I'm going home."

He lowered his chin. "Easter, have you thought what a terrible long way it is?"

"I have. It won't be easy."

"Alone out there, a woman, in that big country? You'd never find your way."

"Once I get onto the plains, I think I know the watering places. I've traveled with the tribe. I'll find them."

"Some stray Indian see you, he'll shoot you for a white woman without ever knowin' the difference."

"No," said Easter, "up there I won't be a white woman. I'll be Comanche. I didn't throw my Indian clothes away."

"You've lived long enough here to get to feeling the white man's way. Do you think you can live again like an Indian?"

"To find my baby, I'll live any way I have to."

"Would you take another Indian husband?"

"Not by choice."

"What if you had no choice?"

She shook her head in determination. "I want my baby."

"I won't let you do it, Easter!"

"How will you stop me? Chain me to a post? You

may stop me once; you might stop me twice. But sooner or later I'll find a horse, and I'll get away. Don't try to stop me, Cloud. One way or another, I'll go!"

Defeat lay heavy in Cloud. "If I can't stop you, I guess I won't try. And talkin' won't do any good either, will it?"

"No."

"Then I'll go with you!"

She stiffened. "Cloud—"

"No, don't try to talk me out of it. If you're goin', I'll go with you as far as I can."

Fear colored her voice. "The Indians will kill you!"

"I won't go all the way. But I'll stay with you till I know you can make it in alone."

"Cloud, please—"

"Hush, Easter. If you go, then I go too."

Resigned, she asked, "When?"

"Tonight, if you're ready. If we wait, the captain may send me out on a patrol." He knew that in such an event Easter would try to ride off and leave him.

"What about the captain? What'll he do when he finds you gone?"

Probably order me shot on sight, he thought. But he said, "I don't know. I guess I'll find out. Now you go get ready, throw together the things you need. I'll be back directly with a couple of horses."

As he started to turn away, she rose from the chair and caught his hand. "Cloud." He stopped and faced her. She said, "You're a foolish man." She turned her face up, stepped to him and kissed him. "But I *do* love you."

After Cloud came with the horses, Henry Lawton regretfully helped him put together a sackful of supplies from the store. Tying a string around the top of the sack, he stared gravely at it and said, "Too bad we got no dried beef to let you take. You're goin' to need it."

Cloud said, "There'll be game enough, I reckon. We won't be hungry."

Lawton drew on his pipe and cast a worried glance at Easter. Dressed in her buckskin clothes, her brown hair in braids again, she stood silently by the closed door, barely touched by the weak glow of the lamp. "You couldn't talk her out of it?" he asked.

Cloud shook his head. "Tried."

"How'd you get the horses?"

"Told the guard the captain had given me orders to go out on scout. No trouble there."

"Be trouble when you get back. Aaron'll want your hide."

Cloud reached for the sack, gripping it so tightly that the cords stood out on the back of his hand. "I know, but I'll just have to face that storm when I get to it. I got another worry right now."

"I'll tell Aaron I advised you to take her back. Maybe that'll help some."

Cloud shook his head. "Not likely. The captain's got a strong mind. Whatever he sets it to, that's the way things've got to be."

Henry Lawton bit down hard on the stem of the

pipe and leveled his gaze at Cloud. "There's one way out, Cloud. You don't have to come back."

Cloud straightened. "You mean run?"

Lawton turned up his hands. "Not run, exactly, just not come back. Head west to New Mexico or Arizona—even California. This war keeps on, it's goin' to be more and more unhealthy for a man with Union sympathies anyhow. You watch, before this thing's over there'll be burnin' and lynchin' and the like. The smart man would git!"

Cloud swung the sack over his shoulder. "Texas is my home."

"Just advice, Cloud. It don't cost you nothin', and you don't have to take it."

Easter said a tearful good-bye to Mother Lawton and Hanna while Cloud put her Comanche saddle on her horse. Then she and Cloud rode out across the creek and headed northwestward.

They rode steadily through the night and all the next day, slowing down only occasionally to let the horses rest. Cloud turned periodically in the saddle to look over the back trail.

"You never know about the captain," he told Easter. "We got to keep ridin' and put a lot of miles behind us. If he decided to come after us, he'd let Miguel do the trackin'. That Mexican could trail the shadow of an eagle clear across a mountain."

Before them stretched the great brown vista of the lower plains, swelling and falling gently beneath the late-summer sun, a dry land begging for rain, the smell of fire clinging to the scorched carpet of brittle grass. In vain they searched for a waterhole that hadn't long since dried up in the summer drought. The horses had slowed. Cloud's mouth was so dry that his lips were cracking. But he was saving the short canteen of water he had, saving it for Easter.

"Somewhere way up yonder," said Easter, "is a spring that flows all the time; good, clear water. If we could find it, I'd have no trouble getting home. I've been there several times, and I know the trail. But down here, this land all looks the same to me."

"To me, too," Cloud admitted glumly. Here he had only his frontiersman's instinct to depend on, and he hated to trust it with his life. True, it hadn't often been wrong. But it only took once. . . .

So weary they could hardly climb down from their saddles, they stopped to make camp a while before dark. Cloud found a spot where a buffalo bull had pawed out a hole, and he built a small fire there so it would not spread out into the dry grass. He had picked up dead limbs of a mesquite at a dried-out natural lake a couple of hours earlier and had tied them behind the saddle. Firewood was scarce in this country.

At a prairie-dog town he had managed to bring down one animal and recover it. Actually, he had shot a couple more, but they had rolled back down their holes so he couldn't get their bodies.

He had gutted the animal at the time. Now he finished skinning it and spitted the tiny carcass on a stick, holding it out over the fire.

"Hungry?" he asked the girl. She sat on the ground, legs gathered up, head against her knees. She nodded. "A little. Mostly I'm tired."

By the time the prairie dog was done, Cloud saw that Easter was dozing. Gently he shook her shoulder. She looked up, startled. Then she eased again and smiled at him.

"Supper's ready," he said. "It's not much, but it beats grass."

The animal wasn't large enough to satisfy the hunger of either one, much less both of them. There were some dried biscuits in the sack, and Cloud handed a couple of these to Easter. He started to take one for himself, then changed his mind and dropped it back into the sack.

Things might get worse instead of better, he thought. He'd keep these for Easter. Instead of the biscuits he munched on a few dry mesquite beans he had picked up earlier. He hated the taste of them. Far as he was concerned, they were meant for horses, not for men. But they could keep a man from starving to death.

Finishing the meager supper, Easter took a small drink of water from her canteen while Cloud pushed dirt over the fire to put it out. He didn't want to risk its being seen in the darkness. But if anyone had followed after them, he'd be having the same kind of trouble. That, at least, evened things up.

By the time Cloud got through, he saw that Easter had stretched out in the grass, her blanket beneath her and her head on the saddle. He picked up his own saddle and blanket, and he was conscious of the girl watching him, wondering where he was going to put them. He walked out away from her a few feet and spread the blanket, then put the saddle down and eased his long frame wearily to the ground.

"Good night, Easter," he said.

In the gathering darkness he thought he could see her smile as she answered, "Good night."

With dawn they were up and riding again. For breakfast they had eaten a little cold bread and had broiled bacon on a stick. Cloud had used enough of the remaining water to boil each of them a little coffee.

Into the hot day they rode, the sun climbing on their right, burning ever more relentlessly as the day wore on. Still no water. The horses were suffering now. Cloud picked up his canteen and shook it. He heard the slosh of the meager supply of water. "How much left in yours, Easter?"

"About the same," she said.

"We're goin' to have to let the horses have some of it, or we're liable to find ourselves afoot."

Dismounting, he took off his hat. He pushed the crown down and poured water into it. He held it up to his horse's nose. The horse quickly drank. Cloud repeated for Easter's horse. He could tell the horses wanted more, much more.

"Sorry, boys," he spoke, "that's all we got for you."

He shook his canteen again. Hardly any left. Easter was staring at the canteen, her lips tight. Cloud handed it to her. "You just as well finish it," he told her. "It'll evaporate anyway." It really wouldn't, in that tight canteen. But he could tell she badly needed a drink.

"What about you?" she asked.

"I'm used to it, goin' on these long scouts. And you've lived a white woman's life long enough to get spoiled." He smiled thinly and looked northwestward. "Somewhere yonder there's got to be water. We'll never find it standin' here."

He swung back into the saddle, lips burning and his body aching for the drink he hadn't let himself have. He touched heels to his horse, and the animal grudgingly started walking.

Late in the day he came upon the first sign: a pair of mesquite trees alone out here in these open plains. It wouldn't be too far to a waterhole, he figured. Where there were mesquites, water could usually be found someplace. Reason was that mesquites were most commonly spread by the wild mustangs which roamed these plains. Left alone, the horses never strayed too many miles from water. They ate mesquite beans from trees around the watering places. These beans later were spread out on the prairie, to sprout and grow more trees.

Presently Cloud came across a thin, almost invisible old buffalo trail, nearly grassed over. His heart gave a glad leap. He pointed it out to Easter and said, "The only question is, do we go up the trail or down it?"

Easter frowned. "There's another question, too."

"What's that?"

"Is there still water in the hole, or has it dried up like the others?"

He took a chance and decided to go up the trail. It angled westward, not far off their regular course.

It was a very old trail, not used in a long time. But even when it was hard to spot beneath his horse's feet, he could see it meandering along ahead of him, a tiny thread of shadow in the dry grass.

At last he saw the cluster of mesquites far ahead of him. He grinned, though it hurt his parched lips. "Yonder it is," he pointed. "Just you hold on a while longer."

The horses plodded along in a walk, and it took them a long time to reach the place. Ahead, Cloud could see the small natural basin that caught the runoff from the rains, the runoff that would seep clear and clean from this heavy mat of protective grass.

He reined up on the rim of the basin and felt his heart plunge.

Dry!

He looked back at Easter, who had fallen behind. He felt a wave of pity come over him. How many times, traveling with the nomadic Comanches, had she come up thirsty to a waterhole like this and found the sun had drained it dry? Many times, no doubt. Yet each time it made a person die a little inside. It was something you never got used to. Thirst was worse than hunger. You could hitch up your belt a little and think of something else. When you were thirsty, your mind dwelt always on water.

He saw the bitter disappointment shadow her face.

Then he looked out across the dry lake and got an idea. "There's still a little green out in the middle of it, Easter. Maybe there's water there yet, under all that dried mud."

"It'll be bad water," she said.

"But it'll be wet."

He wished for a shovel, but that was one thing he hadn't thought to bring. Digging into his pack, he found a tin cup. This in hand, he walked out into the dry lake. In the center, where the grass and weed growth still showed some green, he dropped to his knees and began to dig.

It was slow, but after a while he found mud. Digging farther, he found water seeping into the hole as he took the mud out. He kept digging until he had made a hole about as deep as he could reach with his arm.

He raised up then, breathing hard from his exertion in the hot sun. The dank odor of the mud upset his stomach a little. Easter sat in the lacy shade of one of the mesquites watching him. He walked to her and flopped down on the ground.

"Got a slow seep workin'," he said. "We'll have to boil it before we can drink it, and even then we'll have to hold our noses. But it's water, and maybe it'll do till we can find somethin' better."

He boiled the water in a small bucket he had brought, then took the first swallow to be sure it wasn't poison. It wasn't, but it couldn't have tasted much worse if it had been. Involuntarily he spat out the first mouthful and exclaimed, "Damn!" He wiped his mouth on his sleeve.

Then he handed the cup to Easter. It was gyppy water which would leave them feeling almost as thirsty as before. But it was wet, and it would take care of the body's needs. After they had drunk all they could stand of it, he boiled enough to fill the canteens. The horses didn't like the water, either, but they drank it as Cloud poured it into his hat.

They rode on awhile. That night they made another dry camp. They did better for supper, because Cloud had shot a couple of rabbits near the lake. With darkness, they lay down again on the grass, their blankets apart. Cloud felt thirst working at him again, but he didn't want to open the canteens. They might need them far worse tomorrow.

He said, "The hell of it is that in this country we could pass by only a mile or two from water and never know it. Never been people up in this country much."

"There've been Indians here," she corrected him.

"I wasn't countin' them."

With a little of accusation in her voice, she said, "The white man *never* counts the Indian. Never thinks of him as human."

"Does the Indian think of the white man as human?" Cloud asked. "He couldn't, or he wouldn't kill and butcher the way he does."

Sadly Easter replied, "That's the whole trouble, I guess. I can see it now, because I've been on both sides. The Indian doesn't know anything about the white man's way and doesn't care to learn. The white man figures the Indian is some sort of wild animal, and all he cares about is killing the Indian out."

"Don't look like there's much chance for improvement," Cloud observed. "Neither side has any inclination to do anything except fight."

"In the long run it'll end the white man's way,"

Easter said. "There aren't many Comanches—a few thousand, maybe. But there are more white men than there are blades of grass along the river. The Indian moves around from place to place. But where the white man goes, he stays. He takes the land, and he keeps it." Sadly she asked, "What will become of my people then?"

Cloud had no answer. Hard for him to remember, sometimes, that in ways she was more Indian than white. He could sympathize with her concern, even though he couldn't see his way clear to agree with it. He had seen too many murdered men to have any particularly soft feeling toward the Indian.

"I'm like the others," he told her. "I can't help but hate. Maybe I'm wrong—likely I oughtn't to be that way. But that's how it is, and I can't stop it. They hate us as much as we hate them. Who's to say which side is wrong?"

Trying to change the subject then, he said, "It'd sure be worth a lot if somebody was to explore this country and map the waterin's."

"You've been over quite a bit of the country now," she said. "Maybe *you* could draw a map."

"And show all the waterin' places I haven't found?"

"You'll find one. That spring I was telling you about, it's somewhere up ahead of us. I don't know how far; maybe a few hours, maybe another day. But it's there."

"I ain't sure these horses have got another day. We've punished them somethin' awful."

"We'll find it."

They lay in silence awhile then. In the darkness

Cloud could make out the shape of Easter Rutledge lying on her blanket, the curve of her hips, the gentle swell and fall of her breasts as she breathed. He knew he should turn away and sleep, but he couldn't. He kept staring at her, wishing things could have been different, wishing . . .

He sensed that she was looking at him, too. He heard her soft voice say, "Cloud?"

"What is it, Easter?"

A long pause, then she said, "Nothing, I guess. Good night."

He turned over, facing the other way. "Good night."

Next day was as bad as the last one had been. Even coffee didn't make the brackish water taste much better, although its color helped hide the mud. They broiled their bacon, sipped the foul coffee, then swung into their saddles and started out.

The sun beat down without mercy. Cloud didn't know just what day it was, but he knew the peak of summer should have passed. Soon, now, the smell of fall should be in the air. He rode with shoulders slumped, his eyes and mouth burning. His lips were dry and chapped, and when he tried to talk, it felt as if they were cracking. Easter rode much the same way, her head down, her slender shoulders pinched in. Glancing at her often, Cloud could see her tongue run over her dry lips, trying to wet them. But her tongue was dry, too.

He took his canteen from the saddlehorn and extended it to her. She shook her head. "Wait till I need it," she murmured.

It came to him then that he hadn't heard a word of complaint from her. White woman or not, the Indian training had made her strong as leather.

They stopped a while at noon out on the bald, open prairie. Strangely, the brackish water didn't taste bad at all anymore. Cloud didn't try to eat, for he feared that would make him even thirstier. He sat beside Easter in the shadow of the horses, resting. Even with the shade, the sun's heat rose up from the ground and wrapped itself around them like a stifling blanket. He looked down at the woman, marveling at the silence in which she had borne her misery.

This is a woman! he thought. *One in a thousand, and I'm lettin' her get away!*

He put his arm around her shoulder and said, "We'll make it, Easter."

She leaned to him, her head on his shoulder. "Cloud, I'm sorry I brought you to all this."

"If you'd known, would you have changed your mind about comin'?"

She shook her head. "No, but I'd have come alone. I wouldn't have told you and made you share it."

At midafternoon Cloud squinted into the shimmering heat waves on the horizon and reined up quickly. "Hold it, Easter," he exclaimed. "There's somethin' up yonder. Indians, maybe."

Before he could stop it, his horse raised its head, ears pointed forward, and nickered. From ahead came an answering nicker.

If it's Indians, Cloud thought with a stab of desperation, *our bread is dough!*

There was no need to run, for the horses couldn't

have done it. Besides, there was nowhere to go. Cloud blinked, trying to clear his eyes.

"It's not Indians," he said at last, a thin whistle of relief passing between his cracked lips. "It's a bunch of mustangs, wild horses."

As they came closer, he watched them carefully. They were taking their time, pausing to graze. "They've already been to water," he said. "If they was just goin' to water they wouldn't be stoppin' along thisaway."

The mustangs broke into a run as the two riders neared them. They warily circled far around and paused on a rise to look back.

"Easter, all we got to do now is backtrack them. It won't be far to water."

He rode with the rifle across his lap, for where there was a waterhole there might be Indians. He doubted that the mustangs would have watered had men been around, but he didn't want to ride in unprepared.

Ahead he could make out a grove of cottonwood trees, their leaves a welcome green against the brass of a hostile summer sky. From the way the horses picked up, Cloud knew they had smelled water. He felt his pulse quicken as they moved nearer the trees. His dry tongue touched parched lips, and all he could think of was a pool of clear, sweet water—deep and cool.

He held up his hand for Easter to stay back as he eased up to the water, hand tight on the rifle. He looked around, anxiously scanning the trees, the rim of the pool, the rolling prairie which stretched on beyond. Finally he nodded and said, "It's all right, Easter."

Cloud stepped down and loosened the cinches. He dropped the reins and let his horse drink. He reached up and helped Easter down.

"There's a spring right over yonder," he observed. "It'll be a little cleaner than drinkin' after the horses."

Easter replied, "I'm too thirsty to let the horses worry me." He took out the cups and dipped water from the spring, handing the first cup to Easter. He gulped down most of his without stopping for breath. For a moment a spell of weakness passed through him. Then a sigh escaped him, and he smiled.

"Never was nobody ever distilled a drink to match good, cool water."

Easter drank thirstily. Cloud was tempted to warn her to go slow, but he figured she knew. When her cup was empty, he took it and dipped it full for her again. "Just this one more," he said, "then we wait awhile. People have died from drinkin' too much water."

When they had finished for a while, Cloud led the horses away from the water and unsaddled them, staking them in the shade. They wanted more water, but he said, "Just you-all wait awhile, boys. You'll get back to it directly."

He walked around the pool, still feeling dry and wanting more water himself, but knowing he had to hold back. He found where the pool drained off at the far end into a creekbed that meandered out across the prairie, probably to disappear a few hundred yards away. He heard a footstep behind him and turned.

Easter said, "This is the place I told you about.

We've camped here several times. From here on, I know my way."

Cloud nodded, sorrow drifting over him. "Then I expect you'll be wantin' to leave me now."

"It's too dangerous for you to come any farther. You've already come too far, I'm afraid."

"I wouldn't have done otherwise."

She nodded, her eyes level with his. "I know."

"I don't want to see you go, Easter."

She nodded again. "Some ways, I hate to go. But I have to, and you know I have to."

He took her hands. "You can't leave now. You're too tired, and your horse is too tired."

"We'll rest the night. We'll go in the morning." He felt the pressure of her hand. "You'll stay with me?"

"I'll stay."

Taking his rifle, he walked off down the creek out of sight. Then he set the rifle down within reach and took off his clothes. He eased into the creek and gave a long sigh as he slowly sank his body into the cool water. He sat where the creek was shallow, leaning back on his elbows with only his head out of water. There he sat a long time, soaking. There was a strange thing about going for a long time without water: the body seemed to sap itself of moisture, drying the skin, shrinking the man. Yet, when water was found, it did almost as much good to soak in the water as to drink it, for the body would absorb moisture like a sponge.

Cloud sat this way a long time, knowing Easter was doing the same up at the main pool, and not wanting to disturb her.

When at last he climbed out, most of his thirst

was gone. He was fresher now, the weariness lifted from his shoulders. He tried whistling, but found his lips still a little dry for that.

When he had put his clothes on again, he walked on down the creek, looking for game. To his surprise, he came upon a small group of buffalo. Nearsighted, they had not seen him. He knelt in the protection of the brush and took careful aim on a fleshy young cow, leveling his sights on her lungs. From experience he knew that was the best place to hit a buffalo. Squeezing the trigger, he saw the dust puff as the bullet struck where he had aimed it. The cow's hind legs folded. She swayed on her forelegs a moment, slinging her head, then fell heavily on her side.

Shying away from the shot, the other buffalo trotted off, then turned to look back. In a moment they caught the smell of blood and broke into a run that left a fog of dust. When they were gone, Cloud walked out and slit the cow's throat. He waited for her to die, then cut away a hindquarter and threw it over his shoulder with the hide still on it. Back bent under the weight, he carried it to the spring.

Easter had already started a fire. Cloud said jokingly, "Behold, the mighty hunter brings meat to camp," somewhat as he had heard it bragged a couple of times in the camp of friendly Tonkawas.

He could tell by a quick frown of disapproval that she didn't appreciate it. She evidently thought he was making fun of Indian ways, and he knew he *had* been, a little.

She said, "I saw the buffalo run, and I knew you wouldn't miss."

He hung the hindquarter from a tree where Easter could slice it. While she set about fixing supper for them, he watered the horses again, then hobbled and staked them on the grass. The man and the woman ate silently, their eyes dwelling upon each other, and sadness in both.

By the time they had finished eating and putting the camp in order, it was dark. Cloud laid out his saddle and spread his blanket. He sat on it and stared off into the darkness, wrapped in thought. Easter watched him a while, then moved to him and sat down beside him.

"What're you thinking, Cloud?"

"Thinkin' I'll never see you again. It's a bitter thought, Easter."

Leaning to him, she said, "There'll be another woman, Cloud. Just keep looking and you'll find her."

He shook his head. "You're the one I want, Easter, the only one I've ever really wanted. Don't you have any of the same feeling for me, any of it atall?"

Easter's hand lifted slowly and rested on his shoulder. She turned her face up, her lips parted as if to speak. He touched her cheek and found it wet with a tear.

"Kiss me, Cloud," she whispered.

He pulled her close. Her lips were warm and eager, her hands pressing against his back. He held her that way a long time, crushing her as the powerful want boiled up in him like a thunderhead.

"Cloud," she whispered, "we won't think about tomorrow. Let's think only of now—of *us!*"

11

Cloud was the first to leave the spring. Riding south with the morning sun just breaking across the prairie, he paused a moment to look back. Over his shoulder he saw Easter sitting on her horse at the spring, watching him go. He lifted his hand, and she waved back at him. Then she turned her horse about and disappeared.

Cloud clenched his fist and felt his throat go tight again.

"Well, I tried," he murmured. "But a white woman is stubborn enough, and I guess a Comanche is worse."

He touched spurs to the horse and angled southeastward, toward the settlements. He tried to put his mind on other things, like the old days before the war when he ran his own cattle on open grass to the east—not easy times, but enjoyable times when a man had freedom. He thought of old friends he had known, many of them gone now to the battlefields of Virginia. He thought of the Texas Mounted Rifles, of Aaron Barcroft and Quade Guffey and Miguel Soto.

But try though he did, he could not push Easter from his mind. Again and again she came back to him until he gave up and let her take over. He remembered how he had first seen her, running like a deer, turning on him in defiance. He remembered her as he had seen her that day she went into Brush Hill, bewildered, trying not to show her fright. He remembered his own awakening to the magic of her and wondering if she felt any of it for him. Most of all he remembered last night, when she had shown too late that she loved him just as he loved her.

Too late! Many a time in his life he had wanted something, or had thought he wanted it—a horse, cattle, land of his own. But now he knew he had never wanted anything before the way he wanted Easter Rutledge.

He rode with his head down, blind to everything but the sorrow in his heart.

After a long time he knew he had to think of other things. Easter Rutledge was in his past now. He had to forget her—or *try* to.

A movement on a rise made him snap to attention, grabbing instinctively at the rifle, jerking it half out of the scabbard before he realized that what he had seen was only a few antelope, running to get ahead of him. He watched them cut in front of him and cross over from his left to his right. *Wake up!* he told himself roughly. *Life ain't over, but it could be if you don't keep your eyes propped open. They could've been Indians just as easy as antelope.*

It came to him then that where there were antelope, water probably was not too far away. He hadn't given much consideration to water yet, for the canteen was full and the morning heat had not yet begun to make him thirst. But he realized how important it might be if he could find water up here, could remember it and make a decent enough rough map so that others might also find it. That spring back yonder was a good starting place. He knew the direction he had been riding and how long it had taken him to cover the ground. Now, if he could find the water. . . .

He watched the horizon, and he watched the ground at his horse's feet. He watched for wild-animal trails that might lead him to water, and finally he found one: an old buffalo trail. It hadn't been used in a long time. He couldn't be sure whether to go up it or down it. He took a chance and rode down it awhile. Presently another old trail cut in and joined it. Eventually the trail he followed joined another, which had been used recently by animals. He stopped to study the signs. Buffalo, antelope, a few horses.

The latter worried him. Mustangs, probably, but how could he know?

He came upon the seep unexpectedly and found himself alone there. No Indians. Relieved, he dismounted and loosened the cinch to let the horse drink. Now that he saw the water, Cloud felt thirsty himself. He knelt above the horse and drank as closely as he could to the point where the water seeped out. It had a tang of gyp that made him wrinkle his nose. But it was wet, and its taste was not nearly so bad as the mudhole he and Easter had found on the way up here.

Water like this was hard on men's bowels when they weren't used to it. Many a time Cloud had boiled a strong tea out of cottonwood bark to cure diarrhea. It wasn't the best medicine—it was almost as bad as the ailment—but it was often the only one to be had. Here there weren't even any cottonwoods.

He had beep afraid either he or Easter would sicken on the muddy water they had been forced to drink. Luckily they hadn't.

After that stuff, nothing can kill me now, he thought wryly.

Riding again, he thought how glad Aaron Barcroft would be to get his hands on a map that would guide him to the waterholes and lead him up onto the open prairie of the lower plains.

But, came a chilling thought, *he'll probably be even gladder to get his hands on me!*

Up to now Cloud had not given much consideration to the captain. There had been Easter to worry about, her problem to be solved. Purposely Cloud had shoved aside any thought of what the captain might do. Now he could no longer ignore Barcroft.

At best, he'll court-martial me. At worst, he'll hang me!

He felt of his throat, and gooseflesh rose on his skin. Damn! The man just might do it. Fact of the matter, he was more likely to than not.

He's got a back stiff as a poker, Cloud thought. *He's not much given to compromise when he believes he's in the right. He took a woman's baby from her when he thought it was the proper thing to do. He's been through enough hell of his own that no matter what the other man might be tangling with, it looks tame to the captain.*

So, he considered, *if I ride back there now, it'll be my neck.*

Desertion, Barcroft would call it. And delivering a white woman into the hands of the Indians.

Lord, how could I expect him to figure it otherwise?

Maybe the Lawtons could talk to him. Cloud pondered that, then shook his head. Nobody'd ever been able to tell him much. Cloud had seen the captain really unbend only once, when he rigged the escape of the young conscription-dodgers after one of them saved his life. And that had been a weak moment. Later, given time to think, he might not have done it.

If I'm smart, I'll just keep right on riding. I won't stop for Barcroft or anybody.

A man could ride south into Mexico and just sit there till the war was over. Lots of them were doing it. He might have to be a little careful about meeting people on the way down—might even have to tell some outrageous lies.

Bet a feller could make himself a living out of cattle or something down in Mexico and have something to bring out with him when the war was over.

He had heard there was a little trouble down in Mexico, too; some kind of ruckus with a bunch of Frenchmen. He wondered what business a Frenchman had in Mexico anyway. But no matter, an American could stay clear of that if he tried.

Mexico! Man, that was a long way to go—a long way from Easter Rutledge. But what difference would it make, when he could never see her again anyway? Wouldn't matter if he went twenty miles or a thousand, she was lost to him. Maybe she would be easier to put out of mind if he knew she was far away.

Well, sir, that was the thing to do—head south and not stop till he pulled up to dry the muddy water off of him on the far side of the Rio Grande.

But a worry tugged at him. Conscience first, for he would be leaving the frontier service at a time when it desperately needed men. Still, he would rather leave it this way than at the end of Barcroft's hang rope. Second, there was the idea that any knowledge he might gain of the waterholes, the plains route, would be lost with him if he left. No telling what it might be worth to somebody else to know what Cloud was finding out up here on the lower edge of the high plains.

Well, there was one way to fix it. He'd go by Lige Moseley's and draw a map. He'd let Moseley pass it on later, when Cloud had time to get far enough south so that he no longer had to worry about pursuit.

Badly as Aaron Barcroft might hate Cloud after this, he would be glad to get the map. And he wouldn't be ashamed to use it.

Maybe if I leave them this much, the rest of the bunch won't think too bad of me.

It took longer to get back than it had taken to ride out, for Cloud and Easter had been pushing hard at first. With little to go on but instinct, but with full faith in that, Cloud headed as straight for Moseley's as he knew how. He made a dry camp, then found another waterhole. It was muddy, and he could almost smell the gyp in it. He didn't drink any of it, but in a tight place he could have. So could anyone else.

Not far from Moseley's, he came across the tracks. His heart jumped as he stepped down for a look. Plenty of them—riders and loose horses—headed northwest. And from droppings he could tell the trail was not more than a few hours old—perhaps as little as one or two.

The short hair lifted at the back of his neck. Indians! It wasn't that he had any real way of knowing, but a man developed an instinct for it sometimes, like a dog. He wondered how he had been lucky enough to miss them, for their trail was almost parallel to his. There was just enough divergence that somewhere back yonder they had passed one another, unbeknown.

He thought then of Lige Moseley. If these Indians hadn't changed direction, they had come right by his place. A worry built in him, putting a burning knot in the pit of his stomach. This wasn't any little raiding party. This had been a large band of warriors, enough of them to accomplish just about anything they set their minds to.

He spurred into an easy lope. He backtrailed the Indians, watching all the while for sign of captives or white victims along the way. At length he came upon a dead horse and stopped for a look. Moseley's brand! A chill passed through Cloud. He swung back into the saddle and spurred again, no longer sparing his horse.

A spot of color ahead of him caught his eye. Even

before he got there, he knew what it was. His horse shied away as wind caught in the cloth of a skirt and rippled it gently. Heartsick, Cloud stepped to the ground and walked up to the still form of the girl, lying limp in the grass, arrows bristling from her breast. Choking, he knelt a moment with hat in his hand, his eyes burning with tears.

Samantha!

He swayed, the shock hitting him in the stomach like the kick of a mule. He remembered Samantha as he had seen her before, her pretty eyes filled with curiosity—with a vague longing—as she watched him, her long blond hair hanging about her shoulders.

Somewhere up yonder a Comanche brave carried that hair now as a trophy.

Cloud found himself murmuring a prayer. Then he looked about for something to cover her body. Finding nothing, he took the slicker from behind his saddle and used that.

"I'll be back, girl," he said.

He rode on, his heart heavy as lead, for he knew what he must find now at Moseley's. He rode into the clearing and saw the vague drift of smoke being carried southward by the wind. The cabin was only half burned, for the Indians had not done a good job of setting the fire. In the grass around the house Cloud could see several patches of blood.

"They didn't take you easy, old-timer," he breathed.

He found Lige Moseley—what was left of him—beside the corral fence, his body riddled with bullets, cruelly hacked and slashed.

They hated him, Cloud knew. They took it out on him this time.

Mouth drawn tight, Cloud walked on to the cabin. In the front yard by the door lay the oldest boy, Luke. Mrs. Moseley lay in the doorway. Carefully Cloud stepped over her and walked inside the smouldering cabin. In a moment he was out again, retching.

The Indians hadn't missed a thing. Moseley's escape tunnel had not helped his family this time.

Blinded, Cloud leaned against the wall of the cabin and buried his burning eyes in his arms. He clenched and unclenched his fists, praying one moment, cursing the next. Finally he sat down heavily upon the ground, shaking his head and swallowing the huge lump that choked him.

"Lige, Lige . . . what an awful price to pay!"

He wondered then how many others had paid this price for the right to try to build a home, the right to move out and claim a raw land and try to make it grow. How many had died on this one raid?

"Lige," he spoke then, looking toward the still body of the old man, "I was fixin' to run off to Mexico. Fixin' to run off like a cur dog and let you-all do your own fightin'. Shameful thing for a man to figure on, ain't it?" His face twisted. "Well, I ain't goin' to do it now. Somebody's got a lot to pay for, and I'll do my best to collect it, I promise you that!"

He got to his feet then, fists tight, color high in his face. "I swear to God, Lige, I'll stay here and fight!"

It occurred to him that he had not tried to account for all of the Moseley children. He had taken one look, then had fled. Now, he knew, he had to go back and take count, to be sure whether all were dead, or if possibly some were missing. He forced himself to the door. There he hesitated a moment, stiffened his back and went in.

Presently he was out again, face gray and sick. One missing, the little girl named Joanna. Two years old, she was—maybe three. Cloud was certain he hadn't overlooked her body on the trail, and it was not here. He searched around the cabin afoot, around the clearing.

They had taken her prisoner, then. It didn't seem likely, the way they had butchered the rest of the family, but there could be no other explanation. The Comanches were like that sometimes. Maybe one of the warriors had taken a fancy to the little girl's looks. Maybe she had tried to fight them, and they had liked her spirit. They often honored those who fought hardest against them. Whatever the reason, she was with them. She *had* to be.

"Lige," he said, "it'd be better if she was dead. But I'll find her if I can. I'll go after her by myself and steal her back if there's any possible way to do it."

And if he couldn't get her back? He knew the grim answer to that. He'd kill her, even though it meant his own death.

He looked around the ruins of the cabin for anything he might take along in the way of supplies—food, powder, lead. But the Indians hadn't overlooked much. What they hadn't taken, they had slashed to ribbons, spilled or poured out. Even the Moseley's old family Bible had been ripped apart. Cloud found the binding lying on the dirt floor, with a few of the loose pages scattered around. Indians often took all the books they could find. They used the paper to stuff inside their bull-hide shields, for they had discovered that tightly packed paper would sometimes stop a bullet.

Cloud picked up one of the Bible pages the fire hadn't singed. It was the Moseley family record, the birthdates of the children carefully written with goosequill and ink, and the dates of a couple of their deaths, noted afterward.

The tears came back to Cloud as he looked at this record. He could write the rest of it now, if it would mean anything. But it wouldn't. Carefully he folded the page and put it in his pocket. Someday, perhaps, he would come back and put up a monument of some kind.

He looked around him a last time. All this, gone for nothing. All these lives thrown away, with little left to mark their passing except these names written so carefully in an old family Bible.

He stepped outside and walked to his horse. "Well, old friend, looks like we've got all that ride to do over again. It may kill us both, but we'll do it."

He put his foot into the stirrup and lifted himself into the saddle again. He was about to pull the horse around and head him northward when he heard the sound of hoofs and saw the riders break out of the timber and move toward him in a long trot.

In front rode Miguel Soto. And just behind him, Aaron Barcroft.

12

Captain Barcroft gravely rode up to Cloud, his eyes like flint. "Cloud, I never expected to see you here. In fact, I never thought I'd see you again anywhere."

Uneasily Cloud said, "I reckon not, sir."

Barcroft held out his hand. "You're under arrest, you know. I'll take your gun."

Cloud reached for it, then hesitated. "You can have it if you really want it, Captain. But don't you reckon you'll need all the guns you can get?"

The captain lowered his hand, his eyes probing at Cloud. "That's the truth, I will. I'll want your word—"

"I'll promise you anything you ask for, Captain," Cloud said earnestly. "When this is over you can have my guns, do what you want to with me, and I won't whimper none. But right now I want to take part in whatever the Rifles do about this." He made a motion with his hand, toward the ruins of the Moseley home. "I owe it to Lige."

Barcroft shrugged. "I can't spare anybody to take

you back to the settlement, and I know there are enough Unionists in the outfit to see that you got a gun anyway, if you wanted one. So you keep yours, Cloud, for now. Later . . . we'll see." He turned to look over the carnage. His eyes pinched half shut. Cloud saw the man's jaw ridge. Barcroft asked huskily, "All of them dead?"

Cloud nodded. "All that's here. The oldest girl, I found her a ways up the trail—dead. There's a little girl missin'. I reckon them Indians took her along."

"How old a girl?"

"Three, or thereabouts."

Barcroft said, almost in a whisper, "Three . . . like mine." His hand knotted on the saddlehorn. "I told Moseley," he gritted. "He wouldn't listen." He looked down, face saddened. "They tried to tell *me* once, and *I* wouldn't listen. You're a frontiersman, Cloud, so you ought to know. What makes a man do it? Why does he stay when the odds are so heavy against him?"

Cloud shook his head. "I can't rightly say, Captain. All I know is, if it wasn't for men like Lige—and families like his—we'd still be sittin' around Plymouth Rock, afraid to go out in the woods."

The captain nodded grimly. "You've said what's true. All civilization is built over the bones of men like Moseley."

Cloud said, "Lige believed the Lord intended for white men to have this country. He told me once it was like when God sent the children of Israel into the land of Canaan. Some would die, but the most would make it. Maybe Lige was right; maybe the

Lord intended it that way. Maybe He gives men like Lige a divine call, the way He does a preacher."

The men who had come with Barcroft were scattered about inspecting the ruins. The shock of what they saw held their voices down almost to a whisper and splotched their faces an angry red. There were more men than Cloud had seen ride with the captain before. Most of the regular Rifles were there, as well as a dozen or more civilian volunteers. They led packhorses, well provisioned.

Came ready this time, Cloud thought. *Captain must figure to stay on the trail however long it takes to get the job done.*

The men began gathering around the captain again. Cloud could sense a grim, smoldering anger in them. They sat their horses or stood on the ground, watching the captain expectantly, impatient to be on the move.

Barcroft picked out a couple of youngsters from among the volunteers, boys still in their late teens. He said, "Lads, I've got a job for you. We can't just leave these poor people this way. They deserve a decent burial. You'd do me a great service if you'd volunteer to stay here and give them one." When the boys showed hesitancy, he added, "It won't be an easy job. It'll take all the manhood you can muster. Will you do it?"

Approached that way, the boys could do little but consent.

Cloud said, "Captain, we ought to get the boys to go along with us a ways and fetch back Samantha Moseley. We can't just leave her out there."

The captain nodded. He turned then to the men who gathered around him. "Men," he said in as grave a voice as Cloud had ever heard him use, "here you see the nature of our enemy. You see why, this time and every time, we need to follow him till we catch him, no matter how hard it is, no matter how long it takes. We need to show him we're prepared to answer his savagery with a bloody vengeance. This may be a long, hard ride with an awful fight at the end of it. It could be a costly fight that some of us won't come home from. But this I swear to you: we won't turn back till we've gotten it done. If there's anyone here who doesn't feel he can stay all the way, I want him to leave us right now."

He looked about him at the hard-set faces. No one spoke or moved. Satisfied, he said, "I thought that's how it would be. I've never been one to brag on men, but I'm proud of you. You're all sure now? From the time we leave here there'll be no turning back. If you ride away from here with me, you've committed yourselves to stay until it's finished."

Some men nodded, some just held still. But none pulled back. "All right, then," said the captain, "we'll water our horses, then we'll ride." He turned for a glance at Cloud. "Your horse worn out?"

"He's been a long ways, sir. Reckon if he had to, he'd go some more."

"Swap with one of the boys on the burial detail. Their horses are fresher. I'm not going to leave you anywhere along the way, Cloud."

"I have no intention of *bein'* left, sir!"

He moved his saddle to one of the boys' horses

and pulled in beside the other men. Seward Prince, who had fought with him over the Union, just gave him a quick glance of dislike. Quade Guffey shook Cloud's hand gravely, knowing how Cloud felt about the Moseleys.

Barcroft said, "Cloud, you'd just as well take the lead with Miguel."

"You mean you'd trust me up there, Captain?"

The captain grunted. "Rather have you up there where I can watch you."

They strung out across the prairie, following the clear trail the Indians had beaten into the sod with their stolen horses. They came to the body of the girl. The men dismounted silently to stand with hats in their hands. A gray-haired rider who was a part-time preacher bowed his head and spoke a prayer that started with a quiet plea for mercy upon the innocent soul of the girl and ended in an impassioned promise of bloody vengeance.

"She was Thy child, Lord," he declared, his angry face lifting to the summer sky, "and the hand of the heathen smote her down. But Thou shalt have Thy vengeance! Deliver the heathen into our hands, O Lord, and we will be Thy messengers of judgment!"

Cloud held himself apart from the others. His eyes were squeezed shut, but he could still see the girl in his mind.

Miguel Soto moved over to him and spoke with sympathy, "She was a most pretty girl."

Conscience-stricken, Cloud only nodded. He couldn't speak.

She was in love with me, or she thought she was.

And all I felt was embarrassment. I wish it could have been different. She deserved a better man than me. She deserved a better fate than this.

Riding away, the captain pulled up beside Cloud. "That's what they did to one woman. Yet you turned another one over to the Indians."

Cloud didn't feel like arguing with the captain. He didn't feel like talking at all. "It wasn't the same with Easter, sir; you know that. Besides, I didn't turn her over to the Indians. She turned herself over."

"You took her there."

"It wasn't my choice. I couldn't stop her; she was goin' anyway. I wanted to see she got there alive."

"How far did you go?"

"A good ways up yonder, sir."

"Up on those plains? There's no water up there."

"There's water, sir, if you can find it. It's scarce, and a lot of it's bad. But it's there."

"Could you find that water again?"

Cloud tapped his forehead. "I made maps up here, sir. I could find it."

The captain chewed his lip a minute, eyes squinting into the northwest. They were calculating eyes, and Cloud could see hope growing in them. At length he turned again to Cloud. "What you did was a hanging offense. Any court-martial would call it desertion in time of war. If I'd found you at another time, another place, I'd have conducted a drumhead court-martial and hanged you in twenty minutes.

"But now, after what we saw at Moseley's, and that girl back there, what you did doesn't seem important at all anymore. Maybe we'll even be able to use some of the knowledge you gained. No telling what we may need to know before we get through this trip."

They rode without stopping until it was too dark to follow the tracks. The captain ordered a dry camp with no fires. No picket lines were set up for the horses. Each man slept with his horse staked close by him, ready to ride in a moment. Barcroft posted a heavy guard, half expecting the Indians to double back and try for the pursuers' horses. It had happened before.

But the Comanches didn't come that night. Next morning the Texans came across the camp where they had halted to rest, pushing on with dawn.

"Bound to know they're bein' followed," Cloud observed to Miguel Soto.

Soto said, "Somebody always follow them this far. But not many times anybody he ever go much farther than this. Most times, we have to turn back when we get about here."

Miguel added grimly, "I wish now when I live with the Comanche we come this way just one time. Then maybeso I could take the company there—all the way!"

All that day they followed the trail. It began to meander a little, then abruptly straightened again.

Cloud said to Miguel, "They probably figured there wasn't anybody after them anymore and they got careless awhile. Then one of them scouted back and saw us. They sure yanked up the slack."

The riders pushed their horses all they dared. It was hard to resist spurring into a hard run and trying to catch up all at once. But every man knew how futile that would be, how disastrous to the horses.

Dusk caught them, and it was difficult to tell whether they had actually made much gain on the Indians or not. Weariness had settled over the men. They didn't talk as they rode. They just sat slump-shouldered in the saddles and moved doggedly on, hating the colors of fading sunset because this meant they soon had to give up the trail until tomorrow.

Barcroft held up his hand and stopped the men. "We'll hold here a little while. We all need coffee, I expect, so we'll stop early enough that we can afford to build fires. Hurry it up. We'll need to put the fires out again before it turns full dark. Then we'll ride on a little way farther before we camp."

Cloud didn't know how tired he really was until he stepped down and felt his knees buckle. He almost fell.

Soto grinned sympathetically. He appeared to be holding up better. Funny, thought Cloud, how a Mexican so often seemed to have more stamina, always seemed born to the saddle.

"Cloud, my frien'," said Soto, "you got any coffee?"

Cloud shook his head. "Haven't hardly got anything, except an appetite."

Miguel said, "I got plenty. You and me, we share together."

"Poor trade for you. About all I can give you is gratitude."

"That," said Miguel, "is plenty much."

Engrossed in their coffee, their slim supper, the chance for a few moments of rest, the weary men lost their watchfulness. Barcroft had not posted guard because he didn't intend to be there long and expected no counterattack. If the Indians came for horses, he had reasoned, they probably would do so after dark.

Therefore the raiding party was almost upon them before anyone saw it. Someone shouted the alarm as the Indians suddenly showed up on a rise and came riding as hard as their horses would run.

The first thought of every man was to grab his own mount and keep the Comanches from getting it. Men jumped away from the fires, spilling coffee, hurling food aside as they grabbed at bridle reins. In seconds the Texas line bristled with guns. But the dozen or so Comanches didn't try to strike the whole line. They knifed down toward a thin end of it, arrows streaking, guns aflame. Outflanked, most of the Rifles were unable to return effective fire for fear of hitting their own men.

At the very end of the line with Miguel Soto, Cloud grabbed his horse, then dropped to one knee and began to fire at the swift Indian party. He saw Barcroft's lieutenant, Elkin, go down with an arrow in him. He saw Captain Barcroft run to the man's side, then pitch forward, hand to his chest.

An Indian whirled around to stab at the captain with a lance. Cloud brought his pistol up and fired. The lance tipped and drove into the ground. The Indian was hurled off his horse by the powerful leverage of it. Jumping to his feet, Cloud let his horse go and sprinted to the captain's side, pausing to fire again as the downed Indian struggled to his feet. The Comanche went down to stay.

Another Indian drove at them, but Cloud fired on him and forced him to pull away. He knelt by the captain's side, the smoking pistol in his hand, his anxious eyes peering through the smoke for signs of another threat.

As suddenly as they had come, the Indians were gone. The smoke drifted away and the dust settled. Cloud turned the captain over and saw the spreading stain on the man's dusty shirt. He ripped the shirt away to get at the wound. The captain gritted his teeth.

"How many dead, Cloud?" he wanted to know. "How many?"

"Don't know yet, sir. You just lay still."

"Dammit, find out how many!"

"Captain, you ain't in no shape to be worryin' yourself about it one way or the other."

He saw Miguel Soto walking up with Cloud's horse. "Thanks, Miguel," he said. "Figured I'd lost him."

"*Por nada,*" shrugged the Mexican. "I share with you my coffee, but I don' share with you my horse."

Cloud found the captain's wound to be low in the

shoulder. "Close, Captain," he said. "A little lower and it'd have been in the heart."

"Well," the captain breathed tightly, "it wasn't, so let me up. I've got to see about the company."

Cloud shook his head. "Captain, the company's goin' to have to do without you, or else turn back. You've gone as far as you can go."

The doctor, Walt Johnson, showed up with his bag. He glanced in dismay at the captain, then forced a thin smile. "They told me you were dead, Captain. No such luck, eh?"

"Patch me up so I can ride!"

"Shape you're in, Captain," Johnson said, "you'd be lucky to ride in a wagon."

"We have no wagon."

"Sort of narrows it down, doesn't it, sir?"

The captain seemed to give up then. He sank back, hopelessness in his eyes. "Damn them, what were they after? They knew they couldn't whip us all. What did they come for?"

Cloud said, "Fun, maybe. Thought they'd hit us a lick and get the hell out. And they probably figured they could get away with some of the horses, too. Been spyin' on us a spell, more'n likely. Seen us stop for supper and thought they'd bust in and run off all the horses they could. Leave enough of us afoot and there'd be nothin' left but for all of us to turn back."

"Did they get many horses?"

"No, sir, not hardly a one."

"And men . . . I asked you once about men."

"Just one dead that I've seen, sir."

Barcroft's face fell. "Elkin?"

Cloud nodded. "Yes, sir, Elkin. Way he went down, I don't reckon he hardly felt a thing."

Barcroft shut his eyes against a surge of pain that stiffened him hard as a rock. When it passed, he opened his eyes again. They were glazed now. He spoke tightly: "Elkin . . . best man I had. Always figured if anything happened to me . . . he'd be the one to take over."

The doctor broke in, "Captain, that bullet's got to come out, and pretty soon. Longer we wait, the worse it'll be."

Barcroft whispered, "Get on with it, then."

The doctor warned, "It'll hurt pretty bad. I've got some whiskey along—brought it for just such an emergency. Drink enough of that and maybe it won't seem quite as bad."

"No whiskey," Barcroft said flatly. "I can't be drunk and command."

"You can't command now anyway," said the doctor. He glanced at Cloud. "Get me some hot water started, will you?"

The doctor went after the whiskey, and Cloud got some water on to boil over a fire. The doctor brought the bottle and handed it to Barcroft. "I'm the doctor," he said firmly, "and I'm telling you to drink it!"

The captain took a long pull at the bottle and swore at the fire of it. "Where'd you get this?"

"Just drink it . . . sir!"

Even with the whiskey, the captain fainted before they got the bullet out. He spent a restless night, tossing in fever. By morning, though, the fever had subsided to some extent. The captain's eyes seemed to be sunk far back into dark hollows. He tried to sit up, but he couldn't make it.

The doctor told him, "You've got to go back, sir, there's no alternative."

Barcroft said in a thin, fevered voice, "I vowed we wouldn't stop this time. I promised to follow the Indians all the way."

"The company might be able to go on, but *you* can't."

The captain's pain-ridden eyes studied the worried men gathered around him. At length his gaze settled on Cloud.

"Cloud," he said, "Likely as not those Indians'd throw you off the trail sooner or later, and you'd have to go by instinct. Could you find the watering places you told me about?"

Cloud frowned and looked at the other men. "I think I could, sir."

"Thinking isn't enough. You'll *have* to do it."

Cloud shrugged. "All right, sir, I *will* find them."

"Have you ever led men? Commanded them, I mean?"

"Never no bunch like this."

"You'll have to do it now. I'm turning the company over to you!"

Cloud rocked back on his heels. "*Me,* Captain?" He took a deep breath. "Why *me?*"

"It's not that I want to, Cloud. If I had a choice, any choice at all . . ." He scowled. "I've watched you. Unionist or not, you know what you're doing, and you've got an advantage over everyone else here. You've been up into the edge of the high country where these Indians are heading. It just seems to fall into your lap, doesn't it?"

"Captain," Cloud pleaded, "why don't you turn it over to somebody else? Just let me be a guide—a scout—like I've always been. I never figured to be no officer, never had no trainin' thataway."

"You know what you need for *this* job, probably better than any man here. It hurts me worse than it does you, just having to give it to you. So take it and go on. That's an order!"

Cloud rubbed the back of his neck, still unable to accept what had happened to him. "Captain, I don't know much about the military, but I thought I was under arrest. You sure don't turn a command over to a man who's under arrest."

Barcroft scowled again. "Then you're not under arrest anymore. You forget about it and I'll try to."

Cloud looked around him, worriedly studying the faces of the men, wondering how they would accept him, especially those strongly Confederate. "Boys," he said, "I don't really want this job, and if you-all don't want to follow me, I won't take it. It's up to you."

The captain protested, "It's not up to them. *I* gave the order."

Miguel Soto grinned thinly and nodded. Red-haired Quade Guffey said, "All right, new captain, you just tell us where you want us to go to."

Cloud looked at Seward Prince, the staunch Confederate. Prince frowned and dug his toe into the ground. He finally said, "This ain't no time to be fightin' over politics. Them Indians don't know one side from the other. Later, maybe, I'll fight you to hell and gone. But right now I'll follow you."

Cloud expected some vocal opposition, for he could see it in a few of the faces. But when Prince accepted him, the rest of the opposition seemed to dissolve.

"Just lead out," somebody spoke, "and let's go."

Cloud couldn't just ride off and leave the captain alone. He had a couple of men who had received slight wounds in the sudden raid last night. These he detailed to take the captain home. An hour's ride back, he had seen a grove of trees late the day before. He told the men to go there and cut a couple of long ones, then make a travois to carry the captain home.

As Cloud started to leave, the captain waved him over. "Cloud," he said, "the main thing now is to try to get that little girl back. I don't expect I'll ever find mine anymore. But get *this* one!"

Cloud promised, "We'll sure try, sir."

13

They found where the Indians had stopped to rest briefly during the night. On the run, Indians seldom rested any more than they had to. From this point, the single trail splintered into half a dozen.

Cloud cursed under his breath and said to Miguel Soto, "Been afraid all along they'd do this. When they couldn't run our horses off, they figured to get rid of us by splittin' up. We can't follow them all."

Quade Guffey suggested, "We could split up ourselves."

Cloud shook his head. "Mighty little I know about soldierin', but one thing I *do* know is that you don't want to divide your forces. We'll just have to pick one trail and stay with it." He turned to Miguel. "Reckon they'll all meet again farther along?"

Miguel said, "Sometimes they do. Not every time. With Comanche, is nothing ever sure."

Quade asked, "How we goin' to know which trail to stay with?"

"We don't. Just shut your eyes and pick one."

Quade took one that appeared most nearly to follow in the same direction as they had been riding. It was the one Cloud would have chosen.

They followed the trail an hour or so before this one split, too.

"Indians," Guffey growled. "They'll wear you to a nub, just makin' decisions."

Cloud gritted his teeth. Anybody could follow a hundred horses moving in a bunch. But it might not be easy to follow three or four ridden by men who knew how to hide their trail.

The late-summer sun built to a deadening heat as the riders moved along, the main body of horsemen staying to one side of the trail to prevent obliterating it in case Miguel and Cloud lost it and had to do some backtracking. They jogged in silence across this open, rolling prairie of brown grass that stretched on to infinity, fading from sight in waves of heat that writhed in ceaseless torment on the vague, brassy horizon.

As the day wore on, Cloud found himself looking back often at the men. He saw their shoulders begin to droop. He saw some of them turning for a wistful look over the back trail. At times the trail was so dim that the men had to ride along in a slow walk while Cloud and Miguel bent in the saddle, straining for sight of something to go by. Now and again they had to halt altogether and circle back for another try, picking up the trail somewhere behind and following it again, careful lest they lose it once more.

Finally, late in the day, the trail played out altogether. Miguel tried hard to pick it up, even got on his hands and knees and probed with his fingers at what he thought might be a horse track. It wasn't.

Until dark they hunted, but the Indians had covered the trail too well. Cloud felt a momentary wave of despair. "Led us right out to the thin edge of nothin' and then dropped us off."

He signaled the men to stop and fix supper. Sharing a fire with Miguel and Quade Guffey, he morosely stared into his coffee cup.

Guffey said, "No use blamin' yourself. Wouldn't have been any different if the captain had been in charge."

"Wasn't blamin' myself, or anybody. Just wonderin' which way to jump next."

"Don't look like we got much choice. We lost them. We'd just as well head home."

Cloud frowned. "Maybe we could find them again." To Guffey's questioning glance, he said, "I got a hunch where them Comanches might be headed. I been thinkin' about just goin' there ourselves, as fast as we can."

Guffey and Miguel straightened with interest. Guffey asked, "Where's that?"

"A spring Easter showed me. Best, she said, anywhere down on this part of the plains. Said the Indians use it a lot as a jumpin'-off place when they sashay south to plunder, and they meet there sometimes when they come back after a raid."

Guffey pointed out, "You don't know that they'll use it *this* time. That bunch we followed when we rescued her—*they* didn't meet on no spring. Why don't we go back to the place where we first found her?"

"They know *we* know where it's at. They *don't* know we know where the spring is."

Some of the men had begun to gather around and listen. Finally Seward Prince spoke up: "Cloud, how far is it to that spring?"

"Can't rightly say. It's a far piece yet."

"How do you know you can find it? You don't even know how far it is."

Chewing his lip, Cloud said, "I can find it, that's all. I've always had a good sense of direction. Ever I'm at a place, I can find my way back to it. Kind of an instinct, I guess."

"You feel sure of yourself, but how can we be sure of *you*?"

Cloud sought an answer but didn't find it. "The Lord gave me an instinct, and I've got faith in it. You'll just have to have faith too."

Prince grumbled, "I got faith in what I can see—a good horse, a gun. I ain't keen on somethin' I *can't* see, like somebody else's instinct."

Guffey stood up and heatedly faced the man. "You got somethin' better?"

Cloud held up his hand to stop the argument. "Boys, ain't no use us gettin' in an argument over this thing. I'm not takin' anybody someplace where he don't want to go." He stood up and looked around. By this time all the men were close enough to hear him. He drained the coffee cup and dropped it.

To all of them he said, "I'm not Captain Barcroft,

and I won't even try to act like him. I got a proposition to make you. Them that don't want to go with me can turn around and head home, and no hard feelin's. Them that does choose to stick with me, I want them to know what the odds are. We've lost the trail. Chances aren't good that we'll pick it up again. Ahead of us, way off yonder, is a spring where I think the Comanches may be figurin' to meet up with one another. I can't guarantee to find it, but I *think* I can. And even if we find the spring, we can't be plumb sure that's where they're headed this time. All we can do is rely on the odds. And the odds are, that's where they'll go.

"Another thing: we know the Indians left a rear guard to spy on us last night. That's why they hit the camp the way they did. Now, they may still be out yonder watchin' us, seein' which way we're goin' to go. So if we do cut out across this prairie and head straight toward the spring, I think we ought to start in the night. With a little luck, we can be a long ways before any spies they've left catch on. That way, we'd be in better shape to surprise the bunch when we do find them."

Dr. Johnson said, "Sounds reasonable to me. If the captain had enough confidence to leave you in charge, I'll go with you."

Other men agreed with the doctor. In a minute almost no one was left except Seward Prince. Cloud stared levelly at him. "How about it, Prince?"

Prince looked around him and saw how the temper of the others seemed to be. He shrugged his heavy shoulders and said, "Well, it's a cinch I don't care none about goin' back by myself. I ain't got your instinct, Cloud; I'm *already* lost. So it looks like I got no choice."

Cloud warned him, "If you go, you'll take orders like everybody."

"I'll take orders. I'm liable to whip you later, but right now I'll take orders."

Cloud nodded in satisfaction. "Fair enough. Whip me later, if you can. Right now we better try to get a little rest. After a while we'll get up and head out in the dark." He paused and added, "And this time we'll do what we came for, boys. I can feel it in my bones."

They rode in starlight. It was barely bright enough to see each other and not become separated in the night. Cloud felt the weariness weighing in his own body and could see it in the sag of the other men. They hadn't rested long enough. Before long they would feel the horses giving out too.

They jogged along in silence, no one talking lest voices carry. They denied themselves the comfort of smoking tobacco, lest the glow be seen from afar. Some men who normally smoked were chewing their tobacco now, trying to defeat the craving that gnawed at them.

Cloud picked a course by the stars and followed it arrow-straight across the gentle roll of the dark prairie. He listened to the muffled thump of hoof-beats in the blackness behind him and was reassured. He knew he was riding across land he had never seen before, land east of the route he had ridden with Easter. Yet within him burned a certainty that he knew how to reach the spring. It was an instinct which came to many frontiersmen who spent their lives in a land beyond trails, beyond civilization. He never questioned the source of it. His faith was simple. As he saw it, the Lord put the instinct in a man with the intention that he use it. Either the man believed in it or he didn't. Cloud believed in it.

After long hours the sun came up, breaking across the right shoulders of the men. There had been no visible change in the prairie. The land over which their long shadows lanced in the golden glow of dawn was the same as they had seen at sundown, the same as they had ridden across all day yesterday. There seemed to be no end to this open land. Its unbroken sweep stretched out all around them, even seemed to move along with them, boundless as the rolling sea. Just grass—the short brown grass of the buffalo range—as far as man's vision reached.

Riding in moody silence, Cloud could not help wondering if eternity itself might not be like this, like a great endless plain of grass stretching on and on, a plain upon which a man might ride and search forever and never find a way to leave it.

He shook his head and tried to put his mind on something else. Just sleepy, he thought, and tired. *Letting my imagination run away. Got to keep my mind on my business.*

All day they rode like this. Occasionally Cloud stopped for a glance over the back trail, as if he expected to find Indians following them. He knew he wouldn't see any, even if they were there. Yet he couldn't keep from looking—looking and wondering.

By midafternoon he could see worry nagging at the men, too. He could feel dust-burned eyes turned upon him, could sense the doubt that began to build in the riders. Tired now, and thirsty, their canteens light because most of the water was gone, they were beginning to wonder if Cloud had led them astray.

The strain began to tell upon Cloud, too. It wasn't that he doubted himself, for he did not. He felt sure the spring lay somewhere ahead, and that he could find it. But he was afraid the men might give up—might turn against him before they reached it.

What would he do if they did? He knew what Captain Barcroft would have done—draw a gun and force them on. But Cloud could never do that. It wasn't his way. From behind him he began to hear grumbling. It wasn't general yet. It was scattered among the same men who always grumbled first. But like rottenness in a barrel of apples, it could soon spread.

The voice he feared most was that of Seward Prince, for he knew there were many who would follow Prince in whatever the man decided to do.

And at last, late in the day, he heard that voice.

"Well, Cloud, how about it? You still sure that instinct is workin'?"

Cloud turned, his face as calm as he could force it. "You haven't seen me alter my course any."

The answer was not one Cloud expected to hear. Prince said, "Then just keep a-ridin'. We'll stay with you."

After that, the grumbling quieted. Cloud felt a gratitude to the big rebel, and at the same time a wonder. If there was to be trouble, he had fully expected it to originate with Prince.

The buffalo trails were the first sign of water. Somehow, sight of it lifted Cloud's shoulders, and he wasn't so weary anymore. It had the same effect upon the men. They followed one of the trails awhile, and the horses began to get the scent of water.

Warily the men balanced rifles and shotguns across their saddles, ready in case there should be Indians at the waterhole. But they found the place clear. Cloud looked it over a moment, and his spirits soared.

"I know this place," he said to Miguel Soto. "I was here." He turned back to the men. "Boys, I'd go kind of sparin' on this water. It's all right in small doses, but too much of it'll sure bust the pucker-string."

This wasn't the spring he sought. It was the somewhat gyppy seep he had found on his way south after leaving Easter.

The men drank sparingly, twisting their faces and swearing at the sharp taste of the water, but filling their canteens anyway. Last they brought the horses up, a few at a time, and watered them. The sun was setting, and Cloud called a halt. He figured they had gone far enough for one day. A little more of this and neither men nor horses would be much good in a fight.

They scattered out around the water to fix their suppers. Cloud ate silently, watching the men and listening to Quade Guffey give his appraisal of this country.

"It never will be worth two cents an acre," Quade declared to all who would listen to him. "Me, I like a place to have plenty of wood and water. You don't find no wood here hardly atall, and what little water you can get is so gyppy it'll go through you about as fast as you can drink it. No, sir, a hundred years from now there still won't be anybody livin' up here but Indians, and they just don't know no better."

Cloud walked over to where Seward Prince hunkered down with a coffee cup squeezed between his two hands.

"Prince," he said, "I was fixin' to have trouble this afternoon, till you spoke up. I'll tell you the truth—I never would've expected it from you. I'm much obliged."

Prince shrugged. "We've done come too far and put in too much misery to turn back whipped. I didn't see nobody comin' up with a better idee than yours. There's enough of us here to fix your plow if you didn't find the spring you was talkin' about."

A crooked grin crossed Cloud's bearded face. Sort of a left-handed support, this was. But it beat having no support at all.

Cloud and Miguel Soto rode in the lead, with outriders detailed on either side of the company. Men and horses had had a good rest, and Cloud held them to a steady jog trot. Such a gait could cover many miles in a day, yet not wear the mounts down. They had to protect the horses, for the horse was the common denominator. Whatever else a man might have was worth nothing to him in this big country without a horse.

Late in the morning Miguel Soto straightened and lifted his hand, pulling his horse to a sudden stop. He pointed ahead of him. Cloud squinted but saw nothing.

"It is down now behind a rise," Soto said. "Wait, maybeso it come back."

Cloud blinked. Heat waves were beginning to wriggle along the horizon line, looking almost like water. "Mirage, maybe," he said. "This country'll fool you that way sometimes."

Miguel shook his head. "No mirage. Maybe a horse, maybe a buffalo. But it is real. Look, there it is again!"

Cloud saw it this time. It moved toward them in a steady, deliberate pace. "Indian, I'll bet you. Better look sharp; there may be a lot more of them."

He had the captain's telescope in his saddlebag. He took it out and stepped down to rest it across his saddle.

"Rider, all right," he said finally. "Fact, it looks like two, ridin' double."

He lowered the glass and looked about for a depression, anything that might give the company some semblance of cover. He found nothing. The plain was unmarred by even so much as a buffalo wallow. He turned toward the men and made a circular motion with his hand. "Spread out in a circle and keep a sharp watch all around," he called. "Could be more than just the one of them."

The men deployed, and Cloud went back to the telescope. "What the . . ." He blinked and looked again. "It's a woman—a squaw. And she's got a child on the horse with her." He shook his head in wonder. "She can't help seein' us," he told Miguel, "but she's comin' right at us."

He kept watching, then he lowered the glass, his jaw dropping in astonishment. "It's *not* a squaw!" he exclaimed. "It's Easter!"

He telescoped the glass and dropped it back into the saddlebag, then swung up quickly onto the horse. "Hold your ground!" he yelled at the men, and spurred out to meet the woman.

Still wearing her buckskins, she dismounted as he neared. She lifted the child down. Cloud jumped to the ground and grabbed Easter in his arms.

"Easter, Easter," he breathed, "I never thought I'd see you again."

He felt the tears on her cheek as she pressed hard against him, her hands strong upon his back. She didn't try to speak.

They pulled apart then, and Cloud looked down at the child. A white child—the Moseley girl!

Cloud dropped to one knee and put his hand under the girl's chin. "Joanna—that *is* your name, isn't it?"

The girl fearfully drew back from him. He realized that the long days' growth of beard and cover of dust made him look like some wild apparition to her. "I'm Cloud, honey," he spoke gently. "Don't you remember me?"

The little girl shook her head and put her arms around Easter's legs. Haunting fear dwelt deep in her wide blue eyes. The child's clothes were dirty and torn, but Cloud could see no sign that she had been harmed. "Easter," he spoke anxiously, looking up, "is she all right?"

"Scared to death but not hurt. She's seen a lot—been through a lot."

"That," Cloud said, "is a mortal fact." He stood up and gripped Easter's arms. "And you, Easter? How about you?"

She dropped her chin. "I'm all right." He saw grief in her eyes.

"What is it, Easter? Did you find your baby?"

She shook her head. "I was too late. It was dead."

He tightened his grip on her arm and said a quiet "Oh" in sympathy.

"It was always a sickly baby," she said. "I told you that. The women did what they could, but they couldn't save it. It was the white blood, they said."

He took her in his arms and held her again, wanting to give her comfort but not knowing how. He expected her to cry, but she didn't. Likely she'd been through that and was finished with it.

He said, "It was our fault, I reckon—mine, for ever findin' you."

"No, Cloud, it's too late now to blame anyone. That wouldn't help. Likely it would've died anyway, even if I had been there. From the first, the women said it wasn't meant to live."

The little girl still held on to Easter's legs. Cloud looked down and asked, "How did you come to find her?"

"They brought her into camp last night. The women sent her to me because they knew I could talk to her." She paused, anxiety in her eyes. "Cloud, they're camped at the spring. I met the band on its way there soon after you and I parted. That's where the raiding parties were to come together."

Cloud nodded. "I had a hunch. That's why we were headin' thataway."

"But, Cloud, they know you're coming. They're waiting for you there."

Cloud looked off in the direction of the spring, his brow furrowed. "Bad luck. I'd hoped we'd shaken them off."

"You didn't. Spies came in last night to report. You've been watched all the way. Now they've prepared an ambush for you at the spring. That's why I slipped out in the night, to warn you. And to bring back this girl." She looked down with compassion, her hand resting lightly on Joanna Moseley's head. "One of the men took a liking to her, wanted to raise her as a daughter. That was why he saved her and brought her along. I think they probably killed the rest of her family."

Cloud nodded. "They did."

"I wanted to save this girl from going through the kind of life I've had, Cloud. At her age, she'd be completely Indian in a year or two. She wouldn't remember anything else. Then someday, if she lived long enough, maybe white men would find her and take her away from the tribe, the way they did me."

She poured out her unhappiness in a thin, breaking voice. "Look at me," she cried. "I'm not a white woman, and I'm not an Indian. I'm a little of both, so now I'm not either one. I was happy enough as an Indian. Life was hard, but it was all I knew, so I thought nothing of it. Then you and the others took me away from that. You wanted me to be a white woman again. But I never was, really, because there was too much of the Indian in me. So I went back to the Indians.

"Those few days in camp at the spring have been enough to show me I'm ruined for that kind of life, too. I've learned too much of the white man's ways to be happy as an Indian again. They're two different worlds. I've got to live in one of them, but I'm not really fit for either one. How can anyone else decide what I'm supposed to be when I don't even know myself? Maybe you can tell me, Cloud; what am I?"

He gripped her hands and looked into her misty eyes. "You're a pretty woman, Easter, and I love you. I know *that,* and nothing else matters to me."

She leaned into his arms again, her head against his chest. "Sometimes I wish they'd killed me years ago instead of taking me with them. At least then I wouldn't have the awful choice to make."

He said solemnly, "It appears to me you've already made the choice. When you left that camp last night and came here with the girl, you burned the bridge behind you. You can't ever go back."

She nodded. "I know. It's finished now." She turned to look gravely behind her. "I wish I could take the best of that life and put it together with the best of the white man's ways. But you can't do that, can you? You can't mix them. You've got to go one way or the other, and burn the bridge!"

Cloud kissed her gently on the forehead. "I'm afraid it's that way. There may come a day when it's different, but not now. We've got to face things the way they are and do the best we can with them. I'll try to make you glad you came back, Easter."

For a moment she remained there in his arms, not saying anything. Then she pulled back. "Cloud, we've got to keep moving. Soon as they missed us this morning, they're bound to've known what I did."

"You figure they'll come after us?"

"I think they will. There are more of them than you know about, because there were men at the spring who didn't make the raid. They want your scalps, and they want your horses. They've got you up here a long way from home. Don't you think they'll try to get you?"

Cloud nodded. "I reckon. Was I *them,* I would." He turned her toward her horse. "We best be movin', then." He gave Easter a lift up onto her horse. He leaned down to the little girl. "Joanna, how's about you ridin' awhile with me? Miss Easter's bound to be tired."

Dubious, the little girl finally nodded. She watched Cloud closely, no longer fearing him but still not ready to accept him as completely human. He lifted her into the saddle, then swung himself up behind her, setting her in his lap. She turned her head to look up into his face. She said, "My daddy . . . we go see my daddy now?"

Suddenly Cloud felt his throat tighten. He looked across at Easter. "Doesn't she know?"

"What does a child her age know about death? How can you tell her?"

Cloud's eyes burned. Unconsciously he leaned down and touched his cheek to the little girl's forehead. "We'll take you home, Joanna."

Once again he saw in his mind the big-shouldered old giant who had been the girl's father. He saw the quiet, determined mother, the brothers and sisters she'd never see again. He remembered most the girl Samantha, with the beautiful hair, the wistful eyes. He said again, whispering now, "We'll take you home."

Riding up to the company, he gave the men time to get over their amazement at the sight of Easter and the little girl. Briefly, he explained how Easter had slipped out of camp during the night, bringing Joanna with her.

"Boys," he said, "this changes things. I know you all came to even some scores. We wanted to square up for Lige Moseley and his family. But the most important thing all along has been to get Lige's girl back. Now we've got her, and we can't afford to take a chance on losin' her again.

"Chances are the Comanches'll be comin' out to get us. Maybe we could whip them and maybe we couldn't. Now, I don't like to tuck my tail and run, but it looks to me like we got little choice now. We got the girl to think of, and Easter. I'll leave it up to you. If you want to stay, and fight, we'll do that. If you want to dust it south, then we'll do that."

He studied the faces of the men. Some of them looked grimly northward, their mouths set in a straight line that said fight. But then they looked at the pitifully ragged little girl, and compassion came into those dirty, bearded faces.

Seward Prince gave the reluctant answer for all of them. "We'd best be a-savin' the girl."

The sun was more than halfway down its western slant when the company once more reached the seep where it had spent the night. As the men rode in, dust lifted in front of them. Cloud spotted a small bunch of buffalo trotting away from the water in their lumbering, head-bobbing gait.

An idea struck him suddenly. "Miguel," he said to the Mexican a little in front of him, "hold up." He turned in the saddle. "Boys, before them buffalo get too far from the water, lope off yonder and shoot several of them."

The men spurred out. *Spa-a-a-n-n-g!* spat a rifle, and a buffalo pitched forward, kicking. More rifles roared. In a minute Cloud could see six or eight buffalo lying in the grass, either dead or jerking convulsively as life ebbed out of them in a flow of crimson. Men and horses and buffalo ran back and forth in confusion. Cloud shouted and lifted his hat, making a circle with it high above his head.

The men began moving back. Seward Prince rode in first, wiping sweat from his face onto his sleeve and leaving a streak of mud. He touched his rifle barrel, then jerked his head back from the blistering heat.

"What's the idee, Cloud? We need some fresh meat in camp, but not all that much."

Cloud said, "I got a purpose. Better go water out."

The men drank all they could stand of the gyppy water and filled their canteens. Then they let their horses in to take a fill. Hot and thirsty, the animals drank better than they otherwise would.

When everyone had finished, Cloud said, "Now let's take some ropes and drag them buffalo carcasses up into the waterhole. Way I figure it, time the Indians get here they'll be plenty dry. So'll their horses. But if we can foul the water, they won't be apt to drink it."

Prince looked northward, his eyes narrow. "Reckon that'll stop them?"

Cloud shook his head. "I don't know. Maybe it won't, but it ought to help slow them down. It might make some of them turn back. And even if they catch up to us, an Indian on a give-out horse won't be near as troublesome. We'll have the edge, because our horses will have watered since theirs did."

Quade Guffey said sorrowfully, "In a country as short of water as this is, it sure does seem like a big waste to mess up a waterhole."

Cloud shrugged. "It'll clean up. But it'll be a long time."

They had ridden until far into the night, then

stopped for a dry camp without fires. At daylight they were up and preparing to ride.

Cloud was moving around, hurrying everybody up. "Come on," he was saying, "Let's get movin'. We got us a long lead, and we sure don't want to lose it."

Miguel Soto appeared, his face grave. "Maybeso we already lose it." He lifted his arm and pointed northward. Cloud turned and heard himself groan.

On a rise behind them he saw two men a-horseback, just sitting there watching them.

Indians!

14

Quade Guffey saw them at about the same time as Cloud did. He stood stiff-backed a moment, staring with his mouth open. He turned to Cloud and asked tightly, "Comanches?"

Cloud's mouth twisted as he watched. "They sure ain't none of *our* bunch!"

"But they *couldn't* have caught us already."

"You don't never want to figure on what an Indian can't do. They could've ridden all night. They knew what direction we were headed in. They could've eaten up the difference in the dark."

"Still, them two could just be a pair of strays that come up on us by accident."

Cloud asked, "You want to wait around and see?"

Quade shook his red head and lifted himself into the saddle, ready to ride. "No, thanks. If they got any business with me, I reckon they'll know where I'm at."

Sight of the Indians was all the group needed. As they rode away, Cloud looked behind him and saw a column of smoke spiral upward. In a moment it had turned into a grayish cloud, and he could see the dancing of flames licking through the dry grass.

Signal to the others, he thought. The main body of Indians must have sent scouts out to locate the white men as soon as it was light enough to see. Now the smoke, visible for miles around, would rally the scattered Comanches.

Looking at the spreading fire, Guffey commented sourly, "Damned prodigal with their grass."

Cloud said, "There's still a world of it left."

They rode steadily, moving part of the time in a jog trot, occasionally spurring up to an easy lope, being as merciful as they could on the horses but at the same time trying to gain on the pursuit. From time to time Cloud rode out to one side and turned to look back. Sometimes he saw Indians, sometimes he didn't. But one thing he knew: they were there, and they were coming as surely as sundown.

He looked apprehensively at Easter Rutledge and at the tiny girl who now sat in front of the doctor, Walt Johnson, in his saddle.

"Miguel," Cloud said, "there's no dodgin' it anymore; we're fixin' to have us a fight. The only thing we got a choice about is where to make our stand."

Miguel swung his hand in an arc. "It makes little difference. All this country, it is the same."

Cloud nodded, glancing back over his shoulder again. "Yeah, all wide open. But somewhere up yonder there ought to be somethin' to hide us a little—even a buffalo wallow if nothin' else."

Miguel humped his shoulders, showing he had little hope. "I do not know this country. I am only a scout. It is not for me to find something which is not there."

They rode on, the smoke of the prairie fire hovering grimly behind them, a stark symbol of relentless pursuit. Cloud could see the growing tension in the faces of the men around him, in the blue eyes of Easter Rutledge. It was not so much the thought that they could not beat back the Indians. In almost any open battle anymore, the white man had the superiority in fire power. That was why the Comanche relied mostly on sneak attacks, on quick stabbing raids and immediate flight. But an Indian attack, even if repulsed, was almost certain to cause casualties out in the open this way. Worst of all, it was just as certain to result in a heavy loss of horses. Even victory in battle would be hollow indeed if many of the Texans were to find themselves left afoot out here in this waterless land, so many days from home.

The only one not showing the strain was little Joanna Moseley, slumped over a-doze in the lap of Walt Johnson. Cloud could feel his own nerves drawn tight. His mouth was dry, and he knew no amount of water could wet it.

He saw the old animal trails without realizing at first what they could mean, for he was too preoccupied with the Indians. Suddenly it came to him: Somewhere there was water, or had been water. The trails had been made by buffalo, drifting in to drink.

And where there was water, there was apt to be a depression of some sort—a hollow, a creekbed. Anything would serve better than this open country.

"Miguel," he said, "we'll stop the company a little

and let them catch a breath. You ride up this trail one way, and I'll go the other. We got to find out which direction the water is."

He veered off to the left and let Miguel take the right. He rode possibly ten minutes. During that time he found two more trails converging into the one he was on. That was enough to satisfy him. He rode up onto a rise, fired his pistol into the air and waved his hat over his head. He saw the company pick up and move his way. On a far rise he saw Miguel Soto pause a moment, then come spurring. A moment after Miguel quit the rise, three horsemen appeared where he had been. Cloud saw smoke puff from a rifle.

He couldn't see Miguel, for the Mexican was behind the rolling hills. He saw part of the company split off and go back after the scout. For a moment the three Indians held their ground atop the hill and continued to fire. Now the sound of rifles began to reach Cloud, muffled by the distance. He never heard an answer he could attribute to Miguel. A premonition struck him. Without seeing, without hearing, he sensed somehow that they had brought down Miguel.

He could see the company sweep up the hill and drive the Indians down the far side. He looked in vain for Miguel's horse. The men turned back, dropping out of sight a minute or two as they came down from the rise. Later, for a few seconds, they came into view again much closer. They were riding fast. But Cloud had time to see they were supporting one man on his horse. Miguel!

Now the main body of the company came up to Cloud. He turned his horse around, leading the way up the trail in an easy lope. He slipped his saddle gun out of his scabbard and held it across his lap, on the ready.

He wondered how far it was to whatever he was looking for. The trail hadn't been used in a long time and was half grown over in grass. If it was a spring, it might have dried up. It *must* have, or there would be fresher sign of game. Even when he got there, it might not be any good for cover. It might be only an outcrop of rock or some such.

But in a time like this a man didn't stop to question. He rode and hoped, and looked to his guns.

Off to the left he saw movement. Indians paralleling him and coming fast!

There *is* something up there, he realized suddenly. *They know it, and they're trying to beat us to it!*

"Come on," he shouted back over his shoulder. "Spur for all you're worth!"

It was a race, a hard race, the grass flying by beneath the driving hoofs of the horses. Cloud stood a little in the stirrups, leaning forward for better balance to give his horse a chance. He looked back again and again and found the company keeping up with him. Those who had gone to help Miguel were coming up behind, perhaps a quarter mile in the rear.

From Cloud's left came a paint-streaked Comanche warrior, desperately quirting a gray horse and heading straight for Cloud. The Indian swung up a short bow and with a quick flip of his wrist brought forward an arrow from the quiver at his back.

Cloud saw the draw of the bowstring, saw the arrow streak toward him. He checked his horse, almost making it stumble. The arrow passed in front of him.

Can't waste a rifle shot, Cloud thought, *for God knows when I can load another.* He shifted the rifle to his left hand and used his right to draw his pistol. He fired once at the warrior and missed. The Indian had another arrow drawn back when Cloud fired the second time. The Indian's horse suddenly plunged forward, driving its nose into the ground. The Indian rolled and came up on his feet. By then some of the riders behind Cloud were in range. Half a dozen shots blazed, and the Comanche fell.

Ahead, Cloud saw what he had been looking for: scrub brush growing along the edge of a narrow dry wash.

No wonder they've tried to beat us to it, he thought. *Good place to make a stand.*

But the race wasn't won yet. The Indians paralleling him were still making a desperate run for it. Cloud turned to urge the Texans to ride faster. But he didn't have to. They'd seen the wash, and they'd seen the Indians. They were spurring, quirting, doing all they could. From here on it was going to be a test between horses.

For a few moments it was close. But gradually Cloud realized his company was going to win. The Indians' horses were playing out, falling back.

Tired out, Cloud knew—tired and dry. Fouling that waterhole had paid off.

Nearing the wash, Cloud reined to one side and stepped out of the saddle, dropping to one knee with his rifle ready. He waved the men on past, trying to get them into the protection of the wash. Some of them pulled up and jumped to the ground beside him, helping give cover for the others while they found a way to get the horses down the four-and-five-foot wall of the wash.

As the first wave of Indians came up—ten or twelve—rifles roared and black powder smoke billowed back into the Texans' faces. The Indians hauled up. A horse and a man fell. One wounded horse began to pitch, the Comanche rider trying to hold on. After several jumps the horse went to its knees, exhausted. In the interval when the Indians drew back uncertainly, Cloud and the others loaded their rifles and began to pull toward the wash afoot, leading their horses. Cloud walked backward, his eyes warily following the Indians.

He heard the pounding of hoofs to the left of him and glanced around to see the rest of his company coming up hard, bringing Miguel. From bellied-down Indians on a far rise, smoke puffed and bullets whined past the fast-moving riders. A horse went down rolling, its rider sprawling helplessly in the grass. Other riders pulled in, helping the dazed man up behind one of them. Cloud waved the newcomers into the wash.

Realizing the Rifles were about to make cover, the Indians began closing in. Cloud heard the whisper of spent arrows, shot from too far away to take effect. Those Indians who had rifles were using them, but the bullets kicked up little geysers of dust and clipped off cured grass, none doing any harm.

Spooked by rifle fire, some of the horses balked at picking their way down the steep sides of the wash. It took two men to get the horses down—one pulling from below, one pushing from above. Once a horse began to scramble and slide, the man beneath jumped back out of the way. Cloud heard a leg snap and knew they'd lost a horse. But they could do much worse if they didn't hurry.

Cloud was the last man into the wash. He dropped to his belly and rolled over the edge, tasting dirt. He held his rifle high in his right hand to keep it clean. He didn't have to give any orders. The men knew well enough what to do. They had scattered out along a hundred-foot width of the wash and peered over the edge, rifles ready. The flush of excitement rode high in their faces, but there was no panic. They'd loosed their horses in the center of the wash, some of the men stringing ropes to keep the animals from getting away.

They had set Miguel down on the ground. Cloud stepped to the Mexican's side and dropped to one knee, cradling his rifle across his left arm. Miguel had caught the wound high in the shoulder. Easter Rutledge knelt on the other side of the Mexican, trying with canteen and cloth to stanch the flow of blood.

Little Joanna Moseley pressed herself against the bank of the wash and screamed for her father, recoiling in terror every time a rifle blazed.

To Miguel, Cloud said, "Too bad, old friend."

Gritting his teeth, his face drained of color, Soto leaned his head back against the side of the wash.

"Is all right, my frien' Cloud. I stomp a many snakes. Is sure thing, someday one of them bite me."

The little girl still screamed. Easter left Miguel to hold the wet rag tight against his own wound, and she moved to hold the little girl in her arms, to comfort her.

"Cloud," she asked anxiously, "what are our chances?"

"We got protection here, better cover than they have. All they can do is come in and try to run over us. Comanches hate to make a direct charge thisaway. They like the odds in their favor. That open country around us gives us the edge."

"There are more of them than of us," she pointed out.

"It ain't always *how many* that counts. Sometimes *where at* means a sight more."

She looked out over the edge. "A lot of them will be killed, I suppose."

He didn't answer, knowing it was pointless. She bit her lip. "I hoped it wouldn't be this way," she said. "I hoped they wouldn't catch us. They're still my people. . . ."

She looked down a moment. "Cloud, if it comes to that, I don't want them to take me back. I've betrayed them. I know better than anybody what they'll do."

A chill passed through him. "They won't take you, Easter."

The rifle fire quickened. Quade Guffey yelled, "Cloud, they're comin' at us!"

Cloud shifted the rifle back to his right hand and

jumped to his feet. He saw forty or fifty Comanches angling toward them in a ragged line. The Indians were still three hundred yards away. The Texans held their fire until the horsemen were near enough for some accuracy. Then rifles began to blaze. Three horses fell, for horses were an easy target. Three men sprawled out on the ground. Two of them got up, one didn't. The Comanche line wavered and turned, sweeping off to the right without ever getting close enough for the Indians themselves to do any damage.

"Testin' us," Cloud said.

Guffey replied, "And I hope they found out what they was after. This ain't no bunch of helpless immigrants."

The Indians moved away from range of the Texans' guns and regrouped. Cloud stood back and wiped grimy sweat from his face and looked to the men. He made a quiet round of inspection and found they were all right.

Easter Rutledge had time now to bind Miguel's wound. Then she again held Joanna Moseley in her arms, gently patting the little girl's head. Joanna still sobbed a little, but no longer with the terror she had shown.

Now, thought Cloud dismally, *who's goin' to comfort Easter?*

The Indians came again, yelping and screaming even before they got in range. They presented an uneven front of painted horses and half-naked, painted men, feathers streaming. Even as he watched, his hands sweaty on the gun and his scalp prickling,

Cloud could not escape the pagan beauty of it, the savage spectacle of these wild horsemen bearing down in a thunder of hoofs, a roll of dust.

Cloud took a look down his own line of waiting riflemen, saw the excitement flare in their eyes. He sensed the men were waiting for him to take the first shot. He picked a Comanche with a long headdress and leveled his rifle. It was going to be an easy shot, for the Indians were coming almost straight at them. It was so easy he almost hated to do it. He squeezed the trigger and flinched at the recoil. He saw the Indian slide off the horse.

Around Cloud the gunfire suddenly blazed, and more Indians and horses went down. But the other Comanches kept coming.

Bound and determined! Goin' to get us or die tryin'!

Close by, Cloud heard a man gasp and turned to see Quade Guffey hunched over, gripping his left arm, cursing softly. Guffey cast a wide-eyed glance over the wash and began trying to reload his rifle. Blood ran down his arm, and he couldn't handle the rifle well enough to get another load in it.

Cloud shouted at Easter. "Easter, Quade's hit! Help him reload!"

Easter stood up and took the rifle. She fumbled with it, then the tears broke and she handed it back to Guffey.

"I can't . . ." she sobbed, sinking to her knees. "I can't. They're still my people."

Guffey, his teeth clamped tightly with his own pain, murmured, "It's all right, ma'am; it's all right."

He drew his pistol and waited for the Indians to get close enough that he could use it.

Fire from the wash was gouging gaps into the Comanche line. The thunder of guns drummed into a man's brain until he could hear nothing except the guns themselves and the ringing sound they left driving in his ears. Cloud could still feel his hand sweaty on the rifle. He could taste dirt and sweat and could smell the warm odor of blood and the sharp biting tang of gunpowder that drifted around him in black clouds of smoke.

Now the Indians were close enough that he could see their painted faces, could see the mouths open in savage screams that barely penetrated his ringing ears. He could feel the vibration of the earth beneath the pounding hoofs. He fired the rifle and saw a man fall and knew he didn't have time to reload. He brought up his pistol and held it steady, waiting for a close shot.

He saw that the Indians were going to try to ride right up over the wash and overwhelm the Rifles by sheer force of numbers.

Now it was short range—rifles empty and no time left to load them. It was pistols against Comanche short-bows. The Texans poured pistol fire into the screaming faces, the painted bodies that bore down upon them. The first of the line was right upon the wash now. The Indian horses slowed, trying to avoid a crashing fall into the gully ahead. The Comanches tried to whip them up, to keep them running. But the horses balked, and as they did, the Texans had time to cut down the Comanches with a blistering fire.

One horse fell, spilling his rider into the wash almost atop one of the Texans. The Texan whirled, grabbing his empty rifle and using the butt of it to brain the Indian before the man could move.

It was an insane swirl of dust and smoke, a bedlam of shouting, cursing men, of blazing guns and screaming horses. Around him Cloud could sense a frenzy of movement, but he forced himself to keep his gaze on what was just ahead of him, what was in range. He sensed that the Indian line had faltered, badly riddled.

He saw a magnificent warrior charging straight at him, a lance poised for the strike. Cloud's mouth was bone dry, his heart hammering. He wanted desperately to fire, but he had no idea how many shots were left in his pistol, if any at all. He couldn't fire until he knew he would not miss, for there might not be a second chance.

A few seconds seemed an eternity. He had time enough to study the Indian's painted face, red-streaked body, the buffalo shield with the scalp tied to it, the long blond hair streaming out.

A cold fury welled up in Cloud. He felt the pistol buck in his hand, saw the Comanche jerk and come off the horse. The Indian hit the ground rolling and came over the edge of the wash, right on top of Cloud. Cloud shoved the pistol into the man's belly and pulled the trigger. There was only a dull click. He went down backward, the Indian's weight on top of him.

He could smell the grease, the woodsmoke odor that clung to the man, and he smelled the blood where he had caught the Indian in the shoulder. But there was strength in the man, even yet. The Indian grabbed at the knife on Cloud's belt and slipped it out of the buffalo-tail scabbard. Cloud gripped his wrist and wrestled with him for possession of the knife. He could feel the sweat breaking on his face, burning his eyes, and he knew the desperation in the Indian. But the Comanche was wounded, and this gave Cloud an edge. He wrested the knife from the man's hand and savagely slashed upward with it. The blade drove into the Indian's stomach. The man screamed and sagged forward. Cloud jerked the knife out and drove it forward again, plunging it hilt-deep between the warrior's ribs.

He pulled away then, letting the Indian slide to the ground. Cloud's eyes were afire from sweat and dirt, his hands desperately feeling over the ground for the fallen pistol. He found it and started to reload it. But even as he did so, he was aware that the gunfire was diminishing.

He blinked away the pain in his eyes and stood up. On the ground before the wash lay a pitiful scattering of dead and wounded horses, dead and wounded Indians. Off to the right, he could see the settling dust as the surviving Comanches retreated.

Quade Guffey stood beside him, holding his wounded arm, his sleeve crusting with blood and dirt, his face slowly paling from shock he had not had time to feel before.

"Reckon they've had a gutful, Cloud," he said thinly. "They could take us, even yet. But they know it'd cost too much."

Already some of the men were climbing up out of the wash, searching for fallen Indians that might still be alive. Now and again they found one and finished him with a shot or the silent thrust of a knife.

Cloud knelt and picked up the buffalo shield where it had rolled into the wash. With trembling fingers he untied the scalp. No question to whom the long hair had belonged.

Seward Prince stepped up to Cloud and watched him finish the unpleasant job. He asked solemnly, "That girl back at Moseley's?"

Cloud nodded.

Prince cleared his throat and looked about uncomfortably. "Maybe she'll rest easy. We sure took that bloody vengeance the preacher was talkin' about." He nodded toward the scalp. "You want us to take that out yonder a ways and bury it?"

Cloud nodded. "It'd be the Christian thing, I suppose."

Prince said, "I'll get the preacher to go with me." He recoiled a little as the scalp passed into his hand. He paused before saying, "Cloud, you done all right. You sure done all right."

"Thanks, Prince," Cloud answered. "You all did." He turned toward Easter Rutledge, who sat in a huddle against the side of the wash, still holding the little girl. Easter didn't look up. She sobbed quietly, her shoulders heaving.

Regret passed through Cloud, and he wished they'd gotten away without all this slaughter.

Her people! And they always will be.

He put his hand on her shoulder and said gently, "It's all over now, Easter. We're goin' home."

The men had ridden wearily, drowsiness in their eyes. But as they came upon the first cabin of the Brush Hill settlement, they began to straighten. They broke their long silence and started talking. They waved at three small children and their mother who stood in the shade of a dog run. A little boy jumped on a horse and kicked him into a lope, moving out ahead of the rifle company to spread the news that the men were coming home.

By the time the men rode into the main part of the settlement, the people stood out beside the road waving, shouting them a welcome.

Cloud swung down as a couple of old men eagerly rushed to shake his hand.

"Glad to have you boys home again," one said with a grin.

"You kill aplenty of Indians?" the other pressed.

Cloud glanced back at Easter. "Enough of them, I reckon." Then, rushing to ask his own question before the two had time to throw another at him, he said, "I been worried about Captain Barcroft. Did he get in all right?"

One of the old-timers nodded. "Yep, couple of the boys brung him. He's over to the Lawton house."

Thanking them, Cloud remounted. He turned to Quade Guffey, who rode along with a stiff arm hanging at his side. "Quade, how's about you takin' the bunch on up to headquarters? I best stop in and visit with the captain first. See you directly."

Guffey nodded and gave a slight wave with his good hand. Cloud motioned for Easter to stay with him. He watched while the Rifles moved on down the dusty road, the settlement people walking out to shake hands with them as they passed.

A long way to Virginia, he thought, *a mighty long way. The war they're fightin' there don't seem to mean much here, don't even seem real somehow. We got our own war to fight, and we got the right men to fight it. Good men, every last one of them, the best men in the country.*

He pulled up in front of the Lawtons' stake fence. Hanna Lawton stepped to the door and saw them. She called back into the cabin, then came running. By the time Cloud had helped Easter down from her horse, Hanna was there, waiting to throw her arms about Easter. Cloud reached up and lifted the little girl down, setting her gently on the ground. They'd stopped at the creek a while back, and Easter had scrubbed the girl the best she could.

Hanna stood off at arm's length, looking Easter over. She said, "Cloud, we never expected to see her again. What . . . how . . . ?"

"It's a long story, Hanna," he said. "We'll tell you later. But first I better report to the captain. How is he?"

Cloud could see happiness in Hanna's smile. "He'll be all right, Cloud. It'll take a while, but he'll be all right."

Mother Lawton came out of the house, and Henry Lawton hurried along from the store. It took a few more minutes to get the howdies said to them. Then Cloud went into the cabin.

He blinked against the darkness and found Aaron Barcroft sitting up in a rocking chair, rocking impatiently, waiting for him. Cloud saluted. "Reportin' in, sir. We did what we went for."

As his eyes became accustomed to the room, he could see that the captain was pale and drawn. His eyes seemed drawn back into his head, but even so, Cloud could see the same spark which had always been there. The captain asked anxiously, "What about the little Moseley girl?"

Cloud smiled a little. "We found her, sir, and we brought her back. We found somebody else, too. We brought Easter Rutledge home."

The captain's eyes widened momentarily in surprise, then Cloud could tell the man was glad. Barcroft asked, "She went after her baby. Did she find it?"

Cloud shook his head. "It was dead, Captain."

Barcroft dropped his chin, regret in his face. "I did that to her," he breathed. He was silent a moment. Then, "How about losses?"

"Two men killed, sir. Several shot up a little—none that won't get over it." He gave the captain a brief review of the campaign, stressing Easter Rutledge's part in it.

At last the captain said, "I guess everybody needs to be laid flat on his back once in a while, just to force him to take time to do some thinking. I've done a lot of it the last few days. One thing I've realized is the wrong I did to Easter Rutledge. Now I'll never be able to right it." He frowned, his gaze on the floor. "I suppose she still hates me. I don't guess she'll ever forgive me for what I did."

"She'll forgive you, sir. You did what you thought was right. She respects that."

The Lawtons came into the room, bringing Easter and the little girl. The captain stared at Joanna Moseley, and Cloud could see Barcroft's dark eyes melt into tenderness.

The captain whispered, "Come here, little girl."

Unsure of herself, the girl went to him. The captain reached out hesitantly and touched her hand and said in a tight voice, "What's your name?"

So quietly the others could hardly hear, the girl said, "Joanna."

"How old are you, Joanna?"

With some deep thought, the girl held up three fingers.

"Three," the captain said. "You know, I had a little girl like you once. Last time I saw her, *she* was just about three. You look like her—a whole lot like her."

Innocently the girl asked, "Where is she now?"

"She's gone . . . far away." The captain paused a long moment, then said, "How'd you like to climb up here in my lap, Joanna?"

Hanna Lawton stepped forward to stop it, worry in her eyes. "Aaron, your wound!"

The captain waved her away. "It'll be all right," he said. Cloud lifted the girl into the captain's lap.

The captain put his good hand on Joanna's shoulder and pulled her against his chest. He said to her, "I've been looking for another little girl to come and live with me, a little girl like the one I had. Would you like to be my little girl?"

Joanna murmured wearily, "It'd be all right, I guess."

The captain began to rock the chair gently while he held Joanna. Presently the girl looked up and said, "You're crying! What're you crying for? Did somebody hurt you?"

The captain shook his head and drew the girl closer. "No, child, nobody hurt me." He kept on rocking, and Cloud turned away.

On the porch outside, Easter said, "I thought I'd hate him as long as I lived, but I don't. I can't hate him anymore. I can only feel sorry for him."

Hanna Lawton said, "He's a good man, Easter. He's hard to understand sometimes, but he's a good man." She held silent a moment, then smiled uncertainly. "Easter . . . Cloud . . . he's asked me to marry him."

Surprised, Cloud blurted, "Well, I'll be damned!"

Hanna said, "It's a cruel thing, but I'm almost glad he was wounded. It forced him to lie still a long time and think. And it gave me a chance to be with him."

Cloud told her, "He's a smart man, Hanna. He wouldn't have overlooked you forever."

"Maybe he would and maybe he wouldn't. It doesn't matter now. He's asked me, and I told him yes."

Cloud said, "Looks like you'll have to be a mother to the little Moseley girl. I hope you won't mind that."

Hanna shook her head. "She'll help. Didn't you see his eyes a while ago? For a few minutes there he was happy—happy like he hasn't been in years. His daughter was one loss *I* never could've made up to him. But maybe this little girl can." Hanna turned then to Easter. "Your clothes are still hanging where you left them. You'll have a home here just as long as you want it."

Cloud took Easter's hand. "Easter's goin' to have a home of her own, Hanna."

Fondly watching the couple, Hanna said, "I'm glad."

When they were alone, Cloud led Easter down to the creek. They stood together beneath the trees, listening to the soft rustle of the leaves, the quiet murmur of the water. Easter looked northwestward toward the land she had left, the home to which she could never return.

Cloud said gently, "You've given up a lot, Easter, and there's some of it I know can never be made up to you. But maybe in time I could help you forget. Maybe I could make you happy."

She leaned to him, her head against his shoulder. Her arms went around him, and she said in a soft voice:

"You will, Cloud. You will."

MASSACRE at GOLIAD

AUTHOR'S NOTE

In the Texas revolution against Mexico, Mexican troops won all the important battles except two: the first one and the last. Between those, the Texians (the early settlers prior to statehood) lost one after another to the numerically superior forces of General Antonio López de Santa Anna.

Everyone knows about the Alamo. Fewer, outside of Texas, know about the massacre at Goliad, where more than twice as many Texians died. The difference was that in the Alamo they fought to the death. At Goliad they were made prisoners, led out, and murdered.

A root cause of the revolution—but by no means the only one—was a vast racial and cultural difference between the native Mexican people and the Americans who had come to settle among them in various colonizations since about 1823. Mexico encouraged these settlers at first, seeing them as a potential buffer against the Comanches and other hostile Indians. Men of good will worked hard for understanding between Americans and Mexicans,

none more diligently than Stephen F. Austin, the Father of Texas.

But even the gentle and trusting Austin finally had to concede that President Santa Anna was a vain and hopeless tyrant. Like many others before and since, he began as a liberator but grasped for power until he became a ruthless dictator, capriciously holding life and death in his hands. Not only the Texas Americans but many Texas Mexicans and citizens of northern Mexican states rebelled against him. Most of the true old Texian settlers continued to regard themselves as loyal citizens of Mexico, in revolt against Santa Anna, not against the country. Indeed, the defenders of the Alamo—Mexican as well as American—fought and died beneath the Mexican flag of 1824.

Texians under spirited old Ben Milam drove federal troops out of San Antonio in the fall of 1835 and dogged them to the Rio Grande. In response, Santa Anna butchered his way across northern Mexico, putting insurgents to the sword wherever he found them, then crossed into Texas.

The determined resistance at the Alamo surprised and slowed him, giving Sam Houston time to strengthen his defensive force. At Goliad, indecisive commander James W. Fannin delayed an ordered retreat until too late and was surrounded by Mexican troops under General José Urrea. After a costly battle, Fannin surrendered his command on Urrea's good-faith pledge of fair treatment. The dictator countermanded that promise. On Palm Sunday some three hundred and forty prisoners were marched out of the old mission in groups and shot.

Because the firing squads were smaller than the number of victims assigned to them, some men were able to break and run between volleys. A few more than twenty are known to have escaped. Some joined Sam Houston in time for his crushing defeat of Santa Anna at San Jacinto.

By then the overconfident self-styled Napoleon of the West had divided his forces and force-marched ahead of the larger body in the hope of catching Houston's little army before it could escape into Louisiana. Santa Anna was contemptuous of his own men, declaring that it was their great privilege to be allowed to die for his honor. He disregarded the suffering they endured by being ill-clothed and poorly equipped for Texas' cold, wet winter. His troops had already been decimated by sickness before Houston's embittered men suddenly turned with a vengeance and drove them reeling into the mud of Buffalo Bayou, where the carnage wrought upon them was horrendous.

In an attempt to escape, Santa Anna donned the nondescript uniform of a common soldier but was captured and brought trembling before the wounded Sam Houston. Most of the Texians wanted to hang him then and there, but Houston counseled peace. Dead, Santa Anna could sign no treaties. Alive, he could—and did—acknowledge that Texas was free.

1

In his later years Joshua Buckalew seldom spoke of Goliad and the terrible thing which happened there. Even in his old age there were nights when the memory returned in a dream and he would wake up suddenly with the cold sweat breaking, the horror as vivid as it had been in his youth.

Yet there was fierce pride in the memory too, for Joshua Buckalew ever afterward considered himself one of the original Texans. He had been a witness to the birth of Texas at Bexar and Goliad and on the marsh-bound prairie of San Jacinto. So, as each of his sons came of age to understand—and later his grandsons—he would tell them the story that they might share his pride in their heritage, and that they might realize and value the awful sacrifice other men had made for Texas.

Always, he began the story long before Goliad. He began it where it had begun for him, one early spring day in Tennessee. . . .

* * *

I could have whipped the Keefer brothers without even breaking a sweat, provided I took them one at a time. But the two together were a mite of excess. They had me staggering in the dust of the crossroads where Gailey's Grocery dispensed everything from harness leather and red calico to raw corn spirits in a jug. Dogs barked. Men and boys cheered and whooped and stood back to give us room. Entertainment was scarce in those parts—a horserace occasionally, a shooting match, a barn-raising or a dance. A good fist fight was usually certain to stir the betting blood. But nobody was betting this time. They could tell that I was fixing to get my plow cleaned good and proper.

I was twenty-one then, five feet eleven and tough as mule-hide. But that wasn't enough. I kept lashing out with my fists at Smiley Keefer and trying with my elbows to knock loose from Snag Keefer's heavy weight on my back. Snag clung like a burr under a pantsleg.

I puffed, the breath coming hard. "This ain't noways a fair fight . . . I didn't go . . . to fight the both of you."

"You got us anyhow." Snag tried to sink his teeth into my ear.

I shifted my weight and threw Snag off balance, sliding him onto his back in the dust. I landed with both knees in Snag's belly. I turned to see where Smiley was and caught a faceful of his fist. These were plowmen, the Keefers, and a plowman's fists are as hard as a hickory knot.

I saw my brother Thomas edge through the crowd.

"Thomas!" I yelled. "Come and help me!"

Thomas was tall and strong, and he had a face that could be as grim as a hangman. He was grim now. He sat himself down in an open spot on the porch and eased the butt of his Kentucky longrifle to the ground.

I never was one to beg for help. Both Keefers were rushing me again. Their weight brought me down and crushed the breath from me. All I had left was a bruised and angry spirit.

"Now, Josh," gritted Smiley, "let's hear you holler quit."

They twisted my arms. The shame of defeat was as bad as the pain. I threshed and pitched. Cloudiness came over my eyes. I heard a firm voice say, "Give up, Josh. You're makin' a fool of yourself." Thomas hovered over me.

I clamped my teeth together tightly to keep from hollering out. Smiley Keefer put more pressure on my arm.

Thomas Buckalew said, "All right, boys, the fun's over. Let him up."

The Keefers waited too long. Thomas grabbed a fistful of hair in each hand, then cracked their heads together. "I said it's over now!"

The Keefers let go and jumped back the way men will jump away from an angry bull that might come up fighting. I arose, eyes blazing, but my knees betrayed me. I knelt, unable to stay up.

Thomas said flatly, "Git your rifle and let's be a-movin'. Pa wants to talk to us."

It was a minute before I had enough breath to speak. "What for?"

"That colonel what's-his-name from Texas has been by the place again. Pa's got that glow in his eyes."

Thomas let me struggle to my feet without help. He stood back, making it plain that he disapproved of my foolishness. The crowd was scattering. I swung around to glare at the Keefers, who leaned against the porch, still breathing hard. Snag was tipping a jug over his arm.

Thomas caught my sleeve and said roughly, "The mail has done left. You lost the fight; now let it go."

"You didn't even ask me how come I was fightin' them."

"I don't reckon as how I care. A man ought to have more pride than to git hisself stomped with half the settlement watchin', and laughin' at him."

"They were pickin' on poor old Muley Dodd."

"*Everybody* picks on Muley Dodd. Besides, I didn't see him."

"He was scared. Minute I hit Snag, Muley lit out arunnin'."

"Josh, you can't spend your life pickin' up after Muley. The Lord chose to short Muley on brains, and it's too bad. But it ain't up to you to be his everlastin' keeper."

"Somebody's got to help him. He can't help hisself."

I limped at first as we walked down the dusty wagon road, each of us carrying a Kentucky rifle. The late-afternoon sun slanted into our faces, for the Buckalew home lay west of the settlement. That was the way it had always been with the Buckalews: always west of the settlement.

Muley Dodd waited for us down the road, his hat in his hand, his eyes afraid. Short, stooped a little, Muley had the first whiskers of manhood soft on his face. Ragged hair touched his frayed collar. He started talking when we were still fifty feet away. "Josh, I didn't go to leave you there. I didn't noways mean to run. The Devil got in me, and I was afeared. It was the Devil made me run."

Impatient, Thomas said, "It wasn't the Devil caused you to light out, Muley. It was the Keefers."

I cut a sharp glance at my brother. "Hush, Thomas." I walked up to Muley Dodd and put my hand on his shoulder. "Don't fret now, Muley. It's done over with. They ain't fixin' to bother you again."

"You sure, Josh?" Muley brightened up. "Did you whup 'em good? You're a real friend, Josh. And next time there's a fight, I won't run away. I'll stay right there and help you."

It wasn't so, but I nodded like I believed it. "Sure you will, Muley."

We walked on down the road, us Buckalews, Muley standing and watching us with his hat still in his hand. Thomas said, "Josh, you know he'll always run. He'll be runnin' the last day he lives. You can't protect him forever."

We came to a field where a mule stood waiting in endless patience, tied to a stump. At the turnrow lay my wooden plow. I had hired out to old man Higgins for a spell of work the year before, and Pa had made me take my pay in this plow instead of cash. Pa had declared: "Every man needs a plow of his own, time he comes of age. Money is soon spent. But give you a plow and you got somethin' that'll serve you for years."

It was true, I would have to admit. But I'd always said I'd rather stand back and admire Mother Nature than scratch her face with the point of a plow. A man got almighty tired sometimes of working up and down the rows all day, staring an old mule in the rear.

Thomas said, "Better fetch the mule."

Thomas was only a couple of years older than me, but times he acted as if the difference was ten. With Thomas, day was day and night was night; wrong was wrong and right was right. You drew a line and you stayed on one side of it. You didn't step over it, ever. I wondered sometimes where Thomas had inherited that stiff-backed way. It hadn't come from Pa.

The Buckalew home was of a mixed architecture. It had begun long ago as a log cabin but had been extended and enlarged with rough-sawed lumber through the years, as the lumber became available and the family fortunes had allowed us to buy or barter for it. At one time a lot of Buckalews had lived there. But gradually each came of age to go on his own. The boys went west, and the girls married off. Now there were only Pa and the oldest son, Lott, who was to inherit the place according to family custom. And there were Thomas and me.

Pa sat hunched on the hewn-log steps, puffing his pipe and taking his rest. He still worked hard, Titus

Buckalew did. But it seemed like he couldn't take as much of it as he used to. He had worn out too many plows, outlived too many mules. He had cleared this land from virgin timber, by himself at first, then with sons to help him as each came along in his own due time. Lott had a large family of his own now.

Pa's old pipe stood black against the white of his beard as he stared at me. I couldn't see any surprise in the pale blue of his eyes. "Mule drag you, Joshua?"

I never did lie to Pa. "No, sir."

"And you didn't fall out of no tree. So I take it you been fightin'."

"Yes, sir."

"Win?"

"No, sir."

The old man frowned and knocked the pipe against the hard heel of his hand to jar the burned tobacco out. "If you got to fight, at least you ought to win."

"Next time, Pa."

His brow twisted into deep furrows, which came easy to him. "That Colonel Ames, he's been by again, talkin' to me about Texas."

Thomas said, "Pa, ain't it a little late in life for you to be thinkin' about faraway places any more?"

"Not for myself. It's you two that I been frettin' about. It's high time you had a chance to take and do somethin' for yourselves, like your brothers have done."

"You wantin' us to leave, Pa?" I asked.

"No, son, it ain't that I *want* you to. A man don't like sayin' goodbye to his young. But it's the way of life. You can see for yourself, there ain't nothin' left here for a growed man. If you ain't already got your land, you never will get it. What we got here will be just about enough for Lott, once I'm gone. Ever since the first Buckalew come across the big water, they've kept a-lookin' west. I done it, in my day. Your brothers have done it. Now I reckon it's your time."

My skin prickled with excitement. "You think we ought to go to Texas?"

"That's for you to say, not me. But Colonel Ames, he talks like it's a powerful good country for a young man to go and build him a life."

The weariness was suddenly gone from me. "Texas! I been hearin' a right smart about it. The Fancher boy went there last year, him and that Whipple girl he married. And the Smith family. And the year before that, old Henry Leech, only he died along the way."

Thomas nodded. The excitement was touching him too, which was a seldom thing. "The Fanchers got a letter from their boy awhile back. He's right taken with the country, Pa."

Pa drew silently on his pipe, enjoying the tobacco. "The colonel, he says this Stephen F. Austin has got him a colony there, and he'll let a man take up more land than he could accumulate here in a lifetime. All that land, just for the askin'. Of course, you'd have to build her from scratch, but us Buckalews, we always done that."

Thomas frowned. "One thing, Pa, you might not've thought about. Texas ain't in the United States. It's part of Mexico. Us Buckalews have been Americans ever since Grandpa froze his feet that winter with George Washington."

"Governments never did mean no awful lot to us Buckalews, son. We always been so far out front that they never was any bother to us. Anyhow, there's been a-plenty of Americans gone there already. I doubt as you'll see much difference." He was silent awhile, studying first one son, then the other. "Something else: you're both of a marryin' age, and neither one has got you a woman."

Thomas shrugged. I didn't say anything.

Pa said, "Colonel Ames tells me a married man gets twice as much land in Texas as a single man. That's somethin' to consider. I don't expect you're apt to find many unattached females down there. Best play the game safe and take one with you. A bird in the hand, as they say." He looked at me. "How about that Merribelle Keefer, Joshua? She's been chasin' around you like a bear after honey."

I shook my head. "She'd be a burden."

"They all are. But think of that extra land."

"She's not the prettiest I ever saw. And I don't love her."

"Love wears off, and looks change. Main thing is that she can cook. You'd be surprised, too, how she can help keep your bed warm in the wintertime."

"Pa, I've tried her." All of a sudden I felt my face turning red. "Her cookin', I mean. She's not for me."

Humor flickered in Pa's eyes. He turned to Thomas. "How about you?"

"I've never seen a woman I'd marry."

"You always expect too much, Thomas, that's

your weakness. You got to learn to bend a little. Women are human. There never was but one perfect man, and I doubt there ever *was* a perfect woman."

Thomas shook his head. "There's still none here I'd want to marry."

Pa shrugged. "Well, that's up to you. Down yonder, you ain't apt to find anything except Mexican girls."

Thomas said flatly, "I know we won't be marryin' one of *them*."

2

We started when the warm spring sun brought the green rise of new grass. We said our good-byes and pointed the wagon-tongue southwestward, angling to cut across a corner of Mississippi.

There had been a brief sadness at the time of parting, and there would be sad moments again when the awful finality of those long miles of separation at last came home to me. Thomas's jaw was set square and sober, for he was thinking on these things. But for me, riding ahead on a sorrel horse, there was too much new to see, a sudden freedom to glory in. There was no time to waste in looking back.

I had come prepared, or thought I had. A gunsmith had reworked my longrifle, making it like new. On my left hip I wore a big cast-steel knife the gunsmith had fashioned, a heavy thing with a hickory handle, a blade two inches wide and fourteen inches long. It was better than a hatchet or a tomahawk for a man in the wilds, the smith had said. I also had a small skinning knife, worn on a belt slung over my shoulder, with a sack of flints and newly-cast lead bullets.

The wagon lumbered along slowly, for its bed sagged with the weight of things we would use in the new land. If left to my own choice, I would have preferred to travel light, perhaps taking a steamboat down the Mississippi to New Orleans, then going by ship to the coast of Texas. Many emigrants were doing it that way. But Pa had argued that this would land us in Texas with only such goods as we could pack. Wagons, plows, and other implements would be hard to come by in Texas, and the price would be high.

To be sure, the wagon would slow our trip. It would mean back-straining labor and galling delay in time of rain, or in passing through the pine forests and the dense cane-brakes which lay ahead.

"But," Pa had reasoned, "it'll be all yours when you get there. You'll have the wagon and the horses. You'll have a plow apiece, and an anvil and tools. You'll have saddles and harness and plantin' seed. Two cows, a heifer, and a bull. Costs money, Josh, to ride a boat. This way you can live off the country, and so can your stock. What money you've got will still belong to you when you get to Texas."

Two strong gray workhorses pulled the wagon, horses that would be worth a-plenty when they got to where they were going. The cows plodded along with infinite bovine patience at the end of their ropes behind the wagon, udders swinging like the pendulum of a clock. Alongside them walked the heifer, and a big bull calf that we were counting on to sire us a herd in Texas.

We would suffer for this burden on the trip, but we would be better equipped than most folks when we finally crossed the Sabine River into Stephen F. Austin's promised land.

We hadn't gone two miles before we saw a man walking down the road in front of us, an old rifle in one hand and an old canvas bag slung over his shoulder. A spotted hound trailed behind him. It stopped and barked at the wagon. The man turned and smiled broadly. He set the bag down and waved, standing in the road until the wagon drew up almost to him. Then he stepped aside.

"Howdy, Josh. Howdy, Thomas. You-all on your way to Texas?" Muley Dodd waited until we answered yes. Then he said, "I'm on my way to Texas, too."

Feeling pity, I swung down from my horse. "Muley, it's a far piece to Texas. You can't go there thataway."

"I got lots of time, Josh. I got grub in the sack, and powder and lead."

The hound came up and licked my hand. It startled me, and I jerked my hand away. "Muley, you don't have enough supplies in that sack to get you to the Notchy country even, much less to Texas."

"I won't go hungry. I can follow bees. Besides, I got money, too. I got three dollars and fifty-two cents." Eagerly Muley reached into his pocket. "Here, I'll show you."

I shook my head and glanced at Thomas as if to ask him what to do. "Muley, you got to go on back home."

"I already left home. Ain't got no folks there no more, and the roof's about to fall in on that old shack anyhow. I'll built me a real pretty house when I git to Texas."

I motioned for Thomas to get down off the wagon and walk with me out to the side of the road. "Thomas, what we goin' to do about Muley?"

"Nothin'. He's not our responsibility."

"He's not *nobody's* responsibility. He's got no folks."

"You've taken care of him for years, Josh. Now let somebody else do it."

"When Muley gets a notion in his head, he don't turn away from it. If he's got it in his mind to go to Texas, he'll keep walkin' till he dies!"

"You fixin' to tell me we ought to take him with us? If you are, you'll just be wastin' your breath."

Thomas climbed back onto the wagon seat. "Goodbye, Muley," he said, and set the team to moving again.

Muley waved good-naturedly. "Good-bye, Thomas. I'll see you in Texas."

I stared at Muley, worried and a little impatient. Thomas was right: I shouldn't have to be saddled with Muley all my life. Something came to me out of the Bible, something about the faith of the mustard seed. Muley had no conception of what lay ahead of him. But he had plenty of faith.

Muley said, "Thomas is fixin' to go off and leave

you, Josh. You better catch up. I'll see you-all again when I get to Texas."

I rode on ahead, catching up to the wagon. But I couldn't keep from looking back. And Muley Dodd kept coming. Sometimes I could hear him whistling at the dog. Finally I said, "Thomas, you'd just as well stop. I'm not goin' without Muley."

All my life I had heard tell of the Mississippi River, but I wasn't prepared. There it stretched in front of us, its lazy brown waters so wide that the river was almost scary to look at. The first money we had spent since leaving home, we spent for passage across on a ferry. It was a long, slow crossing. The ferry heaved, and so did Muley Dodd.

Finally, when we pulled the wagon down onto the west bank and paused to look back across the Big Muddy, I caught for the first time the full sense of parting. It touched me deeper than I expected. Crossing this river was like turning a page in a book. Distance was a relative thing, but a barrier like this was something real, something we could see. It was like shutting a door behind us, knowing we might never cross this river again. It was a sobering thought, as long as it lasted. But it didn't last long. There was a camp to be made, and fresh meat to be hunted.

Crossing Louisiana, we were held up for days by hard spring rains which bogged the wagon to the hubs in black mud that gave way so easily to the iron-rimmed wheels but yielded them up so grudgingly. This was a place where even Thomas was glad to have Muley along. Being as little as he was, Muley had a strong back. He thrived on hard work, as long as somebody told him what to do.

Hunting was poor. Camp meat ran low. We went deeper than we had intended into our supply of ground corn. Muley's own sack had long since run out of grub, so there was a third mouth to feed. But even if we went hungry we would not touch the sack that carried the seed corn, a tough strain that had served the Buckalew family well in Tennessee and would see us through in Texas.

I whiled away the idle hours by studying a map of Texas until I had it memorized in every detail. Muley spent time with his spotted hound, which he had named Hickory, after Andrew Jackson. Muley tried to rename him Texas, but the hound wouldn't answer to it, so finally it was Hickory again.

A friendly sun came out at last to harden the soaked earth. We greased the axles afresh and started the wheels turning once more. Much of the country we crossed now was wild, and we traveled long distances without seeing much sign of people. Some movers would have been tempted to stop here and settle, for it appeared there was plenty of room. But not the Buckalews. We were men of tradition. We always went the whole way.

At length we came out of the thick pine timber to the Louisiana Creole town of Natchitoches, on the right bank of the Red River. This was the jumping-off place for Texas-bound overland travelers. About 120 miles west, across the Sabine River, waited the ancient Spanish settlement of Nacogdoches, the easternmost town in Mexican Texas. It was here in Natchitoches that Stephen F. Austin had disembarked from a steamboat in June of 1821 to make his first trip into that vast expanse of alien country where his father, the late Moses Austin, had dreamed of a rich American colony and a recovery of lost family fortunes.

The Creoles by now were used to travelers, finding them a profitable source of trade. They got little from the Buckalews. Thomas held the purse strings with a tight-clamped hand. What we didn't really need, we would do without. What we did really need, we had brought with us.

"Just a final little jolly, Thomas," I cajoled. "This is our last chance in the United States. Be a sport."

Thomas was resolute. "I've never *been* a sport. You want to dance? Dance around that there wagon and grease the hubs."

I didn't argue with him much. Even if Thomas had been open handed with me—an unlikely development—I wouldn't have spent more than the price of a jug. The weeks of hard, slow travel on dim trails and the painful care we gave our cargo had sobered me considerably. I could understand and respect the responsibility my brother carried.

"Then I reckon me and Muley will go look around some. See what these here French folks have got to offer."

"You watch out," Thomas said sternly. "Don't be gettin' in no fights over Muley. Somebody acts like they're goin' to pick on him, you just bring him on back to the wagon. No arguments."

"No arguments," I promised.

We had hardly left the wagon when we saw the four horsemen. They rode toward the camp in a slow walk, stopping to peer curiously at the wagon from thirty or forty yards.

Muley caught my arm. "Josh, what kind of men you reckon them fellers are?"

"I don't rightly know." Two of them were a lot like the type I had known in the Tennessee settlements all my life—outdoorsmen with sun-browned, tangle-bearded faces. The floppy hats, the homespun shirts, the woolen breeches were familiar enough.

The other two were different, and I guess my mouth was open as I stared at them. They were both small and wiry, hungry-looking. Their faces were dark, but not the same as those of the Negroes back in Tennessee. They wore peculiar hats with tall, pointed crowns and the widest brims I had ever seen. One had an embroidered black vest that must have been something special once, though now it was dirty and threadbare. Both men wore leather breeches and boots, and spurs with huge, wicked rowels. One of them spoke to the other, and the words were foreign. They made no sense to me.

Mexicans, I realized. Yonder, to the west, sprawled the huge Republic of Mexico. It was natural that we might encounter Mexicans here, the first we had ever seen. The strangeness of the men made us hold still in wonder and keep our silence.

At length the four rode closer. One man nodded with some show of friendliness. "Howdy, friends." His teeth were stained from tobacco. "Be you-all headin' for Texas?"

I found myself picking up his manner of speaking. "Yes, sir, we be."

"Where do you-all come from?"

"Tennessee."

The man glanced at his companions. "Hear that, Foley? They be homefolks."

I couldn't keep my eyes from the Mexicans. "*They* ain't from Tennessee."

The man said, "Foley and me, we left Tennessee a mighty long time ago. Miguel and Alfredo, of course, they don't know Tennessee from Massachusetts. They be Meskin."

Excitement stirred in me. I asked the nearest Mexican, "You come from Texas?"

The Mexican glanced at the Tennessean who had done the talking. The Tennessean said, "You got to pardon Miguel. He don't know much English, 'cept a few words like *eat* and *sleep* and *women*."

I felt an awe of these strange men. "You mean you know how to talk *their* language?"

"Sure. You learn it easy when you git to Texas. All you need is a good teacher—a good-*lookin'* teacher."

I grinned at Muley. "It's real lucky, us runnin' into these fellers. They can tell us a right smart that we ought to be a-knowin'." I looked back at the men. "My name's Joshua Buckalew. Just Josh, is all I use. This here is Muley Dodd."

The big man leaned forward in the saddle and took my hand. "I answer to 'Lige'. For Elijah, you know, like in the Book. He was one of them prophets, or maybe it was a disciple—I forgit which. That there is Foley. The Meskins, they got names longer than a hoe handle, but all you need to remember is Miguel and Alfredo. How many with you, Josh?"

"Just us and my brother Thomas. Us three is all."

The man frowned, looking toward the wagon. "Sure got a load of plunder, just for three of you."

"We figured to be prepared. Come meet my brother." I turned and walked ahead. I shouted, "Thomas, come see what's here."

Thomas came around the wagon, halted and stared, a sharp question in his eyes.

I said, "These fellers come from Texas."

Thomas's eyes seemed to harden as his gaze drifted from one to the other. "How do."

His unfriendly manner caught me by surprise. "Thomas, I said they come from Texas. There's a lot they can tell us."

"I already been told a right smart."

For a moment Lige seemed to stiffen. Then he eased again. "How long before you figger on leavin', Thomas?"

Thomas shook his head. "Can't say for certain. Might stay a spell."

That was a lie, for we had planned to leave the next morning. But I held my silence.

Lige rubbed his beard. "Your brother's a cautious man, Josh. And he's right. It don't pay to trust strangers in these parts. Man can't be too careful in a new country." He took a long last look at the wagon and the livestock. "Fine outfit you got. You ought to git off to a good start in Texas." He pulled his horse around. Foley and the two Mexicans followed his example.

I called, "Maybe we'll see you again. There's a heap of questions I'd like to ask."

Lige replied over his shoulder, "Any time, Josh."

When they were gone, I turned angrily on Thomas. "If you'd been civil we could of talked with them. You wasn't like this at home!"

"We ain't at home, Josh."

"But they was homefolks, and they been in Texas."

"Just because a man's from Tennessee don't mean he's gospel-honest." Thomas frowned. "You're in a strange country, Josh. You don't trust nobody till you have time to size them up. And you don't go tellin' anybody what your plans are. Remember that!"

"They been on the trail. You condemned them because of what they looked like."

"Some things, Josh, you learn to take by instinct. Out in the woods, did you ever sense a varmint before you seen it? It was like that with them four. It was like I had come across a pack of wolves. Nothin' you can put a finger on, but the feelin's there. And when it's there, I pay heed to it."

"I didn't get that feelin'."

"It'll come to you. And till it does, we'll go by my instincts."

That should have been the end of it, for Pa had pledged me to follow Thomas in all important things. But I still burned to find out about the country we were heading for. I wouldn't exactly go looking for Lige. But if we should happen to come across him by accident. . . .

Muley and I started to resume our walk down to

the town. Thomas said, "Don't you be late. We want to get started by daylight."

Trailed by Muley's spotted hound, we walked up and down the length of the town, pausing to stare at the river, looking at the small boats, listening with a keen ear to the strange Creole talk.

I shook my head. "I expect it means as much to them as English means to us."

Muley said in all innocence, "I don't understand English neither. I just talk American."

"That's not what I mean, Muley. It's just that . . ." I broke off, for there was no explaining to Muley. I wasn't even sure I understood it all myself. Take for instance the name of the town: *Natchitoches*. Anybody could look at the word and see how it was supposed to sound. But these people called it something like NAK-i-tosh. I figured either the people who had named the town hadn't been able to spell, or the people who lived here now just didn't know how to read.

Muley wasn't satisfied. "Those little kids yonder, how are they supposed to know what they're talkin' about?"

I just shrugged.

Muley said, "Looks to me like it would be simpler if everybody in the world just got together and decided to talk like *we* do. It must be the best language anyhow, or they wouldn't of wrote the Bible in it. Ain't that so?"

"I expect."

"Looks like it sure would save everybody a heap of bother."

After a couple of hours of looking around, we

hadn't seen anything of the four men. We figured they had left town. Then on our way back to Thomas, we stumbled right into their camp. We found ourselves facing them over the flicker of a dying fire. I sensed a vague hostility. "Let's move in closer, Muley. They probably can't tell who we are."

Lige took a couple of steps forward, hand on a pistol stuck in his waistband. Then he smiled. "Well, I'll swear it's the lads from Tennessee. Set down here, Josh, you and Muley. Share some poor vittles with us. We got a little left."

I looked around for their wagon and saw that they had none. There were only four saddle horses and a couple of pack animals, staked out on the grass. "Thanks, but we wouldn't want to put you out none. We'd drink a little coffee, though, if you got any." We'd been using ours sparingly because we knew it would be expensive in Texas.

"Sure," said Lige, all friendship and smiles. He spoke in Spanish. Miguel fetched a jug. Lige said, "Before the coffee, a little drop of kindness. For Tennessee, and fond recollections."

Muley drank first and went into a coughing fit. Then I tipped the jug over my arm. Whatever it was, it felt as if it would burn a hole plumb through me.

Lige said, "That's Meskin stuff, pretty hot doin's. Not as good as old Tennessee makin's, but it don't lack for authority."

I gasped, "That's for certain sure."

The burn was a while in wearing off. I didn't care for another. Lige laughed as I blinked the tears from my eyes. Muley still coughed a little, trying to clear his throat. It came to me that Foley and the Mexicans were staring at us, their eyes hard. All of a sudden I didn't like these men. Lige was probably all right, but the others. . . .

Even disliking them, I kept glancing at the Mexicans. And Muley stared at them in honest curiosity.

"Lige," I said, "I want you to tell us about Texas."

Lige shook his head. "It's a mighty big subject."

"Just the important things, what we ought to know before we get there."

Lige shrugged. "Well, if I was givin' advice, I'd say the thing most emigrants do wrong is to come unprepared. But from the looks of your wagon, you-all come loaded for bear. So the next thing is to decide where you want to settle."

"We talked to a Colonel Ames back home. He said we could get land in Austin's colony. You know Colonel Ames?"

Lige frowned. "Can't say as I recollect the gentleman. I know Austin, though."

Foley hadn't spoken before. Now he put in bitterly: "Everybody knows abut the good Colonel Austin. Him and his damned whip."

That surprised me. "I thought everybody liked Austin."

Lige replied quickly, "Most folks do. Foley there, he's got a personal grudge is all, and he talks too much." He frowned at Foley. "Austin is pretty much the whole law in his colony. A man who strays off of the straight and narrow has got to answer to Austin. He's a little feller, and he looks gentle, but now and again he rears up and shows his teeth. Now, Foley had a friend who done a transgression, and Austin ordered the man whipped and throwed out of the colony. Foley ain't forgave that."

My flesh crawled. "Whippin' *is* an awful salty punishment."

"It beats hangin'. They can't hang a man in Texas lessen they git permission first out of Saltillo, and that's way to hell south. Takes a long time. So usually they just whip a man out of the settlement and hope somebody else'll hang him. They don't appreciate the rough element in Austin's colony."

Lige paused as if a sudden thought had come to him. "By the by, you'll be needin' to be able to show you're of good character. *I* can tell by lookin', but Austin sets a heap of store in seein' it wrote down."

"Thomas and me, we got letters from Colonel Ames and some of the quality folks around home. And *we'll* vouch for Muley."

"It takes a little money, too, to pay down on the land. I hope you got money."

A warning tingle of suspicion touched me. I had never traveled before, but it seemed unlikely to me that quality folks would ask a man if he was carrying money. Muley spoke up with enthusiasm. "Sure, they got money. *I* got money, too." He reached in his pocket for it. "I got three dollars and fifty-two cents."

I said, "Muley!"

Lige grinned. "That's good, Muley. That much money'll take you a long ways in Texas." Lige reached into the fire for a burning stick and used it to light his pipe. His eyes fastened onto me, and I began feeling uncomfortable. "You know somethin', lad? I like you two. Yes, sir, I like you. And I'm fixin' to give you a mite of advice. Between here and Texas there's a heap of unpleasant things layin' in wait for the unwary. You got to cross the Redlands. Lots of hard characters in there. Some been run out of the colony and don't dare go back to the States. Others been run out of the States and can't go to Austin's. So they just squat in the Redlands and turn their hands to mischief. Dangerous for three young fellers alone with one wagon."

I sipped his coffee and hoped my eyes did not betray the suspicion that was boiling up in me. "We'll do all right."

"Been others felt that way and never got to Texas alive."

I made no reply.

Lige said, "You need to join up with others a headin' for Texas. We'll be goin' that direction ourselves pretty quick. We'd be right tickled to have you with us."

My gaze drifted from one man to another. The eyes of Foley and the Mexicans were cold. And so was my back.

Foley was twisted sideways, his right arm bent awkwardly as he tried to scratch along his spine. The truth came to me like the flash of a pineknot exploding in a campfire: Foley's back was sore. It wasn't a friend of Foley's who got whipped out of the colony. It was Foley himself!

Suddenly cold all over, I spilled what coffee was left in the cup and pushed to my feet. "We'll see about it." I handed Lige the cup. "Thomas and me, we decided to camp close by here for a week or so and rest up the stock. We'll think on what you said."

It was a lie, but I hoped they wouldn't sense that.

Lige said, "We'll come around and see you in a few days."

As we walked back to our own camp, Muley protested, "I thought Thomas said we was goin' to leave early in the mornin'. It's a sin to lie. How come you lied, Josh?"

I didn't answer him. At the wagon Thomas sat back from the fire, a plate in his hand. He was impatient. "You been gone a long time."

"We ran into those men who stopped at our wagon today, the ones who said they were from Tennessee."

Thomas's eyes narrowed, but he didn't say anything. "Remember what you told me about bein' able to smell a varmint?"

"I remember."

"Well, I think I smelled *four* of them."

Thomas went back to eating. It was several minutes before he said anything, though I thought I saw satisfaction in his eyes as I told him all there was to tell. At length Thomas remarked, "Four men like that wouldn't have much trouble killin' two, would they?" He glanced at Muley. "Or *three*?"

I shook my head. "Not when the three thought the four were friends."

Thomas nodded. "You're smartenin' up, Josh. Tonight we'll get the wagon ready. Come sunup, we'll be three hours down the trail."

3

We had a map drawn by Colonel Ames, but we found it more useful to follow wagon tracks and tree blazes than to depend upon the map for more than the most general type of guidance. Looking back over our shoulders every so often for sign of Lige and his three partners, we traveled three days through country that looked as if it would take only a little spit to turn it into a quagmire.

The third night the rain started. It was still raining at daybreak when we hitched the team. The wagon moved ten feet and sank halfway to the hubs.

Thomas accepted it philosophically with no more than a shrug of his shoulders and a frowning glance at the heavy timber just behind us. "If we got to bog down, let's do it out in the open where we can see what's comin' around us."

We hadn't spoken to Muley of our suspicions. Muley was like a little boy—easily made happy and easily frightened. No use frightening him now, for he was having a good time.

"You reckon they'll still come?" I asked Thomas.

"They might, if they don't find better pickin's in Natchitoches. I got a feelin' this bunch of cutthroats wouldn't be choosy."

So we fought the wagon out into the open. I tied the sorrel on with the team and used him to help pull while Thomas and Muley threw their shoulders against the mired wheels and pushed. The spotted dog now and again would bark at the straining team as if trying to do his bit. By midmorning we were two hundred yards out into the clear.

"We'll stop now," Thomas said, his chest heaving from exhaustion, rain spilling from the flattened brim of his mud-streaked hat.

We staked the livestock on grass close by and stretched an extra wagonsheet out from one side of the wagon to give us a place where we could stay out of the rain. This precaution came late, for we were already soaked. We huddled over a small fire which was kept alive with dry wood saved inside the wagon.

No one came that day. In the night Thomas and I took turns sitting up on watch. We couldn't trust Muley to stay awake. Next morning the rain stopped. The sun came out from behind the breaking clouds to raise steam from the black, sodden ground. The second day of sunshine we hitched up and made a try. We moved a hundred feet and quit.

"If they come," said Thomas, "at least we're in a position to see them before they get here."

And they came. The four horsemen emerged from the timber in late afternoon. Lige rode in the lead.

They halted, seeing the mired wagon in the open. Lige came riding on cautiously, Foley and the two Mexicans trailing by a length or so. They left two pack horses behind.

Thomas was dozing. I touched him gently. "Thomas, they've come."

He was awake instantly, reaching for his rifle. I saw Muley off in the grass, running with the hound.

"Muley," I yelled, "come here, quick! Run!"

Muley caught the urgency in my voice. He saw the four men and came sprinting. "They Indians, Josh? They Indians?"

"No, Muley, not Indians. But help me bring the stock in and tie them to the wagon. We don't want them run off."

Muley did as he was told. He asked no questions, though his frightened eyes showed a-plenty of them. We tied the team and the milk cows securely. Picking up my rifle, I said, "Muley, you stay right here, tight by the wagon. Don't say nothin' and don't do nothin'."

Thomas stood ten feet out from the wagon, his rifle cradled over his left arm. I joined him.

Lige reined up. He eyed us critically. Finally he said, "I wouldn't noways call this friendly."

Thomas's voice was cold. "Neither would I."

Foley reined up on one side of Lige. The Mexicans stopped on the other. Their eyes were hostile.

Lige made a show of disappointment. "A man would have to take this as a sign of distrust. You must think we're robbers or somethin'."

I replied, "The thought did occur to us."

"Here I been tellin' Foley and the boys that you-all just changed your minds and left Natchitoches a little earlier than you intended to. If I was of a suspicious nature, I might think you just plain lied to us."

Thomas said, "We don't want trouble. You-all just ride on by us and don't be a stoppin'."

Lige's eyes began to harden. "If we *was* robbers, you boys would be in a tough spot now. I judge that you still can't move that wagon. That boy yonder . . ." he pointed at Muley, "ain't goin' to be of no use to you, so it'd be just you two against us four. And you got just one shot apiece."

Thomas's voice was flat. "We'd make those two shots count. You don't know which two we'd kill."

Lige glanced at his companions. "We come to do these boys a favor and see how it turns out! The milk of human kindness has done clabbered."

Foley scowled. "It's a long way to Texas. They got to sleep sometime."

Thus was all pretense stripped away. Lige shed his false friendliness like a shabby old coat. He looked at the wagon with unmasked greed, plainly calculating what it and its contents would sell for in Texas.

"Boys," he said, "there ain't no use you-all dyin' for this. You can always git you another wagon someday. But once you're dead, nobody can bring you back to life till the Angel Gabriel hisself blows on that horn."

I said, "We ain't dead yet."

"And you needn't be, boy, you needn't be. Think it over. We'll be back in the mornin'. You just ride out in the nighttime and forgit you ever seen us, or that you ever had a wagon."

Lige pulled his horse around and started back to the timber. Foley and the Mexicans held a moment, their hostile eyes fixed on us and our rifles. They had expected to ride directly into camp and have the whole thing over within a moment of complete surprise.

One of the Mexicans spat something in Spanish that I didn't understand. But the other was clear enough when he drew his forefinger across his throat. The three men reined around and went off after Lige.

I just stood there, my hands frozen on the rifle. Muley began whimpering, "Josh, what do them fellers want? Josh, I don't think I like them fellers."

I licked my dry lips. "Thomas, what comes next?"

Thomas shook his head. He lowered his rifle. "Depends on *them*. Like as not they'll lay up yonder in the timber and snipe at us. Let's don't be makin' them a target."

"Like Foley said, it's a long trail to Texas. We can't dodge bullets the whole way."

Thomas shook his head again. "No, we can't. So we'll just lay low and see what kind of move they make."

"What if they don't make one?"

"Then we will."

Muley trembled, and it took all the persuasion I could muster to get him settled down.

Every time one of us stepped out into the clear, a rifle ball would buzz like an angry hornet. The first one bothered me considerably. The second one made me mad. "What do they want to do that for? They can't hit us at this range."

"They might," Thomas said, "if they're lucky. Mostly they want to keep us stuck here till they can pick their own time to come and get us. And maybe they think they can scare us into runnin' away and leavin' it all. That's what they want."

"Well, they're scarin' poor Muley to death, and me too, a little bit. All that friendly talk, sweet as sorghum molasses, and then they want to rob us."

The sun went down. I wasn't too hungry, and Muley was so frightened he never even thought of supper. But Thomas was calm. He built up the fire a little and went about heating some leftover rabbit stew. I got the idea somehow that Thomas might even be looking forward to the inevitable conflict with a certain enjoyment.

I made Muley eat, hoping some hot food in his stomach might make him feel better. I forced myself to eat a little, too, though I had no taste for it. As darkness came, the glow of a campfire showed in the timber.

"Eatin' theirselves a good supper," I said with some bitterness.

Thomas only nodded.

"They could stretch this for days if they wanted to," I complained. "And all we can do is sit here."

Thomas's jaw jutted. "Wrong, Josh. That's *not* all we can do." He stared intently at me. "So far, Josh, what fightin' you've done has been of a piddlin' variety. You've fought at the wrong time and in the wrong places for the wrong things. But a bloody nose or a split lip was the worst you could get. Are you ready to fight now when you *could* get a bullet in your gut?"

"Just try me!"

"Way I see it, they either plan on lettin' us sit here and worry all night, or they'll wait till late and try to catch us asleep. Either way, they'll figure *they're* the hunters. I doubt they'll look for us to come huntin'."

"You mean we're goin' after *them*?"

"It sure beats waitin', and our chances are better. Once it turns pure dark, we got a little time before the moon comes up. We can be on them before they know it."

"I'm willin' to try it. But what about Muley? He'll be a hindrance to us, not a help."

"*That,*" Thomas said sharply, "I tried to tell you in Tennessee. But anyhow, he stays here."

"He'll be scared."

"He'll stay if we have to tie him. You tell him that!"

We checked our rifles. Each of us loaded a cap-and-ball pistol. Two weapons apiece meant a total of only four shots, with four targets. That was drawing it mighty fine. If four shots failed to do the job, each of us still wore a wicked Arkansas toothpick strapped to our belts, a heavy hunting knife with a razor-sharp blade of cast steel.

Muley watched our preparations wide-eyed. "What you fellers fixin' to do, Josh?"

"We're goin' huntin' in a little while. Don't fret, Muley."

We smothered the fire, then sat awhile in the darkness, listening. In the timber we could still see the glow of the robbers' camp. Worriedly I whispered, "How do we know they won't be comin' after *us*, and we won't run into them in the dark someplace?"

"We don't. We just have to go on faith and hope, and depend on them not bein' in no hurry. You scared?"

I started to say I wasn't, but it would have been a poor lie. "If I was any scareder I'd have to change breeches."

Thomas said, "Well, it's about as dark as it's goin' to get. We want to be in the timber before the moon comes up. You talk to Muley, and be sure that dog of his is tied to the wagon."

Muley trembled. "You leavin' me here by myself, Josh?"

"Just for a little while, Muley. You got to stay and look after the stock. Don't you leave this wagon for nothin', you hear me? Don't leave it at all."

Muley was dubious. "I ain't goin' to like it here, Josh."

"You stay, though. Don't leave it for a minute, or I'll be real mad at you."

"I don't want you bein' mad at me, Josh."

"Then you mind what I tell you."

We moved out, our soft-leather moccasins noiseless on the wet earth. I stayed close to Thomas, for I could hardly see even the outline of him in the darkness. If we ever strayed twenty feet apart, we would lose each other.

We crouched low and moved softly, pausing often to drop to our knees and listen. Hearing nothing but the night birds and the crickets, we would move on a way, then stop again. Back at our wagon, we heard the dog set in to barking. For an awful minute or two I thought the robbers might be stalking Muley. But the barking stopped. Presently we were in the edge of the timber. Ahead, brighter now, glowed the campfire. We paused again to listen. This time we heard voices.

We nodded at each other, satisfied that the four men were still in camp. Thomas signaled for me to follow him. Cautiously, testing the ground each time we put a foot forward, we moved toward the fire.

Thomas's outline showed against the dim glow, bent low and edging in close. Soon we were in the fringe timber around the clearing where the outlaws had made their camp. Without looking back, Thomas hand-signaled me to come up beside him. We knelt to watch, and to consider.

Nearest us, at perhaps twenty feet, Foley sat with a jug, scowling. "I say we ought to've took them, Lige. How do we know they ain't packin' up right now and movin' out?"

Lige stood beyond the fire, thumbs hooked in the waistband of his woolen breeches. "They'd just bog that wagon. I say let them sweat a little. They'll be easier handled when they git good and scared. A scared man don't generally shoot good."

One of the Mexicans sat silently with a long dirk in one hand and a whetstone in the other. The steel blade made a whispering sound each time it passed over the stone. At length the Mexican pulled up a runner of winter-dried grass, left from the previous fall. He slashed at it. The runner floated back to earth in two pieces. The Mexican nodded his satisfaction and said something in Spanish.

The other Mexican lay stretched out on a blanket, evidently asleep. A small jug sat beside him.

I looked for their weapons. Foley's rifle lay on the ground within easy reach. The Mexican Miguel held the dirk. I couldn't see how the sleeping Mexican was armed. So far as I could tell, Lige had no weapon on him. He was twelve or fifteen feet from any rifle in view.

Thomas whispered in my ear, "Rifles first. I'll take Foley. You take the Mexican that's got the knife. We'll have to get Lige and the other Mexican with our pistols."

"Just shoot them? From ambush?"

"That's what they would've done to us!"

The rifle hammers clicked loud and metallic in the night air. Foley and Miguel jumped to their feet. Foley moved so rapidly I hardly saw him bring the rifle up. In the split second between the flash in the pan and the roar of my rifle, the Mexican sent the dirk spinning toward me. I saw him stagger. Then the blade slashed into my arm.

Thomas made his shot good. Foley's rifle dropped harmlessly to the ground.

The other Mexican was awake instantly, groping desperately for a weapon and tipping over his jug. Thomas dropped his rifle and drew the pistol out of his waistband. The pistol flashed, and the Mexican fell.

Across the fire, Lige stood stunned. He made no move toward a weapon. The nearest was too far for him to reach. He turned and ran into the night.

Thomas shouted, "Shoot him, Josh, quick!"

But I was swaying, the warm blood running down my arm. Instinctively I reached up and pulled the dirk out. I stood with it in my hand and stared in blind shock at the dead Miguel.

Thomas leaped forward, grabbed up Foley's rifle and fired it into the darkness. But he missed, for we could hear Lige's footsteps and the man's heavy body, crashing through the timber.

Thomas stepped back into the firelight and methodically began to reload his pistol. Pursuit would be useless. "Why didn't you shoot him, Josh?" Then he noticed for the first time that I was wounded. "Josh, I didn't know. How bad did he get you?"

I shook my head. "It's bleedin'. That's all I can tell."

Thomas led me closer to the fire for a better look. "It's risky, us bein' close to the fire this way. But I don't expect Lige got away with a gun. He'd of used it already."

My stomach turned over. "Look out, Thomas. It's all coming up."

And it did. But afterward I felt better. Thomas bound the wound tightly, and the bleeding stopped.

We heard footsteps again, a man running. Thomas pulled me away from the fire and into the darkness. He held the reloaded pistol ready.

"Josh!" a voice called excitedly. "Josh! Where you at, Josh?"

"It's Muley," Thomas said. "I knew he wouldn't stay at the wagon."

"He stayed till it was over with. That was the main thing."

Thomas called, "Over here, Muley."

Muley came into the firelight, his eyes wide. He shrank back when he saw the bodies.

"It's all right, Muley." I said. "We got them before they could get us."

Shakily Muley asked, "They all dead?"

"I reckon."

Getting braver, Muley moved close to look. He pointed to the Mexican who had been caught asleep. "This one ain't dead, Josh. He's movin'."

The wounded Mexican had inched himself along on the ground until he had reached a knife. His fingers were closing around it when Thomas leveled the pistol. A faint smile came to my brother's face. The pistol flashed. The Mexican's fingers spread and dug into the mud. Then they went stiff.

A chill ran all the way down to my boots. I stared hard at Thomas, for this was something I had never seen in him before.

Thomas caught the look. "It had to be done."

"You didn't have to enjoy it."

"Was that how it looked?"

I nodded. Thomas said, "I didn't. But on the other hand, I can't say as it bothered me none, either."

From far off we heard a horse running. I knew without having to see. "It's Lige! He's stolen one of our horses."

Thomas swore.

Thinking about it, I shrugged. "Well, maybe it was a fair trade. He couldn't get to his own. We lost one horse but got six."

Thomas shook his head. "No, Josh. We'll pick the best one from theirs to replace the one we lost. We'll turn the rest of them loose."

My mouth dropped open. "Turn them loose? Thomas, we can use those horses. And it's a cinch *these* men will never need them again."

Thomas shook his head again. "*They're* the thieves, not us. We don't steal, even from dead men."

He had a strange sense of values, my brother did. He could smile while he killed a man. But he wouldn't take that man's horses.

He said, "We'll go back to our own camp now. Come mornin', Muley and me will come over here and give these men a plantin'. I doubt your arm will be in shape for diggin'."

He studied the two dead Mexicans, first one and then the other. "A real pair of cutthroats, weren't they? The first Mexicans we ever saw, and they tried to kill us. Gives us a lot to look forward to when we have to live amongst them in Texas."

"Maybe the others won't be like these, Thomas. These were outlaws."

He didn't even seem to hear me. And if he had, it wouldn't have made any difference. Thomas made his mind up in a hurry. And once made up, it never changed. He grunted. "They're a sorry class of people."

"The other two weren't Mexicans," I argued. "They was from Tennessee."

I had as well have kept my silence. Thomas said, "I told you I could smell them just like wolves. I've already decided one thing, Josh."

"What's that?"

"I'll never trust a Mexican!"

4

Among the towering pines at the far eastern edge of Mexican Texas, hardly a horse-lathering ride from the international boundary of the Sabine River, Nacogdoches was the gateway. Once it had been a sleepy Spanish village, site of the Mission Nuestra Señora de Guadalupe, trying to bring the *padres'* message of God to the heathen of the woods. Now it was awake and bustling, the gathering place for hopeful immigrants bound for Texas, and for the wishful ones who had gotten that far on nerve and could go no further. It had also become a gathering place for a lawless element that had been run out of the colonies or never had been able to get in. It was a lonely garrison for Colonel José de las Piedras and a comparative handful of homesick soldiers serving hundreds of miles from the villages of their birth. This ancient Spanish town was legally Mexican now, since Mexico had broken away from Spain. But in truth it was actually much more American.

Not long before, General Manuel de Mier y Terán

had taken a long, painful look and had found Mexican influence all but gone, except that a lax and corrupt municipal government still functioned on old Mexican customs of bribery and self-interest. "The whole population here is a mixture of strange and incoherent parts without parallel in our federation," he had written worriedly. He was right, for criminals from the old Neutral Ground squatted here, along with a scattering of Indians from many tribes, and French and Spanish creoles, genteel American planters, and raw frontiersmen.

Terán wanted to shut off the immigration of Americans before the situation became worse.

True, through here had passed filibusters and freebooters beyond counting. Here in 1812 had come the Gutiérrez-Magee Expedition to invade Texas when it was still a part of Spain. In 1819 Dr. James Long had marched down from Natchez with 300 men and had held Nacogdoches temporarily. In 1826 one Haden Edwards had received permission from Mexico to settle 800 families in eastern Texas but found himself unable to evict Mexican and American squatters and Cherokee Indians from the land which had been given him. He and his brother Benjamin established themselves in Nacogdoches' old stone fort and proclaimed the Republic of Fredonia. This republic crumbled quickly in the face of Mexican troops, bolstered by militia which Stephen F. Austin raised. Austin was for law and order. The law happened to be Mexican, and he respected it.

Terán had gotten his law. Except for the Austin

and Green DeWitt colonies, legal immigration of these blue-eyed foreigners had all but stopped.

Illegal immigration was another matter.

We Buckalews knew little of this as our wagon groaned into Nacogdoches. Colonel Ames back in Tennessee had mentioned that there had been a mite of trouble once or twice, but he had reckoned it was past history. He had written a letter for us which Thomas in turn had given to an Austin representative in Natchitoches. We had been handed an immigration document with Austin's signature on it to guarantee us clear passage.

Lige had stolen my sorrel to get away that night in the timber west of Natchitoches. Now I rode a young bay gelding which had been Lige's. I had talked Thomas into letting us keep one more horse for Muley. I still felt he had made a mistake in turning the other outlaws' horses loose, but I had to respect his version of what was honest.

Though he sat on the wagon seat beside Thomas, leaning forward eagerly for a view of Nacogdoches, Muley usually did his talking with me. "Looky yonder what a town we're comin' to, Josh. Looks like folks is thicker'n jaybirds at acorn time."

I rode close beside the wagon and nodded, excitement building in me too. At the Sabine River crossing we had officially entered Texas, but somehow the feeling wasn't strong. I couldn't tell that one side of the river looked much different than the other. I knew it was a foolish notion, but somehow I had expected the difference to show right off.

I had expected Nacogdoches to have a Mexican look, though I had no clear idea what a Mexican look was. Again I was disappointed, for I saw few people who appeared to be Mexican. Most were light-skinned, like us. The signs were mostly painted in English.

I had no way of knowing these were the same thoughts which had bothered General Terán, for at that time I hadn't even heard of the man. But we were about to be introduced to the results of Terán's observations.

Thomas's voice was sharp. "Get close to the wagon, Josh. We got company comin'."

Half a dozen horsemen approached, wearing uniforms that had been bright when new but now were faded and wrinkled and browned with grime.

"Didn't expect we'd rate a reception like this," I said.

Thomas frowned. "Raggy-lookin' lot. Mexicans."

He pulled the team to a stop as the soldiers came up. One man circled around and halted beside Thomas, touching his hand to the bill of his cap. His face was a deep brown, his eyes almost black. His uniform had been fancier, once, than the others. He was plainly an officer. His moustache was thick and black, but he was still a young man.

"How do," Thomas said stiffly.

"*Buenos días.*" The Mexican took his time, studying the wagon and the animals trailing it. He spoke, but the words were Spanish and made no sense to us. The Mexican turned in the saddle and called. "*Señor* Charters!"

An American was trailing the soldiers. Astride a fine black horse, he pulled around beside the officer. He gave a courteous nod, exchanged a few words with the Mexican, then turned to us.

"Lieutenant Obregón has not yet mastered the English language. Occasionally I help him. My name is Benjamin D. Charters. I hope I can be of service to you gentlemen."

Thomas was not impressed. "What's he need?" he asked bluntly.

"You gentlemen surely know about the law of 1830, which restricts immigration into Mexico? The lieutenant says he trusts you have some documentary evidence of your right to enter this country."

I studied Charters, trying to discover the reason for Thomas's quick and adverse judgment. Charters spoke with the ease and eloquence of a lawyer. His suit was cut of good cloth and well-tailored, though it had seen better days. Thin at the knees and elbows, frayed at the cuffs and collar, it told of a genteel poverty.

Thomas reached back into the wagon and got the document with Austin's signature. Charters passed it on to the lieutenant. Obregón read it critically and handed it back, shaking his head.

Charters listened to the officer, then explained, "He says this is not enough. You must have another permit to go beyond Nacogdoches."

Thomas reddened. "They told us in Natchitoches

this was all we'd need to get us to San Felipe de Austin."

Charters smiled thinly. "This is a long way from Natchitoches. Some of these garrisons make their own laws."

Thomas's eyes hardened. "What else we goin' to need?"

"You need a new order signed by a local military officer to pass you through the guard at the road to San Felipe."

"How do we get this order?"

"It is difficult, usually. The wait is often very long; you know how slow the military can be about these things. However, the lieutenant says he likes your looks and has decided to do you a favor. He has ways of cutting through regulations when the reason is good enough."

Thomas clinched his fist. "He wants money?"

Charters winked. "A bit of coin is like grease on the wheels of progress. All men have their price. I think you'll find that the lieutenant's price is reasonable."

Thomas was speaking quietly now. I could feel the anger rising in his voice. "What he wants is a bribe."

Charters made a pretense of surprise. "I didn't say that. Nobody ever bribes anybody in Mexico. This is simply a sort of hidden tax. Everybody pays it when the occasion arises. They call it *mordida*, the little bite. It is one of the facts of life in Mexico, like ground corn and chili pepper."

"What part do *you* get out of it, Charters?"

Charters began to anger. "You are insulting me, sir. Now, if you don't *want* to go to San Felipe . . ."

"We *are* goin' to San Felipe. And we'll do it without givin' you or this leather-colored parasite a penny."

"I don't see that you have much choice."

"Tell those Mexicans to get theirselves out of our way if they don't want to get run over!"

Charters was livid. "This is Mexico. You're a foreigner here. You'll live up to Mexican laws or suffer the consequences."

"This isn't law, this is a try at robbery. We've been tried once already, on the way down here. It didn't work for *them*; it won't work for you."

"Try to move past these men and you'll be stopped."

"You're not gettin' any money out of *us!*"

Charters regained some control. "Look, friend, you could afford to put a little silver across the lieutenant's palm. The Mexican government doesn't pay these men much way out here, and what it *does* pay is often slow in coming. You can't blame these soldiers for taking a little extra."

"It's wrong. I'll rot here before I'll pay."

Charters spoke to the lieutenant. From his looks I thought Obregón might order his men to shoot us down like dogs. I didn't know a word of Spanish then, but I knew pretty well what kind of language he was spitting at us. He hadn't learned it in church. He reined his horse around, savage as an Indian, and signaled his troops to follow him.

Charters spoke crisply. "You'll get tired of sitting

here, and you'll come begging to pay. Obregón will take a very *big* bite then; you can count on that." He rode off, following the troopers.

I thought we had been whipped, but Thomas had a stubborn look of victory all over him.

I said, "Thomas, we're in trouble now. Wouldn't it of been easier to've just paid the man a little somethin'?"

"That would have been a compromise."

"What would that hurt? We always got to compromise!"

"Not when it's right against wrong. If you come to a fork in the road, you got to turn either to the left or the right. You can't compromise. You do what's right, or you do what's wrong. Bribery is wrong, whether it's a dollar or a hundred dollars."

I shrugged. "A man can get awful hungry, tryin' to be right all the time." The soldiers were about out of sight. But they weren't out of mind. "How do we get out of here *without* payin'?"

"There aren't many soldiers. Ever try to stop a creek flowin' by stickin' your hand in it? The water just goes right on, between your fingers. I'll ask around, find out where they guard the trails. Then we'll go the long way around. We don't have to follow *their* route. We'll just make our own!"

5

I didn't realize it then, but our encounter with Lige, Foley, and the two Mexican bandits, followed by our experience with the hungry Lieutenant Obregón in Nacogdoches, had been enough to start hatred to gnawing at Thomas. He had always been one to make up his mind in a hurry. From this time on he had a cold contempt for all things Mexican. Strange, how some people so easily form a hate, and how hard it is for them to find a liking for the new and different.

We did what Thomas said—took the long way around and got clear of Nacogdoches. It was so easy I felt sure there must be a catch to it somehow, but there wasn't. We didn't know that many others had done the same thing before us. We found out later there was a trail which had been used by so many contraband immigrants that it had even won its own name, the Tennesseans' Road. There just weren't enough Mexican soldiers to patrol the whole country.

As I said, we didn't know this at the time. We

thought the idea was original, and we gloried in getting away with it. Not that what we did was illegal in the strict sense. We had the paper from Austin. We had simply avoided having to pay a bribe. But Mexican views of jurisprudence were different than ours. It could have gone hard with us if we had been caught. That's how it was in Mexico in those days. It wasn't the laws written on paper which really counted; it was the men who administered them. In the end, the law was always what they *said* it was.

If written laws were deceptive, so were maps. A mile doesn't look like much on a piece of paper. But on the ground it is something else. The long, long miles passed endlessly beneath the iron-rimmed wheels, and it seemed San Felipe was still a thousand miles away. I had no clear idea of the vast variety of lands we would pass through on the trip—the rolling prairies abounding in wild horses and many swamps and marshes that bogged the wagons and exhausted kinds of game; thickets and canebrakes so dense that once when we strayed off the trail Muley and I had to walk ahead of the wagon and clear a path with axes so Thomas could pick his way through.

As we crossed the map-marked boundary into Austin's colony, we began to come across small settlements and scattered farms. At once we could tell the difference between the legal colony and the squatter element which had prevailed around Nacogdoches. Plainly, Austin had picked these people with a degree of care. Spring-planted crops were coming up in cleared fields which had been virgin grasslands a few months earlier. Log cabins stood along creek banks where Indians had stalked deer or had gathered the native pecans. Wherever we stopped, we found a welcome, for there was a fraternal element in the pioneering experience which made people draw together instinctively. Most of these early colonists were dirt-poor. Their hospitality was almost embarrassing to us, for they would bake us bread from their scant supplies of corn. They would wrap their precious coffee beans in buckskin and beat them with a rock to brew up a drink for us. They were almost pathetic in their eagerness for news of "the States," and we had so little to tell them.

At last we came through a sandy canebrake river bottom to the edge of the broad and lazy Brazos River. Across the river, atop a high bluff on the west side, perched San Felipe de Austin. Situated at the head of navigation, it was the seat of government for most of colonial Texas.

I was disappointed. "That's it? That's *all* of it?"

Thomas shrugged. "Likely there's more that you can't see on account of the bluff. But I doubt there's really very much. Maybe you been buildin' up too much in your mind."

"I thought it would look Mexican. Log cabins is all I see, the same kind I've seen my whole life long."

Thomas shook his head. "I'd as soon not ever see another Mexican. But they're there, waitin' yonder for us across the river."

I could see them idling at the ferry landing on the other side of the Brazos. An uneasiness started, because I thought this might be where we were going to get caught up with for what we had done at Nacogdoches. But Thomas didn't look worried.

A ferryboat slowly made its way across the river and tied up. Thomas pulled the wagon onto the boat, and we all pitched in to secure it so it wouldn't roll with the motion of the ferry.

The ferryman was one of the swivel-jawed kind. "Sure proud to see young fellers like you-all comin' in. Men of the land. Seems to me like this place has gotten overrun of late with lawyers and the like—soft-handed men. We need more with dirt under their fingernails, the way it was when we first come here with Austin. Yes, sir, I been here pretty near from the first. I was one of Austin's Old Three Hundred. Been a right smart of changes, I can tell you."

I got caught up in his enthusiasm. "It sure is a rich-*lookin'* country, all right. Fish and game like I never saw before. Crops show a heap of promise. And trees—I never knew there was so many different kinds of trees in the whole world. Sure, we miss the comforts we used to have at home, and we may be a long time ever gettin' most of them. But it's a great country for growin' things. You just drop a seed in the ground and stand back out of the way."

Muley took it for gospel and whistled softly to himself. "I sure do want to see *that*!"

The ferryman pointed his chin toward the Mexican soldiers waiting on the west shore. "You-all got to stand inspection yonder."

"We have the papers," Thomas said, frowning. "The Mexicans give you much bother?"

The ferryman spat. "It ain't that they *do* anything, really; it's just that they're *here,* that's all. Used to, when we first come, we had a right-smart of Indian trouble, and we could've used some soldiers to help us. They wouldn't send any. Now that we're strong enough to take care of our own selves, Mexico sends soldiers in. Maybe they're afraid we've gotten too strong. I get the feelin' sometimes that they're watchin' *us,* not the Indians."

I asked, "If the Mexicans are so worried about us Americans, how come they ever let any of us settle here in the first place?"

"To protect Mexican people from the Indians. Americans always did have a reputation as Indian fighters. Mexico figured to put Americans in between the Indians and their own people. Worked pretty good, too. Many a red devil has died of indigestion on a Texian rifle-ball."

That was the first time I had heard the word *Texian.* I sensed it was a way the Anglo settlers here spoke of themselves.

The ferryman moved forward as the ferry neared the shore. "Go see Sam Williams over in Austin's land office. He'll introduce you to Austin."

The Mexican soldiers waited as the wagon pulled out onto the riverbank. The dislike was plain and open in Thomas's face while a Mexican sergeant came forward to look at the paper. It was easy to see that the black-moustached man couldn't read the words. He was going by the official look of it. But he read the dark look in Thomas's eyes. Rapid Spanish passed back and forth among the ill-clad troops.

Not understanding a word of it, I realized for a moment just how helpless and alone an outsider would be. It occurred to me that this was one major barrier between the average Mexican and the average Anglo settler, this difference of language.

"Thomas," I said, "one thing I'm goin' to do as soon as I can is to learn to speak Mexican."

Thomas shook his head. "English is good enough for me."

Muley watched the soldiers with lively interest. "You mean a man can *learn* to talk like they do, Josh? I figured you had to be born with it."

Without friendliness, the sergeant waved us on.

It was more of a town than I had supposed, once we passed through the tall-tree fringe—pecan, oak, ash, cottonwood—and came out over the top of the bluff. There we found a growing settlement situated neatly around an open plaza. It was still a young town, for most of the log buildings had not yet grayed with weathering. The axehewn timbers of many houses remained bright and unstained. A few buildings were of rough-sawed lumber, which indicated that somewhere in the region—downriver, we learned later—someone had set up a sawmill.

Thomas pulled the team onto a street that bordered the eastern edge of the plaza. We began to discover that the town was better in appearance than in reality. Like a funeral procession, perhaps, great on length but somewhat thin.

A townsman directed us to Austin's office in one

end of a double log cabin, which sat near the bank of a small creek. A moss-strewn oak stood in front of it. A roofed-over open section divided the office from the sleeping quarters. A chimney stood at each end of the cabin.

I was a little let down. "This don't look much like the head office of the whole colony of Texas."

Thomas shrugged. "Handsome is as handsome does. I bet the roof don't leak."

Sam Williams met us at the door. We introduced ourselves. Thomas was of a notion to get right down to business, but he had to hold off until Williams heard all the news we had picked up along the trail. In time, however, Thomas was able to hand him the document with Austin's signature. Williams nodded. "To be sure, you'll be wanting a grant of land. Do you have an idea where you'd like to settle?"

I put in, "We've studied the map till we know it backwards. We'd like to go somewheres west."

Williams' eyebrows arched. "Why west?"

"Why not?" asked Thomas. "You still got land to the west, haven't you?"

"Yes, but it's wilder, farther removed from the more settled portions. It puts you in more danger of contact with Indians. In short, it's a long way to civilization."

Thomas said, "We'll just take civilization with us."

Williams glanced from Thomas to me and back again.

He had sized up Muley in the beginning and paid little attention to him now. "If that's your wish, then, we'll go forward on that basis. You understand about the Mexican colonization laws?"

Thomas replied. "Some. Colonel Ames told us."

"What it amounts to is that a family man can receive a *labor* of farming land and a *sitio* of grazing land if he wants to raise stock. A *labor* is 177 acres. A *sitio* is 4,428."

I whistled. We couldn't get that much land together in two lifetimes back home. Here it was almost handed to us.

Williams went on. "There will be some nominal fees, of course, for surveying and other costs. I hope you brought enough cash to cover those."

Thomas nodded. "I hope so, too."

"By law, you two brothers as single men won't quality for a full grant each. We can list you as a family, and you can receive that amount together." Williams pointed his chin at Muley Dodd. "How about *him?*"

Muley spoke up eagerly, "I got money for land, too." He dug into his pockets. "I got three dollars and fifty-two cents."

I shook my head. "Muley, that won't be enough. But don't you fret. You can go with us. Whatever we got, you'll have a share of it."

Muley smiled. "Thanks, Josh. You're a good feller, but there's no need. I got my own money. I want to put in my part."

I glanced at Thomas, but he had nothing to say. I shrugged. "If it'll make you happy, Muley. This way, at least, you got a claim on us." My eyes met Thomas's. "Both of us."

As we pored over Williams' maps, we heard a horse trot up to the front of the cabin. A saddle squeaked in thin protest as a man dismounted. Williams glanced through the glassless window. "It's Colonel Austin."

For weeks now, I had been hearing Austin's name. I guess I expected the man to stand eight feet tall. So, for a moment or two as Austin stood in the doorway, I felt the quick sag of disappointment. In reality, Stephen F. Austin was a rather spare man, and he had to lift his face to look at us, even Muley Dodd. He appeared as if he ate irregularly, and not very well. But strength showed in the care-drawn features, and determination in his dark eyes. Only a strong man would ever have dared start the project Austin had fostered here in Texas, much less carry it through this far against all the adversities of nature, human frailty, and Mexican law.

Williams made the introductions. I shook hands with a certain amount of awe, for Austin was the only famous man I had ever met. I was surprised at the strength of Austin's grip. Those small hands hadn't looked capable of taking hold so tightly. Williams told about the grant we sought, and Thomas had to explain again—somewhat laconically—why he wanted to settle in the west. Austin read the letter of recommendation from Colonel Ames and several other letters from various people back home in Tennessee. He glanced questioningly at Muley.

"Muley's with us," I said quickly. "We'll vouch for him."

Austin seemed to sense Muley's problem without being told. "This can be a fine country for those willing and able to work. It can be death for the incapable."

"Muley's with us," I repeated.

Austin nodded, dismissing the question as having been answered. "You'll not regret that you've come. Texas is wealthy in natural resources—fertile lands, timber, pasturage. I've seen much of the United States, but I've seen nothing as fine as Texas. Nature has supplied us everything we need except population. You, and others like you, are slowly supplying that." He paused, studying us with those dark, keen eyes. "You are unmarried, I see. Later on, as you marry, you can each obtain enough land to fill out your individual allotment to full size. And, of course, as the children come, we get our population. I might add that if you marry a Mexican woman, the law entitles you to even more land."

Thomas said firmly, "No chance of that."

Austin smiled faintly. "I would wager you've seen no Mexican women yet."

Thomas replied, "We've seen some of the men."

Austin's smile broadened. "You would be surprised how many American men have found Mexican women to marry. Some of them are quite pretty. And they have one sterling qualification: they are *here*!" He let that matter drop and frowned as another thought crossed his mind. "Have you men any strong leanings toward politics?"

Thomas shook his head. "We never been noways

connected with politics. The Buckalews have always voted for Andrew Jackson. Past that, we just never was interested."

"I had a good reason for asking. Mexico is still unstable. Governments change like the wind. Politics can be a perilous thing here. I've endeavored from the beginning to keep these colonies free of the political pressures that have been the bane of Mexico. But more and more new men are coming in who will not let matters be. More and more, our people are being caught up in the tides of change. It is a dangerous involvement.

"Out where you're going, you'll have some Mexican neighbors. In many ways you'll find them different from yourselves. In some ways, they are much the same. All humans come from the same mold. Be friendly; get to know them. Accept the differences and be grateful for the things in which you are alike.

"But above all, remain aloof from their politics. They are the natives here, and we are the strangers. Mexico still has turbulent times ahead. It will require a steady hand and a careful silence to see us safely through."

6

The surveyor who tied his horse and pack mule behind our wagon and went along with us was a lean, likeable man named Jared Pounce. He had come with the Old Three Hundred, had a farm of his own, and did outside work ranging from gunsmithing to surveys. There wasn't much loose money around the colonies, except some counterfeit which floated in periodically from the Redlands. A man did whatever honest work he could that would let him clasp his fingers over a bit of coin.

Pounce liked his tobacco. Wadding a home-grown leaf into one corner of his mouth, he studied the wagon with open admiration. "You lads come prepared. I'll sure grant you that. I been here since almost the first, and I still ain't got me a wagon. There's three classes of settlers in Texas these days. The upper class are them that owns a wagon. The next class down uses a sled. And the lower class, they just have to walk and tote their own load. You lads are startin' off in the upper class."

Now that we were getting near it, I began to itch

with impatience for a view of our own land. I begrudged every stop we made. But Pounce wouldn't be hurried along the trail.

"Just take it as it comes, boys. Life's too short to spend it in a lope. There's too much to see and learn and enjoy."

Pounce was a born talker, and we were good listeners, especially when the subject was Texas.

"It's hell on women," Pounce said, "but it's God's own country for a man. You wake up every mornin' to a brand new world, especially when you go west where the people ain't thick yet. There it stands, all around you, as fresh and new as if God had just finished makin' it. Big sky, a whole world of room. Air so fresh that it makes you grow younger instead of older. You never saw such a country for huntin', either. You just step out of your door with a rifle in your hand and there's dinner standin' there waitin' for you. You don't even have to drag it far to the cabin.

"They plan these grants so that they front on the water. You'll want to locate on a clear creek so's to have clear water all the time. The Colorado is a mighty river, but she runs muddy. That's what the name comes from, Mexican for *red*. Man has got to let it settle before he drinks it, or he'll have to lay over to let his stomach settle instead."

Thomas asked, "What about Indians, Jared?"

Pounce squeezed one eye shut and peered off to the north thoughtfully. "They'll bear watchin'. They don't bother folks much anymore in the settlements. But now and again they'll skulk around the fringes and do mischief. You boys'll sure be on the fringe."

Thomas nodded. "Austin said we'd have some Mexicans for neighbors. We apt to have trouble with them?"

Pounce shrugged. "Mexicans have got their own ways. You'll find good ones and bad ones and indifferent, like there is amongst the rest of us. There's saints, and there's sinners. I'd say if you don't bother them, they ain't apt to bother you."

I said, "I reckon a man could even make friends with them."

Pounce replied, "Sure, *I* got some Mexican friends, and I got a few Mexican enemies. It's like anyplace else: you got to judge each man separate. Trust them all and you'll get your fingers burnt. Condemn them all and you'll miss some people that would've been good friends. Out here, you'll need all the friends you can get."

We didn't have to do all our own cooking. Pounce had traveled these trails many times and was acquainted with most of the people. He knew where the good cooks lived. Once he pointed to a low-built log cabin with half a dozen loose hogs rooting in the front yard. "Always pass up this place here. See the black smoke risin' out of the chimney? That old woman burns everything she cooks. And she ain't none too clean, neither."

He was more likely to refer to people by their cooking than by their names. One place was "the corn-dodger woman's." Another belonged to "the deer-meat and honey man."

Deer and wild turkey were so many it seemed the Lord was being wasteful. We always had something to take to a settler's house along with our appetites. Thomas said he didn't like to receive more than he gave, and I reckoned that was an honest way for a man to be. We noted that, particularly among the newer settlers, meat was the main thing on the dinner table, and wild meat at that. A few of the older colonists usually had bread, made of rough-ground corn. We hadn't seen an egg since Louisiana.

I was careful to study the settlers and their ways of living, for their ways would be our ways. Most—but not all—of the men wore buckskins, the women homespun. The houses were mostly of a kind, built of logs. Some, where the family was large, were big double cabins with an open dog-run in the center. Most of the floors were of earth, though here and there we found a cabin with puncheon flooring. That was a mark of comparative wealth. The windows lacked glass but had shutters that could be opened for air or pulled shut to keep out wind, rain, and Indians.

Not everybody had a cabin. At one place we came across a new arrival who hadn't taken time yet to put up any kind of building. He and his wife were still living out of their wagon while they broke the land and got a crop started. There would be a cabin later, when the crop was up.

"That's how it'll be with us, Josh," Thomas said. "We'll likely spend most of this summer sleepin' under the wagon."

"That's what we've done since the day we left home," I said indifferently.

"I like it," Muley put in.

Jared Pounce commented, "Most young men just naturally take to the outdoors. Used to, I could've gone for a year without a roof over my head, and I'd never given it a thought. Now, though, when night comes around I like to look up at the rafters instead of the stars. Sign of age, I reckon."

Time and again we came across grazing bands of wild horses. The best Pounce knew from talking with old-time Mexicans was that these bands had been here for generations. Some said they were descended from horses which had gotten loose or been stolen from Spaniards long ago. Whatever their origin, their reproduction had been remarkable.

"Time or two," said Pounce, "I been reduced to eatin' horsemeat. It ain't so bad, when you got nothin' better to compare by. Some people say it's the heart that rules a man, but they're wrong. It's his stomach."

In due time we hauled up to the Colorado River. As Jared had said, it was red with mud carried in upriver.

"On across," said Jared, "and down to the southwest, is Gonzales. That's the headquarters of the Green DeWitt colony. Above you there's not a lot—a few scattered Americans, some Mexicans. And Indian country."

Standing there, looking out across that muddy river, I felt a deep emotion rolling over me like a flood. I felt a strange joy that I'd never known before, and have never felt again in quite the same way. I sensed that somewhere yonder, not far away now, lay the ground we had been looking for. I knew that soon I would set my boots down on our promised land.

It had been three hours since we had passed the last settler's cabin. We had this all to ourselves. "Thomas," I said, "I got a feelin' about this country. I'm goin' to like it here."

Thomas replied, "We've come too far *not* to like it."

Jared pointed his chin northwards. "Boys, let me make a suggestion to you. One time I was through this neck of the woods on an Indian-chasin' party. Not far from here I came across a place on a creek, as pretty a place as ever I seen. For a long time I kept thinkin' someday I'd come back and take it up. Now I know I never will. It's yours if you want it."

"Show us," Thomas said.

We crossed the river, and we traveled awhile. I knew the place instinctively, even before Jared spoke. I touched spurs to horse and rode ahead across a flat stretch of open ground that one day soon would be a field. Beyond lay an uneven stand of timber along a creek—huge old pecan trees heavy with foliage, rugged live oaks with leaves that would stay green the year around, willow, ash. . . . A buck jerked its antlered head toward me, the startled eyes wide and brown. It bounded away into the timber. Three wild turkeys, disturbed by the deer, moved into a trot, then soared at a low level into the shelter of tangled underbrush.

I rode on without slowing until I came to the bank of the creek. Below me was a deep flow of clear water. Looking around carefully for sign of human life and seeing none, I dismounted and tied the horse to a bush. Then, rifle in my hand, I moved down the bank to the water's edge. I tasted it and found it as good as any in Tennessee.

I returned to the flat and waited there, looking around, until the wagon came up. My spirit soared as it had never done before.

"Thomas," I said, "the trip is over. We're home!"

The surveying job took a while. Jared knew his business, but he didn't rush. "This is for ever," he said. "We can't afford mistakes."

Jared would carry his compass. Muley and I took turns carrying the chain, while Thomas stood watch nearby on horseback, the rifle across his lap. Not once was there sign of a human being. It couldn't have been lonesomer if we had staked out a claim on the moon. We had wanted the "far back," and this was certainly it.

When Jared's job was finished and the new claim plainly marked on his map, Muley and I ground some of our scant supply of corn into meal as a gift to him.

"Jared," I asked, "do they ever have elections here in Texas?"

He frowned, not sure of the reason for the question.

"Sure, we elect what we call an *ayuntamiento*, a local government."

I said, "If you ever take a notion to run, let me know. I'll vote for you twice."

He wished us good luck on this land he had wanted so long for himself, as he set out a-horseback, his pack mule trailing. Jared would eat his way back to San Felipe.

We hated to see him go, but there was no time to worry about the isolation, for too much work was long overdue. First thing we did after Jared left was to begin breaking ground on the big flat. It was hot, back-breaking work. Thomas and I took turns standing guard while the other one and Muley strained, sweated, and swore behind the heavy wooden plows. We couldn't trust Muley to stand guard. We had tried it, only to see him forget his task and go chasing off with his dog after a rabbit or a deer, or hunting a bee tree.

Weather was hot, and a little on the dry side. With summer on the way, we had to get our seed planted and up to a good stand before the full heat came on, or the corn would wither before it ever made a head. So we kept chopping trees, pulling stumps, breaking ground, and putting in seed. It was years and years ago, but I can still remember the rich smell of that fresh-turned earth, opened to the sun after untold ages of darkness.

We didn't allow ourselves to let up from daylight until dark, except for what little time was necessary to hunt game and prepare meals. Thomas was not content with the field. He broke a garden plot near the spot on the creek where we would put up our cabin.

The day finally came when we had caught up, at least temporarily. The corn was rising, and enough rain had fallen so that it would not parch. Now we could begin thinking about a cabin, to get ourselves in from under the wagon. I wanted it closer to the creek, but Jared Pounce had warned us that wherever the wild pecan trees stood, we could expect flooding every so often. Better to tote water an extra distance than to wake up some morning being toted by it.

We built corrals first, for the livestock, and a low-roofed shed open on the south. Then we began felling trees and squaring them up so they would stack and make a neat fit with a minimum of chinking. Because there had been no sign of intrusion, we loosened our reins on Muley, letting him go out after the game it took to keep us fed. Muley was a fair-to-middling shot, though we had to keep warning him about shooting too near the cabin and scaring the game away.

It was Muley who saw the first Indians.

We had begun snaking the finished logs up to the cabin site. Back home we would have made a community celebration out of a cabinraising, but here there was no community. It was a job we would have to do for ourselves. We had laid the foundation logs and were saddle-notching the first logs for the cabin sides when Muley came running across the flat, shouting all the way. The spotted dog loped along ahead of him. Muley fell once, sprawling face down in the grass. But he was up again in a second, hardly missing a step.

"It's Injuns, Josh! It's Injuns!"

I ran for my rifle. Thomas stood soberly scanning the scattered timber beyond the flat. "I don't see nothin' chasin' him, Josh. You got to remember, Muley ain't bright."

Muley reached us and fell to his knees, shoulders heaving. Gasping for breath, he half turned to point behind him. The words wouldn't come. He dragged himself on his knees to the wooden water bucket and drank thirstily from the dipper.

"I saw them, Josh!" The words were still difficult to get out.

Thomas kept squinting into the distance. "I don't see anything, Muley. Maybe it was just deer, or some wild horses."

Muley shook his head violently. "No, sir! They were there, a whole bunch of them. On horseback."

Anxiously I asked, "Did they shoot at you, Muley?"

"No, Josh. They just sat there and looked at me. They didn't move. Didn't even say howdy." He paused. "I didn't say howdy, neither. I just lit out a-runnin'."

Thomas moved toward his rifle now. "It was likely his imagination, but we better go see."

I slung powder horn and shot pouch over my shoulder and saddled my horse. Muley and Thomas did the same, Muley still trembling from his scare. He pointed the way for us to go, but he was careful not to ride out in front. We skirted the newly broken field and moved through scattered oak trees. We kept clear of underbrush where a red man might hide, though we scouted it for tracks. For a time Muley was positive where he had seen the Indians. But after a while he began to fidget uncertainly. I knew the signs well enough: Muley was lost.

Thomas had doubted from the first, and now I began doubting too. Muley sensed it, for he started pleading: "They was there, Josh. They was as real as you and me and that spotted dog. He barked at them. He wouldn't bark if they wasn't real, would he?"

I shook my head. "No, Muley, he wouldn't." But the dog would bark at almost anything that moved. And it could have been anything.

We scouted and circled and saw nothing. At length Thomas pulled up. "We're wastin' our time, Josh."

Muley kept pleading, but I agreed with Thomas. "Sure, Muley," I said, trying to pacify him. "You saw them, but they've gone now."

We started back. I kept my gaze on the ground, looking for tracks. I didn't expect to see them. But suddenly, there they were. "Thomas, here's Muley's tracks when he was runnin' for home. You can see for yourself, he was travelin' pretty fast."

Thomas nodded. I said, "Let's backtrack them a ways. Can't hurt nothin' to do that. We can spare a little time."

Thomas didn't want to, but he gave in. "Let's hurry. We need to be gettin' that cabin up."

Taking the lead, I followed the sign of Muley's head-long rush. Presently Muley shouted, "Yonder's the place, Josh! Yonder's where I seen them at!"

A chill ran down my back, and for some reason the doubt left me. My grip tightened on the rifle. "Hang back a little, Thomas. Keep me covered."

I touched my heels to the horse's ribs and started ahead, nerves tightening.

Muley shouted. "That tree yonder, Josh. That's where they was."

Slowly I rode to a huge old live oak. I found the sign there, plain and fresh. There *had* been horses here—two of them. I called for Thomas and Muley to come up. Thomas studied the sign. "Wild horses, maybe."

I shook my head. "Not wild horses. I can feel it, Thomas."

Thomas nodded, after a moment. "So can I. It was Indians."

I pointed out, "They didn't shoot at Muley. Maybe they were friendly."

Thomas said grimly, "There were friendly Indians in Tennessee too, in Papa's time. But there was a heap of unfriendly ones. You couldn't hardly tell them apart till it was too late. Got so folks quit takin' any chances. The dead ones you could trust."

I glanced back at Muley. "Thomas, you're always too hard on Muley. You'll have to admit, he was right about this."

Thomas shook his head. "You don't have to have any sense to see Indians."

I fingered the rifle a long time. My hands had trembled awhile, but now they were steady again. The excitement had gone. "Well, we oughtn't to be surprised none. Folks told us there would likely be Indians. We won't leave here just because they showed up."

Thomas frowned. "No, Josh. Indians go with new land and westering, just like snakebite and the fever. We come to stay!"

7

After that we built the corral fence a little higher, and we rushed our construction work. To clear the view and help reduce the chance of surprise attack, we cut down most of the trees that stood near the rising cabin. When we weren't using the horses in the daytime, we staked them on fresh grass at the end of a long rope. At night we never failed to bring them into the corral and tie the gate shut with rawhide.

Several nights the spotted dog's barking woke us up, afraid Indian horse thieves were trying to open the corral. But always it turned out to be no more than a skunk or a coon, or at most a grazing deer.

One night the dog did not bark at all. Next morning Thomas went out to milk the cows and found fresh moccasin tracks near the corral.

Why the Indians hadn't taken the horses, we didn't know. "If they come stealin'," he said, frowning at Muley, "the first thing they'll take will be the watchdog. That hound of yours is cowardly and no-account."

Muley threw his arms protectively around the dog's neck. "He's a good dog. Sure enough, he is. You ain't fixin' to do somethin' to him, are you?"

Thomas left it to me to reassure Muley. "No, don't fret over that. But someday when we get time to visit the neighbors we'll see if we can't get him some company. We need a dog around here we can depend on."

The time finally came when the cabin was up, the chimney finished, logs rived for clapboard shingles, and the roof covered over so that it wouldn't leak badly in the rain. They always leaked a little, those days. The field had been hoed and the garden work caught up with. The corn was coming along nicely.

"Thomas," I said, "don't you think we ought to go now and get acquainted with the neighbors we haven't met yet? When the crops start to ripenin', we'll be busy again."

Thomas replied, "We've got along pretty good so far without worryin' about neighbors."

"But we might need them someday, and maybe they'll need us. We ought to get acquainted."

We had met the neighbors on the colony side as we came up here, unless of course some more had come in behind us. According to the map we had copied from Pounce's, the nearest neighbors upriver bore the name of Hernandez. I could tell that wasn't Irish.

Thomas grumbled, "I'd as soon not have any truck with Mexicans. I don't see how any good could come of it."

"They're there," I argued. "I don't expect they'll

move away just because we've come. And like Jared said, we'll need all the friends we can get." The truth was, I was curious.

"Chances are we couldn't understand them noway. We'd have to make sign talk, like a bunch of Indians."

"Our rifles speak the same language. Mexicans or not, we'd want them with us if we ever have Indian trouble."

That kind of talk reached Thomas when nothing else would.

"We'll go," he said reluctantly.

We took Muley along, afraid to leave him by himself. We also took the extra horse, leading him for a pack animal. It wasn't so much that he was actually needed, but it didn't seem wise to leave him at home unattended if somebody with feathers in his hair should drop by to call. Anyway, before we reached the Hernandez place we might shoot a deer or two, as a courtesy. The extra horse would be handy to pack in the meat.

We found the country west of us to be much the same as our own—rolling hills with scattered oak and other timber, wide valleys with the grass so tall the seedheads brushed the soles of our shoes as we rode through it on horseback. The grass was still green at the base but maturing now in the summer sun. It was not as lush as in Tennessee, but the look and feel of it showed it was strong.

The cattle along the way confirmed that. They were in good flesh. These were wild-natured cattle of every color in the rainbow, with long horns and long legs that carried them with almost the swiftness of deer.

"Notice somethin' about these cattle, Thomas? They every one got a fire-brand on their hip. And it's always the same brand. Sort of an H, done up stylish. H for Hernandez, I reckon."

Thomas was not impressed. "This far out, what difference would it make who they belonged to?"

"I'll bet they can drive these cattle down to the settlements and sell them for beef."

Interest sparked in Thomas's eyes. "You may have an idea, Josh. I'd put up my horse against Muley's spotted dog that these are plain wild cattle that was runnin' free. These Mexicans just gathered them and put their brand on them and made them theirs. We could do that too."

"Take them away from the Mexicans?"

"No, I don't mean that. But we could hunt down wild cattle and burn our brand on them and bring them down to our place. With our three cows and a bull, it's goin' to take us a long time to get a herd together. This way, we could rush things a right smart."

One of our cows had dropped a calf just after we had gotten here. Another had calved just a couple of days back. Thomas was right. Nature's way would be slow.

I said, "Maybe the Mexicans will teach us how they do it."

Thomas shook his head. "We can learn by ourselves."

I nodded, but the thought ran through my mind that I was going to ask anyway, if these Mexicans were friendly, and if we could find some way to talk to them.

Muley and I fell to talking. That is, Muley talked and I listened, about the deer and the wild turkeys and a coon that had gotten into the cabin. Gradually we dropped back somewhat behind Thomas. He rode up over a rise and pulled his horse to a sudden stop. He motioned excitedly for us to stay back. Slowly, carefully, Thomas slipped off of his horse. He motioned again for us to stay back, but I wouldn't have done it for a sackful of silver. I dismounted and moved up, leading my horse. Muley's eyes were wide with wonder as he came along behind me.

"What is it, Thomas?" Muley called innocently.

If Thomas could have found a quiet way to kill him, he might have done it then and there. He put his finger to his lips, then drew it slowly and pointedly across his throat. He turned angrily on me. "Why didn't you do what I told you?"

"Because I want to see."

What I saw made the hair bristle around my collar. Down in a flat, two men rode along horseback, side by side, rifles in their hands, ready to fire in an instant. Flanking them rode six Indians, three on each side. Two of the Indians carried lances. One had a gun of some sort. The other three held bows, with arrows strung and ready to loose. They moved in silent, patient menace.

"Cat and mouse," said Thomas. "They know they got those men in a trap, so now they're playin' it like a game."

"Six against two." A chill ran through me. "They could finish it in a second."

"They're wonderin' a little, though. Those two fellers have each got one shot to fire. When they die, they'll likely take a couple of Indians with them. That's what's holdin' the redskins off." He said it with calm detachment, as if what we watched were nothing more than a good checker game.

"Thomas, there's three of us. That would narrow the odds."

"It would if those were white men. But they're just a couple of Mexicans."

"That doesn't make any difference."

"It does to me. When my time comes to die, I want it to be for somethin' important. I say let the Mexicans take care of their own."

I put my foot into the stirrup. "Then you just sit here!"

Thomas caught my arm. "You're not goin' down there. It's not our put-in."

Muley's face paled. "Josh, don't you go and leave me."

I said, "You stay with Thomas."

Muley protested, "I want to stay with you, Josh."

Thomas didn't often swear, but he swore now at me. "You're as simple-minded as Muley is. But if you're bound and determined, I won't let you go by yourself and get killed." He swung onto his horse, his face twisted. "Just remember if these Mexicans slit our throats someday, this was your idea."

We put Muley in the middle, where he might be less of a hazard to himself and to us. Then, riding abreast, we walked our horses over the crest and started down the other side.

One of the lance-carrying Indians spotted us before we got down to the flat. He shouted and waved the lance. The Indians halted. The two Mexicans immediately turned their horses so that the men were back to back, facing out and ready to fire instantly in any direction. An Indian loosed an arrow. It missed us by a long way. I held my breath as we kept riding, the rifles cradled in our arms. I could see Muley's face whitening.

"Don't show them you're scared, Muley."

"I *am* scared."

"So am I, but we don't want them to know it."

"I'll try to grin at them, Josh."

The Indians stood their ground but loosed no more arrows at us. Thirty feet from them, Thomas said, "We better stop here."

We stopped, our rifles pointed at the Indians.

For a minute or two it was a contest of wills. They tried to stare us down. We stared back. At last one of the Indians spoke in a sharp voice. The six pulled their horses around and started away in a long trot.

One of the Mexicans shouted something I couldn't understand. They quickly stepped down from their saddles. "Down!" Thomas barked. Fifty yards away the Indians suddenly stopped and whirled around. The one who had a gun fired it. The ball fell short. The others loosed their arrows. One of the Mexican horses fell kicking and screaming.

Again the Indians wheeled and moved into a lope, away from us.

The horse threshed, an arrow in its flank. The Mexican waited until the horse laid its head upon the ground, then lowered his rifle and fired point blank. He turned gravely toward us and removed his big-brimmed hat. "*Grácias, señores.*"

Thomas made no reply, so I did it. "Mister, I don't know what you're sayin', and I'm sorry about that."

The Mexican was in his early twenties, his face a light brown, his eyes black. The other was much younger, about sixteen. Their resemblance indicated that they were brothers. The older one made a weak attempt at a smile and gave it up. He was beginning to tremble now, the after-shock starting to reach him. "Too much excitement. I forgot, you do not understand."

I glanced at Thomas. "He speaks American."

The Mexican shook my hand, and I could feel the cold sweat on his palm. "I am called Ramón Hernandez. I speak a little, only, of the English."

"I'm Josh Buckalew, and I don't speak Mexican atall. That yonder is my brother Thomas. The other feller is Muley Dodd."

Muley shook hands. Thomas only nodded, staying where he was, aloof and vaguely disapproving. Hernandez turned to his brother. "And this is Felix."

Felix was quivering. The full weight of the experience had come crashing down on him. He settled to the ground and knelt with his shoulders shaking uncontrollably. He crossed himself. The older brother moved up beside him and spoke to him in a gentle voice.

"For Felix," he said apologetically, "this is the first time death is come so close. He can smell its breath."

I remembered how I had felt that night we fought the outlaws near Natchitoches. I could sympathize.

The Indians had disappeared. "You have much trouble with them?" I asked.

Ramón Hernandez shook his head. "Not many times. Most time they just want to steal horses. Today these young Indians, they find two Mexicans and think *Ay*, why not get two scalps to take home, show women. Very easy, he thinks. Comanche, he does not fight much when he is not sure he wins. You come, he goes."

"They might come back."

Ramón shrugged. "Maybe not for months again." He watched his brother as the boy regained his composure. "Where you come from?" he asked me.

I said, "We're neighbors. We got land, yonderways."

Ramón nodded, pleased. "Good to have people here. When some day we have enough people, Indians come no more."

He helped Felix to his feet. Felix gave us a shy, half-ashamed grin. He said something we didn't understand, and Ramón told us he was apologizing for acting like a woman. It would never happen again, he promised.

Ramón said, "Felix and me, we take you home with us. We want family to see you."

I could tell Thomas didn't like it, but I said, "We'd be right tickled."

Ramón smiled. "We will be friends. Maybe you teach me better the English."

I said, "Ain't no doubt about that. Time I get through ateachin' you, there won't be no college professor that talks better. Now, whichaway's the house?"

The Hernandez house blended into the land, and I didn't even see it at first. It was long and squat, almost flat-roofed, its walls of rock and its roof held up by timbers dragged from the banks of a creek nearby. Smaller houses and sheds clustered around the main house, all within easy running distance in case of attack. We rode through a scattering of cattle and passed a band of small native horses and little Mexican mules, these loose-herded on grass by a boy of ten or so. Half a dozen milk goats followed along, eyeing us with curiosity.

In a flat stretch of open ground beyond the house, a man and a boy with wooden plows and a mule apiece worked a field where young corn was up to a good stand. Nearer the house, women and small girls hoed a garden. They all stopped work to stare at us.

Ramón pointed toward an opening in the heavy corral, which was built of live-oak limbs stacked and wedged between pairs of stout posts. We rode in. A pair of boys came running at Ramón's call. He spoke to them in a fast-clipped Spanish that I could only marvel over. That language, I thought, was going to be a booger to learn.

We followed Ramón's lead and unsaddled. As we started toward the house, Felix and Muley somehow seemed to fall in with each other. Thomas followed along behind, making it plain he was not keen on any part of this.

Near the front door were two homemade crates, each containing a game rooster. The Mexican people all loved a cockfight.

"*Mamá,*" Ramón called. "*Tenemos huéspedes.*"

An elderly woman appeared in the open door of the long rock house, her brown hand up over her eyes. She peered out beyond the broad brush arbor that served in lieu of a porch. She greeted us cordially, even before Ramón began to tell her what had happened. I heard her gasp the word, "*Indios,*" and knew it meant Indians.

She came first to me, then to Muley, and finally to the flustered Thomas, kissing each of us in turn.

Hat off, I had to crouch a little to follow her into the house. Mexicans were inclined toward smallness, and so were their houses. Ramón pointed to several hand-made wooden chairs that had rawhide seats. "Please, it is not much. But sit. Be to home. This house is your house." When we were seated he said, "*Mamá* will bring you to drink. I bring the family."

As the gray-haired mother bustled about excitedly, I took a long look at the room. The house was stoutly built but Spartanly furnished. Almost everything appeared hand-built, probably right here. The rock walls were mostly bare, except for a few clothes pegs and a crude carved crucifix prominently displayed. Heavy shutters were hung inside each windowsill, with a bar which could be dropped to secure them. In each shutter was a small leather-hinged porthole, rifle-size.

"This is more than just a house, Thomas. This is a fort."

Thomas shook his head. "It don't look like much to me." Señora Hernandez brought black coffee. Coffee was very scarce out here. I knew she was cutting into a long-saved supply for us.

Ramón came back, trailed by half a dozen youngsters. "I want you to meet my brothers and sisters." He lined them up by ages, ranging from a boy of six or seven up to a pretty, black-eyed girl I guessed to be fourteen, or maybe fifteen. She was still lank and a little awkward, but in a year or two the woman would begin showing through. *Then* there would be visitors a-plenty to the Hernandez' door.

Ramón counted them off. "Here we have Enrique, Consuelo, José, Margarita, Alfredo, and María." He looked back over his shoulder. "Teresa! *Dónde estás*, Teresa?"

My heart leaped as a girl walked in. Girl? She was a woman, the most beautiful woman I had ever seen.

Ramón said proudly, "Teresa is the oldest of the sisters."

Teresa bowed. I started to put out my hand but

didn't know whether I was supposed to shake hands with her or not. I pulled it back, the color rising in my face. "Howdy, Miss Teresa."

Her answer was in Spanish. Disappointment touched me, for we wouldn't be able to talk to each other. Not, at least, until I learned Spanish. And suddenly I knew I was going to learn in a hurry.

A shadow fell across the open doorway. Another brother stood there, one I judged to be nearly as old as Ramón. He scowled, his gaze touching first Thomas, then Muley, then me. He said something in a sharp voice.

Ramón's smile dimmed, but he managed to hold part of it. He said, "This is my brother Antonio. Next to me, he is the oldest. Next to me, he runs the family since our father is gone. *Next to me.*" He said something sharp to Antonio, and Antonio quit scowling.

Ramón retold for the brothers and sisters what had happened to him and Felix. I found Teresa watching me, and my gaze dropped away from her. It was the younger girl, María, who stepped forward and stood almost toe-to-toe with me. She spoke words I could not understand, but I could read the gratitude in her eyes.

Ramón explained. "María, she says she wish to speak English, so she can say to you how much thanks she has in her heart."

I said, "Tell her, Ramón, that I'll come over here as often as I can. I'll teach her to talk American." I glanced shyly toward Teresa. "I'll teach all of those who want to learn."

Ramón translated. María clapped her hands. I found Teresa smiling. This time I kept my nerve and returned the smile.

Antonio did not miss the look that passed between Teresa and me. He spoke in anger. Ramón answered him in words that cut like a whip. Antonio's eyes pierced me with hostility. He pointed first at me, then at Teresa, and said something more. Then he turned on his heel and strode out of the house.

I saw Teresa drop her gaze, hurt.

"What was that all about?" I asked.

Ramón's face was darker than it had been. "Antonio has a strong mind. He does not like Americans."

Thomas spoke for the first time, belligerently. "What's wrong with Americans?"

Ramón shrugged. "For me, nothing. I have *Americano* friends. They teach me this little English I speak. I learn much from them, and I hope teach them a little. But Antonio is like some others of my people—he hates those who are not the same as he is."

I offered, "Maybe some American did him dirty."

Ramón shook his head. "No, but he thinks they will, someday. So he hates *now*."

Thomas snorted. "That's a hell of a thing, hatin' us for no cause."

The thought ran through my mind that Antonio was no different in that respect than Thomas. My brother must have read the thought in my eyes. "It's not the same thing," he said defensively.

"Ain't it?"

I glanced again at Teresa and found she had turned her face away. "Ramón," I said, "Antonio said somethin' about Teresa and me."

"It is not important."

"He must have thought so."

Ramón shrugged. "He says I should tell you Teresa is—how you say?—promised. She has a man who will be her husband."

That came like a dash of cold water in my face. But I tried to keep it from showing.

Ramón said, "Many years ago it is decided, by our father and by the father of Diego Esquivel."

My mouth dropped open. "They decided? Didn't she have any say-so?"

"She was only a child. This is a matter for the fathers."

"It don't hardly seem fair to her . . ."

"Diego is a good man. Good friend of mine."

"Does she love him?"

Ramón shrugged again. "One learns to love, as one learns to speak English, or Spanish. It is the way of our fathers."

Thomas muttered, "I don't see why it should make any difference to you, Josh."

But I looked into the beautiful eyes of Teresa Hernandez, and I knew it was going to matter to me. It was going to matter a lot.

8

The people kept coming, some with proper papers and some without. Legal or contraband, they trekked across Texas in a hungry search for a fresh start, for land of their own. It was a restless time, a reaching time. Men prowled and hunted until they found what they liked, and then they planted their boots there and claimed it. Sometimes Mexican soldiers came and moved them on, but more often no one came, no one challenged, for the land was still broad and open, and there was room for so many more. What did it matter to a man what was written on paper five hundred miles away when he could reach down right here and scoop up a handful of black earth and almost feel the life throbbing in it? Who cared whether government spoke Spanish or English when the sky was big and blue and the land called out to a man in a voice that touched the soul?

They were all kinds, these early Texians. Most of them came to farm and raise their families and mind their own business. They came seeking peace and opportunity, not a fight.

But there were some who seemed to be looking for trouble from the time they dropped their saddles to the grass and claimed their ground. Four miles to the south of us, three men made camp and started clearing the land. Two were young brothers, Jacob and Ezekiel Phipps, late of Kentucky. They had come to Texas for the same reasons we had—their father had sent them in search of a virgin land, just as he himself had searched a generation before. They were a decent pair—loud but basically honest—with one bad weakness: they were easily led.

And leading them was a shouting, cursing, irascible old reprobate named Alfred Noonan. Stocky, red-faced, he had been in Texas several times, off and on, through the last ten years. He told us something he evidently had not chosen to tell any of the authorities who granted him his land: once he had smuggled forbidden trade goods down into Mexico. During this enterprise he had been hounded and hunted and shot at by Mexican soldiers, so he nursed a virulent hatred of Mexicans in general and officials in particular. He had managed to rub off this feeling onto the Phipps brothers, though neither of them had ever seen enough Mexicans to count on their fingers—if, in fact, they could count at all.

Thomas, of course, had already developed a strong dislike for Mexicans. So he fell in with Noonan and the Phipps brothers like a thirsty duck that has found a water hole.

We all went down to help them raise their cabin. By the time that job was done I'd had enough of Noonan to last me for twenty years. I never went back. But Thomas went often, and sometimes they came to our cabin.

I could always predict what Noonan would say. "She's too good of a country to be run by a bunch of ignorant Mexicans. I say the United States ought to wade in here with an army and just naturally take over the whole shebang."

When Thomas and Noonan got started talking, it was always a marathon of sedition, with the Phipps brothers eagerly joining in like a pair of young coon dogs following the older hounds. Seemed Noonan always knew of a revolution brewing somewhere down in Mexico—there had been a lot of them—and he was full of ideas about how he and Thomas and the Phipps boys could smuggle guns in there and get rich.

I tried to tell Thomas he ought to steer clear of the old man. Thomas would simply shake his head. "It's all just talk—you ought to be able to tell that. Ain't none of it ever goin' to come to pass."

"This is dangerous talk. You know what Colonel Austin said about us gettin' mixed up in Mexican politics."

"I'd rather be mixed up in their politics than mixed up in their families. The kind of friends *you* got, you have no call to be talkin' about mine."

The argument always came down to that, sooner or later. I'd been going over to the Hernandez *rancho* often. I always tried to explain to Thomas that I was only going so I could learn to talk Mexican, and to teach the Hernandez family how to speak

American. But Thomas figured all along that my main interest was in Teresa Hernandez.

And he was right.

María, fifteen, was the best learner. She picked up English faster than any of the others excepting Ramón, of course, who already had a fair knowledge of it. María showed so much interest in learning that Ramón helped her when I wasn't there. That way, she had a long head start on the others.

Teresa was learning English, too. But English was only her secondary interest in the lessons, as Spanish was mine.

Muley always went with me. He never did really get the hang of Spanish; his mind just wasn't bent toward learning. Yet, it always amazed me how he got along with the smaller members of the Hernandez family. They communicated through act and expression, rather than through the words they said. In the years since, I've seen Mexican and American kids get along like cousins without either really knowing a word the other spoke. There's an understanding between children that has nothing to do with words. And Muley, in many ways, was a child. He always would be.

Language wasn't important to Teresa and me, either. We understood each other without stumbling over the problems of translation. A glance, a quick touching of the fingertips when nobody was looking . . . we didn't really need to talk.

The trouble was, though, that we were never alone. Always, someone managed to be nearby, letting us know we were watched. Often it was her mother, sometimes one of the brothers or sisters. Occasionally it was the smoldering Antonio, hating me because my eyes were blue and my skin was light, making it plain that he never intended either of us to forget Teresa was already promised.

Neither did Thomas. He pointed it out every time I started toward the Hernandez place, and he would repeat it when I got back.

Back in Tennessee I had usually taken whatever advice appealed to me, and let the rest alone. I didn't change my ways much in Texas. I let Thomas advise me about planting and plowing and such, but when it came to Teresa I just didn't figure he knew much.

Through the long summer I kept going, and I kept learning. I got so I understood Spanish tolerably well.

I learned more than language. Ramón and Felix taught me a lot about their way of handling the wild native cattle. They taught me the fundamentals of using the rawhide *reata* to catch animals, and I practiced it until I was a fair-to-middling hand. I learned how the Mexicans captured wild cattle and took the vinegar out of them, fire-branding them with a hot iron that stamped a permanent claim of ownership on them.

The Hernandez brothers hated working in the fields and did as little of it as they could get by with. They enjoyed breaking wild horses to ride, or gathering wild cattle and putting their brand on them. That was hard work, but it had an excitement to it that a man never found behind a plow.

Even there, I found there were basic differences between my outlook and that of Ramón Hernandez. Sometimes it would be only the middle of the afternoon and there would still be plenty of cattle nearby for the taking. But he would hold up his hand and say:

"Enough. It has been a good day. One does not want to be greedy."

"Ramón," I would argue, "it's a long time till dark. Why quit now?" Usually I would talk to him in English and he would answer me in Spanish, for that way each of us would express himself best and still be understood.

"Work was made for the convenience of man, and not man for the work. Besides, over that hill lies the home of the most beautiful Gloria Vasquez, and I would like to go and pay my respects. After all, she might one day be the mother of my sons."

Other times it might be Catarina Torres, or Silvia Martinez y Flores, or Margarita Sanchez. No matter. He was always watching for the woman who would be his wife. He said he did not know yet what she looked like, but he thought he would know her when she crossed his path.

Felix would smile and shrug as if to say he and I might as well go home.

Thomas never would admit that anything good came from my being around the Mexicans. But he was quick to pick up the use of the *reata* and the cattle-handling skill I had learned from the Hernandez men—Ramón, Felix, and Antonio. Yes, even Antonio. For, to give the devil his due, I guess Antonio was the best cowman of them all, and horseman too. If he hated hard, he also worked hard . . . harder than Ramón.

It was as if his hatred gave him a special drive. Thomas had that drive too. It crossed my mind often that Thomas and Antonio had a lot in common, but of course they would not ever stop and compare.

In time, Thomas and Muley and I had a fair-sized bunch of cattle with our own brand on them, cattle whose ancestors had strayed from the pastures of the Spanish missions and had gone the way of the wild herds. Come fall, we would pick out the fattest and drive them down to the settlements to trade for supplies, and maybe even a little coin.

I mentioned Felix. He was a year older than María, just at the age when he was looking for somebody to follow. One time it would be the grinning Ramón. Another, it would be the brooding Antonio, who had a way of making a sunny day dark. If Felix was dark and morose, he was following Antonio. If he was joking and enjoying himself, it was Ramón day.

A constant rivalry existed between the older brothers, each trying to bring Felix into his own camp to stay. I sensed that there probably had been a rivalry of one kind or another between Ramón and Antonio from the time Antonio had first grown big enough to hurl a rock in anger.

It pleased me to see that Felix followed Ramón more than he followed Antonio. Felix had the makings of a good man, if he didn't choose wrong.

* * *

From what Ramón told me about Diego Esquivel, the man Teresa was pledged to marry, he sounded all right. Under different circumstances I wouldn't have hated him. But I lay awake nights, tortured by the thought of his taking Teresa in forced marriage, closing the door behind them and shutting her out of my life. It didn't help much that Ramón said Diego was none too ready for marriage himself. Esquivel was enjoying all the pleasures and privileges of bachelorhood and, among the gay young maidens of Bexar, these were considerable. He had seen Teresa but few times in recent years and had no more romantic interest in her than he might have had in any pretty girl.

Yet I knew that her beauty would quickly develop that interest, once she was his wife. Worse—she might even learn to enjoy his love, eventually. He would have what I had not even dared hope for. Though the sight of Teresa fired my blood, I had had nothing more from her than her smiles and fleeting touches of her hand. Not once had I ever been able to kiss her.

Except for Antonio Hernandez, I might have had a chance. The rest of the family liked me. There was, of course, the old family tradition of the arranged marriage. Even this we might have worked out in some honorable way, had I been allowed the opportunity to reason with Diego Esquivel.

Always there was Antonio and that implacable hatred, standing like a barred door between Teresa and me. I should have expected the thing he did, but it came as a surprise.

One day when Muley and I rode in to the Hernandez place, we found the family strangely silent. María, who usually met me at the door, smiling, only glanced in sadness, then turned away. Teresa was in the front room. I saw tears as her eyes met mine.

"Teresa, what's wrong?"

She ran, crying.

Ramón took my arm. "Josh . . . friend . . . let us go out into the cool of the arbor. We have something to talk about."

I sent Muley to play with the kids, because that was why he came.

Ramón was grave. "First of all, let us be honest. For a long time we have known of your feeling for Teresa. And we have known she felt strongly about you. But you were told from the first that she was promised, in the manner of our people. Perhaps we should have done something to stop this at the beginning, when there would have been little pain. But you were our friend, and we did not know how. Now there is no choice. The pain has to come.

"Do not ask me why Antonio hates you. Do not even ask him, for he does not know, except that you are of one people and we are of another. He has not liked what has happened between you and Teresa. He has taken it upon himself to stop it. He went to Bexar. He talked with Diego Esquivel, and together they planned the wedding. Diego is on his way here now, with his family and the priest. The wedding will be tomorrow."

It was as if he had slashed me with a knife.

"Ramón, she doesn't love him. She doesn't even know him."

Ramón shrugged. "What can be done? It is the tradition. Love comes, and love goes. But tradition lasts forever."

"To hell with tradition. I love her, and she loves me!"

"She will learn to love Diego. It is our people's way."

"I'll take her away from here. I'll make her one of *my* people."

Ramón shook his head. "You cannot do that. She has too much honor to go against the wishes of her father, rest his soul."

I pushed to my feet and strode into the house, Ramón following. I found Mrs. Hernandez in the front room with Teresa and Antonio, watching me worriedly. I spoke in the best Spanish I knew.

"Teresa, this is not going to happen. I'm not going to allow it. You're going to marry *me*!"

Her mother stood silent, shocked beyond speaking. But Antonio's voice lashed at me. "Away from here, American! Teresa is not yours, and she will never be yours! She stays among her own."

I grabbed Teresa's hand. "Come on, I'm taking you away."

I didn't even see the knife until Teresa screamed. There was a blur of a hand, the flash of the blade. He held the point against my throat. It burned like fire. Antonio's voice was as sharp as the steel. "I would see both of you dead first. Turn loose her hand, American, or you die right now!"

His black eyes seethed. He meant exactly what he said. Teresa jerked her hand away and screamed, "Antonio, no!"

Ramón stopped it. "Put the knife away, Antonio!" His voice was quiet, but it carried an authority that penetrated even the fury of Antonio Hernandez. Antonio lowered the knife. I could see a small spot of red on the point, and I could feel a burning where he had brought the blood.

Ramón turned to me. "Josh, we have enjoyed your company here many times. We had hoped nothing would ever come between us to spoil it. But now we must ask you to leave. We must keep the door shut against you until the wedding is over and Teresa is gone. Please go now, and go quietly."

That was it, courteous but to the point. The Mexican people had a courtly way of telling you to go to hell.

There seemed little choice at the moment. I would have to hurt someone—maybe even kill—to get Teresa out of here now. I backed toward the door.

"Wait for me, Teresa. I'll come for you."

Antonio gritted, "Come back and you will be buried here!"

Ramón said, "Please go, Josh. Lose gracefully, so we may still be friends."

I said, "I haven't lost yet."

All the way home I tried to decide what I was going to do. I couldn't develop any definite plan. All I knew was that after dark I was going back, and somehow I was going to break Teresa out of there. Maybe I could get Thomas to help me. And if he wouldn't, I had friends downriver who would.

It was nearly dark when Muley and I reached the cabin. Thomas had the cow milked and the horses penned. I saw three extra horses in the corral.

Muley saw them too. "The Phipps boys are here. And that old man Noonan. He sure does talk a right smart, don't he, Josh? Half the time I don't know what he's talkin' about."

"Neither does he."

The dog set in to barking and brought Thomas to the door, rifle in his hand. It was always like that with Muley's dog: bark when there wasn't any need for it, and hide when he should be making a racket. Thomas said, "Wasn't lookin' for you back. Thought you'd spend the night with them Mexicans again."

I could tell by the sound of his voice that he and Noonan had been talking, and he was in a mood to argue with me about the Hernandez family. I was in no temper for it.

"Thomas, I got to talk to you, and I got to do it right now." I saw the visitors come to the door, their curiosity aroused. "Out in the corral. By ourselves."

Thomas glanced at his company and said he'd be back directly. He followed Muley and me to the corral. I unsaddled and waited until Muley had done the same. "Go on to the house, Muley."

He protested. "I don't want to have to listen to old man Noonan."

"Go listen to him anyway."

Muley grumbled and walked off. I told Thomas

that Diego Esquivel was on his way to marry Teresa. Thomas nodded in satisfaction. "Well, maybe now you can set your mind on your plowin'."

"But he's not goin' to marry her. I am."

"How you figure that? I don't expect them Mexicans are goin' to throw roses in your path and tell you to come take her."

"I'm takin' fresh horses, and I'm goin' back to get her tonight. I'm goin' to break her out of there. I want you to help me, Thomas."

"Me? Are you crazy?"

"You're my brother, Thomas. I've never asked you for much. I know you don't agree with me about Teresa, but I hope you'll be a big enough man to put that aside now and help me."

A deep frown creased his face. "Josh, goin' over there and lovin' her up is one thing. Actually marryin' her is somethin' else."

"I'm goin' to do it, with your help or without it. I just hoped it would be with your help."

Thomas stared at me a long moment, then turned away. I didn't realize what he was going to do until he opened the gate. Then he turned and waved his hat, shouting at the horses.

Before I could move, they were on their way out of the corral.

"Damn you, Thomas!"

I ran to my saddle and grabbed a rawhide *reata*. I yelled, "Muley, come help me."

Thomas stood in the gate. As I started around him, his fist came at me. It slammed me back against the fence. Thomas called for his friends, and they came running. The four of them moved in on me. I tried to lunge at Thomas, but strong hands grabbed and held me. Thomas's fist drove into my stomach. All my breath left me.

"Now, Josh," Thomas gritted, "just quit it. What we're doin' we're doin' for your own good."

I heard Muley yelp and saw him come running to help me. I tried to yell at him to stay where he was, but no sound would come. He plowed in with fists swinging. One of the Phipps boys backhanded him, then slashed at him with a rock-like set of knuckles that bent Muley back like a small boy. He dropped.

Thomas told them what was happening. "Looks like we'll just have to tie Josh up and keep him awhile. Never thought I'd see the day I'd have to do this to my own flesh and blood."

I struggled against them, but they had me so tight there wasn't a chance to break loose.

Noonan said, "Thomas, what do you say we take them over to our cabin a spell? There's more of us to keep an eye on them there. And if drastic measures is called for, we might come nearer takin' them than you would, bein' his brother and all."

Thomas frowned. "I don't want him hurt none."

"We'll just kind of salt them down, both of them. You won't have to fret none or feel the least bit uneasy. Come tomorrow, Josh'll still be a happy bachelor. And you won't have no Mexican kinfolks."

My breath was coming back. "I'll get you! I'll get all of you!"

Noonan didn't seem impressed. "Sure you will, Josh. But for now you're goin' to come on along like a good boy. Thomas, how about you bringin' them horses back in?"

After a while the horses came. I tried to fight free, and Jacob Phipps fetched me a clout that put me on my knees. He pushed me down onto my stomach and sat on me while the others saddled up. Then he pulled me to my feet. "We'll be a-leavin' now, Josh. It's up to you whether you get on that horse by yourself or if we clout you again and put you up there."

I knew I didn't have the strength for a fight, so I climbed up. I had some notion of being able to pull loose from them down the trail and get away. I wanted to save my strength for that possibility. But I found they weren't going to give me the chance. They tied my hands to the saddle. Then they tied a short rope to the reins. Ezekiel Phipps held the end of the rope in his big hands.

Muley sobbed. "I tried, Josh. I did try."

"Sure, Muley. You did right good. There was just too many of them."

Thomas said, "Josh, don't you do nothin' to make them have to hurt you, do you hear? The time'll come when you'll thank me for this."

In my fury there was nothing I could say that was half enough. So I held my tongue. I'd be back, and there would be a reckoning.

They kept us tied all that night, and all the next day and night. They untied Muley to let him eat. They tried untying me once but tied me up again when I attempted to fight my way out of the cabin. If I had any satisfaction at all, it was that I had left my mark on all of them. The afternoon of the wedding, Noonan rode to the Hernandez place and spied on it from a distance. He came riding in next morning, satisfied.

"It was quite a sight, Josh. You ought to've seen it. When them Mexicans throw a celebration, they sure do it up right."

I knew without asking, but I had to ask anyway, the dread coming up in me heavy and cold. "They're married?"

"Sure enough. Handsome-lookin' couple, best I could tell. You got to understand I was too far away to see real clear. I doubt as she'll miss you much, Josh. Mexican gals have got a talent for lovin', and I expect that boy will keep her too busy to be frettin' herself about some calf-eyed *Americano*." He glanced at Jacob and Ezekiel. "Reckon you'd just as well untie him and let him go."

Jacob went to work on the knots that bound me. "Josh, I hope you'll take this in the spirit we meant it. We was just doin' you a favor."

When my hands were free, I rubbed my raw wrists to get the circulation going. I would need it for what I wanted to do.

Jacob grinned at me. "No hard feelin's, Josh."

I don't know where the strength came from, but my fist caught his nose dead-center. His head snapped back and cracked against the log siding. I whirled and caught Ezekiel in the ribs. He grunted and doubled over.

Noonan hobbled toward the door, his eyes wide. "Now, Josh, you wouldn't go and hurt an old man."

I stopped, for dizziness came over me. Noonan said. "You're sure an ungrateful kind, Josh. No wonder you're such a burden to your brother."

I reached for him but missed. He ran out of the cabin, shouting and cursing at me. I untied Muley. We walked out into the daylight. It hurt my eyes at first, but that was only a small addition to the agony I felt in body and in spirit. The whole world had fallen in on me.

I caught up our horses, trying to choke down the rage which fought for release. I think if I had had a gun I would have gone back into the cabin and killed all three men, or tried to.

"Muley, you ride on home."

"What you fixin' to do, Josh?"

"I'm goin' to the Hernandez place."

"Seems like it's a little late now, don't it? I mean, they said there had done been a weddin' and all that. There ain't nobody but God can undo a weddin', is there?"

"Just go on home, Muley."

"When you figure on bein' back?"

"I don't know. Just look for me when you see me comin'."

Eight days came and went before the night I finally rode up to our cabin. I swung down woodenly and unsaddled, turning the horse into the corral and tying the gate. Muley's dog barked at me. I trudged to the cabin, my head down, my throat in a knot.

Thomas opened the door and stood there against the candlelight, rifle in his hand. "Josh? That you, Josh?"

I walked in past him without being able to look into his face.

"Josh, it's been over a week. Where you been?"

I couldn't answer him at first.

He stared at me. "You're sure makin' it hard on yourself. You've been blinded by somethin' you take to be love. Hell, you don't even know what love is. You never felt it before, and the first time you get a real itch toward a woman you think you're in love with her. This'll all blow over, and you'll thank me. You'll look at her and tell me how glad you are that you're not tied to her."

Voice came to me. "I'll never see her again, Thomas, nobody will."

His mouth dropped open.

I said, "She's dead, Thomas."

I think that was the first time he ever really saw how deeply and honestly I had been in love with Teresa. "Dead? But how?"

"The mornin' after they were married, the two of them set out alone toward Bexar, ahead of the others. When the Esquivel family came along later they found them . . . what the Indians had left of them."

Thomas looked at the floor, his face frozen. "My God, Josh. . . ."

I said, "If I'd gone back that night, she'd still be

alive. I'd have gotten her away from there, and I'd have taken her back toward the settlements, where there wouldn't have been any Indians. That's how it would have been, Thomas, if you hadn't stopped me."

"I was thinkin' of you, Josh."

"Or maybe you were just thinkin' of yourself, and how bad you'd hate to have a Mexican woman for your sister-in-law."

Thomas shook his head. "What can I say?"

"It'd be better if you didn't say anything."

He brought himself to look at me. "Josh, that was over a week ago. Where have you been all this time?"

"Been lookin' for some Indians to kill."

He stared. "Find any?"

I shook my head. "They disappeared like smoke."

"But a week, Josh. How come you to stay so long?"

"Afraid to come back any sooner. Afraid I might kill you." I could see the hurt in his eyes. "I won't do it, though. I got over that much of it. But from now on I'm through lettin' you think for me. I'm through listenin' to you. I don't even want to see you."

Thomas put his hand on my shoulder. "Josh . . ."

I couldn't hold it any longer. I hit him. And when I saw him stagger back, all the anger and all the grief that had banked up in me seemed to explode at once. I tied into him, slashing, jabbing.

It was years before I could think back on it without my emotions getting in the way. Long afterward, remembering, I knew Thomas didn't do much to defend himself. He took all I had to give him, and what I gave him would have killed a lesser man. I fought him until all the strength had ebbed out of me and I lay on the earthen floor of the cabin, sobbing like a little boy.

For a long time I lay there, letting the hurt have its way with me. But finally I pushed to my feet and saw Thomas sitting on a rawhide chair, regarding me gravely. His face was bruised and swollen, his clothing torn. But in his eyes was only sadness.

"Well, Thomas," I said, "which one of us is it goin' to be?"

"What do you mean?"

"I mean one of us has got to go. Will it be you, or me?"

Thomas's voice was hollow. "It's that bad, is it?"

"It's that bad."

He dug into his pocket. "I wish it wasn't this way, Josh." He brought forth a coin. "This is gold. Come all the way with us from Tennessee. You call it."

"Heads I go, tails you do."

The coin caught the candlelight for an instant as it flipped out of Thomas's hand, went up, then fell. It made a faint thump on the floor. Thomas leaned over and picked it up. "Tails."

"I didn't see it," I said.

"That's what it was, though. Tails. The place is yours."

I nodded, too numb really to care which one of us went. "I want you to go tonight, Thomas!"

That shook him, but he shrugged. "All right."

He gathered up a few of his belongings, rolled his bedding, and stepped out into the night to fetch his horse.

Muley said, “Josh, it’s awful dark out there. It ain’t good to turn a man out into the night this-away.”

“I’d have gone, if it had come up heads.”

Muley said with an innocent wisdom that would come back to haunt me in the years ahead: “Maybe it did, Josh.”

9

Hard work has never been popular, but it is a merciful healer.

Since Thomas had left, it was up to Muley and me to bring in the crops that fall. If I hadn't been up moving before daylight and laboring like a gray mule until dark, then flopping on my cot too tired to move, I might not have brought myself through those first dark weeks. Even with the work, I would glance up every so often and see Teresa's face in the autumn-red fringe of timber.

If it had been the beautiful face of those fleeting days we had together, I could have stood it. But always I saw her as I had seen her in death, the eyes and mouth open in horror, the blood dried to a sickening blackish crimson. The heart would drop out of me.

At such times, some men drown themselves in liquor. I had no liquor, so I tried to drown myself in work. There was more than enough of it. Muley suffered, because he tried with all that was in him to keep up with me. It's a wonder I didn't kill him.

Thomas stayed out of my sight. Muley tried to hide it from me, but in his guileless way he let me find out that Thomas would come around now and again, when I was somewhere else. Thomas would look things over, question Muley a little, then fade away before I got back. Much of the time he was staying with Noonan and the Phipps boys, helping them bring in wild cattle the way he and I had done, or helping them harvest their crops. At that time of year there was always work for a man like Thomas who wanted to hire out and didn't balk at hard labor. Usually he was paid in kind, for coin was scarce.

Once, I learned, Thomas went off on a long trip with Noonan somewhere to the south. Not for the world would I have admitted it, but I worried about him. I knew Noonan had him mixed up in a smuggling venture or something of that kind. Trouble and contention were like food and drink to Noonan's breed.

Muley got lonesome sometimes, with just the two of us there on the place. "When we goin' back to see the Hernandez family again?" he would ask.

"I don't know if I can ever go back," I told him. "Teresa's gone."

"The rest of them ain't gone. The kids are still there. I like them kids, Josh."

I could sympathize with Muley's loneliness, for I had my own. But I couldn't bring myself to visit again the place where I had known Teresa. Most of all, I knew I could not bear the sight of Antonio Hernandez. Always turning in my mind was the grim certainty that it had been his hatred—and Thomas's—

which had killed her. Their blind, selfish, senseless hatred. . . .

The long months went by and Ramón came to see us finally, he and Felix. Muley and I were working in the field where our small crop of cotton had matured into a blanket of white fluff. Ramón sat on his horse and watched me.

"You do not look good, friend Josh. You have carried grief badly."

I laid down my cotton sack. I felt resentment at first, for he could have called a halt to the wedding if he had not been so hide-bound to tradition. He could have spoken one word and stopped it.

"How is a man supposed to carry grief, Ramón? It's a heavy burden, no matter how you try to pick it up."

"Ours is the grief, too. We could help you carry it, if you would but ask."

I shook my head. "I'll tote my own load."

"We have not seen you in a long time."

I turned away and picked up my cotton sack. Ramón and Felix got off their horses. Muley ran forward to pump Felix's hand, his face shining with pleasure. Ramón fell in beside me and silently began to help, putting cotton into my sack. He had probably never picked any before, because the Mexicans themselves rarely grew it. Cotton had come in with the Americans. Sometimes I wondered why we tried it, living so far from the market: we couldn't eat it, and we didn't spin it, but we could trade it for coffee and flour and other necessities down in the settlements. The necessities were so hard to come by that they were almost considered luxuries. As for luxuries, there just weren't any.

Ramón and Felix soon had their fingers torn and sore from the hard, dry burs. Ramón said disapprovingly, "I had rather break my neck with the wild cattle and horses than to break my back in the cotton."

I had softened a little, working beside him. "There's not much fun in a cotton field," I admitted. "But cotton sells, and there's precious little else that does."

"What is money, that one must do so many unpleasant things to get it?"

"Why, Ramón, money is . . . Well, I mean, a man's just got to have money."

He shook his head. "Among our people there are some who live a lifetime and never feel a piece of silver cross their palm. A man can live from the land, if he will be content with what the land chooses to give him. This growing of cotton is not a natural thing, like hunting. Do you see the deer or the wolf or the buffalo planting cotton? No, they live as God intended them to, from what the land itself provides. If He had intended that we have cotton, He could have planted it Himself. This kind of work does no honor to a man."

"Work *is* honor. The Book says that by the sweat of the brow shalt thou earn thy bread."

"I had rather sweat my brow running the wild cattle. What could a man want that would make him do dishonoring work to get money? He cannot eat money. He cannot wear it. All he can do is trade it for something he wants. A few beans, a little corn, enough beef—what more could a man want?"

I knew Ramón was purposely working up an argument with me to take my mind away from Teresa. I also knew he was dead serious in what he said.

He went on, "In the Book you learn of the lilies of the field. They do not toil, neither do they spin. And of a certainty you find no lilies in a field of cotton."

I let go my cotton sack while I wiped the sweat from my brow. It gave me a righteous feeling to know I was earning my bread like the Book said to. But it never had occurred to me that there might be conflict between that part of the Word and the passage Ramón had quoted.

I said, "It's all in the way a man looks at it, I reckon. You and me, we just naturally look at it different."

"I think, my friend, this is the big problem between your people and mine. There is little understanding. Perhaps there never will be. Your people say my people are lazy—that they work no more than they have to. My people say your people are greedy—that you work too long and too hard to get money for things you do not need and that you do not take time to taste life for the good flavor that is in it.

"In too many ways we are different. We shall never be alike."

Ramón was wise enough to see it, though it took me a long time to admit he was right. Even then, so long before the final and complete break came to

Texas, the long shadows of the future were beginning to stretch out across the bold new land. No one ever really left the old country when he came to the new. Wherever the settler ventured, he took with him his customs and beliefs, the individual ways of the land he had come from. That applied to both American and Mexican. There was no such thing as a fresh, clean start. He resisted whatever was alien to the things he had known before.

True, the American and the Mexican found some points they could agree on. They might join to face the common enemy—the Indian. They could and did get together when it was to their advantage to trade. Individually, they made friends, as I had done with the Hernandez family. Some intermarried, as Jim Bowie had done in Bexar.

But basically, they remained two different kinds of people in outlook. There had been a time, in the beginning, when they might have stressed the points in which they were alike. Instead, they dwelt upon the differences. It is a human trait—not one of the better ones, but one which usually crops out. Where Mexicans and Americans lived in the same areas, the tendency was to group with their own kind. The dividing boundary might be a river or creek; it might be only an imaginary line. But real or imaginary, it was always there.

Often, in looking back, I have tried to decide for myself who was really to blame for it, who had started it. And always the answer comes up the same: nobody, and everybody. The tendency was there in the beginning, and it was on both sides.

That is the great irony of it all: the fact that we pulled apart and made so much of our difference only proved how much alike we were.

It was a big and open country, but bad news had a way of traveling fast. A foretaste of trouble came when a Texian force attacked the guardhouse at Anahuac, on the coast, to release prisoners who had been wrongfully taken. Excitement rippled through the colonies, and it left its mark even after the Mexican government moved to correct the situation that had brought on the trouble. Shortly afterward came a battle at Velasco, when a Mexican garrison tried to stop the sailing of a Texian ship that carried two cannon. The Mexicans ran out of ammunition, and the Texians persuaded them it would be wise to head south without undue delay.

I didn't see him, but I learned that Thomas had joined Noonan and the Phipps brothers for a fast ride to the coast as soon as they heard. By the time they got there, the smoke had cleared. Diplomatically minded Texians and Mexicans were working to mend the breach that had been torn by their more warlike friends.

If the battles had any good result, it was that Mexico pulled most of her garrison out of Texas. They had been manned mostly by convict soldiers and others of poor repute. They had been a festering sore—a constant reminder that Mexico didn't really trust her new citizens from the north. Santa Anna was a revolutionary leader in Mexico in those days. He took the Texians' side after Anahuac and Velasco. A fresh wave of enthusiasm swept through the old settlers.

Here, it seemed, was a new Mexican leader who understood and liked these blue-eyed foreigners—a Mexican who was going to give us all a fair deal.

There was a time—a short time—when it seemed we were about to get the world by the tail with a downhill pull. Mexico let up some on its immigration laws. More people crowded in. It got so that on an early fall morning when the air was crisp, I could hear a neighbor's ax ringing from across the hill.

But not all the newcomers were farmers and stockmen.

Once in a great while there was reason for Muley and me to go to San Felipe. It had grown, stretching out far along the Brazos. It was crowded with lawyers and land men, promoters of every kind. They worked little—some of them. But they never ceased talking, never stopped agitating. Wherever they found muddy water, they stirred it.

One spring day of 1833, Muley and I were nearing San Felipe in our wagon when we came across a familiar figure astride a bay horse. He rode toward us with head down, lost in his meditation. He didn't seem to see us until we were almost upon him.

Muley called, "Howdy, Colonel Austin."

Austin stopped and brought up his hand in greeting. He studied us, trying for recognition. "I'm sorry," he said. "I was absorbed with some worries of my own."

There had been plenty of them. His face was haggard, his eye bleak.

"I should know you," he said. "The faces are familiar."

"Joshua Buckalew, Colonel. And Muley Dodd. We live up yonder on the Colorado. You granted us the land."

He frowned. "Buckalew? Would you be the one who has been making so much talk of war?"

I shook my head and looked down. "I expect that'd be my brother, sir. His name is Thomas. Him and me, we sort of come to a fork in the road. He seems to've took the left hand."

"That's too bad. But he has a lot of company, these days."

I said regretfully, "I'm sorry, Colonel, that things don't seem to be workin' out the way they ought to for you. Anything Muley and me can do, we'd be tickled to try."

Austin shrugged. "There is a need for so many things, I would hardly know where to start."

"Well, sir, like what, for instance?"

He took a long, frowning look at the countryside around him. It was coming alive with the green of new grass and the bright splash of blue and yellow from bluebonnets and buttercups. "It's a beautiful land. I always thought Texas had the greatest potential of any land I ever set my eyes upon. And it does yet, I suppose, if only these war-makers would cease their everlasting talk of disunity and unrest."

"We live way off yonder in the far settlements. We don't hear much of what's goin' on."

"I imagine you hear enough. We have bad trouble ahead of us if we don't curb these restless spirits. For years I've preached that we should go our own peaceful way. And for years, the people would listen to me. But somehow I've lost control now. Other voices speak louder than mine."

"We've always listened to you, Colonel."

"I wish there were more like you." He studied us keenly. "How go things up on the Colorado?"

"Fair enough, sir. Moisture's good for the spring plantin'. Grass is risin' fine."

"I mean politically. Are they talking as restlessly there as in other parts of Texas?"

Uneasy now, I quit looking into his face. "Well, sir, you'll always find people like my brother. They're dissatisfied no matter what. We have Mexican neighbors, and we get along. The government don't bother us much out there. Too far for office-bred people to ride, I expect." I felt my face coloring. "Not meanin' any personal offense to you, sir. I mean, it's different with you."

Austin smiled faintly. "My friend, I have ridden horseback so many thousands of miles in colonizing Texas that a ride up the Colorado River would be like a Sunday picnic. Even now, I'm preparing for another trip to Mexico City."

"It's a mighty long way down there," I admitted. "Farther, even, than to Tennessee."

"Far in miles and in mind. I never look forward to that journey. It's like going to another world. But I have to. I want to reassure the authorities that we are loyal here. With luck, I may be able to persuade them to take action against some of the conditions which have caused grievances here. There are grounds for grievances; I would be the first to admit that. But we must have patience. The Mexicans move slower than we. Change cannot be rushed upon them."

I thought of the Hernandez family. "No, sir, it sure can't."

Austin gazed intently at me. "You're one of the older settlers here now. It's the old settlers I must depend upon to keep things from getting out of hand. Counsel with the new ones when you can—help them realize how precarious our situation is."

"I'll do all I can," I promised. But even as I said it, I thought of Thomas. I thought how useless it would be to talk to my brother, or to anyone like him. I thought of Antonio Hernandez, too. He and his kind wouldn't listen any more than Thomas would.

"Mexico City," Austin repeated. "It's a long, long way. I hope I can be back again before the summer is out."

He wasn't. It was two years before we were to see Austin. He would come home a shaken and disillusioned man, no longer inclined to soothe the restless ones. He would come home from a long and unjustified imprisonment, certain at last that Texas had no future tied to Mexico, where all life depended upon the whims of whatever one man happened to have his fist gripped tightly around the whip of government.

10

Looking back afterward, we could see that war was as certain as the rising and setting of the hot Texas sun. It didn't explode suddenly like a shell. It built gradually step by step, block by block, as methodically as you'd build a church. But the comparison is a bad one, for this war was something out of hell.

Most of us "old settlers" denied its coming as long as we could. We wanted to plow our fields and work our stock and live our lives by our own pattern, and be left alone. But it inched up like a slow-building thunderhead, and we watched it the way we'd watch a storm cloud, hoping it would go around us instead of coming head-on. It came anyway.

On the one hand was the "war party" of Texians who wanted complete separation from Mexico. Some were honest in their fever for freedom; others were only looking for a way to grab new land, or hoping independence would allow them to gain title to the land on which they already squatted.

On the other hand were venal Mexican officials,

greedy for personal riches and hungry for power, despotic not only with the Texians but also with their own people. Such men had a strong tendency to regard other people as little more than cattle, to be used for their own gain and driven and cast aside. Zacatecas and Monclova were only words to us then, but we were dimly aware that places of those names existed, deep down in Mexico, and that angry revolts had leaped to flame there. Clear up in Texas, we could smell the smoke. Santa Anna crushed those people with a red-smeared fist. Then his ruthless eyes turned northward. He had taken off his smiling mask. The sense of absolute power had gone to his brain like the fire of bad *tequila.* Now he was a stalking wolf that had gotten a taste of blood and liked it.

Mañana was an old Mexican word which translated into "tomorrow" but usually meant some dimly distant time that would never come. It was a lazy answer for the things that had not been done and might never be done.

But for Texas, *mañana* was almost here.

Ramón Hernandez had been on a trip to San Antonio de Bexar with his wife to show their baby to her parents there. She was already with child again, and soon she would not have been able to make the journey. It was no longer the dangerous trip it had once been, for Indians rarely showed themselves any more. Too many settlers had built their log cabins or their stone *casas* along the road. Still, there was always a nagging uneasiness about any traveler until he was home and safe. So I was relieved to see Ramón riding up to our field.

It had been three years since I had set foot on the Hernandez place. The *Señora* Hernandez—Ramón's mother—had gone to join the saints. I had not attended the funeral because it would have meant I would have to visit that house. I knew that just beyond the new wooden cross stood one that by now would be darkened by time and rain, a cross bearing the name *Teresa.*

On a trip to Bexar, Ramón had finally found the long-sought woman who would be the mother of his sons. Miranda was her name. She was tiny, like so many Mexican women, but she could move about like some kind of a spirit, and do work that would break the back of some larger women. What she may have lacked in being a beauty, she made up by being a good cook. Ramón had proudly brought her to our place several times before she became *preñada* and could no longer make the trip. Her meals were a feast after the bachelor cooking Muley and I had endured so long.

What mattered most, of course, was that she was good for Ramón. She could wrinkle her nose or wink her eye and melt him like a slice of butter.

Ramón's Spanish ancestors had spent their lives vainly hunting for treasure. Ramón was luckier. He had found his.

Because she was so tiny, child-bearing was difficult. There was a time when it appeared she might not live through it. But she had, and the trip to Bexar was Ramón's reward to her for delivering him a son, and for promising him another.

"What's the news in Bexar?" I asked after Ramón had slaked his thirst out of my water jug.

Ramón didn't answer me right off. He was too busy explaining to Muley why he hadn't brought Felix along, or some of the younger brothers. Muley hungered after company; he had had so little of it.

Ramón said finally, "Austin is back. It is said in Bexar that he arrived in Velasco aboard the *San Felipe*." His face creased. "It is also said that there was a battle in Velasco harbor, and the *San Felipe* captured a Mexican warship."

I felt a sudden angry impatience. "Why do they have to do it, Ramón? They play with firebrands in a powderhouse!"

Ramón waved the question away. "God made the animals to fight. It is their nature. I am afraid He made the man a little too much like He made the animals." There was acceptance in his eyes, but mixed with regret. "It is born in them. It is beyond them to be able to change the will of God."

"It's not the will of God that we go to war."

"He made men different from each other. He made them to talk different tongues and wear different-colored skins. A great many men have died for that, and that alone." He shrugged with a patience inborn in his people. "It is said that even the Colonel Austin talks now of war. It is said that even he—who always talked of peace—is saying that Texas and Mexico must free themselves of Santa Anna."

"He spent a long time in prison. A gentle man, caged up like an animal and for no good reason. It's enough to make him bitter."

"Or to make him realistic." Ramón's eyes were steady. "He is right, I think. There is far more Americans in Texas than Mexicans. Mexico has always had her Santa Annas. They run in the blood, like some disease passed down from father to son. We Mexicans expect it; we accept it. But you Americans will fight. I think you will cut free from it or die."

"If it comes to that, Ramón, what will you do?"

He gazed out across our fields of ripening cotton, our grain. He looked beyond to the cabin on the timber-lined creek. I could see the love of this land in his eyes.

Sadly he said: "Texas is my home. Yet, I am Mexican. I do not know what I will do."

Muley saw the two horsemen first. "Ramón," he called out, grinning broadly, "I thought you said Felix wasn't home. That's him comin' yonder, with Antonio."

They were riding fast. Antonio usually did; he had little regard for his horses. But somehow I could tell this time it wasn't just thoughtlessness. They rode with a purpose.

Anxiety leaped in Ramón's eyes. "Something may have happened to Miranda."

Antonio cut directly across our field, spurring his horse through our unpicked cotton and breaking down the stalks. Felix held up, starting to go around, then thought better of it and cut through after his brother. I thought, *There had better be a good reason.* I was angrier at Felix than at Antonio, for I would have expected this from Antonio any time.

Antonio pulled up. He had passed Muley without a glance. He flashed me a hostile look, then turned to Ramón. "Come, brother, it is time to fight."

Relief washed over Ramón. "Miranda is all right?"

"There is nothing wrong with your woman. But there is much wrong for your country while you stand here and talk with your *Americano* friend. It is time now for shooting, not for talking."

Ramón's eyes narrowed. "Antonio, you have been drinking."

"I do not drink when my country needs me. Fighting has begun, brother, *por allá*, in Gonzales. There has been a call for men."

Ramón's voice dropped to a whisper. "I had not heard . . ."

"You spent too much time on the road home from Bexar with your woman. You missed the news. The *Americanos* have a cannon at Gonzales, and they refuse to give it up. Against the command of Colonel Ugartechea, they have killed to keep it."

Ramón glanced at me, helplessness in his eyes.

Antonio said, "It is time to decide. Shall we bow down to this plague of locusts, or shall we offer ourselves as patriots? Felix and I have made our choice. What is yours?"

Ramón's face was stricken. "Felix? You would take Felix? He is still a boy."

"He will fight like a man!"

Ramón stepped up beside his younger brother's horse and put his hand on the boy's knee. "Felix, this is not for you."

Swallowing, Felix held his chin high.

I shouldn't have interfered, but I liked this lad too much to stand still. "Felix, you'd better listen to Ramón."

Felix would not look at me. Tightly he said, "Yesterday we were friends, Josh. Today we are enemies. I am a Mexican."

Antonio's eyes were like two black flints. "What are *you*, Ramón? The time has come to choose, and choose quickly."

Ramón shook his head. "Antonio, you are crazy."

Antonio spat in front of him. "I expected as much. Stay at home, then. Stay at home with your woman and your American friends. And when they have you in chains, remember that your brothers had the spine to fight!"

He wheeled his horse around and spurred back through our cotton. Felix paused a moment, eyes fixed on his older brother. He was wavering.

Ramón cried, "Felix, stay here."

But Felix touched spurs to the horse and went off in a lope.

And thus war reached us, even here in the far settlements on the Colorado.

I had a strong feeling now that Thomas would return. And I knew what he would be wanting.

That night Muley's dog set up a racket. Rifle in

my hand, I eased the door open. On the front step stood a familiar figure, tall and angular. "Howdy there, Josh," spoke the surveyor Jared Pounce. "Might I be a-comin' in?"

Muley grinned broadly at the sight of an old friend. I said. "Sure, Jared. Come in and we'll fix you somethin' to eat."

Jared hesitated. "Josh, I got somebody with me."

His look made me uneasy. "Bring him on in."

Thomas Buckalew halted in the open doorway. He said nothing at first. We stared at each other in silence. Three years had passed since we had stood face to face. He appeared to have aged much more than that, for his eyes were grave, his cheeks brown and lean. I could see the beginnings of a silver glint in the long hair that touched his collar. He was too young for gray, but there it was.

Muley's grin had faded to fright. "Josh," he begged, "you fellers ain't a-goin' to fight each other again, are you?"

I said, "No, Muley, we won't fight." I stared at Thomas. "You've changed."

He nodded. "So have you, Josh. Been a heap of water flowed under the bridge."

We didn't shake hands. Neither of us was ready to make the first move, so it was not made at all. Too much stood between us—the bitterness of the parting, and the long empty years since. We had moved apart like the opposite branches of a tree, still bound by the common trunk but each grown in his own direction, away from the other.

Thomas said, "You been well?"

I nodded. "You?"

"Tolerable, I reckon."

The silence was long and awakened again. At length Thomas said, "I expect you wonder why I've come, after all this time."

"I think I know. It's the war, isn't it?"

Thomas nodded, his mouth drawn into a thin, taut line. "Santa Anna's sendin' up troops from Mexico under General Cos. They'll join Ugartechea in Bexar. If they come for us, and find us scattered, it'll be the death of us all. You've heard about the fight at Gonzales?"

"I heard this afternoon."

"The call has gone out for help. We got to band together and whip them before they pick us off one by one. I'm goin', Josh. I'd like you to go with me."

"Thomas, are you sure . . ."

"I know there's been a lot come between us, Josh. I know how you feel about what I done. But we got to quit fightin' each other now and fight together. Else it's all over for the Americans in Texas."

I already knew what my answer had to be, but I dreaded giving it. "Have you seen Colonel Austin?"

He shook his head. "I've talked to people who have. Jared can tell you."

Grimly Jared Pounce said, "They treated him real bad down in Mexico. He says we got no choice any more but to fight. He's goin' to Gonzales himself."

I clinched my fist. "I've got friends who'll be on the Mexican side."

Thomas said, "In war, a man's got no friends except those who are with him."

I glanced at Muley. "I couldn't take Muley. He's got no business goin' into somethin' like this."

"Muley can stay here. There's neighbors enough now to help watch out for him. Been no Indians in a long time."

"I guess you've got other men ready to go?"

Thomas nodded. "We'll all be gatherin' over at Noonan's. We'll ride for Gonzales in the mornin'."

I turned toward the wall pegs where my old flintlock rested. With it, I had brought down more deer than I could count. Now I would use it to bring down men.

"I'll go. Give me time to gather my plunder and talk to Muley. I'll go."

A carnival spirit prevailed at Noonan's. The old rogue was boasting loud and long, telling how he had foretold this trouble the first time a Mexican soldier had shot at him, years ago. He didn't mention what he had been doing to get shot at, and nobody seemed of a mind to ask him.

"They're a bunch of yellow cowards," he declared. "They slit a man's throat when they get the upper hand on him, but they'll squeal like a pig under a gate if things go agin them. Give us fifty good men and this war'll be nothin' but a horse race—them runnin' and us chasin'. We'll all be home and plowin' our fields inside of two weeks."

Old Noonan had never plowed a field to my recollection. The only thing I'd ever known him to raise was hell.

I took my blanket and walked away from Noonan's cabin. I stretched out on the ground by his corral, where our horses were penned. Presently Thomas came out and joined me. He said nothing for awhile. He sat leaning against a post in the darkness, drawing on his pipe and savoring the home-grown tobacco.

"Josh," he said finally, "it's been a long time since . . . since that girl died. Have you got over it all right?"

I shrugged. "I can think about her now without it painin' me so, if that's what you mean. It's only that now and again I get lonesome. I get to thinkin' how things would be now if . . ." I broke off.

"There's some single girls around. You haven't found yourself one?"

"I haven't been lookin'."

"Maybe you ought to. I think you need a woman, Josh. And likely someplace there's a woman that needs you."

I didn't mean to, but somehow I let a little of the old bitterness creep into my voice. "There was one once, remember?"

Thomas said, "She was a Mexican."

I knew he hadn't changed.

11

We reached Gonzales too late to help, for the battle was over. The town's "Old Eighteen" had stalled the Mexicans for three days until reinforcements came from neighboring settlements. Then in a fog-shrouded wood on the Guadalupe, the Texians had touched fire to their cannon and watched it belch forth a load of scrap-iron balls and cut-up chain. Again and again the cannon spoke, the noise echoing and re-echoing up the river in the cool of early morning. When it fell silent, the Mexicans had gone, leaving behind them crippled animals and patches of blood.

The whole affair seemed an improbable parody now, on the face of it. I rode over to look at the cannon which had brought on the trouble. It was an ancient six-pounder mounted on oxcart wheels. In Gonzales, its main purpose had been to make noise that would scare off Indians. As a weapon of war, it wasn't much. As a cause of war, it was ridiculous.

But, of course, it hadn't actually been the cause. It

had been only the spark which had touched off the powder. The fact that Ugartechea had heavy-handedly demanded its surrender and had sent an armed group to take it had been the final indignity, the last of a long series of insults against men of strong pride. The defiant band at Gonzales had stood their ground and run up a flag with the words *Come and Take It!*

Austin had said, "A gentle breeze shakes off a ripe peach. Can it be supposed that the violent political convulsions of Mexico will not shake off Texas so soon as it is ripe enough to fall?"

With this battle won, no one was sure just what should be done next. Men and horses and mules and wagons came pouring into Gonzales, ready for war. But no one agreed just how this war was to be fought. Angry talk and fist fights erupted. A dozen men who had been leaders in their own communities wanted to command this volunteer expedition against the Mexicans. Even narrow-gauge men like Noonan saw themselves as the ones to lead the crusade.

"I been fightin' Mexicans longer than half of you have been drinkin' hard likker!" he shouted at a group of us who had declined to acknowledge his leadership. "I'll take on any one of you now. Choose your weapons—knives, guns . . . I'll even fight you with a chunk of firewood."

I'd had a bellyful of his blustering. "Shut up, Noonan, or I'll get the wind out of you and you'll shrink to where a man could stuff you in a saddlebag."

Noonan railed at me, but I knew he wouldn't fight. The Phipps boys took his side. For a while it looked as though I'd have to do battle with both of them.

Thomas stopped it, the way he had stopped scraps of mine back in Tennessee. "You-all hush up now. We're here to fight Mexicans."

Austin arrived, and just in time. The fury died quickly. Austin was the man who had put these colonies on their feet, the man who had undergone bitter personal hardship and even imprisonment for our sake. Some of the fire-eaters had long preached against him because of his peaceable ways. But now we all gathered to listen. Always in the past we had turned to Austin for counsel. We turned to him now.

Seeing him came as a shock to me. He looked much older than when I had last encountered him, that day on the road near San Felipe. His hair was graying. His face was thinner than ever before, his shoulders stooped. Those strong eyes which used to look a hole through a man were melancholy now, and tired.

"Gentlemen," he said in a voice so quiet we strained to hear it, "we have come upon a bitter time. The tyrant has torn up the good constitution of 1824 which first established us here and started us toward prosperity. He has declared that from now on we have only those rights which he chooses to confer. We have striven for peace but have been given war.

"I know there are some among you who have differed strongly with me in the past. But let us put that aside and bind ourselves together. The salvation of Texas is in our hands. And, perhaps, the salvation of all Mexico. Let us fight for the constitution of 1824."

I heard Thomas speak out. "To hell with the constitution of 1824. Let's cut ourselves loose from Mexico. We'll write our own constitution."

There were some who agreed with Thomas, but the "old settlers" dominated the crowd. Their aim was not so much independence from Mexico as simply to rid themselves of Santa Anna.

Austin was not a well man. The mark of imprisonment lay like a shadow upon him. But hardship had been his constant companion these long years in Texas. He was used to it, and he granted it no concessions.

"We can no longer retreat," he said. "The die has been cast. We must fight and win, or Santa Anna will kill us as traitors."

A council of war was set up. Though Austin protested that he knew little of military matters, he was unanimously elected the general-in-chief.

"Very well, then," he said, and regret was plain in his gentle voice, "I shall accept. And my first order is this: we march at daybreak. We march against Cos and Ugartechea. We shall go to San Antonio de Bexar."

And so we marched, our little "Volunteer Army of Texas." There were less than 400 of us at the beginning. And what an army! Our only uniform was a grim look of determination. Each man wore whatever he had, and most of us had only buckskins, darkened by long wear and smelling strongly of sweat and tobacco and smoke and rancid grease. The richer men—and they were few—wore boots or shoes. For most of us there were only moccasins. There were coonskin caps and Mexican sombreros, Kentucky longrifles and short-barreled muskets. Some men rode big, well-bred horses they had brought from the States. Most of us straddled raw Mexican ponies or mustangs, and a few rode mules.

Along the line we picked up volunteers—a pair of mustang runners here, a beehunter there. From Goliad trooped a group of dark-skinned Mexicans, stirred by reports of the bloodshed in Zacatecas and eager to join us against Santa Anna. Their arrival caused a ripple of uneasiness.

"Spies," Thomas gritted. "I never could trust a Mexican."

But they were accepted, for every gun would count.

With the group from Goliad—long called Bahía by the old settlers—came word that Texians had stormed the fortress there and had captured the Mexican troops, along with a large store of arms and ammunition left by General Cos on his march toward San Antonio. That was welcome news—as welcome as the arrival of Big Ben Milam.

I had never seen Milam before, but his name was heard often in the colonies. He was one of the "strong men" of the war party. He had agitated against Mexico for years. Only recently he had escaped from a Monterrey prison and brought news to Texas of Santa Anna's invasion preparations. A tall man, he had picked up Mexican clothing somewhere along the way to replace the filthy prison garb. And because Mexican people were usually small, the clothes he wore were short in sleeve and leg. His scarecrow looks made it hard to realize the caliber of man he really was.

Travis rode in—another name I had heard often but whose face I had never seen. Six foot tall, blond, still in his twenties, William Barret Travis was a lawyer by profession and a fighter by inclination. His name was at the top of Santa Anna's proscription list, for he had been bitterly opposed to the Mexican government almost from the minute he had set foot on Texas soil four years before.

Then came another whose name had conjured up many a legend. Jim Bowie rode into camp, leaving staring, whispering men in his wake. Fresh from Nacogdoches, he had pushed hard to get here before the fighting started. He swung down from a lithe gray mare, a big man in buckskins, that famous Bowie knife sheathed in a leather scabbard, two pistols in his belt.

I knew him on sight. There could be only one.

Bowie looked older than I had expected, older than he really was. But I knew that if even half the stories told about him were true, he had lived a fuller life than a dozen ordinary men combined. The deep lines in his face, the dark pouches under his eyes, had been gained the hard way. Bowie had tried to drown himself in whisky after cholera had swept away his Mexican wife and family. *Borrachón*, they called him. The Big Drunk.

But now here he was, a strong man still, sober and ready to fight, ready to seek redemption at the cannon's mouth.

And Austin, still an *empresario* rather than a general, and despite his past disagreements with the sentiments of Milam and Travis and Bowie, was glad to see them in camp. He was a quiet man, a builder, and here he was out of his element. But these were fighting men. Austin badly needed their help to control his volunteers. They were eating up all their corn, drinking up all their whisky, killing for beef the work oxen that had pulled the Gonzales cannon all the way to Sandy Creek, then left it there, stuck.

Austin needed the peculiar talents of these three fighting leaders, and they were glad to oblige him. This was their line of work.

Probably none of the four suspected what was to come. Shortly, every one of them would be dead.

We came to Salado Creek, about five miles from San Antonio. Scouting parties went out to reconnoiter, but Austin made no move for an immediate attack on the Mexican force. We had visits by several delegates of the Texas Consultation, which had been called so that the leaders of the various communities could decide what course the settlers would follow in their stand against Santa Anna. It seemed that with all the excitement the Consultation was having a hard time keeping a quorum.

Even Sam Houston, that towering giant of a man,

vastly able and gloriously vain, came to make us a speech. He said that right now he thought we would do better to drill and prepare ourselves than to get tied up in a death battle with the Mexicans. After all, he pointed out, we were citizen farmers, not soldiers, while San Antonio de Bexar was fortified and manned by professionals. That was largely true, though most of us knew that a big percentage of the Mexican soldiers were actually convicts, serving their prison time in uniform instead of within stone walls. Their hearts would not be in it if they came against us.

This was pretty well proven true in the battle of Concepción. Austin called for Bowie and Captain J. W. Fannin, Jr., to take a detail of 92 men and find a good camp site as near the city as possible. I missed out getting into this bunch, but Thomas was with them. He had been restless as a caged cat, lying around camp. A chance to ride—anywhere—was as welcome to him as rain on new-planted corn.

He got more than he bargained for. Bowie and Fannin selected a place near the old Concepción Mission. It being late, they camped their men there for the night. Next morning they found they had been surrounded and were outnumbered by at least four to one. When the smoke cleared, the Mexican troops were in wild retreat for town, leaving their artillery and twenty to thirty of their men behind them dead. The Texian loss: one.

Thomas came back flushed with excitement. The battle had fired his blood like raw wine. "It was beautiful!" he declared, his eyes flashing. "If we'd just been able to get word back here and have the rest of you brought up we could have finished the whole thing. Bowie said we'd have tied Cos's tail in a knot."

The way it was, the situation degenerated into a kind of Mexican standoff. We had Cos and his troops bottled up in Bexar. He couldn't get out, and no help could get in. But our leaders were skeptical about taking us into that town against the Cos cannon, against those soldiers waiting behind the heavy stone and adobe walls. We sat . . . and we sat . . . and we sat.

Sitting, I think, was worse than fighting. Time got to be more cruel an enemy than the Mexican troops who watched us from the flat roofs and the church towers.

Of course, some men always find ways to occupy themselves. There were certain of the Mexican women in town who found the fair-skinned Texians not really so terrible. Sometimes at night they would come strolling out to assure the men that they weren't really that kind of women. And some among the men were always willing to prove that they really were.

Jacob Phipps had found himself one. "I don't care if we never go in there and fight them soldiers," he told us, grinning. "I'd rather just wrestle with Guadalupe." He gripped Thomas's shoulder. "Thomas, she's got a sister. Real little *tamale*, that one. All pepper. Come with me tonight. See for yourself."

Thomas gravely shook his head. With the same hardshell pride he had always shown, he said, "I wouldn't dishonor myself. I would never pollute myself with a woman I wouldn't marry. And I wouldn't marry a Mexican."

I flinched, and he saw it. "Meanin' no offense, Josh. But it's the way I see it."

"None taken."

How could you take offense? He meant every word he said. You could get angry enough at a man like Jacob Phipps to pound his head against a wagon wheel, for he talked one way and acted another. But right or wrong, Thomas always did as he talked.

A few scattered skirmishes were fought, and finally one battle which got to be known as the Grass Fight. Bowie and a patrol of forty or so men jumped a Mexican pack train which they thought was bringing in silver to pay the soldiers. When the fight was over and the blood spilled, the packs were slashed open. There wasn't any silver. There was only grass, gathered to feed the horses.

That wasn't enough action to keep free men happy. Thomas paced restlessly in camp, a war fever burning in his eyes.

Every day the number of men became smaller and smaller. They were pulling out by ones and twos and threes, going home to see about the crops, going to comfort the wife and kids. The word we got in camp was that Austin wanted to march into the town and take it, but others were counseling against him. The longer he waited, the more desertions he suffered, the lower sagged the troops' morale.

I'll admit that if it hadn't been for Thomas I'd probably have pulled out like so many others did. I thought often about Muley all by himself out on the place, probably scared half to death. But Thomas was duty-bound to stay. All hell couldn't have pried him loose.

Word came from the Consultation. Austin was being sent to the United States to try for money and men. We didn't know it then, but he would work so hard on this mission that he would wreck his already frail health, and he would die without seeing the full fruit of his labor.

It looked as though we were going to lose the siege of San Antonio de Bexar by deterioration, rather than by battle.

On the fourth of December—two months after the cannon had spoken at Gonzales—Ben Milam walked among the discouraged men who still remained. A grim determination was in his eyes, and in the hard set of his jaw. Danger was an old acquaintance of his. They had never been far apart since the first time he had set foot in Texas nearly twenty years before.

His strong voice challenged us: "Who'll go in with Old Ben Milam into San Antonio?"

By twos and threes, by tens and twelves, men rose to their feet and reached for their rifles. Thomas spoke not a word, but he tucked the old Kentucky flintlock under his arm and felt for his shot pouch and powder horn. He glanced at me, his eyes asking the question.

"I'll come along," I said.

Commander Burleson had taken over after Austin left. He didn't like Milam's move, but he gave us the support of his artillery, dropping cannon balls into an ancient, half-ruined mission which the Mexicans had long ago turned into a fort. Cottonwoods stood around this once holy place, and around the high stone walls which surrounded it on all but a part of one side. Because of this, the mission had long since lost its church name and had become known by the Spanish word for cottonwood: *Alamo*.

There were some three hundred of us, divided into two companies. Ours was under Milam, the other under Colonel F. W. Johnson. We were outnumbered by three to one.

Six long, hard days we fought. It was toe-to-toe battle, and we moved by inches. Again and again the din of gunfire became so loud that I thought my head would explode from the pain of it. The sharp smell of gunpowder was always there, and the smoke kept my lungs afire. Now and again my hair would bristle at the death scream of a mortally wounded man on their side or ours.

The Mexican soldiers were tired and hungry and scared, but give them this: they fought like men. Surrounded, they could not run. So they stood and fought, and every inch of ground we gained was soaked by someone's blood. Crossing open streets was suicide. Rather than suffer terrible casualties by frontal assault, we bludgeoned our way toward the enemy's strongpoints by taking battering rams and plowing through the stone and adobe walls.

We moved on room by room, house by house, for most of these Mexican houses were built one against another. We would grasp the heavy poles used for rams, swing them a few times for momentum, then drive them into a wall. Sometimes women and children would scream in terror as the wall crumbled away and they stared at us through the swirling dust. Sometimes there would be Mexican soldiers in these rooms. Rifles would roar, knives would flash, clubs would swing viciously, and men would go down never to rise again.

But slowly we made our gains.

The cost was high. The third day, Ben Milam stepped out into the street, and a bullet struck him in the head. He never knew what hit him.

At last we had the crumbling old Alamo itself under our guns. Rifleshots crackled, cannons roared, and dust and gunsmoke hung heavily in the air. Our battering ram smashed through the adobe wall of a small Mexican house. For a second I glimpsed brown faces and excited black eyes before the guns flashed red and bullets went whining. For a minute it was as if we had torn open a hornet's nest. Then, all lay quiet. In the room only the dust and the smoke still moved, suction drawing them out through the gaping hole. Half a dozen of us stumbled into the room, our rifles ready to fire again. Crumpled on the floor lay five Mexican soldiers, all of them dead but one, and he mortally wounded. He cried out weakly to Holy Mary, the Mother of God. I don't know what drew my gaze to the slight figure slumped in a corner. Even before I saw the face, I felt my heart skip.

I dropped to one knee and gently turned the body over. I could tell at a touch that life was gone. A mass of blood had welled out of two holes in the front of the dirty shirt.

I knew that begrimed, crimson-smeared face.

Felix Hernandez.

I knelt there a long moment, my throat tightening as if a huge fist had clamped over it.

I heard Jared Pounce's quiet voice behind me. "Friend of yours, Josh?"

I nodded. "A kid is all he was. I've known him for years."

"Too bad," the old Texian said sympathetically. "He ought to've been on our side."

"At his age," I replied, "he oughtn't to've been on anybody's side."

I pulled at a small chain and found the crucifix Felix had been wearing around his neck. It would be the only thing of value he had on him. The family would want it for remembrance. Carefully I removed it and put it in my pocket.

"Looky yonder," I heard Jared shout. "Look at the Alamo. There's a white flag goin' up!"

I stared in disbelief, but there it was, rising to the top of a pole, the breeze catching it and flapping it wildly. The gunfire slowly died away. And in its place came the wild, jubilant shouting of the Texians.

"We've won! We've won! They're givin' up!"

Six days of hell had ended. I slumped to the dirt floor of the little house and leaned back against the adobe wall, exhausted, numb. Within reach of me lay the body of Felix Hernandez, but I couldn't bring myself to look at him again.

Why couldn't they have raised the flag an hour earlier?

I had thought I knew what it meant to be weary, but until now I never really had. I was sick of San Antonio, sick of fighting, sick of the sight and smell of blood.

A sharp chill had come. The light clothes, the single blanket were no longer enough, for this was mid-December. I stood beside Thomas as we watched Cos march out of San Antonio on the road that led south to the interior of Mexico.

With him went the remnant of his troops. In two weeks there wouldn't be a hostile Mexican soldier left in Texas.

I had looked up Antonio Hernandez among the prisoners after the battle. I had tried to tell him about Felix. He heard me—he had to—but he gave no sign of it. He refused to look at me, to answer me. His face was like something carved out of stone. He was with the troops as they moved south.

"Thomas," I said, "it's over. I'm goin' home."

Thomas shook his head. "It ain't over, Josh. It ain't hardly even begun. They'll be back, and next time there'll be more of them than there was before."

"What do you figure on doin'?"

"There's some of us that want to go down into Mexico and carry the fight to *them*. Burn their towns, spoil their land."

"Thomas, weren't the last few days enough for

you? Haven't you seen enough blood spilled to last you for a lifetime?"

Again he shook his head. "It's them or us, Josh. We're not half done fightin'."

I wrapped my blanket around my shoulders and looked off toward the Colorado. "I've had enough. I'm goin' home."

I had almost rather have taken a whipping at the hands of Santa Anna himself than to have to go to the Hernandez house with the message I carried. I took Muley with me, for he had stuck to me like a bur. Like a pup whose master has been a long time gone, he would not let me out of his sight.

We rode the familiar trail, and I dreaded the first sight of that stone house. When it came in view, I could see that very little had changed in the three years since I had been there. I reined my horse to a stop and looked at the place a long time, trying to get my courage up. Old memories came racing through my mind, memories I had forcibly buried long ago.

Muley looked at me worriedly. "How come we stopped, Josh? I thought we was goin' in."

"We're goin' in, Muley. It's the hardest thing I've ever had to do, but we're goin' in."

The dogs greeted us a hundred yards from the house and gave us a noisy escort. The younger Hernandez kids came running out, shouting joyously. I stepped down and handed the reins to Muley.

"You stay out here with the little ones, Muley. I'll go on in and do what I've got to do."

I gripped the crucifix nervously in my fist. I look a

deep breath, then walked up under the brush arbor to the front door. The door swung inward. The breath all left me.

"Teresa!"

The girl at the door stared in surprise, then slowly shook her head. "Not Teresa. It's been a long time since we've seen each other, Josh Buckalew. Don't you know me?"

It was a minute before the shock left me so that I could answer. "María?"

"Yes, I am María. I've changed since you saw me last. You've changed too, Josh."

I could tell that in some ways she looked like her sister, and in other ways she didn't. The swift first impression had brought the image of Teresa back to me. María was not quite so tall. She was pretty, but she didn't have quite the fragile beauty of Teresa. María looked stronger, surer of herself. I doubted there was anything fragile about her.

"The wind is sharp outside, Josh. Come into the house."

I found myself trembling a little. "I'm sorry if I look like a fool. It's just that, for a second or two, you gave me an awful start."

"I would never take you for a fool, Josh. Please, come on in."

I followed her. Now Miranda came out of the kitchen, drying her hands. On her tiny frame her pregnancy was showing strongly now. It wouldn't be many months before Ramón would have another son—or a daughter.

"Josh Buckalew," Miranda smiled, "this is a

surprise. After all these years, you've finally come to see us. I thought you were off to war."

"I was. Fighting is over now. I'm home again."

The two women looked quietly at each other. "It is over?" María said. "Then perhaps Antonio and Felix will be coming home."

My fist tightened on the crucifix. "Miranda, where's Ramón?"

"He rode out to find a horse. He should be home in a little while."

María pulled out a leather-bottomed chair. "Please, Josh, sit down. Tell us about the fighting. Was it terrible? Were you wounded?"

Gratefully I took the chair. I looked at the dirt floor. "Yes, it was terrible. No, I was not even scratched."

"And it is over now? All the men will be home?"

I shook my head. "Not all the men."

It seemed an eternity before Ramón finally came. I had to keep answering the women's questions while trying not to let them see in my eyes or sense in my voice the message I had come to give them. When I could, I stole glances at María. She was a woman now, not a girl.

At last Ramón came. I gathered all my courage and told them about Felix, and Antonio. I held out my hand with the crucifix in it. I saw María's eyes flood with tears before she turned away and buried her face against a white-plastered wall. Miranda clutched Ramón's arm as he took the crucifix from my hand and tenderly ran his fingers over the raised figure.

"I wish there was something I could say, Ramón, besides that I'm sorry."

Ramón's voice was brittle. He did not look into my face. "Thank you, Josh, for coming and telling us. Now, please, I would like you to go."

12

Muley and I finished the scrapping that was left on the little bit of cotton he had not already picked. Later we planted a crop of wheat for spring harvest. It seemed there was always too much work to do.

We saw nothing of Ramón Hernandez. I dreaded any return to his place, and he evidently felt no wish to visit us. I could imagine his heavy sense of loss and knew it was not unreasonable to assume that he attached blame to me. I had been part of the attacking force.

The war news we received was scant and mostly contradictory but strong rumors kept drifting in that Santa Anna was gathering an army in Saltillo. How large it would be was something we could only guess at. Many Texians were not prone to worry, for they felt sure one American could whip ten Mexicans. After San Antonio, I didn't believe this—if I ever had.

In any case, no one thought Santa Anna would start north before spring. We all figured it would be late March or even April at the earliest before his troops would wet their feet in the Rio Grande.

In the meantime, precious little was being done to get Texas ready. Wrangling in the provisional government left it impotent. Personal feuds and jealousies kept it going in futile circles. Our Texas army was small and badly scattered, ill-disciplined and ill-equipped. Worse, its officers were quarreling among themselves just as the officials of the government were doing in San Felipe. Sam Houston had the command—on paper—but not many of the subordinate officers paid much attention to him. The command was splintered.

It was at this time that Travis, sharing a command with Bowie in San Antonio, wrote to Governor Smith that the people were "cold and indifferent . . . and in consequence of the dissensions between contending and rival chieftains they have lost confidence in their own government and officers." He added with disgust: "The thunder of the enemy's cannon and the pollution of their wives and daughters—the cries of their famished children and the smoke of their burning dwellings only will arouse them."

And that was the way things stood when Santa Anna's advance guard crossed the Rio Grande on the twelfth of February, six weeks to two months earlier than anyone really expected.

He caught us scattered, quarreling, and totally unprepared.

The first word of Santa Anna's advance was much worse than I had any idea it would be.

It was brought by red-faced old Alfred Noonan. Though any Mexican pursuit had been left days behind him, he spurred into our yard as if Santa Anna were reaching for his shirttail.

"Josh Buckalew!" he shouted. "You better go see about your brother!"

I never had felt any respect for the old man, and after the battle of San Antonio I had only contempt. I couldn't remember ever seeing him at any time when the action was heavy. Only when the conflict was over did he present himself, and then he was blustering and posturing as if he had won the battle by himself.

I walked out into the yard to meet him now. I didn't want to offer him any favors, but I could tell that his mount had been badly used. I pointed down toward the creek.

"Muley, go water Noonan's horse for him, will you?"

Noonan stepped down and handed the reins to Muley. "Much obliged." Noonan's face was flushed even more than usual, his eyes bloodshot.

"Now," I said, "what's this about Thomas?"

Noonan swung his arms in a wide gesture. "Old Santy Anna's done crossed into Texas with the biggest bunch of Mexicans that you ever saw in your whole life. He's acomin', Josh. There ain't nothin' goin' to stop him but the good Lord Hisself, and the way things are goin' He must be busy someplace else."

"What about Thomas?"

"Boy, I'm afeered your brother is wounded. Maybe

dead. There was a scrap down on the Rio Grande. A little bunch of our boys got caught by them Mexicans. It was like a panther pouncin' on a mouse. Most of our boys got theirselves kilt. Thomas was with that bunch."

Ice touched the pit of my stomach.

"You sure, Noonan? You're not just scared and excited?"

"They was down there, him and the Phipps boys and some others. Was all fixin' to go and raid Matamoros, but the orders never did come through. So they stayed down there and watched along the river. I was supposed to've been with them, only somethin' else come up."

Bet your life it did, I thought darkly. You hid.

"Jacob Phipps come back, shot in the arm. He said he seen his brother Ezekiel get his head blowed off. The last he seen of Thomas, he was ridin' off into the dust and the smoke to where the big shootin' was. There was an awful scatteration after that. A few of the boys like Jacob come a-limpin' back. Most of the others never did. Far as I know, Thomas didn't."

"As far as you *know*?" I grabbed him by the shirtfront. "Didn't you try to find out?"

"Boy, them Mexicans was acomin'! I'm tellin' you, they wasn't like any Mexicans I ever saw. They was thousands of them, and they was lookin' for blood!"

The terror of it was still naked in his eyes. I realized the old fraud couldn't help himself. Like many a big talker, he had feet of clay. I let go of him and stepped back, my heart sinking.

"If Thomas did come back, Noonan, where would he most likely be?"

Noonan shrugged. "Hard to say. Maybe Bexar, where Travis and Bowie are at. Maybe Goliad, because Fannin is there, and we was sort of under Fannin's command there towards the last."

I clenched my fists. For a moment hopelessness swept over me. Surely Thomas was dead.

And yet again, he might have gotten out.

I knew what Noonan's answer would be before I ever asked him. "You want to go back and help me look for him?"

Noonan shook his head violently. "No, sir, thank you. I had enough Mexicans to do me for the rest of my life. I'm takin' the Sabine chute!" That was a way of saying he was heading for the Sabine River and the safety of the United States.

"You got a farm here," I pointed.

"Old Santy Anna can just have it back."

I was too numb to offer him anything to eat, and he was in too much of a hurry to have accepted it. Soon as Muley brought his horse back, Noonan spurred away. I leaned my shoulder against the log cabin and stood there weakly, watching him disappear over the hill.

"Muley," I said, "I got to leave you again."

Muley cried and begged me like a little boy. But I had no choice except to leave him here. I couldn't take him with me into God knew what.

"Muley, you listen to me, and listen tight. There's no tellin' when I may get back. If the Mexicans come—and they may—don't let yourself get caught by them. You run. Take the best horse we got and run just as fast as you can. If you have to cross the Sabine, you do it, and don't stop to look back. When this is all over, I'll come find you."

"Josh," he cried, "I don't know what I'd do if you was not to come back."

A lump came in my throat. I wasn't sure either what would ever become of Muley. Alone, he would be as helpless as a child.

"I'll come back."

"You promise, Josh? You promise you'll come back?" His eyes brimmed with tears.

"I promise, Muley. Now you take good care of things while I'm gone. And remember what I said. Watch sharp. Don't let the Mexicans find you here."

It was now past the middle of February. Riding for San Antonio de Bexar, I found people still not certain what to do. Some were packing their belongings and getting ready to head east. A few were already on the road. But most were waiting, still hopeful that the Texian forces could turn back the assault.

I rode into Bexar a little less than three months after I had left it. The city still showed all the scars of the awful battle, many of the stone and adobe houses caved in, gaping holes knocked in their sides by cannon balls or battering rams. I rode along the main street and found to my amazement that despite the dozens of rumors that Santa Anna's column was not far from the city, business still went on more or less as usual. Most of the stores were open, peddling whatever stocks they still had after the December disaster.

I rode up to the high old stone walls of the Alamo and found them fortified. If it came to the point of making a stand, I thought, Travis would probably pull his men into the mission. Its enclosure was big and rambling, containing more than two whole acres. In that respect it would be hard to defend with a small force. There was an alternative: the Concepción Mission, where Bowie's men had first come into conflict with the Cos troops back in November. But Concepción was outside of the city. The Alamo was the more likely choice.

A familiar voice called my name, and I looked up at the wall. There stood the tall, stooped figure of Jared Pounce.

"Howdy, Josh!" the old surveyor shouted. "You come to help us fight Santy Anna?"

I waved back at him and pointed to the open front gate. Jared climbed down and met me there as I rode in. We clasped hands. "Jared, you're lookin' good. To me, you always look good."

He smiled. Somehow I could tell he hadn't been smiling much. "Then I look better than I feel." His smile gradually left him. "I reckon you know what's comin', Josh."

"I've heard rumors. All of them bad." I grasped his arm. "Jared, is Thomas here?"

He shook his head. "No, is he supposed to be?"

I knew I shouldn't feel disappointed. I hadn't really expected to find Thomas in Bexar. But the disappointment was there, just the same. I told

Jared what Noonan had told me. Jared listened solemnly.

"Josh, I think you better make up your mind to accept it. Thomas is likely dead."

"There's still the shadow of a doubt, Jared. I can't stop lookin' till I know for sure."

"I was hopin' you'd stay here with us. We'll be needin' all the men we can get."

A short way along the wall I watched Travis supervising the building of an embankment for emplacement of a cannon. The strain of command had left its mark. He was impatient and snappish with the men doing the work.

Jared said dryly, "He's tryin'. But he's fussin' with the wrong men. The ones he needs to crack the whip over are out in town, enjoyin' theirselves. Seems like the men are ready to fight and die with him, but they ain't willin' to follow his orders."

Across the courtyard came big Jim Bowie, walking unsteadily.

"Drunk?" I asked Jared.

"He's been drinkin' a little. Mostly he's just sick. Needs to be in bed. He and Travis don't get along, but they have to put up with each other. Half the men here won't listen to anybody except Bowie."

Travis and Bowie fell to arguing almost as soon as Bowie reached the embankment. They were too different to be able to get along. Travis was a gentleman born. Bowie had acquired the manner of a gentleman, but he had come up in a rough-and-tumble world of brawling and dueling and wild adventuring. Beneath the polish he was still a backwoods-man.

Their quarreling would soon end, for the enemy was almost at the gates. Then they would stand together, shoulder to shoulder, and leave the world a legend that would never die.

Jared Pounce shook hands with me again at the open gate of the old mission. He said again, "I wish you was stayin'."

"I can't. I expect I'll go next to Goliad. Thomas could be there."

"If you don't find him, come back. The Alamo walls are high and stout."

None of us had a premonition then of what would so shortly come to pass. I did remember, though, that one reason General Cos had surrendered his Mexican troops to us in December was that he considered the Alamo indefensible.

Even now, most of the old Texians were not thinking in terms of independence. They were thinking only of defeating the despot Santa Anna and getting a fair shake from the Mexican government.

Jared said, "Josh, I been doin' a lot of thinkin' lately about what I'm goin' to do when the fightin' is over. You remember, it was me that showed you the place that you boys settled."

"I remember."

"There's still some land close by open for settlement. I think when we get the shootin' finished and square ourselves with Mexico, I'll take up some land out there and be neighbors with you. I always did like that country along the Colorado."

"We'll look forward to it, Jared."

I glanced back once as I rode away and caught a last look at the lean old man there by the front of the Alamo. I would never forget it.

The road from San Antonio to Goliad roughly paralleled the San Antonio River. I set out from the city without delay, for I had a strong feeling there wasn't much time. And there wasn't. Not far from San Antonio my horse suddenly pricked up its ears. It turned its head a little to the right, and I glanced in that direction. I saw horsemen, ten or fifteen of them. Texians, I thought, on their way to join Travis's garrison. Then I caught a glimpse of blue, and I knew. These were Mexican cavalrymen.

They saw me about the same time I saw them. There was no point in trying to do battle with that many men, even if I had had the inclination, which I didn't. It was a horserace for awhile. But eventually I lost them somewhere in the timber.

So they were here. I had been lucky in running into this bunch, then getting away. I was still alive, and free. At least now I knew I had to be alert.

I knew I would have to do a lot of hard riding and very little resting until I reached Goliad.

I learned something else, too. The lesson was abrupt and unexpected. I rode up to a Mexican house, expecting to ask for a fresh drink of water, for this was a place where the trail had dropped back away from the river. What I got was a blast from an old *escopeta* in the hands of a Mexican farmer. He missed me, but he taught me that from now on I had to avoid habitations.

A good percentage of the Mexican people in Texas disliked Santa Anna. But he had proclaimed this a holy war, Mexican against American. It was, he said, a racial war, dark skins against the light. Other matters of politics were put aside for the duration of this crusade. A great many of the Mexican people who otherwise opposed him accepted this at face value because they basically disliked Americans even more than they disliked the little Napoleon of the West. Now that Mexican troops were in the country again, I could not afford to trust any Mexican—civilian or soldier.

From this point on, I moved carefully, leaving the road and skirting any houses I came to.

The old presidio at Bahia, generally known as Goliad by the time of the Texas revolution, had changed hands often, usually with violence. It had been a pawn in the Mexican war of independence against Spain. Its grounds had been tramped by the boots of filibusters. Last October it had been wrested from the Mexicans by Collinsworth and Milam. Now it was probably the chief Texian stronghold, for James W. Fannin had between four and five hundred volunteers quartered there.

The town had once held a thousand or so inhabitants, but now most of its brush *jacales* and its mud and stone houses stood empty. The Mexican people had withdrawn from this place of contention to the comparative safety of the *ranchos* down the river. A scattering of abandoned mongrel dogs roamed its deserted streets, hunting for enough food to keep themselves alive. Cattle blundered in and out of the doorless dwellings, some of which had already caved in.

Built on solid rock atop a hill stood the presidio itself, its thick stone-and-lime walls weathered to an oppressive gray by the long years. A chapel stood in the northwest corner, fronted by an artillery emplacement. The parade grounds were all enclosed by high stone walls which ran south and east from the chapel. This was the finest fort the Spaniards had ever built in Texas, for it straddled an important road from Nacogdoches to the interior of Mexico, and it was also near the sea. If there was a fort which could hold out against Santa Anna, I thought, this would be it.

Soldiers stood along the walls and out in front. One patrol stopped me briefly but quickly let me go.

Riding into the fort, I was struck by the fact that most of these men were not actually Texians. A majority were volunteers fresh in from various Southern states. Something else struck me, too—the strong faith in these men that they could whip anything that came along.

"Bring any Mexicans with you?" somebody shouted at me. "We're ready for a fight."

I explained my mission and was taken directly to Colonel Fannin. He didn't give me time at first to ask about Thomas. He insisted on hearing how things stood in San Antonio, and back in the settlements.

I told him San Antonio had still been open when I had left there. Then I told him about running into Mexican cavalry. His face creased. He paced, his hands behind him.

"How many did you see?"

"Just a patrol, ten or fifteen."

"You saw no others? You saw no columns?"

"Nothin' but that patrol. Other than that, all I can tell you is the rumors I've heard. You've likely heard those already."

He frowned. "A hundred of them, and no two alike. We are in darkness here. We don't know what's going on to the south. For that matter, we know very little that's going on to the north and east. We're isolated. Sometimes I think they've all forgotten us."

"I doubt that's so, sir. One story I've heard is that a lot of men are gatherin' in Gonzales. Buildin' up an army. I expect General Houston will take command of them if it's true. And they'll most likely be marchin' in this direction."

Fannin still paced. "I hope so. Meanwhile I wish they'd let me know what's going on. I wish I could tell just what to do."

I told him it looked to me like this fort was situated to stand off a big siege.

Fannin nodded briskly. "You know how Mexicans fight. It'll take a lot of them to dislodge us. We'll never give up the ship while there is a pea left in the dish."

I nodded agreement, but it occurred to me he was overconfident, like his men appeared to be. The Mexican troops he had seen so far had seemed amateurish and even comical to his West Point-trained eyes. He was downgrading them too much. That could be a costly mistake.

"Colonel," I said, "I've come looking for my brother. I wondered if he might be here."

I explained to him what Noonan had told me. Fannin went to his duty rosters and slowly ran his fingers down the pages, shaking his head as he came to the bottom of each one.

A chill passed through me. I knew before he had finished what his answer had to be. "I'm sorry, there doesn't seem to be a Buckalew listed here anywhere."

I swallowed. "Colonel, does what Noonan said sound like anything you've heard of? Do you know of any scrap that fits the description?"

Fannin rubbed the back of his neck.

"Our reports from down that way have been very sketchy, Buckalew. There could have been a dozen engagements and we wouldn't have heard of them." He turned to a big Texas map which had been pegged to his wall. His finger sought out Goliad. "Now, it's possible your brother could be attached to Johnson's force at San Patricio." His finger dropped south on the map. "It is highly probable that Johnson would be keeping patrols out south of San Patricio, possibly all the way to the Rio Grande. And, if the Mexicans have crossed in force, it is likely that some of these patrols have made contact with them. Violent contact." He turned and faced me. "If you're going that way, I hope you find him alive. And, Buckalew," he paused, "if you find out what the Mexicans are up to, find a way to get the information to me."

"I'll do what I can, sir." I left him then and started for San Patricio.

13

It was all strange country to me, for I had never been in this part of Texas before. This was the coastal region. When the wind was out of the east I could smell the Gulf, or fooled myself into thinking I did.

I wasn't interested in seeing the country, though. My immediate concern was to get to San Patricio without falling into Mexican hands. I followed the trail, for without it I wouldn't know the way. But as on the road to Goliad, I took pains to skirt around any Mexican dwellings.

I came at last to a house that was plainly American-built. Here, at least, I would be welcome. I rode up to it boldly.

That turned out to be a grievous mistake. A Mexican civilian stepped into the yard, a blunderbuss in his hand, and fired at me without so much as a howdy-do. I wheeled the horse around and spurred away, thankful for fast horses and poor Mexican marksmanship.

That was my second such experience. Santa Anna's

race war idea had taken hold. I knew now I would have to live by Thomas's old credo: never trust a Mexican.

There were creeks along the way: Blanco, Medio, and some that weren't named on the map one of the Goliad officers had sketched for me. The rations I'd carried with me from Goliad gave out and I ate dry bread until I came across a fat cow, caught, and butchered her. Taking some of a hindquarter, I rode a long way before daring to stop and cook the meat.

I had lost count of time, but I knew it was the last of February or first of March when I ran into the three stragglers.

They could have been Mexicans, for all I knew. I drew off the trail and into a clump of timber, covering my horse's nose with my hand, hoping they hadn't seen me. My rifle was cradled in my arm, ready. The horsemen came directly toward me, one slumped forward, another helping hold him in the saddle.

Their horses sensed mine. One of them nickered. Instantly two of the men slid off onto the ground, thrusting their rifle barrels up over their saddles. They could have been either Mexican or American. I held my breath and brought my rifle to rest across the branch of a tree. My hand tightened on the stock.

One of the men shouted, "Grab Bill. He's fallin' off."

The man who had been slumped was sliding out of the saddle.

The voice had been enough. They were American. I shouted, "It's all right. I'm a Texian." They still didn't trust me. I led my horse out of the timber and dropped the rifle down to arm's length to show I wasn't hostile. The two men on their feet still kept their rifles pointed at me. I saw that one—a man with red hair and a tangled red beard—was holding his leg out stiffly. A dried crimson spot showed on the dirty cloth wrapped around the leg. The wounded man in the saddle had a gray coat bundled around him, one sleeve dangling empty. Bloodstains showed he had been shot deep in the shoulder.

"It's all right," I repeated. "I come from Goliad."

They lowered their rifles. One said, "Lord, it's sure good to see a friendly face. I hope to God you got somethin' with you a man could eat. And maybe a little water? Bill here is burnin' up with fever."

I helped them lower the wounded man to the grass and brought my canteen. While I carefully doled out water to the one named Bill, the other two hungrily tore into what was left of the beef.

"It's been much hidin', little water, and no rations for us since them Mexicans hit us at San Patricio," one man said, his jaw bulging.

I looked up sharply. "San Patricio?"

"They came on us unexpectedly. Killed nearly every man. I never thought there was so many Mexicans."

"I was on my way to San Patricio. Lookin' for my brother."

"Mister, if he was there, I expect he's dead."

"His name is Thomas Buckalew. Do you know him?"

The man frowned, thinking. "Buckalew? I don't believe I recollect such a name as that. There wasn't no Buckalew at San Patricio, was there, Red?"

The red-bearded one stopped chewing. His lips moved as he formed the name quietly to himself. Then he said, "I seem to remember there *was* a Buckalew, but not at San Patricio. He was south, with a patrol that worked down all the way to the Rio Grande."

Excitement began to build in me. "Where would he be now?"

Red shook his head. "In heaven, I expect, or in hell. Most of the boys down on the river were killed by the first Mexicans that crossed over."

"Did you see anybody who said they saw him die?"

"No, but there was only a handful came out alive."

I looked south, my eyes narrowed. "He could be down there someplace hidin' out, maybe wounded. I might be able to find him."

The bigger of the two men said. "You'd be throwin' your life away to try. You know that country down there? Ever been there before?"

I told him I hadn't.

"Well, there's nothin' down there now but Mexicans, thousands of them. They caught even the boys that knew the country. You would go down like a rabbit in a wolf's den."

It took me a long time to decide to turn back north with these three battle survivors. I could think of a dozen reasons why I should go on south, but these man had an answer for every one of them. They stressed that it was unlikely Thomas could still be alive. That I could find him was even more unlikely. And to fall into a Mexican trap was almost certain death, for Santa Anna's orders were to kill.

"I seen one boy that lost his horse throw his hands up and try to surrender," said Red. "They shot him to pieces."

"That's why you got to go back with us," argued the other, named Jimson. "You got no chance atall. And besides, we need help with Bill."

My jaw went tight when I looked down at the worst wounded of the three. He wouldn't live to reach Goliad. That bullet had been in him too deep, and too long.

So when all the talking was done I had to turn my back on Thomas and San Patricio. I had to accept the probability that Thomas had fallen with the others, and that even if he hadn't, there was nothing I could do for him.

Only three of us lasted to reach Goliad. We scratched out a shallow grave for Bill and left him near Blanco Creek. We led his horse on in. At a time like this, horses would be worth more than gold.

Nobody paid much attention to me, for hardly anyone in the fort at Goliad knew me anyway. Most of them hadn't been in Texas more than a few weeks. They were volunteers from the States, for the most part, come to whip the breeches off a bunch of dirty Mexicans. Besides, I hadn't been in any of the recent fighting. But the men thronged around Red and Jimson, eager for details of the battle.

"Battle, hell," Red snorted, favoring his leg. "It wasn't no battle. It was slaughter."

Colonel Fannin sent for us as soon as he heard. We found him in his quarters, worriedly studying a map. He frowned at me. "Aren't you the man who was here looking for his brother?" I said I was, and that I hadn't found him. Fannin nodded sympathetically, as if he had known all along that I wouldn't. He turned gravely to Red and Jimson. "I've already had the bad news from San Patricio. But I'd like to hear it from your viewpoint."

They gave it to him briefly and simply. They didn't have to embellish it any, for the truth was bad enough. Fannin questioned them closely about the Mexican strength. They could only guess, for like the field soldier anywhere, their knowledge of the war was limited to what went on in front of them. The war, to them, was whatever their own part of the battle had been. And for Red and Jimson, it had been bitter.

Fannin said, "There weren't enough of you, and you had no position of strength. So, the Mexicans took you. Here we have one of the best fortifications in Texas, and adequate men to defend it. When they get here, we'll stop them cold. I can use you men—all three of you—if you'd care to stay."

Red gingerly touched his leg. "I'm tired of ridin' with this. I'd sure admire to rest. And I doubt there's a safer place anywhere than Goliad." Jimson agreed. Fannin looked at me.

I nodded, grimly accepting what had to be the truth. "I'll take up where my brother left off. And here is as good a place as any to turn and fight."

So, without ceremony, we were marched into Fannin's command of volunteers inside that gray, grim stone fortress on the hill.

Fannin believed in drill, and he tried to carry it out in West Point style. It honed the discipline of a military command to a fine edge, he said. We were well honed, for we had several hours of it every day. Some of the volunteers complained that they had come all the way from Georgia and Kentucky and Tennessee to fight, not to drill. They drilled anyway. And when we weren't drilling, we were busy strengthening the rock walls, building new emplacements for artillery.

I was at the gate the day a courier came downriver from the direction of San Antonio and spurred up the hill on a worn-out horse. Stiff and weary, he almost fell from his mount as he reined to a stop. I helped grab him. On his feet, he leaned back on the sweat-lathered animal.

"Colonel Fannin," he gasped. "Message for Colonel Fannin."

I said, "We'll take you to him. Where did you come from?"

"From San Antonio de Bexar. The Mexicans have gotten there."

"How bad is it?" somebody asked.

"Bad. Travis, Bowie, and the others, they're forted up in the old Alamo. Travis sent me to fetch help."

We took him to Fannin's quarters. The courier braced himself with a strong shot of whisky while Fannin read the message from Travis, his brow furrowed. At length he said.

"My last orders were to hold Goliad. If I split my

force to go to Bexar, I would jeopardize our position here."

The courier argued, "They're goin' to need help if they hold the Alamo."

Fannin's sense of futility showed plainly as he turned and looked at his map. He ran his finger along the road from Goliad to San Antonio de Bexar. "Ninety miles to San Antonio. Even with a forced march it would take us time to get there if we took the equipment we need." He rubbed his hand across his face. "I wish to God I knew what to do."

I thought he was going to make a decision, but he didn't. He said he needed time to think. He ordered us to leave while he continued to talk with the courier.

Later, Fannin made his decision. Against his better judgment he ordered us to prepare for a forced march to the relief of the Bexar garrison. We hadn't gotten far before we had a breakdown. Still not certain he had done right, Fannin was discouraged. Somewhere to the south—and probably not far—was a strong Mexican force. If it caught us on the road, we might have a hard time fighting through. The officers counseled.

Fannin reversed his decision. The order came to retreat to Goliad. It was a foregone conclusion now that the Alamo would not stand. Better to stay together and hold Goliad, Fannin declared, than to risk the loss of all.

So James Bonham, the courier, disregarded the admonitions of all around him and spurred once again toward San Antonio to carry the bad news to Travis:

Fannin wasn't coming. He could have stayed. To return was death, and he knew it. But he went.

It was a cold grim, gray day when the expected news came from San Antonio. The Alamo had been overwhelmed. The garrison had been slaughtered to the last man.

Even expected, it was a staggering thing. Travis, Bowie, Crockett, Bonham, and all those others . . . men we had fought beside, men we had eaten with and drunk with.

And for me there had been someone special, old Jared Pounce.

A pall of gloom descended upon the garrison at Goliad.

Yet the strange thing was that few really thought it could happen to *us*. Not here at Goliad. When the Mexicans came we'd show them how Americans could fight. We'd repay them for the Alamo.

What began to break our back was the division of our forces. Word came from the village of Refugio, some thirty miles east toward the Gulf, that families there wanted to leave and needed an escort. Fannin sent Captain King of the Georgia Battalion and a company of twenty-three men. Reaching Refugio, they found themselves hard pressed by Mexican cavalry. They took cover in an old mission. A messenger managed to break through the Mexican lines and reach Goliad. This time Fannin sent out Colonel Ward with the Georgia Battalion of about a hundred and fifty men to relieve King.

We didn't know it then, but these men would never come back. We expected their return at almost any time. But a day passed, two days, and still no word.

Then came a courier from Sam Houston, bearing orders to Fannin that we abandon Goliad and retreat to Victoria, to the area of heavier American settlement.

Had we followed the orders when they arrived, things might have turned out differently. But Ward and King were still out. We couldn't just abandon them. We were told that Fannin was restlessly pacing the floor of his quarters, trying to decide what to do. He was between a rock and a hard place, between military obligation to his commanding officer and the moral obligation he felt toward the men he had sent out and had not heard from.

So again we waited . . . one day, two days, three days.

The Mexicans weren't waiting.

At last Fannin found out for certain what we had all begun to feel in our bones: Ward and King and their commands had been taken.

Fannin gave the order to prepare for evacuation. We worked through the night packing up and getting ready to be on the move. We mounted the artillery that we could transport. The heavy artillery, we spiked. The rest we dumped into the trenches we had sweated so hard to dig, and we covered them up. We set fire to everything that would burn.

With daylight we set forth into heavy fog on the road to Victoria, two hundred and fifty or so men afoot, about twenty-five a-horseback, a company of artillery, nine small pieces of ordnance, and a mortar, all drawn by oxen. Because I had a horse, I was attached to Colonel Horton's scouts. We rode ahead to the ford on the San Antonio River, half expecting attack there, for we had seen Mexicans and had even had a scrap with a Mexican patrol. The attack didn't come, but the largest cannon stuck in the river. We lost an hour pulling it out of the mud.

In all the bustle, nobody had thought to feed the oxen. They were hungry and contrary. All in all, it started out to be a hard day.

We were well across the prairie about ten miles from Goliad, and the oxen were still giving trouble. Ahead of us lay Coleto Creek and a heavy stand of timber. But we came across a patch of new grass in an area that had been burned over by the prairie fire. Fannin decided we had better rest and graze the oxen, or they might never get us to the timber. So another order went down the line: stop and unyoke.

I didn't like it, but nobody asked me. Somewhere—not far away—there had to be a large force of Mexicans. We had seen enough of their patrols to have no doubt about it. Even so, few of the men seemed overly worried. There was still that powerful conviction of our own superiority. Most of them agreed we couldn't be beaten by a ragtag bunch of greasy Mexicans.

Our scouting group went out to look around while the command rested. We didn't go far, and we didn't see anything. When we returned, the oxen were yoked again and the march resumed.

We could camp when we reached the timber, the officers agreed.

We never made it. A vague dark line began moving up in timber to the south of us. As it detached itself from the timber, we saw that the line was made of horsemen, and many of them. We looked back. Behind us came another line. Both lines approached rapidly and began spreading out.

"My God," Jimson shouted, "there are thousands of them!"

There weren't, but there were enough to take a man's breath away. We began crowding the oxen, struggling to make the timber.

Colonel Horton shouted an order. One of the six-pounders was quickly unlimbered. A shot was fired at the horsemen, and another, and another.

"That'll scare them off," the colonel said hopefully.

But all three rounds fell short. The Mexicans kept coming.

Our rear guard came galloping up. We pushed on a little farther. The ammunition cart broke down. We lost time while men transferred the load. By then the Mexican cavalrymen had circled around to the front of us. They had cut us off from the timber.

"Circle up, men!" Fannin shouted. "Circle up!"

Some of the volunteers began firing their rifles, but the range was still much too long. Fannin ordered the shooting to stop. No use wasting powder and lead. We formed a hollow square, facing our artillery outward to fire on the enemy from whatever direction they might come.

Now we could make out the horsemen distinctly. We could see the flying pennants. We could hear bugles in the chill of the March air.

They sounded what must have been the charge. The Mexican cavalry spurred toward us from three directions. Our artillery opened up with grape and cannister shot. We could see horses and men go down. The Mexicans kept coming, right into the range of our rifles and muskets. We began to fire, timing ourselves by ranks so that one group was in position to shoot while another was loading. Great gaps were blasted through the Mexican ranks. Still, on they came.

Their forward riders were upon the square itself when the rapid and deadly fire of our volunteers stopped them. The Mexicans reeled back, loose horses running wild, stirrups flapping . . . wounded horses threshing and screaming. Mexicans afoot looked around desperately for comrades to pick them up. Some were abandoned and fell under the Texian fire.

While the Mexicans pulled back, we reloaded and surveyed our own damage. It was heavy. We had already lost most of our horses and oxen. We had several men killed and a number wounded.

To my dismay I found that the man named Red lay lifeless behind one of the cannons, a gaping hole in his chest. He had taken a bullet through the leg at San Patricio but had survived to rejoice that Goliad would be safe for him. Now he was dead. The irony of it was bitter.

Before this was over, he would turn out to be the lucky one.

Overconfidence appeared to curse both sides. The Mexicans evidently had expected to sweep over us with ease. The steel-coated resistance of these volunteers had come as a deadly surprise. They feinted at us several times, but they kept falling back as soon as they reached rifle range. They quit trying to charge and set up a constant fire of muskets and *escopetas*. We answered their fire. Some of the Mexicans began crawling toward us, hiding in the tall dry grass. But a lot of our volunteers were crack riflemen. Any time they saw enough of a man to draw a bead on, they usually hit their mark. The Mexican losses were heavy.

The fire continued until nightfall. Then the enemy withdrew to the timber. That gave us time to look around and consider our situation. The longer we looked, the less we liked it.

Ahead of us, so near and yet so far away, stood the timber we had been trying for. Once in it, we could take advantage of its cover and stand off a force several times our size. Out here in this open prairie, we were paralyzed.

But how could we ever reach the timber now? In the growing darkness we could see the wink of Mexican campfires around us. Our teams were gone, either stampeded by the gunfire or killed by it. The officers took tally and found that we had seven men dead, sixty wounded. A majority of these wounded would be unable to walk.

Among the wounded was Fannin himself. He had taken a rifle ball in the thigh.

What water we had with us was gone. Most of

the ammunition for our cannons was used up. Food supplies were scanty, for the officers had felt confident we would reach Victoria and had not wanted to overload the wagons.

Now night fell upon us, cold and terribly dark. I still had my blanket, but I found that many of the men had dropped theirs when the fighting started. Now they were without. I tucked my blanket around a wounded man who lay shivering from the cold. He cried for water, but I had none.

Fannin called the men around him. Calmly he outlined the seriousness of our situation, something most of the men had become painfully aware of already.

"We still have a chance," he said, "to reach Coleto Creek and the timber. The darkness will help cover us. And I think that if we run into Mexican troops we can fight our way through. But we'll have to go afoot and there are many among our wounded who cannot walk. We can go, and we can reach safety. But if we go, we'll have to leave those who cannot make the journey afoot."

Someone said, "Colonel, what will the Mexicans do to the men we leave?"

Fannin minced no words. "You all heard the report that came to us about the few of Captain King's men who surrendered at Refugio. They were taken out and shot."

"That means," the soldier declared, "they'll probably shoot anybody we leave behind."

Fannin said, "That is the way it appears to me. We can save ourselves by leaving the badly wounded behind to die. Or, we can stay with them and all take our chance together. I won't command you to do either. I'll leave it up to you men to take a vote."

There was a minute or so of hushed conversation among the men. Almost every one of them had a close friend or relative among the wounded. The decision was unanimous.

"Very well," said Fannin, and I could tell that he approved the decision. "We'll stay. We'll build whatever fortifications we can during the night. And then we'll see what the morning will bring."

14

The night was long and black and cold. The groans of the wounded raised the hair on the back of my neck. Not even in the battle of San Antonio last fall had we been involved in a situation as desperate as this. In their fever, wounded men begged for water that no one had. The little bit of water had long since been used up. All of us thirsted, but for the injured the night was torture. A light mist hung in the air, though not enough to afford relief. On the contrary, it made the cold bite deeper.

Hungry, cold, sleepless, those of us who were able worked through the night digging trenches, fortifying ourselves the best we could. It was too cold to rest long at a time. Instead, we worked.

When we had the ditches two or three feet deep, we dragged up the oxcarts and the carcasses of horses and oxen, and placed them for breastworks. Through the long night we listened to the Mexicans blowing their bugles, far out in the darkness. If it was an attempt to keep us awake, they needn't have bothered. We were too cold and hungry and thirsty to sleep.

Once in a while a Mexican sentry would cry out, "*Sentinela alerta,*" a sign that all was well. For them, it might have been.

Daylight finally came. It was Sunday, March 20. As the darkness began to fade, we could see the Mexicans moving. Three or four hundred men were coming up as replacements, bringing with them a hundred or so pack mules. They had two new brass nine-pounders and would certainly have a fresh supply of ammunition.

The cannons roared. We threw ourselves face down into the tramped-out grass and dirt. The shots were too high. They were over our heads. Fannin, wounded and in pain, gave the order to hold our fire. "The range is too great, and our ammunition is too low. Let's wait until we can hit what we shoot at."

The Mexicans fired their cannons several times, not a single shot hitting inside our tight square. Again movement started among the ranks of the Mexican cavalry. We brought up our rifles and muskets, sure the charge was about to commence. Instead, an officer rode out, carrying a white flag.

"Maybe they want to give up," somebody said dryly.

One of our majors and some other officers walked out to meet the Mexican about halfway between our position and the enemy lines. They talked a little, then came back. The major went straight to Fannin.

"That's General Urrea's command out there. The general sends word that he wants to avoid shedding blood without reason. He guarantees that we'll be dealt with leniently if we surrender at discretion."

Fannin exploded. "At discretion? That means unconditional. That means we retain no rights. We turn ourselves over to them to be treated in any way they see fit."

The major nodded solemnly. "I reckon that's what it means."

Fannin looked at us then, his gaze slowly sweeping the whole miserable little band huddled behind the embankment of earth and the upset carts and dead animals. He shook his head. "Go back and tell him we shall *not* surrender at discretion. We had rather die to the last man in these trenches!"

The major delivered his message. The Mexican officer wheeled his horse around and carried the report to General Urrea. Shortly the whole Mexican line began to move again. It looked once more as if the charge would start at any moment.

Instead, a handful of men rode out toward the truce area. Jimson whistled. "Look at the uniform on that Mexican. That must be Urrea."

Fannin, propped against a pack, his injured leg extended in front of him, lifted a spyglass to his eye. "It is Urrea indeed. He wants to parley. Major, I guess this time I had better go. I'll need your help." The major and half a dozen of us moved quickly to aid him.

Fannin, on his feet but favoring the wounded leg, turned and looked again at those of us gathered around him. "Men, I suspect that this time he has a better offer, or he wouldn't have come. I know that as commander I am supposed to make the decisions. But this may mean your lives, and I'll not make the decision alone. If you choose, we'll stay here and fight until we die. But if you vote to surrender, and we are offered acceptable terms, I shall abide by your vote. What say you?"

The officers huddled first. Then they divided us into our own companies for a quick discussion.

When the question came around to me, I said, "Either way, we lose. We're trapped here. If we stay we'll either starve or be killed. We can't break out without leaving the wounded, and the longer we stay the more wounded there'll be."

Jimson took it up. "We couldn't leave the wounded. So it comes to this: we stay here and die for certain, or surrender and hope."

I pointed out, "You know what happened to King's and Ward's men who surrendered. They were shot."

Jimson shrugged. "A chance of war. If it was an easy decision, we wouldn't be standin' here arguin' over it."

In the end, the decision was made. We would surrender if Fannin could get us good terms. Otherwise, we would stay here and die like the men of the Alamo had died.

Fannin went out, the major and some of the other officers with him. Every step he took was agony.

After a long time, Fannin and the major came back. And with them came the resplendent General Urrea himself, bringing several aides. They wrote down the agreement, a copy in Spanish and one in English. All signed it. Fannin folded the English copy and put it inside his coat.

So we gave up our arms and marched out of the trenches, carrying our wounded with us.

It was a slow, painful, pride-killing return to the fortress we had left. Nobody talked much, for the shock and hurt went too deep. Most of these men had come to Texas lightheartedly looking for the grand adventure, the great crusade, to strike a blow for liberty and show a contemptible enemy how Americans could fight.

It was all for nothing. They could fight, these volunteers, but they had been wasted by poor planning and indecision and a fatal contempt for the enemy. The cause was good, the spirit strong; but it had all been thrown away.

The officer who had superintended the surrender of weapons was a German mercenary. Many of Santa Anna's officers were Europeans. In good English he said, "Well, gentlemen, in ten days it will be liberty and home!"

It sounded good at the time. But it would come back bitter as gall.

They put us in what had once been the chapel, and we began to wish we hadn't worked so hard to destroy everything in the fortress before we left it. That first night was torture. We were crowded so tightly that not all had room to lie down. The trapped air was hot and stifling. We gasped for breath.

Our wounded needed attention and fresh bandages, but the Mexicans had few or none for themselves. Contrary to the terms of the surrender agreement, which had guaranteed to respect private property, the Mexican soldiers methodically robbed us of whatever individual possessions we had. In my case, it wasn't much. I had already lost my horse, my saddle, and my blanket.

The wounded suffered severely for want of attention. The Mexicans had taken our few doctors away to treat their own men. Gangrene developed in some of the wounds. The stench and the moaning of the men made cold sweat break out on the rest of us. We had water now, for details were permitted to go down under guard and fetch it from the river. But there was little food, and no chance to make broth for the men who so badly needed it.

Some of our wounded passed away, and death came to them as a friend.

It was the following Friday that a call went up.

"More prisoners!"

The gates opened. More than a hundred men dragged in—I couldn't say they marched—and the gates closed behind them.

"It's Major Ward," one of the officers declared, and hurried forth to meet the new prisoners. With Ward was the tiny remnant of his men who had survived the battle at Refugio. In addition there were a hundred or so fresh volunteers, taken at Copano the minute they stepped down from their ship. They never had a chance to take a rifle in hand, much less to fire it.

Their faces were sad, angry, frustrated. They had tried, and they had failed. Now they were at this dreary hell with us. I couldn't bring myself to look at them. I dropped my gaze, staring at my dirt-crusted moccasins, my ragged breeches.

I thought I heard someone call my name.

"Josh?" It was more a question than anything. I raised my eyes, and my heart leaped.

"Thomas!"

I jumped to my feet and grabbed him. We hugged each other, blubbering like children. At last he groaned, and I saw what I had overlooked in my haste and my joy. He was wounded. His tattered coat was buttoned with his left arm inside, the sleeve hanging empty.

"Thomas," I cried in relief, "I thought you were dead."

He looked as if he wanted to smile but couldn't. "I thought for a while that I was too. Damn it, Josh, I hate to be a-findin' you here."

"I'm glad to find you here, or anyplace. I'd given you up."

Thomas's eyes showed pain. "You shouldn't have gotten yourself into this. You ought to've stayed home."

"Old Noonan came by the place. Said he thought you'd been wounded, or killed. I set out to find you."

Thomas gritted, "Noonan, that old scoundrel! Big talk, but a yellow streak as wide as your hat. Time for fightin' come around, he wasn't to be seen." He looked at me again with those sad eyes. "I'm sure sorry to find you here."

I said, "Where were you? How bad is that wound?"

He shrugged, and the effort hurt him. "I was

south of San Patricio. On patrol. The Mexicans caught me by surprise. Killed most of the boys. They shot me in the shoulder, then killed my horse. He fell on top of me. They left me there for dead. I finally got out from under the horse and started walkin' north. It was mighty slow going." He looked around. "Josh, I sure hope you got somethin' here to eat. I'm starved."

I shook my head. "There's not much. We've all been hungry for days. A few of the boys managed to hide away a little coin when the soldiers looted us. They been buyin' a small bit of bread and coffee from the camp followers. Outside of that, the Mexicans have been bringin' us a little beef . . . nothin' more."

Thomas found an open spot by the stone wall and dropped down to stretch his legs out in front of him. He flinched as pain from the bad shoulder grabbed him.

"Thomas, you better let me look at that shoulder."

He waved me off. "The bullet's out. Time will take care of the rest of it. If we've got any time."

"What do you mean?"

"These Mexicans haven't been takin' prisoners."

I told him we had a guarantee from Urrea. Colonel Fannin still kept a copy of the agreement in his pocket, as far as I knew.

Thomas asked, "Where is Urrea now?"

"He left. Went on to wherever the fightin' is. A colonel by the name of Portilla is in charge now."

"Urrea signed the paper, and now he's gone?"

I nodded. Thomas grunted, then dismissed the

subject. He started asking me how things had been at home when I left. I told him all I could.

It was strange how all our past differences faded away under these cruel gray walls. Whatever bitterness might have lingered in me had disappeared in my relief at seeing him. The trouble we shared now, the oppression of captivity, made us brothers again.

Thomas told me how he had wandered afoot after the battle, the wound causing a fever that set him to staggering, half out of his head. An old Mexican found him, took pity on him, and carried him to his *jacal*. There the old man and his wife dug the bullet out of him. They hid him for days while Mexican patrols scouted for stragglers.

"Josh, I always said I'd never take a favor off of a Mexican, but that pair saved my life. I owe them more than I could ever say. If I get out of this alive, I'll find some way to pay them. If I don't get out and you do, I want you to pay them for me."

"Thomas, you'll get out. The war is over for us. They say they're goin' to send us home."

He grimaced. "Maybe." He told me the old couple's name and how I could find them. "You remember now, I want you to see that those old folks don't ever need for nothin'."

I agreed, to get him to quit fretting. "Sure, Thomas, if it comes to that. But we're both goin' to live. If the Mexicans take Texas away from us, we can always go home to Tennessee. And we'll go together."

15

Palm Sunday, March 27. It was a beautiful morning, bright and shining with the hope of freedom. Some of the friendlier guards had brought us the rumor that a ship was being sent to Copano to take us on board and carry us to the United States. A feeling of vast relief had swept gloom from the prisoners' compound. Now there was rising jubilation.

"Home," the man said. "They're sendin' us home!"

Last night we had all sung, "Home, Sweet Home," and the words brought tears that burned many an eye.

We didn't know that as we sang, a courier arrived from Santa Anna. The general had flown into a black rage when he learned about Urrea's prisoners. So the courier had brought Colonel Portilla a written order that the officer crumpled in horror. We didn't know the colonel had paced in his quarters all night, racked by conscience, praying for forgiveness for what he had to do.

* * *

The gates opened. We stood up—those who could—hoping the guards had brought beef. Instead, a Mexican officer stepped into the yard and signaled for us to gather around him.

Thomas was stiff and sore from his wound. I helped him to his feet. He leaned on me for support a moment, until he had the strength to walk alone.

"Good news, my friends," the officer said. His mouth was smiling, though it struck me that his eyes were not. "You are starting home today. The ship is arriving in Copano. You have but to walk there."

More than three hundred voices lifted in a lusty cheer. I shouted with them, then glanced at Thomas. I saw hope flicker in his eyes, but I saw doubt there, too.

The officer said, "Those who are able to walk will do so. The badly wounded will stay. They will be taken later in carts. It will be necessary for guard purposes to divide you into groups."

He picked out our officers and told them to gather us into their own commands. Because Thomas had been captured alone and belonged to no group here, I kept him with me. The men who had been captured as they got off the ship at Copano had been given white armbands to wear while they were in the fortress. Now this group was all gathered in one section.

I saw Fannin lying on the ground, unable to walk except with the greatest pain and difficulty. He was smiling as he watched us. The Mexicans up to now had not honored all the terms of the capitulation. They had allowed their soldiers to rob us. They had not fed us as they had agreed. But now they were sending us home. Fannin, I thought, must have felt gratified about this. It meant that after all his defeats, at least he had made a decent bargain for us.

"Thomas," I said, "you'd better stay here. Let them bring you in a cart."

He shook his head violently. "I'll make it. I want to get out into the clear air."

I had some serious doubts, but I figured if he gave out they would let him ride.

I got to thinking then about Muley, back there at our place. Not much telling what would happen to him now. It seemed a certainty that the Mexican army would overrun everything in its path. If he didn't run, they would catch him. If he did run, where would he go?

We were marched out the gate, one group at a time. Ours was the third to leave. The last—the men with the white armbands—were still inside. As we moved out into the open, it struck me that spring was coming now. The brush was leafing, the grass turning green. The sky was a light, clear blue. I didn't remember when I had ever seen it so beautiful.

They started us down toward the old ford on the river. Thomas kept looking back over his shoulder.

"Funny thing, Josh. They didn't bring the other two bunches this way."

"What do you mean?"

"They took them off in other directions. This is the road to Copano."

I didn't have an answer. I looked at the armed Mexican guards who marched on both sides of our strung-out line, an uneasiness stirring in me. About a hundred volunteers were in our group. The other groups which had gone out before us had been much the same. There weren't as many of the guards as there were of us. That didn't look like treachery. And yet, Thomas's contagious suspicion began to work on me.

Several Mexican cavalrymen leisurely worked their way down on horseback from their encampment, carrying lances under their arms.

Jimson was in fine spirits. "They must be figurin' on proddin' up the slow ones. But goin' home, there ain't nobody apt to be very slow."

We walked along in silence. I kept watching Thomas now, and I saw his suspicion gradually change into alarm. He turned now and again, counting the guards over and over, seeing where they were. His restless eyes followed the lancers.

"Josh," he said quietly, "if worst comes to worst, the lancers are the ones you got to watch. Half of these guards probably can't shoot. But those lancers will sure run you through."

"Thomas, you're just borrowin' trouble."

"I'm talkin', that's all. But you listen, and listen good. There's lots of brush along the river. A man could hide himself in there, if he ever made it that far. With luck he could hold out till dark. Then he could head out across country. He'd have a chance to get back to our own lines and maybe strike another blow at Santa Anna."

He walked along hunched a little, for the shoulder was hurting him. I said, "You ought to've stayed and ridden in the cart, like I told you."

He shook his head. "If we're really goin' to Copano, I'll make it. If we're goin' to die, I'll die out here where the air is clean."

"Thomas, you quit talkin' about dyin'."

"You remember what I said about that old Mexican couple. See after them, you hear?"

I wondered how he figured—if something was going to happen—that I would live through it and he wouldn't. I guess he knew that with his bad shoulder he couldn't run far.

We had walked about half a mile from the fortress when a Mexican up front raised his hand and shouted. *"Alto!"* We all stopped.

Jimson called in high good humor, "Tell him we're not tired yet. Tell them we want to keep on a-walkin'."

Several commands were given in Spanish. The squad of guards on the upriver side of us began to move. They split, half going around in front of us, half in back of us. In a moment they filed up to join the guards who were stationed between us and the river.

Thomas stiffened. I saw his face turn a leaden gray.

Then, from far off in the distance, came the ragged sound of musketry.

Jimson gave voice to the sudden horrible realization that swept over us all. "My God, boys, they're goin' to kill us!"

I heard someone cry out. Men began to pray. One man dropped to his knees, his head bowed. Someone shouted, "Rush them, boys! It's our only chance!"

Thomas clutched my arm. "The river, Josh! The river!"

Some of the men began to run toward the Mexicans, hoping to overwhelm them. At a command the soldiers raised rifles to their shoulders. I stood paralyzed, my mouth dry, the cold hand of death holding me there in horror. I looked down the barrel of the rifle that was going to kill me.

Thomas moved suddenly. He stepped directly in front of me. The rifles roared. The impact slammed Thomas's body back against me, men fell like wheat beneath a scythe. I could hear the thud of bullets driving into flesh and bone. Some men died without a sound. Some cried out in mortal pain. I clutched Thomas, but my hand was sticky and warm. I knew instinctively that he was already dead.

For a moment I lay there—half pinned down by his weight—numb, unable to move, to think, to speak. Around me men still prayed and cursed and moaned and died.

Then the realization came to me that I was still alive. I had not even been hit. Thomas had taken the bullet that would have been mine.

And it came to me that men who had been missed by the volley were beginning to run. There had not been enough rifles to kill us all with the first shots. More by instinct than by conscious will, I lay still. I lay there and looked into Jimson's open, dead eyes.

The Mexicans were reloading their rifles as rapidly as they could, many of them moving awkwardly forward as they rammed powder and ball down the barrels. In pursuit of those men who ran up the hill, they moved over us and away.

This was my chance, if I had one at all. Stealthily

I eased out from under Thomas's weight. I gripped his hand, saying a silent good-bye, my heart pounding. Then I jumped to my feet and sprinted toward the river.

A ball whizzed over my head. I cut sharply to the left and ran even faster. I glanced back over my shoulder, half expecting to see a mounted lancer bearing down on me. I was lucky, for they were all busy elsewhere. But I saw a rifleman drawing a bead. I cut to the right. Again a ball missed me.

Then there was the brush. I plunged into a thicket, the branches and the thorns clutching at my ragged clothes, ripping into my skin. I could hear a horseman loping toward me. I glanced back and saw him coming, the lance tipped forward.

I would make it tough for him, catching me in this brush.

Something struck my left arm. It felt like a red-hot poker. I reached up with my right hand and touched the arm and felt the thin flow of blood. I had been nicked by a rifle ball. But I kept on running.

I pushed through the brush until I reached the steep river bank. They were still coming behind me. I dived. The icy-cold water paralyzed me a moment. Then I started to swim. My first thought was to try to make the opposite bank, climb out, and keep running. But the current was swift. I let it carry me along and only treaded to keep my head above water. I kept trying to look back, to see if I was being followed. So far as I could tell, I wasn't.

In a few minutes the current carried me to a spot where the opposite bank was not steep, and where a growth of old grass would hide whatever marks I might make as I climbed out. I clambered over the bank as quickly as I could and tried to lose myself in the timber. I dropped down on hands and knees in a heavy growth of underbrush, clutching my arm, feeling the warm trickle of blood. My heart was still in my throat. I could hear firing across the river as the Mexicans found and murdered one after another of the unfortunate volunteers.

The terror of it swept over me in a spasm of shuddering. Unable to control myself, I lay flat on the ground, clenched my fists, and let the bitter tears flow.

When I was able to collect my wits, I realized I was alive but a long way from being free. It was still less than a mile back to the fortress, with many open stretches of prairie to cross whenever I tried to move farther away. Riders splashed across the river. I could hear the horses grunt as they labored up the bank. They were coming toward me. I huddled in the thicket and prayed softly.

I heard the sound of running feet. Thirty yards away a young volunteer was pounding through the brush as hard as he could. The lancers came yelping eagerly behind him, like hunters after a fox. The youth screamed, "No! God, no!"

The first lance impaled him. A second caught him and drove his body to the ground. The lad gave one horrible cry. One of the soldiers got down, put his foot on the body and pulled the lances free. Another soldier dismounted. Together they stripped the dead man of his clothes, laughing as if this were a sporting event, and they had just killed a deer.

Now I could hear firing in the fortress itself. The wounded! They were killing the wounded—Fannin and the rest.

More than three hundred helpless men—slaughtered like cattle!

I had not had time to feel anger. There had been only fear, and horror. Now came the anger, a bitter, driving, helpless rage. I pounded my fists against the ground.

I knew now that I *had* to get out of there.

Thomas, I swore, *someday, somewhere, somehow, there'll come a day of reckoning for this. And I vow to you and Almighty God, I'll be there!*

Soaking wet, hungry, bitterly cold, I huddled in the brush all that day. Now and again patrols passed through the timber, hunting for stragglers. I stayed low. My arm stiffened and burned, but at least it was no more than a deep scratch. The ball had taken a bite of flesh and passed on. I would live. Or at least, it wouldn't be this wound that killed me.

I tried to decide what I should do. Even with the best of luck, it would be difficult to escape from here. With any bad luck at all . . .

I had no hat, no coat, only these ragged clothes between me and total nakedness, with the chill of winter's breath still lingering into spring. My moccasins were thin. They probably wouldn't survive a long walk home, or even farther if the Texian line had retreated beyond it. And if there even was a Texian line. For all I knew, the Mexicans could already have swept to the Sabine River.

I knew that without food I would never get far. I'd nearly starved for a week now on the meager ration they gave us in the compound, and today there had been nothing at all. I wondered about the deserted Mexican *jacales* in the town of Goliad. I might find something there, if I had the nerve to go and look. A coat, a blanket—something. Probably no food, for the people had been gone too long. They had fled downriver last fall to the scattered *ranchos*, where they thought they would be safe from the war. Maybe if I could get to one of the *ranchos* I could steal some food and some clothing.

I had never stolen anything in my life, but now I was going to try without the slightest twinge of conscience. What did it matter? They were just Mexicans, I told myself. I realized I was thinking the way Thomas had always thought.

Well, he was dead now, and Mexicans had killed him. Maybe he had been right all the time, and I had been wrong.

I knew from description where the *ranchos* lay. My clothes had fairly well dried out through the day. Still, I was chilled to the bone. Even walking, I couldn't get warm. So most of the time I kept going, for the cold hurt me worse than being tired.

I had no firm plan, other than to try to sneak into a house and get some clothes to wear, some food to take along. Ahead lay a small rock house, very much like the one the Hernandez family lived in. Around it were scattered several brush *jacales*. A lingering smell of woodsmoke touched my nostrils. My stomach growled, for woodsmoke meant food.

Dogs were one thing I hadn't counted on. It never occurred to me they would pick me up so quickly. They set in to barking and raced out to meet me with a noisy clamor.

"Hush up," I hissed at them. They didn't savvy English. I crouched behind a bush and tossed rocks at them, trying to scare them away. They didn't scare. Presently a man appeared in the doorway, an ancient musket in his hand. I backed away in the darkness without his seeing me. I couldn't go up against that musket. Maybe there would be another house, one without dogs.

A mile farther on, I saw it. I moved in slowly, expecting the same reception. But this house was quiet. No dogs. I approached stealthily, flattening myself against the rock wall. I eased myself up to the open window and listened. Inside, a man was snoring.

It was somewhere past midnight. I didn't know where I had heard it, but a dim recollection came to me that someone had said people sleep soundest in the hours just after midnight. If that was true, I had a chance here.

Something moved beside me. My heart flipped. I jumped a couple of feet, whirling to face whatever it was.

In a square crate made of green willow branches I saw a rooster, one of the fighting breed so beloved by the Mexicans. I had disturbed his rest. I swallowed hard, regaining control of myself.

The door was closed, but it moved easily on its leather hinges when I lifted it slightly and pushed. I opened it only enough to give me entrance. But I didn't rush anything. I stood outside and listened carefully. The snoring continued. On the ground I saw a long chunk of firewood and picked it up. Flattening myself against the doorjamb, I slid through the open door and raised the club, ready to strike against anything that moved. Nothing did.

Slowly I lowered the club, though I kept a tight grip on it. I looked around the tiny one-room *casa* a full minute, getting my bearings. I could see two people sleeping on a cowhide bed, a slightly-built man and a rather stout woman. They had a couple of blankets wrapped around themselves. How I wanted one of those blankets! But any kind of clothes would be an improvement. I saw the Mexican's shirt and trousers and a ragged old coat hanging from a peg. Carefully I reached for them, took what I thought was a firm hold, and lifted. Something fell. It hit the floor with a light thump. Instinctively I reached down and grabbed. It was a knife in a leather scabbard.

The sound stirred the man. He raised up, blinking uneasily. "*Qué es? Qué es?*" His movement awakened the woman. She opened her eyes and saw me. She screamed.

The Mexican jumped out of bed and rushed me. I had no choice but to use that chunk of firewood. It flattened him.

The woman screamed again, her hands against her cheeks. "*Americano!*" Before I could move, she had yanked the door open and was running out into the night crying, *"Americano! Americano!"*

On the floor the man swayed to his hands and knees. I looked around desperately for a gun, any kind of gun. There wasn't any. The man was pushing himself to his feet. Out in the darkness the woman was running, screaming. In a minute or two the neighbors would be on their way. They wouldn't be friendly.

I wanted to ransack the house for food, but there wasn't time now. I clutched their clothes under my arm, determined to get away with at least that much, and hurried out the door. I stumbled over the rooster's crate and sprawled on the ground.

By George, *there* was food. I gathered the stolen clothes under my left arm and yanked the rooster out of his crate with the right. Then I took off in a hard run. I didn't stop running until my lungs ached and my legs seemed ready to buckle. Then I stopped and fell to the ground to rest. The rooster struggled. My first inclination was to eat him raw, for I was hungry enough. I knew I had to kill him right away, or he would more than likely get loose from me. I wrung his neck and waited for him to quit flopping. At least he had died for a better cause than someone's sport.

I put the Mexican's clothes on over my own. They fitted me better than I had any right to expect. And inside the pocket of the trousers I found a flint and steel.

My situation was still bad, but it was improving.

After gutting the rooster and resting for a little, I set out walking, moving in what I judged to be a northeasterly direction. I carried the dead rooster under my arm, for I couldn't afford to build a fire and cook him until daylight came to mask the flames.

When it was light I picked a good thicket and went into the heart of it. Using the flint and steel, and strips of cloth, I eventually got a small fire underway. The rooster was much too thin and stringy to be good eating, but this was no time or place to be choosy. Little as he was, he would be the best meal I had had in a long time. I impaled him on a spit, scorched him a little, and ate him.

Exhausted, I slept most of the day. Terrible dreams of that awful massacre finally brought me wide awake, trembling. I lay there awhile, my eyes wide open. I had a horrible feeling that if I turned over and looked behind me I would find the Mexicans there with their muskets and lances, waiting to kill me. I managed after a bit to roll over. There was no one. I was alone.

My heart pounded from the terror of the dreams. My eyes burned with tears as the awful memories rushed back unbidden like floodwaters breaking through a dam.

My arm was swollen and sore, but that wouldn't slow my walking. Though still hungry, I had at least had a good rest. With the dark to shield me, I would set out walking. I could walk a long way before morning came again.

16

It was well that I had obtained the coat, for a norther blew in, bringing a cold, drizzling rain. With the bite of cold, hunger came back stronger than ever. That rooster had only whetted my appetite. It was a bad time of the year to find berries, wild fruit, or pecans, for the first were out of season and the others had fallen to the ground to be picked up by the wild hogs, deer, and other animals.

That was the ironic thing. All around me flocked an abundance of game—deer, wild turkeys. But without a gun I was unable to bring any of them to hand. The best I could find was some wild onions.

The third night my luck took a brief turn. I came across a tree where some of the turkeys roosted and managed to get one.

Not having seen a Mexican all day, I decided to risk building a fire to cook the turkey. Rain had left the wood wet. It took half the night to cut wet bark away from enough dead timber to have dry wood to burn. I got the turkey partially cooked, then ate it all except the feathers and bones. But much of my safe walking time had been wasted. And there was no telling how far I was from home. There hadn't been any familiar landmarks.

Hunger appeased, I decided to do some daylight traveling. The arm was still stiff but no longer painful except when I put pressure on it. With the new strength that came from a good meal, I was able to put some miles behind me. Instead of looking for a motte of timber when daylight came, I kept on walking.

In due time I came to a river and judged it to be the Guadalupe. It was running high and muddy from the heavy rains. My heart sagged. With this stiff arm, I probably could not swim it.

I gritted my teeth in disappointment. It would be a grim joke if I had escaped the firing squad at Goliad, only to drown here unseen, a hundred miles from home.

Upriver somewhere would be Gonzales, but it would do me no good to go there. Undoubtedly the Mexicans had it by now.

Somehow I had to find a way across that river but I had not the faintest notion what to do. I thought of trying to make a raft of some kind but had never done it before and didn't know just how to go about it. Besides, that current probably would be more than I could handle. It would likely carry me downriver a way and then dump me to drown.

Well, maybe something would turn up. I started walking upriver.

I had walked a long time when I heard the sound of moving horses. Mexicans, I figured. I flattened myself in undergrowth near the riverbank and strained to see. When the horses came in sight, a chill ran down my back. It wasn't Mexicans, it was *Indians*.

Somehow, in my anxiety, I had considered only the danger of Mexicans. Now I realized I had an equally dangerous foe to watch for, because these appeared to be Comanches. Nothing would please a Comanche more than to come across a straggling Texian and lift his hair. I lay flat until they were well past me, moving downriver. Then I arose and left in a hurry.

In one way the Indians were even a greater threat than the Mexicans. They saw more. They were hunters born and bred. Their eyes could read meaning into a boottrack or a broken limb that might be overlooked by a Mexican or a Texian.

I came at length to a log cabin, or rather, the ruins of one. Only a blackened hull remained, with the charred roof caved in. Cautiously, crouching and taking my time, I picked my way through it, alert for sign of life. There was no evidence of battle. The owners probably had fled ahead of the enemy advance. More than likely Mexican soldiers had burned the cabin, or Indians had come along and done it. If there had been anything of value inside—clothes, for instance—it was gone now. I hoped to find something to eat—chickens or a hog or a milk cow's calf—that had been left behind. If there had been such, someone had beaten me to it. For me, the cabin was a total loss.

No, not quite. At the river bank, partially hidden by undergrowth, a small boat lay mostly submerged in the water. A short length of rawhide rope held it to a tree.

My one bad arm made it heavy pulling against the current. A determined effort finally brought the boat up out of the river. I turned it over to empty the water out and examined it carefully for sign of a hole. A few minutes' search produced the oars.

Now, at least, I was able to cross the river. On the far side I hid the boat and struck out walking again.

During the day I saw four Mexican horsemen. I was crossing an open prairie where last year's dry grass still stood tall and coarse. Dropping down in it, I lay unseen while they passed two hundred yards away. Later I saw a small band of Indians, though they were at a greater distance and were more of a scare than a threat.

I considered going back to my original plan—traveling at night and hiding by day. It was safer. But I was still a long way from home. I found myself worrying more and more about Muley, waiting there for me. With that boy's mind of his, he was probably frightened half to death. He might stay instead of running as I had told him to. He couldn't defend himself when the Mexicans came—if they had not already come. Because of Muley I decided to take my chances and keep traveling during at least part of the day.

My worst scare came the second day past the Guadalupe. Moving across the prairie, I spied a small cloud of dust. It was coming my way. Presently I heard hoofs. A troop of Mexican cavalry, or a band of Indians, I was certain. I tried to flatten and hide myself in the grass, but it was too short. It wouldn't hide me unless they were all blind. And they wouldn't be. The hoof beats came closer.

I had my chin on the ground, but gradually I gathered my courage and raised my head to look. It was horses, all right, and they were coming upon me fast. But there wasn't a rider on them. They were wild mustangs, running free. I waited until I was sure no one was chasing them.

Then, afraid they might run over me, I stood up and waved my arms, shouting. The horses slid to a stop. They stood a moment watching me, their ears all cocked forward. They probably had never seen a man afoot. But they didn't care for what they saw. They wheeled around and galloped off, getting well in the clear. Then they stopped and turned to watch me some more, from a safer distance.

That night, just at dusk, I came upon the Mexican camp.

I would have done like the mustangs and gone way around, had I known. But I almost stumbled onto the camp before I saw it. They were cavalry, nearly twenty men. They had their horses tied on two picket lines, feeding them corn which they probably had found at some abandoned settler cabin. The soldiers were building up a campfire and preparing to cook supper.

I lay on my stomach and watched them. The wise thing, I knew, would be to ease myself well around them in the darkness and be long gone before morning. But the horses had caught my eye.

I had been walking for days. I knew I wasn't far

from home now, but it might take me several more days to get there at the rate I was moving. With a horse, I could reduce the time.

The temptation was almost overwhelming. With my knife I could run in there, cut a horse loose, and be gone before the single Mexican guard would have time to lift his rifle. But it would be like punching at a hornet's nest with a stick. They would be after me in minutes. Whether I could get away or not would simply depend upon whether my luck was better than theirs.

I had seen enough of Mexican luck lately not to want to take the risk.

But I wouldn't leave until I had made a try of some kind. I lay and watched the soldiers cook and eat. My stomach growled. I had eaten only at irregular intervals, and the last interval had been a long one. I watched the dirty-uniformed men move about, and my mind inevitably turned back to that awful morning on the road to Copano. There was no way for me to know whether these men had personally had a hand in it. But they wore the same uniform, and that was enough. Hatred stirred in me. I thought of a dozen ways to kill them all, like finding their gunpowder and throwing it into the fire. But they were all crazy notions, too wild to work.

At length, their hunger satisfied, the Mexicans began wrapping themselves in their blankets and stretching out. They left one guard with the horses. The men quickly dropped off to sleep. From that, I guessed they had had a long, hard day. And so, probably, had the guard.

I crawled closer to the lone Mexican awake, who sat with his back to a live oak tree, his musket across his lap. The dry leaves rustled under me. The Mexican looked around, startled. I froze. For a moment it appeared he might get up and investigate, and I tensed, ready to run. But when he heard nothing more, he gradually relaxed. He probably thought it was some night-prowling animal.

The campfire burned low. Out in the darkness wolves began to howl. They had howled every night since I had escaped from Goliad. Once they had come so close that I had finally climbed a tree. The wolves made the horses restless. The Mexican spoke softly to them but didn't get up. After a long while I saw his head begin to tilt forward. It jerked as he came awake, then sagged again. He was too tired to hold out. I knew I had only to wait.

The longer I watched him, the more I thought about the Mexican officer who had come to us on Palm Sunday morning with the report that we were leaving for Copano. He had known what was about to happen, but he had lied to us with a smile on his lips. I fancied I could see a resemblance between this guard and that officer. I found my hand straying down to the handle of the knife. It would be easy to rise up and steal over to him and slit his throat. Hell, he deserved it. They *all* deserved it, I thought. I ground my teeth, struggling against the temptation.

Even dying, he might cry out and arouse the camp.

No, it was more important to get myself a horse. Vengeance could wait.

It seemed an hour before I heard his gentle snoring. His head was tilted forward onto his arms, his arms across his knees. I arose quietly and moved toward the picket line, the knife in my hand. For a long time I had studied the horses, making my choice.

I wanted very badly to cut all the horses loose and run them off. But I knew I could get shot doing it. I might get away with one horse, but not all of them.

The knife was dull. I had to saw on the rawhide. The horses stirred restlessly. I kept glancing back at the Mexican, thinking he would wake up at any moment. The leather finally parted. Carefully I backed my horse out of his place on the line. I led him in a slow walk, pausing only to pick up a bridle, blanket, and saddle which lay there handy to my reach. I held onto them—and onto my breath—until I had the horse well away from the camp. Then I paused long enough to bridle and saddle him, swung up, and was on my way.

The camp never stirred.

17

Once I struck the Colorado River, I had no trouble finding our place. I passed many others first. Without exception, they had been burned. My hopes sagged. The Mexicans had been here. No telling what had happened to Muley.

Though I nursed some faint hopes, I knew pretty well what to expect when I rode across the field. The winter wheat was growing fine. The corn had been planted—Muley's work. I slanted down the trail to our cabin. The cabin was gone, all but its blackened skeleton. I swallowed, anger rising momentarily. I eased the horse toward the cold ruins, looking for signs of Muley. Actually, though I wouldn't have admitted it, I was watching for his body.

I found no trace of him. When I felt safe in doing so, I began to call: "Muley! Muley! It's me, Josh!"

I had some thought that he might have hidden in the timber. It would be like him. He might be there yet, waiting for somebody to come and get him. Waiting for me.

There wasn't a sign of Muley. But on a closer examination I found familiar dog tracks.

"Hickory!" I whistled a few times, then called again. "Here, Hickory!"

The old spotted hound slunk out of the timber, tail between his legs. He crouched uncertainly, knowing my voice but still not trusting.

I called him again and rode slowly toward him. Recognition came finally, and he fell to barking joyously, running at me, his tail wagging so hard he almost fell over. Always a chaser but never a hunter, he was thin and hungry-looking. That settled it: Muley was either dead or gone. He wouldn't have let the dog do without.

Hickory jumped all over me in his joy. He whimpered and cried while I petted him and tried to get him quieted down.

Now the worry I had carried for days turned to genuine fear. I knew from bitter experience what Santa Anna's soldiers were doing to prisoners. They might not have killed Muley here. They might have taken him to be killed somewhere else, on somebody's cruel whim.

Still, there was a chance Muley was all right. He might have run like I told him. From appearances, all the American settlers in this part of the country had pulled out hastily. Lots of people around here knew about Muley. Maybe somebody had taken enough time to come by and get him.

There was one place I might be able to find out. I found my eyes lifting to the trail I used to ride toward the Hernandez *rancho*. I couldn't be sure, of course, that the family was still there. They might have pulled out too. But I had noticed that by and large the Mexican families were tending to stay put as the American families fled. They didn't seem to feel they had much to fear from the Mexican soldiers. After all, they were of the same blood. A goodly percentage of them, as I had found to my sorrow, sided with the soldiers against us.

I couldn't know what reception to expect at the Hernandez place. I'd thought many times of the way Ramón Hernandez had hedged on an answer when I asked him which way he would go if it came to war. I'd remembered often the look in his eyes when I took him the news that his younger brother had been killed in the battle of San Antonio de Bexar.

Ramón might have gone over to Santa Anna's side by now. Friendship is one thing, but blood is another.

I sat on the hill a long while and surveyed the stone house before I touched my heels to the horse's ribs and started him down in an easy walk. Muley's hound tagged along close. He was sticking to me like a mesquite thorn.

The kids—Ramón's youngest brothers and sisters—played outside. A couple of horses stood droop-headed in a corral. Grazing cattle were scattered in the grassy draw and across the field.

The youngsters raised a frightened shout when they saw me. My beard had grown untouched for weeks and now was ragged and tangled and black. My clothes hung on me like they would on a scarecrow. I must have looked like some devilish apparition. There was, in those days, a strong tendency toward superstition in the Mexican people. Whatever or whoever they thought I was, they ran screaming into the house. The door slammed behind them. I heard the bar drop.

In a moment a shuttered window swung open. The barrel of an old musket poked out. A woman's voice cried, *Ándele! Ándele!* It was a way of saying to move along.

I raised my hands. In Spanish I called, "I am Josh Buckalew."

The musket was pulled back out of sight. The door opened cautiously. A young woman stood there, the musket still in her hands but no longer pointed directly at me.

"Josh, is it you? Is it really you?"

Weak, desperately hungry, I almost fell as I slid off the horse. I caught hold of the stirrup and pulled myself up. "Yes, María, it's me."

Hesitant, she came out under the brush arbor. Finally certain, she ran and threw her arms around me, musket and all.

"Josh, Josh, we thought you were dead!"

She hurt my arm, and I flinched. It never had healed completely. She stepped back, eyes wide in concern. "You are wounded."

"Not bad, still just a little raw. It'll be all right."

She hugged me again but went easy on the left arm. Then she studied my face. "You look terrible. Where have you been?" She didn't give me a chance to answer. "You shouldn't be here, Josh. Patrols come by every day or two. If they find you, they will kill you."

"I had to come. I need to talk to Ramón."

She shook her head. "Ramón has gone to the army."

My breath stopped for a moment. "The Mexican army?"

"No, Sam Houston's army. He went to fight Santa Anna."

The relief that came to me was only momentary. "María, I can't find Muley. I hoped Ramón could tell me what happened to him."

"Muley is all right, or was. Ramón was afraid to leave him by himself with Santa Anna's army on the way. He made Muley go with him to join Sam Houston."

I sighed. A terrible weight slipped from my shoulders.

"Thanks to God, María." For a minute all I could think about was that Muley was all right. Then I glanced toward the door and saw Ramón's wife. Miranda stared, still not sure who I was.

"María," I demanded, "why did Ramón leave the rest of you here? Why didn't he take you and run?"

"It was too near Miranda's time. She could not travel. We decided we would be safe here. We are Mexicans. We thought the soldiers would not hurt us. And it has been true. Many have been here, but none have done us any harm."

I frowned, remembering the trouble Miranda had had with her first baby. "You will need help with her, María."

"When Ramón left, it was all arranged. Señora Ramirez is a midwife, and she was going to stay. But her husband became frightened and took her east with the rest of the runaways. So I will have to do the job myself."

"Can you?"

"I have been told what to do. I will do the best I can." She took my good arm. "Come, Miranda and the children are frightened. They still don't know who you are."

Miranda hugged me and cried a little. The children cautiously shook my hand, but the smaller ones were still unconvinced that I was not some kind of devil. María set about cooking beef for me. I took a pair of scissors and clipped away most of my beard. I then borrowed an old razor that had belonged to María's father and shaved my face clean.

As I ate, I told them briefly what had happened to me. I skipped most of the details, for the thought of them still made my blood go cold. I trembled as I told how Thomas had been butchered. The women wept silently.

I intended to leave after I had eaten and ride through the night. But I was so weary I thought I would lie down on one of the cowhide cots and rest an hour or so. When I awoke, it was morning. I sat bolt upright, staring in confusion and alarm. The women were preparing breakfast.

"María," I demanded, "why did you let me sleep?"

"You needed the rest. See, you look better already."

"I've got to move on. I want to catch up with Houston's army."

"You will eat first."

Impatience was like needles prickling my skin, but she was right. I had needed the rest. And I needed another good meal, for it might be a long time before the next one. So I sat on the cot and watched the women. Miranda moved slowly because of her size. María tried to get her to sit down, but she would not. I watched María particularly. It struck me that she had changed a lot since the first time I had seen her. She was a woman now, moving with purpose and sureness. And, she was a pretty woman.

I was eating when one of the boys ran into the house. "*Soldados!*" Soldiers were coming.

I jumped to my feet. "I'd better run. It'll go hard on you if they find me here."

Muley's dog was barking wildly. María glanced out the window. "Too late, they are too close. We'll have to hide you."

I thought of the horse and the Mexican saddle I had stolen. They would be a dead giveaway.

María shook her head. "I had Pepe turn the horse loose. We hid your saddle under the hay. Come!"

She let me out the back door. We glanced around for some place I could get out of sight. I saw nothing but the woodpile. I sprinted around that and dropped flat on my belly. I lay there with the knife in my hand, the only weapon I had. If found, I intended to sell out at a high price.

I heard the horses at the front of the house, and Hickory's barking. One of the soldiers must have hurled something at the dog, for he yelped in terror and ran around behind the house. He caught my scent and came crying to me.

"Get away, Hickory! Git!"

He wouldn't leave me. He tried to crowd in with me behind the woodpile. My mouth went dry, for I was afraid one of the soldiers might follow Hickory around the house to chunk at him again. None did.

"Damn you, Hickory, I ought to cut your cowardly throat."

But he stayed. It was a long time before I heard the patrol start moving away. Hickory ventured forth to bark at the soldiers from a respectful distance. Cautiously I peeked out to watch the horsemen moving eastward, singing. One of them paused to throw a rock back at Hickory.

I stayed put until finally María came.

"They are well gone," she said, as I got to my feet.

"They sure stayed a while."

"They made us cook for them."

"They didn't hurt you?"

"We told them our men had gone to help Santa Anna. They didn't hurt us."

"María, I've got to leave here. The longer I stay the more dangerous it is for you and for me."

She nodded gravely. "I'll have the boys bring you a fresh horse. We had to hide the good horses from the runaways. They took all they could find."

We returned to the house, María gave orders to the older boys, and they hit the door in a run. Turning to Miranda, I found her trembling. "Please, Josh," she said, "do not think I always am this foolish. It is my time and my condition, I suppose. I was frightened to death."

Taking her hand, I tried to give her reassurance. "I'll be gone in a few minutes. Then you won't have to worry."

A twinge of pain creased Miranda's olive face. "I think I have much to worry about. I think the time has come."

María's eyes widened. She glanced at me, then at Miranda. "You could be wrong, Miranda. Remember, there was that other alarm two days ago."

Miranda paled, flinching again. "This time, I think, it is real. The excitement has been too much." She cried out as a sharp pain hit her. It looked as if she would fall. I grabbed her.

"María, what do we do now?"

María's lips tightened. "I suppose we will deliver the baby."

The boys brought my horse up outside, saddled and ready to go. But there was no leaving now.

"María, I've never been around where a woman was having a baby."

"Then we shall both learn together."

Mostly I stood by and did whatever María said to do, while Miranda bit her lips and gripped the wooden edge of the bedframe, fighting against the pain.

The children were kept outside, watching for another patrol. María and I bustled about, making the preparations she thought were necessary. When the time came for delivery, I turned my face away and left that part up to María. I held Miranda's hands.

Or rather, she held mine, digging her fingernails in, gritting her teeth to keep from crying out.

"Cry if you want to, Miranda," I said. "Sometimes it's better."

But she shook her head. She had no intention of giving in to the pain.

Then, suddenly, the baby was there. María clutched it in her hands, a tiny reddish-brown thing.

"Josh," she cried, "Josh, do something! It's not breathing, Josh!"

The breath had not started. I saw the fear in Miranda's eyes, and in María's. I remembered something I had heard about spanking a new baby's bottom. I took the infant in my left hand and tapped its backside smartly with the palm of my right.

I felt a quiver of life, then heard the whimper that lifted into a cry. I looked at María. Relief flooded her face. She smiled, then laughed thinly. Her laugh grew louder, and I was laughing with her, the baby still dangling from my hand. María threw her arms around me. We stood there holding each other and laughed like a pair of fools.

Later I watched María tuck the blanket around Miranda and the baby. "María," I said, "you're a wonder."

I found myself studying her again as I had at breakfast, admiring the quick and easy way she moved, the slimness of her, the pleasant eyes and face. She was conscious of the way I appraised her, for color rose in her cheeks.

I said, "It's amazing to me, the way you resemble Teresa."

"I am not Teresa," she said pointedly. "I am María. I shall always be María. I would never be a substitute for someone else."

"I didn't mean it that way," I said hastily, realizing I had hurt her. "I would always want you to be yourself. I would always want you to be the way you have been today. With all respect to Teresa, I doubt she would ever have been able to do what you've done."

María said, "Teresa was my sister, and I shall always love her memory. But she was weak, Josh. Had *I* loved a man, I would have turned my back on family and all. I would have spit in the devil's eye to have him. I would never have married someone else because it was expected of me and I had not the courage to say no."

"No," I said with admiration, "I don't suppose you would."

The children came in to look at the new baby. One of the smaller ones marveled that he hadn't seen anybody come and bring it. Smiling wisely, an older boy said, "Your horse is here, Josh, and we see no soldiers."

"Thanks, *muchacho*. I guess I'd better leave."

Miranda called me to her bedside. "Josh, if you see Ramón, tell him I will be waiting for him. Tell him I have given him another son."

I squeezed her hand. "I'll tell him. He'll be proud of you."

María walked out with me, carrying a sack of food she had prepared. She also had the old musket.

"We do not need the gun, Josh. You might."

I took her arm and pulled her up close. I didn't

want to leave. "María, if this war ends in our favor, I'll be back. I'd like to come and visit you, if you'll let me."

Her eyes glistened. "Will you be coming to see me, or will you really be seeing Teresa?' "

"Teresa was a long time ago. That is over. I'll be coming to see you, María."

"Then come back, Josh. Come back soon."

She clutched my arm and leaned forward and kissed me.

I swung into the saddle and rode away, looking back over my shoulder.

18

This was a time that would ever after be known in Texas as the "runaway scrape." American settlers packed what possessions they could carry and left the rest behind them as they fled in their wagons or on horseback or afoot—often in panic—before the onslaught of Mexican troops. The news of the Alamo and Goliad had put an icy chill in Texian veins. A cold, hard fury set in, and a desperate desire for revenge. But there were practical matters to be attended to. Family men left Sam Houston's ranks to hurry home and see that their loved ones were evacuated to the sanctuary that waited for them across the Sabine.

It was a cold, rainy time, with mud that mired wagons to the hubs. Open prairies became vast lakes that sometimes had to be forded. Indians and Mexican guerrillas harassed the stragglers, striking and lashing and running away. Sickness swept the struggling caravans of wagons and carts and sleds.

How many died and were left behind in this awful backwash of war, no one ever really knew. The toll was heavy among women and children.

And all this time Sam Houston's dwindling army retreated, seething for revenge, falling back to first one river, then another—avoiding any full-scale clash. Houston was buying time, giving the runaways an opportunity to reach safety, waiting for the chance to strike the Mexicans when the odds were in the Texians' favor. Always outnumbered, always held back by Houston's caution, the Texians wondered if they would ever get that chance. Impatience turned to anger, and slowly anger built toward open mutiny.

But, grim as the crowded bear, Houston stood up to the abuse and the criticism. His was the only fighting force Texas had left. Texas could not stand another defeat. When he committed his men to battle, he wanted to know they had a better than even chance of winning. If they lost, the war was over, and Texas was gone.

I finally caught up to Houston's army opposite Harrisburg. That had been the capital of the newly declared Republic of Texas, though by now the officials of the government had fled. Santa Anna had already been to Harrisburg and had left it in ashes.

I had come across many Mexican patrols and details of cavalry since leaving the Colorado River. I always kept out of their sight. I had trailed the retreating army to Groce's plantation. East of the McCurley place I came to the fork in the road. The left-hand fork was the trace leading toward the Sabine and safety. The right-hand fork led toward

Harrisburg, and a certain head-on clash with Santa Anna. Though it had rained heavily, and two or three days had passed, I could still tell where the army had gone. It had taken the right-hand fork.

I had a feeling I was getting close now. I hadn't seen a Mexican in some time. Sitting in a clump of timber, I watched four horsemen coming my way, rifles across their laps. I took them to be Texians, though I hid myself until they were close enough that I knew for sure. Then I rode out into the open.

They hauled up quickly, their rifles swinging toward me. I raised my right hand and moved on, slower now.

"All right, friend," one of them said, staring at me over the barrel of his rifle, "before you come any closer we want to know who you are."

"I'm a Texian. I was at Goliad."

The man lowered his rifle. I got a look at his face, and a chill touched me. I knew him from somewhere, and it wasn't a pleasant memory. I reached back in my mind to long ago. Natchitoches. That was the face I had seen at Natchitoches so many long years ago. Lige, his name had been.

I knew a bitter moment then. Had I escaped from Goliad, dodged Mexicans and Indians across most of Texas, only to fall into the hands of cutthroats?

Lige squinted. "By George, I do believe I know you from someplace. Where have I seen you at?"

I said, "Try Natchitoches, several years back. You and some friends of yours tried to rob us on the trail to the Sabine."

Recognition came, and with it a moment of astonishment. Then, a broad grin. "Well, if that don't beat all. That was a long time, boy, for the chickens to finally come to roost. Been a lot of changes made."

"I doubt if you've changed much," I said.

He still grinned. "I know what you're thinkin', but I long since give up my sinful ways. You boys kind of give me a push in that direction. We're fightin' on the same side now, boy. A lot of us have had to turn our backs on old feuds and face the Mexicans together. Goliad, you say? And you got away? Rememberin' Natchitoches, I can't say as I'm surprised none. Come on, we'll take you to camp."

My arrival caused a stir, though I found out I wasn't the first Goliad survivor to catch up with the army. Several had made it here before me, individually picking their way across Texas just as I had done.

I was taken directly to Sam Houston's tent. He sat there and stared at me, a huge man with a strong, square face and piercing eyes. He reached into the pocket of his black coat and took out a bottle of salts of hartshorn, which he applied to his nostrils as I told him briefly what had happened to me.

"You've been through hell enough," he said finally. "You should have gone on to the Sabine instead of coming here."

I shook my head. "Not many of us got away from Goliad, General. I figure I owe a debt to all those who didn't."

Houston's jaw ridged. He glanced at his officers. "Has this man been fed?" When they said I hadn't, he ordered, "Then take him and feed him. See if you can find him a decent rifle and something to put in it."

I saluted him and turned to go. Houston called after me, "You can still go across the Sabine if you've a mind to. You've done your share."

"If it's all the same to you, General, I'll stay." In fact, I had made up my mind to stay whether it was all right with him or not.

One of the officers led me to a small company which he commanded. "Here's a man from Goliad. Feed him."

I wolfed the food down. As I was finishing up I said, "Major, I'm lookin' for a friend of mine, a partner. Name is Muley Dodd."

He shook his head. "We have almost eight hundred men in this camp. I couldn't know them all."

"He's supposed to have come with a Mexican friend of mine named Ramón Hernandez. You'd probably remember Muley if you came across him. He's . . . a little slow. He's not real bright."

One of the men said, "Major, I'll bet I know who he's huntin'. There was a little feller came into camp with a Mexican while we was at Groce's. The Mexican joined up with Juan Seguin's company. The little feller stayed with him. A bunch of us tried to talk him into joinin' a white man's outfit, but he wouldn't. Stuck to that Mexican like a pet dog."

I said, "That'd be Muley. Take me to him."

The name Seguin was familiar. The Seguins were a wealthy Mexican family, with large landholdings around San Antonio. General Cos had mistreated old Erasmo Seguin. As a result the Seguin family sided with the Texians with their land, their cattle, their money, and their arms. Juan Seguin, I was told, had been in the Alamo in the early part of the siege, but Travis had sent him out as a courier. There had been no returning.

The officer led me across the camp to where the Seguin company had bivouacked. A shudder ran through me as I looked at the dark faces and listened to the rapid flow of soft-spoken Spanish. Though these men were on our side, and though a few months ago I would have found it easy to call any of them friend, bitter memories stood between us now. I found myself blaming them all for being Mexicans.

"I am looking for Muley Dodd," I said in Spanish.

"The little *Americano*? He is here somewhere with Ramón Hernandez." He called. "*Señor* Dodd! *Dónde está?*"

I saw a slight figure rise up from some muddy blankets and look around wide-eyed. "Muley!" I broke into a run toward him. He jumped to his feet. "Josh! Josh! Josh!" He grabbed me, and we hugged each other. Muley began crying. "Josh, Ramón said you was likely dead. But I told him you wouldn't be. I told him you promised to come and get me, and you didn't never break any promise you ever made. I told him you wouldn't let them old Mexicans kill you if it was goin' to go ag'in your promise."

I clenched his shoulder and stood back to stare at him. He looked about the same as ever, except a little thinner. Rations hadn't come regularly.

Another voice broke in. "Josh, it is good to see you."

I turned to Ramón Hernandez and gave him the *abrazo*. He smiled broadly. "I thought Santa Anna had nailed you up with his trophies."

I said, "He did get Thomas."

Ramón's smile disappeared. He gripped my arm in sympathy. "Now we have each lost a brother. Where did it happen?"

Once again I told it. The Mexicans gathered and listened, those who could understand English.

Ramón said, "And so now you want to fight, to get even."

"It's somethin' I've got to do."

"This is a good company, Juan Seguin's. We would like you to join us."

I looked around me at the dark faces, the black eyes. Again I felt that uncomfortable stirring. I knew it was unfair, but I couldn't help it. Friends or not, when I looked at them I would see those other dark faces at Goliad, peering at us down the barrels of their rifles.

"Thanks, Ramón. But after what I've been through . . ." I tried to find the words to explain and couldn't. "It's nothin' personal, it's just . . . Well, I'd best find a place among my own people. I'll take Muley with me."

Ramón was silent a moment, perhaps hurt a little, though he didn't show it. "In your situation, I would be the same. It took me a long time to decide that my place was here."

I started to go, then turned back. "Ramón, I went by the *rancho*. You have another son."

"She is all right, my Miranda?"

"She came through fine. Said tell you to hurry home."

"We shall soon see if *any* of us go home."

We were waiting to cross Buffalo Bayou when Houston rode into the center of the army on his big white stallion Saracen. Far in the distance we could see smoke. Santa Anna was burning everything as he moved.

Houston sat on that big stud and made us a speech. He said we would win the battle that lay ahead, that we would have vengeance for those who had fallen in the Alamo. For those slaughtered at Goliad.

"Remember the Alamo!" he thundered. "Remember Goliad!"

It became a war cry. It spread through the army like a brushfire. Men raised their rifles over their heads and shouted the words over and over again. "Remember the Alamo! Remember Goliad!"

San Jacinto. Moving down Buffalo Bayou, we reached the San Jacinto River on April 20. Houston ordered us into camp in a grove of live oaks. Buffalo Bayou to our backs, the San Jacinto to our left. In front of us lay a pretty stretch of open prairie, rising slightly toward groves of moss-strewn live oak trees.

Later in the afternoon the cry went up. "The Mexicans are coming!"

We already knew that, for scouts had been bringing in reports at regular intervals. They said this was Santa Anna himself. We prepared ourselves for attack. With the river and the bayou at our flank and our back, and with Santa Anna coming up in front of us, we were in no position anymore to retreat. If the Mexicans came, we had to stand our ground and fight.

They didn't come. Santa Anna went into camp on the opposite side of the prairie, a broad lake to one side of him, the marshes behind him. He sounded us out by sending forward a six-pounder with a detachment of cavalry for protection. The cannon opened up. Some said Santa Anna probably hoped we would reply with musket fire and give him a good idea how we were lined up. On orders, we held our fire and answered him only with a few rounds from the Twin Sisters, a matched pair of cannon recently arrived as a gift from the people of Cincinnati.

There was one brief cavalry skirmish that afternoon as a group of volunteers attempted to rush forward and take the Mexican cannon. They failed to get the cannon but came back satisfied they had drawn blood.

The night was cold but quiet. Our scouts brought the report next morning that General Cos had arrived with reinforcements for Santa Anna. They had us outnumbered now by a little less than two to one.

This, then, was the time to fight, if we ever were going to fight. Some of the officers quarreled over it, but the men were of a temper to go ahead, with officers or without them. It was about three o'clock in the afternoon of April 21 that Houston ordered us paraded and announced that we were not going to wait for Santa Anna to come to us. We were going to go to *him*.

With the Twin Sisters in the center of the line, infantry on both sides, and cavalry on the right flank, we stretched out for some nine hundred yards.

There was a popular song in those days, a simple little tune called "Come to the Bower." A love song, not a battle song. But now the drummer and three fifers struck it up.

Will you come to the bower I have shaded for you?
Our bed shall be roses all spangled with dew.
There under the bower of roses you lie
With a blush on your cheek but a smile in your eye.

Astride the big white stallion, Sam Houston rode all the way across the long line, making an inspection. What he found was a motley gathering of buckskins and homespuns and clawhammer coats, of farmers and hunters, lawyers and locksmiths, preachers and teachers and sinners and saints. Done, he returned to the center of the line. He sat there a moment, looking back, then looking forward. He shouted a command that I couldn't hear. He dropped his arm. The ragged line began to move across that stretch of open prairie toward the camp of Santa Anna.

The cavalry rode far around on the left to create a diversion. The rest of us walked through the grass, our rifles ready. In the center, artillerymen pulled the Twin Sisters along on rawhide ropes.

The order was to hold our fire until we crested the hill and were well within range. We all walked silently, each of us going back over his own reasons for being here. I felt a prickling of my skin. My hands clutched the rifle I had been given to replace the old Hernandez musket. I knew fear, for I had learned at San Antonio and at Goliad how terrible a battle can be. But I knew also a fresh sense of anger, for now once again I saw Thomas, and I saw all those tragic men with whom I had spent that miserable time in the fortress at Goliad. In my mind I heard again the rattle of musketry, heard the screams of the helpless dying men as they fell on the Copano road. I found myself walking faster and faster, the sound of remembered gunfire exploding in my ears. I found myself muttering quietly. "Goliad. Goliad. This is going to be for Goliad."

We topped over the rise. Now there came a scattering of rifle fire from the Mexican camp. But we saw comparatively few Mexican soldiers. Most of their rifles were stacked.

Siesta! We had caught them at *siesta!*

A Mexican cannon boomed. Our own artillerymen stopped and fired the Twin Sisters. They reloaded and came again, pulling the two cannons closer.

Now that the firing had opened up, men began running. They were shouting, too.

"Remember the Alamo! Remember Goliad!"

The Mexicans of Seguin's company took up the cry in Spanish. *"Recuerden el Alamo!"* The shouts rose up like thunder.

On the far left, the cavalry tore into the Mexican line with a crushing fury.

The Mexican fire was still weak, but it was starting to count. Houston's white stallion went down. Almost instantly someone brought Houston another horse. He remounted, only to go down again, this time with a bullet in his own leg.

Shouting at the tops of our lungs, we raged into the Mexican line, firing, slashing with our bayonets, swinging our rifle butts. The Mexicans who had tried to return our fire went down in those first moments. The others, caught asleep, tried desperately to reach their stacked arms. Most of them never made it.

Riderless Mexican horses galloped through the camp, running over tents in their panic, trampling *soldados* who did not scramble out of their way in time.

Here and there soldiers stopped in their flight to turn and fire at us, but their aim was erratic. Most of the Mexicans simply ran, leaving their weapons behind them.

It has been said that the battle of San Jacinto lasted only about twenty minutes, but the slaughter of San Jacinto went on for hours.

The fleeing Mexicans found themselves trapped by the bayou. Some dived in and tried to swim, many bogging down hopelessly in the mud. Others cowered at the bank, turning helplessly to face the Texian fire. And it was merciless fire, for these men were primed to fury by Santa Anna's vicious slaughter across the entire face of Texas. The screaming *soldados* raised their hands in supplication, only to be cut down.

I had been firing until my rifle barrel was so hot to the touch that it was hard to reload it. As I pushed to ram powder and ball for another shot, I saw a running Mexican confront a bayonet-wielding Texian. He dropped to his knees and cried out, "Me no Alamo! Me no Goliad!"

The Texian rammed the bayonet through the man's heart, put his foot against the body, and jerked the rifle free.

It was no longer a battle. It was a hell of shouting, shooting, screaming men, of panic-stricken riderless horses dashing back and forth, of thundering cannon—our own now, altogether.

Through the smoke I saw a rider loping toward me. I could tell by the uniform that he was Mexican. I raised the rifle to draw a bead. He came through the smoke. I saw his face and gasped.

Antonio Hernandez!

I couldn't shoot. I lowered the rifle. He had his sword raised to strike me, but he recognized me and hesitated.

Beside me, another Texian's rifle roared. The bullet took Antonio in the chest. He jerked backward and toppled to the ground as the frightened horse surged forward, almost running me down.

I turned to see who had fired. It was the one-time highwayman Lige. "I swear, boy, you was about to let that Meskin git away!"

I dropped to one knee beside Antonio. The life was ebbing out of him.

I don't know just what had happened to me then. A cold fury swept over me, a fury at this whole useless, senseless war, a fury for what had happened to Thomas, to all the men at Goliad.

In front of me stood a Mexican officer, no weapon left to him but a saber. I fired and missed. He charged at me, swinging the blade. I raised my rifle and let it take the force of the blow. The saber slid down the barrel, bounced off, caught my arm, and ripped into my sleeve. I felt the deep bite of the steel. But I had too much momentum built to stop now. I swung the rifle butt around and caught him in the stomach. Much of the breath burst out of him.

But he managed to bring up the blade again. Once more I blocked it with the rifle, and this time I stepped in close and gave him a blow in the groin. He stiffened.

My imagination swept me away. For a second I looked at that face and thought I saw the officer who had spoken to us that morning at Goliad, the one who had smiled and led us like a Judas goat leads sheep to the slaughter.

The fury took over. I brought the rifle butt up and caught him under the chin. I pounded him in the face until he fell. In a black rage I used the rifle as a club to pound him and pound him and pound him, taking out on this man all the pent-up bitterness I had carried with me these long weeks.

Finally someone touched my shoulder. I whirled, the bloody rifle ready to strike again. It was Lige.

"Boy, he's as dead as he'll ever be."

That voice brought me crashing down to reality. I shook my head and blinked. Through the gray smoke I could see a vague swirling of figures. Texians still moving on in pursuit of fleeing soldiers. I could hear the ragged pattern of shooting, of continued slaughter. It would go on until darkness finally came to bring it to an end.

But for me, the battle was over. Santa Anna had been destroyed. The Alamo and Goliad had had their bloody vengeance.

It was over, and the fury I had brought with me was spent.

I raised my arm and found blood flowing slowly where the saber had taken its cut.

Lige said, "Boy, you better go and get somebody to see after that arm."

I nodded. I dropped the rifle and walked back in a daze, gripping the arm, the warm blood trickling out between my fingers. But I felt no pain. I felt only a vast relief. It was over now. It had to be.

I sat under a big live oak tree, wearily leaning back against its rough trunk while the doctor wrapped clean cloth around the cut to stop its bleeding. Across the way I could see Sam Houston lying on his blankets beneath another tree, his wounded leg stretched out in front of him. Whatever the pain he suffered—and it was great—he must have been feeling an intense satisfaction. This battle, this victory, was a vindication of his long weeks of silent retreat, of watchful waiting.

Slowly the various companies began to re-form. Weak from the shock of the wound, I nevertheless had to satisfy myself that Muley and Ramón had come through all right. I had told Muley to stay behind.

I found Muley alive, whole, and jubilant. "Josh," he announced proudly, "I fought in that battle. They gave me a rifle and I used it and fought and didn't even run. You ought to be proud of me, Josh. I didn't run this time."

I gripped his shoulder. "I *am* proud of you, Muley."

Muley went with me as I hunted for Juan Seguin's company. It was still badly scattered, but after a long search I found Ramón. His face was begrimed, sweat still running down and leaving tiny trails of mud. He was exhausted, but he didn't show a scratch. He looked at me in alarm, but I assured him it was no worse than I had already received once before, at Goliad.

"It's been a hard day, Josh," he said. "But it was a great victory."

I nodded soberly. "A great victory." I tried to find a soft way to tell him, but there wasn't any.

"Ramón. I saw Antonio."

He read the rest of it in my eyes. "Dead?" I nodded. His eyes closed a moment, and his mouth went hard. Then: "He chose his own way. But he was my brother. Do you think you could find him for me?"

"I could try."

We picked our way across that red-soaked battlefield. Mexican soldiers lay all around us, crumpled in a hundred different attitudes of death. Now that the smoke was lifted and most of the noise and excitement were gone, it was a sickening sight. Muley's face was pale, but he found the courage to stick close beside me, and not turn back.

"There he is, Ramón," I said, pointing.

Ramón dropped to his knees beside his brother's body. He lifted the still hand and felt for a pulse. Gently he eased the hand down, removed his hat, and made the sign of the cross. He knelt there a long time, while we stood in patient silence.

"He is of the enemy," Ramón said finally. "But I will ask General Houston to let me take him home and bury him among our own."

They brought in Santa Anna next day. A great hue and cry arose in camp to hang him, but Houston said no. He argued that Santa Anna, for all his bloody deeds, was of more use to Texas alive than dead. Dead men sign no treaties.

Up to the time of the battle, I would have shouted as loudly as anyone else for Santa Anna's death. But somehow San Jacinto had taken the bitterness out of me. Clubbing the life out of that officer had drained me of anger.

Ramón came to me and said, "Josh, I have permission to leave for home, and to take Antonio."

I could tell it was a way of asking me to go without bringing the question straight out.

"Josh," he continued, "I know you have had some bitter times, and you have had terrible things done to you by Mexican people. But I still consider you my friend."

He turned away, leading a packhorse with its sad burden tied securely.

I glanced at Muley. "When did you plant the corn?"

"First of March, just like you told me to."

"It ought to need plowin' about now, wouldn't you think?"

Muley nodded. "I expect it needs it pretty bad."

I called, "Ramón, hold up. Wait, and we'll all go home together."

ABOUT THE AUTHOR

I was born at a place called Horse Camp on the Scharbauer Cattle Company's Five Wells Ranch in Andrews County, Texas, in 1926. My father was a cowboy there, and my grandfather was the ranch foreman. My great-grandfather had come out from East Texas about 1878 with a wagon and a string of horses to become a ranchman, but he died young, leaving four small boys to grow up as cowpunchers and bronc breakers. With all that heritage I should have become a good cowboy myself, but somehow I never did, so I decided if I could not do it I would write about it.

I studied journalism at the University of Texas and became a livestock and farm reporter in San Angelo, Texas, writing fiction as a sideline to newspaper work. I maintained the two careers in parallel forty-two years. My fiction has been mostly about Texas, about areas whose history and people I know from long study and long personal acquaintance. I have always believed we can learn much about ourselves by studying our history, for we are the products of all that has gone before us. All history is relevant today, because the way we live—the values we believe in—are a result of molds prepared for us by our forebears a long time ago.

I was an infantryman in World War II and married an Austrian girl, Anna, I met there shortly after the war. We raised three children, all grown now and independent, proud of their mixed heritage of the Old World on one hand and the Texas frontier on the other.

Kiss Me

To Tami,
It was so great to
meet you :)

Kiss Me

An Avon Books Valentine's Day Anthology

CODI GARY,
CHERYL HARPER,
JACLYN HATCHER

AVONIMPULSE
An Imprint of HarperCollins*Publishers*

This is a work of fiction. Names, characters, places, and incidents are products of the author's imagination or are used fictitiously and are not to be construed as real. Any resemblance to actual events, locales, organizations, or persons, living or dead, is entirely coincidental.

EPub Edition FEBRUARY 2013 ISBN: 9780062273970

Print Edition ISBN: 9780062273987

10 9 8 7 6 5 4 3 2

The Trouble With Sexy

Codi Gary

For my husband Brian.
Thank you for your continuous encouragement,
love, and support, especially on Sundays.

Chapter One

Eight days until Valentine's Day . . .

"No, I really do. I hate Valentine's Day," Ryan Ashton said firmly, her blue eyes serious.

Gregg threw his hands in the air. "Come on! All girls say that so they won't be disappointed when their significant other doesn't measure up to the hype of romanticism. If a woman doesn't get any of those heart-shaped boxes of candy or a dozen red roses, she'll sit in front of the TV with a pint of Ben & Jerry's Half Baked, crying pathetically while watching *The Notebook*."

Ryan tossed him a glare from across the table of the only coffee shop in their little town, The Local Bean. "Well it's a good thing I don't have a significant other to expect things from."

Gregg asked, "So no plans, then?"

She took a sip of her coffee and assured him, "It's not

a big deal. When I was eleven I had to put my horse Shara down on Valentine's Day. It scarred me for life."

Gregg raised an eyebrow at her and replied, "Really? A horse?"

Ryan's glare became murderous. "Are you laughing at my pain?"

Gregg deadpanned, "No, of course not."

She turned her head from left to right and reached out to smack him on the arm.

"Ouch!" he yelped, rubbing the abused area. "I can't believe you hit me."

She hissed back, "I can't believe you're being such a jerk. You're usually so sweet."

Gregg's gaze shifted away from her. "Yeah well, I guess not everybody likes that kind of thing."

Ryan followed the direction of his glance to the petite blonde working behind the counter and snorted. "Seriously, I don't know why you're so hung up on Ado Gracie," she said, referring to the character in *Oklahoma*.

Gregg barked a laugh and asked, "Really? That's the derogatory nickname you're going with?"

She shrugged. "What? I like musicals. And it fits. She's like a jackrabbit; she bounces around from one guy to the next. Plus I thought you were over that. You guys had one date."

Gregg's tone was testy. "I am over it."

Ryan continued as if he hadn't said a word. "Plus I've heard she's dated all the eligible guys in the surrounding areas."

"Listen to you gossiping like one of the girls. Gracie has not dated every eligible guy."

"Okay, not every guy. Only the cute ones," she teased.

Gregg's face split into a teasing smile. "Are you calling me cute?"

She scoffed. "Of course. You know you're adorable."

"Well geez, that's sweet. Next time try not to sound so disgusted."

Ryan had been going for nonchalant, not disgusted. Gregg was far from disgusting and much more than adorable. His sun-streaked brown was a little long at the moment, resting just over the top of his ears. He had olive skin that tanned easily, and his eyes were a rich hazel with flecks of gold and green. They were adorned with thick eyelashes Ryan thought were a waste on any man and she often grumbled about it. His straight aquiline nose sat perfectly centered over full lips and a gorgeous, easy smile. He could have been a cocky ass, but he was actually one of the nicest guys she'd ever met. Gregg was one of the few people that she'd just clicked with instantaneously, and she valued him as a friend.

Not that she was immune to his good looks. Her heart skipped in her chest every time they worked closely together, and she thought he was absolutely brilliant with a camera. She sometimes caught herself staring at that gorgeous mouth, and when he'd give her a curious look, she'd blush from head to toe in embarrassment. She wasn't under any delusions about her appeal or that Gregg harbored a secret yearning for her. It was just sometimes nice to daydream that when he was looking at her he saw her as more than just the frumpy girl from work.

He looked at his watch and took another sip of his coffee. "Well I've got to head out to Andrew's place to take their thirtieth anniversary pictures."

Ryan's heart clenched. Thirty years together? She was only twenty-six but had always pictured herself meeting the guy she would marry in college. That hadn't happened, though. Instead she'd met Matt—*It's not you, it's me*—sophomore year of college. Josh—*I just don't think we're right for each other*—had dated her for seven months before dropping that bomb. And her personal favorite after four months last year, Doug—*I don't want to hurt your feelings, but you're boring.* At least one of them had given her an honest answer about why they were dumping her. She needed to wear a name tag that said, "Hello, my name is Ryan Ashton. I'm boring. Why bother?"

"Earth to Ryan. Come in Ryan."

She blinked away her thoughts and blushed. "Sorry, distracted. I'll walk out with you. I have to get to the studio by ten to take pictures of little Dylan Watson. He's three months old, you know."

Gregg laughed as he stood up, and Ryan admired the way his eyes crinkled at the corners. He called back as he opened the door with a smile and a wave, " 'Bye, Gracie."

Gracie looked up and smiled brightly. " 'Bye, Gregg! Have a good one."

Ryan waved, but Gracie had already turned back to another customer. She knew she shouldn't feel slighted that the wispy blonde hadn't said good-bye to her, but as she followed Gregg out she couldn't help grumbling, "'Bye to you too."

"Are you jealous of Gracie or something?" he asked.

"No. Of course not. Why would I be?"

He shrugged. "I have no idea."

There was something in his tone that made her look up at him curiously. Had he sounded a little grumpy or was she losing it? She dismissed it as an overactive imagination and asked, "So what are you doing for Valentine's Day?"

"The actual day? Nothing yet. I'm taking pictures at the Sweethearts Festival for the Rock Canyon Press on Friday. Afterward I thought I might participate in the singles auction before the dance. You want to come bid on me?" He struck a sexy pose and she laughed, although her heart dropped a bit at the mention of such a romantic event.

The Sweethearts Festival was a large craft fair that ended in a singles auction and a sweethearts' dance afterward. People talked about it in awed tones, whispering about the magic in the air created by dollar kissing booths and homemade love potions. The excitement of winning the man or woman of your dreams, and taking them to the dance, where more than one couple had pledged their love and devotion. Such places were not for drab losers with all the appeal of burned toast.

She pushed through the bitter thoughts and scolded, "Are you seriously going to get up on stage and let a bunch of girls waste their hard-earned money on you?"

He looked affronted. "Waste? I'm a catch! And no, I'm

just going as Mike's wing man. Gracie told him she's trying to convince Gemma to participate, and he wants to win her. He's hoping that once put into a romantic setting, she'll change her mind about them dating. I feel sorry for the poor guy, being put in the friend category for so long."

"What are we raising the money for, anyway?" The friend comment stung a little, but she wanted to keep the conversation going. She loved the sound of his voice.

"I'm not sure; I'll have to read the flyer again. Hey, you never answered me, though, about what you were doing for V-day." He pulled his keys out of his pocket as he spoke, and she wondered if he really cared or was just being polite.

"Probably sit at home with a pint of Ben & Jerry's Half Baked. Maybe cry pathetically while watching *The Notebook.*" She gave him a brilliant smile when he looked up quickly.

He flashed her a sheepish grin. "Touché. Hey, since neither one of us has plans, why don't we grab dinner or something? We could talk about how bitter we are, and maybe watch a horror movie. Anti-Valentine's Day. It could be fun."

Yeah because that wouldn't be awkward. Going out with him on the most romantic day of the year and pretending that she wasn't wishing that they were out on a real date. "Sounds like a blast, but I think I'll pass."

"Well the invitations there if you change your mind. We could mock all the stupid couples in the movie that try to sacrifice themselves to save their lovers." He let out a diabolical evil villain laugh.

Gregg could be such a goofball. She shook her head, still smiling as she said, "Yes because that's not morbid, to laugh when someone dies by an axe to the head."

"That's the point! 'Cause if we were ever in a horror movie, we'd survive because we don't have anyone."

His argument made her even more depressed. "Awesome. I'll remember that when Freddy comes for me in my dreams."

He laughed and patted her shoulder. "That's the spirit! I'll see you later."

"See ya."

Her shoulder felt the weight of his hand even after he turned to walk toward the parking lot. Actually, his gait was much sexier than a mere walk, and she admired the way he moved until he disappeared into the parked cars in the lot. She finally turned away to head toward the studio, her expression grim. She was actually surprised that no one had snapped Gregg up, especially considering how many women stopped by for package pricing but never wanted to speak to her. She crossed the street and walked by the empty shop next door, noticing the lights were on. Inside, she saw a lean guy with dark spiky hair moving boxes around.

He was good-looking, thinner than Gregg, but his arms were nicely defined and they flexed with each box he lifted under the gray T-shirt he wore. He glanced up through the glass and his eyes locked on her watching him. She felt her cheeks flame in embarrassment, turned and hurried toward the safety of the studio.

Great, now the guy was going to think she was some kind of weird voyeur.

Once inside, she moved passed Gregg's desk to her own, sliding her jacket off and over the back of her chair. She walked back to the little kitchen area and pulled a Coke from the fridge. A picture of Gregg and Mike from New Year's caught her eye, and her whole body tingled as her thoughts drifted to their one and only kiss.

She'd been standing in the corner away from everyone, holding a glass of champagne in her right hand, wearing black wool pants, a silver satin button-up top, and her plain black cardigan. She'd only showed up because Stephanie Brown had caught her in a weak, lonely moment, and she didn't want to spend the evening in her I Love Sushi pajamas with a bag of chili-flavored Fritos in her lap.

"You look like you're having a blast."

Her eyes had popped up toward the deep voice, to find Gregg smiling down at her.

She had been tempted to throw her arms around him in gratitude. Most of the people she knew at the Browns' New Year's Eve party had stopped trying to hold onto a conversation with her by their third shot. Recovering from her initial excitement, she quipped, "Oh yeah, awesome. Time of my life."

Then the voices around them started shouting.

"Ten . . . nine . . . eight . . ."

Gregg shocked her when he reached out to trail his hand against her cheek.

"Seven . . . six . . . five . . ."

Ryan hadn't even registered that his mouth was descending down toward her parted lips.

"Four . . . three . . . two . . . one . . . Happy New Year!"

Loud music hummed in her head as the first brush of his kiss made her eyes flutter closed. The music and cheers drained away, and all she'd been aware of was the taste of Gregg, the feel of his tongue as it swept inside to play with hers, and the rough hand that cupped her cheek. She swayed toward his warmth and could have stayed like that forever if he hadn't pulled back.

Her eyes had been unwilling to open and break the spell his kiss weaved over her, until his voice broke through her daze. "Happy New Year, Ryan."

Finally she'd looked up at him, trying to form the words. What did it mean? Was it just a traditional kiss? While her brain tried to form a coherent thought, a petite brunette grabbed Gregg by the arm and threw herself against his body, plastering her mouth on his.

Ryan had brushed past them quickly, before they broke apart and Gregg caught the tears forming in her eyes.

She'd driven home from the party and ended up exactly where she'd been trying to avoid—on the couch, in I love Sushi pajamas, with handfuls of Fritos shoved into her open mouth.

The bell on the studio door jingled, drawing her back to the present, and Ryan took a steadying breath.

Stop dwelling on it. He's your boss and your friend. That's it. Get over it.

"THAT'S GREAT, YOU guys. Now Mr. Andrews, why don't you put your arm around her and give her a kiss?"

Jim Andrews gave his wife a lecherous grin and said, "Come here and give me some sugar."

Marcie Andrews turned her cheek up for his lips and Jim kissed it with a chuckle. Gregg snapped the smiling Marcie and looked down at his camera. "Okay, so I have about a hundred pictures. Why don't you come by tomorrow afternoon around two and I'll show you the top thirty? You can choose your prints then."

"But we're getting a CD right? Can't we just print the ones we want?" Mrs. Andrews asked, her head cocked to the side innocently.

Gregg wanted to growl at her in frustration. He'd told Mrs. Andrews when she made the appointment that it was $125 for him to come out for an hour and snap around a hundred photos. The package she'd picked included twenty prints and the CD. The prints were included, so even if she didn't want them, it didn't lower the price.

"Like I explained on the phone Mrs. Andrews, the prints are free with the package you chose. If you chose not to take them, that's up to you." He tried to stay friendly even though she made him crazy. He knew his photo packages were reasonable compared to some photographers. Plus he normally threw in a little something extra like a framed eight-by-ten, but right now Mrs. Andrews wasn't exactly on his favorite customer list.

Mr. Andrews gave his wife a stern look and she snapped whatever she was about to say back into her mouth with a pout. Mr. Andrews turned with a smile on his craggy face. "That's fine, Gregg, we appreciate it. Thanks for coming out."

Gregg smiled in return, liking the easygoing dairy farmer. "Thank you, Mr. Andrews. Mrs. Andrews, it was a pleasure. You folks have a nice day and I'll see you love birds tomorrow."

The older couple smiled at him as he gathered up his equipment and headed for his blue Chevy Tahoe. He waved good-bye again from the front seat and put the car in reverse, looking over his shoulder. He noticed the scrap of black in the backseat and cursed. He'd meant to give Ryan back the sweater she left in his car after the Wilder wedding, but he kept forgetting. It had nothing to do with the fact that the sweet smell of her perfume reminded him of the one kiss they'd shared at the Browns' New Year's Eve party.

Gregg constantly tried to talk himself out of his feelings, but every time he was with her, he couldn't help liking her. Even when he'd gone on his one and only date with Gracie McAllister, he'd spent most of the evening comparing Gracie's boisterous personality and raw sexuality to Ryan's snarky comebacks and quiet appeal. It had only stung his pride that Gracie had never returned his phone call. He'd just called to tell her he had a nice time, but from what he'd heard around, that was usual with her. It was just more fun for him to tease Ryan about Gracie, since the pretty barrista seemed to annoy Ryan, and Ryan was awfully cute when she was annoyed.

Suggesting that they spend Valentine's Day together had been a spur of the moment thing, but he was surprised when she'd said no. He always had fun with Ryan and considered her a good friend. He'd figured she felt that way too. Had she lied about having plans? Was she seeing someone and just hadn't wanted to share it with him? A little niggle of something unpleasant churned in his abdomen, something that felt a bit like jealousy, and he tried to shake it off. Ryan wasn't a liar, and she had no reason to lie about her plans. Maybe she just wanted to be alone.

He pulled out onto Oak Avenue toward the studio and made the right onto Main Street. Parallel parking, he rushed into the office before the cold wind hit him. The bell chiming overhead and Ryan's voice carried from the back room.

"I'll be right with you!"

"It's just me."

Ryan peeked around the corner, her blue eyes filled with relief. "Oh thank God! Could you hand me my jacket on the back of the chair?"

"Sure, what's going on?"

Gregg came around the corner and nearly swallowed his tongue. Ryan was wearing the same type of wool slacks she wore to work most days, her flame red hair pulled back into a no nonsense bun and her face free of any makeup. Her nose had a little bump on the bridge, and she had a heart-shaped face with full lips. His eyes traveled down to where her buttoned-to-the-neck top should have been and instead, in its place, a slinky white camisole showed a lot more than it covered. It was usually hard to discern what her figure looked like under her drab clothes, but in the tight top tucked into the slacks he could see that her breasts were firm, more than a handful, and it made his palms itch to reach out and cup them. Her waist was slim and indented, and if he had to hazard a guess, they probably flared quite nicely under the sexless pants.

His imagination was taking a dangerous turn and his mouth dried out as he pictured her in nothing but that sexy little see-through top. When he opened his mouth to speak, it came out a little ragged. "What happened to your shirt?"

"Oh good, you brought my sweater." Oblivious to his pained expression, she grabbed the cardigan and slipped it over her arms and shoulders. She buttoned the sweater, covering the upper portion of bare skin he'd been admiring, and said, "While Cammie and Joel picked out the pictures they wanted, I offered to hold Dylan, and the little booger puked on me. I tried to just wipe it off, but apparently baby puke is toxic. I couldn't get the smell to go away and it was making my stomach turn."

He tried to forget about what he'd seen under the dowdy black sweater, and choked out, "So is it just the puke you object to? Or is it the actual kid you find distasteful?"

She shook her head and walked around him. "No, I love kids. I would love some of my own someday, lots of them, but the only puke I want to clean off me is theirs. Or my husband's, depending on how much I love him."

He wasn't sure he'd ever love anyone enough to let them puke on him. He tried imagining Ryan sitting in a rocking chair surrounded by a dozen little cherub faces, and the scene made him smile. She'd make a wonderful mother, being so patient with the kids who came into the studio.

"So how many is a lot?"

She smiled as she sat down at her computer. "I don't know, maybe four? I always wanted a big family. My mom had complications when she had me so she could never have any more kids, and it was always kind of lonely by myself. We didn't live in a neighborhood, so I didn't really get to have friends until school, and I had a few really great ones but I was always a little . . . awkward."

Gregg knew that Ryan had a hard time talking to people outside of her job, and it always puzzled him. She had been a little nervous during her interview with him when she responded to his help wanted ad, but she warmed up quickly. Of course, they had been talking about photography, which Ryan was very passionate about, but after that he hadn't had any trouble having a conversation with her. In fact, she was actually really funny and could give as good as she got.

This wasn't the first time Ryan had brought up her awkwardness, and for some reason, the thought that she couldn't see herself the way he did bothered him. To him she was funny, sweet, and easy to talk to. Their constant banter was one of the things he looked forward to most days.

He leaned over her shoulder and whispered, "Well I don't know if it counts for anything, but I think that you have definitely grown out of your awkward stage."

She looked up at him. "You really don't think I'm awkward?"

He stared down at her, drowning in her eyes. "Not at all."

She swallowed a little. "Gregg, we're friends right?"

He cocked his head and gave her a small smile. "Of course."

She twisted her hands in her lap. "And you'll be honest with me?"

He sat on her desk and nodded. "Sure."

She cleared her throat and whispered, "Do you think I'm sexy?"

He froze above her and his mind started searching for something to say.

She turned away from him quickly. "I'm sorry, please forget I said anything."

He hadn't liked the flash of hurt in her eyes, and blurted, "No! I mean, you just surprised me. I think you have a lot of really great qualities. You're smart. You're funny. You are really artistic. You're attractive. You have a great work ethic. You're a good person." He paused and took in her blank expression. "Yes, you're sexy."

He could tell by the look on her face that she didn't believe him, so he continued, "The trouble with sexy is people have different tastes. Some guys like girls in flashy skimpy clothes with big hair and cowboy boots. Other guys think shy girls that are less obvious are more desirable. Some guys check out a woman's body and others look at her face. It's all about personal preference."

"What kind of girls do you like?"

Was she kidding? He didn't really have a type, unless you counted busty redheads with blue eyes that liked to wear a lot of wool, but he wasn't about to say that. Besides accepting his kiss at New Years, Ryan had been nothing but professional, and a good friend. He wasn't going to jeopardize that by opening his big fat mouth. "I like girls who are confident. They need to be funny and like the same things I do—"

She interrupted him. "Yeah, but that's not what makes you approach her right? Are you a leg man or a breast man?"

"What?" He couldn't help the bark of laughter that escaped.

"It's a simple question. Does a girl that walks into a bar wearing a miniskirt get you going or a low-cut top?"

This conversation was leading into some very dangerous areas, but he answered her anyway. "Low-cut top."

She blushed at his quick reply, and at that moment he'd have given more than a penny to get a real good look at those thoughts.

Chapter Two

RYAN LOCKED UP the studio at five o'clock and gasped as a blast of frigid air hit her face. Maybe it would help to take her mind off the sting of humiliation she still felt from Gregg's good-natured attempt to spare her feelings. Attractive? Great work ethic? Really? Funny how he'd almost choked when he tried to assure her she was sexy. She knew she wasn't out-of-this-world gorgeous, but he could have done better than a gargled attempt to save her ego.

Thank God Mr. Francini had come in to ask Gregg to take pictures of some vandalism he was sure had been perpetrated by Mr. Nelson. The two men had been involved in a vindictive feud for the last fifteen years, and were constantly blaming each other for phantom acts of theft and sabotage. Gregg and Mr. Francini had walked out of the studio, and she was left alone to dwell on her very big problem. If she didn't make a change soon, she was going to end up being the lonely, bitter woman Gregg teased her about: eating ice cream every night, wondering why she couldn't find someone to love her.

She hadn't exactly been honest with Gregg. She would have been excited about Valentine's Day if she had a special someone to share it with. She was tired of being alone, and wanted to find someone. Someone who wanted to get married and have a family, someone who would love her for all her snark and insecurities. But that type of man was hard to come by. Especially when you had the sex appeal of a hermit crab.

She smiled over the analogy and thought of her large cardigans and high-necked tops as her protective shells. Her mother had never thought clothes that were in style were appropriate for her little girl, being too short and too revealing, and she'd urged her to earn respect based on her mind rather than her looks. Ryan had learned the lesson too well. She continued to dress conservatively, even though she'd watched the girls in stylish dresses and boots longingly. She once tried on a tight black dress at Macy's for a date, and loved the feel of the soft material hugging her body, but all she could think of as she stared at herself in the mirror was her mother's voice: *Guys like a little something left to the imagination. Those are the type of girls they want to bring home to their mothers.* She'd put the dress back on the rack and walked out empty-handed.

Her mother failed to mention that mothers might love conservatively dressed girls, but their sons sure didn't.

She walked toward her Rav4 in The Local Bean parking lot and noticed that Gracie was just coming out of the shop. She was dressed in a tight-fitting red sweater dress, black tights, and knee-high black suede boots. Her blond hair was perfectly flipped, and Ryan was sure that her face was just as perfect. She envied the confident way Gracie held herself, and thought if she just had a little bit of that, maybe Gregg would look at her differently.

Girls like Gracie had always intimidated Ryan. It wasn't even that they were prettier or that they always seemed to know what to say or do in any situation to have people hang on their every word. It had nothing to do with them and everything to do with how she felt around them. Tongue-tied. Quiet. Shy. She didn't feel bullied, just never really noticed unless it had something to do with the color of her hair, which bothered her. Her hair seemed to draw teasing comments. More than once she had considered dying the irritating strands, but could never spark the courage.

She'd tried to cope through awkward encounters with other girls with her own sense of snark and humor, but most of them found her strange and off-putting. She'd had a few good girlfriends who understood her, but none of them could help her with her current dilemma. They weren't exactly . . . sex kittens.

Gracie must have heard her footsteps because she turned to see who was walking behind her. After surveying her, Gracie turned back around, apparently deciding Ryan wasn't much of a threat. Ryan didn't know what possessed her, but before Gracie got too far ahead, she blurted, "Excuse me, Gracie? Can I talk to you?"

Gracie turned around, her brow furrowed in confusion. She was probably wondering why Ryan wanted to talk, since they'd hardly had a single conversation since she'd moved to Rock Canyon. "Hi Ryan," the other girl said. "How are you?"

Ryan felt a twinge of nervousness but pushed on. "I'm good, thanks. I was wondering if I could ask you something."

Gracie cocked her head. "Sure. Let's walk and talk, though. It's freaking cold out here."

It was on the tip of Ryan's tongue to mention that if she was wearing more clothes she'd be less cold, but she decided it would defeat the purpose of her little impromptu powwow. "I was just wondering how you . . . well, you obviously . . ."

Gracie stopped at her car and turned to her impatiently. "Spit it out, girlie."

Ryan felt a twitch of temper. Gracie wasn't much older than her. "I want to learn how to be sexy. Can you teach me?"

Gracie looked at her seriously, her eyes trailing up and down her outfit. Gracie's face broke into a huge smile and she said, "Hop in; we can take a road trip."

Ryan started to stutter an excuse and Gracie raised an eyebrow. "Look, I hardly know you. You approached me and I am more than willing to answer your questions, but you've got to trust me. Deal?"

Ryan stared at Gracie as if she had horns and a tail. She was supposed to just go with a woman she barely knew and do what she said, no questions asked?

Gracie shrugged. "Suit yourself."

She started to open her car door, and Ryan cried, "Wait!"

Gracie looked over her shoulder with exasperation. "Seriously, get in."

Ryan walked carefully to the passenger side and hopped in. "Where are we going?"

Gracie smiled at her. "Well, sexy comes with a price tag. I figure it's only five. We have enough time to head into Twin Falls for a little shopping and other beautifying experiences."

Ryan blushed. "I don't know . . ."

"You have your wallet?"

Ryan blinked. "Yes."

Gracie's smile flashed, lighting up her green eyes. "Great, let's go."

Gracie pulled out of the parking lot and headed out of town toward Twin Falls. She glanced over at Ryan. "What made you ask me, anyway? I never really got the impression you liked me very much."

Ryan's face was beat red at Gracie's blunt assessment. "It's not that I don't like you. I just . . ." Her voice lowered an octave. "Gregg's my friend. You hurt his feelings."

Gracie silently stared at the road for a while. "You know, I never meant to hurt Gregg. He's a sweet guy but we just . . . weren't compatible."

Ryan gave a bark of bitter laughter. "Yeah, I get that a lot too."

Gracie glanced over at her. "How's that?"

Ryan looked down at her hands. "I've been told I'm . . .

boring. And not sexy at all." She swallowed hard. "That's why I thought I could get some advice from you. All the guys in town think you're sexy."

Gracie looked positively feline. "And you want to hook a guy? Anyone I know?"

Ryan looked away and muttered, "No."

Gracie made a left turn and said, "Well, girlie, I guarantee you, by the time we're done, whoever you're setting bait for will be good and hooked."

RYAN LOADED THE last of the shopping bags they'd purchased into the trunk and sighed in relief.

Gracie had dragged her into the salon, and after a brief negotiation, Gracie convinced her stylist, Jessica, to squeeze Ryan in for a cut and style. While Jessica worked on Ryan's hair, Gracie snagged Karen, whose five o'clock appointment hadn't shown up, to give Ryan a mani/pedi before she left for the day. Gracie argued Ryan down when she'd tried for just clear polish on her nails and toes. Instead, she picked a vibrant red for Ryan's toes and suggested French tips for her fingernails. When Jessica finished layering Ryan's long red tresses, she took a fat curling iron to them, spiraling curls past Ryan's shoulders. She had stared at the difference in her appearance in the mirror, turning left and right, and after paying both ladies, left a generous tip.

Gracie rushed her from the salon to the car; all the while talking about how being sexy was all about feeling good about oneself. "If you think you look hot, other people are going to notice. It's all about attitude, my friend."

Once they hit the mall, Gracie dragged her into Victoria Secret, where Ryan bought several sets of uncomfortable, overpriced panties and bras, one slinky nightie in black with a matching robe, and a white bustier with little red hearts on it. The corset was too tight, but when she'd said so, Gracie demanded that Ryan let her see. She'd protested from the safe side of the dressing room door, and Gracie merely scolded, "Dude, it's not like I'm checking you out in a sexual way. I just think you don't know what you're talking about because you've never worn one."

Ryan reluctantly opened the door a crack, placing her hands over her overflowing chest. Gracie pushed the door open wider, grabbed her hands and gave her a once over. "Nope, it's perfect," she said. "Your boobs look awesome, and it's super sexy. You're buying it." Ryan had been too astounded to argue.

They'd hit several more stores afterward, and finally finished up at Macy's, where Megan, the girl at the makeup counter, used a mineral type of makeup on her. She tried not to squirm or twitch when Megan brought the eyeliner and mascara toward her eyes. When she finished, Megan turned the mirror around to face her and asked, "What do you think?"

Ryan had stared at the girl in the mirror. The darkly shadowed eyes seemed brighter than usual, and the line of freckles was nonexistent. Her lashes were long and full, her lips plump and glossy. "Wow."

Megan had put everything she'd used on the counter,

and Ryan hardly blanched at the price. She never bought anything she didn't absolutely need for herself and had built up quite a nest egg, so whatever she spent could just be replaced later. She'd smiled as she handed over her credit card, and when she left, fairly danced out the door.

She was brought back to the present when Gracie stopped her from slamming the trunk closed. "There's no sense in wasting that hair or face. Here." She rifled through the bags, pulling out the midnight blue bra and panty set, telling Ryan, "Sexy starts from the skin out. There's no way you're giving off a sexy vibe in granny panties."

Ryan blushed and muttered, "They're briefs and they're comfortable."

Gracie snorted, "Yeah, and so is a muumuu, but guys don't get turned on by those either." She rifled some more and pulled out a clingy blue top with a low neckline, Ryan's new boot-cut jeans, and the black ankle boots she had fallen in love with. Gracie shoved the clothes into her arms and said, "There."

Ryan took the bounty and asked, "Where do you want me to change?"

Gracie rolled her eyes. "In the car, silly. Come on, it's almost nine-thirty. I think we should head over to Buck's Shot Bar for a little fun."

Ryan shook her head. "Gracie, I can't change in the car. Someone might see me."

Gracie reached in and pulled out the slinky pinky dress she'd bought. "I'll do it with you. Here, we'll pull over to the dark part of the parking lot. No one will see."

Ryan didn't protest again. She'd learned over the last few hours that Gracie was pretty much used to getting her way and didn't take well to the word no. She crawled into the backseat and started to change. Gracie climbed into the front and lifted up her sweater dress, tossing it into the back just as a truck drove by, honking. She continued to pull the pink number over her head and fluffed her hair, unfazed by the fact that someone had seen her nearly naked. Ryan shook her head at the woman's confidence.

When Ryan finally finished changing, she stepped out of the car, wiggling about. How did women find the scratchy lace and wedgie-causing boy shorts comfortable?

"How do I look?"

Gracie eyed her from the driver's seat. "Damn girl, I think you went way past sexy."

Ryan's face hurt all the way to Buck's from smiling so hard. Gracie kept jabbering on and on, and Ryan turned to her in the seat. "Thank you, Gracie. For today. I . . . don't have a lot of girlfriends. I'm a little awkward around other women especially . . ."

Gracie gave her a look out of the corner of her eye, "Dumb ones?"

Ryan gasped. "No. Popular types. Pretty ones."

Gracie burst out laughing. "Oh honey, I wasn't ever popular. I was a drama girl in high school and I tended to say whatever I was thinking whenever I wanted. That doesn't exactly endear you to people. I just love the spotlight so much that it just keeps following me." She paused for a minute. "As for not feeling like you belong, I don't think you'll have a problem with that tonight. You'll be the belle of the ball."

GREGG WAS GETTING a beer with his friend Michael Stevens, discussing the latest romantic setback with Mike's friend Gemma, when Mike's eyes caught something at the door. "Damn."

Gregg swiveled his head around to see what had caught Mike's attention and his mouth dropped. He barely glanced at Gracie standing in the doorway in her bright pink clingy dress. His eyes devoured the curvy redhead in the tight jeans and low-cut blue top next to her. "Holy hell."

Mike recovered enough to joke. "I think I covered it with 'Damn.'"

Gracie and Ryan walked toward the bar, and Gregg's eyes were drawn to the shy smile on Ryan's made-up face. Why was she dressed like that? And why was she wearing all that makeup? Gracie was waving to get Eric Henderson's attention, and when Eric approached them, Mike elbowed Gregg in the ribs. "You want to go over and say hi?"

What Gregg wanted was to live in a universe that did not leave him feeling like all the air had been sucked out of the atmosphere. When had Ryan started hanging with Gracie? There was only one way he was going to get any answers, and that was to talk to her. He sucked down the rest of his beer and walked toward Ryan and Gracie, Mike close on his heels. Before the two men rounded the bar, though, a tall guy with spiky hair and earrings approached the two women. It was immediately apparent that Ryan was his object of interest. Gregg's eyebrows slashed in irritation as he watched the guy put money on the bar, obviously paying for Ryan and Gracie's drinks. "Do you know that guy?" Gregg didn't even recognize his own voice, it sounded so dark and gravelly.

Mike shook his head and said, "Nope. He's probably just in town for the night, slumming it with us hicks."

Gregg scowled as Ryan's cheeks flushed with color and she smiled sweetly at the stranger. He watched her glossy lips as she took a sip of her drink, and he wondered if the gloss was flavored.

Mike pushed him forward and asked, "So are we going to go over and talk to them or can I get another beer?"

Gregg moved again, oblivious to everyone he brushed past except the alluring redheaded angel currently inhabiting Ryan's body.

RYAN WAS ENJOYING Chase Trepasso's attention. She'd been horrified when she recognized him as the man in the shop who had caught her staring that morning, but after a few minutes of conversation, she realized that Chase didn't recognize her. He'd introduced himself, bought them drinks, and given both her and Gracie his card. *Jagged Rock Tattoo Parlor* had been written in rough script with his name, number, and the shop address on it. He'd asked them what they did, and after listening politely to Gracie, turned to her. "What about you?"

She wasn't sure if she should've been pleased or irritated he didn't recognize her, considering there weren't very many redheads running around town. "I'm a photographer. I work in the studio next door to your shop."

"Really? I've been thinking of hiring a photographer to take pictures of some of my work. Maybe I could come by your studio for a price quote?" Chase was leaning on the bar next to her, and Ryan felt giddy as she looked up into his cool gray eyes. She'd dated guys before, but never had one actually come up to her with the exclusive purpose of getting to know her. Most of the time they needed help with an assignment and thought she was funny or that under her frumpy clothes there was really a wild woman waiting to rock their world.

It was quite flattering to have such a good-looking guy taking such an interest in her, and her smile widened as she said, "Of course. I could show you my portfolio and give you a list of packages. I'm usually in the studio Monday through Friday until five, and sometimes Saturday, depending on the schedule and appointments, so if you want to set something up, I'd be happy to help." Ryan didn't know if it was the way he was looking at her, but she surprised herself when she added flirtatiously, "Anything you need, you just let me know."

"Maybe you could give me your number. That way I could call you and make sure you're available." He was so close to her now that she got a good whiff of Irish soap, and started to lose her nerve. Chase had the look of a bad boy, and she wasn't quite sure she wanted to encourage him. She wanted to meet a nice man who was looking for a wife, not a hot tattoo artist looking for a fling.

She felt Gracie's elbow dig into her ribs and she made a split second decision, reaching into her purse for a business card and handing it to him. "Here. Now you can call me and I'll schedule a time for us to talk."

He leaned close to her, and there was no missing the suggestive tone as he said, "I look forward to it." Then he stepped back from her with a wink and said, "You ladies enjoy the rest of your night. I've got a lot more networking to do. No better place to advertise a tattoo parlor than a bar with a bunch of drunk people."

The girls laughed, and Ryan watched him move through the crowd. She turned to Gracie with wide eyes when she lost sight of him and asked, "He was hitting on me, right? I'm not making it up in my head?"

Gracie smiled at her and confirmed, "Oh yeah. That was a definite come on. He barely looked at me." Her smile turned into a frown and she continued, "I think I should be insulted. My hotness at least warrants a glance."

Ryan laughed at her new friend and squeezed her arm. "I'm pretty sure he glanced at you. Besides, you have no one to blame but yourself. You did too good a job on me."

Gracie appeared to ponder this. "You're right. I did too good a job. Cover up some, and put your hair back into that prison guard bun."

Ryan was still laughing when Mike came up behind Gracie and gave her a smacking kiss on the cheek. Mike, Gracie, and Gracie's best friend Gemma had been close friends since high school and still did almost everything together. Ryan smiled as Gracie slipped her arm around Mike's waist and said, "Michael, what do you think you're doing? You're going to scare away all my potential conquests."

Mike rolled his eyes. "I think you've already conquested everyone in this bar."

Gracie fluttered her eyes at him. "Not you."

Ryan laughed along with Mike, who turned to her and gave her a thumbs-up. "You look awesome, Ryan. Did you do something different with your hair?"

Ryan felt her cheeks flame with shy pleasure. "Thanks. Yeah, I got it cut. And Gracie took me shopping."

Ryan noticed Gregg standing a little behind Mike. His eyes were focused so intently on her face that she felt the red on her cheeks spread to her hairline. Why was he just staring at her like that, saying nothing?

Why am I just standing here staring? Say something, you idiot!

Gregg shook himself from his mesmerized state and said, "You look beautiful."

He watched Ryan's eyes widen. "Thank you," she said.

"Michael, why don't we go dance?" Gracie nudged Mike, who kept grinning.

"Naw, I think I'm good here . . . yow!"

Gracie grabbed hold of his ear, smiling at Ryan. "We'll see you guys later."

Standing just at the edge of the bar, the sounds of the crowd were loud, but Gregg hardly heard them. He was too busy concentrating on Ryan's pouty lips. He realized they were moving, and he blurted, "What?"

She gave him a curious expression and repeated, "Are you sure it's not too much?" He swallowed. Hard. "No, not at all. I mean, I think you always look great but . . ."

Her eyes looked wary. "But what?"

He tried to find the words, and finally just asked, "Why the change?"

Her chin lifted up a notch. "Why not?"

He didn't have an answer for her yet. He could tell by the stiff line of her shoulders that she was feeling defensive. He knew she didn't take criticism well and that the smallest comment could get her dander up quicker than a dog could tree a cat. Now, her disgruntled look made him smile and relax. No matter how much makeup she was wearing or how different her clothes were, she was still Ryan. She was still the girl who had a secret comic book stash in her desk that he'd found by accident while looking for a pen. She was still the same Ryan whose knees started to shake when she reached the top step on the step stool, and instead usually just waited for him to get whatever she needed from the top shelf. No matter what she did to her outsides, she was still quirky, funny Ryan on the inside.

Gregg reached out to run his hand down her cheek, trailing his fingers over her neck and shoulders. He slid it down to take her hand and commanded softly, "Dance with me."

RYAN LET GREGG lead her out onto Buck's crowded floor and slip the hand he held up behind his neck. He released it and slid both hands over her sides to meet at her lower back, pulling her in close to his body. He opened his hands to press her chest and lower stomach against him and slipped his leg between hers. Their bodies swayed to the beat of a Brooks & Dunn song and he couldn't seem to stop staring at her.

She cleared her throat and said, "You don't like it, do you?"

He shook his head. "That's not it. You just don't look like yourself. It's a little jarring, but I'll get used to it."

As far as compliments, it was definitely lacking in romance. "Gee, great."

His mouth tilted up in a small smile. "I just mean it's a difference, but I like it. I do. Now can you quit being so crabby with me and smile?"

She stuck her tongue out at him, and she felt his body stiffen. She watched his eyes darken as he stared at her mouth, and she pulled her tongue back in self-consciously. She was about to ask him what was wrong now, but when his lips descended toward her mouth, she froze. Gregg was going to kiss her. Feeling like her heart was going to explode from her chest, she caught her breath. His mouth had barely settled on hers with tender pressure when a voice broke the spell.

"Excuse me, Gregg, but I'd like to cut in."

Ryan pulled back in Gregg's arms to see Billy Montaigne standing behind Gregg's shoulder, his white cowboy hat tilted up, showing his wide grin. Billy's lean frame was covered by a loud button-up shirt and tight jeans, and Ryan almost scowled at the poor guy for his crappy timing.

Ryan waited for Gregg to tell Billy to get lost, and was disappointed when he stepped back and told her, "It's up to you."

Why would Gregg just step aside? If he was really interested in her, he wouldn't just step aside for some other guy. And now he'd left it up to her, and Billy was looking at her so sweetly, she didn't want to hurt his feelings, even if he was as dense as a brick.

She smiled in what she hoped was a friendly manner and said, "Sure, I'd love to."

Gregg stepped back farther, and Billy stepped in to wrap his skinny arms around her. He held her respectfully, but Ryan's eyes followed Gregg hungrily as he made his way back toward the bar. Ryan tried to concentrate on what Billy was yammering about, but her thoughts were so absorbed with Gregg that it was hard to keep up. Gregg had told her she was beautiful. He'd asked her to dance. He'd even kissed her in the middle of a crowded dance floor. Then given her up to another guy without protest.

She'd wanted to get a good man's attention. But the only good man she really wanted had walked away from her without a backward glance.

THROUGHOUT THE REST of the night, Gregg couldn't get another dance in with Ryan, and he was past losing his patience.

He felt Gracie lean over and ask, "So are you going to stand here all night festering, or are you gonna do something about that big old torch you're carrying for her?"

Without answering her, Gregg marched onto the dance floor. He should have told Billy when he asked to cut in to get lost, but he didn't want Ryan to think he was a possessive jerk. Now, as he watched Wayne Coulter's hands trying to cop a feel of Ryan's rear end, he wished he'd run the kid off, and told any other man that came tapping at his shoulder to take a hike too. Maybe if he had, he wouldn't be watching Wayne Coulter's hand creeping down Ryan's back. If that hand crept any farther south, he was going to end up with a stub.

He tapped Wayne on the shoulder firmly and said, "Hey, Wayne, I'd like to cut in."

Wayne, who was never quite a gentleman even when he was sober, snarled, "Back off, we're busy."

Gregg felt his blood boil and tapped him harder. "Look Wayne—"

Wayne turned around again and gave him another ornery glare. "Look, Gregg, I don't want to tell you again. Get lost."

Wayne's hand drifted down onto Ryan's butt, and she grabbed his hand, yanking it back up to her waist. "Please keep your hands on my waist."

Wayne gave her a drunken grin. "Sure, sweet thang. How 'bout a kiss, then?"

Gregg's vision blurred into a bright red, and without a second thought, he pulled Wayne around to face him and let his fist fly. Wayne crashed to the floor and Gregg stood over him, breathing hard. The whole bar was silent, and Gregg's harsh tone was a boom in the quiet of the crowd: "You need to learn some manners, Wayne."

When he lifted his gaze and caught Ryan watching him with a horrified gaze, he didn't know who was more surprised by his actions, Ryan or himself.

RYAN DIDN'T KNOW whether to be grateful or angry. She was handling the drunk just fine without Gregg, but somehow the thought of him stepping in to defend her honor was . . . well, exciting.

Gracie pushed through the crowd, stopping when she reached Ryan's side. She took in Gregg standing over the prone Wayne, and her lips kicked up into a smirk. "Are you causing bar fights now?"

Ryan looked at Gracie in surprise, but started laughing when she saw her amusement. "Apparently."

Gracie slipped her arm through hers and squeezed. "That just means you've definitely achieved your goal."

Ryan blushed, pleased with Gracie's words if not with the situation. It had been fun to dance and be told how good she looked, but it hadn't been the same as when Gregg held her so briefly. Every nerve in her body had felt alive in his arms.

Mike came up behind Gracie, and they all gulped when Eric Henderson pushed his way through the crowd angrily. Eric was Buck's son and handled the bar most nights, since his dad was semiretired. He looked from Gregg to Wayne and grunted. Looking around the bar, he hollered, "Who brought Wayne?"

Wayne's brother Walter came forward, looking scared. "We came together, Eric."

Eric nodded toward Wayne. "Get him up and out of my bar. And when he wakes up, let him know that this is the last time. He causes any more problems and he'll have to get shit-faced somewhere else. This isn't the first time I've had to throw him out. If your brother can't handle his liquor, he should stop drinking."

Walter swallowed hard, nodding at the much larger man. "Sure, Eric."

Mike came forward to help Walter lift Wayne up and drag him outside. Eric turned his dark, intense gaze on Gregg, who stared back at the brawny bald man with the tree-trunk-sized, tattoo-covered arms. Ryan was afraid that Eric was going to throw Gregg out too when Eric asked, "I'm assuming you had a reason to lay out Wayne?"

Gregg looked Ryan's way and said, "He was being grabby with Ryan."

Eric looked toward Ryan and Gracie, shaking his head. His gaze focused on Gracie and he snorted. "I'm surprised you didn't start this. It seems like anytime there's trouble in my bar, you're behind it."

Gracie glared and started to open her mouth, but he'd already turned back into the crowd toward the bar, and the music started up again. Gracie turned to Ryan with a dark scowl. "I really hate that guy."

Ryan laughed at Gracie's expression, but her laughter died when she caught Gregg watching her with an intensity so out of character with his usual easygoing manner. Gregg broke the spell by clearing his throat.

"It's late. I think I'll call it a night."

Gracie protested. "Oh come on, it's not even midnight."

Gregg smiled ruefully. "I have to get up early. It was great to see you, Gracie. This was fun." He looked at Ryan with a heavy expression. "I'll see you tomorrow."

"Yeah, see you."

Gregg turned away from her to walk toward the exit, stopping when he met Mike at the door. She watched the two men say good-bye and her eyes followed his broad back as he disappeared outside.

Gracie nudged Ryan with her elbow. "Well? Aren't you going to go after him?"

Ryan looked over at Gracie, nibbling on her lip. "Why would I?"

Gracie rolled her eyes. "Oh please. You were all pissed at me for not calling him, and your eyes follow him everywhere he goes. You are totally into him."

Ryan tried to form a denial. "No I'm not. He's a good-looking guy, but we're just—" She stopped and turned embarrassed eyes toward the floor. "Is it really that obvious?"

Gracie made an exasperated noise. "About as obvious as the way the man watches you. He is crazy for you, Ryan." She gave Ryan a little push toward the door. "Seriously, the puppy dog stares are painful to watch. Go get him now, before I take all your sexy points away. And remember, attitude is sexy."

Ryan smiled nervously at Gracie's prodding and moved away from her to walk outside.

The cold air hit her like a ton of bricks and she shivered violently, searching the dark parking lot for Gregg's Tahoe. Her eyes finally caught movement in the second row and she started toward him.

"Gregg, wait."

He turned toward the sound of her voice, his face shadowed in the dim light. She walked carefully, afraid of tripping in her new boots. When she was a few feet away she stopped, wrapping her arms around herself. "I wanted to say thank-you. You didn't have to step in like that, but I appreciate the gesture."

Gregg's expression was guarded. "The guy was all over you. I didn't like it."

Her breath caught a little. "Why?"

Gregg gave a snort. "Because you told him to stop and he didn't. He needed to learn a little lesson in how to treat a lady."

She stepped forward. "Is that it? You were just being the good guy?"

He shrugged. "That's me. Just another knight in shining armor." He noticed her shivers and shook his head. "Why don't you go back inside and have fun? Enjoy your new look."

Her eyes narrowed. "Really? You wouldn't mind?"

He gave a growl. "Of course not."

"Hmmm. All right then. See you tomorrow." She turned to walk away, heard him curse behind her and turned back, ready to unleash her temper about his mixed signals. But she never got a word out.

Suddenly, his rock hard arms were around her and his mouth had slammed down on hers. She reached up behind his neck and made a soft sound as his tongue swept out over her lips. She pressed herself against him as he slipped his tongue inside her mouth, mating with hers. His fingers kneaded into the small of her back and she felt his hard length pressed against her abdomen. He pulled back a little, softening his kiss and nibbling at her full bottom lip. Her stomach felt like a thousand moths were flying around inside, and when his mouth slipped along her chin to kiss the pulse at her neck, she let her head fall to the side to give him better access.

A round of catcalls broke them apart, and Ryan wanted to cry out in protest when Gregg pulled away from her. She watched him take a deep, shaky breath, and her heart thumped when he whispered, "God, I've thought about doing that for over a year."

Her chest rose and fell, desire still coursing through her body. "Then why didn't you?"

His small smile flashed in the dark. "I did. On New Year's."

She shook her head. "But you turned away and kissed that other girl."

He slipped out of his jacket and wrapped it around her. "She pounced on me. By the time I got her off, you were gone."

She swallowed hard. "Really?"

He stepped into her again. "Yeah really."

She cuddled against his chest, listening to his heart slowing against her cheek. "But you never brought it up afterward."

His deep chuckle vibrated against her cheek. "Neither did you."

She leaned back, looking up into his handsome face. "But . . . I thought you liked Gracie."

He smiled back at her. "Not as much as I wanted you to think."

She raised her eyebrow. "Oh, so it was just some kind of ploy? To make me jealous?"

He shrugged. "Did it work?"

She shook her head and lied. "Not in the slightest."

He grinned again, and slid his hands over her back. "Do you maybe want to take this someplace warmer?"

She swallowed hard. It was one thing to kiss him in a parking lot, with no way to go much further than that without being seen, but if she went back to his house, he would think that meant a green light for sex. Her fear of disappointing him weighed heavily in her mind and a knot formed in her stomach. "Actually, I'm a little tired. I'm going to go see if Gracie is ready to take off."

He caught her as she started to pull away. "I can take you home."

She swallowed hard. "Well, the thing is, we went shopping this afternoon and all my stuff is in her car. And my car's still in The Local Bean's parking lot, so . . ."

He smiled at her patiently. "Can't you get your stuff tomorrow?"

"I'd like to have them tonight and wash them."

"Ryan, if you aren't interested and trying not to hurt my feelings—"

"No!" she blurted. "It's not that. I just don't want to move too fast."

He touched her cheek gently and assured her, "I won't push you for anything you don't want."

She went back into his arms and hugged him. "I know."

He kissed her hair and they just stood there, wrapped up in each other's warmth. Ryan thought about how just a few hours ago he'd had a rough time telling her she was sexy, and tonight he'd invited her home. She was already regretting her train of thought when she said, "Gregg? If you'd been thinking about kissing me for over a year, why didn't you ever say anything? And don't say New Year's, because that doesn't count."

She waited with bated breath for him to answer, and let it out slowly when he said, "Honestly, I just never got that vibe from you. That you were into me, I mean."

She snapped her head up and stared at him in disbelief. "Are you crazy? I could barely form sentences around you for weeks after you hired me."

He shrugged. "I just thought maybe you were shy."

"I'm not that shy! You're just that intimidating."

He leaned down and kissed her nose. "Flattery will get you everywhere, sweetheart." He gave her another lingering kiss, and whispered, "You should probably go find Gracie before I change my mind about taking you home. I'll see you tomorrow."

She felt bereft as she watched him get into his car and pull away, but didn't have the nerve to stop him. She wrapped her arms around herself and realized she was still wearing his jacket. Bringing the warm fabric up to her nose, she breathed him in with a smile, and with a lightened step went back inside to find Gracie.

Chapter Three

Seven days until Valentine's Day . . .

"SERIOUSLY, WHY DIDN'T you let him take you home? Gregg is a sexy beast."

Ryan shook her head at her new friend's description. "It's hard to explain."

Gracie raised her perfectly plucked eyebrow. "Try me."

Ryan hadn't slept well last night and needed coffee in a bad way when she left the house. She'd walked into The Local Bean early to grab some coffee before her first appointment, and saw Gracie sitting down with a pretty brunette Ryan recognized as Gracie's best friend Gemma Carlson, the object of Mike's unrequited love. Gemma was a single mother who'd had her son at nineteen, and although speculation ran like a mountain spring all over town, no one knew for sure who the father was. One rumor said he was a random guy she'd met on the Internet, and another said that Travis Bowers, country music's hottest bachelor, had done the deed and dumped her right after.

Despite what most of the older generation described as a major transgression, Gemma worked hard for her community and loved her son and her business, the little used bookstore next to the coffee shop, Chloe's Book Nook. Ryan felt instantly at ease with Gemma when Gracie had invited her to join them, until Gracie brought up the Gregg situation.

Ryan glanced at Gemma, who attempted a rescue. "Gracie, it's probably very personal. Ryan doesn't have to tell you just because you're nosy."

Ryan shot Gemma a grateful smile, which Gracie waved off. "I hate to break it to you, but I'm your friend now. And I know you haven't had very many girlfriends so let me tell you the first rule of friendship." She took a sip of her coffee, pausing for dramatic effect. "All girls are nosy. Eventually I will pry all secrets from you. It's futile to resist."

Gemma laughed at her. "I still have some secrets you don't know about."

Gracie narrowed her eyes at Gemma. "I'll deal with you later." She turned her attention back to Ryan. "Seriously, it took a huge set of balls to ask me for help yesterday. I respect that. Maybe if you tell me why you're so freaked out by Gregg, I can help you."

Ryan looked from Gemma's reassuring smile to Gracie's eager one. She thought about continuing to protest her right to privacy, but why bother? It didn't take a lifelong friendship to realize that Gracie would just pester her until she gave in and spilled her guts. "Okay, well I told you yesterday about how my last couple of relationships hadn't gone so well?" Gracie nodded, and Ryan continued, "Well, I think maybe I'm just not good in bed."

Gracie shook her head and snorted. "You dated Doug Dooly. No one can enjoy sex with that selfish pig."

Gemma grinned at her. "Didn't you go out with Doug?"

Gracie glared at her. "Yeah, when I was eighteen and crazy. No offense, you didn't know better when you went out with him. Doug has the sensitivity of a gnat and I'd be surprised if he cared about anything more than getting drunk and getting off."

Gemma gasped. "Gracie!"

Gracie shrugged off Gemma's horror and Ryan hid a grin. Gracie was outrageous and said basically everything that came to her mind, but Ryan already adored her. Every misconception she'd had about the pretty blonde made her think that Gracie probably wasn't the first person she'd misjudged, if Ryan's ex-boyfriends were any indication.

"I'm just saying that all Doug cares about is Doug, and if I had to guess, I'd bet your other boyfriends were the same. I mean seriously, if you don't enjoy sex, how are you supposed to be good at it?"

Ryan thought about that for a minute and realized Gracie was right. Majority of the time, she didn't even orgasm during sex, she was so busy trying to make the guy she was with happy. In fact she never remembered having one orgasm with Doug, mainly because he was pretty quick on the draw. She bit her lip to hold back a laugh but Gracie caught her look. "Hey, what's the laugh about?"

Ryan shook her head. "Nothing, I was just thinking."

Gracie watched her for a minute, as if weighing whether to press for the joke. She must have decided to just let it go because she pointed her finger at Ryan. "You just need to relax and let nature take its course. I highly doubt Gregg's the type of guy to leave a girl hanging. He's one of the good ones."

Ryan felt her stomach tighten with a little twist of jealousy. "Can I ask you something?"

Gracie smiled and volunteered, "No, I never slept with Gregg."

Gemma rolled her eyes and Ryan blushed. "No, that's not it. Why did you blow Gregg off after your date?"

Gracie's smile dimmed a little and her eyes clouded. She sat back with a sigh and replied, "I just knew we weren't a good fit. I mean, Gregg is hot, don't get me wrong, but he needs someone like . . . well like you. I would have just run roughshod over him and ruined him for any other decent girls."

Gemma smiled at Ryan and said, "What Gracie's trying to say is she's a little boy crazy. She tends to break nice guys' hearts to the point that all women become the evil enemy."

Gracie glared at her. "Hey, I just haven't found the one yet, okay? And it's not like I sleep with all of them."

Ryan grinned at Gemma and asked, "Have you ever seen *Oklahoma*?"

Gemma grinned back at Ryan, her eyes twinkling. "Yeah I've seen it."

"What are you two babbling about?" Gracie glared between them, and both women burst out laughing.

Ryan tried to stop laughing and said, "You just remind me of Ado Annie."

Gemma waited for Gracie to scowl or get angry, but was startled instead when Gracie started singing, " 'I only did the kind of things I orta, sorta . . .' "

Startled patrons and employees turned to stare at them, and the three of them burst into fresh peals of laughter.

RYAN LOCKED UP the studio and looked at the surrounding shops, scrunching her nose at the red hearts and cupids that decorated the store windows. She really didn't think Valentine's Day was a big deal. She'd never had a boyfriend on the actual day, unless you counted Troy Grover when she was in fifth grade and he gave her a Power Ranger's Valentine. Most of the time it was everything that happened before Valentine's Day that made her despise the overwhelming pressure the world of marketing drummed into her brain through every avenue of communication and visual stimulation. Watching all of the happy couples making gooey eyes at each other and the men rushing around to buy cards and bouquets last minute just added to the problem, and made her shake her head in disgust.

She reached her car and started to open the door. When she felt a hand on her shoulder, she jumped a foot in the air and turned to find Gregg smiling apologetically. "Sorry, didn't mean to startle you."

She shook her head. "It's okay, I just didn't hear you."

"Well I just wanted to catch you and see if maybe you'd like to have dinner tonight?"

Her face broke into a relieved smile. "I was afraid you were mad at me."

He shook his head. "No, I understand why you didn't want to leave with me last night. I meant to call you earlier but got caught up with Sally Barrett wanting me to drive around with her and take pictures of some of her property listings. I'm okay with taking things slow." He stuffed his hands into the pockets of his coat. "So what do you think?"

"I'd love to go to dinner with you."

His face split into a gorgeous smile and he smoothed his thumb across her cheek. "I'll pick you up at seven-thirty?"

Her heart hammered at his touch. "Sure. That works."

His hand dropped slowly and his eyes held the same heat they had the night before.

"All right, I'll see you then."

Ryan watched him walk toward the Tahoe and couldn't stop the tingles radiating across her cheek from where his thumb had been.

GREGG KNOCKED ON her door at 7:27, a dozen red roses that Nancy at Hall's Market had wrapped up for him in his hand. He was dressed in a blue-collared shirt, khakis, and brown dress shoes. His jacket was brown corduroy with a thick, warm lining and he'd already messed up his hair by running his fingers through it nervously.

Ryan opened the door and Gregg sucked in his breath. The light from the living room illuminated her from behind, making her mane of red hair darker and her smile brighter. She wore a soft-looking cream sweater that fell off one shoulder, revealing rich pale skin down to the soft rise of one breast. A wide black belt was attached to her sweater, accenting the indent of her waist and the flare of her hips. Her legs were encased in tight boot-cut jeans, and short black boots gave her an extra two inches in height.

"Hey Gregg." Her voice was soft, and he felt a stirring below the belt when her little pink tongue reached out to smooth over her lip nervously. "Are those for me?"

Gregg tried to yank his eyes away from her exposed flesh and cleared his throat. "Yeah."

He held them out to her and she took them with a smile. "Do you want to come in while I find a vase for these?"

"Sure." Gregg stepped over the threshold and closed the door behind him, his eyes on the sway of her hips as he followed her into the kitchen. There was something different about the way she was moving. She seemed taller, and her shoulders weren't rounded forward. Usually she walked with her eyes downcast and moved in a quick, no nonsense fashion. Tonight she glided across the floor to the kitchen like it was made of ice.

When she bent down to pull a vase from the bottom cupboard, he gripped the counter behind him to keep from gripping her butt. The way the sweet round flesh bobbed up and down as she searched made his mouth go dry.

"Here we go." She stood up with a tall glass vase in her hands and went about cutting the stems and filling it with water. "So where are we going tonight?"

He cleared his throat again. "I was thinking Carolina's, if you're in the mood for Mexican."

She shrugged, bringing all that creamy flesh higher. "Sure, that's fine with me." She finished arranging the flowers and with another wide smile said, "Just let me get my jacket." She picked up the black trench coat and turned. "You ready?"

He moved past to open the door for her, and was awarded another flash of white teeth behind perfectly glossed lips as she moved toward him.

Confidence.

That's what he saw shining in her eyes. Ryan had always been a bit like a scared mouse, but something inside her had blossomed with the new clothes and hair. She laughed and smiled more than he had ever seen before. She was still his funny friend Ryan, but she was so much more now. The awkward little duckling had transformed into a proud, beautiful swan. It wasn't the clothes or the makeup that made her beautiful, though. It was the fact that wearing them had given her the little push she needed to come out of her shell.

Suddenly his graceful swan was pitching forward. He reached out to catch her, pulling her tight against his chest. "Are you okay?"

Her face was pressed against his chest and he couldn't see her expression, just heard a muffled "Damnit."

He reached down to lift her face up and noticed the red hue on her cheeks and the wet drops on her lashes. "What's wrong?"

She took a breath and said, "I'm such a klutz."

He chuckled, and the look she shot him was so pained it cut his mirth short. "Everybody trips. If I was wearing boots with heels like that, I'd have broken an ankle by now. It doesn't make you a klutz. In fact, I was just thinking how graceful you were."

She scoffed at him. "Yeah right."

He squeezed her until she looked up at him. "Why don't we just pretend it was a clever ploy on your part so that I'd be forced to hold you tight?"

Her mouth twitched. "That's awfully chivalrous of you."

He shrugged. "What can I say? My mama raised me right."

She laughed and started to pull away. "Thanks. For catching me."

"Any time." He followed her out the door, and when they reached the porch he reached out and took her hand. She looked up at him, and he simply said, "Just in case I need to catch you again, I have an advantage."

DINNER WAS DELICIOUS and Ryan finally started to relax as she kept reminding herself that this was Gregg, the guy she had spent endless hours with at weddings and anniversary parties snapping pictures, laughing at and complimenting their photos in front of the computer. The guy who liked to eat peanut butter from the jar with a spoon when he missed breakfast, and who tapped a pen on the desk when he was concentrating. The guy who had taught her how to salsa in the studio when she told him she was a hopeless dancer, and after fifteen minutes of toe-stomping fun, he agreed with her. He was more than her boss, he was her friend.

They'd laughed all through dinner, and although the lacy underwear still bugged her and made her jump around in her seat, she started to understand what Gracie was saying. She felt good in the clothes she had on, and when she went to the bathroom to touch up, she looked at the smiling woman in the mirror and finally felt like she was who she was meant to be. She still had her faults and insecurities, but today when people passed her on the street, she hadn't lowered her eyes to avoid the contact. And when Chase waved to her from inside his shop and gave her an appreciative glance, it had made her walk taller. She thought about Gracie and Gemma, with the easy way they laughed at her humor and accepted her, all because she had finally opened her mouth and asked for what she wanted. Maybe she wasn't really that awkward but she'd never been able to grow into herself. She'd only ever been herself with one person in this sleepy little town, and that was Gregg.

And when his hand reached out to take hers across the table, he didn't release it until he opened the car door and helped her inside to take her home. Once he hopped inside the cab, he reached across the seat to take her hand again, and she felt the bubble of giddy, girly laughter rising in her throat and covered her mouth to hide the sound. It was the same noise she made during romantic movies as the hero confessed his love for the heroine and the two kissed passionately before the fade-out.

Kiss. Would he walk her to the door and kiss her? Or would he start kissing her in the truck? Or should she invite him in for coffee? Was that too soon?

He pulled up to her house a little after ten. He parked the car, and she tried to breathe normally as he walked her to her door.

Ryan nervously twisted her hands as she asked, "Would you like to come in for some coffee? Maybe watch a movie?"

"I would but I've got kind of an early day tomorrow."

She tilted her head in confusion. "But we're closed tomorrow."

"Yeah but I've got some stuff going on. I figured I'd go for a run early. Get some stuff done afterward."

She tried to hide her disappointment. "Oh sure, I understand. Thanks again for dinner, it was fun."

He nodded. "No problem. I'll see you Monday. Do you want to meet for coffee before we open?"

She gave him a small smile. "Sure, that would be great."

He shoved his hands in his pockets. "Well good night, then."

"Good night, Gregg." She waited a bit to see if he would kiss her but he just backed off her porch. She turned to go inside, trying to hold back her tears as she closed the door with a click, locking the dead bolt.

GREGG CURSED AND kicked the wheel of his truck. Going slow sucked. He'd wanted to kiss her again so badly, but knew that if he put his hands on her, there was no way he'd be able to stop. After kissing Ryan last night, the memory of the way she'd responded had kept him aroused all day. It had been downright uncomfortable to drive out to River Road with Sally Barrett, having a semi half the time because of one kiss. He opened the door of the Tahoe, hopped in and slammed the door. His grip tightened on the steering wheel as he watched the porch light go off. He hit the steering wheel with the palm of his hand and was about to start it when he saw her lift the drapes and look out at him.

All night he'd watched that hair catch the light, like live flames dancing. He'd already fantasized a thousand times during dinner about sliding his fingers into the thick curls while he kissed her good-night. But she wanted him to go slow, and kissing her the way he wanted wouldn't lead to slow and steady.

It's only a kiss good-night. That's all it needs to be.

It wasn't like they were strangers still getting to know each other. And it wasn't like they hadn't already kissed. She still stood at the window watching him, and another thought occurred to him. What if she thought he didn't want her? What if she'd been waiting for the kiss and when it didn't come thought she'd done something wrong?

"Shit."

He pulled his keys out of the ignition and got out, loping up the steps. Just as he hit the top step she opened the door and stepped out. He'd meant to just give her a gentle peck, something to let her know he wanted her but still respected her. But her wide eyes looked glossy in the light from the house, and her lips glistened invitingly, and he couldn't help himself. Without a word he reached for her and was surprised when her lips met his hungrily. He pressed her back against the wall of her house and lifted her up. Her legs and arms wrapped around him, his erection pressed snuggly against the juncture of her thighs. Her hands tangled in his hair as he supported her sweet little rear end with one arm, his other pressed against the wall for balance. He made love to her mouth, and their breathing became ragged and loud in the quiet stillness of the night.

Gregg felt her shiver and pulled back. Leaning his forehead against hers, he whispered, "You're cold. You should go inside, before we let all the warm air out of your house."

She laughed a little. "It would probably be easier if you put me down."

He let her slide down his body, her hands running down his neck and over his chest. He started to drop his arms from around her but she reached around to hold them in place.

He stopped, and she whispered, "I like them just where they are."

He ran his hands over her waist and asked, "Do you want me to leave?"

She shook her head slowly and that was it. He pulled her back to him, kissing her roughly as he maneuvered her toward the open door. They tumbled through and he kicked it shut, never breaking the passionate embrace. He backed her up to the sofa, and she ran her hands down his chest again, fingering the buttons loose one at a time. She mumbled against his lips, "The bed would be better."

With a frustrated growl he threw off his jacket and picked her up, cradling her in his arms. "I thought you wanted to go slow."

She kissed the pulse on the side of his neck, her soft breath against his skin making him quake. "Slow is overrated."

He carried her down the hallway, not giving her a chance to change her mind. "Which door?"

She bit his earlobe and whispered, "On the left."

He twisted the knob viciously and pushed into the darkened room. He laid her back on the dimly lit bed and leaned over her, kissing her deeply. He ran his hands over her curves until they reached the fly of her jeans, then moved quickly and unceremoniously discarded them, thanking God she'd already kicked off her boots. Her hands were working the last button open on his shirt and then sliding over the warm skin of his chest and abdomen. He growled like a rabid wolf when he couldn't get her sweater off without ripping it because of the attached belt. He fumbled with the buckle and she reached down to help him. Slipping the belt open finally, he yanked the sweater up over her head.

Clad only in her lacy red boy-cut panties and matching bra, he had to keep himself from drooling. She sat up and slipped her hands over his shoulders, sliding the shirt down his arms and licking at his skin. He moved his hands to get the buttons on the cuffs of his shirt undone, and once his hands were free he gave into his fantasy and buried his fingers into the fiery curls. The pressure of his hands pulling gently brought her mouth up to his, and her hands slid down to his belt. She pulled the leather through the metal, her mouth busy parrying with his. When she slipped her hands inside the waistband of his pants and wrapped her hands around him, he thought if he died right then, he'd be almost perfectly happy.

SHE HOPED THE sounds coming from Gregg's mouth were happy ones and that she hadn't grabbed him too hard. She wasn't exactly a rock star in the bedroom, but for the first time ever, she didn't feel like she was playing a role with someone. She didn't have to act like she couldn't wait to have him, because that was exactly what was making her slip her bra down her arms so eagerly.

She wanted him more than she'd ever wanted any

man, and when he pushed her backward onto the bed and came over her, she giggled with pure joy until he closed his mouth over her puckered nipple. Her giggle turned into a moan as his mouth and tongue worked her sensitive flesh, her fingers slipping into his hair and holding his mouth in place. His hand slipped down under the scrap of lace and into the moist folds of her femininity. He found the tiny nub with his thumb and forefinger, pulling and rolling it between the two digits.

At the first electrifying zing of pleasure, Ryan cried out loudly. Gregg manipulated her flesh, pulling, rubbing it quickly back and forth, and the pressure built between her legs. She couldn't control the high-pitched sounds escaping from her mouth as she begged for more. She'd never had anyone work her like this, and when he slipped his finger inside and up, flicking over the hidden patch of sensitive tissue inside, she exploded. Her whole back arched, her breast pushed farther into his mouth, and she shook with the effects of her orgasm. Tiny little stars flickered behind her closed eyelids and she let out another cry as he slipped his finger out.

Gregg pulled her panties down slowly over her thighs, grazing the sensitive skin with lips and teeth. She jerked at the sensations, her body still throbbing. He pulled the panties all the way off and stood up. The loss of his warmth caused Ryan's eyelids to flutter open, and she watched him dreamily as he slipped off his shoes and socks. After those were discarded, he reached jerkily for the snap of his khakis. He pulled them and his boxers down in one motion, stepping out of them. She licked her lips in anticipation and reached down to take off her socks, the last piece of clothing left on her body.

His lips twitched as he crawled onto the bed with her. "Not a fan of making love with your socks on?"

Her laugh escaped with a raw, smoky edge. She reached out her hand to touch him and he stopped her. He reached over the side of the bed for his wallet, pulling out the little foil package of a condom. She reached for it and opened it swiftly, sliding it over his length with shaking hands. He took her wrists when she finished and pulled her hands up and over his neck.

"If you touch me anymore, I'm going to explode."

She let out another laugh as he laid her back again, sliding his firm muscular body over hers. Her breasts pressed against his chest as he adjusted himself to fit his hard length against the opening at the center of her thighs. She placed her feet on the bed and lifted her hips to give him a better angle. At the feel of the round tip slipping inside her wet warmth, Ryan started trembling again. Gregg was moving slowly, slipping inch by glorious inch into her tight wet folds, but the slow pace was making her crazy. She slid her hands down his back, over his tight butt, and gripped his cheeks in her palms. His eyes popped open with surprise, and she gazed back at him, eyes pleading with need. "Please, Gregg, I need all of you."

He leaned on his forearms and thrust home, causing her to cry out loudly as he stretched her. He slipped halfway out and pushed forward again, catching her next cry in his mouth as he thrust his tongue inside the warmth.

She slipped her arms back up and held onto his shoulders as his pace increased. Ryan's moans were coming closer together and her fingers gripped his muscular arms as he swirled in and out, in and out. The pressure inside her built again with every stroke. He shoved inside her one more time, his hard cock sliding over her pleasure spot. She came again, lifting her body off the bed, and tore her mouth from his. "Oh my God, yes. Yes."

She came back down from heaven to feel his mouth trailing kisses along her neck and chin. She felt his rhythm start to slip, and lifted her hips to meet him as he came, his body stiffening on top of hers. He caught himself before he put all of his weight on her, and she kissed him. She still had a hard time believing it had happened, that she'd had the most mind-blowing experience with a man. A man she had fallen hopelessly in love with.

Her whole body tensed as that crazy thought settled in and took root. She'd been in love with him as a person, as a friend, and her crush had always been that. A hopeless infatuation with a man she would never have. Now that he was attainable, her heart had taken that last leap over the edge and it belonged to him. She'd wanted him for so long, and now that he was hers, she had a hard time slowing her heartbeat.

Is he really yours, though? He says that he's always wanted you, and maybe that's true, but what if it's not? What is he's just here because he likes the Gracie version of you?

She nibbled her lip and tried to push the little voice of doubt from her mind.

She caught him watching her in the dim light and flushed. She moved her hand up to run her finger over his mouth and whispered, "That was wonderful."

He let out a breathless chuckle. "Just wonderful?"

She smiled softly and offered, "Amazing?"

He flashed a grin in the dark. "Better."

"Mind-blowing?"

"Keep 'em coming."

He covered her laugh with a kiss and rolled to his side. He leaned up on his elbow, looking down at her. She lost her smile and whispered softly, "How was it for you?"

He reached out to stroke her face, leaning over her again, his lips hovering. "You are the most beautiful, intoxicating, and extraordinary woman I have ever been with."

She caught her breath and whispered, "Really?"

His mouth took hers deeply, making the moths dance and her eyes flutter. When he pulled away he whispered back, "Really."

Chapter Four

Six days until Valentine's Day . . .

It felt like she had only been out for a few minutes before the feel of warm hands on her stomach woke her up from a weird dream about puppies eating her socks. She smiled sleepily, her eyes still closed. "Are you ever satisfied?"

She felt his lips against her neck, and he breathed his reply across the sensitive skin, "No. I'll never get tired of feeling you come apart in my arms."

She felt her body tighten at his hushed words and pressed back into him, only she felt rough cloth instead of naked skin. Her eyes popped open in surprise and she turned over to find him fully dressed. He laughed at the wide eyes and slightly opened mouth. "I went out to get breakfast."

Her stomach rumbled at the mention of food, and he

kissed her open mouth quickly. "Come on lazy, I've got plans for you."

She grabbed the blanket and held it to her breasts. "I thought you had things to do today?"

He grinned at her. "I'd rather be with you."

Sweet warmth spread over her and she reached out to him. She climbed onto her knees and pulled him into her arms, kissing him softly, running her fingernails along his neck. He groaned aloud and pulled back gently. He stared down at her, his eyes stormy. "Ryan, if you don't stop that, we'll never leave this bedroom again and we'll starve to death."

She sighed and started to climb off the bed. "Okay, I'll go take a shower."

He pulled her back into his arms and glowered at her. "Wow, that wasn't much of a fight. Did I wear you out already?"

She gave him a sultry smile and slid her hands down his body, sliding one hand over the hard bulge under the fly of his jeans. "Hmmm, somehow I don't think so."

He grabbed her hand and pulled it up, kissing her palm. "Come on, you hussy. Daylight's a-wasting."

Ryan smiled as she stumbled into the bathroom, wrapped in the blanket for modesty's sake. She stared at herself in the mirror and gasped in horror. Mascara and eyeliner were smeared around her eyes like a raccoon's mask and her lips were swollen from kissing. She scrubbed her face with bar soap, cringing when some of the stinging liquid got into her eye, frantically rinsing it. Then, looking at her face again, scrubbed clean and her hair looking like rats had been living in it, she couldn't believe she was standing in her bathroom after a night of mind-blowing sex and the most gorgeous, wonderful man was waiting in her kitchen with breakfast.

Humming to herself, she pushed all the little niggles of doubt to the back of her mind as she turned on the shower. She scrubbed her body, her hand trailing over places that Gregg had spent extra time kissing, her eyes closing and a smile spreading over her lips as flashes of the night before made her body sizzle. The hot water sprayed over her skin, loosening tight muscles that had stretched and flexed in ways they hadn't before. But it wasn't just what he'd done to her body. He'd told her things about himself, about his mother and sister, and how hard it had been after his dad left. He'd talked to her like he never had when she'd been just Ryan the friend. That had to mean something, right?

She turned off the water and climbed out of the shower. She tried to get ready quickly, drying her long tresses and brushing her face lightly with the mineral base and a little mascara, trying to separate the black lashes like Megan at Macy's had shown her. Satisfied that she looked presentable, Ryan slipped out of the bathroom wrapped in a towel and went back into her bedroom, where she opened the dresser drawer and pulled out a pair of white briefs and a cotton bra, shrugging off Gracie's advice for today, at least. There was no way she would be comfortable running around with scratchy lace creeping up her hind end.

After clipping the bra into place she called through the door, "So what are we doing today?"

"What?"

She heard his footsteps coming down the hallway and cried, "Don't come in! I'm not dressed."

She could hear the grin in his voice when he replied, "So what? I've already seen and tasted most of you."

Oh man, the moths were back and wreaking havoc. "It was dark."

He started to open the door. "Not that dark."

She rushed to stop him, leaning against the door. "Stop it! I just asked what we were doing so I know what to wear."

He stopped trying to open the door. "Dress warmly, and I'd wear snow boots."

"Snow boots?"

He didn't answer, just whistled his way down the hallway. She finished throwing on a T-shirt, jeans, and a sweatshirt, and made her way out to the kitchen. Gregg stood by the counter with a cup of coffee in his hand, chewing on a muffin as he held out a white bakery bag to her.

"Gracie said to tell you hi." His smile was sheepish, and she groaned out loud. Gracie was going to be hell-bent on yanking all the gory details from her. Awesome. She pulled a muffin out of the bag and took a bite, moaning when the sweet swirls of flavor hit her taste buds.

"I swear, Gracie is a nosy pain in the butt, but she bakes the most orgasmic things." She caught his weird expression and wiped at her mouth. "What?"

"Did you just say, 'orgasmic'?" His eyes were wide, and she blushed.

"What? It's a word. Gracie said it the yesterday when we were shopping." When he burst out laughing, she glared at him, preparing to give him a severe tongue-lashing, but the phone rang. Instead she stuck her tongue out at him as she answered, "Hello?"

"Hi, honey! How are you?" Her mother's voice was loud and cheery.

Ryan turned her back on Gregg and answered, "I'm good, Mom. What's going on?"

"Nothing, I just hadn't heard from you in a few days and wanted to make sure you were still coming over tonight for dinner."

Crap. She'd forgotten about dinner. "Yeah, of course I remembered. Can you hold on a minute?" She covered the phone with her hand and whispered, "I'm supposed to go to my parents for dinner. Will we be back before four?"

He shook his head. "I was thinking we'd head out to the City of Rocks and take some pictures. Even if we left right now, we wouldn't be back until almost five-thirty."

She bit her lip with regret. "Can we do something closer to home? I promised my parents that I'd come over."

"Ryan? Who are you talking to?" Her mother's voice had taken on a shrill note.

"Hold on, Mom." She covered the phone again and asked, "Is that okay?"

He shrugged. "Sure, although we could just compromise. We'll go somewhere close to home and then I'll go with you to your parents later. That way I can spend more time with you."

Ryan's eyes widened and she whispered loudly, "You really want to go?"

"Unless you think they'd mind."

She uncovered the mouth piece and said, "Mom, would it be okay to bring a friend to dinner?"

"Who is this friend? You haven't mentioned you had a friend." Her mother's voice had a disapproving tone.

"It's my boss, Gregg. I've told you about him."

She glanced over at Gregg and blushed when her mother whispered, "Is he handsome?"

She lowered her voice and hissed back, "Yes."

"Then by all means, bring him along. You know I always make enough to feed the whole county."

Ryan said good-bye quietly and hung up.

"So what were you whispering about?" Gregg asked. She turned toward him, noting the wicked gleam in his eye.

"Nothing, just mother-daughter stuff." She backed away from him as he reached out to her ribs. "What are you doing?"

He wiggled his fingers. "It isn't nice to tell lies. And I'm prepared to use torture if necessary."

She squealed and tried to run, but he caught her around the waist. She was laughing and gasping as he wreaked havoc on her ribs. "Handsome! She asked if you were handsome!"

He stopped tickling her and kissed her swiftly. "There. Now was that so hard?"

She pretended to slap at him, and he grabbed her wrist gently, bringing her palm to his mouth for a light kiss.

The air around them heated up, and she reached out to bring him close so her lips could exact their own form of torture. Muffins and coffee forgotten, it would be a while before he would again care that daylight was being wasted.

THEY PULLED UP to the large ranch house and Ryan hopped out with a nervous smile on her face. They'd had such an awesome day, and now that they were standing in front of her parents' place, it seemed she was more nervous than Gregg. Most guys freaked about meeting parents, but he simply came around the Tahoe and took her hand in his. They walked up the steps to the porch and across the wooden planks to the whitewashed front door. Gregg was about to knock when Ryan reached out and turned the knob.

"We don't have to knock," she said, pushing the door open and hollered, "Mom? Dad?"

"In the dining room!" a merry voice called.

Ryan led him through the entryway to a large room with a long oak table and high ceiling. Her mom appeared and held out her hand to Gregg. "I'm Brianne. One thing Ryan forgot to mention was what a good-looking man you were."

Ryan rolled her eyes. "No, actually I didn't, Mom . . ."

Her mother turned to look at her and gasped, "Ryan! You cut your hair!"

Ryan shifted uncomfortably. "I just got a few layers."

Her mom looked her over, and Ryan relaxed when she

smiled. "It's very becoming," her mother said. "Is that a new top?"

Ryan had pulled on a purple long-sleeve blouse that bared her left shoulder. It covered everything important, but still she could hear the touch of disapproval in her mother's tone. "Yes, my friend Gracie and I went shopping for some new clothes."

Her mother clucked her tongue. "Well the color is very nice on you."

Ryan was disappointed by her mother's lack of enthusiasm, but her attention shifted when her dad came around the corner. "Was that my baby I heard?"

Gregg laughed as Ryan's face flamed. "Geez . . ."

Ryan's dad pulled her into a tight bear hug. She hugged him back, inhaling the cedar smell that always seemed to cling to him. She loved her parents deeply and enjoyed the close relationship they shared.

Her father set her back from him and gave her a critical eye. He whistled low and said, "Well well, now I could have sworn you were my little girl, but I see I was mistaken. What have you done to yourself, dear heart?"

She thought that if there was ever a time that lightning should strike and incinerate her, it was now. She glanced at Gregg, who seemed oblivious to her humiliation, and said, "I just got a haircut and put on a little makeup. Do I really look that bad?" Home ten minutes and both of her parents had already made her feel like an eight-year-old who had raided her mother's makeup drawer.

Her father gave her another hug and patted her back. "I think you look lovely. It was just a bit of a shock, that's all." He turned to eyeball Gregg. "And who might you be?"

"I'm Gregg, sir." He held his hand out to her dad, and she sighed in relief when her father reached out to take it.

"Gregg, you can call me Zach." He released Gregg's hand quickly and asked, "So you're Ryan's boss?"

Gregg nodded. "Yes sir. She's a great asset to my studio."

Ryan beamed with pleasure and her dad grunted. "I suppose business is good, since you can afford to keep her?'

Ryan ground her teeth. "Dad . . ."

Gregg gave her a smile and said, "We do really well, sir. We have plenty of repeat clients and I run specials every month to bring in new ones."

Her dad stroked his square jaw. "Well why don't we head into the living room and talk, Gregg?"

"Absolutely, sir."

Ryan sent her dad a warning look as he passed, which he returned with a wink. Gregg took her hand and squeezed it, making her insides turn to goo, before following her dad out of the room.

Once the men disappeared, Ryan turned to her mother and rolled her eyes. "Dad is so ornery."

Her mother laughed. "Oh, let your dad have his fun. He wouldn't tease you so bad if you didn't rise to the bait every time."

She followed her mom into the kitchen and her stomach growled at the array of smells wafting around her. "Hmm, so what's for dinner?"

Her mother pulled down the oven to peek at something, and shut it gently before answering, "Pot roast, mashed potatoes, and mixed vegetables. Are you hungry?"

Ryan's stomach growled again. "Starving." She paused before asking, "Mom, I know that you don't really like my clothes, but do I really look that bad?"

Her mother reached out and touched her face. "I only care that you're happy. If you like your new clothes and you feel good about yourself, then I'm happy." As if it was an afterthought, she pulled a wooden spoon from the drawer and slapped Ryan's thigh.

"Ouch! Mom! What was that for?"

Her mother pointed the spoon under her nose and said, "That's a warning. I see you wearing skimpy miniskirts or hooker heels, you won't be able to sit for a week once I get through with you."

Ryan laughed at her mother's stern mouth and twinkling eyes, and knew she was teasing.

"Deal."

"So MY PARENTS seemed to like you," Ryan said as they drove back to Rock Canyon. "Especially my dad, and he hates every guy I bring home."

Gregg smiled in the dark and reached out for her hand. "I guess that means I'm a good one. You should probably be very, very nice to me."

She slid her hand over his thigh and smiled seductively, "Oh I plan on being very, very nice to you."

His pants were suddenly a little tight across his lap and he grabbed her hand to stop her exploring fingers. "Want to stay over at my place tonight?"

She brought his hand up to her mouth, running her tongue over his thumb. He felt every flick as if they were happening all along his body.

"But I don't have anything to sleep in," she teased him softly.

He pulled their linked hands away from her mouth and bit her thumb gently. "Who said we're going to be sleeping?"

Chapter Five

Five days until Valentine's Day . . .

"I DEFINITELY THINK I'm going to do the auction on Friday," Gracie said, running her hand over her hot pink apron with black letters that read, CALL ME CUPCAKE ONE MORE TIME . . . and had a picture of a sprinkled cupcake making an angry face.

Ryan and Gemma looked at each other in amusement. Gracie looked between them, her eyebrow raised. "What? I think it will be fun. Plus, it's kind of romantic."

Gemma laughed. "Romantic? Being bid on like an object is romantic? And possibly having to spend the entire evening with someone you can't stand? You're nutty."

"I'm sure whoever bids on me won't be that bad."

"What about Eric Henderson?" Ryan smiled at the scowl Gracie shot her.

"Okay, so there are exceptions to every rule."

Gemma laughed. "Seriously, what is the deal with you two?"

Gracie made a face of disgust. "The guy is an ass."

Ryan gave her a little smile. "I always found him a little gruff, but still nice."

Gemma nodded. "Yeah, he's always been good to me."

Gracie groaned. "Okay, enough about him please." She turned to Ryan and smiled slyly. "So, how was your weekend?"

Ryan looked down at her coffee cup with a small smile. "It was wonderful."

Gracie squealed. "Oh my God! Tell us!"

Ryan's head snapped up in shock. "I can't!"

"Gracie," Gemma scolded, "she doesn't need to share intimate details! You need to respect other people's privacy."

Gracie rolled her eyes. "I'm not asking for details about that! I just want to know what they did. Last I heard was you were going on a date! Then Gregg comes in Sunday wanting breakfast for two and I just figured that everything had gone very, very well."

Ryan smiled dreamily. "We went to dinner at Carolina's on Saturday, and on Sunday we went for a drive around Hagerman and Thousand Springs Resort, taking pictures. After that we went to my parents' house for dinner."

"So he spent the night?" Gracie asked.

Ryan blushed and Gracie squealed, doing a little

dance in her seat. "I am so awesome! I am the queen of the cupids!"

Gemma rolled her eyes. "What did you do?"

Gracie gave her an incredulous look. "I took her shopping! I helped her set the bait."

Ryan couldn't stop smiling. "He actually said he's been into me for a long time but didn't think I was into him."

Gracie scoffed. "That's ridiculous. I've watched you two in here for months. You gave him big sappy 'I love you' eyes."

Ryan's face flamed up in embarrassment. "I did?"

Gracie grinned. "Yep. It's how I figured out all the death eyes you sent me were because I'd gone out with Gregg."

Ryan's face burned brighter. "I did not send you death eyes!"

Gemma laughed. "You two are amusing and all but I've got to get going."

Gracie stood up to give her a hug. "Are you going to do the auction with me? It's for a good cause."

Ryan stood up too. "What's the cause?"

"It's going toward the extracurricular budget for Rock Canyon Elementary," Gemma said. "The fourth graders want to go to Craters of the Moon for their end-of-the-year trip, but they're short three hundred bucks, and it's too cold to do a car wash. My son, Charlie, is really excited about it, but Gracie, I do not want to stand up there and let a bunch of men bid on me like I'm a slab of meat." Gemma's expression was grim as she made her point.

"You're just afraid Marcus Boatman will bid on you and you'll have to spend the evening with him. Don't worry; I have it on highest authority that Michael can top anything Marcus bids." Gracie's face was innocently blank, and Ryan covered her mouth to hide her grin when Gemma's eyes narrowed.

"Do not even think about getting all cupidy on me, Gracie. I still have those pictures of you from sophomore year. I don't know how many times I have to tell you, Michael and I are just friends."

Gracie gasped in outrage. "Maybe you should tell that to him, then! And you said you'd burn those!"

Gemma gave her an evil grin. "I lied. I knew that there would be times only blackmail would curb your outrageous behavior. And I have told him. I've told you, I've told him, I've told Charlie. I am not interested in Michael that way."

Ryan laughed, and both women gave her sheepish looks. Gemma hugged Ryan, whispering in her ear, "Don't let her bully you. Just tell her to mind her own business."

Ryan whispered back, "I'm sorry, but have you met her?"

Gemma was still laughing as she walked out the door.

Once she was out of sight, Gracie turned to look at Ryan expectantly and said, "Okay, she's gone. Now give me the dirty details!"

GREGG COULDN'T WAIT to see Ryan. He'd been out with Sally Barrett again all day taking pictures of the rest of her real estate properties and was sick of driving around. Now that he knew she wanted him as much as he wanted her, it was like his whole body itched with anticipation whenever he thought about her and all he wanted was to get her back to his place and keep her close. It didn't even have to be about sex, although being with Ryan was beyond anything he'd ever experienced. Just holding her close to him, stroking his hands down her sides as he listened to her talk about her childhood, left him with a joyous contentment.

He climbed out of his Tahoe and walked up to the front of the studio. He saw Ryan standing inside by her desk, talking animatedly to a tall guy with short dark hair. He couldn't see the guy's face but saw Ryan's big eyes twinkling, her body showcased in a long purple sweater dress with black leggings and boots. He could see the confidence vibrating from her, and wished she wouldn't stand so close to the guy. Jealousy was a relatively new experience for him, but his whole gut burned with it as he opened the door and marched inside.

Her eyes strayed behind the guy's shoulder and her whole face brightened like a hundred watt light bulb, making him feel better. "Gregg! This is Chase Trepasso! He moved here from Elko a few weeks ago and is renting the store next to us. He just bought the Sandersons' place."

Chase turned to him with cool gray eyes, and Gregg recognized him as the guy with the earrings who had been hitting on Ryan at Buck's on Friday. Gregg resisted the urge to plant his fist in his pretty face.

Chase held his hand out. "Good to meet you, Gregg."

Gregg took his hand reluctantly. "Yeah, likewise. Why'd you move to Rock Canyon?"

He shrugged. "Seemed like as good a place as any. I like small towns and the scenery is nice to look at."

Gregg noticed that Chase looked toward Ryan when he said the last, and he stiffened. "Yeah, the area is beautiful, but there are still dangers," he said. "You should probably ask around to see which areas to steer clear of."

Chase gave him an assessing look. "I'll be sure to do that before venturing out. I'm actually here to see about hiring Ryan to take some pictures for me."

Ryan gave Gregg a wide smile. "Chase is a tattoo artist. He wants us to take some artistic pictures of his work to hang in his shop."

Gregg nodded. "Sure, we can do that. You have some models already?"

Chase shook his head. "Right now I just have a few, but I'm sure to have more in a couple of weeks. I just wanted to get an estimate and take a look at your work."

"Chase was very impressed with my outdoor shots and was thinking about going for a sexy feel to it." Ryan looked so twinkly and bright, Gregg felt his irritation mounting, and held back a sarcastic, *I'll bet.*

He nodded his head instead, and replied, "That would definitely bring people in. Aren't you worried you won't get a lot of business out here? We're kind of small town conservative."

Chase shrugged. "Not really. I'm far away enough from any other tattoo parlor and my work is excellent. I also illustrate and write comic books in my spare time, so I figure I'll be okay."

Gregg didn't like the interested light in Ryan's eyes as she said, "Oh really? I love comic books! What have you done? I'd love to read them."

"I'll bring you over a copy of my first comic, *Destructo Boy*. It's a little rough but they get better."

Gregg took a step closer to Ryan and wrapped his arm around her shoulders. She shot a surprised look up at him, but Gregg just ignored her as he said, "Well I'm sure you've got lots of unpacking to do. Just give us a call when you're ready to shoot those photos. You can't do better than Ryan for a photographer. She's got a keen eye for detail."

Chase's gaze flicked back and forth between them. "Well that's good to know. It was nice to meet you, Gregg. I'll call you a little later to set something up, Ryan."

Ryan smiled at Chase brightly, her best customer expression on. "It was nice to see you again, Chase."

RYAN LOOKED UP at Gregg from under his arm and said clearly and sarcastically, "Well that was better than you peeing on me, I guess."

He dropped his arm from her shoulders. "What are you talking about?"

She let out a bark of mocking laughter. "The arm thing and you glaring at Chase all puffed up like an angry bear."

He scowled at her. "I wasn't glaring at him."

She shook her head as she walked away from him, not knowing whether she should be amused or furious. "Um, yeah you were, but I think he just shrugged it off."

His scowl darkened. "I didn't like the way he was looking at you. Maybe you should dress more conservatively at work."

Ryan froze and turned toward him, feeling rage bubble up inside. Amusement left the freaking building and her voice came out strained as she said, "Excuse me? I am covered from head to toe; there is nothing about my outfit that is inappropriate or revealing."

"It fits you like a second skin."

His oblivious reaction to her tone told her that he either really believed what he was saying or was too upset to care. Either way, if he thought she was going to take a bunch of double standard crap, he was out of his ever lovin' mind. "You didn't seem to mind my new clothes over the weekend."

"Yeah well, that was in your free time. When you're here, you need to be professional."

Her eyes narrowed and she hissed, "Is that a suggestion or an order, boss?"

His eyes met her fiery gaze and he tried to speak, "Ryan—"

She waved her hand to cut him off. "I just can't seem to get it right, can I? Either I'm a boring prude or I'm just asking for it, right? I can't just do what makes me feel good, because people always want something else. I have been here, working with you, apparently giving you all kinds of signals, but you never picked up on anything until Gracie got ahold of me. Which begs the question Gregg . . . did you really have feelings for me or was it just Gracie's influence that made me so desirable to you?"

He reached out to her and she slapped at his hands. "Do not touch me. I'm so angry I can't even see straight. I'm such an idiot! You have no idea who I am. You think just because I dress differently, that I'm not still me? If you knew me at all, you'd know that no matter who flirted with me or how cute a guy was I would never hurt you."

He tried to reach out to her again but she snatched her jacket and jerked away. "Be sure to lock up, boss."

It was amazing how easy it was for her to avoid Gregg for the next two days. She'd gone about business as usual on Tuesday, and went straight home after her last appointment. She'd ignored his phone calls and curled up in front of the TV to watch *Private Practice*, a bowl of kettle corn in her lap. She finally turned her phone off after he sent her a text that said, *We need to talk.*

Thank God she hadn't done something stupid like tell him she loved him. Well, at least not when he was awake. She might have said the words quietly while she watched him sleeping next to her. He'd looked so relaxed and handsome, and she'd just needed to say the words. And then she'd proceeded to wake him up in the naughtiest way she could think of. Her stomach hurt thinking how awful it was that you could go from blissfully happy one day to crawl-in-a-hole miserable the next.

Wednesday morning, Ryan drove by The Local Bean

and saw him sitting inside waiting for her, so she just kept going out to her first appointment. She tried not to think about him, but throughout the day flashes of his smile or the image of him naked under her as they made love had her stomach in knots. She hadn't meant to lose her temper with him, but he'd deserved a set-down after insinuating she was dressed unprofessionally. That she was somehow asking men to flirt with her. She had just wanted to feel good about herself, and yes, to be more appealing to the opposite sex, but the minute he kissed her outside Buck's, no one else had even crossed her mind. But she knew needed to talk to him, and no matter what he said, she needed to just get past it and be professional. She could work next to him even if they weren't together.

After driving back to the studio, Ryan went into The Local Bean to get the coffee she'd missed that morning. Gracie saw her and gave her a guilty smile. "Hey sweets, just the girl I wanted to talk to."

Ryan raised her eyebrow. "I know we haven't been friends that long, but I've seen your 'I've done something bad' look enough with Gemma to think maybe I should get my coffee before you say anything."

Gracie made her usual coffee with room for cream and handed it to her quickly. "So Gregg was in here this morning and he kind of told me what happened between you guys."

Ryan stiffened, irritated that Gregg would talk to Gracie about their quarrel. "He shouldn't have done that."

Gracie shrugged. "Yeah well, I only got the edited guy

version so I knew there was more to it. But I may have made a slight error in judgment."

Ryan smiled a little. "You? No."

Gracie glared. "You need to stop talking to Gemma. Anyway, it's not that big of a deal, but I might have said that he should probably apologize quickly because you volunteered for the singles auction on Friday."

"You told him what?" Ryan's voice roared in the quiet coffee shop.

Gracie looked sheepishly around. "I was just trying to speed things along so you guys could kiss and make up."

Ryan groaned. "The fight started because of a client Gregg thought showed too much interest in me. Then he suggested maybe I shouldn't dress so provocatively at work."

Gracie gasped in outrage. "What an ass! That's not even close to what he said happened."

Ryan raised her eyebrow. "Oh really?"

"Yeah, he said you two just had a misunderstanding and he was going to give you time to cool down."

Ryan's eyes narrowed. "Oh I need time to cool down, do I?"

"Yeah, and that's when I mentioned the singles thing. I was just trying to speed the makeup sex along."

Ryan groaned. "Gracie . . ."

"Okay, okay, sorry. I'll take your name off the list."

Then Ryan had an idea. A wonderful idea. "No don't. I'll do the auction."

Gracie's jaw dropped. "Really? Are you sure?"

Ryan grinned over her coffee cup. "Definitely. It's for a good cause right?"

After two days, Gregg was spitting mad. He'd shown up at Ryan's house on Wednesday night with a handful of roses, hoping to catch her, but she wasn't home. He'd debated over waiting for her, but it was too freaking cold outside. Plus, with the mood he was in, he'd probably have just made the situation worse.

What had possessed her to do the singles auction after she told him she was still the same Ryan she'd always been? The old Ryan would never have volunteered for a singles auction, let alone when she wasn't single.

Technically she is single.

The thought was like getting splashed with cold water. They hadn't discussed feelings or whether their relationship was exclusive. Maybe she thought that he wasn't serious. Wait, how could she not think he was serious? He'd met her parents, for God's sake! And to avoid him like they were kids and he was just an irritating guy she wanted to blow off was beyond immature.

He was waiting at her desk when she walked inside on Thursday, and she looked so amazing it made him grit his teeth with irritation. She'd swept her hair up in a clip, loose curls escaping around her face and neck. She wore her baggy black cardigan over a cobalt blue top with enough flesh showing to make him adjust his body in his chair. She walked right past him and headed back to hang up her purse in the closet.

He stood up and followed her. "Don't you have anything to say to me?"

She turned and cocked her head. "Good morning Gregg."

Good morning? His eyes narrowed. "I called you several times."

She smiled serenely. "Yes, I know. I got your messages."

The muscle in his jaw ticked. "I also left some roses on your front porch."

She nodded. "Yes, they were lovely. Thank you so much for thinking of me."

He exploded. "What the hell is going on? I have tried to apologize to you, and you keep avoiding me. And then you show up today like there's nothing going on between us."

She blinked at him innocently. "I'm just trying to be professional. I even incorporated some of my old wardrobe to make myself less provocative. Thank you so much for your advice, by the way. I totally agree that I was not being appropriate. I feel much better now."

He stalked closer, backing her against the closet door. "Messing with me right now is not a good idea, Ryan. I am beyond furious with you."

Her tone was sickly sweet as she replied, "But why are you angry with me, Gregg? I took a few days to really think about what you said, and I agree with you. Isn't that you wanted?"

"Why are you doing the singles auction? Because you knew it would piss me off?"

She looked bored and said, "It's for a really good cause. Besides, if it bothers you so much, you could always come bid on me."

His eyes were dark as he placed his hands on either side of her head against the door. "I'm going to beat you."

"But Gregg, that's not very professional."

He growled as his mouth took hers, pushing her back toward the wall, feeling the softness of her body from chest to hips. He felt her mouth soften and her hands push against his shoulders weakly before she slid them over his shoulders and kissed him back with a little moan. He pulled away to drag her into the empty studio closest to them and shut the door behind him. She backed away from him, and he felt raw male satisfaction coursing through him.

He'd never been so angry at anyone in his whole life.

Her tone was low and breathy as she started, "Gregg, you know, this isn't very—"

"Shut up, Ryan." Before she could respond, his arms wrapped were around her like steel bands and his mouth crushed hers again. His hands slid over her back to grab her butt, and she gasped against his mouth. When he felt her body surrender and her lips play against his, he softened the kiss, running his hands over her lightly. His hands slid up under her shirt to skim the soft skin of her lower back when the bell rang, warning them that someone was in the studio. He pulled back reluctantly and looked down at her hungrily.

"Hello?" they heard a feminine voice call out.

Ryan took a shaky breath. "That's Mrs. Cranston. She's here for her prints."

Gregg released her with a growl. She turned to flee the room but his voice stopped her. "This isn't over, Ryan. Not by a long shot."

She turned around and smirked, "See you at the auction."

Before he could grab her again, she was gone.

Chapter Six

One day until Valentine's Day . . .

"How's everyone doing tonight?"

The crowd of men and woman cheered with enthusiasm and Buck Henderson grinned wide, his shiny bald head gleaming in the town hall lights. "All right folks, we all know why we're here, so gentleman get out those wallets because as always, ladies first. Our first lovely lady owns her own salon, and if you can win this little darling, gentleman, you'll get a pretty woman and free haircuts for life." The guys in the crowd laughed. "We'll start the bidding at twenty-five dollars; let's give it up for Katie Connors."

Ryan felt sick having to stand in front of all these men, and it reminded her of what Gemma had said earlier. She did feel a little like a cow at the fair.

Buck went through the names quickly, and when

Gracie took the stage, the flurry of bids was downright aggressive until Eric Henderson offered four hundred dollars. Buck pounded the gavel after three "Goings," and Eric swaggered up to the stage grinning. Ryan couldn't hear what Gracie said to him, but Eric just shrugged and unceremoniously dumped her over his shoulder. Gracie hollered at him while Gemma and Ryan watched in horror as the large grinning man left the hall with his prize.

Ryan turned to look at Gemma, who was covering her mouth, and she realized that Gemma was giggling uncontrollably. Gemma was still laughing when Buck called her up on stage.

Marcus Boatman and Mike had an intense bidding war, with Marcus bowing out once they reached $375. Mike came up to the stage to lead Gemma down with her hand resting in the crook of his elbow.

A few more women "sold" before Buck called Ryan up onto the stage. She smiled nervously as he introduced her, and she pressed her hands against her stomach, trying to quiet the moths as she searched the crowd for Gregg. She didn't see him in the sea of faces and started to panic as Buck called for the opening bid. Twenty-five. Fifty. One hundred. One hundred and fifty.

Her eyes focused on the last bidder's voice, and Chase Trapasso gave her a wide smile. Another voice upped the bid to two hundred, and Chase countered at two fifty, and still she couldn't see Gregg. Chase was a good-looking guy, but she didn't want some just any guy. She wanted the man she was crazy about, although at the moment she was pretty sure *she* was the crazy one, for loving such a jerk. She'd hoped he would have been standing right in the front row, ready to plop down all his money. Maybe she'd pushed him too far and he didn't want her anymore.

Another voice yelled out three hundred. Chase held his hand up and said loudly, "Three fifty!"

Panic overwhelmed her, and suddenly she reached out to take the microphone from Buck. He was so surprised he didn't even stop her as she shouted, "Greggory Phillips, where are you?"

The crowd parted a little, and she saw him standing there next to Mike and Gemma, smiling lazily. He gave her a little wave and she saw red.

"Are you going to bid on me or not?"

He shrugged and shouted, "I'm not sure yet. Three fifty is a pretty steep price."

Her face turned scarlet and she sucked in her breath before yelling: "Why, you lousy, no good . . . . you know what? Fine! Don't bid on me. I'm sure someone else would love to see my tiny white corset."

The whole room sounded at once, between gasps of surprise and male shouts of approval. Buck tried to take the microphone from her, and she shot him a look so dark the big biker backed up. She turned back to Gregg and nearly choked on the lump in her throat. He was staring at her calmly, and she blurted, "What's a reasonable price for a woman, then?"

He had the audacity to shrug again. "All depends."

"On what?" Obnoxious man. How was it she ever thought he was nice? He was awful. He needed to be slapped.

He looked at her squarely. "On whether she loves me or not."

Her eyes narrowed. "I told you I loved you, jackass!" She handed the microphone back to Buck and started to march off the stage.

"Five hundred dollars!"

Ryan turned around and found Gregg pushing his way toward the stage. She stood frozen as Buck banged the gavel when no one challenged his bid, and Gregg took the steps to the stage two at a time. When he reached her, he pulled her close and whispered, "When did you tell me you loved me?"

She couldn't look away from his intense expression. "The other night before I . . ." She blushed.

He scowled. "It doesn't count if I'm sleeping."

She smiled softly. "Why not? I still said it."

He put his mouth close to hers and urged, "Can you tell me again?"

Her smile spread impishly and she wrapped her arms around his neck. "If you say please."

His scowl melted into a resigned smile. "Please."

She pressed closer and whispered, "And say really loud how sorry you are for being such a jerk."

"I'm sorry I was such a jerk!" He shouted it loudly and impatiently.

The whole room laughed and cheered. Ryan laughed along with them, and Gregg nudged her. "Are you going to tell me?"

She ran her hand over his cheek, looked into his eyes and said, "I love you, Gregg."

He picked her up against him and spun her around, making her dizzy. When he set her back on her feet, he cupped her face and kissed her like she was air and he was drowning. The kiss ended when Buck tapped Gregg on the shoulder.

"I love a romantic gesture as much as the next guy, but maybe you folks could move it off the stage?"

Ryan buried her face in Gregg's chest in embarrassment. He grinned at Buck apologetically, swept her up into his arms and carried her off the stage. She lifted her face up and cleared her throat. "You can put me down now."

He stopped at the back door and looked down at her with a grin. "Maybe I want to keep holding you."

He turned to bump the door open with his hip and she protested. "Wait! Where are we going?"

He looked down at her like she was crazy. "I'm taking you back to my place so I can see that pretty little white corset you taunted the masses with."

She struggled out of his arms until he set her back on her feet. "Don't you have something you might like to say to me?"

He cocked his head thoughtfully. Her happy face popped into a scowl and she turned away from him, only to be caught back against his hard chest. He leaned his face into her hair and whispered, "Can you contain that crazy temper of yours for a minute? We've already caused enough gossip to last our lifetime. I'd like to have some special moments between just you and me."

But there were some moments that couldn't wait, and

to hell with the gossip. She whispered back, "Tough. I want to hear it now."

He leaned down to take her lips again. "I love you."

She sighed. "Say it again."

He laughed softly and complied. "I love you."

She sank into him. "I love you too."

"How did I get so lucky?"

She smiled against his mouth and whispered, "Beats the hell out of me."

He pulled back and watched her smile teasingly up at him. His mouth twitched. "You'll pay for that."

She laughed. "We should go get some food and head over to the dance. Gracie and Gemma are expecting me."

"Really? Because I was thinking instead of spending the night with a bunch of sweaty dancers listening to bad love songs, we could go back to my place, where I could do a private photo session of you." His eyebrows wiggled up and down rapidly.

She pulled away, shaking her head with a smile. "No way! You are not taking naughty photos of me."

He chuckled wickedly. "All right, no naughty photos. But if we skip the dance, I promise I'll make it worth it for you."

She really had no interest in attending the dance, but there was no sense in letting him know that. "Prove it."

And he did. Thoroughly.

Chapter Seven

Valentine's Day

RYAN WALKED THROUGH the door of her house with a smile. She was slowly wearing Gracie down about what happened with Eric after he carried her out of the auction. Gracie still protested that nothing happened except a good ear blistering from her to him, but Ryan and Gemma had their doubts. However, it was a lot more fun making Gracie uncomfortable for a change.

Ryan stopped just inside the door. Little red arrows were taped on the floor about a foot apart, leading into the kitchen. A smile tugged at her mouth as she followed them to the fridge. Red cut-out letters on the freezer door commanded, OPEN ME. She pulled the handle, and inside sat a pint of Ben & Jerry's Half Baked. She laughed out loud, seeing the scrap of paper next to the ice cream, pulled it open and read:

Hello Sweetheart,
Go to the DVD player and press Play.

She kept the note in her hand as she walked to the living room and saw the TV was on DVD mode. She bent down to press Play and already had a feeling about what he'd put inside.

Ryan Gosling and Rachel McAdams stood drenched on the wooden dock, yelling at each other. It was her favorite scene. Suddenly the screen went black and words were streaming across the blackness.

Come to the bedroom for one last surprise.

Ryan could barely contain her excitement as her shoes tapped across the wood floor. She pushed open the door to her bedroom and gasped, dropping the note.

The whole room was filled with flowers, in vases and pots, and petals were scattered across the floor and bed. Ryan's eyes caught a last note amidst the red and pink petals and walked forward to pick it up.

Turn around.

She turned to see Gregg coming through the door in a button-down white shirt and the Valentine's tie she'd left on his desk this morning. It was light pink with a big red heart in the middle that lit up like a strobe light. She had found it at Spencer's gifts and thought it was hilarious.

Gregg came forward, but instead of embracing her like she thought he would, he kneeled in front of her. She held her breath as he reached into his pocket and pulled out a little black box. He popped it open with a snap and a lovely three-stone diamond ring glittered up at her.

She looked into his nervous face with wide eyes as he said, "Ryan. I love you. I love you for your snarky comments and your playful teasing. I love you for the way you bite your lip when you're nervous and the way your eyes flash when you're angry. I love your beauty and your strength, and I want to give you all of me for the rest of our lives. I promise in turn to be the best husband I can be for you, if you let me. I want you to give me every part of you to love, all your insecurities and your doubts, and I will spend the rest of our lives kissing them away until all you see is the wonderful woman that I love. Please make me the happiest man alive."

Ryan's eyes filled with tears. "You are asking me to marry you, right?"

He gave her a funny smile, "Was that not obvious?"

She reached out her and took the tiny box from him, holding it in her palm. She stared down at the beautiful ring and pulled it out, then held it out to the equally beautiful man on his knees before her. "Will you put it on me?"

He took the ring and slipped it onto her ring finger slowly. It fit perfectly, and her tears spilled over with abandon. She smiled through them and chided, "You still have to ask the question."

He shook his head, his smile never faltering. "Ryan Marie Ashton, will you please put me out of my misery and marry me?"

"You know, you could be a little—"

He stood up and pulled her tightly against him, cutting off her teasing. He kissed every piece of exposed flesh he could find, finally settling his mouth over hers. She kissed him back for all she was worth, and they were both breathing heavily when he pulled back enough to ask, "Can't you just say yes?"

"Yes," she said, her voice hushed. "Yes I want to marry you. I love you."

He kissed her again. "I love you. Do you like the ring?"

She nodded enthusiastically. "I adore it."

He smiled widely and squeezed her affectionately. "So did I ruin your hatred of Valentine's Day?"

She laughed huskily. "Not fully. It took me almost twenty years for my hatred to fester. I figure it's going to take at least twenty more years to counter act all that loathing."

"Twenty years of Valentine's Days? I suppose I could do that."

About the Author

CODI GARY has been an obsessive book worm for twenty years and dreamed of writing romance since her first Sweet Valley High book. She writes best with a white mocha in one hand and the sound of female country singers in her ears. She lives in Idaho with her family.

Visit www.AuthorTracker.com for exclusive information on your favorite HarperCollins authors.

Love Me Tender

Cheryl Harper

Chapter One

Are You Lonesome Tonight?

Julie Dillon prayed under her breath while she did a particularly active form of airplane yoga. She contorted her nearly six-foot frame into this position and that to wrangle the seat belt and buckle out of the seat before cramming her twenty inches of hip into a seventeen-inch seat.

"Please don't let anyone sit next to me. Please, God, let's leave this one seat empty, okay?"

This had been the day from hell, if hell was a frozen wasteland that sent freezing precipitation across half the country. So far she'd gone from Atlanta to Chicago to Charlotte and right back to where she started before dawn. After a quick race through the airport, she'd been one of the last people to board the final flight of the day. It would take a miracle for her to make it to Dallas tonight but she wanted to get home. She was staring Valentine's Day in the face, and if she didn't make it home tonight, she'd be at the mercy of the world's romantics tomorrow.

Maybe the good luck that had gotten her to the gate on time would hold and that seat would be vacant for the hour and a half it would take to fly from Atlanta to Dallas.

As Julie leaned back to take a deep, calming breath, she kept an anxious eye on the front of the cabin and the still-open door. *Really wish I'd taken this jacket off before I buckled in.* With her knees crammed up against the seat pocket in front of her, she decided there was no way she'd ever be comfortable on this flight, jacket or no jacket, and besides, she didn't have enough energy to repeat the process and take it off. Instead, she waved her hand limply around her glowing face and decided to cool herself by sheer force of will. She closed her eyes to concentrate and kept whispering "Please let it be empty" under her breath.

"Sorry, darlin', but that prayer isn't going to be answered."

At the deep, soothing voice, Julie's eyes snapped open and she swallowed a groan. She didn't want anyone in that seat, but she sure as heck would have picked just about anyone else besides Luke Pearce. She should have expected him. They'd both been in Atlanta for client meetings.

The Dillon Agency specialized in sports law, and business was very, very good, especially for Luke. His latest client was a University of Georgia linebacker ready to go pro. Julie had been in Atlanta to review and discuss employment contracts with her biggest client, a minor league baseball team. If only she'd known how good Luke was at his job when he'd asked her out in the first place. She might still have questioned her luck but "No" would never have crossed her lips. At the time, all she could picture was the last time she'd been fooled by a man who was really just looking for approval from her father, Big Jack Dillon. And now . . . well, now she just felt like an idiot around Luke most of the time. Not that she'd let him know that. Living and working with her father for this long had taught her the value of a good poker face.

Now they both had to get home to Dallas somehow. She tried to pretend she was unaffected by him when they happened to work together. It happened so infrequently that it wasn't hard to keep up the pretense. Being shoehorned together into a space that might fit one human comfortably was going to test her powers of indifference.

He slowly shrugged out of his suit coat and put it in the overhead compartment before folding himself neatly in beside her. Somehow it looked like his hips were a perfect fit. His wide shoulders nudged and jostled her with every move he made to get buckled in. When he snapped the buckle, he turned a lazy grin her direction. She was in awfully close quarters to absorb the perfection of his wavy dark hair and brown eyes without reacting. His smile was hard to ignore.

She wanted to smile back. So badly. Instead she cleared her throat. "Was I saying that out loud?"

"No, but I think every person who flies has probably prayed, 'Please let that kid sleep all the way through, let the toilets work, let the flight be smooth and my connection on time, and don't let that guy sit next to me.'" He wiggled his arms a bit, each shift rubbing across her right arm and thigh. "These seats get any smaller and we're actually going to have to get a butt cheek removed to get in."

Julie's lips twitched but she wasn't going to laugh. He made that difficult. "Listen, maybe we should try to get someone to switch with one of us. We'd probably both be happier."

He waved his hand. "I am in no way complaining about being wedged in with you. Besides, I don't think the right combination exists to fit us into a spot like this comfortably."

As the flight attendant closed the door, he added, "I just think that's the next machine that ought to go up at security. Maybe they could call it the Ass Minimizer 2000 or something." He waggled his eyebrows at her. "Let's get to work on that. An invention like that would make us a buck or two."

Her smile fought its way to the surface before she snorted. "Believe me, I've been trying to lose some portion of my"—she licked her lips—"rear end for most of my life. If I could have invented something like that, I'd have already done it."

And then she wanted to smack her forehead. Or maybe die. Calling attention to the size of her rear was never a good idea.

When a wicked smile spread across his face and his eyes heated, she knew that a mental smack to the head would never be enough.

"I think that might be a shame, darlin'. I wouldn't change a thing."

Julie rolled her head on her shoulders to try to ease

some tension. "Luke, can we not do this? The very last thing we need to be talking about is my rear, overabundance or not. It's not appropriate for coworkers. Maybe stick to something you do know very well, like the flight attendant's measurements, the latest stats on your fantasy football league, or . . . maybe we just shouldn't talk at all." The bitch defense. It usually worked pretty well for her, yet it shouldn't have surprised her that it had very little effect on him.

His shrug jostled her again, and she fought off the urge to lean closer. "Well, I'm pressed pretty tightly to a portion of it right this minute," he said, "so I do feel qualified to make a judgment. And you know I'm always right. Now, which flight attendant do you want me to measure?" His voice was mild, like maybe he was humoring the crazy person. And smacking her forehead became a viable option again. Biting her tongue would have been better but it was too late for that.

"Sorry. It's been a long day and I'm not at my best, but none of this is your fault. I shouldn't take it out on you." The bitch defense was the nuclear option. He didn't deserve it. And now she felt awful. Worse, she felt frumpy, frustrated, and mean. If only he'd snapped back at her. She had a lot more experience with handling her father being angry and unreasonable than Luke being even-tempered and amused. Since he'd never once shown her another side, she'd come to the uncomfortable conclusion that Luke was just a good guy. Sometimes that was as irritating as it was attractive.

He waved off her apology. "No worries. It's nice to have a little heat. Most of the time you're so . . ." He paused and then winced. "'Frosty' is the right word."

He was right. Again.

Julie looked out the window before sliding the panel down. Every snowflake that fell whispered that she would not be sleeping in her own bed that night. "Did you go on a tour of airports too?"

He frowned. "Nah, missed the first flight this morning and decided to take my time. I was talking with the gate attendant when you shot past me. I figured you were already in Dallas and fully provisioned for at least two weeks."

"So you've just been taking it easy all day?"

"Pretty much." He stretched a long leg out in the aisle. "I didn't see much of a reason to wear myself out with all the cancellations, but Fran convinced me to give this flight a try. So here I am."

Julie shook her head and crossed her arms over her chest while they listened to the safety instructions and then taxied down the runway. How he could be so laid back about the whole thing amazed her. She'd fought her way through airport after airport trying to make things work while Luke had gone with the flow, and they ended up smashed together on the same flight. There was probably a lesson there. Maybe she'd get lucky and some of his coolness would be passed to her through osmosis. If that was ever going to work, it was now. They were pressed together from shoulder to knee at this point.

After takeoff Luke leaned down to say, "Are you a good flier?"

As her elbow bumped his on the armrest between the seats, she said, "I don't have much trouble on short flights like this one. Long flights make me antsy, mostly because of the tight space. And I can be a bit of a dictator inside the airport because I have a thing about missing my connection. But the worst I have to deal with on the plane is a little bit of nausea." She grabbed his hand. "But there's nothing you have to worry about. No airsick baggy needed."

He glanced down at her hand on his. "It was a dumb question. You do everything well, right? I would *not* want to get between you and the gate, though."

His compliment sent her already uneasy stomach into a full-on tumble. He both recognized her abilities and had a healthy respect for her quirks. Both were attractive qualities in a man.

Julie squeezed his hand then yanked her hand away as soon as she realized what she'd done. He'd obviously understood, as she had, that while a blizzard might be threatening half the United States, many places would feel like sub-Saharan Africa with blazing heat, and Luke had dressed accordingly in layers. His short-sleeve polo left lots of muscular, tanned, beautiful forearm exposed.

"Why is it that men think they can claim the armrest, every armrest?" She pointed down at his legs, which were spread and encroaching on her space. "And extra leg room too?"

She tried to make herself as small as possible while he seemed to grow. He winked down at her. "I'm okay to share, darlin'. Come closer."

More than anything, she wanted to rest her head on his shoulder. He was the kind of man who inspired confidence. If she had any idea how to loosen up at this point, she would. She'd probably be doing the world a favor. She thanked the beverage gods as the flight attendant rattled to a stop next to him.

"Something to drink?" The attendant was looking straight at Luke. Of course. And she had an avid, ready-to-please look on her face. Out of principle, Julie wanted to tell her to go open a window, but more than that she wanted something to drink. Flying really did bring out her worst side.

Luke's smile was charming and nearly angelic. Julie bit her tongue and tried to figure out how he could pull that off. Luke Pearce was very good with people but he was no angel. Thanks to his people skills and powers of persuasion, he'd made partner in her father's law firm faster than anyone before, and he was very comfortable as her father's right-hand man. She still couldn't figure out why she'd ever thought he needed her help. If their last names weren't the same, her father would probably have overlooked her existence in the firm. He liked flash. He liked success. Luke had them. She'd learned a long time ago to keep her head down. She might never have the huge success Big Jack Dillon demanded, but she was pretty safe from his disappointment this way too.

Luke patted Julie's leg. "Nothing for me, thanks, but my wife would like a ginger ale."

The flight attendant looked her way, and Julie was no mind reader but her face was all headlines and no subtext. She was surprised, disappointed, and definitely wanted to spit in her drink.

She didn't. The woman precisely filled the glass with ice and ginger ale, peeled off one napkin, and handed Julie both in one efficient maneuver. As she made to roll on down the aisle, Luke stopped her. "I sure could use something to snack on, darlin'. Got any peanuts in there?"

The attendant unstarched enough to smile at him before reaching down to pull out a tiny package of cookies. When she handed them over, he shook the package at Julie. "Look, honey, we can share!" He winked at the flight attendant and off she went.

"Now you've done it."

Luke bit into the package to pull it open as he turned to face her.

"You certainly won't be getting a second cookie," Julie told him. "I hope you can live with the consequences of your actions."

He tilted the package toward her, then tilted it up to empty it in his mouth when she shook her head. He chewed for two seconds and swallowed. "If by 'second cookie' you mean an actual second cookie, I think I can. I could probably have gotten something sweeter from her later, and I miss that a bit more."

Julie laughed. "I think you might be right. Why would you introduce me as your wife anyway? You had to know I'd cramp your style." Fidgeting in her seat to try to make room, she muttered, "And your leg."

He shrugged a shoulder. She could feel the weight of his eyes as she crossed her arms over her chest. Every move he made detonated a flash of heat across her body. It was embarrassing. And something else that she wasn't going to think about here. She could still feel the heat of his hand on her leg. She didn't need anything else to overheat.

Luke said, "I thought you might squawk. Makes me wonder why you didn't." She very studiously poured more ginger ale in her nearly full glass.

Finally he winked. "She's not really my type."

Nodding, Julie looked over at the miffed flight attendant. "Sure, what man in his right mind would be attracted to a thin, petite blonde?" She shivered. "Yuck."

He bent his head down closer to her ear. "Some guys, smart guys, like tall curvy women. Nothing against her, but I prefer a different type."

He pointed out the dark window. "Too bad we can't see what's happening down there. Think we'll make it home tonight?"

Julie shrugged as she pulled her tablet out of the pocket in front of her and opened up Angry Birds. "After the day I've had trying to get there, I'm not holding my breath. I tried to cover my bases before I got on the airplane, made reservations in likely spots . . . Tulsa, St. Louis, Chicago."

"Of course you did. Probably a good policy." He

watched her for a minute before he pulled the airline magazine out of the pocket. "So, are you one of those people who don't like to talk on planes?"

She sent a yellow bird flying at a stack of wood blocks and then took a sip of her ginger ale. "I need the distraction. If I start to worry about where I'll be sleeping tonight, it could get ugly in here."

He shrugged. "One place is as good as another if it's not Dallas."

She put her drink and tablet down on the tray table and cursed as the next bird bounced off rock. "Aren't you worried about finding a place to sleep tonight?"

"Nah, I'll find a place." He flipped the magazine open.

Luke's world was a nice place to be. He had no doubts about his ability to land on his feet, no matter what city they landed in. And he would. That was how it went for him. He announced his intent, and problems parted like the Red Sea before Moses. It was annoying. She had to rely on superb planning and logic. Thank God she was good at both.

As she restarted the game level, she leaned forward to escape the constant pressure and heat of his arm. He held the magazine in front of him with one hand and turned the pages with the other. She could sit here and watch him read for a while. The thing about Luke Pearce was that she knew he was smart. Everyone did. It was impossible to miss, even working on the periphery as she did. It didn't seem fair that he should be tall, muscular, good-looking, charming, *and* so intelligent that he was able to outsmart opponents without breaking a sweat.

When he'd asked her out two months after he joined the firm, she was suspicious. Clearly, he was ambitious. He wouldn't have been the first man to approach her with an eye on getting into her father's good graces. And long before she knew he was the last man on earth who needed her father's favor for any measure of his success, she'd blown up any chance she had with him. Worse, she froze it off. She'd pulled him into her office, shut the door, and coldly informed him that she knew what he was up to and that she didn't date coworkers. Ever.

Luke had proven to be a total gentleman about the whole thing. That somehow made it the worst. When she was being an idiot, she normally preferred someone to call her on it to prevent future episodes.

Now, he closed the magazine and dropped it back in the pocket. "It'll all work out," he said. "Fabulous Fran is on the case. She's watching the flight and the weather. No matter where we land, she'll have a hotel room for me." With an easy sigh, he leaned his head against the seat and tried to stretch out in his seat.

Fran was his assistant. Top performers like Luke got top assistants. Ever since Fran walked in the door, Julie had been trying to come up with her own nickname for her, something like Frumpy Fran or Freckled Fran or Frightening Fran. At five feet even, chipper as a former pom-pom shaker could be and all-American cute, the only way Fran was frightening was in her ruthless effectiveness. And since only Flawless Fran really worked, in her mind Julie preferred Freaking Fran, though she never said it out loud.

With a powerful jab, she sent another bird flying, and her elbow followed, clipping the ginger ale and sending it flying. In slow motion, she watched the cup crash-land in Luke's crotch. Maybe a mental slap to the forehead had been the right response for bringing up the size of her butt in mixed company, but that embarrassment didn't hold a candle to this one. Here, now, death was the only choice.

Chapter Two

All Shook Up

One minute he was resting his eyes and doing his best to come up with a conversational gambit that would keep her in the game, and the next his crotch was a cold, sticky mess. He jerked up, grabbed the world's smallest napkin she was waving in his face and tried to mop up the spill while he picked up ice cubes and dropped them in her empty glass.

When he'd done the best he could, he set the glass down on her tray table with a snap and took three deep breaths. That had always been all he needed to cool down. And he had a lot of experience. It probably helped that he could hear his mother say, "Now, you go sit down, take a few deep breaths, and come back with a better attitude or you don't come back." She must have said that to him a thousand times when he was a teenager. It was good advice.

When he slowly opened his eyes, he glanced over at Julie. She looked mortified, like maybe she would throw herself out a window if she could pry it open. Her face was bright red. That did nice things for her blue eyes, and she had her bottom lip clenched between her teeth.

"God, I am so sorry! I can't believe I did that." She reached up to punch the button to call the flight attendant. When the woman appeared, Julie stuttered, "I—I . . . could we get some napkins?"

With one smugly happy look, the flight attendant pulled a stack out of her pocket. "Here you are." She shot a glance in his direction, and he pasted a smile on his lips.

Before she could turn away, he picked up Julie's empty glass and handed it to her. "And could you be a big help and bring her another ginger ale?"

She turned sharply on her heel and marched back down the aisle. Luke kept up his deep breathing and refused to look at Julie until the flight attendant returned. After Julie whispered "Thank you" and took her drink to set it carefully on the far side of the tray, he handed the flight attendant the stack of used napkins with a smile. "Thanks, beautiful. I don't know what we'd do without you."

That worked just like he thought it would. The flight attendant was old enough that it was clear she'd been flying the friendly skies for some time, and pretty enough that she was used to admiring men. The exception to that rule would not be popular. His smile and easy compliment had gotten him a flash of dimple. After she left, he glanced over at Julie to see her huddled in her seat with her arms clenched over her chest.

Finally she met his stare. "Why did you do that? I'm obviously never going to drink anything ever again."

She looked miserable. It was cute, and a nice change from the ice queen who was normally the bystander instead of the main event. "You need it, right? Flying upsets your stomach."

She reached up to rub her forehead. "Probably not as much as dumping a drink in a perfectly nice man's lap does." She shook her head. "I can't believe you even remember that I said that. Or care."

Nice man? Things were thawing nicely here. Who knew all it would take was a blizzard and a shot of ice to his crotch? Didn't matter. He just had to figure out how to keep the magic alive. He leaned forward. "It was an accident. And it'll dry. No big deal."

"Why are you so nice to me? Do you ever lose your temper?" The color was starting to fade from her face, but she still looked like she wanted to crawl into an even smaller space than an airplane seat. He couldn't imagine what that might be. Maybe a bread box?

"Sure, I lose my temper, but never with people. When you're as big as I am, control is real important early on. I've seen other people lose it and that's never going to be me. Unless you're a broken machine, maybe something electronic. Then you might feel my wrath. I had a television in college that required regular maintenance in the form of a swift kick to the side now and then."

When her eyes met his again, he smiled slowly. He said in a singsong, "You think I'm a nice guy."

She raised her chin and stared him down. "Clearly. You should be trying to shove me wheels first into an overhead bin right now."

He cleared his throat. "Like I said, it was an accident. We both know those don't happen much around you, so I don't think it'll happen again."

Whatever she started to say was lost when the captain came on. The first part of his speech was impossible to understand, but after he was done, she turned to him and said, "He just said we're not going to Dallas, right?"

"Yes, the airport's shut down." He tried to stretch again. The wet denim was annoying but he didn't think she'd catch that in her distress. "They're going to land in Memphis if possible. The weather's bad there, but they're clearing the runways to get us in before the airport closes."

"Of course. Memphis wasn't on my list." She closed her eyes for a second. "So that means we probably won't make it home tomorrow either, then."

He nudged her shoulder to be annoying. He really did enjoy that. "Romantic plans for the big day?"

Her face wrinkled in a good display of disgust. "God, no, I'd planned to spend it like I did last year, holed up in my apartment with my Valentine, Larry."

Luke tried to convince himself he wasn't disappointed. When she'd icily informed him that she didn't think they should go out, his deep-breathing technique had been seriously tested because she was able to offer no good reason, not even that his face made milk curdle or his breath could sink spaceships. Neither was true, but even a lie would have been better than nothing. When he could count two coworker couples and at least one set of exes at the Dillon Agency, her "I don't date coworkers" hadn't held a whole lot of water. He couldn't argue against someone who didn't even care enough to make something up. And she'd done everything quietly, respectfully. Julie Dillon didn't do scenes. Unfortunately, a boyfriend would be hard to argue against. He could only play the waiting game at that point.

He rubbed his neck as he muttered, "I'm sure he'll be happy to reschedule."

"Sure. He's a dog."

He'd been wrong. Being dumped for some jackass who didn't treat her right, that was worse than no cause. Still, he wasn't too proud. He spent too much time thinking about her. "Maybe this is a sign. You shouldn't waste time on a guy who doesn't treat you right. Call him. Dump in. Spend tomorrow with me getting so very even."

He watched her wheels turn for a minute before she frowned. "No, he's a literal dog . . . four paws, floppy ears, Milk-Bone breath. And the best company to have on Valentine's Day. I wouldn't step foot out in public given the option. Too much pink. Too many hearts. Emotion all over the place. I prefer to sit it out, pretend it's any other day and the only way to manage that is to draw the blinds and start a movie marathon. I was going to go with *Die Hard* this year."

He tried not to smile at how disappointed she sounded.

"My neighbor's keeping him for me. And I was worried about having to extend his stay, but . . . he's a pretty flexible Valentine."

So here he was, being a total idiot in front of her again. She managed to do that to him more often than anyone else he'd ever met. She was always a step ahead, never reacted like he expected her to, and kept him guessing. Maybe that was because so little showed on her face. He hated looking stupid, but there was nothing to do at this point but laugh. He tried not to, but when it escaped him in sputters, he let go and laughed hard and loud and long. When he finally wiped the tears from under his eyes, he felt better than he had in a long time. She was his captive audience and she was unattached. It was going to be a good blizzard.

When he finally noticed she wasn't having as much fun as he was, he looked over to see her eyebrows frozen near her hairline. Her look said "What the hell's so funny?" better than a scrolling marquis across her forehead.

After he cleared his throat, he muttered, "Sorry."

Julie tossed her hair with a haughty sniff. "I'm sure it's amusing, the sad spinster whose only devotee is a dog. He doesn't bring me flowers, candies, or cards, but he loves me and that's more than I can say for some people who desperately hook up so as not to be alone for this invented 'holiday.'" Her fingers made air quotes around the word before she slammed her arms around her chest in a tight, angry ball.

There was something about her. She never reacted the way other women did. "Listen, I was just . . ." When she refused to return his stare, he trailed off and watched the flight attendants prepare for landing.

The closer they got, the better they could see, even in the darkness, how much snow had already fallen. As they taxied for the gate, he scrolled through Fran's messages.

The last one said *Rock'n'Rolla Hotel, reservation confirmed, yes, it's a real place, shuttle waiting curbside. Will try to book first flight out on Thursday.* That was Fran, short and to the point. And he owed her a raise.

When they'd reached the gate, he looked over at Julie. She was studiously ignoring him, working down a list of hotels she'd gotten from a call to information. And it did not look good.

Once the door was opened and people started filing out, he stood to let her out of the seat. When she struggled with her carry-on in the overhead, he smoothly pulled it down, earning him a drop-dead look. And then she did her best to smoothly exit. He lost count of the number of times her bag flipped and she had to right it before walking three more steps and hitting a seat. He shrugged the strap of his own bag over his shoulder, and as soon as they were both off the plane, he tugged the handle of her suitcase out of her hand.

She lurched to a stop and watched him walk away with her bag for a moment before she caught up. "What are you doing? I can do that!"

He raised an eyebrow at her. "Don't you need to be making phone calls?"

She rolled her head on her shoulders. "Not sure it will do any good. We aren't the only flight rerouted to Memphis. I may have to rent a car to drive somewhere."

He turned and looked out a window at the snow flying before he nodded. "Right. Or come with me to my hotel."

She pinched her lips as she thought. "Do you think Fran could get a second room?"

"Probably not now." He shrugged. "But you don't need to be driving in this. We'll get a room with two beds."

He headed for the ground transportation area and listened to her alternate between protests that she'd be absolutely fine on her own, that he didn't need to take care of her, and that surely there would be one room left for her somewhere close by. He listened but didn't let go of the handle of her suitcase, and she followed along like he was pulling her on a leash.

When they made it to the shuttle, he was glad he'd managed to get her that far. Snow fell in heavy flurries but in no way obscured the bright pink shuttle covered in music notes and gold records. If he'd thought they had a lot of choices, he might have reconsidered and tried for a nice Hilton somewhere in the neighborhood. When she shivered, he wrapped a hand around her wrist and sized up the long line of people trying to get on. No matter how this turned out, they were in this together, whether she knew it or not.

The driver held up his hands. "Sorry, folks. Hotel's completely booked. If you don't have a confirmed reservation, I can't take you." He pulled out a cell phone and dialed. "Step up and tell me your name. If I have a reservation, on you get, and hold your bags please. Weather's bad. We need to do this quickly."

She looked at her wrist, securely wrapped in his hand, and back up at him. "I'll be fine, really. I take care of myself."

He shook his head. "Not this time. Come with me. Or I'm coming with you, but if I get ginger ale frostbite on my very important pieces of anatomy, you may see me lose my temper for the first time in ever."

Her shoulders slumped. "Fine. Get me on the shuttle. And I'll owe you one."

While he had a small surge of interest at the idea of her owing him one, he shook his head. He negotiated the driver with skill and charm and they both collapsed in seats near the front. The driver made quick work of the rest of the line and thudded up the steps to plop down in his seat. He buckled his belt, closed the doors, and off they went. The hotel couldn't have been more than five miles, but the trip took thirty minutes. Snowy roads, stalled cars, and blinking red lights meant traffic moved at a crawl.

When they tumbled out of the van, he grabbed her hand again and made a quick jog to the front desk to beat the rest of the passengers. While waiting in line to check in, he surveyed the reception area, which was apparently modeled on Graceland's Jungle Room. Natural fieldstone and lush vegetation sprang up all over the room, nearly hiding the solid wood counter of the reception desk. Heavy wood and leather armchairs were scattered around, and he counted three different monkey carvings. He could hear the trickle of a stream from a waterfall in the corner. And it looked like there was a pretty decent bar restaurant, appropriately titled Viva Las Vegas, modeled with the glitzy neon of Vegas along the back wall. Food would be a good thing, but not before he got a solid eight hours. He idly wondered if they performed marriages somewhere on the property too.

Key in hand, he walked over to where Julie slumped against the wall. She looked like someone who'd been flying all day. She looked worn-out.

"C'mon, top floor." When she made a feeble attempt to take her suitcase from him, he turned her toward the elevator. "Go."

Chapter Three

HEARTBREAK HOTEL

WHEN HE NUDGED her, Julie stumbled to a stop. If she didn't get to a bed soon, she'd fall asleep on her feet somewhere, but there was something she was trying to remember, a reason this was a really bad idea. She grabbed his arm to pull him up beside her and then leaned against him as they walked to the elevator. He sighed as he reached over to push the button.

"No staring at my ass," she said. "It's been a long day and I don't have it in me to control all the jiggle and bounce, you know?"

He shook his head as he watched the numbers over the elevator. "If it's not me staring at your ass, it's someone else. Does that make it better?"

She yawned widely and rested her forehead on his shoulder. "As long as he keeps his mouth shut about it, it's better."

"I stand by my earlier judgment. Never change that

ass, okay? If you think you might, call me so I can talk you out of it."

Julie knew her mouth was hanging open but there was absolutely nothing to say to that. Her teeth clicked as she snapped it shut.

"You know, Luke, I like you, but it's okay to let the flirting go."

He wrapped an arm around her to urge her onto the waiting elevator. "Thanks. I appreciate your kindness. I like you too. I like your ass. I wouldn't mind taking either or both out on a date but you've got your reasons."

She ignored his added, "Wish I knew what they were," and watched the doors close. Before they shut, she saw the long line at the reception desk and was glad she'd hooked up with a sprinter instead of a distance runner. His speed was going to get her into bed sooner rather than later.

At that thought, she snorted.

He raised an eyebrow and she shook her head. If she made it through this night without losing her mind, it was going to be a damn miracle. When the elevator doors opened, they stepped out on the top floor. It had to be the luxury floor because the carpet and walls were all covered in leopard-skin print. With a sinking feeling, she followed Luke down the hall. When he paused in front of a set of double doors, she took the handle of her suitcase from him and leaned against the wall.

Luke whistled as he stepped inside, and she tried to take a fortifying breath but it whooshed out as she stepped into a room decorated exclusively in white and purple. The walls were white. So was the carpet. The chair and love seat in front of a large television were purple. So were the bedspread, the lamp, the curtains, and even the telephone. The bright neon of the Elvis alarm clock and the movie posters on the walls were nice additions.

As he flipped on the light in the small bathroom beside the door, Luke whistled again. Biting her lip, Julie took a deep breath and peered into the room. It was pink. Every bit of it. Tiles, toilet, sink, shower curtain . . . all in pink.

"I hate pink!" she moaned as she dropped the handle of her suitcase, which toppled over and landed with a thump. Completely understanding the sentiment, she collapsed against the purple velvet sofa and started to laugh.

"Good thing I'm pretty secure in my manhood." Luke picked up her suitcase. "Uh, did you notice? There's only the one bed."

Lurching up, Julie shook her head. "Does that mean we have to leave this . . ." She looked around and tried to come up with a good word. She couldn't. "Do we need to go back downstairs?"

He propped his hands on his hips and stared at the bed for a while. Finally, he shrugged. "That's up to you, darlin'. I've got no issue. It's a king. Should be able to share without too much trouble, but I don't mind going back down to see if they've got anything else."

She knew they were both thinking about the long line at the reception desk. The chances of there being anything else were slim to none.

She laid her head back on the couch. "Nah, I'll sleep here. In fact, if you'll stop talking, I'll give it a try right now."

Before he could answer, there was a tap on the door. When she made no move to answer it, Luke rolled his eyes and yanked it open.

The young man wore a black suit jacket and his hair was slicked back like the King. The ratty black high-tops were probably not part of the uniform. When he spoke, his lip quivered. Julie thought it wasn't a bad impression, but she had spent all day traveling.

He handed Luke a tray. "Valentine's package, Mr. Pearce. I hope y'all enjoy."

Julie leaned up on her elbows when he was gone. "What's inside a Valentine's package?" she asked Luke. She hoped her voice showed more righteous disdain than curiosity. She had both, but was only willing to cop to one of them.

He shrugged. "Who knows? Since I know how much you hate the day, I'll just drop it in my bag and take it home."

Deflated, she collapsed again. "Oh. That's good, then."

When she turned her head, Luke was watching her. His lips were twitching but he didn't say anything. He took tiny, slow steps toward his bag. "I mean, that's okay, right? You didn't want to know what was inside or anything?"

She shook her head. "No, it's your room anyway. Your package."

He nodded once and set it on the nightstand. "Right. So . . . I'm done for the day, ready for bed. You?"

Her eyes slid shut and she nodded. "Yep, out like a light."

"You want to use the bathroom first?"

"Go ahead. And be quiet on the way out." She reached up to flip off the overhead light and then rolled over on the couch.

"You aren't sleeping on the couch, darlin'."

She mumbled something, and he sighed. He sounded exasperated. A couple of hours in wet jeans and an unexpected roommate would do that to a man. She couldn't force herself to care.

After he shut the door and she heard the shower start, she turned her head slowly to consider the black velvet box on the nightstand. She really shouldn't care what was inside. She was comfortable right here on the couch. No matter what was in there, she was going to stay right here.

She looked up at the ceiling for a minute as she considered her willpower. Then she raced across the room to flip open the lid. Inside were two small, snack-sized bottles of champagne, chocolates individually wrapped in red foil, and gold-plated condoms. Well, not really, but they were wrapped in shiny gold packages with black lightning bolts and the letters TCB, so that ought to count for something. Luke could have the Valentine package. She might like to have some champagne, but the chocolate would just make Larry sick.

Deflated, she trudged back to the couch and her breathing slowed until the sound of running water put her right to sleep.

After what seemed like hours but had to be minutes, Luke leaned over her and said, "C'mon, Julie, change your clothes and come to bed. You'll be more comfortable."

When she didn't move, he put one hand on her arm and started rubbing up and down. "C'mon, we're both tired, but I'm going to stay right here and talk to you until you do what I want you to do, and you know I'm stubborn enough to keep us both awake all night long if I have to because you're being a—"

"Fine." She pushed him away and laughed as he landed with a thud next to the couch. "Don't be such a bully."

While stepping around him, she thought she heard him mutter something about it being such a good thing he never lost his temper, but she couldn't be sure. And she needed to go to the bathroom anyway.

As she stumbled into the door frame, he said, "The bully put your suitcase in the bathroom for you."

She mumbled, "Thanks," and shut the door behind her. Then, seeing her reflection in the mirror, she said a quick prayer that it had been dark in the room. She had pillow rash on her face, some crazy pattern of diamonds. The original kind of bed head, not the sexy, tousled, three-different-styling-products-required look, but the rat's nest of tangles perched on her head. And her smudge-proof mascara had lied.

She started the water in the sink and rifled through her clothes. There was nothing suitable to wear for a coed hotel room. There were work clothes. And there was the nightgown she packed. It was entirely too short, too thin, and too . . . not a long-sleeve turtleneck and sweatpants, which was what she needed to wear to be completely comfortable.

As she washed, combed, brushed, and pondered,

she lectured herself. She was a grown woman. He was a grown man. He'd seen scores of women in a whole lot less than her perfectly suitable nightgown. He was probably already asleep. All she had to do was get up first in the morning so she could put on slacks and a blouse. And even if he did catch a glimpse, he'd forget all about her short but perfectly respectable nightgown soon enough.

Julie imagined that his usual type fit in the airplane seat perfectly, slept naked, and had never been betrayed by her beauty products.

She banged her toothbrush on the sink and made a mental note to add sweatpants and sweatshirt to her packing list for all future trips. Then she dropped her travel weary clothes, yanked on the silky nightgown, and flipped off the light before she walked out into the bedroom. The warm glow of the table lamp lit the bedroom, but she moved quickly to dart under the covers and pull them up to her neck.

"Comfortable?" His voice could raise goose bumps under normal conditions. In a dark room and a warm bed, he was lucky she didn't spontaneously combust.

She had to cough to clear her throat before she could answer. "Fine. But I don't mind sleeping on the couch."

Before she even heard his answer, she was dead to the world.

LUKE LISTENED FOR her answer before he leaned up on an elbow to look more closely at her face. When he saw the smooth forehead and even breathing, he shook his head and lay back down. He stared up at the shadowed ceiling and wondered how he'd gotten here.

He was snowed in on the eve of Valentine's Day with the only woman who'd ever completely shut him down. She'd told him then she knew he was only asking her out to get ahead. He wondered what she thought now, when he was clearly already ahead. He could pin her down here and get some answers, maybe even give the whole thing another shot. A merger between the two of them still made perfect sense to him, but he didn't *need* her. Never had, really. He still wanted her. He almost always got what he wanted, and had for a very long time. He couldn't keep the stupid grin from crossing his face. Thank God she couldn't see it. She'd know he was up to no good.

The gentlemanly thing to do was keep his hands to himself. The "nice guy" worked for her, so he'd do that. Probably. But that didn't mean he couldn't take this golden opportunity to press his luck. When he'd first met her, he liked her looks, her attitude, and her general outlook. Then he found out she was related to the boss, the best manipulator and most goal-oriented man he'd ever met. And he still didn't care. Maybe he wasn't her usual type, which appeared to be Ivy League with a cotillion upbringing, but he had lots of incentive to pester, annoy, and infuriate as much as possible. With her, the easiest way to do that was laugh at the occasional tantrums. And ignore inconveniently spilled drinks, apparently. He'd worked his way up from lower middle class obscurity with as much help as his single mother could provide. He'd faced harder battles than Julie Dillon. Staying as far away from any comparison to her father would be critical.

She was hard to read, one of those quiet people who listened, absorbed, and then let loose with an insult or an idea so perfect that the room was amazed. That reserve was probably a defense. Breaking through it would be tough.

Luke was glad he was damn good at it. And happy to have a distraction.

As a yawn took over, he decided he'd get right on that. Tomorrow.

Chapter Four

A Little Less Conversation

As she stretched in her warm spot in the bed, Julie was happy that even in a place like the Rock'n'Rolla Hotel, situated right on Elvis Presley Boulevard in the shadow of Graceland, the world still held that quiet stillness only a blanket of snow produced. And then she remembered that snow was going to keep her in Memphis.

She inched up against the headboard and looked around the quiet room. Her roommate was missing, and she was glad to have a minute to wrap her head around the idea that she'd slept with Luke Pearce. In a bed. All night long. And couldn't remember one single blessed minute of it.

She heaved a sigh as she picked up her cell phone to check her e-mail, scroll through her tweets, and check the weather: below freezing, but the snow chances and amounts would be tapering off. Dallas was the same. She was obviously going to have one more shot at sleeping beside Luke. This time she'd force herself to stay awake for five minutes so she could experience the magic.

Remembering her commitment to reaching business casual before Luke got a good look at her perfectly respectable nightgown, she slid from the bed. It was late, lunchtime. As she replayed the hellish day before, she realized it had been almost sixteen hours since she'd last eaten. She had to get dressed and then go on her own foraging expedition. Pausing beside the window, she yanked back the curtains.

Being on the top floor had its advantages. In addition to the luxury of leopard-skin hallways, the view was nice. With a shiver, she leaned her forehead against the glass to see what she could see. From here, the world was fresh and clean and white. An easement behind the hotel showed snowy trees, and there were footprints marking the paths of a few adventurous souls. The cars were mounds of white, and nothing moved on the street in front of the hotel. It was pretty. It also posed the problem of what in the world she would do cooped up in a hotel room with a man all day.

She thumped her head lightly on the window. It would totally be the best Valentine's Day in the whole world history of Valentine's Days if they did what she wished they could. But, no. She'd had to be the principled idiot who jumped to conclusions, and the socially inept type with no idea how to dig her way back out. No matter how badly she wanted to say, "Never mind. Now let's take our clothes off," she couldn't. Every time she considered it, the memory of her father's sneer floated to the surface.

At the quiet click of the door, she froze. And when Luke swung the door open and stepped inside, she stopped breathing. The door slammed shut. It was the crack of thunder that accompanied the lightning sizzle of his eyes meeting hers. They both stopped, and no matter how badly she wanted to make a crazy, humiliating scramble for the hated pink bathroom, her feet wouldn't cooperate. She could feel the cold draft of the window at her back, but the heat from his eyes was intense as he looked her over.

He let out a slow whistle. "Damn, I'm sorry it took me so long to get food."

Julie wrapped one arm in front of her to clutch her elbow. Then she tried to motion to the bathroom. "I was . . . it's time for me to . . ." She cleared her throat. "I'm going to go put on a nice pair of slacks and the closest thing I have to a turtleneck right now."

He set the bag he was carrying on the table in the small sitting area before he moved to stand in front of the bathroom door. One corner of his mouth twitched as he said, "Hey, I'm a firm believer in dressing to be comfortable. If that makes you happy"—he swept his eyes in one more comprehensive tour over all the skin exposed by the stupid nightgown—"I am very happy."

She waved the free hand in an abracadabra flourish, hoping that he'd either get the clue or be magically removed from her path to safety through multiple layers. She was going to put on every piece of clothing she'd managed to cram inside her suitcase. For warmth. Right.

He didn't budge. Of course.

In her very best Ice Princess voice, she said, "Please step aside. I need to get dressed so that I can find lunch."

"No need to search." He pointed at the table. "Lunch for two is served, right here in the comfort of your own room where you can lounge around with your . . ." He paused. " . . . legs hanging out." When she narrowed her eyes at him, he said, "I only want you to be comfortable, Legs."

"Please don't call me that." She waited for him to agree. He didn't, but she decided she'd fight that out with him when she was fully clothed. "I'll join you as soon as I have everything covered."

He tilted his head and put on a sad face. "Really? But I like this look."

She shook her head. "Stop teasing. If I don't get on a pair of wool slacks soon, I'm going to die of overexposure."

He moved to sit on the couch. "Forget that. Slip on some sweats. We aren't going anywhere today. Waiter said he heard the airport was still shut down here and Dallas was still getting ice."

As she pawed through her suitcase, she muttered, "If I had sweats, do you really think I'd be wearing this nightgown?"

Her mutter must have been louder than she thought. He appeared in the doorway with a pair of sweatpants and a green T-shirt. "Remember how nice I am? I'll be happy to loan you these."

Biting her lip, Julie straightened, holding the pants she didn't wear often because they were too tight and the shirt she hated because the sleeves were too short.

She wanted to put on sweatpants. She wanted to turn back time so that she was back in her house, with Larry stretched across the pillows of her bed while she sorted through needs and wants in the attempt to pack for a two-day trip in a carry-on bag. If she could go back to right before that crucial moment where she'd gone uncomfortable business instead of comfy too-casual, she wouldn't need Luke's help.

His bag was smaller than hers, but he'd been in Atlanta for the same two days and somehow managed to cram in not one pair of casual comfort, but two. That seemed an unsolvable mystery, but she figured needing to be able to choose between this boring pantsuit and the other boring dress according to her mood explained part of it. Plus, shoes. She had heels, she had flats, and she had flip-flops. Dumping one of those options probably equaled sweatpants.

But she couldn't. She itched to reach for the clothes he held out, and even had a proper sheepish grin of thanks building. And he was offering them to her out of the goodness and kindness of his . . .

"On one condition."

Julie curled her hands into fists and clenched her arms tightly over her chest to keep from jerking the pile of clothing from his hands. To show how completely unaffected she was by standing in front of him wearing a nightgown that was about six inches too short and seriously sleeveless, she rubbed her forehead and waited.

He smiled in what might be considered a helpful and friendly manner.

"I'm bored. Let's play Twenty Questions. You have to answer honestly whatever I ask." He leaned against the doorjamb. "What do you think?"

She shook her head. "Do I get to ask questions too? And the same rules apply?"

He nodded, and tossed the clothes on the pink bathroom counter behind her. "Sure." The expression on his face said the whole thing would be a piece of cake for him, he had nothing to hide, and he had the upper hand. She wasn't so sure about that.

Julie took a step closer on the cold pink tile to put one hand on his chest. She met his stare and licked her lips. When his breathing hitched, she gave him a hard push and slammed the door shut in his gaping face.

She turned to face the mirror and did a little happy dance in celebration of how awesome she was. She didn't think many people caught Luke off guard. It was fun to be one of them. As she changed into soft, slouchy cotton, she wondered what he'd do if she told him how stupid she'd been to turn him down. She'd slept next to him. Now she was wearing his clothes. The chill of the drafty window was long gone.

She ran her hand over her stomach and down one thigh and told herself that they were just clothes. Maybe they smelled like a powerful combo of clean laundry and hot man but they couldn't actually be warmer than other, regular, normal clothes. Borrowing someone's old T-shirt shouldn't make her heart race and heat spread up over her face. Wearing Luke's did, and the heat didn't stop at her face. She fidgeted with the edge of the shirt and considered taking it all off. Wearing her own clothes would be safer. Less comfortable, yes, but now she felt surrounded by Luke. And she liked it way too much.

She held up the pants she was going to wear and stared at the waistband that would make her miserable as long as she wore them before tossing them back in the suitcase. As she brushed her teeth and tried to tame the wild brown curls on her head, she told herself that no matter how appealing Luke's flirtation was, dating a coworker was a bad idea.

But what if it wasn't dating? How bad could a fun night with a coworker while she was stranded in a hotel far from home be, really? Other people did it. Right? Julie leaned against the counter and stared hard at her reflection before she shook her head.

With one last steadying breath, she yanked open the door and marched out. He'd recovered from his stumble across the floor and had made himself useful by putting out everything he'd brought. She could see huge sandwiches, fries, and what looked like chocolate cake.

"So you think I eat like a lumberjack?"

He glanced up before he pointed at the seat across from him. "I didn't take you for a girl who picks at her food."

Julie knew her eyebrows had nearly flown off her forehead at that remark. There wasn't much she could do to prevent it, unless she ran crying back to the bathroom instead. It might have been what she wanted to do when he implied she could enough food to feed all the starving children in Africa in one sitting, but she wouldn't.

She forced her eyebrows back down into an unperturbed mask and sat precisely in the middle of the cushion across from him as she murmured, "Nice."

She could see him replaying the scene in his head, and then the light come on. He waved a hand. "Now, wait a minute. I was saying that in only the most complimentary of ways."

Julie's lips twisted as she took the plate and considered what he'd said. She met his stare and shook her head. He was going to have to try harder.

After he shoveled in a handful of fries, he nodded and held up a finger before taking a sip of coffee. "Got it." He cleared his throat and put on a sincerely hopeful face. "Legs, I just didn't want you to get hungry."

Her lips twitched. "Don't call me that."

He handed her a huge plastic cup. "Diet Coke, right?"

Her heart gave a little flutter as she took it from him. Remembering her drink of choice seemed like . . . something. She wasn't sure what it was yet, and decided not to make another thing out of him bringing her a meal only a linebacker could put away and a diet drink to wash it all down. Not this time, anyway.

"How'd you remember?" They'd probably sat through a hundred lunch meetings together, but she wouldn't think her drink choice was memorable.

His lips tilted up. "I can remember a lot of things if they're important."

She paused with a fork raised. "Important like my drink preference?"

He nodded. "I remember a lot of things about you." He set the plate down on the table to tick off facts on his fingers. "Thirty-one, Dallas native, graduated from Baylor with your law degree, worked at the Dillon Agency since." He narrowed his eyes. "I'd guess right at six feet tall, weight around—"

"Nice. I'm impressed." She took a bite of the sandwich and did her best to chew nonchalantly. If he'd been wrong about what she weighed, she'd have either had to kiss him or kill him. But if he'd been right, she'd have had to kill herself. She and her doctor knew what she weighed and that was enough.

He shook his head. "I wouldn't have guessed you'd be one of those women who cared what she weighed."

Julie snorted and nearly strangled on a fry. After a quick drink, she said, "You mean one of those women like every woman?"

He shrugged. "Everything you've got is very well arranged. Why worry about it?"

"Are you still trying to dig out of the first hole in the conversation? If so, I'd warn you to tread carefully. You're on very dangerous ground here." She tried not to smile at the threat, and they managed to polish off most of what he'd brought, although she made sure that he took care of more than half. It was only right.

"So, my Twenty Questions . . ." He raised an eyebrow.

She leaned back in her chair and thanked God for loaner elastic-waisted pants. "Let me save you some trouble. No, I never played basketball. Six feet even. Yes, I've dated shorter guys. Tall pants and jeans are hard to find but there several online places that sell nice things. And two inches is my limit."

He leaned his head back against the couch and stared up at the ceiling. "I might have asked those questions, so I'll allow it. The only one I'm unsure of is the last one." He tilted his head up. "Two inches? I'm actually morbidly curious to know what question might get that answer. Also, I think you should raise your standard."

She scratched her forehead and felt her own lightbulb go off. Inches. She got it. "I meant shoes. People ask if I ever wear high heels." She sniffed. "Get your mind out of the gutter."

"I have no idea what you're talking about." He picked up the television remote and started flipping through the channels. At least he was absolutely normal in this one way. If he hadn't felt the draw of a remote, she'd have wondered if he was a fully human male.

When he flipped past a sports show replaying clips from the week's pro basketball games to stick on a romantic comedy, she felt her mouth drop open. "You know, it's okay if you want to watch sports. I hate those kinds of movies anyway."

He tossed the remote control aside. "Too bad. I happen to love them. Tom Hanks is my idol."

Confused, she said, "Really?" She might have guessed Tom Cruise, pre-Oprah couch jump. Or maybe Tom Selleck in the Magnum years. Or even Tom Hardy in almost any movie he made, but Tom Hanks seemed strange.

He leaned back to stretch out on the couch. "Does that count as one of your questions?"

She really didn't see much of a downside. "Sure."

"In the movies, he's always a likable nice guy. He makes you laugh and usually gets the girl. I love his movies."

She curled her legs beneath her and leaned on the arm of the chair. "Even the one in the airport? Or the one with the volleyball?"

His look said he couldn't imagine that there was anyone who wouldn't love those movies too but he nodded once. "Plus, he seems just as normal, just as funny, and just as lucky in real life."

"O-O-kay, I'm a little concerned about how much thought you've put into this."

He shook his head. "You just thought I'd say Chuck Norris was my favorite actor or maybe some other action figure. Sylvester Stallone. Bruce Willis."

She raised a hand. "Okay, now Bruce Willis I could support one hundred percent."

He mimicked her voice. "Even that one with Tracy Morgan?"

She couldn't argue with that. "Really good point."

He pointed at her. "Favorite action star."

She pointed back. "The Rock."

When he didn't sneer or sigh or answer, she looked over at him. He was biting his lip.

"What?" When he still didn't answer, she held up two fingers. "For these reasons. Number one, he is funny. And number two, he is hot."

Luke raised an arm and flexed. "Glad to hear it. I am funny and I am hot."

She wrinkled her nose. That was impossible to deny. And for some reason she wasn't even going to try it here. "Yes, you are. You could make a fabulous action star."

She cleared her throat and fired out, "Let me see what I can remember . . . Tulane, top of your class, only child to a single mother, played basketball in high school but you have season tickets for all Cowboy games at home, drive a blinged-out SUV, and blast country music when you pull into the parking garage."

He nodded. "Don't you want to guess my height and weight? Shoe size?"

"I'm not a very good guesser."

"But you got some really interesting details."

She blushed. "I'm really careful with details about things that I think are important." And then she wanted to move right on. "Next question."

While he rubbed his forehead, pretending to be in deep thought, she enjoyed the sight of him stretched out on a purple velvet couch wearing black sweats and a long-sleeve gray T-shirt. It was a good look for him. She had yet to see a bad look for him. Whether it was a suit, jeans, or worn fleece, he looked strong and healthy. And hot. It was just wrong. She probably looked like a frumpy thrift store reject. She didn't care. She loved wearing his clothes.

Dangling her legs over one arm of the chair, she stretched back to watch Tom Hanks typing on a computer. There was no way she should be this comfortable with Luke. She usually dated the kind of guy who waited for orders. There'd be no ordering Luke. That was a really sexy trait in combination with an easygoing personality and what seemed to be a good heart. More than anything she wanted to brain herself all over again for turning him down.

Caught up in the drama of her own thoughts and the short and sweet trip to happily ever after of Tom Hanks and Meg Ryan, she didn't realize she'd been waiting for his next question for a long time. When she rolled her head on the arm of the chair to see if he was still burning valuable brain cells, she saw that he'd burned them all right out. He was asleep with his arms folded behind his head, long body completely relaxed, and white athletic sock-covered feet crossed on the other arm of the sofa.

Julia Roberts and Hugh Grant were up next in the all-romantic-comedies, all-day marathon, so she definitely needed to get up to grab the remote. Surely Maury was running paternity tests somewhere or there was a string of real housewives or Honey Boo Boos that needed to be watched. A wide yawn convinced her to settle back for just a minute. Maybe the actress and the bookstore owner would be a more realistic love story. She drifted off to sleep with a smile on her face.

Chapter Five

Don't Be Cruel

Luke leaned over Julie sprawled in a purple velvet chair and, in a low voice, said, "Legs, you better wake up. I think you're going to have an awful neck ache as it is."

When her eyes blinked open, he was struck again by how pretty they were. This close, he could tell the light blue had a darker ring around the outside. And she smelled sweet, sort of like flowers. Probably it was shampoo. Her hair was a bedraggled mess of falling down ponytail, and she didn't have on one single speck of makeup. He wanted to kiss her awake. Instead, he ducked a flying elbow.

She struggled to sit up and immediately cringed. "Ow, ow, ow." One hand reached up to rub at her neck and she frowned up at him. "How long was I asleep?"

He shrugged. "I'm not sure. I slept through at least one 'adapted for television' romantic comedy. Depending on how much you saw of *Notting Hill* and most of *Bridget Jones*, you did too."

She wrinkled her nose. "One and a half, apparently. That stinks. I actually like *Bridget Jones*."

He brushed her hand away and put his own hands on her shoulders. "Also there's this pain in your neck." As he massaged, her head dropped forward and she let out a relieved sigh. He tried to concentrate on the sight of her lopsided ponytail instead of how hot she sounded as she whimpered when he hit a good spot. If he thought about that too much, he'd insist on finding other ways to make her whimper, and since they were snowed in together that thought had never been very far from his mind anyway. Fleece did very little to hide an erection.

"You can't help it, right?" she said. "And I'd say you've been a pretty good roommate so far. You did bring lunch." At first he froze, certain he'd said something aloud about his oncoming erection, but he resumed his slow kneading when he realized she was just insulting him. Again. Or really, just teasing. Maybe he'd rather they did something about his erection, but it was still nice to have some reaction from her.

He huffed out a breath. "That's sweet, Legs. All I've done is bring you food and give you a shoulder rub. And you repay me by calling me a pain in the . . . neck."

She laughed. "You're right, and I appreciate it, but I'd really like it if you'd call me Julie or even 'Hey, you' instead of your new favorite nickname."

He worked on the side of her neck, gently rubbing the muscles there to ease the knot. He murmured, "That's really too bad. No plans to change it. I like the memory it pulls up, you know?"

The minute she realized how close he was, she froze. He could lean forward and kiss her. It would be easy. If he'd been able to guess whether that would get him a sigh or a slap, he might have done it. He knew it would be one or the other. She was quiet but she was intense. Here he was, uncharacteristically hesitant, and just like that his chance slipped away.

Whatever tension he'd managed to ease out of her shoulders marched right back in. Her shoulders were raised nearly to her ears at this point. Fighting his natural inclination to do what he wanted anyway, he leaned back and ran his hands down her arms. "You know, it's probably not a good idea to sleep in the chair like that."

She did her best to meet his stare head-on but couldn't hold it. Finally, she cleared her throat and looked away. "Traveling wears me out."

No matter what he wanted to do from this position, she wasn't going to go for it. With a mental sigh, he scooted back to sit on the coffee table. She had a clear path of escape, and took it. As she flipped on the switch in the bathroom, he heard her gasp and say, "Good grief, my hair." He did his best not to chuckle.

"So, what should we do about dinner?" she asked. "I haven't been out of the room." When she ducked her head back around the door frame, her ponytail was back in place, high and perky as it should be. "Any place to eat?" She disappeared again and he could hear her rummaging in her suitcase.

"There's a bar downstairs, Viva Las Vegas. We could

head down to see what they're serving. Otherwise, we could try room service."

He could hear muttering and then she slammed her suitcase shut again and stepped back out. "So, I'd like to go on a walkabout, but"—she pointed down at her feet—"I have no shoes. I'll either look like a social reject in sweatpants and flip-flops or a social reject in a pencil skirt and heels." She wiggled her toes. "What do you think?"

He shrugged as he stepped into the running shoes he'd toed off by the door. "Do what you want. You'll never see these people again."

She wiggled her toes again. "I guess you're right. It's probably deserted anyway."

He glanced over at the alarm clock on the nightstand as he pulled the door open. Nearly six. She had no idea what time it was, but he wasn't about to remind her about the dinner rush. As he followed her down the hall, he wondered what the people at the Dillon Agency would think if they could see her now. He ought to figure out some way to take a secret photo that he could use for blackmail as needed. She'd hate there to be permanent photographic evidence that she'd ever worn his sweats or had a bedraggled ponytail.

When the elevator dinged, he realized a smart man would have done so while she was asleep and defenseless in the bordello chair. But he'd gone neck rub instead. And that was the story of his life with her. He had a shot here to win her over. He had to get his head in the game. The clock was ticking, and he had a feeling they'd both be sorry if they didn't take advantage of this timeout in Tennessee.

The problem with her was that she made him a better man than he was used to, slowed his killer reflexes, made him go neck rub instead of kiss. His career, his success, depended on getting people to do what he wanted them to, but he couldn't pull the trigger with her. Instead he was floundering around, trying to predict what she wanted. It wasn't natural. He pulled strings to get people to give him what he wanted. That's the way it worked. Except with her.

"After you." He watched her struggle to come up with some way to get him in front of her but she couldn't so she flip-flopped as fast as she could and spun around to punch the button for the bottom floor.

The television display in the elevator showed a listing of the day's events. There was only one. "Trivia contest in the bar . . ." He glanced at his watch. " . . . in about ten minutes. Are you up for it?"

When the doors opened, he motioned her ahead of him. She had to be distracted by the green and leafy goodness of the wild lobby because she didn't hesitate this time. When he walked beside her and rested his hand in the small of her back to guide her to the bar, he didn't sense any tension. But when they stepped in the open doors of the bar, she snapped to attention. The place was packed.

Apparently they weren't the only ones to choose the bar over romantic comedies and room service.

A chipper blonde dressed as a modest showgirl, if

there was such a thing, met them at the hostess station. What she lacked in va-va-voom she more than made up for with silver sequins and large red feathers that waved as she grabbed two menus. "Good afternoon. Y'all here for the trivia contest or dinner?"

He looked down at Julie, but she was in sensory overload. And he could totally understand. It was as if the Jungle Room and the Vegas Strip had produced a love child inside the Rock'n'Rolla Hotel. Foliage jumped out at them from all sides but the bar was one blinking, flashing sight to behold. The lightbulb inventory of the place must be huge.

"Maybe both?" He wasn't sure they'd be able to eat here. He hoped Julie wasn't subject to seizures. The flash of lights around the bar was impossible to avoid.

The hostess nodded. "We can do that. We'll just put you close to the stage so you can hear and I'll send a waitress over for your order. Burgers are real good here but you can't go wrong with the peanut butter and banana sandwich either."

When Julie made no move to follow the hostess, he grasped her hand and towed her through the tables. When they reached the stage area, he pulled out a seat and put his hands on her shoulders to guide her into it. He wanted to laugh at the look on her face but could understand her shock. She didn't have the look or attitude of someone who'd spent a lot of time in tourist traps like this one. The only music she probably listened to was opera.

"Have you ever visited Graceland?" he asked. His parents had taken him when he was ten. It wasn't an easy place to forget.

She shook her head vaguely but her eyes didn't stop roaming over the bright flash of the bar.

When he waved the menu in front of her face, she took it, and he watched her read her choices very carefully. His lips twitched as he looked around. Maybe he was wrong. Somebody who loved the Rock and his movies probably had a better grip on pop culture than he imagined, but Julie had probably never seen another place like this. To be fair, the only other place like it was Graceland itself. Whoever decorated the bar had decided to try to one-up the extravagance of Elvis's home. He had to admire the effort.

"Welcome to Viva Las Vegas, y'all." A frazzled brunette wearing half the sparkles but twice the feathers of the hostess paused beside their table. "Lucky'll be starting the trivia pretty soon, but I'll go ahead and take your order."

Julie smiled sweetly up at her. That made him happy. He couldn't stand women who were rude to waiters. He'd worked his way through high school at the local burger joint. There were a lot more rude people in the world than he'd have guessed going into it.

"So, I've got to have the Elvis and a Diet Coke."

If anyone had asked him to wager on what she would order, that would have been his last pick. But he was happy she went for it. No way in hell was he doing the same. "Burger. Sweet tea."

Just as the waitress walked away, the emcee bounded

through the small group of tables to leap up on the stage. For his attire, he'd gone jumpsuited Elvis, complete with impressive faux sideburns that did not match his hair seamlessly, but Luke thought he deserved points for effort.

Julie nodded her head once in a *Would you get a load of this?* way before focusing on the stage. "Hound Dog" blared through the speakers as the vertically challenged impersonator gyrated around the small stage.

When the song ended, he said, "Afternoon, lovely ladies and lucky gents, thanks for joining us on this snowy afternoon. See a lot of couples in the room." He tilted his head down and peered at an older couple on the other side of the stage. "Not a bad way to spend Valentine's Day, snowed in with the one you love. Am I right?"

The couple smiled politely and then there was silence. The clanks and clatter of the kitchen were the only sounds until he cleared his throat and said, "Well, now, here's how it's gonna go. I'll be playing some of your favorite Elvis songs and we'll follow up with some questions. Answer correctly for a chance to win a free dinner right here at Viva Las Vegas. Who's ready?"

Luke looked around and it seemed that dinner had been the bigger draw. Very few people were paying any attention to the guy at all. Finally he whooped and clapped his hands.

Julie and everyone in the place turned to look at him. Luke called out, "Hit us with a question, Elvis."

"Elvis" reached up to smooth his sideburn down.

"Will do." He picked up a card. "Sha Na Na covered 'Hound Dog' for what 1978 movie?"

Julie looked around the room. A few more people were interested but there didn't seem to be much happening. Luke nearly choked on his tea when she cupped her hands over her mouth and shouted, *"Grease!"*

"Whoa, now, got an answer on the first try from the . . ." He paused to give her a long look up and down. " . . . sharp-dressed tall drink of water here in the front row. What's your name, honey?"

Luke wasn't sure she was going to answer. She sure looked like she wanted to crawl under the table, so he answered, "Julie." And the "King" typed *Tall Julie* into a computer, and the display screen at the right side of the stage showed one check.

As the waitress approached with their food, Julie muttered, "And I'm never doing that again. Tall drink of water. If I had a nickel for every time some clever man used that . . ."

Her disgust at Lucky's attempt at witty banter was clear. She was cute when she was only mildly disgruntled like this.

Luke waved off the waitress's question about what they needed and then squeezed her hand. It just seemed the thing to do. When "Jailhouse Rock" blared, conversation was impossible. And Julie managed to sit on her hands and ignore all the wrong answers being shouted out from the few tables participating. And every answer, wrong or right, got some teasing and/or creepy commentary from Lucky. Still, Julie had the look of someone who knew the answer.

He leaned closer. "If you want to tell me, I'll shout it out, save you the attention."

A small flush lit her cheeks. "Thanks."

"How's the sandwich?"

She smiled. "Better than you think it is. Yours?"

"Good, I guess." They listened to the next song. When it was over, he said, "Wouldn't have guessed you for a big Elvis fan."

She shrugged. "Big *Grease* fan is more like it. Plus, I like trivia. It sticks in my head."

"Okay, so how many questions did I use up?" He took a bite of his burger.

She pretended to think. "I'm pretty sure it was nineteen. Make the last one good."

He shook his head. "Be good or I'll tell the King you want to come up on stage with him."

She narrowed her eyes at him. "You better not. I know where you sleep."

When they could hear each other, he fired off first date questions. Favorite movie, musician, color, where she went to high school, dogs versus cats . . . he covered all the basics in between Elvis's greatest hits.

"All right, ladies and gents, we've reached our final song. Got lots of people with points, but this is it, the final question, last shot to get your name in the drawing. Ready?"

Luke looked around and the crowd was paying marginally better attention when "It's Now or Never" blared out of the speakers. Julie's lips moved along with the song as she shoved her empty plate back. When the song ended, she took a sip of her drink. When "Elvis" started his patter, Luke tore his eyes away from her happy smile.

"Now, then, this was one of Elvis's biggest international hits. I need to know what song the melody is based on."

It was completely the wrong season, but Luke would have sworn he heard crickets. He'd also have bet every dollar he had and both pairs of sweatpants in his possession that Julie knew the answer. She fiddled with her straw wrapper and sent anxious looks around the tables.

"Come on, fans. Hit me with it and we can all get back to shaking and shimmying in the privacy of our own hotel rooms with our very own Valentines. Anybody?"

The King's shift must have been drawing to a close. He marched across the stage and in a clumsy kung-fu move knelt at the edge of the stage and pointed right at Julie. "Hit me with it, Stretch."

Julie looked at him and finally shook her head. She licked her lips and glanced around again before saying, "O Sole Mio."

Elvis jumped to his feet with a loud "Whoooooeee!' His hips shook and his arm made huge clockwise circles. "Got it in one!"

He ran up to the stage and shook a big fishbowl before he jammed a hand in and drew out a name. "And the winner of a nice dinner for two right back here is . . ." He drummed on the top of the small table on the stage.

"Howard!" The gray-haired man at the table on the other side of the stage stood and waved at the smattering of claps.

Julie's face settled into a disgruntled frown and Luke motioned for the check.

Chapter Six

Hound Dog

And that was the story of her life. Publicly humiliated and she still couldn't win a free dinner. "Tall Julie" ought to be used to it by now, the winks and nudges about her height. She still hated it. She could have answered almost every one of the Elvis questions, but she didn't want to draw Lucky's attention.

She eyed the empty glasses stacked up on Lucky's table. He was still pretty sharp. Obviously he could hold his liquor.

As Luke signed the slip for their lunch, his phone rang. After he read the caller ID, he waved the phone and said, "Be right back."

Up until this point she'd done pretty well at fending off the black cloud of doom over the stupid holiday. She'd been able to pretend that it was actually only a snow day, like many other snow days, even with a romantic comedy marathon. But there were a lot of couples trickling out of Viva Las Vegas. It was enough to make even a sane woman mutter. She could do sane 364 days a year, but holding onto her mental health was hard on this day. At least she wasn't at work to see rose bouquets and flower arrangements paraded through the office.

When Luke didn't immediately return, she decided to wander around to see what other wonders the Rock'n'Rolla Hotel might hold. She stood and walked out into the lobby before turning down a small hallway that advertised the pool area and workout room. Slowly flip-flopping in that direction, she perused the various album covers and photos of Elvis lining the hall until she became aware of footsteps behind her.

She glanced over her shoulder with a smile to see Lucky, the terrible impersonator, standing behind her. She motioned him around. "I'm in no hurry. Just waiting on the room key. Go ahead."

He stepped closer, so close that her eyes watered at the smell of booze and she could see where the glue holding his sideburns on had squeezed out beneath whatever sort of hair it was.

His sleazy grin never made it to his eyes. "I just wanted to tell you your husband's a lucky man." His stare burned her from head to toe and back to meet her eyes. "He must be a leg man, like myself."

Julie stepped back but bumped her elbow on the wall. Pulling her arms between them, she rubbed it and looked over his head. When he inched closer, she said, "Not my husband. A coworker stranded here just like me, but I should probably catch up with him. Don't want to keep him waiting."

When she moved to scoot around him, he moved with her to lean a shoulder against the wall. He reached up to run his other hand down her arm. "So you need a Valentine too, then. Am I right, Legs?" He wiggled his eyebrows. "If it's a free dinner you're looking for, I could probably hook you up. We could go back to my room and"—he licked his lips in what was probably supposed to be a seductive maneuver—"see what happens."

When Julie realized she was holding her breath, she forced herself to breathe deeply. Her heart was pounding and she was scared to death, but that was ridiculous. She outweighed this creep by fifty pounds. She could take him if she had to.

She straightened to her full height and looked down to meet his stare. "No, thank you. I don't celebrate the holiday. It's against my religion."

His pointing finger came to rest in the middle of her chest. "Fine. Forget the holiday. Let's just have some fun, Legs. You're a little bigger than I normally like them but I'm in a generous mood."

The little idiot was completely unaware of Luke approaching. But Julie wasn't. And as much as she hated that he'd found her here, with this worm, and heard what he'd said, she'd hate it more if he had to rescue her. So she ran her hand down Elvis's face.

"Listen, Elfish." She shook her head. "Nah, that's probably too subtle, isn't it? Elfish? Shoulda gone with Shorty. Because you're the runt in the litter. Or maybe living under a rock too long has stunted your growth. Whatever." Jamming one finger on her chest, she said, "Have you got any idea how many people in my life have called me some version of Legs or Stretch or Tiny? Too many, that's how many. My father called me Bigfoot for the first twenty years of my life. You name it, I've already heard it. The least you could do was put some thought into your insult. I appreciate creativity, Elfish." She pasted a smile on her face. "I know you have a lifetime of pent-up rage from not being able to reach any top shelf, but don't take it out on me." She could see the anger in his eyes. And Luke looked ready to bust.

She pushed Elvis's shoulder with one hand while she gripped and yanked a firmly glued sideburn right off of his smugly smirky face with the other. His strangled yelp filled her with satisfaction. The moment deserved a victory dance but Lucky was quickly recovering. She darted around him and froze as he grabbed her T-shirt. He must have seen Luke at that point because he let go slowly and held up his free hand. The other one was clutching his face.

"Fine. Never mind. All you had to do was say you weren't interested."

Luke took an angry step forward while Lucky cowered. She stepped around him and grabbed Luke's hand to haul him down the hallway toward the elevator. "Let's go. There's nothing more to see here."

When Luke refused to move, she yanked hard on his hand and he followed. She punched the button and then pulled him onto the elevator before she started to laugh. When the elevator opened on their floor, she stepped out and then looked back at him when he followed slowly. "Are you coming?"

He nodded. And then shook his head as he crammed a hand in his pocket to pull out the room key. "I can't believe you're not taking this seriously. There's no telling how far he'd have pushed it back there where there was no traffic. What if he'd hurt you?"

When the door opened with a snick, he pushed it open and then shut and locked it behind her. She flopped down on the couch. "I guess it's relief, Luke. I was really worried but then I realized I could probably take him if I had to, if I was smart enough to think it all through and breathe instead of panicking. And then I saw you. I knew you wouldn't let anything bad happen to me." She hammered her feet against the carpet. "Plus, did you hear me? I got to use one of the put-downs that I've always thought of five hours too late. It was great!"

She tried to get serious when she saw the dark frown on his face. "You were worried. But I'm happy I finally got to put a bully in his place." She waved her hand in the air. "And I have his sideburn as a souvenir because I *rock*."

Luke sat down across from her and rubbed his forehead with one hand. She had no idea what he was thinking. His face was unreadable. When his strangled cough escaped, she smiled. And when he started to laugh, she did too. When she was gasping for air and wiping the tears off her cheeks, she said, "Elfish was pretty good, though, right?'

His smile slowly disappeared and he leaned forward to rest his forearms on his knees. "I'm sorry."

She waved her hand. "You've got nothing to apologize for. Who knew a five-foot entertainer would attempt Mount Julie?"

When he didn't answer, she tilted her head to look at him.

"I'm sorry about stupid shit like that," he said, "but more than that I'm sorry for calling you Legs. You said you didn't like it, but I didn't really understand why. So I'm sorry for calling you that."

He looked sorry. There was a sincere apology on his face and it was nearly too much for her to handle. As always, she downplayed her feelings. "No worries, Luke. You couldn't have known."

He ran both hands through his hair. "Uh, yeah, well, at the very least I could have asked you why. Instead, I used it because I knew you didn't like it. Also, your father . . . he's clearly a bigger ass than I knew."

She rolled her eyes. "Okay, I know I haven't used up all of my questions. Why would you do something to annoy me on purpose?"

He stood and slid around to sit on the coffee table, so close his knees brushed the edge of her shirt. Well, his shirt, but the one she was wearing. And at his closeness, her heart started to pound.

"Why wouldn't you go out with me when I asked?"

He didn't touch her but she could feel his heat, and she either wanted to run for the pink bathroom or pull him down on top of her. When she made up her mind, she was totally going to do one or the other.

Julie licked her lips. Suddenly her mouth was dry, dry, dry. "You didn't answer my question. Wasn't that the deal?"

He shrugged. "I tried being all grown up first, asking you out, declaring my interest in an up-front manner. That didn't work. So then I fell back on what used to work in fourth grade. Negative attention is still attention, you know?"

She sat up and crossed her legs underneath her so she could face him head on.

He shook his head. "I mean, you're so reserved. Shaking you up . . . it's like the only way to see the real you, know what you're thinking." He muttered, "And when I think about who your father is, it all makes so much sense."

Her heart was definitely pounding and she could feel the heat on her face. Flop sweat was breaking out and she thought she might have to go stick her head in the snow to recover. Trying not to think about how uncomfortable another night in a bed with a man who had every reason to be mad at her might be, she raised her chin and said, "I was afraid."

When he said nothing, she pinched at the fleece pulled tight over her knee and looked away. "When I was younger, just starting with the firm, I wasn't as . . ." She wanted to think of a better word but nothing would come. " . . . careful, I guess. I believed the wrong man, one of my father's employees, and when I couldn't get him the recognition from my father, he dumped me." She shrugged a shoulder. "You've seen how much my father appreciates my input and courts my love and affection. Once he finally calmed down, I promised I'd be more careful. And I have good reason to. It's been five years and he hasn't let me forget it yet."

"So because of one jackass, you can't give a perfectly respectable gentleman like me a chance? That's harsh." He was smiling as he said it, but she didn't get the impression that he was only joking.

She crossed her arms over her chest. "He wasn't the only one, Luke. He was the only one to get to me. But my father's been pretty powerful in Dallas since . . ." She shrugged. "I don't know, since Noah saw the rain forecast."

His lips twitched. So did hers. And they both laughed.

"That's a long time."

She nodded. "It really is." She shook her head. "I hate being the poor little rich girl cliché with daddy issues. I really ought to be past this by now, you know? College was a whole learning curve of weeding out boys who liked me from boys who liked my family tree. Eventually, I just got pretty cynical."

He traced a finger over her knee. "And tough."

She waved a hand. "Not really. Just good at hiding the emotions."

He nodded. "You're pretty good at that, except anger. You're pretty good at letting that one fly."

"Yeah, I can handle anger. Also irritation." She met his stare. "Which is why you like picking at me."

He nodded again.

"Got it." She leaned her head back against the couch. "Since you've asked for complete honesty, I'm about to lay it on you here, Luke." When his tracing finger stilled on her knee, she squeezed her eyes shut and said, "There's only been one time I regret shutting a guy down."

When he didn't answer, she forced her eyelids open to see a smug smile on his face.

"And what just happened is a good example of why I regret saying no to you. You didn't accuse me of being an idiot for going down that hallway or tell me I should have stayed where you put me." She wiped her hands down her thighs. "And I'm wearing funny clothes, bad shoes, and answering silly trivia questions that draw attention while doing so." She shrugged. "I don't think I could do that with anyone else I know. And I like it. I appreciate you and the way you make me feel. I wish I'd done things differently. I wish we were celebrating Valentine's Day in the traditional way."

"It's not too late." He settled a hand on each of her knees and leaned forward. "So, say . . . if he were to ask you again. If that guy called you up and very respectfully said, 'New Nickname, would you go out to dinner with me tonight?' What would your answer be?"

She leaned forward until her nose could touch his. Their breaths mingled as she stared into his eyes. Finally, she gave a small shake. "I'd have to say no. Tonight I'm going to be busy."

His eyebrows shot up and he licked his lips. "Busy? Doing what?"

She smiled slowly. "That depends on how good you are with your hands."

Chapter Seven

Shake, Rattle, and Roll

Luke knew that he shouldn't ask questions or in any way show concern. He who hesitates loses the chance to get the woman he can't get out of his mind naked. And he had never been that guy. He was too smart and all his body parts functioned superbly. But he couldn't get the idea out of his head that Julie was different. She'd always seemed different.

Right now she seemed insistent too. She'd slithered around him to stand, pulling his hand as she went. When he reluctantly stood, she towed him toward the bed, spun him around and launched herself at him. They both tumbled to the bed and Luke had to take advantage of her straddle to wrap both hands around her ass. It was a really good ass. That might have weakened his position on the moral high ground.

She braced both hands on his shoulders and smiled down at him.

He smiled back and then shook his head. "Wait. I'm not sure this is what—"

Her lips were soft on his at first, tentative in their exploration until he opened his mouth. Her tongue darted in to tangle with his and every nerve in his body sat up and said "Hello." He tightened his hold on her butt and pulled her closer, tighter, until his erection pressed against soft, fleece-covered heat.

When she pulled back and they gasped for breath, he surrendered his hold and moaned as every shift of her body rubbed them together. He had died and gone to heaven. This was heaven. Luke had left the building. He was about to meet the King in person. He had no doubt.

He wrapped one hand around each of her wrists to still the hands that were questing under his T-shirt. She frowned as she struggled against his hold.

"Just wait a minute, Julie. I want to talk." And he wanted to roll his own eyes. He sounded like some Victorian maiden and his erection was draining every bit of his will to go on reasoning. He only had one shot. "We don't have to do this tonight."

Her shoulders drooped and the nasty smile she'd been wearing slid away. "You don't want to have sex tonight?" She looked around the room. "I mean, really?"

He teased the soft skin of her wrists with his fingers as he memorized every bit of her, disheveled, flushed, wearing his clothes, and straddling his lap in one of the most unusual hotel rooms he'd ever visited. "Of course I want to have sex!"

He took a deep breath to calm down. "But, there's no rush for us. When we get back, maybe we go out. We can get here, but just take some time with it and get to know each other better first." He tried to smile. It might have been more like a grimace, but he expected points for effort. Being a hero was a damned nuisance.

When she shifted her hips against his, he squeezed his eyes shut and bit his lip to keep a moan from escaping.

When he opened them again, she was smiling down at him. "Thank you. I really appreciate the offer." She squirmed around to reach the Valentine's package he'd left on the nightstand before she settled back against him. He counted it a success that he hadn't died or exploded in the experience.

She flipped open the box and pulled out one of the condoms inside. She waved the shiny gold wrapper and said, "But for the first time, I have a Valentine. And I want to celebrate the holiday properly. Forget the future, what happens when we get home. I don't want to miss this chance. Join me?"

Luke frowned. "How did you know that was in there?"

She shrugged a shoulder, and he bit his lip. "I peeked."

He rolled her over and slid off the bed. He held up one finger. "I give up, but I'll stick with my own condom."

"Fine." Julie plopped it back in the box and shoved the box off the bed. "I love a take-charge kinda guy."

When he made it into the bathroom to dig through his shaving kit for one of the two condoms he always traveled with, he paused to look in the mirror. The face looking back at him was not one of a man about to make a mistake. His lips twitched as he fought a smile. The face in that mirror belonged to one lucky bastard.

He grabbed the condom, and flipped out the light on his way back to the bed.

WHEN LUKE SAUNTERED back to the bed and crawled over the mattress to stretch out beside her, she was happy to see he looked more certain. She'd battled her own nerves by seizing the opportunity to set the scene a little more to her advantage. She'd turned down the lights, and now only the bedside lamp illuminated her and the purple bedspread. She hadn't been able to force herself out of her clothes. Not yet. She'd burned through just about every bit of bravery she possessed getting him this far. Surely his instinct would carry them through the rest.

When he reached behind him to yank the T-shirt over his head, Julie couldn't look away. The ripple of his muscles was amazing even in the shadowy room. He had golden skin and a light dusting of chest hair. Helpless to resist, she slid her hands over his stomach and up to his shoulders. When he cursed under his breath, her building nervous tension melted into a warmth between her thighs.

This was going to be all right.

Luke moved to straddle her hips and quickly yanked her own shirt up over her head. Before she even had time to bemoan the fact that she'd worn her best, most supportive bra instead of prettiest, most seductive one, it was gone. He slid the straps over her arms and reached under her to unfasten it and then tossed her bra away, into the shadows.

She made a mental note to examine how she felt about his aptitude. Later.

When he leaned back to stare down at her, she fought the urge to cover herself and instead ran her hands up and down his thighs. Hot fleece molded the muscles there perfectly, and she kneaded, scraped her fingernails along the inside of his thighs. His hands were firm when he grabbed hers and his voice was raspy. "Stop."

He bent forward to kiss her before scattering kisses down her neck, over the ticklish spot where her neck and shoulder met, past her collarbones, and down the center of her chest. Julie shivered at the gentle seduction and her nipples hardened, begging for his attention.

"I know I've made my feeling about your ass clear, but we've never talked about these beauties." When his mouth touched her nipple, teasing with a tongue before he sucked it into his heat, she gasped. And when he repeated it with the other nipple, she moaned. Shots of heat from each tease swept through her and pooled between her thighs. As he teased and tormented, she yanked her hands free. She curled one in his hair and then the other returned to his leg.

Goose bumps covered her arms when her nipple slipped out of his mouth. He mumbled, "Perfect," before he scooted back, pulling her sweatpants and panties off as he went. His eyes never left her as he pushed his own pants and underwear down.

Julie wanted to agree. He was the perfect one, all golden

skin, lean muscle, and an erection that removed all doubt about his attraction to her, but her tongue stuck to the roof of her mouth. She struggled to sit up so she could properly memorize every inch of his athletic build, but he was too quick. She had a flash of a wicked smile and then he was in motion. She didn't stop him. She wanted to touch.

He crawled back between her legs and ran his hands in tickling caresses over her calves and up the inside of her thighs before he rubbed the outside with hot, hard palms. The waves of cold and hot that went over left her confused, shaken, and anxious to have her hands on him.

Shadows got in her way but his body was strong and hard. The hair on his muscled thighs tickled and scratched the inside of her thighs, and when he leaned forward to kiss her again, his erection was hot and hard against her stomach.

He smiled as he teased her lips. She smiled back but lost her breath as one of his hands ran up her thigh to tangle in the curls covering her heat. As one finger traced her wetness and toyed with the bundle of nerves that made her jerk and gasp before answering her ache with cautious exploration and then tension-building thrusts, his eyes swept over her body.

His voice was a low rumble when he said, "Legs is a stupid nickname."

She tried to concentrate on his face. She really did, but her eyes wouldn't cooperate. She closed them and did her best not to beg out loud as she moved her hips to meet his finger's thrust. At this point the friction was a torment. She wanted more.

He laughed softly. "You're paying no attention."

Julie twisted her head on the pillow. "Can't we . . . talk about this . . ." She grabbed his arm and held on as she felt the tension building. He pressed harder and faster, answering the jerk of her hips. "Later" escaped on a long moan as her climax arrived. Her body tightened and then spasms left her weak, strung out, and so content.

She sighed as Luke brought his hand up to lick his fingers. And she nearly died. But the heat came back with a vengeance. She shifted her legs anxiously.

He watched her. "Got your attention now?"

She still had trouble focusing on his face but she nodded.

He shook his head. "Never thought I'd be the deep thinker in this couple."

She wanted to answer but her tongue was still caught up in the afterglow.

His eyes were hot as they swept up and down her body. He scratched his nails lightly down her thigh and Julie shivered again. "Know what your new nickname will be?"

Julie licked her lips and managed to say, "I'm afraid to ask."

One corner of his mouth curled up. "In my head, I'm going to call you 'Heaven' because I'm never going to forget the sight of these long legs stretched out, those curls, or the feeling of sliding into you for the first time."

When he settled between her thighs and then slid into her slowly, she gasped. And then squirmed. And then caught on fire as he muttered, "Never want to forget this."

Julie knew what he meant. His chest was a hot, hard weight against her that teased and tickled with each slide in and slow retreat. She wrapped her hands around his back to memorize the feel of the muscles in his shoulders and hips working. He hissed as she squeezed his hips to pull him closer, tighter against her.

Julie forced herself to focus on his face. His eyes were locked on her, and she wanted to smile and laugh with her unbelievable luck, but he leaned back. His voice was rough when he said, "Watch." They both watched his hips working between her legs, and his movements became harder, faster, while he whispered hot blessings and curses in her ear. She moaned as their bodies worked together to climb, the tension building again until he said, "Now, Julie." The demand and the rough emotion in his voice sent her over the edge just as he jerked against her and then collapsed on top of her.

And she thought maybe he was right, maybe this was Heaven right here at the Rock'n'Rolla Hotel. He stretched as she rubbed her hands up and down his back, savoring the feeling of his warmth and strength. Breathing was a challenge, but she didn't want to move from this spot.

When his phone dinged, he muttered, "Text message." He kissed her lips before sliding off the bed. On his way back from the bathroom, he snagged the phone off the nightstand before urging her under the blankets on the bed. He wrapped one arm around her to pull her next to him and then checked the message.

"Fabulous Fran has us booked to Dallas on an eleven

o'clock flight," he told her, then dropped the phone on the bed with a tired sigh.

"Both of us? Did you ask her to do that?" Julie thought he looked even better now than he had before. She carefully lifted the sheets and comforter to get another look at what he'd been hiding under his clothes. He snorted but gave her a minute to memorize his charms, then tugged her hand down to rest on his chest. He was rumpled and a huge yawn split his face, but he was close and he was warm. The arm he had wrapped around her made her feel safe. And maybe even . . . no, not loved but maybe . . . cared for.

He lazily slapped her hip. "Duh. Of course. And she's good that way. Tomorrow night we'll be asleep in our own beds."

His breathing evened out and Julie did her best to memorize how nice it felt to rest next to him. She didn't sleep much. The thought of returning to her own bed, alone, since it didn't sound like he was planning to join her anytime soon, was depressing. And this was still the best Valentine's Day she'd ever had.

Chapter Eight

Suspicious Minds

When the phone alarm went off the next morning, Julie slid out of bed and escaped to the bathroom while Luke dug around to find it on the bed.

As she shut the door, she could hear him muttering about the damn phone. And it was funny. She'd spent a little too much time worrying about what Luke wanted after he'd drifted peacefully to sleep, so she had a headache of monumental proportions, but was determined to be casual. It might be a good idea to figure out what she wanted first. She'd take her cues from him and make it home without incident and then she might fall apart. But not before then. Nope. He'd said "maybe" they'd date. And now that he wasn't on the verge of hotel sex, maybe he'd change his mind. If he'd only been looking for a good night with a convenient partner, then so had she. Really, what had she lost? Nothing. And she'd gained a lot of fun. And a nice Valentine. It was all good.

That calm acceptance lasted until he knocked loudly

on the door. "Good morning, Heaven. I need to get in there before you take over."

It was the stupid nickname. That was a place, not a person. He really sucked at nicknames. "Just a minute and it's all yours."

She turned the lock on the door and started the shower. She tried to enjoy it for twenty minutes but felt a little bit guilty. And that lasted as long as it took her to get dressed and open the bathroom door.

"No, I'm glad you called." Instead of doing an urgent dance, Luke was stretched out on the couch. Wearing only his boxer briefs. It was a really nice look for him. She forced herself to look away.

"I'm looking forward to seeing you too. I missed you yesterday, but I don't think you need to come out to pick me up. The weather . . ." He ran a hand down his chest and winked at her.

She froze in place as she tried to remember if she'd ever asked him if he was dating anyone. What an idiot. Of course she hadn't asked. She gritted her teeth and stomped back in the bathroom to dry her hair. While she did so, she alternated between righteous anger and horrified embarrassment. *What if he has a girlfriend?* played over and over in her mind. Of course they'd both go back to their own beds when they got to Dallas. He probably had somebody doing roll call on his.

As soon as she clicked the hair dryer off, he invaded her space. He leaned down to kiss her neck while his hands wrapped around her shoulders. She was desperate to blurt out the question but didn't want to hear the wrong answer. He slowly turned her and urged her out the door before he pushed her suitcase out the door and closed it in her face.

Julie lectured herself on the proper morning-after etiquette while she threw everything she could find in her suitcase. He'd never said he wasn't already dating someone. He'd also never said they'd have an exclusive relationship. He had tried to slow her down, maybe because his Valentine was his ride home from the airport. In Julie's mind, she was wearing only a bikini and a dozen roses.

When the water stopped running in the shower, she tapped and said, "Want coffee?"

He cracked the door open. The water running down his chest nearly killed her. She almost fell over into a faint right there on the white carpet. But she didn't. She was made of sterner stuff.

Luke frowned and then said, "Sure." When she walked sedately over to the door to pull it gently open, at great expense to her frayed nerves, he stopped her. "Everything okay?"

She smiled brightly and nodded. "You bet. Be right back."

He didn't buy it, but time was ticking already and they needed to make the trip to the airport pretty soon. Missing this flight home would send her into a full-blown melt-down, and she wasn't going to do that until she'd made it home. In the privacy of her perfectly acceptable three-bedroom bungalow, she'd clutch Larry and cry about how stupid she'd been because of this idiotic holiday that caused her to do something she'd never do because she knew better. First, she'd figure out how to ask him whether he was seeing anyone. Of course. And then, if the answer was yes, she'd go home, crawl under her bed, and never come out.

Hot coffee was the great equalizer. When she made it back to the room, Luke had already dried, dressed, and packed. He was staring out the window when she came in.

He smiled as she handed him the coffee. When she had a hard time meeting his eyes, he grabbed her hand to stop her retreat. "All right, Julie. What's wrong?"

She made an obvious glance at the Elvis alarm clock. "Nothing, but we should probably get going. The roads might still be trouble and I will harm someone if I don't make it home today."

He looked away while he considered her answer. "Is this about the phone call?" His hand slid off of hers. "Or is this about regrets?"

Julie jammed the last of her stuff in the bathroom in her suitcase. "Maybe both. A little."

He crossed his arms over his chest. "I hate to say 'I told you so' but . . ."

She rolled her eyes. "No, you don't."

"Nope, you're right. We moved too fast." He pursed his lips and then shook his head. "Not that I didn't thoroughly enjoy every single minute of it."

Julie slung her purse over one shoulder, yanked the handle of her suitcase out, and picked up her coffee. "Let's just get to the airport. We can iron all this out then."

Luke nodded once. "Fine."

Checking out and the long, slow ride to the airport were both quiet, chilly affairs. When they made it to the gate with time to spare, Luke plopped down in a seat and pulled her down beside him. To be fair, she'd been impressed how he hadn't complained once at her dictatorial commands in the airport. Now that they were at the gate, she could breathe again.

And he'd clearly reached the end of his patience. "Talk. Or I'll call you the nickname you hate right here in front of all these people."

Julie slapped a hand against the empty seat next to her. "You know, the problem with you is that you're too damn smart. And charming. It's hard to stay mad at you even when it's in my best interest."

He shook his head. "Nope. Still don't understand."

She said, "I'm pretty good at protecting myself. I've done it for a long time, pretty well. A few bobbles maybe, but nothing I couldn't recover from."

He rested his elbows on the armrest and dared her to say a word.

"With you, I mean, I was cautious, took my normal precautions not to be taken advantage of." She huffed. "I mean, you could be the first man in my world who, instead of needing me to get my father's approval, might actually boost his opinion of me. After a lifetime of not measuring up, that's attractive, you know?"

He stared up at the ceiling of the waiting area for a moment. "So . . . you're saying, what? You used me?"

She wanted to say yes. She wanted to shrug the whole

thing off, just so she didn't feel like a total idiot. Again.

But she couldn't. He wouldn't have believed her anyway.

"I wish." Julie rubbed her forehead. "Who was the phone call from, Luke? Your Valentine?"

He didn't answer at first. Finally he nodded. "That phone call was from my mother."

The look on his face said it was the absolute truth, and for the first time that morning she took a deep breath. "You tried to slow me down. I have no one to blame but myself. And I don't know what you want for us, maybe you don't do serious relationships, but that's the only kind I can do." She shrugged. "Maybe when we get home, we can go back to the beginning, start over, and do things the way we should have in the first place. The way you wanted to."

Julie covered her face with both hands, acutely aware that she was having a very sensitive conversation in a busy airplane terminal. And hating every minute of it.

He held up one hand and counted down on his fingers. "So, I was right. You were wrong. You hate to give up on someone who might get you some extra cachet with your father, and you're not mad at me because there is no other woman so we can just go out on a date now because you're ready."

Julie replayed it in her head. She thought it sounded right but he was clearly pissed over the whole conversation. "Ri-i-ght." The answer was drawn out and was as much a question as a statement.

"And instead of just asking me about it this morning

and saving me the wear and tear as I tried to figure out what was up with you, you decided to stick with what you know: chilly civility. You didn't ask. And you obviously thought I might be the kind of guy who'd sleep with a woman even though I had someone waiting for me. I hate that." He rubbed his forehead. "But here's the thing. I've been a nice guy for a long time. I've waited for you, puzzled over you, and thought about you since you told me you didn't date coworkers. I'm done with that. I get you and your . . . baggage, but right now, here, we're past that." He scratched his temple as the gate attendant announced they would begin boarding. "So, okay, here's what you need to do."

Julie arched her eyebrows. This was not going at all the way she thought it would.

He stood and put his bag over his shoulder. "You need to really think long and hard about two questions."

Julie stood beside him, but as she was about to demand where he got off with his high-handed . . .

"I'm going to ignore your comments about what I could do for your reputation because that was just a stupid comment. You didn't mean to hurt my feelings. I believe that still, and I'm going to operate there until you explain it differently."

He shook his head as she started to speak. "Nope. I want you. I've never had any trouble saying that. Now, if you decide it's too much trouble or whatever to be honest about what you want, to take a chance and give me a shot even if it means your father might explode, fine. Your loss. Again. That's the first question."

He grabbed the handle of her suitcase and swung it around to get in line to board. He had a small smile on his face as he leaned down and said, "That second question you need to figure out is how far you'll go to apologize for assuming the worst about me."

Chapter Nine

Who's Sorry Now?

Luke lifted her bag into the overhead bin while Julie buckled herself in and then tossed his in behind. She watched him the whole time, clearly confused over whatever his issue was. So he flirted. He chatted up the nice grandmother across the aisle and managed to talk the flight attendant out of three bags of cookies during the trip. And he didn't share. He felt good about that decision too.

After they deplaned, he dragged her suitcase through the airport and walked with one hand on her back. He'd fussed and fumed and there was one thing he was pretty sure of: he wanted her. He didn't cheat. Ever. His mother taught him better, and she'd murder him if she ever thought he did. Julie should know that, and she would with more time. If she wanted to show him off to Daddy, he didn't care one way or the other. She deserved to have her father's respect because she was a damn good lawyer and a better person. If he had to help get it for her, that was more about what an ass her father was than about either one of them.

She'd kept him waiting a long time. Now that he'd had her, held her in his arms, watched her come apart, he was done with that.

JULIE KNEW A few new things after the flight to Dallas was over. One, Luke didn't cheat. His mother was his Valentine. Of course. He just didn't have it in him. Sure, he'd flirted up a storm, but he'd been courteous with her, even though she could see the temper in his eyes. He'd helped her and every other lady who struggled with too much to carry on. He'd matched his pace to hers and stopped at the first restroom he saw. That went beyond good manners or general friendliness. He understood women and, more important, he wanted to take care of her. After she washed her hands and slowly walked back out to where he waited, she fidgeted with her jacket as he straightened from his lean against the wall.

He didn't look ready to chew nails when he asked, "Ready?"

Julie sighed unhappily. "Not really. I need to talk to you first." She pulled him out of the flow of business traveler traffic. "I want to make excuses and then a sincere apology."

He snorted and leaned back against the wall. When his lips twitched in an almost smile, she thought he might already be over the only display of temper she'd ever seen from him.

She twisted her fingers together. "I'm not sure how many excuses it will be. You might want to count." She arched her eyebrows at him until he held up a hand.

"I didn't sleep very well last night." He nodded and flipped up a thumb.

"I was worrying because you said something about sleeping in our own beds when we got back so I thought maybe last night was . . . it, you know, the whole goal." He flipped up a second finger and shook his head.

"I didn't even think about your Valentine dinner plans until everything was all over." He flipped up the next finger.

"And that made me feel like some two-timing Jezebel. I couldn't imagine you without a hot Valentine. Because you are awesome. I wasn't really mad at you, but at myself. If only I'd spent two seconds thinking about whether you would do that, cheat on anyone, I'd have come up with a better answer, I know it. I don't have any excuse for that except that letting down my guard doesn't happen very often." He flipped up another finger.

"My number one goal for a long time has been to protect myself. I never measured up for my father and then there were all these guys who I just couldn't trust. To protect myself, I wanted to lump you in with them." He waved all the fingers on one hand and held up the other.

Julie grabbed both. "I think that's all the excuses I have. Here's part of my apology: I should have asked you, probably before my clothes came off but definitely before I jumped to conclusions, about whatever this relationship should be. I apologize."

Luke tilted his head as he stared down at her.

She rubbed her forehead. "For the longest time I've wanted to figure out a way to tell you 'never mind' on the whole not dating coworkers but I just couldn't get there. Thank you for not letting me screw this up again."

He let out a deep sigh and squeezed her hands. Finally he straightened. "Let's get out of here, then."

As she walked beside him, Julie stared up into his face, but he was impossible to read. "So do you accept my apology?"

When he met her stare, he didn't smile, but she thought she could see warmth in his eyes and her heart lifted. "Almost."

As they cleared Baggage Claim, Julie heard someone shout "Luke! Over here!" and she turned to watch him trot over to grab a woman who looked suspiciously like him and twirl her around. With a sinking heart, she grabbed her suitcase handle and tugged it behind her to go and meet Luke's mother.

She was tall, well-dressed, and had the same brown hair and twinkling eyes. Julie heard her say, "I was so sorry to miss a special dinner with my son, but I'm glad to have him home finally."

Luke motioned toward Julie. "Mom, let me introduce you to Julie Dillon. We work together, but it's probably more important to know that we're dating. Now." Luke stared into her eyes and waited for her nod.

Julie held out her hand. "Mrs. Pearce, it's so nice to meet you."

Luke's mother held her hand for the briefest second

before glancing up at her son. "Dillon as in the Dillon Agency?"

He nodded. "Yep, dating the boss's daughter."

Mrs. Pearce's mouth quirked up as she winked at Julie. "As smart as he is handsome, right?"

Julie licked her lips and then nodded. "Oh, yes, ma'am."

"We're going to go have lunch since we missed our dinner last night. Why don't you come with us?" Mrs. Pearce motioned over her shoulder and then turned to lead them out of the airport. "Ever since Luke's dad died when he was teenager, he's been my Valentine. We started out celebrating at McDonald's but his good taste has grown along with his bank balance."

"Oh, but . . . I wouldn't want to . . . I was just going to call a cab and—"

Luke just wrapped his hand around hers and pulled her along. His mother probably thought she had some hideous skin disease, as she could feel the heat of a flush on her cheeks and a slight but very present film of sweat building. It wasn't a good look for her.

He nodded as she mouthed, I'm sorry, I'm sorry, I'm sorry.

When his mother hopped into the driver's seat of her comfortable sedan, Luke stopped Julie and leaned forward to say, "Remember the second question? I hope you're working on the answer. I want romantic comedy, meeting at the top of the Empire State Building big."

He tossed their luggage in the trunk and then opened the front passenger door for her. When she was buckled in, he shut the door with a wink and slid into the back.

"All right, now, what sounds good for lunch, honey?" In the restaurant his mother did her best to keep the conversation rolling, and Julie contributed what she could. Which were mainly embellishments of Luke's description of the hotel. He didn't quite do it justice but that wasn't his fault. Pictures were worth a thousand words and that would have been the only way to explain the Rock'n'Rolla Hotel. Mrs. Pearce laughed in all the right spots and it was clear that she was happy to see him. Every story she told confirmed that Luke Pearce was better than sliced bread. He started to look a bit embarrassed before the waiter delivered the bill. And with each funny story and fond pat of his hand, Julie sunk lower in her seat, the combined weight of guilt over doubting him and stomach-churning jealousy over his relationship with his mother crushing. Her own father treated her like hired help at best and as the dog who pooped on the living room rug when he was on a roll. Thank God Luke hadn't let her off the hook here. She'd said no the first time because of her father and his disapproval. She wasn't going to say no to Luke Pearce ever again.

When lunch was over, Mrs. Pearce dropped her in front of her modest house. Julie thanked her sincerely and followed Luke up the sidewalk. When she opened the door, Larry bounded out to greet her. Black from head to toe, Larry was more legs and tail than anything else but his excitement was contagious. Her neighbor across the street, Larry's babysitter when she traveled, waved from her window. And Luke and Larry bonded. That wasn't saying a lot. Larry loved everyone, but Luke was also universally adored.

"How'd you come up with the name Larry?" he asked. They both looked down at the dog who was nosing through the bushes.

Julie laughed. "That was the name on his cage at the animal rescue where I found him. I always hoped that the name Larry was the worst abuse he suffered before he showed up there."

Luke stood up and watched her. Ready to apologize profusely and for quite a long time, Julie propped her hands on her hips. Luke stopped her with a kiss.

He leaned back a bit and said, "Now that everything's cleared up, I think we should spend the night in our own beds." The look on his face was as close to a smirk as she'd ever seen in real life. "I mean, my mother is taking me home, you know?" He waved at the car waiting in the driveway. "Grand gestures take careful planning. I happen to know that you're very good with careful planning. This should be a Valentine no one will forget." He gave her a quick peck, reached down to ruffle Larry's ears, and trotted back to his mom's car. They both waved as she backed down the driveway.

When she was safely inside her cozy home, one devoid of all pink, hearts, and the threat of Valentine's Day, Julie banged her head against the door for a minute. When Larry tilted his head at her, clearly worried about her sanity and where his treat was, she laughed.

"C'mon, Larry. Treats first. Then we need to plan a grand gesture."

Chapter Ten

It's Now or Never

Luke glanced at his wristwatch one more time. It was nearly eleven. He and Julie had been held prisoner in the firm's glass-walled conference room for more than an hour now, while Big Jack Dillon quizzed them about the client calls they'd made and next week's plans. Right now Jack was tilted back in the chair at the head of the conference table, one arm propped behind his head and legs crossed on the table while he droned about . . . something. Luke had pretty much stopped listening after Jack had told Julie how lucky she was to have had him along to rescue her. The longer they sat there, the more annoyed Jack got and the more Julie fidgeted. There had to be a way out short of bomb threat. He ground his teeth in what he hoped was a smile as he slapped his leather portfolio closed.

Before he could interrupt whatever his boss was saying, Fran walked in front of the long line of glass that separated the conference room from the cubicles in the center of the office. Paralegals, interns, and administrative support clustered out there. Fran, in a class of her own, had an office next to his. And she was often the first line of defense against the unexpected. It was a natural fit for her.

"Hey, boss!" She stuck her head in the door. "I think you need to see this." She was looking at him and her eyes were speaking but he couldn't translate. Still, he'd been looking for a way out. He just had to take Julie with him.

"Are we done here, Jack?"

Jack tilted forward and landed with a thud. He wasn't used to anyone interrupting him.

When Julie said, "I think we both need to go up to reception, Luke," and stood, Jack's mouth dropped open.

Jack's eyebrows lowered in a V but he gestured them out. "Let's all go take a look-see, then, at whatever's so damn important the flighty receptionist can't handle it."

Julie waited for Luke just outside the conference room door. As she wrapped her hand around his arm, he had an inkling. He was about to witness the grand gesture.

When they rounded the corner, he was a bit sorry he'd ever dared her. A huge pink and red banner asked, LUKE, WILL YOU BE MINE? Bouquets of roses and carnations covered every flat surface, all of them containing some combination of pink and red or white. Silver balloons littered the ceiling. And a quartet of Elvis impersonators stood in front of the elevator bank. Before anyone had a chance to react, they launched into an acceptable rendition of "Love Me Tender."

When he glanced down at Julie, he was afraid she

might literally combust right there. It was a lot to absorb, and the whole company was watching, each person frozen in place. He could feel a little bit of heat in his own cheeks, but she looked so damned uncomfortable and proud at the same time. It was adorable. He never could have imagined she had it in her. He'd be more careful with every dare from now on.

When the last note died out, she went to shake the lead Elvis's hand, and they waved as they got on the elevator. Before the doors shut, the Elvises launched into "Teddy Bear," and after they left, the lobby was one living, breathing ball of silence.

No one spoke. Luke shrugged and turned to Julie. "Yes."

She whooped and launched herself at him. When she'd wrapped her arms around his neck, he kissed her and said, "And you win this round, darlin'."

She leaned her forehead against his for a quick second. "I think you're absolutely right."

At a loud harrumph, Julie stepped back and her arms slid away.

Luke grabbed her hand before she could step back and smiled at Big Jack Dillon.

"What kind of idiot move is this, Julie?" Jack demanded. "Throwing yourself at a coworker, and in front of the whole damn company? We've talked about this and you swore you'd be smarter." He held his hands out. "Luke, son, let me apologize—"

"Big Jack," Julie said, "there's no need! This *is* the apology." She tilted her head. "I mean, aren't you impressed at how much smarter I've gotten?" She pointed at Luke. "This time I picked one that didn't need my help." She shrugged. "He doesn't even need *your* help. Great, right?"

Big Jack's face was bright red and he was clearly stunned.

Julie marched up to him and raised his chin to close his mouth with a click of teeth before she patted him twice on the cheek. Luke thought it might be a good thing Big Jack didn't have Lucky's luxurious sideburns. Julie might have tried for another souvenir.

"You were right, Big Jerk." She paused for the insult to sink in. Every eye in the place widened. Except for Big Jack's. His narrowed in anger. "I was lucky Luke was there to rescue me, but it didn't have a damn thing to do with the weather." Big Jack reached out to grab her arms, and she stepped back to Luke's side.

"I could have spent my whole life trying to make you happy. And we both know that's not possible, right? Bossing people around, that's not really happiness. Luke helped me realize two important things. I've made some mistakes, but one, I'm a damn good lawyer. I make good decisions. You'd do well to let bygones be bygones at this point. And two, not every man's an asshole." The look on her face clearly communicated who was in the top slot of her Assholes of the World list.

Luke smiled when she spun to face him. "Big Jerk? Another play on words?"

She grimaced. "I know. Apparently it's my thing."

Luke tilted his head back and laughed. Jack was at a loss for words and Julie had found her voice. With a vengeance. And it was hot. She seemed as proud of herself as the rest of the company was stunned. Big Jack looked like he'd stopped breathing all together.

The crowd watching them erupted in hoots and claps as he leaned forward to kiss her.

"Do you forgive me?" Julie wrapped her arms around his waist to slide her hands into his back pockets. Thank God she didn't show one bit of doubt about the answer. Ruining such a grand gesture at that point would have been a sorry shame.

After he glanced around the lobby and enjoyed the confusion and excitement on every face but one, he shook his head. It was good to be the king.

"Yes. I can't help falling in love with you."

gence. And it was true; she seemed so proud of herself as the rest of the company was stunned. Big Jack looked like he'd stopped breathing all together.

The crowd watching them erupted in laughter and claps as she leaned over to kiss him.

"Do you forgive me?" Julie wrapped her arms around Big Jack and slid her hands into his back pockets. Thank God the actual show couldn't be aired about this interview. Soothing such a grand gesture at that point would have been a sorry shame.

After he glanced around the lobby and winked at the [illegible] and [illegible] everyone [illegible], he shook his head. It was good to be the king.

"Yeah," [illegible] with you."

About the Author

CHERYL HARPER is often entertained by the goings-on and saddened by the serious lack of shopping and restaurants in her small southern town. In her spare time she's mesmerized by Gordon Ramsay and most televised cooking competitions, British dramas and actors, and just about any show people will be talking about the next day. When it comes to reading and writing, Cheryl prefers a few laughs and a happily-ever-after ending.

Visit www.AuthorTracker.com for exclusive information on your favorite HarperCollins authors.

About the Author

CHERYL HARPER is often entertained by the goings on and sometimes the serious lack of shopping and restaurants in her small southern town. In her spare time she's a member of the Garden Club and [illegible] cooking competitions, [illegible] drinking [illegible] and just about [illegible] people will be talking about the next day. When it comes to reading and writing, Cheryl prefers a fast pace and a happily-ever-after ending.

Visit www.AuthorTracker.com for exclusive information on your favorite HarperCollins authors.

Love, Guns, and Heart-Shaped Chocolate

Jaclyn Hatcher

To my family for being so supportive of my dreams
And to my friends: Britney, Melanie, Steffanie, Lindsay,
and Zach for encouraging me, brainstorming with me,
and for listening to me whine about writer's block.

Chapter One

The fluorescent lights of the supermarket flickered overhead as Katie Quinn considered the bag of Dove chocolates in her hand. Thirty percent more for free, she noted with a satisfied nod. That was good because she was at least thirty percent more depressed at the moment. Valentine's Day was always a kicker, but getting dumped by her boyfriend two days before just seemed to bring the agony of the holiday into razor sharp, mind-numbing focus.

"He just didn't want to have to buy you shit," her best friend Tracy had said when Katie told her about it over a steaming mug of coffee at her kitchen table. In all the years Katie had known her, Tracy had always been a bit of a ballbuster. However, at five feet eight inches of slender, polished, Grace Kelly–like beauty, men still kept lining up to get her attention.

"No really," she said when Katie shot her a glare.

"Guys do that. They break up with a girl right before any gift-related holiday so that they can save a buck. I had one that dumped me right before Christmas. One of his buddies told me later that it was because he didn't want to buy me a present." Tracy poured about a liter of vanilla creamer into her mug. "And don't even get me started with commitment-phobes. He probably got all freaked out about the significance of a box of cheap chocolates just because they come in a little heart-shaped box. Like we're gonna expect a diamond ring inside of it or something."

Whether it was a fear of commitment or just a way to save cash, she would probably never know. Either way, it didn't change the fact that she was alone on Valentine's Day. Alone. The hardest day of the year to be alone and that's just what she was.

Alone.

With an eye roll and a sigh, Katie dropped the bag of chocolates into her basket, throwing in some peanut butter cups for good measure while purposefully avoiding the red velvet heart-shaped boxes. They sat on the clearance shelf looking jumbled and picked over. One was poised on the edge as if it were trying to jump. The poor dateless chocolate wanted to end its misery, she thought. Whereas she had a nice, relaxing, romance-free night planned. No swan dives off the clearance shelf for her. She was going to drink a bottle of cheap wine, gorge herself on chocolate, and watch *Jurassic Park*. It truly was the perfect movie for tonight. There was no love plot and all the men got eaten by pointy toothed monsters. Now if only that were real.

The store was mostly empty and quiet. A modern version of "The Way You Look Tonight" echoed through the aisles as she headed over to the wine section. How romantic, she thought with a sneer, wanting to hurry home.

"There is nothing for me but to looove you," Michael Bublé's voice sang. The soft, smooth jazz seemed to float, weightless and seductive, in the air. It made her want to heave. They had to be playing love songs right now? Really? She shook her head and got her mind back onto her task. Should she get the big bottle of wine? Or the smaller, less expensive bottle? If she wanted to be really cheap she could go for a box of wine instead. Nah, not a box. She wasn't that low just yet. She picked out a bottle and slid it in her basket, wanting to hurry away from the lovey-dovey music.

She was turning to head for the checkout counter when something large and heavy slammed into her back. The basket threatened to fly from her hands as she stumbled forward a few steps. "Hey, watch it!" she said, rubbing her shoulder.

The sound of a man's laughter filled her ears, and as she righted herself she noticed the guy who had bumped her. He was in his late twenties, just under six feet, with dirty blond hair and a face full of scruffy stubble. He had the stunted vacant expression of a man who hadn't matured much past fifteen. Katie shoved a handful of dark blond hair off her face and hoisted her purse back up her shoulder.

"Not cool, Will," another man said to the moron.

"What?" The moron, Will, adjusted his grip on a six pack of beer, still grinning like an idiot. In his other hand he held a box of chocolates and a card with Valentine's sentiments written in red scrawling letters. "It's not like I ran into her on purpose."

"No, you're just too obnoxious to look where you're going," the second man said, before turning toward her. "Are you all right?" he began, then saw her, surprise flashing on his face. "Katie?"

She looked at him in confusion, wondering where she knew him from. He was handsome, that was for sure. How could she forget someone this good looking? Of course, she *would* run into someone she knew when she looked so disheveled. She had thrown her clothes on with no thought as to how they matched, she wore no makeup, and her hair hadn't seen the business end of a brush in about twelve hours.

She looked closer, trying to place him. He was taller than his friend, with sleek black hair combed back from a face that was all sharp angles and strong jaw. His eyes were dark and kind, with brows that framed them in thick slashes. His build was slim, but even with a heavy wool coat, she could see the bulge of biceps and wide shoulders that a girl would want to hold on to. Where his friend was brimming with puppy-like excitement and energy, this man had an air of calm about him conveying that not much got under his skin. He didn't seem ready to give freshman wedgies, like his doofus of a friend, which made her wonder how he could stand to be near the guy.

"I'm sorry," she said, shrugging helplessly, her cheeks

coloring in embarrassment at not being able to place him.

"It's Logan," he said. "You probably don't remember me. Why would you, it's been years."

"Logan?" she said, shock registering on her face. The only Logan she knew was Tracy's twin brother, but this couldn't be the same guy. Granted, she hadn't seen him since he left for college, out of state, over ten years ago. Afterward, Tracy told her it had been impossible for him to find a job in Michigan so he'd remained away. In fact, with the exception of a holiday here and there, he hadn't been back, and she had only seen him in pictures. Which had *not* done him justice.

It was difficult for her to reconcile the man standing before her with the teenager she remembered. He had been a scrawny boy with a mop of thick dark hair falling in his face. He almost never ventured out of his room, so she hadn't known much about his personality save for the fact that he was shy, quiet, always working on some math problem or watching a science documentary. Tracy had joked about him not actually being related to her because she couldn't fathom his interest in deeper pursuits, seeing that hers lay firmly in the shallow end of the pool. To say the years had been kind to him was an understatement.

"Logan Cross?" she asked.

"Yeah," he said, his mouth curving into an amused smile. Cute dimples, she thought. It was strange that mere minutes ago she would have welcomed the death of all men, yet one crinkly eyed, dimpled grin from this guy and her stomach was fluttering. For the love of God, were her palms sweating, too? She tried to discreetly wipe them on the rough wool of her winter coat. What was wrong with her?

"Dude, can we get going?" Will asked. "I'm already late. Savannah is going to kill me."

Looking over at that guy, her desire to see genetically engineered dinosaurs bent on gobbling up men came back. She was glad to know she hadn't lost her edge. For one sweaty palmed second she'd been worried about that. Logan turned to his friend, giving him a pointed glare, and her eyes fell on the little muscle working in his jaw. The beer bottles clinked together as Will put his hands up and took a step back in mock surrender.

Logan turned back to face her, stuffing his hands in the pockets of his jeans. "So how have you been?" he asked.

Great, just what she needed. Small talk. He was pleasant to look at and she was sure that he was a very nice guy, but small-talking with a man was not on her list of things to do tonight. Getting a stomachache and cursing her rat of an ex-boyfriend was her list. She mentally checked her list again. Nope, flirting with a new guy definitely wasn't there.

"I've been good," she said, trying to remain pleasant. It wouldn't be fair to take her frustration out on this poor guy. Especially since this poor guy was her best friend's brother. If she were rude, she'd never hear the end of it. Besides, from what she could remember, Logan had always been a sweetheart. Geeky, awkward, and quiet, but sweet. "How long have you been back in Michigan?" she asked.

"A few weeks, I got a job teaching math at the college," he said.

"That's great," she said. Then silence fell, as she couldn't think of anything else to say. "I actually was going to meet up with someone, so I have to get going," she lied. "It was nice seeing you."

"Yeah," he said, his voice laced with disappointment. "You too."

She turned to walk away, already feeling guilty for blowing him off, when her phone let out a shrill ring. With a frustrated breath she fumbled to fish it out of her bag, shifting her basket to the crook of her elbow. The zipper on her purse was being stubborn as she struggled to open it without dropping everything, then she felt the basket being gently taken from her.

"Let me," Logan said.

She murmured a quick thanks and got to her phone just before it went to voice mail.

"Thank God," she heard Tracy say. "You have *got* to save me."

"Tracy?" Katie said, concern flooding through her. "What's going on? What's wrong?" She noticed Logan tense up beside her. "Are you all right?"

"Yeah yeah," she said. "Right as freakin' springtime rain." In the background Katie could hear the sound of running water and the flush of toilets.

"Where are you?"

"I'm at the movies," Tracy said. "I ducked into the bathroom. You have to save me."

"And you need rescuing because . . . ?" Katie drew out

the last word, hoping to prompt Tracy into giving her a direct answer.

"Is Tracy okay?" Logan said, leaning closer. Katie held up one finger.

"Who is that?" Tracy asked.

"No one," Katie said, wanting to speed this along. "Why do you need me to save you?"

"Because I'm on the blind date from hell," Tracy said.

"Geez, woman, don't scare me like that," Katie said, pushing one hand through her hair. "I thought you were in real trouble."

"I *am* in real trouble, Katie, you don't understand just how terrible this date is," Tracy said, coming as close to a whine as Tracy ever got.

"She's fine," Katie said to Logan, moving the phone away from her mouth as she said it.

"Who are you talking to?" Tracy asked, impatience dripping from her voice.

"No one," Katie said. "If it's so bad, then why don't you just ditch the guy?"

"See, normally I would, but Charles is the one that set me up with him," Tracy said. "It's his son."

"What?" Katie said. "Are you crazy, going out on a blind date with your boss's *son?*"

"I know, I know," Tracy said. "But what was I supposed to do? I couldn't tell Charles no. I really really really want that promotion, and if I have to kiss his ass to do it, then I will. Besides, I didn't want to be alone on Valentine's Day. I figured a bad date was better than no date at all. Boy was I wrong."

"First of all, you do not need to date his son to get promoted. You are the best sales rep that they have," Katie said. "Second, is there any such thing as a *good* blind date? Besides, I don't have a date and I'm fine."

Logan made an almost imperceptible jerk, straightening his spine, and she shot him a squinty glare. *That's right, Katie, announce to the world that you're dateless.*

"Are you kidding me?" Tracy said. "You've been about as upbeat as a Nicholas Sparks movie marathon lately. It's what made me depressed about today."

"Do not blame me for this," Katie said. "I am fine with today." *Mostly. Not really. Stupid Valentine's Day.*

"Dude," she heard Will saying behind her. "Savannah is blowing up my phone. Can we go?"

Logan shot him another look that shut Will up. Logan, apparently, was busy shamelessly listening in to her conversation.

"So why don't you just make up an emergency and leave?" Katie asked.

"Well, I didn't drive myself," Tracy said.

"First rule of a blind date, Trace," Katie said, a smile curving her lips. "Never allow yourself to be stranded."

"I can hear that smile in your voice. Do not laugh at my distress. Just come save me. Show up and say there was some kind of emergency, blah blah blah. He can't blame me if you yank me away, now can he?"

"Well, he probably can blame you," she said. "Tracy, can't you just ride out the date? I have . . . plans."

"Eating chocolate and watching movies alone is not plans," Tracy said. "Seriously, this guy is ridiculous. He's a mouth breather and he chews so freaking loud that I feel bad for the popcorn he's torturing. He has pit stains, Katie. *Pit stains.* Stop laughing, it's not funny. It's like death, and I'm stuck here. Come get me. I'm already thirty minutes into the movie, but he's taking me to dinner at Lucky's. Rescue me there?"

Katie let out a loud sigh. "I'm on my way. Just try to get through the appetizer and I'll be there before dessert."

"Don't make me wait till dessert," Tracy said. "He keeps making hints about seeing his 'authentic' *Battlestar Galactica* memorabilia or some geekery like that at his place afterward."

A snort of laughter escaped her, and Katie clapped a hand over her mouth.

"Shut up and drive, woman," Tracy said, and disconnected.

LOGAN WATCHED KATIE as she talked. She was just as beautiful now as she had been when they were seventeen. If she had makeup on, he couldn't tell, but her skin was smooth with a natural blush and her full pink lips begged to be kissed. Beneath her long wine-colored coat she wore faded blue jeans tucked into knee-high boots. A sash was cinched tight around her slender waist, and the top few buttons of her coat were left undone, showing the hint of some pretty spectacular cleavage. It was just enough that he wanted to take the time to undo every button until all that soft, warm skin was exposed. He watched her graceful fingers as she brushed a lock of long ash blond hair off her face. Her big green eyes lit up as she talked to Tracy. And when she smiled, she was the most beautiful thing he'd ever seen. Years, he thought, it's been years since I've seen her and I still can't stop staring at her like a teenager with a crush.

She gestured as she talked, even though she was on the phone and Tracy couldn't see her. Every second was filled with movement, and she was so alive, so animated, that it made him want to be near her. He wanted her to look at him like that and make him feel alive again. His life wasn't exactly exciting. He had dates, and he had fun, but there was no spark to anything. Hell, it was Valentine's Day. He could have a meaningless date and a night of easy-to-get sex like most of the other single men he knew. Instead he was helping his best friend pick out a Valentine's Day card. Why? He just couldn't seem to feel a connection. There was no thrill. But when he looked at Katie, he felt it. A spark that rocketed through his gut and drew him to her.

Katie hung up her phone and dropped it back in her purse. "I have to go rescue your sister from a mouth breather," she said to Logan. "It was nice seeing you, though."

Don't just let her walk away, you idiot.

This was his chance. He didn't think he could let her leave and then not see her again for another ten years. "I'm worried about Tracy," he blurted out, knowing it sounded lame. Even Will let out a barely audible groan behind him. He wasn't worried about his sister. It was just a lousy date. His sister was a little overdramatic, so he figured she was probably exaggerating anyway.

Judging by the way Katie was looking at him, she thought he was crazy, but he was going to grab onto any excuse he could get if it meant having a chance to spend time with her. He could always just ask her out, but there was no way she would say yes. It was clear in her body language. In the cute little way her brows drew together and her forehead wrinkled when she looked at him. To her, he was probably the same hopeless geek from high school.

"Oh, don't be," she said. "It's nothing, she just needs a ride."

"I'll go with you," he said. "Just to be sure."

KATIE LOOKED AT Logan, wide-eyed. "You really don't need to," she said, an edge of panic in her voice. She did not want to have him, and worse, his friend tagging along. Her man-hating Valentine's Day would be ruined if she was forced to spend it with two men. One of whom she was finding annoyingly attractive. Yep, that was just what her day needed. Acting like a love-struck Barbie doll who had just seen her first GI Joe and making a fool of herself.

"Sure I do," he said, flashing a winning smile at her. "I just want to protect my sister."

Bullshit, she thought, but wasn't sure why. There was no reason for him to lie to her, and yet her "full-of-crap meter" was going off. To say she was curious was an understatement. But was she really curious enough to let him come along?

"We *really* don't need to," Will said, coming closer to stand beside them. A soft whoosh of breath escaped when Logan's elbow connected with Will's stomach. Katie eyed them with one brow cocked. This is just strange, she thought.

"I don't have time for this," she said, finished with trying to guess what Logan was up to. Without waiting for them, she turned and started to walk away. The sooner she picked up Tracy, the sooner she could go home and wallow.

"Then you don't have time to talk me out of not going," Logan said, setting down Katie's basket and following her. "Come on, Will."

"Are you shitting me?" Will said, but followed Logan's lead.

"You're serious?" she asked as Logan caught up to her with no effort at all.

"You wanna drive or do you want me to?" he asked.

"Why?" she said, and stopped, coming to a sudden halt as he almost bumped into her. "You know what, I don't need to know why. To be honest, I don't really want company right now. I've had a rough week and I want to be left alone. I don't want to be rude but I'm not in the mood to be around people." Being around a man she found attractive made her uncomfortable this soon after her breakup. And being around Will, whose phone kept buzzing every two seconds, made her want to cringe.

"I want to help," Logan said, and she wasn't sure if his sincerity was real or not. "Let me come with you?"

If he had demanded, she would have told him flat

out no, but he said it like a question. She didn't have the energy to argue with him so she gave in and they waited in line with Will while he bought his last minute gifts. She did inform both of them that if they bothered her, she had no problem dumping them on the side of the road and making them walk. It was an empty threat, and they all knew it, but she was hoping they wouldn't bother her that much.

Chapter Two

"YOUR CAR SMELLS," Will said from the backseat of her two-year-old Impala.

"It does not," she snapped. The heavy acrid smell of a lit cigarette filled the air, and she looked back and saw the spark from the tip glowing in the darkness. "Do not smoke in my car."

"Jesus," he muttered as he rolled down the window, letting frozen February air rush over them before he flicked the cigarette out. "Damn, Logan, Savannah is really freaking out."

"Who's Savannah?" Katie asked, slowing down at a stoplight.

"Will's girlfriend," Logan said, not sounding thrilled about it. "You need to get away from that woman," he said to Will. "Dump her."

"On Valentine's Day? Do you want her to chop off my

balls?" Will said as his phone vibrated and lit up again. "Women kill men for that shit."

Logan glanced over as Katie shifted uncomfortably in her seat, her gloved hands tightening on the steering wheel and her lips pursing.

"Dude, I have to go talk to her."

"Right now?" Logan said.

"Yeah, right now," Will said. "She's going nuts. If I'm any later I'll be a dead man, for real. Turn left up here."

Katie leaned away as he reached his hand over the console to point at the next intersection. "You have got to be joking," she said, narrowing her eyes and glaring at Will's outstretched arm. "I am not your chauffeur."

"You'll just be dropping me off. It'll only take a few minutes, I swear," Will said.

She considered telling him to shove it but then thought better of it. She wanted to be rid of him. He was so obnoxious that she was sure her eye would start twitching if she spent much more time with him. What were a few extra minutes if it meant not having to deal with Will? Tracy was still at the movie, so she had some time to spare.

"Lead the way," she said, and followed Will's directions, heading farther into the middle of who-the-hell-lives-out-here-anyway. The only sign of life was a tiny family-owned gas station with flaking paint and flickering lights.

Will had her turn down a darkened side street. There were no streetlights and even the moon and stars were covered by night clouds and scraggly tree branches. Frost-covered gravel from the dirt road crunched and crackled under her tires. The headlights cut through the heavy darkness, illuminating brown sludgy snow and rough tree trunks. She slowed down when she saw bright little eyes glowing from the brush on the shoulder.

"It's right at the end of the street," Will assured her. She sure hoped so because this road was giving her the creeps.

"Are you sure?" Logan asked. "I don't see any driveways."

"It's right there." Will pointed, and Katie turned onto a narrow driveway. It was lined with pine trees that were missing half of their branches. The sight reminded her of a mangy old squirrel after a fight. At the end of the drive there was a run-down ranch-style house. It was difficult to see in the darkness but she could make out a beat-up front porch that was missing the railing and shutters which had fallen off and were hanging askew.

"This is it," Will said, shoving his phone into the pocket of his jeans. "See you later, Logan."

Logan opened his mouth to speak but was cut off by the sound of something slamming on the hood of the car. Katie jumped and let out a small scream of surprise, gripping Logan's arm.

"Will! What the hell is going on, you bastard?" a woman shrieked, both of her hands splayed on the hood.

Where had she even come from? Katie wondered.

"You asshole," the woman said. Another loud bang filled the air as she beat down on the car to emphasize her words. She made eye contact with each of them through the windshield, her scowl intensifying when it landed on

Will in the backseat. The glass fogged in front of her as she huffed out angry breaths. Glancing over, Katie caught Logan's stricken gaze. Apparently he didn't know what to make of this, either.

"And that would be Savannah," Will said before climbing out of the car, the box of chocolates in his hand.

"What a lovely woman," Katie said as she watched Will approach Savannah, who removed herself from the hood and turned to face him.

The two of them stood in the beam of the headlights with a light dusting of snow falling around them. A heap of shining platinum hair fell over Savannah's shoulders and heavy but meticulously applied makeup covered her face. She wore tight gray sweatpants that had LOVE spelled out with tiny red hearts on her booty and were tucked into a pair of tan Ugg boots. Even though it had to be less than ten degrees, she only wore a thick zip-up hoodie and wasn't so much as shivering. Shaking with rage maybe. But with cold? No.

Realizing she still had her hand on Logan's arm, Katie gently tugged it out from under his grip, feeling awkward and unable to meet his eyes. Savannah was screeching about what a horrible boyfriend Will was, which did not surprise Katie at all. She would probably want to scream, too, if she were dating Will. Still, it was not very becoming. Especially once Savannah started dropping F bombs every other word. Katie couldn't hear Will's response, but it looked like he was trying to calm her down by giving her the chocolate. Putting her hands on Will's chest, Savannah shoved him, throwing all her weight behind it, and let out a loud cry. Savannah was not a large woman, so Katie was surprised when Will slipped and fell backward onto his ass.

"Stay here," Logan said, got out and moved to the front of the car. His back was blocking Katie's view of Savannah, making it impossible to see what was happening. But she did see Logan jerk to a stop and hold up a hand in a placating gesture.

What was going on? she wondered, craning her head to see past him. A moment later she figured it out, because Savannah strode past Logan and over to her window.

"Get your dumb ass out of the car, *right now*!" Savannah yelled, and Katie realized the reason for Logan's abrupt stop as she looked down the barrel of a gun.

TRACY TRIED TO focus on the movie, but Dustin, better known as the date from hell, kept leaning in, his doughy shoulder bumping against hers. His hand crept closer. Again. Every time his fingers brushed the back of her hand, she jerked it away and grabbed a mouthful of popcorn. *Pace yourself, running out is not an option.* Without the popcorn as a buffer, he would expect to hold hands for sure. Bile rose in her throat at the thought. If he so much as attempted the yawn-and-put-his-arm-around-her trick, twenty ounces of ice cold Coke might "accidentally" fall straight onto his lap. She felt a tickle on the back of her hand again.

There was no way she could make it through this movie. The urge to escape was becoming nearly uncontrollable. Waiting until Dustin was about to make another pass, Tracy reached for the soda and purposefully collided with him, tipping the cup and pretending to spill it on her own pants.

"Oh no," she whispered. "I'm just gonna go to the restroom and clean myself up."

Not a second passed after the hallway door swung shut that her cell phone was whipped out and the call was going through. Katie would have to haul ass to the theater, because there would be none of this waiting until the end of the movie crap.

Tracy's frustration mounted as the phone kept ringing. Where was Katie while she was going through this hell?

Chapter Three

KATIE HAD A gun in her face. Blood pounded in her ears and her breathing was coming in short puffs as she got out of the car. With the gun, Savannah gestured for her to stand over by Logan and Will, and then opened her mouth to speak. Whatever she'd been about to say, however, was suddenly overridden by the sound of Katie's cell phone.

"Give me that," Savannah said, reaching her free hand out and wrenching Katie's purse away. With a pointed look, Savannah repeated the gesture for her to move and Katie made her way to stand by Logan. "You guys, too. Phones, now." She looked at the men, who then tossed her their phones. Savannah dug around in Katie's purse and pulled out her wallet. "Let's see what we have here," she flipped it open, plucked out the small stack of bills and tucked them into the pocket of her hoodie.

That bitch.

"Katie Quinn, huh?" Savannah said, looking at the driver's license in her wallet. "Well isn't that just the most precious little name. Katie Quinn." She spat the words out. "Aren't you the cutest fucking slut I ever did see?"

"Excuse me?" Katie said, drawing back from the pure venom coming from the other woman. Savannah's eyes were like lasers burning into her. Crazy radiated off of her in almost palatable waves.

"Savannah," Will said. "What are you doing? You need to calm down and put the damn gun away."

"Shut up, Will," Savannah said, turning back to Katie. "What the hell do you think you're doing with my boyfriend?" she asked, taking another step closer.

Logan angled himself in front of Katie, putting an arm across her body, with one hand resting on her hip.

"Don't fucking move!" Savannah said, waving the gun at him.

"I'm not moving, Savannah," Logan lied, his voice steadier than Katie would have thought possible.

She was shaking from head to toe and she clutched a handful of the back of Logan's coat. The feel of his body heat clinging to the fabric was a small comfort, and she wanted to pull him in closer, close her eyes and pretend this wasn't happening. That, of course, wasn't an option. She settled for focusing her mind on the hand that rested protectively on her hip. On the heat that burned through her jeans to her skin underneath. It anchored her. It kept her from running away from the crazy lady who would shoot the first person who moved.

"Savannah, babe, you have it all wrong," Will said with

forced patience, as if he were talking to a stubborn child. If Savannah heard him, she made no indication of it.

"Shut up and tell me what you think you're doing with my boyfriend!" she shouted at Katie.

"Will?" Katie said around Logan's shoulder. "I'm not doing anything with Will. To be honest, I don't even like him." She glanced over at Will. "No offense."

He just shrugged, keeping his eyes on the barrel of Savannah's gun. Evidently he had more important things to worry about than his ego.

"I just met him," Katie said, and Savannah shot her a look that asked if she were born yesterday. "I was just dropping him off. Really. If I were sleeping with him, don't you think I would have at least let him ride shotgun?"

"Are you kidding me?" Savannah asked. "Shotgun?"

"Trust me, I know how you feel," Katie went on. "My boyfriend dumped me two days ago."

"Why? Did he catch you fucking my boyfriend?" Savannah said, gesturing to Will with her gun.

"Katie," Will said. "Stop helping."

"Men," Savannah said with distain, the gun shaking in her hands. "Of course he's fooling around on me. Of-*freaking*-course. Men are incapable of keeping their pants zipped for two seconds, aren't they?"

Katie almost nodded in sympathy, then looked with horror at Savannah. Was this where she was headed, herself? This blinding hatred for men? Was she one bad relationship away from waving a gun in people's faces and shouting about lying, cheating men? Her stomach knotted and it wasn't because of the danger. That, of course, didn't help, but she felt a tightening in her chest and an anxious churning in her belly that was born of self-realization. She did not like it.

"I can't trust anybody, can I?" Savannah continued. "The sad thing is that I didn't even see this coming. Well, Will, you're gonna wish you had never even looked at this slut here."

"I'm not cheating on you, Savannah," Will said.

"Goddamned men," she went on, like she hadn't heard him. "They take and they take and they take. It's *my* turn. They *owe* me! *You* owe me!" she yelled at Will. "I'm so done with men. I'm so over this *crap*. I'm taking all the money and I'm getting the hell out of here. To think I was going to take you with me!"

Money? Katie wondered. What money was she talking about? There probably wasn't enough in any of their wallets for her to "get the hell out of here." *It must be something else.*

"Why the hell did you have to bring these two into it?" Savannah said. "What am I going to do with them?" She began pacing back and forth. Confusion showed on Logan's face as he glanced over his shoulder and met Katie's eyes. He appeared just as puzzled as she was. Katie shrugged. She didn't know what the hell was going on. What she did know was that they had better come up with a way to get out of this soon because Savannah was all kinds of batshit crazy.

So far she was not impressed with Logan's social circle.

Although to be fair, it was shaping up to be a much

more interesting night than she had originally intended. I could use a little less interesting, she thought, never taking her eyes off the gun. Savannah was barely paying attention to them now, lost in her own thoughts. Katie thought longingly about the evening she should have been having. If Tracy hadn't called her tonight, the helicopter would probably have just been arriving in *Jurassic Park*. She'd be safe and warm in her Snuggie instead of freezing her fingers and toes off in this tundra they called Michigan with the threat of death hanging over her head.

Pressure on her hip drew her attention from the gun to Logan. Every muscle in his body was tense, his jaw clenched, and he glared at Savannah with murder in his eyes. He looked like he was going to charge her at any second. Trying for silent communication, she tugged on the arm of his coat. When he tore his eyes off Savannah and met hers, she shook her head, hoping he saw the fear on her face. She didn't think she could handle it if he got shot.

With a curt nod, Logan removed his hand from her hip and laced his fingers with hers, giving a reassuring squeeze before slowly trying to inch them closer to the safety of Katie's car. At the sight of movement, Savannah's head snapped up. Evidently she was paying closer attention than they had thought. With lightning speed Savannah reacted, and before Katie even realized what was happening, she'd raised the gun and fired.

A bullet whizzed past them, hitting the ground a few feet from where they were heading. For such a small gun it was shockingly loud, and Katie was impressed with herself that she didn't pee her pants as Logan once again shoved her behind him. She had a death grip on his arms, with her forehead pressed against his back and her eyes squeezed shut as the bang reverberated in her ears.

"Don't move!" Savannah yelled. "I can't *think* when you're moving!"

Katie had to remind herself to breathe again. The sound of tires slowly crunching their way down the driveway brought her back from her paralyzing fear. Since she couldn't spend the rest of her life with her face buried in Logan's coat, she muddled up the courage to at least look at what was happening.

Headlights cut through the darkness, blinding her, as a black Ford Escape pulled to a stop next to her car.

"*Damn* it, they're early," Savannah hissed under her breath, then let out a groan of frustration as her eyes darted back and forth between the vehicle and her hostages. Having a poker face did not seem to be one of her strong suits. Even so, the gun never wavered, so Katie held out little hope that whoever was in the SUV was going to be of any help.

The driver killed the ignition and three men stepped out. Had they not been in this situation, Katie would have thought they looked normal. Like professional businessmen, late thirties, polished and well-groomed. She half expected one of them to have a briefcase and a short presentation about their company's quarterly earnings.

"What the hell is going on?" one of the three said. He was good-looking and square-jawed, but Katie could tell that he was going soft. Beneath his open coat she could see the paunch of his belly where a button-down shirt was tucked into his pants.

"What?" Savannah asked, stalling.

"This?" another one of the men said, pointing to Logan, Will, and Katie, then back at the gun. He was the youngest looking of the three, with short dark hair and a boyishly handsome face.

"This?" Savannah repeated. "Well, they . . ." She paused, thinking. "He," she said, stronger this time as she pointed straight at Will, "stole the money."

"What?" Will said. Even in the darkness Katie could see the whites where his eyes widened.

"He's my boyfriend, or was, anyway," she said to the men, who were tensing up, scowls forming on their faces.

"Boyfriend?" the young-looking one said, his stare shifting to Savannah, outrage clear in his voice.

"He found the money and took it this morning while I was sleeping," Savannah said, ignoring his protest. "I'm just trying to get it back. I'm getting him to tell me where he hid it. I was hoping that I'd have it before you got here."

If Katie wasn't mistaken, she thought she heard a dose of damsel in Savannah's voice. Oh, she was trying to play these men so bad. And if they believed her, Logan, Will, and herself were going to be shot dead in the process.

"What are you talking about?" Will asked.

"Shut up, you bastard," Savannah said. "You know what I'm talking about. These men are not going to be as nice as I've been. Just tell us where you put the money and they might not kill you."

"Shit, Savannah," the third man said, rage making his voice shake. "How could you let this happen?" The look of steely anger in his cold blue eyes sent a terrified shiver down Katie's spine that had nothing to do with the chilly air.

"Well, what are we supposed to do with them, Clint?" The man with the paunch said.

"Get the money back and get rid of them," Clint said.

Get rid of them? Katie sucked in a quick gasp of breath. Logan made eye contact with Will and gave a small jerk of his head. Katie followed the direction he indicated to the line of trees beyond the house. Oh dear God, they were going to make a break for it. She hoped these guys were sucky shots. Logan reached his hand back, and she locked her fingers with his.

"Get rid of them? I'm not a murderer," Paunch said. "I didn't even want to steal this money in the first place, and now we're killing people, too?"

"Jesus, Rich, grow a pair," Clint said, stepping closer to Rich and lowering his voice so Katie had to strain to hear. "I don't see any other options. Either they have the money and we need to get it back, or they'll go to the cops and we're screwed. What's your solution?"

"Now wait a minute, we don't even know what's going on," the youngest one said.

Suddenly all three men turned to look at Savannah, who started shrieking again. "You don't believe me? *He* has our money," she said, pointing at Will. "Ask *him* what's going on! Just shoot *one* of them. The others will probably tell us what we want." A sly half smile formed on her face. "Oooh, how 'bout we shoot the girl? See if she cries."

That must have been their cue to book it, because Logan tightened his grip on her hand, nodded to Will, and all three of them took off running. She heard shouts from the men behind them followed by the *pop pop pop* of guns. Thank God it was dark, because they needed all the help they could get.

"Get off your lazy, wide loads and get them," Savannah shouted. "They're getting away!" Risking a backward glance, Katie saw two of the men starting forward, but Savannah stayed put.

Puffs of breath rose in the cold air in front of them as she, Logan, and Will ran. The ground was icy and she was terrified that she would slip and fall and everything would be over. She'd be left for dead, and over what? Some money that she knew nothing about? This didn't make any sense. An hour ago she was bummed about not having a date, and now she was running through some backwoods in the country being shot at by businessmen?

Katie couldn't tell for sure, but she thought the bullets were getting closer. This was doing nothing for her internal panicking, and she fought to stay calm. The inky blackness of the night and the scattering of trees provided some cover, but odds were they wouldn't escape unscathed. She grabbed Logan's arm and pulled him with her behind the trunk of a huge tree just as a bullet zinged past, narrowly missing him.

"Where's Will?" Logan whispered, looking around. He was pressed against her side and she could feel his warm breath on her cheek. Her heart was beating so fast she thought it was going to take off like a rocket and shoot out the top of her head.

"He must've kept going. I think that's him up there," she panted, pointing where she thought she saw movement ahead. "I don't think he got hit." She gave a quick tug on Logan's sleeve. "We can't stay here, though."

Still glancing around, Logan nodded, and they started moving farther into the woods, the trees becoming denser and their pursuers' voices more muffled. Her eyes had adjusted pretty well to the darkness, but even so, she kept stumbling over tree roots or twiggy little dead shrubs. Logan was surprisingly agile, his steps sure. He was having no problems, which was good because he kept her from falling over, but aggravating at the same time because she hated not being able to keep up. Her balance sucked. This snow sucked. These stupid skinny trees sucked. Valentine's Day sucked.

They heard footsteps behind them and the gruff panting of an out-of-shape stockbroker type on their heels. It must have been the one with the paunch, she thought. Rich, the scary one had called him. It was hard to judge how close he was because she refused to look back. That was all she needed, to lose focus, trip, and face plant in the snow. Rich was right on them but he wasn't shooting. That's good, she thought, always one for that silver lining.

Without warning, Logan stopped, turned, and slammed his fist in the man's face. A surprised grunt of pain came from Rich as he fell to one knee. Rearing back, Logan punched him again, this time with enough force to knock him out cold. Rich fell onto the soft snow with a plop. Well, that was unexpected. Having not stopped when Logan did, she had skidded a few feet ahead and could barely see through the darkness. However, the man on the ground did not seem to be moving, which was enough to bring a tiny flare of hope into her chest.

"Come on," Logan whispered, grabbing her upper arm and guiding her forward. "There's another guy close by."

"Of course there is," she moaned. That flare was awfully short-lived. "Are there things that will eat us in these woods, too?" She was sure she had seen glowing green eyes. It was probably a rabid, bloodthirsty, feral dog. She was eighty percent sure that it was either Cujo or some other form of slobbering monster. A Yeti maybe? That would be her luck.

"Nothing's going to eat us," he said impatiently. "But I do know there are some guys who want to shoot us, so *shhhh*."

She wanted to snap back with some stinging retort, but he was right, and she was out of breath so maybe later. She concentrated on putting one numb brick of ice foot in front of the other. Her boots were adorable. Maroon suede, knee high with little silver buckles. Very fashionable. Practical? Not even a little bit. Traction? Zero. She was cursing the day she bought them. Who lived in Michigan and bought boots for looks? If she lived through this, she was treating her feet to thermal socks and Eskimo boots. With extra traction. Cleats, even. Or maybe those snowshoe things that looked like tennis rackets. Bet she wouldn't slide around like Bambi on this damn ice if she had herself a pair of those.

WE HAVE TO stop, Logan thought as he righted Katie again. She kept slipping, every time letting out a small frustrated sound that he would have thought was adorable if they hadn't been running for their lives. "Are you all right?" he asked, hauling her upright again.

"I can't feel my feet," she said, looking down at the offending feet like a sea captain whose crew was committing mutiny.

Since the moment Savannah had pulled out that gun, all Logan could think about was getting Katie someplace safe. With grim determination, he silently vowed that he was going to get her out of this. But having resolve was all well and good, except he had no idea what he was going to do. It's not like he'd ever dealt with a situation like this before. He was a college math professor, for Christ's sake. This kind of stuff didn't happen to him. To think he had been feeling bored with his life lately. Complaining about a lack of excitement. Well, this was sure exciting. He should have kept his big mouth shut. Putting that out into the universe had just screwed him over.

And now Katie was drawn into the middle of this mess. To be honest with himself, he had no idea how to get them out of this. He just knew he had to.

They were winding their way through the trees in what he hoped was the opposite direction of the men with guns. But Logan was pretty sure that one of them was still close, and that was making him nervous. The silhouette of a small building appeared in the distance, so he changed course and began moving toward it. When they got closer, he realized that it was a toolshed.

"I'm going to burn these shoes," Katie muttered under her breath after she slipped and fell to one knee.

"I'll give you the match," Logan said, grabbing her around her waist and hoisting her up. This caused her to fall against him, and even in these circumstances he could appreciate the feel of her curves pressed to his side. "Let's go in there," he said, motioning to the shed, and they hurried toward it.

Logan tried the door but it wouldn't budge.

"Is it locked?" she asked, looking around.

"I don't think so," he grunted, and slammed his shoulder into it. It groaned beneath the force but stubbornly refused to open.

"Hurry up, I think I see something moving," she whispered, squinting. "I definitely hear voices."

Taking a deep breath, Logan rammed his shoulder into it again. This time the wood splintered with a cracking sound that was amplified in the silence. The door scraped open and got stuck on something behind it. Katie helped him push, and after what seemed like an eternity they had it open wide enough for them to squeeze inside. Then Logan cracked the door about an inch so he could peer out.

Shit, he thought, squinting through the thick flurries of snow, seeing two men appear in a clearing about thirty feet away. Unfortunately, Rich hadn't stayed unconscious, and now Clint was with him as well. A scattering of trees lay between the shed and the men. Hopefully, it provided enough cover to keep them from being noticed.

The sound was muffled, so he couldn't make out their words but he could tell they were talking to each other in heated tones. Clint pointed in the opposite direction of their hiding spot, giving Logan hope. Maybe they wouldn't see the shed. Rich shook his head and spoke. Logan vaguely heard the word "No," and a little of his hope faded away. Whatever Rich said must have been something that his friend didn't like, because Clint grabbed him by the lapels, getting in his face before shoving him aside. Glaring at each other and bristling with enough hostility that Logan could see it even from his vantage point, they left, heading off the way Clint had indicated.

Logan breathed a deep sigh of relief. "They're going the other way," he said, glancing over his shoulder at Katie. She was sitting on a box with her arms folded over her stomach. "Are you okay?" he asked, crossing the few feet to her side. "You're shaking."

"Oh, I'm fine," she said with a faint smile. "At this point I'm honestly not sure if it's from being shot at or just because I'm freezing." She was shivering so hard, he could see it even in the limited light. Grabbing both of her hands in his and drawing her to her feet, he pulled her close. The feel of her small frame shaking in his arms made a wave of fierce protectiveness rush over him, and without thinking, he squeezed her tighter.

"I'm going to get us out of this," he said into her hair, which was pressed smooth as silk against his cheek. He inhaled her scent, and sweet vanilla rushed his senses, making him light-headed. "Do you trust me?"

"I want to," she said, her voice small. She slid her arms around his waist, and his heart beat heavier at the thought of her returning the gesture. It could just be because she was cold, he told himself. He shouldn't read anything into it. But that didn't keep the pure pleasure of her touch from sinking into his chest. There was nothing he wanted more in the universe at that moment than to keep her safe. And not just right now. Not just from the men who wanted them dead. From everything. He didn't want her to feel any pain ever again. He had never felt this way about anyone else, and the intensity of it frightened him. Maybe it was just the adrenaline talking. He didn't know her. He hadn't seen her in years, and yet he wanted to protect her forever? His brain felt foggy. He wasn't thinking clearly.

"You have no idea how much I want to," she said and he had to strain to remember what she wanted to do. *Mind out of the gutter, Cross.* Trust. Right. Her trusting him.

"But you don't?" he asked, wounded that he was having these huge feelings and she wasn't. He sincerely wanted to keep her safe and she didn't trust that he could. He realized that she didn't know him any better than he knew her and had no real reason to trust him. It was irrational, but he wanted her to anyway.

"I have . . ." She paused, having a hard time spitting out the words. "I have a difficult time trusting people. Men in particular."

Understanding that this was a sensitive subject for her, he wanted to tread lightly. "I will get you out of here. Safe and sound." He felt her nod, her forehead bumping softly against his shoulder.

"When Savannah was raving about men earlier, about how she can't trust them and how she knew Will would hurt her, I wanted to agree with her," she said, her hands clutching harder onto the back of his coat. "I wanted to give her a little 'Amen, sister.' Then I stopped and thought about it. I—I'm kind of terrified that that's where I'm heading. Angry and bitter. Unable to trust or open up." She drew back to look up at him. Her cheeks were rosy from cold, and even in the dark he could see a spark in her eyes. She was tired and scared, yet still had a fire inside of her. It drew him in. It made him want to know everything about her. "I don't want to end up like that. So, yeah, I want to trust you."

Unable to stop himself, he lowered his lips to hers. He couldn't help it. His brain shorted out and he was drawn into her. Katie, his fantasy since he was fifteen, the woman he'd secretly been comparing all other women to for years, was looking up at him with her big bright eyes telling him she wanted to trust him. It was either kiss her or keel over dead. At least that was how it felt. There wasn't time for this. He knew he needed to come up with a plan to get them out of there but he couldn't stop himself. Her lips were soft and her warm breath mingled with his, and he deepened the kiss, letting his tongue sweep into her mouth, tasting her sweetness with startling urgency. He couldn't get enough. Every nerve in his body came alive.

With a soft moaning sound she rose onto her toes to get closer. His blood surged and pounded in his head, making him dizzy with lust. It was like a drug, seeping into his system and driving him higher. He needed to touch her, to feel the smoothness of her skin. Without breaking the kiss, he reached both hands behind her back and ripped off his leather gloves, feeling the ice cold bite of air on his fingers. Shaking with the intensity of his passion, he brushed his knuckles along her cheek, making her shiver, before gliding them down to rest on her neck. He could feel the slamming of her pulse beneath his fingers, glad that he was not the only one who felt this overwhelming need.

His hand cupped the back of her head, tangling in her hair as he kissed her harder. With his other hand he undid the buttons of her coat and tugged on the tie at her waist. Pushing the rough fabric apart, he slid his hand along her side, the heat from her body seeming doubled to his cold fingers. He brought his hand up to cup her breast, feeling the weight of it, so full and heavy and round. Even with the layers of her clothes between them, it gave him a rush of pleasure feeling how soft she was. She gasped as he gave it a gentle squeeze, wishing he could do more, wishing that he could rip the clothes right off her body and bare her beauty to him. He wanted to take her nipple in his mouth. To slide his hand between her thighs, feel the wet heat of her core, and make her writhe underneath him moaning with pleasure. To make her come screaming his name.

He broke away, brushing her hair back with a gentle tug that elicited a soft groan from deep in her throat, and bent his head to trail hot kisses down her neck. The sharp intake of breath and the shiver that ran through her body when he found a particularly sensitive spot spurred him on.

"Logan," she moaned, her hands running up his chest and grasping his shoulders. He was thrilled to hear his name coming from her mouth.

"You're driving me crazy," he breathed, his heart pounding faster.

Chapter Four

KATIE FELT ALL the tension drain out of her as his lips traveled over the delicate skin of her throat. Needing to feel those lips on hers, she grabbed a handful of his hair and dragged him back up to her mouth, melting helplessly into his kiss. Logan was so solid and warm that she wanted to stay pressed against him forever. His hands were a miracle, moving over her body, caressing her. Millions of tiny sparks were flickering and jumping in her stomach, and her head felt light. Heat flared all over her body, starting in her chest, radiating down her spine and gathering between her legs.

Surprising herself with her own abandon, she gave him everything she had, pressing her lips harder against his, deepening the kiss. It was like she was awake and alive for the first time in a long time. Like she had been pulling away from everything, going through the motions, until now. In this moment she was connected to someone, excited about something. She hadn't realized how much she'd missed this feeling. The feeling of everything being right, of someone else being so close.

It wasn't like she hadn't been kissed recently. She'd even gotten laid not too long ago. But it had never felt like this. There hadn't been this sense of urgency, this need, this fire, this passion. How had she gotten along without it for so long?

She parted her legs, allowing his thigh to settle between them, pressing intimately against her. She couldn't get close enough to him. More, she wanted so much more.

With a sudden jerk, Logan lurched forward, pushing her back, then whirled around, ready to fight.

"Ouch," Katie muttered. *What the hell?* Something had slammed into Logan's back. Peering over his shoulder, she strained to see. The door was partially open, letting in faint bluish light and an icy breeze.

"Jesus," came Will's voice from inside the doorway. "I'm running for my life and you two are in here making out?" He shoved the door open farther, smacking Logan in the shoulder with it again for emphasis.

"Hey," Logan said, rubbing his arm and glaring at Will.

"Are you two done?" Will said. "Should I leave you alone for a while? Did you forget about our friends with the guns? I covered for you, man. They were headed right to you in this stupid shed and I got them to chase me. I did not risk my life so you could get laid."

"Come on—"

"No, Logan, I got shot for you," Will said, and Katie noticed Will clutching his arm.

"Holy shit," Logan said, starting forward to see for himself. "Are you all right? *Shit.*"

"I'm fine, it just grazed me," Will said, pushing Logan away, while Logan regarded him with a wary look that said he didn't believe it. Will's face was tense, but Katie could feel how annoyed he was. "I cannot believe that I'm out there getting shot and you're in here gettin' the girl."

"How about we fight later," Katie cut in as she began to button her coat back up, then tied the sash with a vicious tug. "Right now we should probably get out of here before the three stooges find us."

"There's only two of them chasing us," Will said, "and last I saw they were still heading the wrong way." He stepped inside the shed. There wasn't much room, and Katie ended up squashed against Logan's side. Now that the kiss was over and she had some of her brain power back, she was feeling a little uncomfortable about it. She wished she had some space so she could clear her head. She couldn't think with Logan this close. But even though her mind might have been feeling awkward, her body still thrilled at the contact. Traitorous body.

"Where's the third guy?" Logan asked, and Katie brought herself back to the situation.

"I think he stayed with Savannah," Will said.

"Speaking of which, why the hell is your girlfriend shooting at us?" Katie asked, shifting to get at least on inch of room between herself and Logan.

"Hell if I know," Will said, anger seeping into his voice.

"Are you trying to tell me that you know nothing

about this? You're dating her, you probably see her all the time, and you don't know what's happening," Katie said, crossing her arms over her chest. "Why would she say you had their money? This doesn't make any sense."

"Calm down," Logan said, putting his hands up and looking from Will's angry face to Katie's confused one. "Getting pissed off at each other isn't going to help."

After a long moment Katie let her hands fall to her sides. "You're right, getting upset isn't going to make anything better. I'm sorry." She said the last bit to Will, who gave a terse nod in response.

"Will," Logan said, looking at his friend. "Do you even have a guess about the money she was talking about or who the guys chasing us are? She's never mentioned anything to you?"

"Well, she never hinted that she was gonna try to shoot me, no."

"Be serious, Will," Logan said.

A hiss of frustration escaped Will's mouth and he ran a hand through his hair. "I honestly don't know. She works at a bank." He shrugged his uninjured shoulder. "It's the only place I can think where she'd get enough money to kill over."

"Okay, that makes sense. And those men helped her steal it, then?" Katie asked, piecing together what she remembered of Savannah and the men's conversations. "She looked pretty surprised to see them. Why? A double cross?"

Logan nodded. "She was gonna take the money and

cut them out. But they showed up early so she used us as a distraction."

"Yeah, that was fun," Katie said with a shake of her head. "So what now?"

"I wouldn't hate having Katie's car back," Will said.

"Do you think we can get it without your girlfriend shooting us?" Katie asked, because she wanted her car back, too. She loved her car. And more important, she loved the thought of driving away to safety in her car.

"I think we have to try," Will said.

"No," Logan said. "That's the first place they'll look if they don't find us in the woods. And Savannah might still be there. What about that gas station we passed on the way here? I think it was only a mile or two away. We could walk to that."

The thought of walking in the snow held no appeal for Katie. Of course, the thought of getting shot going to her car held less appeal than that. "That could work," she said.

"I still think we should go for the car," Will said.

"It's too risky," Logan said.

"I'm risking it," Will said, unmoving. "Please tell me you still have the keys?"

"Savannah took my purse," Katie said.

"You took the time to put them in your purse?" Will asked. "She had a gun in your face."

Honestly, she couldn't remember what she had done with her keys. She had been so focused on the gun that she could have left them in the ignition and not remembered. Stuffing her hands in her pockets, she dug around. "Huh, what do you know," she said, feeling the uneven metal of her key ring. "I did put them in my pocket."

"Okay, I'll go try and get the car," he said. "You two can go to that gas station for help." He held out his hand. "Give 'em." Katie held her keys out to Will, but Logan snatched them out of her hand instead.

"No," he said. "It's too dangerous."

"I'll be careful," Will said, his tone curt. "If there's no way to get to the car without being seen, then I'll meet you at the gas station."

"I don't like this," Logan said, but handed the keys to Will.

"Tough," Will said, then poked his head out the doorway. Evidently the coast was clear because without another word he took off running.

TRACY SAT IN the restaurant and listened to Dustin talk about golf. Well, pretended to listen anyway. He didn't notice that she wasn't bringing anything to the conversation besides the occasional sound of agreement. Trying to keep her mind off him, she attempted to hear the lyrics to whatever love song they had playing. She was pretty sure it was "Love Me Tender" but couldn't quite hear. Her eyes focused in on his face. Tiny bubbles of spit were forming on the corners of his mouth and she tried not to cringe. While she was staring in horror, he caught her looking at his lips and smiled. *Great, now he thinks I want to kiss him.* Flecks of spit sprinkled the table as he said something about the importance of the right club. Like she gave a single crap about golf.

Their soup arrived and Tracy dug in with pleasure, grateful to have something to divert her attention away from Dustin. Glancing over at him, she wasn't sure but he might have been adjusting himself when he thought she wasn't looking.

"Excuse me a minute," she said, pasting a fake smile on her face. "I just have to fix my makeup."

And for the third time that night she made her way to the ladies' room. At this rate Dustin was going to think she had an overactive bladder or something. He was the type that would mention that, too. She sat through the entire movie with that creep and would be damned if she was going to sit through two more courses with him. She was going to kill Katie if she didn't show up soon.

FRESH, LIGHT SNOW was piling high on the road as Katie and Logan walked through the slush on the shoulder. Snow was a beautiful thing when it was freshly fallen. Like something out of a Christmas card, all white and fluffy, sparkling like thousands of glass shards in the light. But by February the snow had been driven on, shoveled, plowed, and walked through so much that it was nothing but brown slush. Just because it had a fresh cover of pure white over the top did not mean it wasn't nasty underneath. It was dirty, wet, cold slush that was soaking through her shoes and making her socks soggy. It was probably a good thing, then, that she couldn't feel her feet.

Hoping he wouldn't notice, she stole a glance at Logan. The memory of his hands on her caused an uncomfortable wave of heat to creep up her neck and into her cheeks. She had no idea what to make of that kiss. Or of him. He was difficult to read. Because she thought he felt something for her, but with her track record of bad boyfriends she didn't really trust her judgment. It was rare when she was actually right about how strong a man's feelings were. It always ended up with her thinking he had real feelings, and getting way too invested, only to find out that he was just having fun. There was no way she was going down that road again. She envied people who could just open themselves up over and over again. She wasn't quite there yet. And she was so sick and tired of being hurt all the time.

Why was she so stuck on this? It didn't matter anyway, because she didn't even care about him. Just because she couldn't look at him without fantasizing about his hands didn't mean anything. She didn't have feelings for him. That would be crazy. Silly, even. Just because she wanted to be near him. Just because he gave her the best kiss she had ever had. She felt nothing for him but lust. Sex appeal. That was all.

"So when we go our separate ways," she said, "is there a girlfriend you're going home to?" A flicker of emotion crossed his face, but she had no idea what it meant. She wanted to kick herself. Why was she asking? She didn't care. Really.

He looked at her like she had slapped him. "If I had a girlfriend, there's no way that I would have kissed you tonight," he said. "I'm glad you have such a high opinion of me." She blushed and started to speak but he overrode her. "Not all men are complete douche bags, Katie."

"I know that," she said, crossing her arms over her chest.

"I'm not so sure that you do," he said, sounding irritated. Which, in turn, made her feel irritated. What right did he have getting annoyed with her? So she asked if he had a girlfriend. So she didn't want to just assume that a kiss meant something.

"Well then, maybe I'm on to something with that," she snapped, using the same tone that he had adapted. She lengthened her strides to walk ahead of him, holding her arms stiff at her sides, not wanting to talk to him anymore. Apparently, he wasn't thinking along the same lines because he quickened his pace to match hers.

"Just to be clear, are you saying that after tonight you don't want anything to do with me?" he asked.

"I'm saying I don't want to talk to you right now." She tried to walk even faster.

"Are you literally running away from me?" he asked, his irritation sounding like it had morphed into amusement. Great, now he was *laughing* at her. He caught up to her easily. Since she was running short of breath, she decided to just slow down.

"You are making it difficult to," she said, wondering why she wanted to smack him and at the same time grab the front of his coat and pull him down into a kiss. She had never had this reaction to a man before.

"Why are you so upset?" he asked, a smile quirking his lips. He was looking at her with an odd expression on his face, like he was figuring something out. That worried her. She didn't want him figuring anything about her out. If he did, he might jump to conclusions, and she did not want that. Especially since she didn't even want to analyze what she was feeling yet.

"Because you're annoying the hell out of me," she said, making a point to look straight ahead. If she looked at him, she would have mixed emotions again, and she did not want to deal with that.

"You didn't have plans tonight, did you?" he said. The abrupt change in the conversation made her forget that she was ignoring him.

"What makes you say that?" she asked.

"My first clue was when you told Tracy on the phone that you didn't have a date. Then you also mentioned something about being dumped," he said. Was he purposefully trying to tick her off? "And back at the store you were buying a basket full of chocolate and a bottle of wine. If you'd had a date, he would have been bringing you those things. That, and you sounded like you were just trying to blow me off."

"And yet," she snapped, "it obviously didn't work."

"So who was the moron that dumped you?"

"Why do we have to talk?" she said, her strides becoming angry and kicking up flecks of slush as she went. "Is there a way that we can get there without speaking?"

"The conversation is keeping my mind off of frostbite," he said, looking down at the snow that was hitting his pant legs. "So what happened with the boyfriend?"

"You are not going to let this go, are you?" she asked.

"It's not like I have anything else to do."

She punched her hands into her coat pockets and shook her head so her hair covered her ears, in an attempt to block out some of the cold. "To be honest, he was nobody. I had only been dating him for a few months and we weren't all that close. I didn't dislike him but it's not like he made my heart beat faster or anything." Not like you, she thought. "Not that I really expect that fairy-tale bullshit. I was hoping to have a date for tonight, though," she said. "He dumped me a few days ago, so that was fun."

"That's harsh," Logan said, gently putting his hand on her elbow and steering her around a crater-sized pothole that she was too lost in thought to see.

"Thanks," she muttered, then pulled her elbow from his grip and stepped away from him. He gave her that look again. "Stop looking at me like that."

"Like what?" he asked as the corner of his mouth tipped up. Katie hated it when people laughed at her, and he was getting awfully close. She pursed her lips and let out an angry breath.

"Like you can see in my brain and read my mind. It's awkward." Mostly because she didn't want to dwell too much on her thoughts, let alone think that he knew all of them. He looked away with a shrug, the smirk still on his face.

"So do you have plans for tomorrow night?" he asked.

"You mean if we're not dead?" she said, and he let out a short chuckle and nodded. "I don't know."

"Do you think you'd want to make plans with me?"

"What? Oh, I don't know," she said, her voice going up as the words rushed out. "I don't—I mean I'm not—I'm not dating right now." All she needed was to get involved with her best friend's brother. No matter how great at kissing he was. How awkward would that be when they broke up? He would do what most men did and get bored and move on and then where would she be? She would probably go crazy like Savannah had. It had only been two days since her last relationship ended, and she was obviously going to be bitter for a while, so why start something when she knew it wasn't right for either of them? "Can we just drop it?" she said.

He looked back and opened his mouth like he was going to say something, then snapped it shut.

"What?" she asked, not so sure she wanted to know.

"You're scared."

"Well, doy," she said. "There are people trying to kill us. Of course I'm scared."

"That's not what I meant," he said. "You're scared of this." He motioned between the two of them. "Of us. Of starting something new."

"I am not," she said, her brows knitting together. He was on her last nerve. "One kiss doesn't mean anything to me. Stop acting like you know me, because you don't.

I am not afraid. I don't know you. The kiss was great, mind-blowing even, but that's all. I just got dumped. I would not be good for anybody right now. What's the point of starting something when you know it's not going to work?"

"Those are some nice excuses," he said, and sped up to walk ahead of her.

Hey, why does he get to do that and I don't?

Chapter Five

The fluorescent glow of the gas station lit up the night, making the blackness surrounding it stand out in stark contrast. There were no cars and the windows of the store were dark.

"Great," she said as they approached it. She stood next to pump number three and leaned against a metal pole. "They're closed." What were they going to do now? The enormity of the situation was sinking in, and she just wanted to slide to the ground and cry. She didn't because that would have been counterproductive, but she seriously considered it for a moment.

"Maybe there's a pay phone," he said.

"Hi, Logan, welcome to the twenty-first century," she said, knowing she sounded cranky and not really caring.

"Aren't we pessimistic," he said, then nodded to his right. "I see one right there." He walked over to it, leaving her standing under the creepy greenish lights at the pump.

"Then why did you say 'maybe'?" she muttered to herself, crossing her arms. She watched as he picked up the receiver and tried to get it to work. After a moment he turned around and shrugged. "Doesn't work," she said to herself. "Shocker." She was about to start toward him when she saw fast approaching headlights coming down the road. Since they hadn't seen a single car the entire time they were walking, she was almost certain it was not just a passerby.

"Logan," she called as loud as she felt she could get away with. When he looked over at her, she pointed to the road. She couldn't hear what he said, but judging by his body language and the set of his jaw, she assumed that it was not a good word.

Katie hoped beyond hope that it was Will with her car coming to save them, but when was she ever that lucky? Deciding not to chance it, she found the best hiding place she could under the circumstances. Which was not a good one. There wasn't much time, so she ducked behind the pump and hoped they kept on driving. She noticed Logan crouching down behind a garbage can on the side of the building and wished that she could go hide with him. His hiding spot was better than hers. Hers sucked.

She held her breath as the vehicle turned into the lot. "Hang on to your butts," she muttered, wishing she were at home hearing Samuel L. Jackson say it instead.

Now that the vehicle was closer, she could see that their luck was not getting any better. It was the Escape, and she had a feeling they weren't here to fill their tank. From her hiding spot she could see Logan through a small gap between the wall and the garbage can, but the angle was wrong for the men in the car to see him. She and Logan made eye contact, her own worried look mirrored on his face.

The SUV stopped and two of the men climbed out, slamming the doors shut behind them. It was Clint and Rich, and they did not look happy. Especially Rich, whose eye was already swelling where Logan had hit him. That probably hadn't endeared Logan and herself to them. The muscles in her legs were already starting to tremble as she crouched lower. She wondered where the third guy was. Maybe he was still in the car. Or he could have been back with Savannah. Or they could have killed him. Probably not, but it would be one less guy to worry about so she was secretly hoping for that one.

The men moved forward, and she realized that if they looked her way she'd be completely visible, so with careful steady movements she slid around to the other side of the pump, praying the entire time. She almost fell backward when there was a step down but righted herself, glad when she managed to bite back the girlish scream that threatened to pop out.

"I thought I saw something over there," Rich said. She risked poking her head out to see where he was pointing. Right by Logan's hiding spot. *Shit, maybe my spot is better after all,* she thought, her mind racing.

Logan was backed against a wall. Literally. If they found him, he wouldn't have any place to run. There was at least three feet of snow built up in the field behind him, a wall to his right, and the two men in front of him. He was not in a good position, and they were heading right toward him.

She had to do something.

She had to do something now. Any closer and they would see him for sure. The thought of something happening to Logan made her chest tighten and her breath leave her body. She could not just stay hidden when she knew he was about to be caught. Catching sight of his face through the gap, she saw him shake his head with a glint of warning in his eyes. She was starting to wonder if he really could read her mind because she knew she had no choice but to divert their attention.

She popped up from her hiding spot then, standing still until she was sure they saw her. The movement caught Clint's eye and he spun around to face her. "There's the girl," he said, smacking Rich on the arm and nodding toward her. Following his comrade's movement, Rich turned and pulled his gun from the waistband of his pants.

Aw, shit, she thought as she turned tail and ran, trying to stay behind the pumps for cover. A bullet dinged off of one, making her shriek and duck, but they didn't have a clear shot so she kept running. As her feet pounded on the pavement and nearly slipped out from under her—*stupid boots*—she heard them approaching and knew that hers was not the best thought out plan. The cold air was already making her lungs burn, and her eyes stung, tearing up, as the wind blew in her face. Deep male voices filled the silence, shouting over one another with an indiscernible jumble of words. This was followed by the sounds of fists hitting flesh and grunts of pain.

Curiosity overcame her and she made the mistake of looking back. A fresh surge of fear hit when she saw that Clint was almost on her. Farther back she noticed that Logan had tackled Rich. Now they were on the ground struggling, red-faced and straining, for possession of the gun.

Bad idea. This was a bad, bad, bad idea, she thought, picking up her pace and running faster. Maybe Logan could take out that guy and she could lose this freak. Clint was pretty big, so she didn't think she could take him in a fight. Her best bet was outrunning him. And her best bet did not seem to be working. As she hit the street, she felt an arm wrap around her waist and Clint haul her back up against him. A surprised scream wrenched itself from her lungs and she struggled like crazy, kicking her feet and thrusting her elbows back. She connected an elbow in his ribs and he let out an *ooomph* of pain.

"Knock it off," Clint said, and tightened his grip as he brought his gun up to her head.

She stilled, holding her breath and hoping with everything she had that he was not about to pull the trigger.

He didn't. "Where's the money?" he asked, his voice a low growl.

"I don't know anything about any money," she said, trying to keep calm.

"Bullshit," he said in her ear, spitting a little when he said it. She flinched as it hit her cheek, and leaned away from him. Removing his arm from her waist, he clamped his hand painfully around her bicep and dragged her back toward the SUV.

As Clint pushed Katie forward, the sounds of fighting made her wince. Logan was on top of Rich, his fists making a sickening sound as they connected with the other man's face, slamming relentlessly down, over and over again. The crisp white snow beneath them was flecked with blood and the gun lay, tossed aside, just out of reach. Between blows, Rich kept trying to dislodge him, looking about for his weapon, trying to connect a hit anywhere possible. Logan didn't falter or show any sign that he felt it.

"Enough!" Clint yelled. Neither man looked over, too absorbed in their battle to take note of anything else. Lowering his head, Clint spoke into Katie's ear: "I'd rather not risk hitting Rich, but if I have to I will shoot your boyfriend anyway. Call him off. Now."

"Logan," Katie yelled, her voice shaking in fear. "Stop!"

That got his attention, cutting through the violence long enough for Logan to raise his head. Seeing the gun pressed to Katie's temple, every muscle in his body went rigid. With his opponent distracted, Rich surged upward, knocking Logan to the ground before jumping to his feet.

"You bastard," he yelled as he reared back and kicked Logan in the ribs. Logan curled up and let out a grunt of pain as the guy kept kicking him.

"Stop!" Katie yelled, forgetting all about the gun and struggling against Clint. Every kick, every sharp intake of breath, was like a punch to her own gut. "Logan!"

"Rich, knock it off," Clint said as he fought to keep his grip on Katie, who was struggling like a wild animal. After one final heel to Logan's stomach, Rich stepped back, using his sleeve to wipe blood and sweat from his face. The fury in his eyes made it clear he wanted to keep going and didn't want to stop until Logan was dead. Clint gave her a shake that was really more of a violent jerk. "I still have a gun," he said.

Katie stilled, but the look she shot him was pure hatred. Her eyes narrowed and her breath came out in a sharp hiss, but she kept her mouth shut because she didn't feel like having her head blown off. It would almost be worth it to be able to get at least one good hit in. Anger welled up inside of her chest and she was shaking with it as she tried to tamp it down. It burned in her stomach and filled her head with the rushing of her own blood. She wanted to see these men bruised, and bloody, and laying in a heap of agony writhing in pain, and suffering. She tore her eyes away from her attackers, knowing she would be unable to control her anger if she kept thinking about how much pain she wanted to inflict on them. Looking down at Logan, her heart ached at seeing him in pain.

Clutching his stomach, he struggled up to his knees. "It's okay," he said, glancing up at Katie and letting out a cough. "He kicks like a bitch."

Rich surged forward, like he was going to attack Logan again.

"Rich, you can beat the hell out of him later," Clint said, and Rich stopped to look at him. "Right now we need him to tell us where our money is."

"Go to hell," Logan said, getting to his feet. And Katie wished she could go to him. She wanted to put her arms around him. She wanted to take his pain away. She wanted this whole night to go away.

"Yeah yeah, you hate us, we hate you," Clint said to Logan. "Now tell us where our money is or I'll blow her pretty little brains out."

Logan clenched his fists at his sides. "I don't know where your damn money is," he said. "If you hurt her, I swear to God I'll kill you."

"Before I shoot you, too?" Clint said. "I don't think so. You only have one option if you want her to live. I'll give you three whole seconds to tell me or I'll shoot her. Three . . ." Clint brought the gun closer to her head. "Two . . ."

Katie squeezed her eyes shut and waited for the end.

"Wait," Logan yelled, and the man drew the gun back a few inches. Katie let out the breath she had been holding, watching it rise in front of her like smoke. It wasn't her last one, she thought, watching another puff of air fan out from her mouth. Never before had she been so grateful to see her own breath. To know she was still alive to take another one.

"I'm waiting," he said when Logan didn't speak.

"I don't have your money," Logan said.

"Then you are no good to me and I have to kill you both," Clint said.

"I can get it, though," Logan said.

"I thought you could," the man said, sounding like he was losing patience. "Where the hell is it?"

"I don't know personally," he said, then held up his

hands in surrender when Clint jerked on Katie's arm again. "But Will can get it. I just need to find him."

"I guess that makes two of us," Clint said, and dragged Katie closer. "Rich, grab your damned gun then call Tom and Savannah. See if he found that guy yet."

Taking a few steps to his left, Rich retrieved his fallen gun, stuffed it in the waist of his pants and pulled out his cell phone. Logan was shifting his weight from foot to foot and his hands were clamped in angry fists at his sides. She could see his breath coming out in sharp pants and had to look away from him. Her body shook with the control it was taking to stay still when everything inside of her wanted to go to him. "I'm getting voice mail on both of their cell phones."

Katie could feel Clint tense up behind her. "Then try Savannah's house phone," came his curt reply.

Rich held the phone up to his ear and waited for an answer, then got a confused look on his already dumb-looking face. "Who is this?" he asked, then paused, his expression unreadable.

"What the hell is going on?" Clint asked.

"Umm," Rich said, holding the phone away from his ear. "It's that Will guy."

"What? What the hell is he doing answering Savannah's phone?" Clint said. "Take her and give me that." He shoved Katie away from him, causing her to stumble into Rich, who grabbed her arm, his grip even tighter than Clint's had been, then passed the phone off to Clint.

"Ow," she muttered, but Rich didn't ease up. Logan's

eyes narrowed, and she thought she heard him growl but he remained still.

"Where the hell are my partners and my money?" Clint said into the phone, then waited. "I don't believe you. I have your friends, you bastard, and I will kill both of them if you don't tell me where my money is." He paused, then let out an angry sigh before holding the phone out and pressing it to Katie's ear. "Say something, princess."

"Will, what are you doing there?"

"Shit, they really do have you," Will said. "No one's even here. I was about to call the damn cops but now I have to ransom you guys instead? 'Oh it's way too dangerous to go and get the car,' blah blah blah." He was swearing, but Katie didn't have to hear any more because Clint yanked the phone back.

"You had better get your ass over here with my money in the next five minutes or I start shooting," Clint said, anger making his voice deeper. "And keep in mind that the police won't make it before I kill you all, so don't even bother calling them, got it?" He listened for another second before ending the call. He looked up then and said to them: "You'd better pray he gets here soon."

The next five minutes were the longest most uncomfortable minutes of her life. No one moved, no one spoke, they just stood there waiting. A hair before the deadline, she saw headlights approaching and breathed a sigh of relief that Will was on time.

Will pulled into the lot, and Katie wished with every

cell in her body that she and Logan were about to drive away. She took a moment to close her eyes and pretend that she was leaving. The car would be warm and toasty. Nobody would have a gun. She would be safe. They would go back to her apartment, and the second the door closed he would pull her into his arms and— Whoa, buddy, those thoughts weren't getting her anywhere. She opened her eyes again and things were still just as bad as they had been before.

Will pulled the car up behind the Escape and slowly got out. Clint turned Katie to face him, making sure Will could see his gun pointed at her head. "I trust you have my money?" Clint said.

"In the five minutes you gave me?" Will said. "I don't have it here."

"That does not make me happy," Clint said, a frightening edge of panic buried in his tone.

"Let Katie go and we'll go and get it for you," Logan said, and Clint turned to look at him.

"Do you think I'm a moron?" he asked, and Katie sincerely hoped Logan wouldn't answer because yes, they all did think he was a moron. How could he not see what was happening? How did he not realize that Savannah had played him? Why couldn't he see that they had nothing to do with his stupid money? "You're going to get me my money, and I'll keep the girl as collateral." Katie's heart skipped a beat. *Collateral?* As in he was going to take her away? The acid in her stomach churned, making her feel sick.

"No," Logan said, and started forward.

"Logan don't," she said as Rich pulled out his gun and trained it on Logan.

"You have one hour. Understand? One hour. Rich," Clint said. "You go with them and make sure they do what they say they're gonna. No point in letting them turn around and run to the cops. Just don't kill them, okay?" Rich nodded but didn't look happy. "Call me as soon as you get the money. I'm gonna take her someplace they can't get to her. And keep trying to get ahold of Tom and Savannah," he said, then opened the passenger door to the SUV and none too gently shoved Katie inside. Being tossed around so much was really starting to get on her nerves, she thought as she rubbed her bruised arm.

"One hour or she dies," Clint said before getting behind the wheel and driving away.

Chapter Six

Logan couldn't breathe. His mind whirled with pure, undiluted fear. His hands were shaking and he was standing on legs that felt like rubber. The air was too thick and the ground was spinning. His body was itching to follow the SUV like a dog chasing after its owners. That wouldn't work; Rich would shoot him before he took two steps, and at any rate, the SUV would lose him in a matter of seconds. What was he going to do? Clint had Katie. The only thing he knew was that he had to get her back. What if she died? He couldn't live with himself if anything happened to her. He had failed her. He promised her that he would get her out of this, that he would keep her safe, and he hadn't.

"Well?" Rich said, looking at them expectantly. "Are we gonna go find that money, because I'm freezing my balls off out here."

Logan looked up at the man who had tried to kill

him several times. The man who helped kidnap Katie. His mind came into sudden sharp focus, bent on only one thing: getting Katie back and getting her back safely. The pain that he had felt from his beating earlier dropped away. He couldn't feel a thing. He vaguely heard Will say his name and ask him a question, but he wasn't focused on his friend.

"Get in the car," Rich said.

"All right, let's go," Logan said to Rich, taking a step closer. He was within arm's reach now.

"Lead the way," Rich said, gesturing toward the car with the gun. For the split second that the barrel was pointing away, Logan saw his opportunity. Without a moment's hesitation he stepped to the outside of Rich's arm and grabbed the wrist with his right hand, keeping the barrel away from himself.

A loud bang erupted, echoing through the night, as Rich accidentally squeezed the trigger. Will yelled a curse and scrambled behind the car to safety. While still holding the wrist, Logan clamped his left hand onto Rich's bicep and with bone-breaking force brought the arm down, connecting with his knee, snapping Rich's arm at the elbow. Rich howled and dropped the gun. Jerking away, he stumbled to the side, clutching his arm and taking in short, pained gasps of air.

A look of panic mixed with the agony on Rich's face, and he jabbed his uninjured arm forward, reaching for the gun. Not about to let that happen, Logan launched himself at Rich, tackling him to the ground and rolling him away from the weapon. Rich fought like a scared animal, with no control, screaming in pain and flailing wildly around. Most of the blows he threw missed entirely. The ones that did connect were so unfocused they made little impact.

This was growing old fast, Logan thought. There was no time to waste. The longer he fought with this guy, the farther away Katie was getting. Pulling back, he slammed his elbow onto Rich's temple, connecting with a sharp thud. It was enough to make him slump to the ground, unconscious. Hopefully, he wouldn't get up again for a while.

When Logan looked up, Will had moved from behind the car and retrieved the gun, holding it at his side. Panic was beginning to settle into Logan's stomach. His breathing was coming faster and faster and he had to fight to calm it. He had to keep cool and figure this out, otherwise he really would have failed Katie, and he was not about to let that happen. He could still fix this. He could still keep her safe.

"Keys," was all he said as he rushed to the car. Will fished them out of his pocket and tossed them to him. Logan caught them without missing a beat, yanked the door open and jumped in. The car was in gear and starting to move before Will even had the passenger-side door closed.

"You might wanna put your seat belt on," Logan said. The tires spun and the rear end fishtailed on the slick pavement before shooting forward. He swerved around Rich's inert form and rocketed ahead.

"What exactly is the plan here?" Will asked, clutching the "oh shit" handle as Logan peeled out of the lot.

"I'll let you know when I know," Logan said, stepping on the gas.

"Dude, it's been snowing. I get that you're worried, but we won't catch up to them if we're dead in a ditch." Logan ignored him and kept going.

"How'd you manage to get the car anyway?" Logan asked, nearly sliding off the road when they went around a curve. "And what were you doing answering Savannah's phone?"

"It was abandoned when I got there," Will said. "I was gonna just take the car and leave, but I looked around and Savannah's car was gone. She must have taken the money and run. So I decided to go inside and call the cops. I was just about to pick up the phone when it started ringing. By the way, I loved having to come out here and save your ass."

"By the way," Logan said, "I love that you're dating a girl that embezzles money and gets people to try to kill us."

"Touché," Will said.

"Where do you think she and Tom went to anyway?" Logan said, righting the car again as the tires lost traction across some ice. Will sat up ramrod straight and put one hand on the dashboard.

"I actually called Savannah," Will said, and Logan shot him a look of surprise.

"You called her?" he asked.

"Could you please look at the road, dude," Will said, sucking in a breath.

"When?" Logan said, turning his attention back to driving.

"Right after I hung up with psycho-kidnapper guy," Will said. "I asked her what she thought she was doing, where was she, and I think I yelled and swore at her quite a bit."

"Understandable," Logan said, wishing he could wring that woman's skinny little neck.

"She just laughed at me and told me how she was sleeping with Tom so he'd the steal money for her. I think she was trying to make me jealous," Will said, not sounding jealous at all. "We were right, they all work with her at the bank, and according to her, she talked them into embezzling five million dollars but wanted it all for herself. She was going to take me with her and leave tonight, before her . . ." He paused, trying to think of the right word. " . . . associates came looking for the money. But I was late. That's why she was blowing up my phone earlier. Then I showed up with Katie, and Savannah is psychotic and went nuts. So she decided to blame me to distract the goons. She's gone. As soon as their backs were turned she took the money and left. I assume Tom went with her, even though she didn't say anything about him. She was on the road when she was talking to me."

"And you had no idea about any of this?" Logan asked. "How long have you been seeing her, again?"

"Two months," Will answered with a shrug. "Gimme a break, she hid her crazy pretty good up till now. She was a pain in the ass but she's a fucking miracle in bed."

"You have great taste in women," Logan said. He saw the faint red glow of taillights down the road and knew it was them. He sped up as Will held his breath and closed his eyes.

"COULD YOU NOT point that gun at me while the car is moving? Or at least put the safety on?" Katie asked as they hit a bump in the road. "I saw *Pulp Fiction*. I don't wanna end up with my brains sprayed across the back windshield by accident. Besides, it's not like I can go anywhere."

"That's fair," Clint said with a shrug, putting the gun in his lap. "That was a good movie."

"I was supposed to be home watching movies right now," she mumbled, settling deeper into her seat like a sulky kid. At least it was warm in the car. She could feel her fingers and toes for the first time in what felt like years.

"Oh yeah? You and the boyfriend gonna watch some chick flicks?" he said, and snickered. Really? Now she was discussing movies with the guy. To be fair, she did bring it up. It was a little surreal, though.

"Nope, no boyfriend," she said. Even this guy liked to rub it in.

"I don't really want to get too involved because I'm probably just going to kill you anyway," he said, twisting his hands tight on the wheel, brimming with nervous energy. "But that asshole back there looked like he was going to kill us for you. You're saying he's not your boyfriend?"

"That's just what my Valentine's Day needs," she said,

crossing her arms over her chest. "To discuss my love life with my kidnapper." She cocked her head to the side listening. His radio was playing something upbeat with way too many saxophones. She realized it was "The Way You Look Tonight." Was that song the official sponsor of Valentine's Day or something? It was annoying the crap out of her. As much as she loved Frank Sinatra, he sounded too happy to be real. He didn't sound like he meant even one of the words of love he was singing. She wished Clint would turn it off.

"Trust me, this isn't how I imagined spending my Valentine's Day either," he said, scowling at her. "My wife is waiting for me at home and she is probably not happy right now, let me tell you. I was supposed to be bringing her the best gift of her life: a boatload of cash. But no, I'm stuck cleaning up this mess. Which makes me hate you *that* much more."

"Hey, I don't want you to shoot me for saying this or anything, but you can thank Savannah for this," Katie said, watching the streetlights flash across his face every time they drove under one. "She's the one that has your money. We were just in the wrong place at the wrong time." It looked like they were moving into a more populated area. She might be able to work with this. She just needed to find a way for him to stop the car.

"Yeah, I'm gonna believe you," the man said.

"When was the last time you heard from Savannah or your friend?" she asked, giving him a pointed look.

"That doesn't mean anything," Clint said, clenching his fingers on the wheel. Maybe she was pushing him too far. Maybe she should back off. But damn it, she was annoyed that he was so stupid. At this point he probably knew that he had screwed up but didn't want to admit his mistake. Either way, it didn't look good for her because if she got away that meant he'd go to jail for sure. And he knew it. She had no idea where he was taking her, but she knew that she didn't want to let him get there. Every instinct she had said that as soon as they were where he wanted to be, he was going to kill her. Simple as that.

"Knowing that slut, Savannah, they're probably just having sex," Clint muttered under his breath, thinking out loud, and she had to strain to hear him. "It's what got us in this whole damned mess to begin with."

They were in a downtown area coming up to a busy intersection. Katie saw a crowd of people bustling to get inside of a nearby brick building. Loud music spilled out from the doors and people were lined up, waiting on the sidewalk. It looked like some kind of party. This is it, she thought with growing excitement. This was her best chance of getting away. This was the only place they had passed where she'd seen people. She had to get out of this car, now. If the light they were approaching would just stay red, she could hop out when he stopped and make a break for it. No sooner had she thought this than the light ahead turned green. They were going to breeze right by what was probably her only chance at finding someplace populated. What was she going to do now?

Her heart leapt as she saw a vehicle stopping up ahead for a group of people crossing the street. Katie had never been happier to see the hazy glow of red brake lights.

Clint was forced to slow the car as her hand crept up to clutch the door handle, ready to yank it open and take off the moment he stopped. But the people made it across the street and the other car took off again before Clint had come to a stop. He was beginning to accelerate. As she watched the speedometer slowly creeping upward, she saw her chance of escape dwindling to nothing. If she didn't get out of this car now, there might not be any other chance. And if she had no other chances, she was a dead woman. She would have to jump.

The back end fishtailed in the snow as he sped up. She said a short prayer, and with a deep, shaky breath, popped the door open. The wind whipped her hair into her face and she could hear Clint yelling at her. But she couldn't hesitate. If she did she would lose her nerve, so she launched herself out of the car.

The fall felt like it lasted for minutes as she sailed through the air, instead of mere seconds. Closing her eyes, she braced herself for impact, landing with a wet thud on the snowy curb and rolling to a stop. *"Ooomph!"* The breath was pushed from her lungs and the cry of pain that emerged came out as more of a low croak. Holy crap, I can't believe I just did that, she thought, forcing herself to take in gulps of air, coughing and wheezing as she pushed herself up onto her hands and knees. That was going to leave a bruise.

The ground was slick and she slipped and faltered as she got to her feet. Every muscle in her body protested and there was a sharp twinge in her left wrist, but nothing seemed to be broken. On weak trembling legs she scurried away, making a beeline for the crowd of people down the street. It had dissipated some since she first noticed them, but there were still a few people piling in through the building's double doors. No one seemed to have even noticed her action-movie-style escape. She was a little bummed. How often, really, did someone get a chance to jump out of a moving vehicle?

She glanced behind her, hoping that Clint wasn't right there. Nope, he had pulled the SUV over to the side of the road and was stuck inside it as a string of traffic passed close to his door. Perfect, she thought with a wan smile, and shoved her way inside, only to stop with a gasp of horror.

LOGAN HAD LOST them. Somewhere along the twists and turns of the country roads the taillights had disappeared. Swearing, he slammed a hand on the dashboard in frustration and dread.

"Just keep going," Will said. "They can't be too far ahead. We'll find them."

What if they didn't? What if Clint had made a turn and he'd missed it? Katie would be at that psycho's mercy, and he would have no way of helping her. Going with his gut, even though it was a wreck of nerves at the moment, he sped up to the next light and careened around the corner toward downtown, hoping it was the right way. If it wasn't then Katie's death would be his own fault. He refused to let that happen.

TRACY WANTED TO kill herself. She stared at her steak knife longingly and for a moment seriously considered ending it all. Dustin was still talking. Did this man ever shut up? What was that about his car? The exhaust? What made him think she wanted to hear about his exhaust?

"My ex-girlfriend hated my car," he said. *Oh no, don't start in on the ex.* "She hated everything, actually. She was so picky and demanding. Not like you." He looked at her like a five-year-old girl meeting Prince Charming at Disney World. He reached across the table and grasped her hand with his. This was just how she envisioned spending her Valentine's Day. With a sweaty-palmed, never-ending story teller. She let out a small breath and plastered a fake smile onto her face, hoping to ease the rejection as she pulled her hand from under his. She tried to cover it by grabbing her glass and taking a sip of water.

"You are so warm. So beautiful."

Apparently he didn't notice a little rejection.

"I'm the luckiest man in this restaurant. It makes me glad that Ellie dumped me."

"Oh," Tracy said, her fingers idly playing with the handle of her knife. "Thanks."

"Can you believe she dumped me for another guy?" he said. *He's still talking. Why, God? Why is he still talking?*

"I sure can't," she said, glancing at the clock. She was actually starting to worry about Katie. What was taking her so long?

A wide grin cracked his face as a thought seemed to occur to him. "Do you like foreign films? Because there is this Swedish documentary playing at the museum that I am just dying to see. We should go there for our next date."

Tracy looked down at her steak knife longingly.

KATIE HESITATED IN the doorway for a moment, caught off guard by the god-awful decor. It looked like Valentine's Day had thrown up. It was so ghastly that she actually forgot she was being chased for a moment. The small entrance room was decked out for the holiday. Paper hearts and cupids hung from the ceiling as a canopy of red and pink balloons bobbed about, their strings trailing behind them brushing the tops of people's heads. There were people dressed in red from head to toe, wearing white-feathered cupid wings and holding toy bow and arrows, standing in front of the only other door in the room. A long table was set up right in front of the entrance, and the crowd of people had to stop there before they could get to the cupid-manned doorway. The table was covered with a crimson cloth and scattered with tiny, glittering, heart-shaped pieces of confetti, and on top of those were stacks of HELLO MY NAME IS stickers.

Katie had no idea what this was all about, but she did not have time to wait in line and get signed in. She barged through the line of people, past the table, and walked right by the cupids by pretending to be with a group of name-tag-wearing people. The main room was even worse than the lobby. It followed the same puking-up-Valentine's theme but maxed out on steroids, to the point of pink lights shining hearts onto the walls, more balloons, and a huge cupid chandelier dangling over a buffed and polished dance floor. A banner hung from the farthest wall saying WELCOME FINDURLOVE.COM MEMBERS TO THE 2ND ANNUAL VALENTINE'S DAY SINGLE MINGLE. *Oh dear God.* The dance floor covered most of the room, and to the side were tables filled with refreshments and what looked like an open bar. Quite a party, she thought. People already seemed to be hitting the bar heavily.

Katie rushed inside, sliding in between groups of people, trying to blend into the crowd. Exhaustion and fear clouded her mind as she tried to come up with a plan that did not involve crying in the fetal position. She needed to call the police, and wondered if Clint had called Rich and told him she'd escaped. She wondered if her stunt would put Logan and Will in extra danger. Probably not yet. Probably Clint would want to try and get her back before raising the alarm.

"Oh, hey there." The sound of a man's drunken slurred voice caused her to jump. When she turned her head, she was right at eye level with him. He looked to be in his late thirties with thinning blond hair. Normal enough, however, he had swiped a pair of cupid wings from an employee and the feathers were poking into her shoulder as he swayed.

"Hi," she said, distracted, rubbing the wrist that was still sore from her fall. Her eyes continued to dart around the room for signs of Clint. What was she going to do?

"So," the man said, sliding a hand around her waist

and resting it on her hip. "Want me to get you a drink?" He pulled her closer until she was pressed up against him. A pungent wave of alcohol breath hit her full force and she leaned away.

"No thanks," she said, trying to step away, but he held on tighter.

"Oh, come on, I know why people come to these things," he said. "We're all here to get laid."

"Not me," she said, shoving him away. He let her go and stumbled backward.

"So I'm not good enough for you?" he said, his voice rising in volume. Shut up, she thought. The last thing she needed was to attract attention to herself. Clint would find her for sure. "You don't want any of this?" He came toward her again.

"Not me," she said, keeping her voice soft. "But I think I saw a woman over there eyeing you up. Better go get her," she said, pointing in a different direction.

Katie felt bad siccing this guy on an unsuspecting woman, but he was probably harmless, and she couldn't afford to be seen right now. The drunk tottered off the way she was pointing. She looked past him and felt a spurt of panic as she saw Clint pushing his way into the room. The only thought that crossed her mind was to hide. She was running on pure adrenaline and instinct took over. It was fight or flight, and flight won out, so she hurried away in the opposite direction.

"Hey where ya goin'?" she heard the drunk guy say from behind her, and she shot a look back at him. He looked really confused, like he wanted to follow her and at the same time find the woman that she had pointed at. Instead he stood in one spot, shifting his weight from foot to foot.

Clint hadn't seen her yet, she realized, breathing a sigh of relief. It wouldn't last long, though. Not if she didn't do something. She needed a moment to think. She reached the wall, seeing a long panel of bright paper hearts strung together to create a banner. They sat a few feet from the wall and fell from the ceiling, brushing the floor. There were several of these lining the wall, and she noted that other people had the same idea as her, except they were using the cover to discreetly make out. She slid behind an unoccupied one and tried to think over the pounding of her heart.

"Hey, sexy?" she heard the drunk guy call from the other side of her banner. He was far from keeping his voice down. "Where'd ya go?"

She poked her head out to see where Clint was.

Looking right at her. That's where he was. He was still across the room, but the drunk guy was attracting so much attention that just as she peeked her head out, Clint's cold angry eyes zeroed in on hers. His face was a mask of pure fury, which did not bode well for her.

"There you are!" the drunk guy said, throwing his hands in the air and starting toward her. What the hell is wrong with this guy? she wondered, and noticed a door farther down the wall. A couple was pressed up against it kissing like the apocalypse was coming, but they wouldn't be a problem.

She darted forward and pushed the kissing couple out

of the way. They glanced at her, let out an offended "Hey!" then continued kissing. Gripping the cool metal knob with shaking fingers, she twisted. Her gloves slipped and refused to grip the handle, so she ripped them off, letting them fall to the ground, and tried again. A sigh of relief whooshed past her lips as it gave no resistance. She ripped it open and flung herself inside, taking note of her surroundings.

It proved to be a dim stairwell with dirty, stale-smelling carpet. There was only one way to go, so without hesitation she bolted to the stairs and gripped the railing hard for fear that her terror would make her clumsy. Her feet had just hit the next level when she heard the door above her open and close again.

Panic threatened to seize her, making it difficult to breathe, but she pushed through it and tried to think calmly. She was in another hallway, fluorescent lights flickering and humming overhead. The walls were paneled in dark glossy wood that reflected the dim lights and cast a yellow glow through the hallway. There were several doors on each side that appeared to be offices. The first one she tried was locked. Tears pricked her eyes as she tried the second one.

Clint's footsteps slammed down the stairs, and Katie knew she was out of time.

Chapter Seven

LOGAN FELT LIKE a giant hand was squeezing at his lungs when he saw the Escape parked empty on the side of the road, its passenger door hanging carelessly open. Where was she? What if Clint had decided to pull off, drag her someplace private, and kill her? There were barely any people around, and because of the thick, wet snow the roads were quickly becoming deserted.

He pulled Katie's car over to the curb in front of a darkened storefront. The street was lined with them, all dark except for the building at the end of the street that looked and sounded like there was a raging party going on inside.

Will must have noticed his ashen, pained face. "She's all right, Logan," he said. "Keep it together and we'll find her."

"You're right," he said, the words feeling as thick as peanut butter in his mouth. "Do you think she ran or did he take her from the car?"

"I can't see why he would take her out of the car here,"

Will said. "Why not just wait until he got wherever he was going?"

"Right, so if she ran," Logan said, "she would have gone into that party for help."

"And if she didn't run?" Will asked.

Logan sucked in a sharp breath. "Then he would have dragged her someplace no one would see them," he murmured, his lungs feeling tight again.

Logan got out of the car, oblivious to the biting cold of the ankle deep snow, or the thick flurries of it coating his hair and seeping through the fabric of his coat. Will followed suit, getting out of the car and looking to Logan for a plan.

"Will, you look around out here, check behind the buildings," Logan said already starting off. "While you're at it, borrow someone's phone and call the police. I'm checking that party."

Once inside, he charged past the employees at the front table, ignoring them when they called out that he would have to sign in. Frustration mounted in his stomach mixing with pure terror and raging fury. He was surprised he could function with so many turbulent emotions threatening to overcome him. And as he scanned the crowd of people all dressed in fancy clothes tossing back cocktails like it would save their lives, he saw no signs of Katie or Clint. The dance floor housed only a few brave couples, and the rest of the crush seemed to center around the small bar. He made his way to where people were clustered, hoping that he would find her blending into the safety of the crowd.

KATIE ALMOST SOBBED with relief when the second door was unlocked. She slipped inside and closed it behind her, wincing at the click it made. She did a quick scan of the door and her heart dropped into the pit of her stomach when she saw that it could only lock with a key. There was nothing to keep him from coming right inside. She was backed into a corner. Trapped. She could hear his muffled footsteps hitting the carpeted floor of the hallway as she scanned the room for a weapon. There was no time to barricade the door. Even if there were, the only furniture in the room was a large metal desk that would be way too heavy for her and a rolling computer chair. She heard him rattling the knob on the first door in the hallway and knew that he would be on her in a matter of seconds.

There were two options. The first was to hide under the desk and hope he didn't come inside. This was flawed, though, because he would have to be missing half of his brain not to find her in the only unlocked room in a dead-end hallway. The second option was to stand her ground and fight. The problem with that was she would probably end up with a point-blank hole in her chest.

She had a split second to decide. As if disconnected from her mind, she grabbed the slender metal garbage can from the corner of the room, ignoring the throb in her wrist. It was lighter than she thought it would be, and the metal felt smooth and cool in her hands. She stood next to the door, clutching it tight to her chest and steeling her nerves for the fight.

Katie gave a brief thought to Logan. She had finally

found someone she could see herself falling for, and now she would probably die before she got her chance with him. And maybe it wouldn't have worked out. Maybe he would have broken her heart. But all she wanted was the chance to find out. She wanted to be with him. To see his face every day. To get to know him and to let him know her. To let someone love her without being afraid to believe it was real. She wanted to put herself out there and trust in another person. It figured that she would know what she wanted now, she thought with a sardonic shake of her head. In what might very well be the last moments of her life. Katie felt a vicious stab in her heart as she realized that she probably would never see him again. The thought made her eyes sting with tears.

She sucked in a slow, shaking breath, the will to fight burning deep inside her. The next few seconds took years. Time stopped and the only thing on the planet was the drumming of her heart and the amplified, echoing sound of his footsteps drawing near. She could see him in her mind: gun drawn, his sharp blue eyes blazing with fury, his jaw set, shoulders steeled, and ready to put an end to all of this. Ready to put an end to her.

KATIE WASN'T IN the crowd.

Searching frantically, Logan pushed people out of his way. Every moment that passed when he couldn't find her, he felt her slipping away from him. Images of what that bastard would do to her were racing through his mind, each worse than the last. He decided to do one last sweep of the room before looking outside. He started with the perimeters, hoping he might have better visibility of the entire room. Before he got very far something made him stop in his tracks. A man was standing by the wall droopy-eyed with drink and teetering like a weeble wobble. What made Logan take note, though, was that he seemed to be rubbing a black glove on his face. A glove that looked identical to the ones Katie had been wearing.

He approached the man. "Where did you get those gloves?"

The man looked at him. It seemed to take a lot of energy for his eyes to focus on Logan's face. "They're soft," the man said. "Wanna feel?"

"No," Logan said, wanting to take the man by the lapels and slam him against the wall until he told him what he needed to know. This would probably only make the guy either pass out or throw up on his shoes. "Where did you get them? Was it a woman? Thin, with blond hair?"

"She was so hot," the man said, the glove slipping from his fingers as he leaned against the wall, his head lolling to the side. "But she left."

"Left?" Logan asked, losing patience.

"Over there," the man said, taking on the Herculean task of lifting his arm to point at the wall. "She ran away from me." Tears started leaking out of his eyes. "They all run away from me." He slid down the wall and plopped onto his bottom, sniffling.

Logan didn't stick around to watch the grown man's breakdown. Down the wall he noticed a door that was cracked open the slightest bit. He tore it open and hurried inside. The sound of a woman's scream made his stomach lurch with fear and he ran faster.

KATIE DIDN'T FLINCH as the door banged open and hit the wall. Without a wasted second, she hauled back and swung the trash can, aiming high. With a satisfying crash, she connected with Clint's head, sending him reeling backward into the hall. He let out a shout of surprise and pain, fighting to catch his balance as he pushed off the wall, trying to right himself.

With a war cry, she brought the can up and bashed him a second time, his head snapping back and his legs buckling under him. The gun flew from his hand as he hit the ground, skittering silently across the carpet. He groaned and clutched his nose as blood spurted out, running between his fingers. Tossing the can to the side with a clang, she stepped over his legs, intent on getting the gun. She thought he would have been so preoccupied with his face that he wouldn't even notice her. She was wrong. One blood-slicked hand shot out and clamped onto her ankle mid-stride. She fell forward, unable to stifle the scream that burst from her lips, and landed on the ground, hitting her shoulder and hip. Sharp pain spiked through her body and panic seized her when she couldn't find her breath.

"You bitch!" Clint said as he lurched to his feet, looming over her. She coughed and managed to suck in a deep wobbly breath, tossing her hair off her face to look up at him. "You're gonna pay." He grinned down at her, the promise of pain clear on his bloodied face. "And I'm going to enjoy every second of it."

Katie pushed herself onto her elbow, bringing one knee up as if to protect herself, never taking her eyes off him. She masked the fear on her face, unwilling to give him the pleasure of showing weakness. *Where is that gun?* she wondered, afraid that if she looked around it would break the fragile stalemate they seemed to be in. She was fairly certain it was close, within a few feet.

A snarl of pure rage erupted from behind them, breaking through the silence. Startled, Clint whirled around, but Katie didn't look to see who it was. She didn't care. Using her legs, she pushed herself across the floor, twisted onto her stomach, and lunged for the gun as she heard the sounds of chaos erupting above her. The cool slick feel of the metal under her outstretched hands caused her to sob with relief. Swinging around into a sitting position with one hand braced on the floor, she brought her other arm around and pointed the gun straight at him.

Immediately, she lowered it again. Logan was there and had Clint pinned against the wall, his hands around Clint's throat.

"I told you I would kill you if you if you hurt her," Logan growled, his face clouded with stark fury as Clint's face turned purple. Katie rose to her feet gripping the gun with both hands, her face grim with resolve, her body shaking with the aftereffects of the fight.

"Logan!" Katie yelled, afraid he wouldn't stop until Clint was dead. But he stilled at the sound of her voice, every muscle in his body taut and vibrating with suppressed anger. "You need to stop, now. If he moves I'll shoot him." She was surprised to find that she meant it.

"Katie," Logan said, loosening his grip, and Clint doubled over coughing. "Are you all right?"

"I'm fine," she said. "We should just tie him up or something. Then the police can deal with him. Don't do anything stupid." *Like murder him.*

Logan narrowed his eyes at Clint. "You know, I wasn't a violent person before tonight," he said, stepping away. Logan held his hand out for the gun and Katie hesitated. "I won't use it unless I have to," he assured her, and she set it in his waiting hand.

Sure that he had Clint under control, she went to find something to tie Clint up with. After rummaging around a few minutes she managed to find duct tape in a supply closet. They taped Clint to the computer chair in the office, with another piece of tape over his mouth.

"What now?" Katie asked when they were back in the hallway with the door shut behind them. Logan swept her into his arms and pressed his mouth to hers in a quick, urgent kiss, gathering her tight against him.

"I was so terrified," he said, running his hands down her back then over her arms, as if making sure she was actually there. "If something had happened to you . . ." He left the thought unfinished, as if it were too much to contemplate.

She looked into his eyes and felt safe for the first time that night. Everything was going to be okay, she could feel it. She was still alive and he was here holding her.

That was all she wanted. If this moment never ended, that would be perfectly okay with her. She wrapped her arms around him and buried her face in his shoulder as he whispered soothing words in her ear, telling her that everything was all right.

"I thought I was going to die," she said into his coat. "I didn't think I'd get a chance to see you again." She felt his hand beneath her chin tipping her face up to his. He looked like he wanted to say something, but the words wouldn't come out so instead he lowered his lips to hers in a hard, deep kiss. The air left her lungs and she clutched at his arms, afraid she would fall over otherwise. Groaning deep in his throat, he let his tongue enter her mouth, exploring, caressing, demanding.

He pulled back, breaking the kiss and holding her at arm's length as she leaned back against the wall, looking dazed. He took a deep, calming breath.

"Let's go get this mess sorted out and get you home," he said, taking her hand in his and leading her to the staircase.

"Okay," she said, sounding breathless. "Oh," she said, shaking her head, remembering. "What about Tracy? We have to go get her."

"Really?" he said, looking at her with one brow raised. "She can deal with having to finish her crappy date."

"Hey," she said, poking him in the chest. "Rescuing her was the only reason I got into this mess. If I don't go, then it was all for nothing."

"I'd say having to cut in on her blind date is a waste of time," he said. "You need to rest."

"I'll rest after we go get Tracy," she said, though the temptation to go home and sleep nearly overwhelmed her. But Tracy was her best friend. Her night had been hell so far, and there was no way she was going to betray her best friend's trust on top of everything. She was sure that Tracy would understand if she was a no show, given the circumstances, but she wanted to be there for her. Besides, if she didn't go, then this whole evening need never have happened, and that was just too frustrating to deal with right now. "We're going."

AFTER WHAT SEEMED like an eternity, Katie was finally behind the wheel of her car.

"You really still want to go pick up my sister?" Logan asked from the passenger seat.

"You know," Will said from the back, "I'd rather just go home. Your friend can deal."

She looked over at Logan as he ran a hand through his already tousled hair and let out a weary sigh. After having made their way out of the party, they were greeted by the flashing blue and red lights of a police car. Will had been talking to an officer, frantically gesturing to the building, then stopped when he saw them approaching. The rest was kind of a blur to Katie's exhausted brain.

Logan had held her hand throughout the questioning, and she would be forever thankful for his strength. Especially when they brought Clint out with his hands cuffed behind his back. His cold eyes had locked onto her, the loathing clear on his face. She had tightened her grip on

Logan's hand as everything caught up to her. Looking at Clint, she remembered how he had held the gun to her head. Shoved her around. Chased her. Loomed over her, thinking he'd won, thinking she was helpless as she lay on the ground at his feet. She wasn't weak, she had told herself. She was stronger than Clint in every way. With these thoughts running through her brain she had leveled her eyes with his. Her gaze unwavering, her chin tipped upward. Then, just to piss him off, she let the corners of her mouth turn up in a grin. She wouldn't have thought it was possible for him to look angrier, but her gloating seemed to do it. That made her feel so much better.

Then they followed the police back to the station, left their statements, and promised to be available for further questioning, even though they had already answered plenty already.

"She's probably not even there anymore." The sound of Logan's voice brought her back to the present. She shook her head to focus as she eased away from the curb and pointed her car toward the restaurant.

"Her movie just got out about an hour and a half ago and it's Valentine's Day; it can take that long just to be seated at a restaurant. She'll still be there. And if she's not, we can get some cheesecake to go and call it a night."

"Can you believe Savannah called me to try and bail her out of jail?" Will asked. Earlier, while the EMTs were bandaging where the bullet grazed him, he had gotten a call from his now ex-girlfriend. It turned out that shortly after leaving her house, Savannah was pulled over for reckless driving. When the officer heard sounds coming from her trunk, he did a little investigating and found her partner in crime, Tom, bound and gagged inside. In the backseat there was a duffel bag filled with stolen money. Suffice it to say it was not long before Savannah ratted out the other two men. Add that to attempted murder, and those four were looking at a lot of legal troubles.

"I can believe anything from that psycho," Katie said. She was slowing the car for a traffic light when the radio caught her attention. Soft piano music was drifting out of it and she turned the volume up. For some reason this song felt soothing to her, and she was surprised when she heard the words. It was "The Way You Look Tonight," the song that had been driving her batty all evening. It was beautiful, and sincere. It wasn't too sultry, like the Michael Bublé version, or too jaunty, like Sinatra's. It felt real and heartfelt, like whoever was singing it was truly in love. "Who's singing this?" she asked, interrupting Logan and Will as they argued about Savannah.

"This?" Logan paused, listening to the music for a few beats. "I think it's Fred Astaire."

"Dude," Will said, sounding disgusted. "How do you even know that shit?"

Katie rolled her eyes. Going through this ordeal with Will still hadn't endeared him to her.

"My mom loves him," Logan said, visibly bristling that his manliness was called into question. Katie shushed them both so she could hear the rest of the song, and let out a little sigh when it was over. She was starting to understand all this romantic stuff.

Chapter Eight

KATIE STRODE PAST the protesting hostess and rushed straight to Tracy's table.

"Tracy!" she shouted, laying on the drama a little thick. After the night she'd just had, there was no energy left for decent acting skills.

At first Tracy shot her an annoyed glance that clearly said, *Where the hell have you been?* But when she saw Katie's disheveled appearance, worry clouded her features. Katie had been avoiding her own reflection as much as possible, but judging by her friend's reaction, she knew she wasn't looking too hot. She ran her fingers through her hair in a futile attempt to right herself but got stuck on a tangle halfway down, so she tugged it out and tried not to think about it.

"Is everything okay?" Tracy asked, her voice filled with genuine concern.

"No," Katie said.

"And what is my brother doing here?" Tracy asked, just noticing Logan standing behind Katie.

"There's no time to explain," Katie said, and heard Logan cough back a laugh behind her. "I'm so sorry," she said to Tracy's date, "but we have to go. Now." Katie grabbed Tracy by the arm and started to haul her away.

"So sorry," Tracy said, as she snatched her purse off the chair back and stumbled after Katie. "It appears to be an emergency."

"I'll call you," her date called to their backs.

"Can't wait," Tracy mumbled. As they walked out into the parking lot, Tracy gave Katie a once-over. "Nice touch making yourself look like you've been through a hurricane."

"Thanks," Katie said, still dragging Tracy. "I'll tell you about it later."

"You know you can let me go now," Tracy said, looking at Katie like she was certifiable.

"Oh," Katie said. "Sorry."

"Logan?" Tracy said. "What are you doing here? I didn't realize you and Katie were even in touch."

"Ran into her earlier," he said. "It's a long story."

"Okay," Tracy said to Katie, her brows furrowed in confusion as she climbed into the passenger seat. "You're acting weird." When they were all inside and Katie had started the car, Tracy slipped her heels off. "Oh man, that feels good. You have no idea how bad my night was."

Katie caught Logan's eyes in the rearview mirror and they shot each other a smile. A little burst of butterflies erupted in her stomach and she had to remind herself to look ahead and drive.

"Hi, there, I'm Will." He thrust a hand out and leaned into the center console to see her. Jarred by the sudden movement, Tracy took it with a wary look on her face. "*Very* pleased to meet you," he said, and Katie shot him a scowl that she hoped stated clearly not to hit on her friend.

"Okay, I'd say that right now is 'later,'" Tracy said, turning back to Katie and dropping Will's hand. "Tell me what's going on? Why were you so late? I was worried."

Katie did not feel like rehashing the whole evening. "We ran into Will's ex-girlfriend and she went a little crazy," she said. Looking in the mirror, she saw Will shoot a smile at Tracy. Then his eyes drifted farther south to take in her friend's cleavage. "We've kind of been dealing with that all night."

"Oh, poor thing," Tracy said, glancing behind her with an appraising eye. "She must have been *really* angry."

"You have no idea," Will said.

"Was your date really that bad?" Katie asked, in an attempt to change the subject and Tracy gave her a pointed look that said she wasn't fooled.

"Yes. It was. Do you realize that we had finished eating nearly twenty minutes ago? He was gonna keep me there, talking at me all night, I swear! But he did get me these," she said, pulling a red velvet heart-shaped box out of her purse. "What do you say we go back to my place and watch movies and polish off these chocolates?" Tracy asked.

Katie met Logan's eyes in the rearview mirror again. The heat in his gaze was enough to send a tingle shooting down her spine. "You know, Trace, I'm really beat tonight. Maybe tomorrow."

Tracy popped a candy in her mouth and grumbled about her horrible night the entire ride home, while Will made sympathetic noises and craned his neck to look down her shirt.

BY THE TIME both Tracy and Will were dropped off, Katie was about ready to rip her hair out with frustration. She was so glad to finally be alone with Logan as she slid the key into the door of her apartment. Anticipation raced through her body, making her heart beat faster. The hairs stood up on the backs of her arms as she felt Logan's presence behind her. Her awareness of him heightened until she shivered just thinking of his mouth on her.

"I'll see you tomorrow, then?" he asked, and her heart dropped. *He isn't staying?* Disappointment settled in her gut. She pushed her door open and flipped on the light.

"Do you wanna come in?" she asked, letting her intention hang heavy in her voice. Maybe he wasn't sure she wanted him to stay. She gestured that he should step inside.

"Katie," he said, letting out a breath. "You need to rest, and I need to let you. You've been through a lot tonight."

"I'm not tired," she lied. She was tired but she wasn't dead. She had been painfully aware of him all evening and wanted to do something about that so badly she ached with it. Finally she wanted to be with someone, to trust him with her heart, and he didn't want to stick around to let her? Stepping in closer to him, she whispered, "I want you to stay with me tonight."

"Katie," he groaned. "I won't take advantage of you. Go in and rest before I change my mind."

"Logan," she said firmly, "I want you to take advantage. I want you to change your mind." She reached her hand out and ran it up his chest before gripping his collar and giving it a little tug. "Don't you want me?"

"God," he said, his hands coming up to rest on her hips. "You know I do."

"Then what's the problem?" she asked with a smile. She rose onto her toes and pressed a feather soft kiss onto his lips.

"I don't remember anymore," he said, looking at her face as if trying to memorize every detail for later. "I know there was one, though."

With a sly smile, she walked backward into her apartment, grasping his hands and leading him inside. "I am not sleeping alone tonight," she said, pulling him close and pressing her body along his, loving the feel of his strong, solid chest against her. "Don't be all honorable. That's no fun for anybody."

"Whatever you say," he said, lowering his mouth to the curve of her neck, nuzzling kisses to the soft skin there. She let her head fall back and groaned because it was him, and because it felt so right. Bringing her hands up, she sank her fingers into his hair, pressing him closer.

Logan kicked the door shut then whirled her around,

pushing her back hard against it, and a thrill shot up her spine. The warmth of his breath hit her cheek as he exhaled slowly, as if to calm himself, and the need she felt for him rose up into her chest so strong she was nearly choking with it. She wanted more, she wanted everything. Excitement rocketed through her veins as she looked up at him with anticipation burning inside of her and heat twisting and pooling between her legs. A lock of hair fell over his forehead, and his eyes went dark with lust.

"You are so beautiful," he said, brushing his lips across her cheekbone, and in that moment she realized that this was more than a physical urge. She needed him, wanted him, in every way possible.

She felt it everywhere, hot and warm, radiating from her chest, and she never wanted it to end. Letting her hand glide behind his head, guiding him to her lips, she kissed him, falling into him, letting herself go light-headed. Sensation flooded her body, leaving her shaking and weak with need. She pushed his coat roughly off his shoulders and let it fall to the floor, sliding her hand down his chest and over his stomach to the front of his pants.

"Whoa," he said, catching her wrists, "slow down. I wanna do this right."

Katie savored the smooth taste of his mouth as he kissed her gently. Too gently. It was a lovely kiss but she wanted more. She wanted him to take her hard, and fast, and now. But he seemed intent on going slow, letting his hands smooth over her hair and cup the curve of her cheek as his lips moved softly on hers. It was sweet and it felt nice, but she wanted the passion they had shared in the woods earlier. She wanted that heady sense of losing control. Of being so overcome that they couldn't think of anything but devouring each other. She let out a frustrated sigh and clutched at his hips, pulling him close, feeling his erection against her stomach. Now that's what I want, she thought, but he was still touching her like she would break. Katie understood that he was concerned for her after everything that had happened, but she was in no mood to be gentle. She wanted some head-banging, screaming, pounding, mind-blowing sex. She wanted to feel alive.

"Don't go slow on my account," she panted, and felt his arms tighten around her, his muscles tensing. "I want you more than I've ever wanted anything in my life. So don't go slow. I want it fast, and hard, and right now."

"Thank God," he moaned as his control visibly shattered. He ripped at her clothing, pulling her shirt over her head, cupping her breasts through the thin material of her bra as he teased her nipples into taut peaks. Whimpering in pleasure at his touch, she arched her back to press herself more firmly into his hands. The heat from his hand burned into her skin, setting her on fire. She undid the snap on her jeans and helped him pull them down before kicking them away. But it wasn't enough. They tore at each other's clothes and within moments were naked together. She shivered at the contact, gasping at the feel of his warm skin and tense muscles under her hands.

Sinking down onto the carpeted floor of her living room, Logan angled himself on top of her, his chest rising and falling in sharp pants. He filled her entire world, and she was dying to feel him pounding hard and slick inside of her. He kissed his way down her neck, nipping at the cushion of her cleavage before drawing a nipple into his mouth, and she writhed beneath him, letting out a small moan when his hand slipped between her legs, stroking her sensitive flesh, driving her to the brink.

"Logan," she cried, overwhelmed with sensations. "I need you inside of me. Now."

A sound of protest escaped her lips when he stopped touching her, reaching over her for his jeans and digging in the back pocket.

"Don't stop," she urged, so close to an orgasm she was quivering with it, before she realized that he had been getting a condom.

She spread her legs wider, allowing his hips to settle more firmly between her thighs. Gripping her ass hard, his fingers digging into her soft skin, he slowly eased himself into her, and she lifted her hips to take in every delicious inch of him. He drove into her with long, powerful thrusts, the movements of his body growing more urgent with each passing second. The sound of her name being ripped from his mouth excited her, took her higher, brought her closer to the moment she was craving. Every thought was pushed out of her mind as she arched up to meet his rhythm. His taste, the masculine scent of his sweat-slicked skin, the feel of his mouth and tongue on her body, were all she could focus on. Raking her nails down the hard muscles of his back, he let out a rough groan, pushing deeper, filling her completely. *Right there, yes, there!*

"I'm not going to last much longer," he managed to say. "Oh, God, you feel so good." The pressure built inside of her, tightening and clenching, until she cried out his name, sobbing in pleasure as she came, trembling with the force of it. Logan rocked inside her faster, harder, over and over, until he closed his eyes and went rigid, shaking and shuddering in his own climax. He fell against her then, exhaustion overtaking his body. The sounds of their panting and gasping filled the room as they lay in the aftershocks of ecstasy.

"Wow," was all Katie could say.

"That about sums it up," Logan said, rolling onto his back.

"That was just . . . wow." She smiled, snuggling close to him, and his arm went around her.

They stayed that way for a few minutes and she began to fall asleep, floating on wave of warmth until he pressed a kiss to her forehead, whispering for her to wake up.

"Don't wanna," she mumbled sleepily.

"Come on," he said, rising to his feet, pulling her along with him.

"Fine," she sighed, then led him to her bed, where they curled up under the covers together.

As she drifted off, Katie noticed the clock read after midnight. Well, I survived Valentine's Day, she thought, closing her eyes and letting sleep claim her.

When she woke up the next morning, her first thought was just how warm and cozy she felt. Logan's arm was draped over her waist and the muscled length of him was pressed against her back. The feel of soft flannel sheets against her bare skin was like heaven after spending the entire evening outside in the cold. Soft, buttery sunlight filtered in through the sheer curtains. She lifted her arms above her head to stretch and winced at how sore all of her muscles were. Well, fighting for your life would do that to a person, she supposed. She glanced at the clock and was shocked to see that it was already noon.

She shifted to face Logan and he made a sleepy sound and tightened his arm around her. She sighed looking at his face, peaceful in sleep, and wished she could stay like this forever, but something was nagging at the back of her brain, making it difficult to relax. A dark bruise colored Logan's jaw, reminding her of the terrible ordeal they had shared. Being careful not to wake him, she slid out of bed, grabbed her fluffy pink robe from the hook on the door and slipped it on. She left her bedroom and went straight for the coffeemaker. If there was something that she was going to have to think through she wasn't going to be able to do it without being caffeinated.

As the rich, life-giving coffee smells started filling the kitchen, she sat down at one of her mismatched bar stools and leaned her arms on the marble counter, letting her head fall into her hands. She hoped that Logan would want to stick around. She knew that last night had been stressful and she wouldn't blame him if he woke up and realized that his attraction to her had all been a product of danger and a damsel in distress. She knew how some men were suckers for that shit. Hopefully it was more than that. It was for her.

And, on another note, was it too early for brownies? She wondered, eyeing the batch she had made a few nights ago.

By the time Logan woke up and joined her, she was on her second brownie and sipping from a steaming mug of coffee. He smiled and leaned in to kiss her.

"Everything all right?" he asked, seeming to sense her unease.

"I think so," she said, looking up at him and feeling warm inside. "About last night, there's no pressure."

"Okay?" he said.

"I would understand if it was a one night thing. I mean with the near death experiences, and the fighting, and it's all very swash-buckle-y, and I guess I'm saying that I would understand if you wanted to go your separate way—" He cut her off with another swift kiss. "Or we could do that," she said against his lips, a smile tugging at the corners of her mouth.

"Was it a one night thing for you?" he asked, pulling back.

"No." She shook her head. "No, it really wasn't."

"Me neither," he said, running his hand along her cheek and cupping the back of her neck. "I've always wanted you, Katie. It wasn't just last night. I've been crazy about you since we were teenagers. I've never wanted anybody as much as I want you."

"Seriously?" she asked, and in that moment she knew that everything was going to work out.

"Seriously." He pulled her to her feet and leaned in to whisper in her ear. "Let me show you how much I want you."

And he did.

Six months later he proposed.

One year later, on Valentine's Day, with Fred Astaire singing "The Way You Look Tonight," they had their first dance as husband and wife.

About the Author

JACLYN HATCHER has always held a love for romance and adventure, and with an imagination that won't shut up, what else is there to do but write? She's an artist, a black belt in karate, and a lover of all things coffee. She lives in southeast Michigan but vows she'll never get used to cold weather.

Visit www.AuthorTracker.com for exclusive information on your favorite HarperCollins authors.

SEDUCED BY THE GLADIATOR

By Lauren Hawkeye

An Excerpt from

SEDUCED BY THE GLADIATOR

by Lauren Hawkeye

In Lauren Hawkeye's second erotic romance featuring the fierce gladiators of Ancient Rome, Lilia is the rarest of commodities—a champion female gladiator. When Christus, a warrior with the body of a god, is sold to the *ludus* that owns Lilia, she finds herself forced to defend her position and guard her body against the erotic sensations only he can bring. But beneath the tantalizing flesh of the gladiator, Lilia finds a man determined to protect her—and to love her—no matter the cost.

AN AVON RED NOVEL

"What are you doing?" My words were a hiss as I looked frantically around the room. We were alone for the moment, thank the gods, but someone could come in at any moment.

Weak was the least of the things that I would appear to be if someone were to come upon this scene, me flushed from the steam, Christus' sure fingers lightly massaging the purpling skin of my ankle.

Every touch of his fingers sent a lick of fire straight between my legs. Though I tried to swallow it down, a groan escaped my lips.

His touch felt so incredibly *good.*

"I cannot let myself be seen like this." There was no point in denying that I found his touch pleasurable. Against my better judgment, I closed my eyes for a moment—just a moment—and let sensation wash over me.

When I again opened my eyes, Christus' fingers had

trailed upward to my calf. His eyes burned brightly and were fixed on my own.

"I told the men that anyone who bothered you while you bathed would find himself without a cock." My mouth fell open at the words, and inexplicably a giggle bubbled up from my throat.

I clapped a hand over my mouth as it escaped. I never giggled. I rarely even laughed.

Sobering myself, I tried to tug my leg from Christus' reach. "That does not mean they will listen."

"I assure you they will." Christus did not allow me to pull my flesh away, instead trailing his fingers ever higher. My breath caught in my throat as he stroked the tender skin beneath my knee.

"If it eases you, Darius is keeping watch. No one will disturb you. No one will disturb us."

I heard the double meaning in his words, and though I felt as though I should run, I found myself doing nothing of the sort. Instead I reached out, my hand shaking, and ran uncertain fingers over the stripe of his cheekbone.

I shuddered as my fingers made contact with his skin. It had been so long since I had been touched with anything but violence or desire that was twisted at its root. Darius touched me sometimes, but his caresses were friendly and reassuring.

They did not affect me in nearly the same way that these small caresses did.

"Christus. I cannot do this." I wanted to. I could no longer lie to myself. I wanted this man, wanted the moments of pleasure that he could bring to me in this strange life that I called my own. "If the men found out that I took you as a lover, we would both be under attack."

My voice had a breathless quality to it, one that I had never heard before. I was feeling things that I had never felt before, too, as Christus lowered his head and laid his lips on my knee.

When he again looked up, the expression on his face—the longing, the desire—was my undoing.

"Why should anyone find out? It is no one's business but our own." The fingers that still softly stroked the skin beneath my knee moved with excruciating slowness, tracing a stripe up and up, until they found the edge where my leather wrap met my skin.

"Christus." What was happening to me? I was not weak—I made my own decisions. Yet I could no more have stopped this encounter than I could have stopped breathing.

Slowly, giving me time to say no, Christus worked at the knot in my leather. When the fastening was loose, he pulled the garment away from my body, hanging it on the edge of the tub.

Leaving my skin bare from the waist down.

I felt my lower lip tremble, but apart from that small movement I was still, tensed, my breath caught in my throat with anticipation. With his eyes on my own, drinking in every nuance of my expression, he inched his fingers up, then up again, trailing them over my inner thighs as the muscles beneath quivered.

I inhaled sharply when those fingers grazed over the heated skin between my legs. Christus paused at the noise, again giving me time to say no.

I waited a long moment, my innermost thoughts whirling through my head in a great rush. Sex had been tied up with violence for so long, it had made me feel cheap at best. The idea that I could embrace it for pleasure was strange and oddly thrilling, if I could but take that leap.

My eyelids lowered, I looked down from the edge of the bath, where I still perched, looked at the god of a man who was rising out of the water at my feet. He was golden and sleek and beautiful, and he wore an expression of reverence and of need that looked to be nearly painful.

It was this exact combination that pushed me the last step. With an exhalation of the breath that I had been holding, I covered his wrist with my hand, holding his fingers in place even as I arched my hips to meet his touch.

"You are certain that we will not be disturbed?" I could not quite believe that I was prepared to accept his word when he nodded. The Lilia of even a day before would never have taken anything at face value, would have had to see for herself.

But this man inspired trust. Trust, as well as lust.

For the first time since I had come to the ludus, I decided to embrace the sensations.